STAR WARS

THE FORCE UNLEASHED II

SEAN WILLIAMS

BASED ON A STORY BY
HADEN BLACKMAN

 DEL REY

BALLANTINE BOOKS
NEW YORK

 LUCAS BOOKS

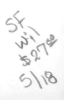

Published in the United States by Del Rey, an imprint of The Random House Publishing Group, a division of Random House, Inc., New York.

DEL REY is a registered trademark and the Del Rey colophon is a trademark of Random House, Inc.

This book contains an excerpt from *Star Wars: The Old Republic: Fatal Alliance* by Sean Williams.

ISBN 978-0-345-51154-6

Printed in the United States of America

www.starwars.com
www.lucasarts.com
www.delreybooks.com

2 4 6 8 9 7 5 3 1

First Edition

For Robin Potanin,
fellow lover of
champagne and good sci-fi

ACKNOWLEDGMENTS

With thanks to Haden, Brett, Sue, Frank, Leland, David, Shelly, Evan, the Mount Lawley Mafia, and my wonderful wife, Amanda, as always.

THE STAR WARS NOVELS TIMELINE

OLD REPUBLIC
5000–33 YEARS BEFORE STAR WARS: A New Hope

Lost Tribe of the Sith*
Precipice
Skyborn
Paragon
Savior

3650 *YEARS BEFORE STAR WARS: A New Hope*

The Old Republic
Fatal Alliance

1020 *YEARS BEFORE STAR WARS: A New Hope*

Darth Bane: Path of Destruction
Darth Bane: Rule of Two
Darth Bane: Dynasty of Evil

RISE OF THE EMPIRE
33–0 YEARS BEFORE STAR WARS: A New Hope

Darth Maul: Saboteur*
Cloak of Deception
Darth Maul: Shadow Hunter

32 *YEARS BEFORE STAR WARS: A New Hope*

> ### STAR WARS: EPISODE I
> #### THE PHANTOM MENACE

Rogue Planet
Outbound Flight
The Approaching Storm

22 *YEARS BEFORE STAR WARS: A New Hope*

> ### STAR WARS: EPISODE II
> #### ATTACK OF THE CLONES

22–19 *YEARS BEFORE STAR WARS: A New Hope*

The Clone Wars
The Clone Wars: Wild Space
The Clone Wars: No Prisoners

Clone Wars Gambit
Stealth
Siege

Republic Commando
Hard Contact
Triple Zero
True Colors
Order 66

Shatterpoint
The Cestus Deception
The Hive*
MedStar I: Battle Surgeons
MedStar II: Jedi Healer
Jedi Trial

Yoda: Dark Rendezvous
Labyrinth of Evil

19 *YEARS BEFORE STAR WARS: A New Hope*

> ### STAR WARS: EPISODE III
> #### REVENGE OF THE SITH

Dark Lord: The Rise of Darth Vader

Coruscant Nights
Jedi Twilight
Street of Shadows
Patterns of Force

Imperial Commando
501st

The Han Solo Trilogy
The Paradise Snare
The Hutt Gambit
Rebel Dawn

The Adventures of Lando Calrissian
The Han Solo Adventures
The Force Unleashed
The Force Unleashed II
Death Troopers

REBELLION
0–5 YEARS AFTER STAR WARS: A New Hope

Death Star

0

> ### STAR WARS: EPISODE IV
> #### A NEW HOPE

Tales from the Mos Eisley Cantina
Allegiance
Galaxies: The Ruins of Dantooine
Splinter of the Mind's Eye

3 *YEARS AFTER STAR WARS: A New Hope*

> ### STAR WARS: EPISODE V
> #### THE EMPIRE STRIKES BACK

Tales of the Bounty Hunters
Shadows of the Empire

4 *YEARS AFTER STAR WARS: A New Hope*

> ### STAR WARS: EPISODE VI
> #### RETURN OF THE JEDI

Tales from Jabba's Palace
Tales from the Empire
Tales from the New Republic

The Bounty Hunter Wars
The Mandalorian Armor
Slave Ship
Hard Merchandise

The Truce at Bakura
Luke Skywalker and the Shadows of
  Mindor

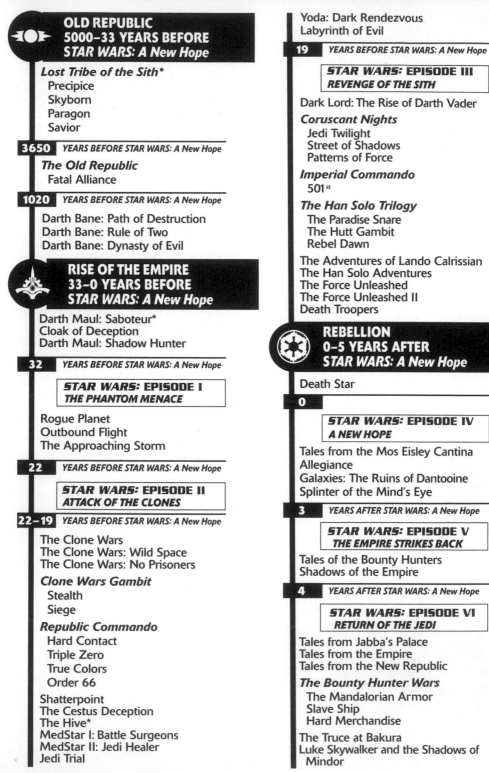

NEW REPUBLIC
5–25 YEARS AFTER
STAR WARS: A New Hope

X-Wing
Rogue Squadron
Wedge's Gamble
The Krytos Trap
The Bacta War
Wraith Squadron
Iron Fist
Solo Command

The Courtship of Princess Leia
A Forest Apart*
Tatooine Ghost

The Thrawn Trilogy
Heir to the Empire
Dark Force Rising
The Last Command

X-Wing: Isard's Revenge

The Jedi Academy Trilogy
Jedi Search
Dark Apprentice
Champions of the Force

I, Jedi
Children of the Jedi
Darksaber
Planet of Twilight
X-Wing: Starfighters of Adumar
The Crystal Star

The Black Fleet Crisis Trilogy
Before the Storm
Shield of Lies
Tyrant's Test

The New Rebellion

The Corellian Trilogy
Ambush at Corellia
Assault at Selonia
Showdown at Centerpoint

The Hand of Thrawn Duology
Specter of the Past
Vision of the Future

Fool's Bargain*
Survivor's Quest

NEW JEDI ORDER
25–40 YEARS AFTER
STAR WARS: A New Hope

Boba Fett: A Practical Man*

The New Jedi Order
Vector Prime
Dark Tide I: Onslaught
Dark Tide II: Ruin
Agents of Chaos I: Hero's Trial

Agents of Chaos II: Jedi Eclipse
Balance Point
Recovery*
Edge of Victory I: Conquest
Edge of Victory II: Rebirth
Star by Star
Dark Journey
Enemy Lines I: Rebel Dream
Enemy Lines II: Rebel Stand
Traitor
Destiny's Way
Ylesia*
Force Heretic I: Remnant
Force Heretic II: Refugee
Force Heretic III: Reunion
The Final Prophecy
The Unifying Force

35 *YEARS AFTER STAR WARS: A New Hope*

The Dark Nest Trilogy
The Joiner King
The Unseen Queen
The Swarm War

LEGACY
40+ YEARS AFTER
STAR WARS: A New Hope

Legacy of the Force
Betrayal
Bloodlines
Tempest
Exile
Sacrifice
Inferno
Fury
Revelation
Invincible

Crosscurrent
Millennium Falcon

43 *YEARS AFTER STAR WARS: A New Hope*

Fate of the Jedi
Outcast
Omen
Abyss
Backlash
Allies
Vortex**
Conviction**

*An eBook novella
**Forthcoming

DRAMATIS PERSONAE

ACKBAR; Rebel leader (*Mon Calamari male*)

BAIL PRESTOR ORGANA; Senator and Rebel leader (*human male*)

BERKELIUM SHYRE; repairman (*human male*)

BOBA FETT; Mandalorian bounty hunter (*human male*)

DARTH VADER; Sith Lord (*human male*)

GARM BEL IBLIS, Garm; Rebel leader (*human male*)

JUNO ECLIPSE; Rebel captain, *Salvation* (*human female*)

LEIA ORGANA; Princess and Rebel leader (*human female*)

MON MOTHMA; Senator and Rebel leader (*human female*)

PROXY; droid

RAHM KOTA; Rebel general and Jedi Master (*human male*)

STARKILLER; Rebel and apprentice to Darth Vader (*human male*)

YAT-DE VIEDAS; Rebel leader (*Rodian male*)

YODA; Supreme Master of the Jedi (*nonhuman male*)

A long time ago in a galaxy far, far away. . . .

PROLOGUE: Cato Neimoidia

Juno Eclipse stood with her hands behind her back and stared down at Cato Neimoidia. From the bridge of the *Salvation,* the densely forested world shone a brilliant green against the star-dusted black, and she was keenly reminded of other forest worlds she had visited during her career as an Imperial pilot.

Callos was the first. There she had obeyed orders that had resulted in the death of the entire planet's biosphere.

Felucia was next, and that world, too, had been left poisoned in her wake.

Kashyyyk, the last and most difficult to recall, had not been damaged at all. In fact, the prospects for its forests' continued survival had taken a sharp turn for the better following the destruction of the skyhook that had threatened to enslave every last Wookiee and to ensure the planet remained part of the Empire forever. The resolution made in the ruins of a jungle hut, where a handful of people had vowed to rebel against the Emperor and free the galaxy's tormented trillions, was bound to help, too.

Given luck, then, the forests of Kashyyyk would survive, but Juno remembered wondering how she herself possibly could. The pain she felt had been too great, the sense of loss too deep. Every living thing reminded her of the part of her that had unexpectedly wakened within her and then died just as suddenly. Her heart beat with a heaviness that hadn't been there before—not even when she'd been held captive for months in the *Empirical,* expecting to be executed at any moment.

Sometimes she woke in the night, still feeling *his* lips against hers. They had kissed just once, but the memory of it was burned in her brain. He had died, and she lived on. It had taken a year before she finally felt as though she might be over him. So why was she letting a bunch of trees bother her now?

She told herself to get it together. Juno Eclipse had bigger things to worry about.

"Excuse me, Captain," barked a voice at her elbow. "Our probe droids are picking up an atmospheric disturbance in the vicinity of the target."

She turned away from the view to face her Bothan second in command. "What kind of disturbance, Nitram?"

"Explosions."

"Show me."

The circular display screen in the center of the bridge zoomed in tight on the city closest to the Imperial stronghold. Secondary screens flashed infrared images conveyed by heavily encrypted transmissions from the droids on the ground. The bridge city hung like a vast urban hammock from its overarching stone spire. Several thick supporting cables were glowing red. One was actually burning.

"Looks to me like nothing more than local insurrection," she said. "If it keeps Baron Tarko off our backs, all the better."

"Uh, yes, sir." Nitram cleared his throat.

Juno studied his long face. "Speak your mind. That's an order."

"Well, there were some unusual heat readings immediately prior to the blasts. You can see them here, and here." He pointed to a recording time-stamped an hour earlier. "It looks like a ship's exhaust."

"So where's the ship? I can't see it."

"That's exactly my point, sir." He looked around the bridge, then leaned in closer to whisper, "I think it might be General Kota."

Juno didn't know whether to be annoyed or amused. For such

a young officer, Nitram was good: he had, in fact, stumbled across the truth of their mission with impressive and inconvenient speed. Fortunately, Juno had learned fast under her Imperial masters to keep every emotion well concealed.

"You've been listening to too many stories, Nitram," she said, clearing the incriminating secondary screens. "Wherever Kota is, he's not slumming here with us."

That was a lie, of course: She would recognize the signature of the *Rogue Shadow* anywhere, even when it was fully cloaked.

"Yes, sir."

Nitram had no choice but to accept it as the truth. She was, after all, his superior officer. But that didn't have to be the end of it.

"Sound the alert. I want twelve fighters strafing that city in the next five minutes. Let's take the chance to strike while the Baron is busy."

Nitram saluted. "Yes, sir." He swiveled briskly on one heel and snapped out a string of orders.

Juno turned back to the window, hiding a smile. The EF76 Nebulon-B frigate *Salvation* was a valuable part of the growing Alliance navy, and she had no intention of putting her inexperienced crew in serious harm's way. But it *was* a training run, she told herself, and what better way to learn than in the thick of combat? She was sure, anyway, that the infamous Baron Tarko would soon have more to worry about than her green hotshots.

Sirens wailed through the ship. Feet thundered on bulkheads. With a string of distant thuds, a dozen Y-wings launched and, wobbling only slightly against the starscape, grouped in two six-ship formations rocketing down into the atmosphere.

"Take us out," she told Nitram. "No point hiding now."

The *Salvation*'s seven ion engines roared into life, thrusting it from its redoubt behind the planetary system's smaller moon. The deflector shield generator was running at full capacity, ready for immediate reprisal. Baron Tarko's facility on the ground wasn't heavily enforced. It consisted of a slave processing plant with a number of ancillary buildings, including barracks, laser batteries, and TIE fighter launchpads, all suspended from the bridge city over a giant sinkhole. A constant stream of freighters came and went from the world, redistributing the Empire's ill-gotten prisoners. Intelligence made very clear that the Baron thrived on bribes from high-ranking Imperial officers keen to obtain the best "stock," while at the same time selling excess numbers to the Hutts and other criminals. What he did with his wealth, exactly, no one knew. But all could guess at the suffering he was responsible for. If someone *were* to put an end to his brutal regime, they would be doing the entire galaxy a favor.

That wasn't the *Salvation*'s job, however. Juno's orders were strict: Prick the Baron's defenses and see how strong they were; shake her young crew into battle readiness; and under no circumstances risk the integrity of the ship. The official line was that resources were more valuable to the Rebellion than tiny victories—at least at the moment. When the navy was big enough and the lines of supply more secure, *then* the fight could begin in earnest.

Not everyone agreed with the official line, though. Some thought the fight had already begun and could be pursued by a small force as readily as by something larger and therefore less defensible. Take out the right target, the naysayers said, and entire star systems could be disrupted. Like the ripples that spread across a pond's surface at the drop of a single stone, every Imperial facility and process that relied on slave labor would be slowed down by a successful attack on Cato Neimoidia.

Juno had heard the argument a thousand times. She knew just how much difference even a single person could make. The newly formed Rebel Alliance wouldn't exist at all, most likely, but for *him*.

She shook her head, annoyed at letting herself be distracted again. Kota needed her. She wouldn't let him down.

News of the frigate's presence spread fast through the freighters orbiting the plant. Many vanished into hyperspace, taking their slaves with them. Others broke orbit and began to descend dirt-side. Her fighters dodged among them, increasing the chaos of the skylanes. Red dots on the display screen signaled the launch of a TIE defense squad: ten ships, exactly as expected. Laser batteries swiveled to track the Rebel squadron.

She tuned half an ear to the star pilot chatter even as she monitored Nitram's handling of the crew.

"Watch that tower, Green Six."

"On your tail, Blue Four."

"Arm turbolasers. Target those batteries."

"Keep it tight, Green Two. Keep it tight!"

"Fire at will."

The *Salvation* rocked as its powerful lasers unleashed their deadly energies onto the planet below. Juno felt a rush of cautious pride. Her people were nervous, excited, and occasionally frightened—as was perfectly appropriate. Cato Neimoidia might be an outpost, but it was fundamentally connected to the Empire as a whole. Stick around too long and the whole weight of the enemy would come to bear on them. Everyone understood that they had to be in and out fast, or they'd never get out at all.

The turbolasers missed, but someone else didn't. The ground-based lasers exploded into a million pieces, destroyed by unknown fire.

Juno gave silent thanks to Kota and his invisible militia, and readied herself for Nitram's excited announcement that his theory had been confirmed. Kota was indeed active in the galaxy, striking hard and fast against the Alliance leadership's express orders. They couldn't stop him, and they had many reasons to be grateful for his activities. Baron Tarko would soon regret ever coming to his attention.

Instead of gloating, Nitram said in a worried tone, "Launches—ten more TIEs!"

"That can't be right," Juno said, leaning closer to check the data. It was all too right, unfortunately; intelligence had gotten the fighter strength wrong. Worse still, the TIE fighters were coming their way. "Launch all remaining Y-wings. And put someone else on turbolaser control. I want the roof of the barracks in flames in the next two minutes if I have to come down there and press the button myself."

"Yes, sir!"

The crew's energy level ramped up a notch. There was no time to hold back out of nerves or uncertainty. Intel flooded through the ship like an invisible gas. Within moments, they would be under attack, and all were aware of the frigate's strategic disadvantages. It was well armed and well shielded for a vessel of its size, but the slender midsection connecting the engineering and crew quarters could be ruptured by concentrated enemy fire. Were that to happen, the atmosphere would vent immediately, killing everyone aboard.

The turbolasers fired again. Targets on the ground burst into brilliant balls of fire. Juno caught glimpses of the cloaked *Rogue Shadow* ducking and weaving among the TIE fighters below. It looked like the general was trying to find a place to land. Once he and his commandos were on the ground, the ship could automatically retreat to a safe location and wait for a signal to collect them when the mission was over.

Juno hadn't flown the *Rogue Shadow* since the events on the Death Star, but she still knew its specifications by heart. Better than she knew the *Salvation*'s, in fact. Here she was just the commander. In the *Rogue Shadow* she had been captain *and* crew. There was an important difference.

Rebel and Imperial starfighters met in the vacuum between the frigate and the planet. Energy weapons flashed and ricocheted. The screens were full of light. She wished she was out there with the pilots, breathing acrid cockpit air, thumb growing tired on the firing stud. Her heart beat faster for them even as she reminded herself of her new duties. War was simpler in a starfighter, but it wasn't better. The bigger picture was what mattered. Winning the war, not the battle.

In that sense, she had some sympathy for those who opposed Kota's way of thinking. Going in too hard, too fast was a sure way to be encircled and wiped out. A degree of caution never went astray. That was why she surreptitiously helped him—to keep him in check as much as to watch his back. Someone needed to make sure he didn't go AWOL as he had before. The Rebellion needed him.

Thinking of the downsides of Kota's campaign made her frown. What was taking him so long? The *Rogue Shadow* should have been on its way ages ago.

"Nitram, concentrate fire on those cannon emplacements there and there." She indicated two locations near the barracks. The fire coming from both was much greater than intelligence had indicated it should be. Maybe that was the problem.

"Yes, sir."

Rebel starfighters changed course to attack the targets. The exchange of weapons fire intensified.

Juno squinted at the data, worrying at the inconsistencies between the intelligence gathered from Imperial sources and what lay evident before her. "Get those probe droids closer to the barracks. Something doesn't look right to me."

Finely balanced forces jockeyed for position on the ground and in orbit as she waited for the data to trickle in. From a distance, the Imperial installation looked perfectly normal. It possessed a spaceport, shield generators, security compound, and so on—all the same as on any occupied world. But it was better defended than most, and the spaceport was crowded. Why land so many ships on commercial territory when there was plenty of space over by the slaving compound? More important, why were Imperial records on Cato Neimoidia so wildly different from what was actually here?

There was little to tell from the data, so she turned her attention to the starscape around them. No sign of Imperial reinforcements.

"Why hasn't the Baron called for help yet?" she asked Nitram.

"I don't know, sir. We've been monitoring signals closely."

She cupped her chin and thought hard. It was only a matter of time before the Imperial fleet showed up, whether Baron Tarko called for it or not. All it took was just one fleeing freighter to sound the alarm and the Emperor's boot would descend to crush the Rebels. Really, with forces evenly matched and Kota dragging his heels, she should already have sounded the retreat rather than risk the *Salvation*.

"Give me the comm," she said. "Don't listen."

Nitram's ears went up and then flattened down against his skull. "Whatever you say, sir."

She selected a little-used channel. "Blackout to Blackguard. Respond, please."

The line crackled for a moment, and then Kota's gruff voice came on. "I don't have time to talk."

"Bad luck. This is taking too long. You need to pull out."

"Negative, Blackout. Leave if you want to. I'm staying to finish the job."

She ignored the implied reproach in his words. "How? You're never going to get close enough to the barracks to get Baron Tarko. It's too well defended."

"That's no barracks," he said.

"Then what is it?"

"I don't know, but it won't be anything by the time I—"

Kota's signal disappeared into static in time with a bright flash of light from below. Two of the probe droids winked out. The *Rogue Shadow*'s heat signature disappeared into an expanding ball of fire. Someone had dropped something big on Cato Neimoidia, taking out several Rebel and Imperial starfighters at once. Fire licked at the walls of the Imperial compound, making them glow bright red.

The crackle over the comm intensified.

"Respond, Blackguard. This is Blackout. Do you need help down there, Blackguard?"

Nothing.

Juno tried again, forcing herself to speak calmly. Nitram was watching.

"Blackguard to Blackout. Respond immediately!"

Nothing. The bridge was silent.

She stood, frozen, with one question echoing in her mind: What would the man she had loved have done now?

She knew the answer. He would do everything in his power to rescue his friend and Jedi Master. He would fight with every drop of energy in his body. He would let nothing stand in his way.

But she wasn't him. She didn't have his powers and she did have responsibilities he never had to consider. Besides, *he* was dead, and now there was no sign of Kota, either. What was she supposed to do—rescue a ghost? If she knew how to do that, she would have done it a year ago.

An alarm sounded. The bridge came to life around her.

"We've got company," said Nitram, gaze dancing across the rapidly filling display screen. "Two frigates, a cruiser, and—yes, a Star Destroyer, *Imperial*-class. Could be the *Adjudicator*. It's launching fighters. Captain?"

Everyone on the bridge was looking at her.

"Recall our pilots," she said in a clear and level voice, knowing that her hand was being forced. There was only one responsible decision open to her now. "Bring everyone aboard, then get us out of here, fast."

"At once, sir."

Juno stepped back from the display screen in order to let her officers go about their work. Tiny dots converged on the *Salvation* as its starfighters broke off their engagements with their enemy and raced for safe harbor. She counted eighteen, which meant six pilots wouldn't be going home. In exchange for what?

Again, the answer lay before her. Her crew was functioning perfectly well, and they knew through hard experience that Cato Neimoidia was better defended than they had expected. The *Salvation* had pricked the Empire and forced it to respond. Someone, somewhere, would be grateful for the *Adjudicator*'s unexpected absence from their skies.

But where did that leave her?

"Take us the long way to the rendezvous," she told Nitram. "We don't want anyone on our tail."

"Yes, sir."

Nitram didn't question her order, even though the reason she had given him was meaningless. The truth was that she needed time to think.

Kota was gone. How was she going to explain *that* to the alliance leadership?

Farewell, old friend, she thought. *What kind of mess have you landed me in this time?*

"Calculations complete," said Nitram.

"Ready the hyperdrive," she responded automatically. The shields were taking a heavy pounding, making the floor sway beneath her. Just two starfighters remained outside. When they were aboard, she gave the order.

"Jump."

The *Salvation* rushed into hyperspace, leaving the ill-fated world, its mysteries and its ghosts, far behind.

Part 1

REVOLUTION

CHAPTER 1

Present day . . .

FROM THE DEPTHS OF MEDITATION came a man's voice.

"You're running out of executioners, Baron!"

Starkiller opened his eyes. He knew that voice. It tugged at parts of him that had lain dormant for a long time—or never genuinely existed at all, depending on one's viewpoint.

He shied away from both memory and contemplation. There was no point wasting energy on either when his very survival was at stake. How many days he had been down the pit he no longer knew, but in that time he had neither eaten nor slept. His enemy wasn't physical in the sense of a foe he could strike down or manipulate. It was himself—his fallible body, his weak mind, his faltering spirit. He would endure and emerge whole, or never emerge at all.

Such was the life of Darth Vader's secret apprentice.

"He is dead."

"Then he is now more powerful than ever."

More voices. He closed his eyes and shook his head. Kneeling, he placed his manacled hands on the slick metal surface below him and concentrated on hearing the world outside.

Long stretches of isolation had attuned him to the cloning facility's many moods. Through the metal he heard a relentless hiss that could only be rain. Sharp cracking sounds were lightning, coming and going in staccato waves. Rolling rumbles were thunder, and a deeper note still was the song of seabed-hugging currents that circled the world.

He was on Kamino. Starkiller was sure of that much. He had been reborn on the distant waterworld, where a significant percentage of the Emperor's stormtroopers were grown. Here it was that he would live and grow strong, or die weak and unmourned. Every hardship, every hurdle, was one step closer to full mastery of his fate. That was the lesson underlying all lessons.

A new note entered the planet's endless song: the scream of a TIE advanced prototype starfighter. Angular and fleet, with bent vanes, it entered the atmosphere with a whip-crack sonic boom and descended on a bold, high-energy descent toward the facility.

Starkiller tensed. He knew that ship's sound and could sense the well-practiced hand behind its controls. He heard stormtroopers marching quickly in response to their master's electronic summons, calling orders to one another as they went. Blast doors opened and closed with booming thuds. The facility woke from its unattended slumber.

He didn't move as the TIE fighter landed. He didn't open his eyes as two heavy, booted feet dropped onto the platform and began the long walk through the facility. He breathed at a steady pace through the whine of the turbolift and the hiss of doors opening. A ring of red lights at the top of the pit came on, and although he felt the light against his hunched back, he didn't look up.

He heard breathing, mechanical and regular. Heavy footsteps came to the very lip of the pit, and stopped.

"You're alive," said Darth Vader.

At the voice of his former Master, Starkiller looked up, blinking against the light. Vader's boots were three meters above him, barely visible behind the lights and the grate that separated the pit from the dark room beyond. The Dark Lord loomed like a shadow, a black hole in the shape of a robed man.

Starkiller's throat worked. It was so dry he could barely talk at all.

"How long this time?"

"Thirteen days. Impressive."

The compliment was hard-won. It ground out of the triangular grille covering Vader's mouth and fell on Starkiller's ears like dust.

"The Force gives me all I need."

"The Force?"

The hint of praise turned to warning, as it did so often.

Starkiller lowered his head. He knew what was required. The weeks of training and isolation he had endured made that exceedingly clear.

"The dark side, I mean, *my Master*."

One gloved hand moved. The grate flew open.

"Come," said the dark figure above him.

The metal floor beneath Starkiller lurched and began to ascend. He forced his leg muscles to unlock from their long kneeling position, and stood to meet Darth Vader upright and unbowed.

The room above was sparsely furnished, with no windows, just one exit—the turbolift—and little light. Shadows cast by terminals and floor lamps made its very dimensions ambiguous, but Starkiller knew from long training exercises that the room was circular and its walls were impenetrable. He flexed his fingers, yearning for a lightsaber to hold. Muscle memory was keener than any other kind. Even with the new skills Darth Vader had taught him, his hands wanted to fight the way he knew best.

At the very edge of his vision stood several skeletal PROXY droids, awaiting activation. If he was lucky, he would be unshackled and allowed to duel some of them. If not . . .

The lift ground to a halt. Vader stepped back to study him. Starkiller felt the keen eye of the Sith Lord on his gaunt form even through the layers of durasteel, obsidian, and plasteel that covered the man's face. Something was different. Although nothing had been said, he could tell that this was no ordinary training session.

He waited. There was no hurrying Darth Vader.

"I have a mission for you."

"Yes, my Master."

"Starkiller's former conspirator has been captured."

He experienced a moment of confusion. Then his memories stirred, providing a name. The name of the one who had lured him away from the dark side and to his death.

The same voice that had disturbed him from his meditation . . .

"Vader thinks he's turned you. But I can sense your future, and Vader isn't part of it. I sense only . . . me?"

"General Kota," he said, struggling to keep himself anchored to the present.

"Yes. You will travel to Cato Neimoidia and execute him."

"And then will my training be complete, Master?"

"You will not be ready to face the Emperor until you have faced a true Jedi Master."

The voice was Darth Vader's, but again from another time, another memory. The present-day Darth Vader hadn't spoken at all.

Starkiller put his manacled hands to his head and turned away, lest his disconcertion be exposed. No matter how he tried, no matter how he concentrated, the past simply wouldn't leave him alone.

Vader's close attention hadn't ebbed. "You are still haunted by visions."

"Yes." There was no point denying it. "Yes, my Master."

"Tell me what you see."

He didn't know where to start. Thirteen days, this time, he had stayed motionless in the pit, subjected to visions and hallucinations through all his senses: strange odors, fleeting touches, voices calling him, sights he could never have imagined. He tried to ignore them, and when he couldn't ignore them, he tried to piece them together instead. Neither was entirely possible, and every attempt hurt so badly he despaired of it ever ending.

"Sometimes," he said, falteringly, "I smell a forest on fire."

"Continue."

"I see the general falling, and feel the ground shake as a starship crashes around me. And I hear a woman—a woman's voice—when I try to sleep." He swallowed. This was the most painful

recollection of all. "I can't understand what she's saying. Do you know who she is?"

A pleading note had entered his voice, and he hated himself for it.

"They are the memories of a dead man." Vader came closer, his physical presence lending weight to his words. "A side effect of the accelerated cloning process and the memory flashes used to train you. They will fade."

"What if they don't?"

"Then you will be of no use to me."

Starkiller straightened. For the first time, that fact had been said aloud. He had always known it was so; Darth Vader wasn't renowned for his charity. But to hear it stated so baldly—that this Starkiller, this clone, would be disposed of like some faulty droid if he didn't pull himself together soon—had a profoundly focusing effect.

Not for long.

"Try the Corellian razor hounds."

That was a new voice, one he hadn't heard before. He winced, and knew that by wincing he had effectively doomed himself.

"Starkiller's emotions made him weak," the Dark Lord said. "If you are to serve me, you must be strong."

What form of service that might take, Darth Vader had never said. To take the former Starkiller's place, he presumed, as a weapon that could be aimed at the Emperor then Vader's enemies whenever he commanded. From treacherous commanders to perhaps the Emperor himself—that was how it had been, and how he assumed it would be now. For the moment, however, that didn't matter. The new Starkiller wanted only to live.

"I am strong, my Master, and I am getting stronger."

Vader stepped behind him and waved a hand. Metal complained as the manacles dropped from Starkiller's wrists and hit the floor with a boom.

"Show me."

Numerous pairs of eyes lit up in the shadows. The PROXY droids were activating. Starkiller's fists balled in readiness. He had defeated their training programs over and over again. There wasn't a Jedi simulation that could beat him.

But this was different. Even as Darth Vader provided him with his weapons—two lightsabers with matched crystals, producing identical red blades—he saw that he wouldn't be fighting Jedi Knights this time. The targets stepping out of the shadows wore uniforms not dissimilar in color to the Sith's ancient enemy, but these were ordinary men armed with nothing more than blasters.

He had seen such armor before, in the memories of the original Starkiller's life. Men like this had fought him in a TIE fighter factory high above Nar Shaddaa. They had been on Corellia, too. He remembered the places clearly, even if he couldn't put them in context. The uniforms weren't Imperial. That was the only thing he could be sure of.

More voices came to him, a veritable babble of overlapping statements that went some way to filling one hole in his memory.

"We'll join your alliance."

"All we needed was someone to take the initiative."

"Let this be an official Declaration of Rebellion."

And he did remember now. The PROXY droids were wearing the uniform of Kota's militia, later adopted by the Rebellion—the Rebellion the original Starkiller had brought into being through a mixture of deceit and something that felt, through the obscuring veils of the cloning process, remarkably like sincerity.

"You must destroy what he created," Darth Vader intoned.

Starkiller ground his teeth together. If he was going to survive the coming minutes, he had to concentrate. He wasn't really destroying the Rebellion, just an imitation of it. And what did the Rebellion matter now, anyway? It existed. The original Starkiller was dead. He needed to move on.

The troopers rushed him from all sides. Twin red blades flashed as he met their advance, spinning and slashing with an easy grace that belied the strength behind it. Mastery of the Jar'Kai

dual-lightsaber fighting style hadn't come easily, even given his in-
herited knowledge of the Niman and Ataru techniques. Using two
blades came with both advantages and disadvantages. Although he
could attack or defend himself against more than one opponent at
once, he could only wield his lightsabers one-handed, reducing the
power of his blows.

Building up his physical strength had therefore been a key part
of his training on Kamino, starting with simple weights and grad-
uating to combat training with droids like these. Dueling the Dark
Lord himself had come last of all, and he had clung to that ultimate challenge even as his mind played games with him. He might
not know who he was, but he could learn—and had learned—how
to *fight*.

Fight he did, deflecting every attack the faux-Rebels dealt
against him, singly or in pairs and trios. Holographic limbs and
blasters were no match for his blades. Sparks flew. Droids fell in
pieces. Brown uniforms turned red with illusory blood.

More droids issued from the wall, crowding him, coming at him
in waves of four or more. Starkiller went into a fighting trance, stabbing and sweeping complex arcs through the air. His nostrils were
full of smoke. The stink cleared his head. No more voices assailed him,
and no doubts, either. He was who he was. Born to kill, he killed.

With a roar he forced his way through a wall of Rebels, slashing and hacking as he went. They fell apart on either side, leaving
just one standing before him. He raised both blades to strike him
down.

Not him. *Her.* She was a slender, blond woman in an officer's
uniform clutching a blaster in both hands.

Starkiller froze.

He knew that face.

He took a step toward the woman.

*"You're still loyal to Vader! After all he did to us—branding
me a traitor and trying to kill you—"*

"No," he said.

The words in his head wouldn't be drowned out.

"I saw you die. But you've come back."

"No," he repeated, raising his blades.

"Don't make me leave another life behind."

"No!"

The woman cowered before him. "Wait," she said in a voice identical to the one in his head. "Don't!"

"Now the fate of this Alliance rests only with you."

He lowered his blades, stunned out of his fighting trance. The voices were the same!

Memories stirred in his mind. Images of the woman before him came in a bewildering rush. Vader wanted him to destroy everyone the original Starkiller had fought with, and that meant this woman, this Rebel officer, this . . .

"Juno?"

"Yes," she said.

"Strike her down" came the command from Vader.

"I—I can't."

"You must learn to hate what he loved," said Vader, and suddenly it was just the three of them in the center of the droid-strewn training ground. Starkiller, the Sith who had created him, and a woman from the first Starkiller's past.

Conflicting impulses warred within him, triggered by the ongoing cascade of recollections. Juno was Juno Eclipse, the woman Starkiller had, yes, loved. But he wasn't Starkiller, so what did he owe her? He was just a clone, and she was only a droid, an illusion fashioned to test him. What did it matter if he did as he was told, as he had been bred to do?

His hands trembled. The twin red blades wavered. They grew steadier as he drew his elbows back, preparing to strike.

"I guess I'll never need to live this down."

He remembered a tender pressure against his lips, the feel of her body against his, a heat he had never experienced before, in this life or any other . . .

He couldn't do it. He couldn't kill her.

With a double click, he deactivated his blades. His arms came down and hung at his sides.

"It is as I feared."

Darth Vader lashed out, channeling the dark side with practiced ease. Starkiller winced, but it was the training droid the Dark Lord had targeted. His lightsaber sliced it neatly in two. The image of Juno Eclipse vanished in a shower of sparks.

Starkiller held his ground. No more *my Master*. No more pretense. "What will you do with me?"

Darth Vader strode to face his former apprentice, kicking the body of the droid out of his path.

"You will receive the same treatment as the others."

"What others?"

"Those who came before you went mad within months, tormented by emotional imprints I was unable to erase. Some would not kill their father, others their younger self. With you, it is this woman. Now you will suffer the fate they did."

Starkiller bowed his head, rocked by the revelation that he wasn't the only Starkiller Darth Vader had re-created. This he had never been told. The possibility hadn't even been insinuated— although he should have guessed.

How many had come before him? How many had died before they had ever truly lived? Could his creator possibly be telling the truth about their stubborn emotional imprints? He spared no feelings for the father he could no longer remember or the boy he had stopped being long ago. It didn't seem remotely possible that any version of Starkiller could do anything other than share that love for Juno Eclipse.

Another vivid memory tore through him.

Staring down in shock at the sight of his Master's lightsaber protruding from his stomach. Unbearable pain. Falling heavily to his knees with a choked scream.

And another woman's voice, the dying words of a Jedi Master he had killed.

"The Sith always betray one another—but I'm sure you'll learn that soon enough."

His mind cleared, and he stared in new understanding at the Dark Lord before him.

Vader was lying. There had been no other clones—or, if there had been, they had felt the same way as him. The original Starkiller had loved Juno Eclipse, and so did he. He was sure of it. He felt it in his bones, in the genetic machinery of his cells. It was the one thing he was sure of.

Vader wanted to weaken that certainty, to turn him back into a weapon, by implying that this feeling was spurious.

And worse—the act of killing Juno Eclipse was symbolic only, here in the Vader's secret cloning laboratory. How long until that became Juno's *actual* slaughter? Would that have been the next stage in his training?

The hum of the Dark Lord's lightsaber changed pitch slightly as Vader shifted position.

Before Vader could strike, Starkiller turned. He didn't activate his own lightsabers. Vader would expect be expecting that—a defensive pose, or at best a halfhearted attack. Starkiller would surprise him with the one weapon Vader couldn't wield in return.

A burst of lightning arced from Starkiller's fingers. Too late, the Dark Lord raised his lightsaber to catch the attack. Lightning crawled up and down his chest plate and helmet, provoking a painful whine from his breathing apparatus. The servomotors in his right arm strained.

Starkiller had only a split second before his former Master repelled the attack. The Force flowed through him. Droid parts and debris rose up and spun around the room. With a harsh rending sound, the metal wall burst outward, letting in the fury of the storm.

But even in the grip of his passions he knew that there was a difference. He was intimately familiar with what being driven by negative emotions felt like. His original had been a slave to the dark side until Juno and Kota had shown him how to be free. That legacy remained even now. He would choose the emotions that ruled him. He would not be a slave to them.

The dark side tugged at Starkiller, and it was hard to resist. He hated his former Master. He feared for Juno. He doubted the very fact of his existence. Killing the man who had created him would go some way to solving at least two of those problems. The temptation was very strong.

Vader's blade caught the edge of the lightning. The Dark Lord began to straighten.

Starkiller leapt for the hole he had torn through the wall and entered the storm. He jumped high and long, aiming for the landing platform he had located by hearing alone, weeks ago.

He came down with a solid thud on the slick metal platform, just meters from Vader's TIE fighter. Lightning split the sky into a thousand pieces. Thunder boomed. Far below, and all around, the sea raged.

The rain and wind scoured him clean. He opened his mouth and felt moisture on his tongue for the first time in thirteen days. After so long in the pit, it tasted like freedom itself.

His arrival took the squadron of stormtroopers guarding the facility by surprise, but they reacted quickly enough. Sirens sounded. Blaster rifles came up to target him. Three AT-STs standing guard over the landing platform clanked and began to turn.

Starkiller bared his teeth. His heart beat with an excitement he hadn't felt since his awakening in Vader's laboratory. This was why he had been made. This was why he existed.

He reached out with his hands and flexed his will. The Force responded, swelling and rising in him like an invisible muscle. A nearby communications tower groaned and twisted. Sparks flew. He wrenched the tower down and sideways, sweeping it over the platform, knocking the AT-STs into the ocean and crushing the stormtroopers gathering to rush him.

Something exploded—a generator, pushed far beyond its capacity. Through the exploding shell of shrapnel stalked a black figure holding a red lightsaber. Vader was moving with surprising speed.

Starkiller almost smiled. Vader's rage was not so easily escaped. But he had done it once before. He would do it again.

The starfighter behind him was unharmed by the devastation he had wrought. Starkiller ran to it and leapt inside. He worked its familiar controls with confident speed, activating systems still warm from its last flight. Its ion engines snarled.

An invisible fist gripped the starfighter. Starkiller increased the thrust. His determination met Darth Vader's rage, and for an instant he was unsure which would win.

Then all resistance fell away, and the TIE fighter leapt for the sky. He fell back into the seat and watched the black storm clouds approach him. Electrical discharges danced around the cockpit. Darkness briefly shrouded him.

Then he was through and above the clouds and rocketing high into the atmosphere. The planetary shield surrounding Kamino was designed to keep ships out, not in, so he passed easily through their visible barrier. Stars appeared, and Vader was far behind.

Now what?

He didn't dare believe that he was entirely free, or that Juno was entirely safe. He had to find her before Vader did. He had to be with her.

Every breath he took filled him with the certainty of that fact. This was the emotion that would rule him, not revenge or bloodlust or despair. But how to pursue this mission? Where did he start looking for one woman in an entire galaxy?

"Starkiller's former conspirator has been captured."

General Kota. If anyone knew where she was, it would be him.

As the cloud-racked face of Kamino receded behind him, Starkiller locked in a course for Cato Neimoidia.

CHAPTER 2

Four days earlier . . .

THE *SOLIDARITY* SHONE like a miniature star in the reflected light of Athega system's blazing primary. The streamlined, organic-looking star cruiser, a recent Mon Calamari model, hung in the shadow of volcanic Nkllon, a small world about as inhospitable as any Juno could imagine. There the *Solidarity* and its small flotilla of attendant vessels were simultaneously hidden from any passing gaze and shielded from the blazing, hull-stripping light of the deadly sun.

"Your request to come aboard has been granted," Juno's second in command said. Nitram spoke cautiously, as though reluctant to intrude on her mood. "The shuttle is ready to launch."

Juno didn't blame him. Knowing what she faced, she had been tense throughout the journey, and her crew had left her alone, which was exactly what she had needed. She had a lot to consider where the Alliance leadership was concerned.

"Thank you, Nitram. You have the helm until I return."

He saluted, touching his left ear with the tip of one paw-like hand. "Yes, sir."

She strode unhesitatingly from the bridge, keen to give the impression that she had no doubts at all about her return, when in fact there were no certainties at all. She had put her ship at risk to assist Kota on one of his unauthorized missions. In the past, the success of Kota's missions had protected her from disciplinary action. This time, she had no such recourse. Officers had been demoted for much less.

The short hop in the shuttle seemed to pass in seconds. She saluted the escort awaiting her at the other end, keeping the fear that it was there to take her prisoner deeply concealed.

"Welcome aboard, Captain. Commodore Viedas is expecting you. This way, please."

The detail fell in around her, and she matched their pace step for step. Around them, the ship hummed with industry and discipline, its white fittings clean and well maintained. Her ship, the *Salvation,* seemed old and clunky by comparison. It had been liberated from the Empire during a skirmish over Ylesia and renamed in the style of the fledgling Rebellion. The *Salvation* still bore the scars of battle, unlike the *Solidarity,* which looked brand new.

The issue of the ships making up the Alliance's fleet occupied more than her own mind, as she discovered on being admitted into the commodore's secure conference room.

Yat-de Viedas was a Rodian, and a natural for enlistment with the Rebel forces, given the Empire's xenophobic stance on non-humans. A privateer of some standing, he had risen quickly through the ranks of the Corellian Resistance, ultimately to be hand-picked by Garm Bel Iblis to lead the attack group Juno belonged to. He was short, and his Basic became increasingly accented under stress, but he was liked and respected by his officers. Juno had served with him briefly after the birth of the Rebel Alliance on Kashyyyk, and she knew that, whatever came next, it wouldn't be born from maliciousness or ill feeling on his part.

"I'll hear nothing bad said about the MC-Eighty." Viedas was pacing from one end of the conference room to the other, addressing the rest of the small gathering. Present via hologram were Mon Mothma and Garm Bel Iblis, presumably from their respective homeworlds. The Senators looked stressed and didn't notice Juno's entry. Princess Leia Organa attended in person. She returned Juno's salute with a respectful nod.

So far, thought Juno, *so good.*

"The redundancy of its shield system is of prime advantage," Viedas was saying. "I cannot overemphasize how important this is in conflicts against the Empire. We will always be outweaponed, so defense should always be our first priority."

"I understand, Commodore," said Mon Mothma. "But the simple fact is that we can't afford any more of them. Not at the moment. Our resources are stretched too far as it is."

"If the Mon Calamari won't give them to us," said Bel Iblis, "then we must take them."

"We're not pirates," said Leia. "My father would not agree to this."

"Your father isn't here. Perhaps if we had greater access to *his* resources—"

Juno cleared her throat, and the commodore turned to face her.

"Ah, good. Captain Eclipse, would you care to report the outcome of your mission to Cato Neimoidia?"

"Of course, sir." She came deeper into the room, trying to take the measure of the meeting. Clearly something had leaked. Someone on her bridge, or perhaps in the starfighter squadrons, had let slip what had happened, so the people before her already knew part of it. The question was: Would they give her a fair hearing, or had they already made up their minds?

"My orders were explicit," she said, deciding to draw the picture in black and white herself and thereby disallow any enemies she might have the advantage. "Gather intelligence, shake up my crew. That's all. When the opportunity came to assist General Kota in his mission to kill the Imperial administrator on Cato Neimoidia, I decided to do so."

"What kind of assistance did you provide?" Bel Iblis asked without any sign of prejudgment. She knew that he would be interested, first and foremost, in the military angle.

"We acted as a distraction for the ground forces, primarily by launching starfighters, but also by making the frigate's presence known. We jammed signals in and out, inasmuch as we could. The *Salvation* engaged directly with the enemy only when it became clear that General Kota required our active support."

"Did he know you were going to be there?" asked Mon Mothma, who no doubt cared less about the tactical details than the circumstances under which the brief alliance had come about.

"He did, Senator," Juno said.

"And how did he come to be privy to this information?"

"Because I told him two days in advance."

"I see." Mon Mothma's lips tightened. "Would you care to explain why?"

"I wasn't aware that I was required to keep secrets from a general in the Rebel Alliance."

"But you *are* aware, no doubt, that the general's actions are not always sanctioned by the Alliance."

"Yes, Senator."

"Do you consider yourself to be part of his renegade campaign?"

"No, Senator."

"Yet you disobey orders in order to help him. How do you explain that?"

Juno felt as though the deck were slipping out from beneath her. She wondered again who had sold her out, and if she would get the chance to find out why before she was decommissioned, maybe worse. "Permission to speak freely, Senator."

"Granted," said Garm Bel Iblis.

Mon Mothma glanced at him in surprise and some annoyance, but didn't countermand him.

"I have helped General Kota before," Juno said, "on Druckenwell, Selonia, and Kuat. Each time, his missions were successful in helping the Alliance. Each time, my assistance cost the Alliance nothing. I took no orders from him, and he accepted the limitations of our arrangement. He knew that the responsibilities of my command took precedence over the success of his mission." *At least I hope he did,* she added silently to herself. "We were on the same side, Senator, and I am not ashamed of helping him. I would help him again, in a heartbeat." *If I could.*

Everyone started to speak at once, but it was Mon Mothma's voice that carried the moment.

"Did you know about this, Commodore?"

"No, Senator, but I take full responsibility." Viedas's green skin had turned faintly purple around the edges. Juno hoped that didn't mean *anger* among his species.

"Commodore Viedas couldn't have known," she said. "I was careful to keep it a secret from him, because I knew that he would not approve."

"Did you take any losses, Captain?" asked Mon Mothma.

"Six starfighters," she said. "That's less than our last official mission, which was considered a success."

"I want more details," said Bel Iblis, leaning forward in the hologram to steeple his fingers. "What did your collaboration with Kota gain us?"

"Well, we know that Cato Neimoidia is better defended than we initially thought. It's taken some hits and brought in reinforcements. The Empire knows we're watching the slave industry now. Baron Tarko will be more cautious in how he mistreats his 'stock.'"

"So he's still alive?"

"I'm afraid so."

"You said *were*," put in Leia. "You and Kota *were* on the same side."

Juno couldn't meet the Princess's observant eye. It was she who worried Juno more than the others. Her father had been an old friend of the general. They had known each other longer than Juno had been alive.

"Kota fell on Cato Neimoidia," Juno said. "His end of our joint mission was not successful."

The air in the conference room seemed to solidify as the news sank in.

"Did you *try*—" Bel Iblis began, but cut himself off. The thought didn't need to be finished.

"You were constrained by your orders," said Mon Mothma, nodding. "That I understand. But do you see where you have left us? By assisting Kota—by actively *encouraging* him in his reckless solo campaign against the Empire—you have cost the Rebel Alliance our most experienced general. Can you honestly say that we have benefited from this outcome?"

Juno met the Senator's accusatory stare without flinching. "I believe he would have died anyway—perhaps long before now—without my help. You know his history as well as I do. He was never going to sit around and watch as opportunities came and went."

"She's right," said Bel Iblis. "The longer we wait, the more people like Kota we're going to lose."

"But if we attack now, we might lose *everything*." The passion in Mon Mothma's voice was naked. Even by hologram, the mixture of grief and determination could not be mistaken. "Renegades like Kota would have us die by degrees or burn in one final conflagration. There must be another way!"

"There is," said Juno.

All eyes turned back to her.

This was the moment she had prepared for all the way from Cato Neimoidia. She wasn't going to let it slip through her fingers.

"We've lost a general," she said, "and we must mourn him. But we can't let a setback like this knock us off course." She said the words with a faint sense of déjà vu, remembering the traumatic times after the agreement on Kashyyyk—except then they had been Kota's words, not hers. "We must find a replacement for him—a military leader who will rally people to our cause—someone who comes with his own resources, as Kota did, but someone who also captures the perfect balance of action and caution we need to embody, if we're going to win this war."

"Do you have someone in mind, Captain?" asked Mon Mothma.

She was ready for this, too. "I've been hearing about a Mon Calamari called Ackbar, a slave we rescued from the Eriadu system—"

"Captain Ackbar has pledged his support of the Alliance. We already have him on our side."

"But we don't have his people," Juno persisted. "They were among the slaves Kota tried to free on Cato Neimoidia. If we can earn the support of the Mon Calamarians, then we get their soldiers and their ships with them. Didn't I just hear you talking about the MC-Eighty star cruisers as I came in? Imagine if we had the resources of the entire Mon Cal shipyards at our disposal! Wouldn't the Emperor have to sit up and take notice of us then?"

Viedas nodded, and so did Bel Iblis. "He would have no choice," said the Senator from Corellia.

"There are no guarantees the Dac resistance movement will ever join our cause," said Mon Mothma. "We've approached them several times. They remain unconvinced we mean business."

"Actions speak louder than words," said Bel Iblis.

"I agree," said Juno. "A decisive strike against the Empire on Dac, with the support of Captain Ackbar, and they'll come around for sure. It's exactly the opportunity we need."

"And what if it goes wrong?" asked Mon Mothma. "What if this mission fails, as Kota's did, and we lose Ackbar, as well? Then we'd be even worse off than we are now."

Juno felt some of the frustration that must have boiled inside Kota, ever since the optimistic early days of the Alliance. She wasn't afraid for herself and the fate of her career. The Alliance itself was at stake now, bound up in endless bickering and disputes.

"Princess," she said, "you're very quiet."

Leia looked up at her. "I don't feel that I can offer an opinion without further consultation."

"But your father has the deciding vote, and you represent him, so—"

"So I would like to consult with him before I cast that vote, if you don't mind."

The firmness of the rebuff took Juno by surprise. She had felt sure that Leia's opinion would be the same as hers. It was she, after all, who had cemented the agreement on Kashyyyk, she who had chosen *his* family's crest to represent the hope they all had felt, then, for the future.

It didn't help that Bel Iblis looked as frustrated as Juno felt.

"We mustn't rush in, Juno," said Mon Mothma, her tone ameliorating now that it was clear she had the upper hand. "Kota has barely been gone a day, and threats close in on all sides. Let us choose carefully. Let's not be blinded as Kota was by the dream of an easy victory. We learned the hard way that this will never be our lot."

Juno knew she was thinking of the Death Star, still lurking somewhere in an unknown state of readiness. They had come so close to the Emperor and failed to take him down. Had they only succeeded then, they would never have been having this conversation.

Juno forced herself to use the only name she could bear to think of *him* as, anymore.

"You wouldn't be saying that if Starkiller were here."

Mon Mothma's expression hardened. "He's not here, so the point is irrelevant."

"I think you've said enough, Captain Eclipse," interrupted Commodore Viedas with a pronounced Rodian lisp. "Leave us now, while we discuss what happens next."

"I'm prepared to resign my commission over this," Juno said, reaching up to tug off the four red pips of her captain's insignia. The very thought of it pained her, but to stand aside and do nothing, to wait while a golden opportunity slipped them by . . .

"Don't be so hasty," said the commodore. "We might well court-martial you first."

She dropped her hands to her sides, feeling nothing but defeat. Of course: That was what he had meant by *what happens next.* Adding impulsive defiance to her case wasn't going to help the matter of her disobedience with regard to orders.

"Yes, sir," she said, snapping off a quick salute. "I await your decision."

"Corporal Sparks will show you to the officers' mess."

The door opened behind her, and she exited quickly, without glancing at Mon Mothma or Leia. Garm Bel Iblis gave her an encouraging look, but he was as powerless as she was, outvoted by his co-leaders of the Alliance and hemmed in by logistical realities. Without ships, they couldn't fight; if they couldn't fight, they'd never get any more ships. At this rate, the Rebellion would either tear itself apart or die of attrition before another year was out.

She was shown to the mess by a bright-eyed young woman who looked barely old enough to be a private, let alone a corporal. Advancement came quickly in any movement afflicted by heavy losses. In the mess, Juno was offered refreshments and a chance to rest, but she declined everything. She simply stared out the viewport at the vistas of molten Nkllon and its fiery sun. She imagined that she could feel the heat even through half a meter of transparisteel, burning her defenses away.

Finally she felt a hand on her shoulder. She turned to find none other than Commodore Viedas standing behind her.

"I thought I'd better come myself to give you the news," he said. "I'm sorry, Captain, but we're standing you down from the *Salvation*. The demotion is only temporary, while Senator Mothma goes over the case again, and may not last longer than a day or two. Both of you just need an opportunity to cool down. I hope you understand."

She bit down on her disappointment and the urge to argue. Viedas was going out of his way to explain, something he was under no compunction to do. "Yes, sir. I understand."

"In the meantime, the Princess sent you this," he added, patting the head of a blue-and-white astromech droid she hadn't even noticed at his side. "She hopes that you will put it to good use."

"I'm sorry, sir?"

"She understands that you have a faulty droid in your possession. He's being brought from the *Salvation* as we speak. The corporal will show you to a maintenance suite that has been put at your disposal. You have the time to see to your droid now, and I suggest you don't waste it."

With that, he left her. Juno watched him go, frowning. What did he care about her droid? What did the Princess?

"Is it possible," she asked herself, "that I'm dreaming all this?"

The R2 unit burbled something electronic she couldn't understand. It didn't help.

"This way," said the perky corporal, reappearing at her side.

"After you," Juno told her. The R2 trundled patiently in their wake.

PROXY was already waiting for her when she arrived, stretched out on an examination table in a private workshop. His familiar, skeletal form was dented and scarred by countless rough patch jobs and the occasional field welding. His yellow eyes were extinguished now, as they had been for months. Just seeing him made her uncomfortable for reasons she found difficult to express, even to herself. Surely she should be over it all by now?

"Let's fire him up," she told the R2 unit when the corporal had gone, "and see what you can do."

She reached a hand into PROXY's innards to reactivate his power supply, but instead of moving to help her, the R2 unit rolled back a step and projected a hologram onto the floor between them.

"I apologize for the deception, Juno," a miniature version of Princess Leia told her. The recording had been taken not long ago: She was still wearing the clothes she had worn to Juno's interview; only the background had changed. "I hope you'll forgive me for not standing up for you before. I cannot speak freely, even when I know what my father would have me say. While he is in hiding, it's my job to keep the Alliance together, and I know you appreciate how hard a job that is. Mon Mothma is my friend and teacher; I would not defy her openly, when we all know that what she says is at least in part correct. We *must* proceed cautiously. But at the same time, we must act decisively. No agreement is possible—so it's better that she doesn't know what you are about to do."

Juno squatted down in front of the hologram, feeling a faint revival of hope within her.

"Artoo-Detoo here will do what he can for your droid," the

Princess went on. "You'll need help convincing the Mon Calamari and the Quarren to join our cause, even with Ackbar on your side. I've arranged for one agent of the Organa household to meet you and PROXY at Dac's Moon and coordinate the rendezvous, but that's all the help I can spare you, I'm afraid. From here on, it's up to you." She smiled. "I'd wish you good luck, Juno, but I'm hoping you won't need it."

With that, the recording fizzled out, looped back to the beginning, and started to play itself again.

"That's enough," Juno told the R2 unit.

She settled back onto her haunches to think.

Leia wanted her to bring the Mon Calamari to the Alliance table without Mon Mothma learning of it. Did Garm Bel Iblis know? Probably not, since he was elsewhere in the galaxy and even private transmissions could be overheard. But Commodore Viedas had to be part of the scheme. It was he who decided how officers in his attack group were disciplined—in Juno's case by relieving her of her command—and he who had delivered the droid to her. He was definitely a conspirator in the plan to give Juno not just the means to complete this mission, but the opportunity.

Yet without the *Salvation* behind her, she wondered, what could she possibly achieve in the fight against the Empire?

She snorted at her own cowardice. What *couldn't* she achieve, without that great lumbering mass of responsibility hanging over her head? Kota had been a master of this kind of work, employing small teams of handpicked militia in fast strikes to achieve well-defined outcomes. If he could do it, so could she.

"Hello, Juno," said a familiar voice from the table. "I can't tell you how relieved I am to see you again."

She braced herself to look at PROXY, but the sight still came as a shock.

Sitting on the table was a perfect replica of *him*. Of Starkiller. Of the man she had loved, who was now stone-dead—but recreated down to the last detail by the droid that had served him.

"Artoo-Detoo, was it?"

The droid beeped happily.

"See what you can do to fix his faulty holographic circuits," she ordered. "His primary programming is gone, too, but I can live with that if you can fix the other. It's been getting worse, ever since we found him on Corellia."

"Thank you," said the perfect image of Starkiller as the R2 unit moved in. He was wearing the same Jedi uniform the real one had worn during the attack on the Death Star. "I am aware that I cause you distress. It would please me to serve you again, as my master wished."

"Stop," she said, raising a hand and turning away. "Just stop."

"Yes, Captain Eclipse."

She held her breath until the little droid went to work, and the crackling of an electric arc banished all possibility of conversation.

CHAPTER 3

Present day . . .

CATO NEIMOIDIA'S ORBITAL LANES buzzed with nervous activity. A strong Imperial presence vied with a steady flow of freighters to and fro, many of them escorted by TIE fighter or mercenary squadrons. Even from orbit, Starkiller could see evidence of recent military activity, particularly a deep black scorch mark near one of the planet's famous hanging cities. Some kind of heavy munitions had been in play, although probably not nuclear. There was no sign of evacuation of the nearby populace.

Starkiller had never had cause to come to this world before, not during his brief period of recruitment for the nascent rebellion, nor during his first apprenticeship to Darth Vader, when his role had been as much assassin as apprentice. Indeed, surviving and defeating those who challenged his former Master had been as important a part of his former self's training as anything on the *Executor.* Those challengers had been his first real targets, apart from PROXY droids. Only when he had proven himself capable had the Dark Lord deemed him worthy of combat with him.

Starkiller orbited Cato Neimoidia once, safe in Darth Vader's TIE fighter, and simply stared. He had been down a pit on Kamino for thirteen days, and in Vader's clutches for what felt like a lifetime. He had forgotten what sunlight looked like. He had forgotten what it felt like to be a free agent. There was so much he had forgotten, and so much that was slowly coming back to him.

Juno.

She felt strangely close, even though he had no reason to suspect that she was nearby. In his mind, she was coming clearer with every hour. He couldn't believe that she had almost slipped away. Oh, he understood it well enough. He knew all about Darth Vader's mind games and the power of the dark side. He had lived with it, and prospered from that, too, in his original lifetime. He could exert his will over others in order to get what he wanted, but he didn't doubt that . . . didn't doubt that Vader had almost succeeded in driving every last memory of the woman Starkiller had loved from his mind.

Now she was back, and it seemed incomprehensible to him that she had ever gone away. Even when he had lost everything in his former life, when every last hope of victory had been taken from him, he had thought of her. His demise had meant nothing compared with the knowledge that she had escaped safely from the Emperor's deadly space station.

Then . . . death. And revival. And forgetting, powerlessness, and fear.

But now he was back. Nothing could stand between him and Juno. Not for long, anyway. With her ahead of him, leading him on, he felt stronger than ever.

From the depths of his memory, he heard the murdered Jedi Master Shaak Ti: *"You could be so much more."*

Then his own voice, speaking not to her, but to Juno, in another place, another time: *"The Force is stronger than anything we can imagine. We're the ones who limit it, not the other way around."*

Starkiller breathed deeply and closed his eyes. His mind was just one speck in the endlessly shifting sea that was the galaxy. He felt the eddies and currents of the combined life force of every living thing sway through him—and with only a small effort he detached himself from himself and joined that flow, seeking the one he needed.

The roar of a crowd filled his mind. Movement scattered his

mental vision, made it hard to make out anything specific. Was that fluttering wings, or banners? He couldn't quite tell. Figures that might have been beings glowed blue all around him. Above him hung a giant eye, staring downward.

Are you still with me, Kota?

His vision shifted, became red-tinged—*deeply* red, as though someone had cut the throat of a giant beast and drained it onto the ground. Something snarled. Something roared. There was a flurry of limbs, a wild rush of violent intent.

"It's all in your mind, boy," said Kota from his memory.

Green light flashed. More blood. Severed limbs fell onto the dirt. The crowd roared.

General Rahm Kota, leaning back on his heels, breathing heavily, surrounded by a ring of corpses. How long had he been fighting now? Six days? Seven? Fatigue was taking its toll. With every wave he came closer to making a mistake—and when that happened, it would all finally be over.

Starkiller opened his eyes. His lips were pressed into a thin line.

"Hold on, old man," he whispered, and brought Darth Vader's TIE fighter smoothly out of orbit.

The Imperial forces on Cato Neimoidia were clustered around one particular bridge city suspended over a deep sinkhole that led an unfathomable distance into the planet's crust. Why? Perhaps the local dictator liked to throw his prisoners off the edge so they would serve as examples to their friends. Starkiller didn't care. He wasn't going over the edge. He was coming for just one thing: to rescue General Kota, or at the very least learn from him where Juno could be found. Nothing else mattered. Not even the endless vistas of space, or the light of an unfamiliar sun.

His ship had been noticed the very moment he had arrived. On descent, it was immediately joined by a full escort of TIE fighters, acting on the assumption that the being piloting it was Darth Vader, the Emperor's chief enforcer, as its transponder code suggested. Starkiller didn't disabuse them of this notion. Anything that eased the path ahead was fine by him. The TIEs broadcast warnings and cleared a landing bay ahead of him, and then peeled off to resume their regular duties. He brought his stolen starfighter safely to a halt on the swaying platform, conscious but not caring that there was nothing between him and the sinkhole below but several layers of metal. It might intimidate others, but it made no difference to him.

Several skiffs parked on the platform had scattered as he approached the waiting hangar. A squadron of stormtroopers stood to attention in two perfectly parallel lines, their weapons honorific, not threatening. If Vader had guessed that he was coming here, word had not yet reached the local potentate. That was good.

He landed, shut down the engines with smooth efficiency, and climbed out of the pilot's seat. The hatch opened with a hiss. His booted feet hit the hot metal of the landing deck with a ringing boom.

A new person had arrived, a balding man dressed in heavy robes with Imperial insignia mixed with Neimoidian trappings, standing at the head of the double line of troopers. He looked nervous, but that soon turned to puzzlement as Starkiller strode into view.

Starkiller realized only then how he must have looked. The flight suit he wore was torn and filthy, thanks to weeks in Vader's pit and ceaseless combat training. In the former Starkiller's life, he had had the art of stealth and invisibility drummed into him, but he was in too much of a hurry now to worry about that.

"I was expecting Lord Vader," said the robed man—the potentate himself, judging by the air of authority he thought he radiated.

Starkiller recognized his voice; he had heard it in a vision on Kamino, saying, *"Try the Corellian razor hounds."*

This was time for neither small talk nor mystical catch-ups.

"The Jedi," Starkiller said. "Where is he?"

"He's alive, for the moment."

"I asked *where* he is."

The robed man straightened, sensing a challenge. "What are the security codes for this sector?"

Starkiller ignored the question and kept walking between the double lines of stormtroopers.

"The security codes!"

With a rattle of plastoid, the stormtroopers shifted their weapons to point at him. The robed man drew a blaster and aimed with a steady hand.

The Imperials stood between Starkiller and Kota. With a tightening of his lips that might have been a smile, Starkiller ignited his lightsabers.

"Kill him!" ordered the potentate, snapping off two precise shots. Starkiller deflected both of them harmlessly into the floor. The troopers opened fire on both sides, and he turned to deflect the incoming blaster bolts. In the corner of his eye, he saw the potentate heading for the turbolift.

Not so fast, he thought, reaching out to pull the man back.

The lift doors opened, and a pair of heavily armed troopers emerged, already firing. Pressed on three sides, Starkiller forced himself to forget about the potentate and concentrate on the immediate threats. Blaster bolts ricocheted wildly around him, deflected by his double blades and hitting neck joints, visors, and breathing systems. Missiles from the newly arrived pair peppered him, filling the air with smoke. His Force shield kept the worst of their effects at bay, and he pressed forward, reaching out to telekinetically crush the missile launchers and trigger the remaining charges. With a bright flash and a deafening boom, the last of his obstacles disappeared.

A powerful excitement thrilled through him. For the first time, in the middle of combat, it came to him that he was truly alive. He wasn't a shadow lurking in a hole somewhere, dreaming of being. The Force was with him, and he was free. He was free, and he had a mission.

The potentate was long gone. Starkiller tore his way into the turbolift shaft, bypassing security codes by means of sheer power, and rode to the upper levels. The transparisteel walls revealed the hanging city in all its glory, curving away from him to his left and right, but he wasn't interested in taking in the sights. He studied the buildings looking only for tactical information. The vision of Kota had hinted at an open space and a large gathering of people. The scans he had taken from orbit hadn't showed anyplace like that. The largest structure in the city was the Imperial barracks, a circular building at its direct center.

When the turbolift reached the summit and the doors opened on the city, he was greeted by the distant roaring of a crowd.

He stepped out and listened closely. The roar was coming from the barracks.

He set off on foot, running swiftly through the streets. They were only sparsely populated, with the occasional green-skinned Neimoidian scuttling by, determinedly staying out of his way. He could hear no audible alarms, but had no doubt that they were ringing somewhere. That suspicion was confirmed at the sound of booted feet stamping along the streets behind him.

He shifted to an aerial route, climbing to the top of the nearest building and leaping from it to the next in line. That way he could avoid the roads entirely. He felt weightless as he swung from hand-hold to handhold with the Force thrilling through him like the purest oxygen. The city's lower levels clustered around the bases of several broad, circular towers, connected by looping tramlines, and it was a simple matter to travel from one to the other into the city's heart, as light as air itself.

When the Imperial security forces got wise to his plan and ac-tivated gun emplacements in the city's upper levels, things became considerably more interesting.

Dodging weapons fire from tram-track to building and back again, Starkiller felt a familiar calm creeping over him. It was a calm born not of peace or tranquillity, but of violence and anger. Countless hours of meditating on the dark side, fueling the nega-tive energies that Darth Vader encouraged him to embrace, made this kind of combat trance almost second nature to him. Fighting people was harder than fighting PROXY droids, but there was a greater pleasure in it too, more of a challenge. A warrior who fought only rationally and without emotion fought exactly like a droid. People were stranger, more unpredictable, and therefore fundamentally more difficult to defeat. He swung his lightsabers as though in slow motion. He watched reflected energy bolts creep between him and his targets with a laziness that belied their deadly power.

Once, in his other life, he had been sent to Ragna III to quell an uprising of the hostile Yuzzem. Barely twelve years old, he had been betrayed by the weapons his own Master had given him. All had failed on landing, along with his starship, leaving him armed only with the Force and his wits. Singlehandedly, he had fought to the nearest Imperial installation and escaped off-world, expecting either rebuke for failing his mission or praise for having survived. He had received neither—and the memory of his puzzlement came to him now, as clear as the crystal in the heart of his first lightsaber. The lesson hadn't been to survive, he had eventually come to understand: it had been to come to terms with his own destructive power. In his wake, he had left dozens of Yuzzem injured or dead. Until it had been forced upon him, he had never known just what he was capable of—and just how little praise he needed to keep on doing it.

Later in that other life, Starkiller had raged against all the deaths he had caused in the service of his dark Master. Starkiller had been Darth Vader's weapon, aimed squarely at the Emperor's enemies, and nothing, he had sworn, would stand in his way. Only at the last minute had he swerved aside, deflected by Juno's love from his former purpose, to another he had been unable to complete. He was no one's weapon now but his own, but he still felt an echo of that remorse, that nagging feeling that killing wasn't the answer, despite the calm acceptance he felt while waging war on Kota's captives. Trained for violence, remade in violence, he struggled with the concept that anything other than violence might constitute a solution to any problem, but he was willing even in the heat of his familiar battle trance to entertain the possibility.

The crowd noise grew steadily louder as he approached the barracks—chanting, roaring, filled with mob fury. The weapons fire concentrated on him intensified, too. Jump troopers equipped with jetpacks were beginning to converge on his location. He angled toward a slender tower connected to the barracks by several high-rise accessways. When he was within leaping distance, he jumped for one of its transparisteel viewing platforms, lightsabers stabbing ahead of him. The window shattered.

He rolled across the platform and came up running for the stairs. Bystanders leapt out of his path, waving their upper limbs and screaming for help. They were extravagantly dressed, and few of them were Neimoidians. Humans vastly outnumbered aliens. They didn't look like Imperial officers, though.

Starkiller ground his teeth together as he entered what looked like nothing so much as a casino. That was why there were so many extra ships around the Imperial compound: the potentate was running a decidedly non-official credit-making venture on the side. He was no different from the many Starkiller had rooted out for Darth Vader while still in the service of the Empire. Venal, self-serving, and cruel, they squeezed their minions with an iron grip while at the same time currying favor from those like them higher up the chain.

The Empire's well-being was no longer his concern, but the galaxy as a whole would be better off if he took another corrupt Imperial down along the way.

He could feel the crowd's roar through the soles of his feet. He was close now, very close. The casino's defenses were tight but no match for him. What he couldn't fight through, he simply destroyed. At the final juncture, he guided a sky-tram off its tracks and into the side of the building, tearing a hole large enough for an army to burst through. He jumped into the maelstrom of sparks and molten metal and ran to where he could sense Kota, still fighting for his life in the potentate's theater of death.

One long, straight corridor led to a double door made of durasteel. It was guarded by six stormtroopers. Starkiller didn't bother stopping to fight them. With a gesture, he pushed them aside, then burst open the doors.

The full-throated roar of the crowd hit him hard, like a physical blow. He slowed to a walk as he passed through the door and found himself in a giant stone arena—a combat zone painted red with blood, exactly as he had seen in his vision. The steep sides were full of spectators, but only a handful were present in the flesh. The rest attended via hologram. Their blue, flickering fists, claws, or tentacles were upraised, chanting in numerous languages at once.

Starkiller didn't understand what they were saying, but he could work out the gist of it.

"Kill, kill, kill!"

In the center of the arena, surrounded by a legion of dead and wounded assailants, was Rahm Kota. One fist was wrapped tightly around the throat of a dying stormtrooper. His green lightsaber blazed as he raised it to deliver the killing blow. Starkiller felt the stirring of another memory: he had been in such positions before, tossed into arenas and forced to kill everyone who came against him. That was for training, though. He didn't think there was anything remotely educational about this spectacle.

"Kota!" he cried.

The aging general raised his head, searching for the source of the voice over the baying of the crowd. "It can't be . . ."

Starkiller ran out into the center of the arena. The crowd howled and hissed.

From far above came a booming command. "Send out the Gorog!"

Starkiller came to a halt in front of his second Master.

"By the Force," Kota whispered, staring at him with eyes that no longer worked—thanks to an injury Starkiller himself had delivered—but seemed to see regardless. His exhaustion radiated from his filthy skin like the heat of a sun. He was battered and weary and on the verge of collapse. He staggered back, looking almost drunk with fatigue. "I saw you die . . ."

"You saw me in your future, too."

"I did, but—"

A series of thudding clangs came from a vast gate on the other side of the arena, and the huge metal doors began to open. From the darkness on the other side came a vicious snarl.

Starkiller turned to face the latest threat.

"Why don't you sit this one out, General?"

Kota gripped Starkiller's shoulder and bared his teeth. "Never. I've got a score to settle."

Something moved on the other side of the gates. Something heavy and bestial and very, very big.

Starkiller grinned back, although he didn't know what was funny. He wanted to ask about Juno, but just then wasn't the time. "You were never very good at taking orders."

Out of the darkness thundered a bull rancor, roaring and spraying drool. Starkiller came forward three paces, putting himself squarely between the beast and Kota, feeling nothing but confidence. On Felucia, his former self had defeated just such a beast. This one, he was sure, would prove to be as significant a foe. He raised his lightsaber to strike.

There was something wrong with the way it was running, though. Its eyes were wide and staring, but they weren't quite focusing on either Starkiller or Kota, and the light he saw in them wasn't fury. It was something else, something Starkiller didn't immediately comprehend.

"I don't care whether the restraints have been tested or not," boomed the voice a second time. "Open the Gorog gate now!"

Starkiller recognized the voice as belonging to the potentate who had "welcomed" him on the landing deck, and heard another loud clang. The bull rancor glanced over its shoulder, and Starkiller realized then that it wasn't running toward him, but away from something else.

The look in its eyes was *fear*.

Through the open gate behind the rancor came a giant hand, attached to an arm as thick as a small cruiser. Each clawed finger was as long as a starfighter. With surprising speed, it reached out and snatched the bull rancor off the floor of the arena, right in front of them, and pulled it screaming back into the darkness. Something crunched, and the screams were cut off. Bones cracked and splintered with a sickening sound. Sinewy tissue stretched and tore.

The crowd was utterly silent, now. Not a soul moved.

Starkiller backed up a step, staring up into the shadows in shock. What exactly had he just seen? Was it a hallucination?

An earsplitting roar came from the darkness, and he braced himself to find out.

CHAPTER 4

·

Two days earlier . . .

DAC'S MOON, Juno very quickly discovered, was as unexciting as its name suggested. It was a gray, airless rock tidally locked to the waterworld it orbited, so its back side pointed endlessly outward at the stars. Juno had spent several hours watching those stars—and the faint specks that indicated ships traveling to and from the Mon Calamari system—waiting for the Organa operative she was slowly beginning to believe wasn't coming at all.

"I have completed my scan of Dac's traffic control," PROXY told her. "There is no mention of a ship or ships intercepted on suspicion of anything related to the Rebel Alliance."

She irritably tapped the controls of the two-seater R-22 Spearhead interceptor she'd found waiting for her in the *Solidarity*'s hangar bay. How long did she have to wait before she gave the mission up as a waste of time? She had better places to stew over her lot than the back side of this sterile dustbowl.

At least, she told herself, PROXY was working properly now. The damage to his holographic camouflage systems that had frozen him in the image of his former Master had been successfully repaired by R2-D2. Only occasionally now did he adopt one of his many stored templates—including Juno's—but most of the time he was just his skinny metal self, with glowing yellow eyes and an unflinching desire to serve her. The latter was the one remaining fragment of his primary programming, given to him by his deceased

Master. The rest had been burned out of him by the Core on Raxus Prime.

"Ten more minutes," she said, "and that's it, Princess or no Princess."

"Will we attempt this mission on our own, Captain Eclipse?"

She had been giving that a lot of thought. "Dac won't save it-self."

But she wasn't Starkiller, and she didn't want to become him. All her life, she had been part of a system. It suited her, the hierarchy of command and her place in it. Yes, she argued sometimes, and she especially didn't like being reprimanded, but on the whole she preferred it to going alone. Nothing had made her happier than when the Rebel Alliance firmed up its command structure, with Bel Iblis providing strategic and tactical advice, Bail Organa or his daughter supplying access to crucial resources and intelligence, and Mon Mothma presenting the public face of the Alliance to those beings who required inspiration. The Alliance fleet didn't have a Supreme Commander per se—it didn't actually have much of a fleet to speak of yet, just a ragtag accumulation of ships—but the fact that a vacancy existed had reassured her. Someone would eventually step up to fill it, she had been certain.

And for a while, the system had worked. Orders filtered down from one commander or another, and the Alliance had held intact. Now, though, with Bail Organa absent and something of a schism developing between Mon Mothma and those of a more military bent, including Bel Iblis, nothing was certain anymore. Who exactly *did* tell Juno where her duties lay? Did the leaders have to take a vote now before making any kind of decision? If Leia Organa felt compelled not to take sides while her father was absent, what happened next time there was an emergency and the Alliance needed to act quickly?

These thoughts circled endlessly through Juno's mind as she waited.

It was an improvement, she supposed, over wishing Starkiller would come back to shake everyone back into line.

"I have detected an approaching vessel," said PROXY.

Juno was instantly alert. "Where?"

Information on the screens in front of them enabled her to locate the tiny dot in the endless starscape. It grew brighter by the second until the blocky outlines of a cargo shuttle became identifiable. Markings on its hull identified it as belonging to a small mining company on the inward face of the moon. It had no visible weapons, no shield, and offered no explanation for its presence. As it neared the surface of the moon, the cargo hatch on its port side opened wide, revealing nothing at all within.

Juno's hands rested on the R-22's controls, ready to fire or flee as circumstances demanded.

Dust puffed as the cargo shuttle touched gently down. From the brightly lit interior unfolded a reticulated loading arm. It pointed once at her starfighter, then once into the shuttle's hold. Juno examined the prospect with a critical eye.

"We could shoot our way out of there if we had to, right?" she asked PROXY.

"I foresee few difficulties on that score," said the droid. "There appears to be no armor on the inside of the shuttle, and its crew space is small."

"Lucky we didn't come in a Y-wing," she muttered as she activated the starfighter's attitude controls, "or we'd never have fit."

The arm folded back into its niche as the R-22 hovered gently across the rocky gray terrain. Juno took it as a personal challenge not to ding either vessel as she slid inside. Such maneuvers were unfamiliar to her after years of fighting combat and recon missions—and, more recently, simply telling the staff of her frigate where to go. She was pleased to feel old reflexes stirring, guiding her hand as much by instinct as by anything her head could identify.

With a gentle thud, the metal surfaces of the two ships met. The cargo shuttle's hatch slid closed. Juno took her hands off the controls and waited.

When the space inside the shuttle had repressurized, a small hatch opened and a tall human male stepped out of the crew chambers. He wore a gray-green pressure suit, minus its helmet, and could have been any one of a million unskilled cargo shufflers from anywhere across the galaxy.

Only he wasn't. Juno recognized him the moment the R-22's landing lights caught his features.

It was Bail Organa.

The starfighter's hatch swung open above her, and he helped her out of the pilot's seat.

"You're a little overqualified for this, aren't you?" she said.

His Serene Highness, Prince Bail Prestor Organa, First Chairman and Viceroy of Alderaan, patted down his oil-smudged outfit. "What, haulage, or convincing the Dac resistance to join the Alliance?"

"Maybe both."

"Well, I offered you a job once, and you said you'd think about it."

"You called me a pilot with a conscience," she said. "I'd never work for someone with such poor judgment of character."

They grinned and shook hands.

"Nice to see you, too, PROXY," he added as the droid unfolded from his own seat. "Come on through."

"So this is how you stay out of the Emperor's scopes," Juno said as he led them into the cramped, ozone-stinking cockpit. He was the shuttle's only occupant.

"Part of the time." He tapped the outdated instrument panel with some affection. "In this I can go practically anywhere, anytime, and no one gives me a second look. Same with this." He indicated the mirror-finished helmet hanging on a rack behind the pilot's chair. "Cheaper than a cloaking device, and no messing around with stygium crystals."

"Tell me about it."

"Oh, yes, you've had experience with them, on the *Rogue Shadow*." He sobered. "I heard about Kota. That's terrible news."

She took the copilot's seat. "It was bound to happen eventually. The man had crazy luck, but it couldn't last forever."

"He made his own luck. As we're about to."

He operated the controls with the ease of recent practice, lifting the cargo shuttle off the surface of the moon with the starfighter safely inside and sending it on a long arc around to the Dac-lit side. Juno noted with approval that he didn't fly *too* well: Anyone watching would see the occasional jerk and misdirection, as they would expect from a clumsy grunt.

"I presume Leia explained the situation," she said.

He nodded. "We're meeting Ackbar in an hour."

"What's the plan?"

"We don't have one yet."

"Where's the rendezvous point, then?"

"A mining colony called Sar Galva."

"Sar Galva is located on the Murul Trench," said PROXY. "We are not designed for aquatic environments."

"No, but the Quarren are, and we need them if we're ever going to get the Dac resistance movement into the Alliance."

Dac rose over the moon's forward horizon—a crystalline blue world streaked with high-altitude clouds. The cargo shuttle glided slowly upward until it broke free of the moon's gentle gravitational pull and began powering for the planet. Its main drive was inefficient and noisy, making conversation difficult. Juno settled back into the seat, thinking over everything she'd learned about the world and its resistance movement before leaving the *Solidarity*.

Home to numerous sentient species, although predominantly the deep-ocean Quarren and the semi-aquatic Mon Calamari, Dac had a long history of conflict with the Empire. With the Declaration of a New Order and the beginning of the Imperial regime, their Senators had been arrested and a new, corrupt regime had been installed, helped by indigenous collaborators who had sabotaged Dac's planetary shield. The takeover of the shipyards and the subjugation of the native population hadn't broken the planet's spirit, however. A resistance movement had struggled on for many years, and then foundered when the Empire destroyed three of the planet's floating cities in reprisal. Since then, Quarren and Mon

Calamari had squabbled more often than they had worked together, and the Empire's grip on their homeworld remained crushingly tight.

Ackbar had been one of the failed resistance movement's earliest and most promising leaders. So impressive had been his fight against the Imperial forces that the officer who had eventually captured him had presented him as a trophy to the Grand Moff in charge of the occupation, who had kept him as a slave for more than a decade. Rescued in one of the Rebel Alliance's earliest coordinated attacks against the Empire, Ackbar had returned to Dac to stir up revolt—and met surprising resistance. Discredited by historians, their shipyards nationalized, and their leaders enslaved, the population of Dac had very nearly lost their spirit. It would take a show of strength to whip them into the proper frame of mind to retake their world.

The shuttle rocked from side to side as it hit atmosphere. Organa pulled back on the throttle, allowing them to talk again.

"Dac has no aerial defenses to speak of," Organa said. "The planetary shields have never been repaired, and the remaining cities suffer constant bombardment. An entire fighter wing is stationed here, its mission to terrorize and to crush any signs of an air force forming. Ackbar has tried, but he can't get so much as a recon droid in the air without it being shot down and his equipment destroyed."

"So where do the Quarren fit into this? They live underwater, not in the air."

"The fighter wing only patrols the air, not the oceans, and particularly not the deep trenches. By following those trenches, the Quarren can go anywhere without being seen. They can construct supply lines, establish headquarters, even build submersible launch platforms that would be less vulnerable to attack than anything on the ground. With the Quarren on their side, the Mon Calamari would have a real chance."

"So what's the problem?"

"You'll see."

Ahead of them, the ocean was rising up rapidly to meet them. Organa did nothing to slow their descent. All he did was tip the shuttle in order to present the smallest possible cross section to the approaching wave tops. At the last instant he fired the forward thrusters on full, not to stop the shuttle but to turn the water ahead of them to steam, cushioning the impact.

Even so, Juno was thrown forward against her harness. A rushing, swirling sound enfolded them, and the deck rocked beneath their feet. The main drive cut out and repulsors kicked in. Instead of pushing up, they pressed the shuttle down against the resistance of the water.

Her ears popped as they dropped rapidly into the depths. Darkness fell outside. The shuttle's many joints and seams creaked under the rising pressure.

Juno felt queasy but refused to let it show.

"I'm guessing," she said, "that the plan is for the resistance to take out the fighter wing and thereby show the locals what they're capable of."

"Spot-on, Captain."

"What's the wing's designation? Would I have heard of them?"

"Quite possibly. It's the Hundred Eighty-first."

She shook her head. "Never come across them before. Just be glad it's not the Black Eight."

"Your old command?"

"I'm sure it's gone downhill since I left," she said, "but I doubt its methods have improved."

She thought of the forests of Callos melting into black sludge and tried not to imagine what Dac would look like after such an attack. Oceans were different from forests, but the principle was the same. Where life got in the way of the Emperor's plans, its very existence was forfeit.

The scopes showed the hard surface of the seabed approaching. Undulating hills punctuated by the occasional sharp spire stretched off into the murky distance, covered with fields of thick, waving weeds. Organa leveled off and headed north. They hadn't traveled far when an enormous chasm opened up before them. The Murul Trench, Juno presumed. Clinging to its side was an artificial structure that projected out over the depths. Several thick cables and pipes stretched vertically downward. What lay at the bottom, Juno couldn't tell. The scopes didn't even show a bottom.

"Welcome to Sar Galva," Organa said as he guided the shuttle to a halt near a docking tube. "This is nominally an Imperial station, but just in case . . ." He handed her a fake ID, which she affixed to her flight uniform. "If anyone asks, my name is Aman Raivans. You're Pyn Robahn."

When the docking tube was empty of water and full of breathable atmosphere, they headed back to the air lock and cycled through. Juno stepped warily into the station, testing the air and finding it more than a little fishy. Literally. Sar Galva stank like an aquarium that hadn't been cleaned for a decade.

Organa led the way. PROXY took up the rear. They passed a checkpoint without incident and headed deeper into the station through a maze of tubes and spherical-shaped compartments. Vast machines chugged and bubbled all around them. Juno didn't have the first idea what the station extracted from the depths; fearing that asking might expose her as an outsider, she stayed quiet.

They passed several bulging-eyed Mon Calamari, but by far the majority of workers here were Quarren, with their tentacled faces and clawed hands. Juno didn't suffer from speciesism as many of her old Imperial colleagues had, but she was still getting used to the variety of beings she encountered through the Alliance. Mon Calamari looked cheerfully guileless to her, while the Quarren were utterly unreadable. The language they used when talking to one another was unlike any other speech she had ever heard. She hoped the individuals she would be dealing with could at least understand Basic.

"Through here, I think," said Organa, waving her ahead of him into a cramped mess.

"You're not sure?"

"Let's just say that down here, everything's uncertain."

The room contained a long table and several individuals. Five orange-skinned Quarren huddled in a group at the far end. Closest to them was a slender Mon Calamari who looked up as they entered. Juno recognized him instantly from holos.

"Senator Organa," Ackbar said, reaching out with one long-fingered hand. "Thank you for coming. And you must be Captain Eclipse."

Juno returned the handshake. Ackbar's skin was damp and cool, and his grip surprisingly strong.

"Don't close the door," he said to PROXY, who had turned to do just that. "We're expecting someone else." The five Quarren looked up, and he introduced them in turn as Siric, Nosaj, Rarl, Cuvran, and Feril. "Siric is an underwater explosives expert," Ackbar explained. "He lost his family during the destruction of the Three Cities. He and his assistants are keen to help in any way they can."

"We're grateful to you for meeting us here," said Organa, offering them a brisk bow. "I'm as keen to see your planet freed as you are."

The Quarren exchanged a handful of short words, none of them in Basic.

"Are they always this conversational?" asked Juno.

"Don't be discouraged," said Ackbar. "They're a brave and proud people, like my own, when roused."

A tenth person came into the room from behind them, and instantly the five Quarren were on their feet, bulbous eyes staring, tentacles waving and fingers pointing. They tongue-spat and snarled in their alien tongue, as much at Ackbar as to the new arrival, who was another Quarren, as impenetrable as the rest.

"This was a mistake," this one said in heavily accented Basic. "I knew I should not have come."

"Stay, Seggor, stay." Ackbar put a hand on the Quarren's arm and turned to the others. "He's here at my invitation," he told the others. "Don't you think I have as much to be angry about as you?"

An uneasy silence fell. Juno studied the dynamic closely as the newcomer eased farther into the room and Ackbar encouraged everyone to sit with him at the table. He introduced the people who didn't know one another in a matter-of-fact way, downplaying the dramatics with his brisk, no-nonsense tone. Juno felt some of the tension ebb, even though it was never remotely close to vanishing.

When it was Seggor Tels's turn to be introduced, he offered a brief explanation regarding his fellows' outrage.

"A young fool I once was," he said. "A fool who thought my enemy's enemy must be my friend. It was I who sabotaged our world's planetary shields, resulting in our home's occupation and my people's enslavement. In the many years since, I have learned to regret that action, and to understand that my kind is not alone in its persecution. We must put aside our differences and work together to reclaim our world. We must stand together."

He addressed them with a conviction that spoke more of necessity than real commitment, but Juno admired the attempt. In the face of years of animosity between his species and the Mon Calamari, plus the very personal antagonism displayed by Siric and the others, he was bravely standing his ground when it would have been much easier simply to go into hiding and never emerge.

"We're here to help you," she said. "If you'll let us."

Siric said something in the Quarren tongue, which Tels translated.

"He says you're only here to help yourselves. You care about starships, not the oceans or the people who live in them."

"The right of all beings to live freely and in peace," said Organa, "is what the Rebel Alliance cares about. Ships will help us, yes, but that's not our primary objective in coming here. We need leaders and soldiers; we need people who will spread the word; we need translators and medics and all manner of specialty. What we need most of all, though, is to know that the people we're fighting for are behind us. We're risking our lives—and the lives of our families—every time we so much as speak out against the Emperor. Forgive us if we ask for a little commitment in return."

Organa's expression was severe, and Juno could tell that he was thinking of more than himself. Now that the Emperor knew he was a traitor, Leia was in constant jeopardy. Only a constant pretense of innocence and compliance had saved her thus far—that and the fact that even the Emperor balked at murdering such a well-known and well-liked young woman.

Tels translated Senator Organa's words, and some of the aggression left the five. Siric looked down at his hands, which were splayed out in front of him. Juno noticed that two of his digits were missing from his right hand. *Explosives expert,* she remembered, and wondered what efforts he had already made to repel the Empire from his world.

"The Hundred Eighty-First fighter wing is based in Heurkea," Ackbar went on, producing a datapad and displaying images as he spoke. The first was a map of the southern territorial zone, with the floating city appropriately marked. "We can approach from the east, behind the cover of Mester Reef. The Hundred Eighty-First patrols every three standard hours, in groups of two, with a ten-minute overlap, but there's a period once every five days when all the pilots are recalled for debriefing. That can last anything up to an hour. The next such briefing is in six hours."

Siric said something in his native tongue.

"I know we have no air force," Ackbar said. "Ask yourself what a frontal assault would achieve. Reinforcements would arrive within hours, and any advantage we gained would be quickly reversed. And more. The Empire does not take kindly to insurrection."

"As we know all too well," said Tels.

"You've got something else in mind," said Juno, relieved she wasn't going to be asked to mount a single-handed assault on the fighter wing, and thinking of Siric's missing fingers.

Ackbar outlined the essence of the plan in a few brief sentences, and Juno learned why his mind had been so highly prized by the Grand Moff who had made him a slave. The plan was within their means, yet certain to have a far-reaching effect on the

Imperial forces in the region. If it succeeded, they were bound to galvanize the resistance into a single force. If it failed, no one would ever know.

"I like it," she said. "Count me in."

"And I," said Tels.

All eyes turned to Siric and his assistants, who conferred in a series of hurried whispers. Siric asked Tels a question, and he translated it for the benefit of Juno and Bail Organa.

"Siric wishes to know how he can be sure that he can trust you."

"He can't," said Ackbar. "He can only take as a form of assurance the fact that I will be fighting alongside him."

"We all go down together, in other words," Juno said, "or we all give up and go home."

The Quarren conferred again, and this time they agreed. Five nods indicated their willingness to be part of the mission.

"Thank you," Ackbar said. "We will never forget your decision today."

"Neither will the Rebel Alliance," said Organa. He glanced at his chrono. "Six hours, you said, Ackbar? If we're going to make that window, we'd better get started."

"You're coming with us?" Juno asked him.

"Of course. I didn't come here just to make introductions and pretty speeches."

"But you're not trained for this kind of work. I wouldn't want to answer to your daughter if you were killed."

"Don't worry about that, Captain Eclipse," he said with an expression that was part smile, part grimace. "I think you'll find that I can handle myself."

Juno didn't press. Organa's experiences with the Emperor stretched farther back even than the formation of the Empire itself. No one lasted that long on luck alone, she supposed.

Ackbar stood and, with a powerful sense of gravitas, shook hands with Seggor Tels. Only then did the mission truly get under way.

CHAPTER 5

Present day . . .

STARKILLER STARED UP in awe at the massive beast that emerged from the shadows. All muscle and bone and teeth and claws, it walked with a hunched, thundering gait that made the stone beneath him shake. Its thick, powerful legs looked disproportionately small compared with the reach of its arms, but the strength they contained—capable of propping up a creature larger than most spacecraft and actually propelling it, too—was almost beyond comprehension. Were it to raise itself upright, its hands would brush the arena's distant ceiling.

Thick duranium shackles that pierced its dense flesh down its back prevented it from coming any farther than the center of the arena. It strained against the chains, roaring. One mighty fist lunged forward to take out its frustration on the tiny creatures standing before it, with their bright blades raised in futile defiance.

Starkiller went one way, Kota the other. The stone cracked beneath them. Dust and splinters of rock flew like shrapnel. Starkiller rolled on landing, then jumped again as the Gorog groped after him. It missed by barely a meter, amazingly fast for a creature so large. He slashed at it, but although his blades parted the red-black skin, he couldn't cut deep enough to do any real damage.

He was going to have to fight the Gorog some other way.

"You're a Jedi!" said Kota from his memory. *"Size means nothing to you!"*

The Gorog's heavy, domed head swung to its left, looking for the general. Starkiller drew its gaze back to him, pushing through the Force at its nearest foot. It barely moved, but the effort didn't go unnoticed. Keeping its center of gravity low and stable probably took much of the creature's resting energy, so the last thing it would want was to be nudged off balance in the middle of a fight. Whether it reasoned consciously or simply reacted by instinct, Starkiller didn't care. He definitely had its attention now.

Both fists came for him, converging with enough force to crack a moon in two. He stood his ground, adding his defiant shout to the creature's angry roaring. The fists came together, making Starkiller's world shake, but he went unharmed behind the strongest Force barrier he could muster. When the fists lifted, he found himself buried almost a meter deep in a gravel pit of shattered rock.

The Gorog stared down at him in slow-witted surprise. He took the opportunity to leap onto one of its arms and run along it all the way up to its mountainous right shoulder.

It swiveled from side to side, trying to track him, and scratched blindly at its back. The heavy chains clanked and rattled. Starkiller leapt onto one of the anchors that bit deep into the creature's flesh and braced himself against the filth-stained metal. His arms could barely reach from one side to the other. Starkiller took a moment to concentrate, and then poured a powerful stream of lightning through the thick metal teeth, directly into the rippling muscle tissue.

The Gorog flailed and roared. It rose up and up until the surface Starkiller was clinging to became very nearly vertical. He ceased shocking it and climbed from anchor to anchor, heading for its head. Its hands groped blindly, swinging the chains from side to side. He dodged claws longer than his entire body and leapt, finally, onto the great bald skull. A metal plate sealed shut a massive rent in its skull, where some genetic defect or wound had left its brain exposed.

He didn't know if it could feel him yet, but he didn't doubt that it would soon. Raising both lightsabers blade-down, he stabbed deep into the metal plate and ran forward, melting a double line downward, toward its hideous face. At the same time, he shocked it with lightning, using the plate and his lightsabers to conduct the electricity directly to the creature's giant neurons.

The Gorog's fury doubled. The head whipped from side to side with a great grinding of vertebrae and sinew. Huge ropes of spittle splashed from its slavering mouth. The sound of its roars was deafening at such close range.

Starkiller leapt onto one of its thick, plated eyebrows and clung tight to a branch-like hair with one hand. The other pointed down into the creature's nearest eye, ready to send a shock along its optic nerve, right into its brain.

The eye rolled, fixed him in its black stare. The pupil tightened. It had seen him. Before Starkiller could move, one mighty hand came from behind him and, with the force of a mass-drive cannon, swept him from his precarious perch.

For a moment he was both weightless and stunned. The world turned around him, and he thought he heard Juno saying, *"Have you done this before?"* and himself responding, *"Trust me. I'm doing the right thing, for both of us."*

Then he hit the stadium, and only a Force-barrier reflex honed by thousands of hours of punishing training stopped him from breaking every bone in his body.

His senses only slowly returned. Holograms flickered and sparked around him as he climbed groggily to his feet.

He was halfway up the side of the arena, surrounded by spectators from afar, chanting for one side or the other. Starkiller wondered if it mattered to them exactly who was fighting, and why. The promise of violence was all they cared about.

Well, he could give them that.

The Gorog hadn't given up on him, either. It had broken half of its chains during its frenzied writhing, and it pulled free of the rest to follow him into the seating. The few spectators who hadn't already fled Starkiller's vicinity now did so, fearing what might come next. The stadium's walls shuddered as the huge creature applied its full weight to them.

Starkiller took a moment to look for Kota. The old man was neither lying squashed on the arena floor nor foolishly rushing in to help, and both relieved him. He needed Kota alive, if he was going to find Juno soon, and he didn't want to be distracted by keeping the old man that way. But he didn't want to lose him, either.

A quick search through the Force revealed him to be climbing upward through the stands, slashing at anyone who stood in his way. Settling that score he had mentioned, Starkiller assumed. Then there wasn't time to ponder the matter any further.

The Gorog approached, dark blood running down from the gash on its scalp and dripping into its gaping mouth. The taste seemed to enrage it.

One arm swept across the stands, destroying hologram generators and snapping pillars by the dozen. Starkiller ran in the opposite direction. Someone was shouting orders from the skybox above, but he didn't pay any notice.

The creature followed him around the stadium, making it shake and reel.

A huge slab of stone, dislodged by one of its wild grabs, came down just in front of him. Starkiller leapt higher, to the very top of the stands. There he found a ramp along which the very last of the spectators were fleeing. He followed it to the roof of the stadium, and waited to see if the Gorog was following.

It was, using its arms to drag itself higher and kicking out with its legs to gain extra thrust. Through deep rents in the stone floor of the stadium, Starkiller could see the open air below.

He ran from the ramp onto the roof. The Gorog followed without hesitation, shouldering through an opening barely wide enough for its arm, let alone the rest of its body. It blinked in the daylight. All the lights and buzz of the suspended city meant nothing to it when its quarry stood just out of reach, tantalizingly still.

It lunged, and missed. Lunged, and missed. It didn't care what damage it caused. Metal supports bent. Guy wires snapped and whipped away. A handful of jetpack-equipped stormtroopers buzzed about its head, trying to bring it back under control, but it had eyes only for Starkiller.

He led it halfway around the arena before he felt the first lurching from below. A number of supports and stanchions were broken, ruining the integrity of the entire arena. The Gorog just kept on coming. Only when they had returned almost to their point of origin did it seem to notice the way the surface beneath it was sinking, beginning to drop.

The broad disk of the arena roof shuddered. Starkiller jumped to the only structure still attached to the city above: the skybox from which the potentate, he assumed, had enjoyed the best possible view. He landed on the roof just as the last support for the arena gave way and began the long tumble to the sinkhole below.

The Gorog howled as it, too, began to fall.

Starkiller cut a hole in the roof of the skybox and jumped nimbly inside.

There he found the potentate standing his ground in front of an ornate gold throne. A half circle of slain Neimoidian aides lay at his feet. He held his blaster on Kota, who was approaching with lightsaber at the ready, unhindered at all by either fatigue or blindness.

Starkiller's arrival distracted the potentate, who snapped a quick shot at him, easily deflected.

Before Kota could strike—settling the score for a week of endless slaughter—the whole skybox lurched, sending all three of them flying. Metal squealed. Transparisteel shattered. The roar of the Gorog filled the air. Starkiller clutched a console as the skybox lurched again, tipping the floor steadily closer to vertical.

"You fool," cried the potentate, spread-eagle on the floor. "You've killed us all!"

Starkiller peered warily out the nearest window. It was immediately clear what had happened. The Gorog had arrested its fall by catching hold of the skybox with one hand, and now it was try-ing to climb to safety. In doing so, however, it was steadily de-stroying the skybox itself.

The gold throne broke free from its restraints and slid toward the shattered viewport. It scooped up the potentate as it went, dragging him down with its considerable mass. He clutched at the floor but could do nothing to arrest his fall. He screamed as he went out the window and fell straight into the Gorog's gaping mouth.

The tiny meal galvanized what was left of the Gorog's facility to reason. It looked up into the skybox, seeing it for the first time as a container, not simply something to hang on to. It saw the shin-ing of the energy weapons that had stung it. With its free hand, it lunged for them, but succeeded only in bringing down still more of the structure. There was no way now to avoid falling. It knew that in the depths of its deranged mind. With the last of its strength it lunged again, and caught its enemy at last.

"Kota!" Starkiller shouted as the Gorog ripped the Jedi gen-eral from the skybox and dragged him down with it.

"Turn away, boy," he heard Kota saying in his mind. *"Get on with your mission. There are some things you aren't ready to face."*

He blinked. The words were another memory, not an instruc-tion from the falling general. He wasn't going to take orders from the past—especially when he hadn't followed them the first time around.

There's nothing *I can't face,* Starkiller thought.

He let go of the console and took a running jump through the shattered window.

It was surprising just how far the Gorog had already fallen toward the gaping mouth of the sinkhole, but he refused to be dis-couraged. He dived in a straight line, using the Force to propel him through the whipping wind. He remembered with perfect clarity his former self's plummet to the surface of the incomplete Death Star, and hard on the heels of that memory came the sensation of

Juno's lips against his. Longing for her filled him, driving him downward even faster.

The stench of the Gorog's fear and rage came heavily on the air as he approached it. The beast was tumbling. The fist containing Kota flashed once in front of him, then a second time. The general was slashing at the fingers holding him pinned, to little effect. Starkiller had to get him free before Kota's strength gave out and he was crushed to a pulp.

Selecting his point of landing with as much care as he was able, Starkiller came down on the creature's back, close enough to one of the duranium anchors to take hold of it. He braced himself with both feet against the spine, ignoring the way the world was spinning around him. The Gorog didn't know he was there. It wouldn't be expecting an attack from this side.

He took a deep breath, reaching deeper into the Force than he had before. He had never journeyed to the center of a planet, where the molten metal raged and burned under pressure hard enough to make diamond out of dust, but he imagined something much like that. This time, he wanted to do more than just enrage the Gorog. He could feel the web of veins thudding a panicky beat beneath the skin. He concentrated on that beat, on the rapid pulsing of life that would be extinguished when it reached the bottom of the sinkhole. Why wait that long, when Kota's life was at stake as well?

For a moment, he faltered. He had never killed anything this big before.

But it was just one life, and it stood between him and his goal. He had no choice.

Instead of a wild crackle of lightning, he discharged a single pure bolt into the metal anchor, stabbing deep through the creature's chest into its heart.

Its back arched. A strange, fluting cry emerged from its mouth. Starkiller rode out the spasm, maintaining the electric shock for as long as he was able. Muscular waves rolled back and forth, twisting him from side to side. It felt like a groundquake—a *fleshquake* on a planet-sized monster.

The pulsing coming through the soles of his boots ran wild, faltered, ceased.

He sagged as the mountain of flesh finally grew still. The fight was over, but darkness enfolded them as they entered the mouth of the sinkhole and went into free fall.

Starkiller used rough pits in the creature's skin to pull himself up to the shoulder, then down the limp arm that had held Kota captive. The general was clinging to the slackened thumb, head cocked as though he could see the sinkhole walls sliding by. He shouted a greeting over the sound of the rushing wind.

"I hope you've got a way out of this, boy."

Starkiller put an arm around Kota's shoulders. Together they leapt off the Gorog's hand. Starkiller could slow their fall somewhat, but he couldn't fly. The beast fell ahead of them. Maybe, he hoped against hope, it would go some way toward arresting their impact.

"If you're wearing a comlink," Kota said, "hand it over."

Starkiller did so, even though that was as faint a hope as his own. "The whole city's jammed."

Kota punched keys on the comlink. "Let's hope she can reach us in time."

Starkiller's heart quickened. *She?*

He glanced down into the shadow, wondering how deep the sinkhole could possibly be. Above, he saw only the shrinking circle of cityscape. He stared until it was occluded by something solid. He thought he recognized the silhouette. The roar of a starship's engines echoed down the sinkhole, as the familiar angles and planes of the *Rogue Shadow* dived down toward them, and then overtook them so it could intercept them from below.

Though Starkiller pushed down against the starship's hull with the Force to cushion their fall, they still hit the surface hard. Starkiller blinked away stars and groaned under the return of gravity.

Kota was faring no better, clutching his shoulder and struggling to sit up. A hatch popped open nearby, and the old man waved the younger man ahead of him.

Starkiller was already moving. His entire being thrilled at the certainty that Juno was here at last. He could practically see her already, waiting at the controls for him to arrive, ready with some quip about being late to his own funeral.

He dropped down through the hatch and ran breathlessly to the cockpit.

"Juno!"

He stopped dead. The cockpit was empty. All he heard in reply was a ghost of her voice, speaking from the depths of his memory.

"Please don't make me leave another life behind."

CHAPTER 6

One day earlier . . .

JUNO TOOK ONE LAST look at the fluted domes of Heurkea a floating city, before diving under the waves. Its shell-like buildings gleamed red and gold by the light of Mon Calamari system's primary, looking more like something grown than built—much like the coral of Mester Reef beneath her. None of the reef protruded above the water, and she was submerged up to her waist, buffeted by the alien sea as she stared at the city. She wanted something beautiful to hold in her mind before entrusting her life to air that stank of rotten rubber.

Ackbar ducked under without hesitation, followed a second later by Bail Organa, who had donned an old clone subtrooper breathing apparatus like hers. In a wet suit and mismatching white helmet he looked about as ridiculous as Juno felt. For the first time she didn't worry that her weapons would be sealed in their packs until they emerged at the other end. If anyone saw them climbing out of the water at the far end, they would certainly not regard them as any kind of threat.

The Quarren were already underwater. Holding her breath instinctively, Juno took a single step forward, off the rough coral surface, and let herself sink into the water.

It was blue and clearer than she had expected. The cargo freighter was moored safely out of sight at the base of the reef, guided there by remote control once the ten conspirators had disembarked. She could see its featureless nose almost as though through air. She couldn't, however, see their destination. Trusting to the Quarren's sense of direction, she followed strongly kicking feet around the bulk of the reef and into the open ocean. PROXY took the shape of Seggor Tels, using repulsors to swim rather than sink straight to the bottom. Juno kept careful track of which Tels was which, just in case.

Strong currents favored them half the way, then shifted direction as the seabed grew nearer, making progress much more difficult. Heurkea was a true floating city, with no structural connections to the bedrock, but several chunky cables did run from its undulating base down into the sludge. Ferrying waste one way and geothermal power another, she guessed, but just then wasn't the time to wonder about the city's inner workings. As its underside came into view, she kept her eyes open for the vent Tels had described. PROXY had sliced into plans of the city and confirmed that it was still there. The vent had been sealed up early in the Imperial occupation of the city, but laser-cutting equipment designed for underwater use would make short work of that obstacle.

There: a dark patch against the city's white underbelly. She waved to catch the others' attention, and pointed. She could have used the subtrooper gear's comlink, but they were maintaining strict radio silence.

White light flared as one of Siric's apprentices activated the cutting equipment. Bubbles of steam spread upward and flattened out against the city's hull, forming rippling streams and threads. Juno waited for lights to flash and alarms to sound, but nothing happened. The Imperials had clearly grown complacent about security, at least in this damp corner of the galaxy.

With one last flash, the white light died. The grille fell out in a single circular piece and dropped to the ocean floor far below. Tels went through first, staying carefully clear of the still-hot metal. His feet disappeared. A minute later his hand reappeared, giving a definite thumbs-up. One by one, the rest of the team followed him into the pipe.

Juno swam ten meters to a ladder that led up to a level deck. There the water was below knee height and the atmosphere was breathable. She gratefully dispensed with the breathing apparatus and took in a chest full of sweet, if slightly scum-tainted, natural air. The deck was illuminated by faint down-lights that flickered weakly with age. It didn't look as if anyone had visited that level in at least a decade. Still, she moved as quietly as she could to a higher section, where the way was completely dry.

There she slipped off the wet suit and straightened the flight uniform she'd been wearing beneath. PROXY flickered back to his usual form and followed her, yellow eyes flickering in the dim light.

"Are you feeling all right?" she asked the droid. Apart from an occasional flutter, his chameleon circuit remained stable, but he had hardly spoken since his awakening. "Is there something I should worry about?"

"Oh, no, Juno. I am simply processing my lack of a viable primary program."

"Does it seriously impair your function?" she asked, wondering if she had made a mistake involving PROXY in the mission.

"No," PROXY said, "but it does concern me. I have been de-activated twice since Raxus Prime, and each time it seems a miracle that I have returned. Who am I, if not my primary program? What am I, if I have no reason to function?"

That seemed a very human concern, and one that had no easy answer. "I guess you're just you," she said. "And you seem okay to me."

"Thank you, Captain Eclipse. That is of some small reassurance."

"Every being is the sum of its experiences and actions," put in Bail Organa, coming up alongside them and dropping his dis-carded wet suit next to Juno's. "Sometimes we don't know what our primary program is, or was, until we've lived long enough to look back at our lives."

"I'm afraid I do not understand how to function under such circumstances," the droid said. "Droids are not designed to program themselves."

"I'm sorry, PROXY," Juno said, with real feeling. "I didn't realize you felt so strongly about this. Do you wish I hadn't woken you up this time?"

"Not at all, Captain Eclipse. I am glad to be in the world again, and I remain optimistic that I will be assigned a new primary program one day. I cannot be the only example of my class in operation."

Juno wasn't so sure of that. She'd never seen a droid like him before, and assumed that he was something Darth Vader had commissioned years ago to act as plaything and tutor to his young apprentice.

The thought of Starkiller darkened her mood. Why was she thinking about him so much? Sometimes she wished *her* primary program could be changed as easily as a droid's. It would certainly save her a whole lot of grief.

When the Quarren were ready, they gathered at the top of the ramp, where a corridor led off into two opposite directions.

"This is where we split up," said Ackbar. "Siric, you know what to do?"

The bomb expert and his assistants patted their waterproof packs and nodded.

"All right, good luck. Make your move on Seggor's signal."

The five headed off into the gloomy distance, feet slapping softly against the floor. Ackbar guided Juno, Organa, PROXY, and Seggor Tels up the other way. They moved silently, conscious of the fact that the city was entirely in Imperial hands. They could trust no one, and carried blasters openly in case they happened across anyone so deep in the basements.

Around them, the city hummed and shifted on the surface of the endless sea. There was no sense of motion, just a constant creaking and groaning of welds. Juno wondered if any of these floating cities ever sprang a leak, but didn't think right then the time to ask. That was the least of their problems.

Ackbar and Tels swapped positions when they reached the upper levels. The Quarren had the codes for the fighter wing's secure compound—obtained, he said, by bribing a maintenance team who had worked briefly for the city administration. Tels padded softly ahead of them, moving with stealthy confidence along the metallic corridors. If he was nervous, it didn't show.

They reached the checkpoint, one of seven scattered across the city. This was the least frequented but still under heavy guard. Seven stormtroopers patrolled the area, keeping a close eye on anyone who approached.

"Your turn to shine, PROXY," Juno said. "You've assimilated the Imperial files?"

The droid's holographic generators flickered and flashed, hiding his true appearance behind another—that of a rotund, balding white human male dressed in an Imperial uniform.

"Yes, Captain Eclipse." His voice changed, too, to match that of the fighter wing's commander. "If you will follow me . . ."

"Sorry about this," whispered Juno to Ackbar as she aimed her blaster at him. Organa did the same for Tels. "You know it's just for show."

"No hard feelings," said Ackbar, slipping his own blaster out of sight.

PROXY strode confidently into view, leading the two humans and their Dac native "captives" to the checkpoint. The guards looked up as they approached and stood to attention.

"Commander Derricote?"

"Indeed," said PROXY, not breaking step.

The trooper who had spoken raised a hand. "I'm sorry, sir. I just need to record your companions."

"Of course. Two informants and two members of the Dac resistance for urgent interrogation. I have reason to believe that an attack is imminent."

The troopers exchanged nervous glances.

"Security codes?" asked the squad leader.

Juno hid her anxiety. Why was a stormtrooper asking the flight wing commander for security codes? Something was going wrong. She tightened her grip on her blaster.

"Twenty, thirty-five, nineteen, sixty-seven," said PROXY without hesitation, quoting the information he had sliced from the Imperial network.

"Thank you, sir. Move along."

The troopers parted ranks, allowing the group of five an unobstructed path through the checkpoint. Juno held her breath as she passed between the troopers. All it would take now was for PROXY's holographic impersonation to flicker and the ruse would be exposed.

"Commander Derricote, hold a moment."

PROXY stopped in mid-stride but didn't turn. "What now? Can't you see I'm in a hurry?"

Juno didn't learn what had made the trooper suspicious. A bolt of blasterfire from Bail Organa caught him in the throat, throwing him backward. A second bolt took out the trooper closest to him, and a third spun the next one along in a circle. The speed and accuracy of the three shots was as impressive as they were unexpected. She took two shots of her own as the opposing groups scattered, leaving just four troopers to return fire.

Bolts of energy flashed back and forth. Small explosions threw fragments of plastoid from the walls and ceiling. Smoke thickened the air, made her eyes water.

It didn't last long. Ackbar and Tels took out three of the remaining troopers, and the last soon keeled face-forward across one of his compatriots, hit by Juno and Organa from two sides at once.

"Nice shooting," Juno told the Senator as she emerged from cover. The compliment was sincerely meant. Shot for shot, he was both faster and more accurate than she was.

"I'm a little out of practice," he said, checking up and down the corridor for signs the ruckus had been noticed. "You should've seen me during my Academy days . . ."

They dragged the bodies into a storage locker. With luck, no one would notice the breach in security before their mission was complete. PROXY maintained the illusion of Commander Derricote as they resumed their hasty march into the secure compound.

It was more crowded than the city proper had been. Droids and techs hurried through the corridors, but thankfully no more troopers. They received the odd askance look, and Juno wondered why. What about PROXY's impersonation didn't ring true?

When they reached the flight wings' empty barracks, she began to understand what PROXY had got wrong.

"It's filthy in here," she said, staring at the messily draped uniforms and unpolished boots. Weapons parts lay on bunks, next to scattered rations. Because grunts took their lead from their superior officer, she had no doubt that this reflected the real Derricote through and through. "Who are these guys?"

"I don't know," Organa said, "but we have to hurry. The briefing starts in ten minutes."

They found a passerby and grilled him on the whereabouts of the real commander.

"In the n-nursery," stammered the tech.

"They have *kids* here?" Juno's sense of outrage reached a new peak. She would never have allowed such laxity under her command.

"For his p-plants," the tech managed to get out. "The nursery's what he calls the g-greenhouse."

When he had provided directions, Organa knocked him out with a deft tap to the back of the skull.

"Tels and I will deal with the commander," he told Juno. "You and Ackbar go with PROXY to the briefing. Make it convincing."

"We'll do our best," Juno said, even as one growing doubt niggled at her. If Derricote was as slovenly as his pilots, that had to be what was giving them away.

They split up. Hurrying to the briefing room with Ackbar, she directed PROXY to look more like the real Derricote did. She hoped.

"Undo another button. Loosen the collar. Roll up the sleeves, too, and mess the hair more."

"Are you sure this is an improvement, Captain Eclipse?" the droid asked her.

"As sure as I can be, PROXY. Let's keep our fingers crossed."

There was no guard at the briefing room entrance. Ackbar and Juno slipped to the back of the room as PROXY strode to the podium at the front. Pilots slouched in their seats and didn't rise to attention when their commander entered. Although she had left the Empire more than a year ago, Juno's blood still boiled. These guys were giving pilots everywhere a bad name.

No one looked twice at PROXY's modified disguise. His pre-amble was brief. "Forget the flight schedules you already have," he said. "I'm giving you a new assignment—practicing honor rolls over the city. All of you."

There were groans from pilots who had only just come off an active shift. "Is this something to do with the shuttle that arrived last night?" asked one.

"That is classified," said PROXY without missing a beat. "I want you in the air in five standard minutes. Dismissed."

The pilots complained and griped but slowly began to move. Some even managed a semblance of urgency. Five minutes would have been a very quick turnaround even for a well-practiced flight wing. Juno wouldn't have put a credit on this lot making ten, maybe not even fifteen.

Still, time was tight for the conspirators to get to where they needed to be next.

"Good work, PROXY," Ackbar told him when the room was clear. "Now back to the rendezvous point."

They retraced their steps through the secure compound, past the still-unnoticed checkpoint and into the city proper, where PROXY returned to his normal appearance. No alarms sounded;

no shouts rang out. Everything appeared to be going according to plan, so far.

The five Quarren were waiting for them in the shadowy lower levels, rehydrating themselves in the rippling water. They communicated by hand signals that the charges were laid and the triggers set exactly as required.

So far, thought Juno, *so good.*

"Bail and Tels should've been here by now," she said, checking her chrono and counting off the minutes. The TIE fighters of the 181st would be in the air soon, even by her most conservative estimate. "Search for them in the city's security grid, PROXY. Maybe they've been picked up somewhere—"

"No need," called the Senator himself from the top of the ramp. He jogged down to meet them with Tels in his wake, pushing their prisoner ahead of them. "Sorry to hold you up. Our friend here moves more slowly than we planned for."

"What is the meaning of this?" blustered the real Evir Derricote, commander of the 181st fighter wing. He looked even scruffier than PROXY had portrayed him, although perhaps that was a result of his capture. "You'll never get away with it!"

"Take those binders off him," said Ackbar when the commander was before him. "We have a message for the Emperor. Get off Dac, and stay away from the Mon Calamari system, or—"

Something moved in the shadows. Ackbar reached for his blaster, and so did Juno. The Quarren huddled in closer to one another.

"Who's there?" called Organa. "Come out!"

"I think they've said enough," called a voice. "Take them."

"It's a trap!" gasped Ackbar.

Two dozen stormtroopers stepped into the light, weapons trained on the knot of conspirators they encircled. At their head stood a tall, thin man in the uniform of a senior officer in the Imperial administration. So senior, in fact, that she had never seen the insignia in person before. He had a nose like a knife-blade and eyes to match, and his cruel mouth was practically lipless.

It was clear that Ackbar knew him. He instantly raised his blaster to shoot at him, but a well-timed blaster-bolt from one of the troopers knocked the weapon from his hand.

"There's no point resisting, Ackbar," said the stern figure in a chillingly polite voice, striding confidently toward them with his hands behind his back. "You're quite outnumbered. Please drop your weapons, or I will have you executed right here. All except you, Ackbar. I'm looking forward to having you back in my employ. That'll remind my other slaves that escape is simply not an option."

Ackbar's mottled skin had turned a sickly yellow. "I will never be your slave again, Tarkin. *Never.*"

Grand Moff Wilhuff Tarkin smiled coldly. "That choice is now well and truly out of your hands."

Derricote pulled free, rubbing his wrists. "Thank you, Grand Moff. Thank you for rescuing me."

"I won't say it was my priority, but I will accept your gratitude. Be careful it doesn't happen again." Tarkin turned to face Bail Organa. "Your weapon, Senator. I asked you to drop it."

Organa obeyed, and so did the others. All except Tels. His gun remained in his hand, and none of the Imperials moved to force the issue. Slowly, without saying a word, he walked to join their numbers.

"*Why?*" Ackbar asked him.

"Once a traitor, always a traitor," answered Tarkin for him, with a gloating tut-tut. "You Rebels should choose your friends more carefully. He contacted me a day ago, offering to return my slave in exchange for greater freedoms for his people and a place in the civil administration. He won't get either, of course. I'm not known for changing my mind, particularly when it comes to negotiating with aliens."

It was Tels's turn to go pale. "You mean—"

"Yes, put your blaster down and stand with the others while I decide if you're important enough for the Emperor to kill himself, or whether I should just dispose of you now. I'm leaning toward the latter, simply to spare the mess—"

At that moment, a series of explosions rocked the city. The floor moved beneath them.

"What's that?" asked Tarkin of his nearest trooper. "Find out!"

Another trio of blasts brought part of the ceiling down. Tels raised his blaster and fired at the lights, extinguishing them. Utter darkness instantly fell.

In the confusion, Juno dived for her blaster. She heard a stormtrooper say, "It's the Hundred Eighty-first, sir. They're firing on the city."

"Impossible!" blubbered Derricote. "I gave no such order!"

"To me!" Tarkin ordered his men from the ramp. "To me!"

Juno fired in the direction his voice had come from. Her shot went wide, revealing his high-cheeked visage in the flash. She rolled before the stormtroopers could return fire. Soon the space was a maelstrom of light and sound as more explosions rocked the city, one after the other, and the two sides exchanged blasterfire. She found Organa and stood with her back to him, admiring the elegant precision of his shots. When he fired, he nearly always hit, even in the dark.

The stormtroopers retreated up the ramp, following the voice of the Grand Moff. Juno and the others stayed exactly where they were, waiting for the echoes of the last explosion to fade away. When it did, there was blessed silence, apart from the tinkling of debris and the lapping of water.

A torch flared, held high in Ackbar's hand. "Are we all here?"

Juno took a quick head count. Everyone was accounted for except PROXY and one of Siric's assistants, who had been hit in the chest by a stray shot. Organa found Derricote huddling in a ball in the corner of the room with his hands over his head. He didn't seem to notice that the firing had ceased until the Senator pulled him upright, blinking and fearful.

There was no sign of Tarkin.

"He must have slipped away in the skirmish," said Ackbar, looking disappointed.

"Never mind," said Organa, patting his shoulder. "That we *almost* got him sends the same message."

"And we still have this one," said Tels, squeezing Derricote's face between his long fingers and peering close. "For what he's worth."

"You mean you're not—" stammered the flight wing commander, looking from face to face in confusion. "And you are—"

"All on the same side, yes," the Quarren said. "Thanks for your help."

"But I didn't—"

Juno almost felt sorry for him. "Explosions, timed to coincide with the honor roll you didn't order. It won't fool anyone for long, but it had exactly the right effect in the moment, don't you think?"

Footsteps sounded on the ramp above. They looked up to see PROXY returning, the Tarkin disguise he had adopted during the battle slipping away with an electric crackle.

"I led the troopers, in the opposite direction from the real Grand Moff," the droid said. "They are currently on their way to the landing pads, with orders to arrest the pilots responsible."

"Good work, PROXY. It went almost perfectly."

Derricote stared at the droid in shock, clearly beginning to piece events together.

"What are you going to do with me?" he asked.

"Nothing," said Ackbar.

His eyes narrowed. "Nothing?"

"Tarkin will accept your explanation," Organa explained, "but I'd say your career is pretty much ruined here regardless. Grand Moffs don't like inferiors who draw attention to themselves. You might want to pull your head in for a while, if you still have one."

The Senator released him, and Derricote stepped slowly away, as though expecting to be shot at any moment.

"You're really letting me go?"

"Yes," said Ackbar. "You are a witness to what happens when one interferes with the Dac resistance."

The commander was too busy hurrying up the ramp to promise anything, but Juno didn't doubt that the message would get out. With one short action, the Empire had been humiliated and the local resistance strengthened. It was the very embodiment of Kota's methods.

Juno wondered if Mon Mothma would see it that way, when she found out.

When they were alone, Organa put one hand on Tels's shoulder, the other on Ackbar's. "I don't think I need to say anything," he said, echoing Garm Bel Iblis's philosophy: *Actions speak louder than words.*

"In this case, yes," said Tels, tentacles curling tightly in gratitude. "Thank you from the free people of our world for showing us that we can fight together—and must fight together in order to remove the Emperor's net from our world. We will join your Rebellion as one world, in the spirit you have shown us."

"Does he speak for you, too, Ackbar?"

"You know he does, my friend. And I thank you, too." Ackbar's large, golden eyes took in Juno and PROXY. "We owe your Rebel Alliance much already."

"It's not ours," said Organa, and for a moment Juno feared that he would declare it to be Starkiller's, as Kota had on Felucia, once. "The Rebellion can't belong to any one person, or it's no better than the Empire. It's yours. Everyone's. It belongs to all of us."

"Our dead, too," said Tels, acknowledging the body his fellows had lifted in preparation for leaving the city. "We have lost so many already."

They stood in silence for a moment, Juno thinking of Kota and Starkiller and wondering what they would make of this strange moment of communion among three species in a waterlogged basement.

There was no way of knowing, now. No way at all.

Part 2

REVELATION

CHAPTER 7

The same day.

"WHERE IS SHE?"

Kota stumbled into the cockpit behind him. He was covered in blood and dirt and looked on the verge of collapse.

Starkiller didn't care.

"Where is she?"

"I don't know."

"Why not? This is her ship."

"It was. It isn't now. She's moved on." Kota slumped into the nearest seat and put his scarred face in his hands. "The Rebel Alliance fleet is scattered across the Outer Rim, constantly on the run. She could be anywhere now."

Starkiller frowned. It just didn't make sense. "She wasn't with you when you came here?"

"She was, but I had my own squad on the ground." Kota's blind eyes came up. "All dead now, of course. I was the only one Baron Tarko 'spared' when he captured us. The ship went into hiding, awaiting my signal. Then you came. Thank you." The last was said with great gravity and sincerity. "I don't know how much longer I would've lasted."

Starkiller dismissed that with a wave of one hand and checked the controls. Now that his anticipation at seeing Juno had been punctured, more mundane concerns took priority—like making sure the ship wasn't being followed by any of the deceased Baron's underlings.

The *Rogue Shadow* had brought itself out of the sinkhole and was heading for orbit, where it would await further orders. He didn't know what those orders should be, now. And he wasn't ready to take the empty seat at the controls where Juno should have been sitting.

Should have been, in his previous life. But now Kota had his own squad and Juno had "moved on," whatever that meant. Things had changed in ways he had never considered.

"Tell me exactly what happened."

The general related the circumstances of his capture with his usual economy. An unofficial raid on a local despot had gone unexpectedly wrong, thanks to bad intel regarding the size and capabilities of the forces on Cato Neimoidia. Under other circumstances, that might not have been the complete disaster it had very nearly turned out to be, but with no backup to speak of, apart from a small frigate in orbit, there had been no second chance for Kota and his squad.

"She tried her best," Kota concluded, "and I don't blame her for leaving. She couldn't take on the entire Empire herself, although I'm sure she wanted to."

"She *was* here?"

Kota nodded. "She was the captain of the frigate. Mon Mothma recognizes talent, even if she won't always put it to good use." He leaned forward excitedly. "But now you're back, and she will *have* to see what an opportunity this represents. We must capitalize on it immediately—a major strike to take the fight back to the Empire—"

"Wait." The return of Kota's vigor took Starkiller by surprise. One moment he was half dead; the next he wanted to wage war on the entire galaxy with Starkiller leading the charge. Kota's faith in him was touching, but it needed to be tempered with a little reality. "Don't you want to know where I came from?"

"Why? You're back; that's all that counts."

"But I'm *not* back. I'm not *him*."

Kota shook his head emphatically. "I may be blind, but I'm still connected to the Force. I know what I'm sensing."

"I'm not Starkiller!" It was vitally important that Kota understand that much, at least. The general wasn't his Master, and couldn't be until he was certain who he was. They couldn't just pick up where they had left off. "Not the original Starkiller, anyway. I'm a clone, grown in a vat by Darth Vader to take the old Starkiller's place at his side. That should worry you, shouldn't it?"

Kota leaned forward and scratched at his filthy beard.

"I figure I already know the worst you can do," he said, tapping the corner of one dead eye, "but I've experienced the best, too, so I'm prepared to take my chances."

Starkiller backed down, wondering if Kota was referring to his blinding alone or to something much worse?

"You should know that Shaak Ti is dead," he heard Bail Organa say, out of the past. *"She was murdered by Vader or one of his assassins."*

"Probably the same one who did this to me," Kota had replied, making much the same gesture Kota had in the present.

The guess had been correct, but had Juno told him? Had he furthermore connected Shaak Ti's death to the disappearance of Kazdan Paratus, whom Starkiller had also murdered? Kota had forgiven Starkiller for blinding him, but the deaths of two Jedi— one of them a former Jedi Master on the High Council—were an entirely different magnitude of guilt. Could such a thing ever truly be forgiven?

"Light, dark," Shaak Ti had said. *"They are just directions. Do not be fooled that you stand on anything other than your own two feet."*

Even from the grave, she had something to teach him, as Kota had taught him in life. He was no longer a creature of the dark side, or the light side. The only direction he cared about was the one leading to Juno, where his emotions led him.

Kazdan Paratus, moldering on Raxus Prime in his junkyard

version of a living death, was another educative example for him, courtesy of one of his victims: If he were to avoid living entirely in the past, he would have to focus on what really mattered.

"Help me find Juno. That's all I'm asking you to do."

Kota studied him with senses that had nothing to do with his eyes.

"Head for Athega system," the general finally said. "That was the last rendezvous point. When we get there, maybe we'll find some hint of where they've gone."

"They could still be there now, couldn't they?"

Kota shook his head. "If there was any chance I or one of my squad could have survived, the fleet would have had to move. Even Mon Mothma would see the sense in that."

That was the second time Kota had downplayed Mon Mothma's role in the Rebel Alliance. Starkiller filed it away for future consideration.

"I'm going to the 'fresher," Kota said as Starkiller turned to the controls and began plotting the jump. "And then I'm going to sleep. Wake me when we get there."

"All right."

Kota paused on the brink of leaving the bridge. "I'm glad you're back, boy."

Before Starkiller could say, *He's not,* the general turned and limped away.

THE *ROGUE SHADOW* had been modified since he had last flown it, and not entirely for the better. Its shielding was heavier, giving it a different feel when under thrust, and some of the compartments had been expanded to make room for Kota's squad. That left several critical components crushed uncomfortably together, at constant risk of overheating. Starkiller kept a constant eye on the instruments as the ship jumped through hyperspace, waiting for a warning light to flash.

Amazingly, none did. Whoever had rejigged the systems had

made absolutely sure to push the envelope, but never cross it. Someone with extensive battlefield engineering experience was responsible, he suspected. He also assumed they had died with Kota's squad on Cato Neimoidia, so he would never be able to ask how they had done it.

Ultimately, it didn't matter. They were under way, and that was the main thing.

He had time to think, too, although that wasn't necessarily something he welcomed.

His brief exchange with Kota had stirred up a whole raft of anxieties he hadn't even known he possessed. *"I've already seen the worst you can do . . . a major strike to take the fight back to the Empire . . . I'm glad you're back."* He hadn't considered what might happen after finding Juno. Did the rest of the Rebels know about Shaak Ti and Kazdan Paratus? Had they forgiven him for the trap he had unwittingly set on Corellia? Would the stain of Darth Vader's Mastery ever wash off him?

"He stinks of Sith, all right," Kazdan Paratus had said. *"You reek of that coward Vader,"* Shaak Ti had agreed. Only Kota had sensed the goodness within him. Did he really sense it now, or was that just blind hope speaking? Starkiller would have to wait until Kota woke up to ask him.

The issue of what came next connected inevitably to what he had been created *for*. Until Vader had pushed him too far, he had assumed that his purpose was to serve at his former Master's side, killing his enemies and possibly assisting him one day in making a grab for the Imperial throne. That was how he had been trained in his former life, after all, and it was easy to default to that status.

But now, with his memories gradually piecing back together, and more and more of the former Starkiller's life becoming clearer, he began to question that assumption. Darth Vader had plans within plans, making them hard to unravel.

Starkiller's first resurrection had been on the *Empirical*, after the Emperor had ordered Vader to kill his secret apprentice—the betrayal Starkiller had remembered on Kamino, when Vader had declared him a failure, fit for the same fate meted out to the others he had made. Starkiller remembered the almost-blackness of something much like death, and then awakening on an operating table to receive new instructions. Vader said that he had faked Starkiller's death in order to make him a free agent, free to target the Emperor more directly. That had seemed plausible, for that was what Sith did, according to Shaak Ti: betray each other as a matter of course.

But then, on Corellia, Vader had revealed that this had never been his plan, that his intention—the *Emperor's* intention—had been to use him to gather all the Empire's enemies into one spot, in order to destroy them once and for all. And then, Vader had hinted, it would be time to take on the Emperor, but not with Starkiller.

"I lied, as I have from the very beginning," Vader had said.

Vader *always* lied, Starkiller now realized, but somewhere underneath the lies there had to be a measure of truth. A cloned Starkiller must serve *some* purpose, otherwise why go to the trouble? Did he exist to continue one of Vader's previous plans, or an entirely new one? Was Vader still following the Emperor's orders? Or was the Emperor's enforcer making it up as he went along?

That didn't seem likely. One thing Starkiller *did* know was his former Master's nature. Darth Vader was meticulous and controlling. He would leave nothing to chance. His motives and intentions might be hidden for the moment, but they would have to become visible sometime. Perhaps, with enough thought, the clone of his former apprentice might be the one to work it out.

"Without me, you'll never be free," he had told Vader on Corellia. On the Death Star it had seemed that only death would release his Master from servitude, for the Emperor himself had so thoroughly steeped Vader's mind in the dark side—and there had been a moment when the Dark Lord's life had literally been in Starkiller's hands. He could have released his Master from a life of torment had he chosen vengeance over the lives of his friends among the Rebels. If he hadn't, he might not have died and been reborn as a clone. Or he might have died for good.

He wasn't sure which would have been better.

"Do not forget that you still serve me," Darth Vader had said.

In the back of his mind, ever present, was the fear that this would always be the case. That any semblance of freedom he might find would only be an illusion. That at any moment his Master would walk back into his life, as he had on Corellia, and destroy everything he had built.

He swore to himself that it would never happen. He hoped it was a promise he could keep.

And if only he *could* forget. His mind was full of so many things . . .

The controls beeped at him. Time had passed with uncanny speed while he sat in silent contemplation. The *Rogue Shadow* was due to arrive in Athega system at any moment. Starkiller thought about waking Kota, but decided to let him sleep. After fighting seven days straight, the old man deserved his rest.

The blue-white streaks of hyperspace vanished. Blinding yellow radiation took their place, making the ship shake. Starkiller's hands danced over the controls, raising shields and frantically scanning the environment. It felt as though he'd landed right in the middle of an explosion, but what could produce so much force without ebbing in intensity? This was no isolated blast. It was a sustained rage.

The answer was simple: a sun. The sun at the center of Athega system, to be precise. It was huge and highly active, throwing off corona loops longer than most ring systems and deeply pitted with sunspots. Hull temperature was rising fast. Even with the extra shielding, the *Rogue Shadow* wasn't going to last long.

Sensors indicated two rocky planets. A cluster of small dots sheltered behind one of them. He grinned and punched in the coordinates as fast as he was able, assuming that he had indeed found the Rebel fleet.

The relative calm of hyperspace enfolded him. His ears rang in the sudden silence. He took a moment to catch his breath while the ship ticked and pinged around him, slowly shedding its excess heat into the infinite vacuum of an empty universe. He eyed the countdown on the chrono, sure that conditions would be more temperate in the world's shadow. Why else would the Rebel fleet hide there?

The hop was a short one. Barely a minute passed before the ship emerged from hyperspace again, and this time the ride was considerably smoother. The ship's shields were more than adequate to keep the worst at bay. He scanned the ships around him, hoping to find the frigate Kota had mentioned. The *Salvation:* Juno's ship.

None of the transponders matched that name, however—and very quickly another hard fact became apparent. None of the ships belonged to the Rebel fleet. They broadcast the standard transponder signals of the Empire. The fighters swarming around him matched, too. TIE fighters, in their dozens.

He had landed in the middle of an Imperial fleet!

"Identify yourself, unknown vessel," snapped a voice from the comm. "Cease accelerating and prepare to be boarded."

Starkiller wasn't going to sit around and let his ship be taken over. He was already driving hard for the edge of the planet's shadow cone. *Rogue Shadow*'s engines roared as the TIE fighters came about in pursuit. He frantically piloted while at the same time calculating the next jump.

He hit the sun's blazing light the very instant the ship jumped.

Then it was quiet again.

"I told you," Kota said from behind him. "They always find us, no matter where we hide."

Starkiller turned to face him. "Spies?"

"Informers, traitors, lucky guesses—the Force, even, if Vader is looking." Kota fell into the copilot's seat with a weary sigh. His armor was marginally cleaner, but still dented and scratched beyond recognition. "Nowhere is safe."

The ship traveled smoothly to its next destination—the empty shadow behind the second moon. There Starkiller performed a more thorough sweep of the system. He found no signs of a pro-

longed space battle, which came as a relief. The Rebel fleet must
have moved on before the Imperials arrived. But there was no sign,
either, of where they might have gone next.

"The fleet doesn't leave coordinates behind," Kota said. "They
could be decoded too easily. The only way to find the fleet again,
once you've lost it, is to work back up through Rebel contacts."

"That'll take too long."

"What's your hurry? The Empire isn't going anywhere."

Starkiller didn't know how to explain. If Kota didn't already
understand, maybe he never would.

Instead, he closed his eyes and reached out with the Force.

Juno.

He could see her in his mind's eye as clearly as if she were
standing before him. Blond hair, blue eyes, strong jaw, proud
nose—he would carry her face with him for the rest of his life, now
that he had escaped Darth Vader's dire influence. When they were
together again, they would never be separated. It was just a matter
of closing the gap between them—and what was distance but an illusion of the mind? To the Force, all things were one.

Faintly, he heard the *Rogue Shadow* creaking and swaying, but
he didn't let himself be distracted. He was out among the stars,
seeking, searching. There were quadrillions of minds in the galaxy,
and he was looking for just one of them. He sensed fear and great
tragedy, cruelty and petty hate. He saw death everywhere, and life,
too, ebbing and flowing in that eternal tide. The Force surged
within him, primal, powerful, potent—like a beast one never entirely tamed. He felt Kota next to him, full of anger and impatience. He sensed—

A hint of Juno flashed through his mind.

*"I don't trust that kind of power. A lesson learned the hard
way is hard—perhaps impossible—to unlearn."*

They weren't her words, and it wasn't her voice, but she was
near their source, which was itself a tantalizingly familiar presence.

Water.

Kota's urgency flared, pulling Starkiller out of his meditation. A dozen floating objects fell to the floor with a loud clatter.

"What is it?" He checked the scopes for any sign of the Imperials, but they were empty. "What's wrong?"

"I didn't say anything," said the general. "Or do anything. I'm just sitting here, waiting."

There was no denying what he had felt. Kota was impatient, and that impatience was throwing Starkiller off. "You think I'm wasting my time. You don't think I can do it."

"You're right on one point, boy. The galaxy is a big place, and the whole point of the Rebel Alliance is to stay hidden—but I'd never try to guess what you're capable of or not."

"So you think I'm wasting my time."

"I think your priorities are wrong."

"Like Mon Mothma's."

"Yes, exactly so. You're letting your own fears cloud your judgment."

Starkiller turned to face Kota. "What do you think I'm afraid of?"

"Being yourself. Being Starkiller. Being Ga—"

"Don't say that name. I'm not him. I'm a clone, a copy—and a bad one at that."

"Is that what Vader told you?"

"Yes."

"I don't believe it." Kota spoke with surety and great force. "No one can clone Jedi. It's never been done."

"That you know of."

Kota grabbed Starkiller by the shoulders. "I can sense how powerful you are—and here you are wasting it—"

"By rescuing you? By looking for Juno?"

Kota stalked to the far side of the cockpit and rubbed at his forehead with his right hand. "Listen. The Alliance leadership is deadlocked. It can't agree on our next move. We don't have the firepower to take out a meaningful Imperial target, but nobody wants to risk lives making small hit-and-run attacks, either. We need to do *something,* anything. We need somewhere to start."

He stopped and turned his blind gaze back onto Starkiller.

"With your power we can—"

"No."

"Why not?"

"Juno is more important."

"Why is she more important?"

"Because . . ." Starkiller swallowed. He had never admitted this to anyone, not even Juno. "Because . . ."

Kota waved the question away. "It doesn't matter. We both know the answer—and still I have to ask you what difference that makes. She's one person. We're fighting an entire galaxy."

"The Emperor is just one person."

"And so is Darth Vader, and so are all their minions. They add up, boy."

"But we have to defeat them one at a time."

Kota made a dismissive noise and resumed pacing. "Don't try to trap me in riddles. You're no philosopher. You're a fighter like me, and you hold the fate of the Rebel Alliance in your hands."

"*Nobody fights the Empire and wins.* You told me that once. Do you remember, Kota?"

"Yes, I remember." Kota dismissed that, too. "I was a different person back then. You brought me back to myself, back to the Force. You showed me what was possible."

"Maybe I'm really showing you now," Starkiller said. There was a very large, very complicated thought in his mind that he struggled to put into words. "Maybe—maybe where we begin is as important as what we do."

"You sound like a teacher I once had, and you make about as much sense as he did. Do you think *she* cares one bit about that?"

Starkiller hadn't considered that point. He had no idea what Juno was thinking. He couldn't even find her.

So much time had passed. He felt disconnected from everyone he had known best: Juno, Kota, even himself. He felt the world around him slipping away, as though he were becoming a ghost, insubstantial and irrelevant.

"I just want . . ." *Juno*. There was no point saying that again. "Kota, listen to me. I rescued you so you could help me, but you're not helping at all. I need a place to think this through on my own. To meditate without you distracting me."

Kota stared at him, a disbelieving expression on his face. "We're at war, and you want a quiet place to *think*?"

"It's important to me to find her. I won't stop until I do."

"And meanwhile the Alliance will be destroyed. Is *that* what you want?"

Starkiller stood, tired of being loomed over and yelled, "You talking like this is why I have to go!"

"Fine, then. Go to the forests of Kashyyyk or the caves of Dagobah, or wherever you think you'll find what you need and let the galaxy die."

"What are you talking about? I'm not going to let the galaxy die. I want what she wants—what you want, too, just in a different order."

Kota faced him, standing straight and tall. "Is that true?"

"Yes."

"Can I believe you?"

Starkiller hesitated. His feelings were muddied on everything beyond finding Juno. But he meant Kota no harm, and he was certainly no ally of Darth Vader and the Emperor.

"Yes," he said. "Yes, you can. I'm not a coward, Kota, and I will *come* back."

Kota shook his head and seemed to deflate. He looked old and tired, and for a moment Starkiller wished he could take back everything he had said and give Kota, his mentor and friend, everything he wanted. But there was no doing that now, and it would have been a lie. Juno came first. Then the Rebellion. That was how it had to be.

"All right." Kota headed toward the exit of the cockpit. "Go wherever you want. Take the ship: It's always been yours anyway.

Just drop me at the nearest spaceport before you get lost in the stars, so I can find someone who will *fight*."

Starkiller swiveled the pilot's chair toward the console and stared, without really seeing anything, until he was sure Kota had gone. Then he lowered his head onto the blinking instruments and closed his eyes. The face of the empty moon rotated far below, unnoticed, irrelevant.

He was doing the right thing. He was sure of it.

The only question remaining was: where to start?

Water.

He looked up and began calculating a course for the first waterworld he thought of—Dac, the home of the Mon Calamari.

CHAPTER 8

THE CARGO FREIGHTER TOUCHED DOWN on Dac's moon with a dust-softened thump. Bail Organa, back in his grunt pilot's pressure suit, released the controls and set the instruments to standby. No one had followed them on the short journey, and no one would look twice at an authorized vessel in such an utterly uninteresting place. For as much time as they could spare, they would be unobserved and unsuspected of anything at all.

"Nice spot for a summer palace," Juno said as PROXY went aft to warm up the R-22. "You should think about moving here."

"The quiet is tempting." Organa's wry tone perfectly matched hers. "But I don't think I'll be settling anywhere soon. The Emperor will get tired of looking for me eventually, and that's the time to reappear. There's a lot of work to be done out there."

On that last point Juno heartily agreed. They had discussed the Senator's plans on the way from the surface. He believed that he was too well known to be assassinated in public. Robbed of the hope of quiet, out-of-sight murder, the Emperor, Organa said, would stick to the philosophy of keeping his enemies close and rely on other methods to deal with the growing Rebellion.

Juno supposed that he knew the Emperor better than anyone alive, except Darth Vader, but she wondered if he was secretly as worried as she would have been. Painting a target on one's head and sticking it out into the firing line had never struck her as being particularly life affirming. For oneself or one's family.

"Any idea," she asked, "what this work you're planning to do might actually be?"

"I know what you're really asking. You want to know which way I'll side with respect to Mon Mothma and Garm Bel Iblis."

"Spot-on, Senator."

"Well, it's a tricky question at the moment. With the Dac resistance movement on our side, we'll soon have more ships, but that doesn't mean we can afford to be complacent. One shipyard doesn't make us the equal of the Empire. And for that I'm glad. I don't trust that kind of power. A lesson learned the hard way is hard—perhaps impossible—to unlearn."

"Assuming we don't all get killed along the way."

"Assuming that, yes." He looked at her with one hand cupping his cheek. "Where do *you* sit on this, Juno? You're not afraid of action, but I don't see you running off to start your own revolution."

She didn't dodge the question. "I think we need to act decisively, but smartly, too. What we did here, for instance—it made a difference. And if we'd taken Tarkin hostage, it might have made a *big* difference."

"Do you think the Emperor would have cared if we'd threatened to shoot Tarkin? I don't."

"No, but those around him might have. When the ruler of the galaxy doesn't lift a finger to save a Grand Moff, what kind of message does that send?"

"True." He nodded. "For what it's worth, I agree with you. There are tipping points and levers we can use to apply force all through the Imperial administration, and the sooner we start applying them, the sooner the Emperor will start to feel the pressure. But the importance of a symbolic victory should never be downplayed, and neither should the risks. Too many choices, too much at stake, as ever. The future will judge us, not each other."

"If we *have* a future."

"Oh, there's no doubt about that, Captain Eclipse. The question is: What sort?"

Juno smiled, noting how cleverly he had avoided giving a direct answer to her original question. But she didn't pursue it. It had been good seeing him, and she didn't want to spoil the moment with politics.

"Pleasure serving with you again, Senator Organa," she said, extending her hand.

He gripped and shook it. "The feeling is mutual, Captain Eclipse. I hope this won't be the last time I hear from you."

"And vice versa."

"That job's still going, remember."

She rolled her eyes. "The best you could offer at the moment would be low-pay haulage. I did enough of that when I was with the Empire."

He laughed and saluted as she retreated to the cargo bay. PROXY had the R-22's landing lights on and the repulsors thrumming. She climbed up into the cockpit and slid easily into the pilot's seat next to him. When the hatch was sealed, Organa opened the bay doors and she guided the fighter outside, into the gray, lunar light. Juno lifted a hand in farewell, knowing that Organa would be watching through the forward observation ports. The cargo freighter lifted off, hatch slowly sealing shut on its empty hold.

"All systems are fully operational," PROXY advised her. "We are ready to return to the fleet and report."

She wasn't looking forward to that. The question of what she should tell who remained very much open. Should she debrief with Leia or report on developments with the Rebel Alliance leadership?

"First we have to find out where the fleet is, exactly," she said. "Plot a course for Malastare. That's the best place to start looking."

"Yes, Captain Eclipse."

Juno tapped her index fingers on the instrument panel while PROXY performed the hyperspace calculations. The mission on

Dac had been an unqualified success, but it had left her with a faintly empty feeling, as though opportunities had been missed and the obvious overlooked. She didn't know where that feeling came from, exactly. Perhaps no more than because every time she worked with Bail Organa one-on-one it reminded her of Starkiller.

On Felucia they had discussed the mystery surrounding his past and whether she trusted him. On Corellia they had been looking for PROXY, lest information the droid contained fell into the enemy's hands. This time, there had been no mention of Starkiller, but thoughts of him had been unavoidable. If he hadn't died, Kota wouldn't have died; if Kota hadn't died, they wouldn't have been on Dac in the first place. The shadow he cast still stretched long over the Rebellion, a year after his death.

She physically shook herself. How much longer would it take before she got over him? Hadn't she grieved enough?

"Coordinates prepared," said PROXY. "Are you well, Captain Eclipse?"

"Yes," she said, rubbing her eyes and telling herself to get a grip. "I'm all right. Give me the controls. I'll take us there."

"Yes, Captain."

The R-22 hummed under her hands, ready for dust-off. She took a deep breath. This was what life was about, she reminded herself: the roar of engines; the flow of data; the magical yet utterly mechanical routine of traveling from A to B through hyperspace. She had missed being directly behind the controls of a ship. That was the one thing she regretted about accepting the commission to command the *Salvation*.

She wondered briefly how Nitram and *her crew* were faring without her. They felt unimaginably distant, like a dream she had once had.

Like the past she couldn't call back.

"Enough," she told herself, and hit the repulsors with a firmness that surprised her.

* * *

SHE SLEPT BRIEFLY during the hyperspace jump, in several short bursts. It was a long journey, from the Outer Rim on one side of the galaxy to the Mid Rim on the other. First they followed the Overic Griplink to Quermia, where they joined the busy Perlemian Trade Route. The risk of discovery was greater where traffic flowed most readily, so at Antemeridias they took a side route, following the Triellus Trade Route around Hutt space all the way along the galactic arms to the Corellian Run. There they took a series of complicated legs incorporating parts of the Llanic Spice Run, the Five Veils route, and the Sanrafsix Corridor to an uninhabited world called Dagobah on the Rimma Trade Route. They followed that particular route to the Hydian Way, and thus came to Malastare from the opposite direction to the one she had originally set out on.

Juno stretched as far as she could in the cramped cockpit when the high-gravity world hove into view. Orbit was a mess of ships displaying Imperial and independent transponders. The world's last Chief Magistrate had been transferred thanks to his habit of shooting the locals for sport, and the Empire's rule had been contested ever since. High-gravity AT-AT walkers hunted for Rebel outposts in deserts while insurgency groups picked off Imperial officials in the city. Both indigenous Dugs and settled Gran fought fiercely alongside each other to maintain their independence. Juno hoped the citizens of Dac would look to Malastare as an example of how to proceed in the coming months.

Even here, she realized with a sinking heart, was a reminder of times past. The former Chief Magistrate had been Ozzik Sturn, who had moved from Malastare to Kashyyyk, where he had come last in an encounter with Starkiller.

Ripples in a pond, she thought, as she had over Cato Neimoidia. Starkiller had been a particularly large pebble . . .

She took the controls and descended on course for Port Pixelito, the world's capital city and largest spaceport. A trio of TIE fighters buzzed her, but she easily outflew them. Unlike Dac and

Cato Neimoidia, Malastare had little the Empire actually wanted; otherwise there would have been Star Destroyers descending en masse to remind the world of where its loyalties should lie. The low-level campaign against its citizens was just enough to remind them that they shouldn't get too comfortable. Their time would come.

Port Pixelito was a tangled sprawl of low, squat buildings, as befit the higher gravity. Air traffic was lighter and less regulated than elsewhere, and Juno guided her straining R-22 to an empty berth without needing to register with the local authorities. Malastare was, effectively, a free port for non-Imperials, making it a perfect place for the Rebel Alliance to reallocate goods and staff. She had visited several times prior to gaining command of the *Salvation,* and made several important contacts, as well. The man she was coming to see was just one of them.

The repairman.

When the starfighter was in its berth, she shut down the engines and popped the hatch. City smells rushed in, prompting her to pull a face. A crumbling civil administration had disadvantages, too.

"Stay with the ship," she told PROXY. "If anyone comes near it, do your best Wookiee impersonation and scare them away. I won't be long."

"Yes, Captain Eclipse. I will inform you of any unexpected developments."

She checked the charge on her blaster and hurried off, scowling at a number of unsavory characters checking out the R-22's well-maintained lines. Poor security was another problem Malastare suffered from, thanks to the ongoing urban conflict. Starfighters were valuable machines that could be easily adapted to other purposes. Left unguarded, the R-22 wouldn't last an hour.

Juno emerged from the spaceport and checked her bearings. The streetscape had changed somewhat since her last visit. At least one of the major landmarks was gone, probably demolished during a strike from either side. People brushed by her, grunting impatiently. She spotted a dozen different species in the first ten seconds.

There. She found the sign she was looking for and cut a path through the crowd toward it. In blinking yellow and green pixels, it promised REPAIRS—NO QUESTIONS ASKED and hung above the entrance to a green, two-story building that might once have been a small theater. Graffiti advertising the latest Podrace covered the walls almost entirely from ground to roofline. She had watched one of the planet's high-speed extravaganzas the last time she had visited; it had made even her pulse race.

Juno walked through the door, brushing past an elderly insectoid Riorian clutching a dented gyrostabilizer to his chest. He chattered something to her in a dialect she didn't understand then hurried away.

"Another satisfied customer," said the Gran behind the shop counter, smiling hopefully. Its three stalked eyes blinked at her in the low light. Two Kowakian monkey-lizards, possibly a rare breeding pair, chased each other across the tops of shelves stuffed with dusty machine parts. Their squawking voices were loud in the claustrophobic space.

"I'm looking for your boss," she told the Gran. "The repairman."

"Lots of people looking for him. Who says he's here?"

"He never goes anywhere. Tell him it's Juno."

The Gran hesitated, and then lowered its snout to speak into a comlink fixed to the counter. Its native tongue was another Juno couldn't interpret, but she heard her name mentioned at least twice.

A voice answered in the same dialect, and the Gran nodded and pointed at the shelves.

"You know the way?"

"Unless you've changed it, sure."

The Gran pushed a concealed button, and a section of the wall slid aside. Juno went through it and waited for the panel to close behind her. There was a moment of absolute darkness and silence, and then the inner panel clicked. She slid it aside and walked into the workshop.

It was a mess of starship components, droid limbs, photo-receptors, sensors, wires, core processors, field generators, environmental units, and more. Stacks of parts stretched high up to the distant ceiling, while some hung suspended in nets cast from corner to corner. Several ramps led up and down to farther layers, and Juno knew that the deepest levels contained the components required to make weapons and targeting computers. Many of the broken machines that came through the store contained information relating to the Empire's activities in the system and beyond, and the Rebel Alliance had gained valuable data by tapping into this inadvertent leak, as well as sourcing much of its military matériel from reclaimed or completely rebuilt items.

She looked around, standing on the tips of her toes to see over the piles.

"Over here, Juno," called a familiar voice. "Come on through."

A mop of blond hair was just visible on the far side of the room. She wound her way through the close spaces of the workshop to where its owner was working. The main workbench had moved, but it looked about as messy as it had the last time she'd been here. Myriad fragments of a multitude of machines covered its surface, mixed with all the delicate tools of the trade, material, sonic, and laser. As she approached, the owner of the tools put down the blue-spitting lance he had been working with and flipped back his visor.

"Well, well. It *is* you! Pull up a seat and tell me where you've been. You don't write, you don't call—I was beginning to get worried."

She dragged a stool over to the bench and gratefully perched herself on it. Her calves were killing her in the high g. The so-called and literal repairman, Berkelium Shyre, was a human technician who had been living on Malastare for more then a decade, and—after an initial hitch or two—had successfully ridden out the transition from Imperial to independent rule. He was broad-shouldered and very strong, thanks to the local conditions, and his loyalty to the Rebellion was matched only by his skill with machines. Juno couldn't tell how old he was, for the freshness of his features and skin were matched by stress and worry lines, the origins of which she had never asked about. They had become friends over the months she'd helped the Rebellion strengthen its hold on the planet. She'd lost count of the number of late nights they'd spent discussing tactics and drinking cheap Corellian whiskey. He'd sent her the occasional cheerful message since, letting her know that all was well on her old patch. She'd always been too busy to respond.

"I'm looking for the fleet," she said. "Do you know where it's moved to?"

"Hey, not so fast," he said with a grin. "I mean it. Tell me what you've been up to. I won't let you go without having at least a half-hearted conversation."

She caught a faint edge to his tone and wondered if he suspected she might have turned traitor. That was a reasonable concern, and a reassuring one. He shouldn't hand out the fleet's location without proper cause, even to someone he thought he knew.

"Well, you know I was promoted," she said.

"You told me that when you were last here. We've missed you in the sector. How's it going?"

She didn't want to tell him about her contretemps with Mon Mothma, but she found herself doing it anyway. It felt good getting it off her chest. Shyre had always been easy to talk to. There was something so direct and open about him. She saw no judgment at all in his cheerful blue eyes.

"Suspended, eh?" He pushed a couple of fuses around his workbench with the tip of magnetic screwdriver. "That must be hard."

"Well, I've been keeping busy."

"I bet. You couldn't help yourself. That droid of yours still playing up?"

"Actually, he's on the mend now. No more visual glitches,

mostly. He worries sometimes about his lack of a primary program, though. I don't suppose you could help me with that?"

He shook his head. "Afraid not. Specialized units like PROXY,
you probably need to replace the whole core."

"That's what I figured, and they're thin on the ground. Thanks
regardless."

"Anytime, Juno."

There was a small but awkward silence.

"So," she pressed him, "the fleet . . ."

"It's not far from here," he said, not taking his eyes off her. "In
the Inner Rim, just off the Hydian Way. Ever heard of a place
called Nordra?"

"No," she said, "but I'll find it."

"Stick around the area and they'll find you."

"Thanks, Shyre."

She hopped carefully down from the stool, mindful of twisting
an ankle.

"Wait," he said, taking her arm. "Do you really have to go so
soon?"

"Places to be, Emperors to overthrow," she quipped.

"But you've only just got here. You haven't told me about
what you're feeling these days, where your head is."

She didn't remember ever talking much about that kind of
stuff, with anyone, and it was her turn to wonder what was going
on. Could he have notified Imperial agents who might already be
converging on her location?

She tried to pull away, but his grip was too strong. She did
throw him off balance, though, and the gyros of his stool whined
in complaint. From the waist down, he was entirely machine. His
legs had been lost in the early days of Malastare's independence,
when a thermal detonator had gone off in the middle of a squad of
saboteurs he had been helping, leaving him crippled. He had built
the prosthetic himself and traded active combat for offering support behind the scenes, professing perfect satisfaction with his lot.
But there were those worry lines . . .

Was that what this was about, she wondered—turning on those he felt were responsible for ruining his life?

"Let go of me, Shyre."

He did so immediately. "Sorry, Juno. I don't mean to be pushy. I just wish you'd stay."

"I'll be back. Don't worry about that."

"No, I mean *stay*. Here. With me."

Understanding suddenly dawned, and she felt like an utter fool for misreading the cues so badly. *Betraying* her was the last thing on his mind.

"Don't," she said, backing away.

"Hear me out," he said. "I have to say this now. You left too quickly before, and you never responded to my messages."

"I don't want to hear it. I can't hear it."

"But maybe you *need* to hear it," he said with much more than simple entreaty in his voice. "You've been in a funk ever since that friend of yours was killed. I don't know who he was or what happened to him, but I can tell what he meant to you. I can read you, and I know you needed to grieve for him, for what you lost; believe me, I understand that all too well." He rapped the knuckles of his left hand against the metal of his mechanical stool. "But it's been over a year now. Don't you think it's time to move on?"

She turned away to hide the pricking of tears in her eyes. Was it time? Yes, probably. Was she able to? No, it didn't seem that way. Starkiller came so readily to mind. It was like he was still with her, even in death. She couldn't move on until he was gone.

But when would that be? Maybe never, and she didn't want to give Shyre false hope. He was a good man—handsome, smart, loyal, brave, and good-humored. He deserved better than her. She couldn't even speak to him now, let alone give him what he wanted.

"I'm sorry," she said. "I think it might be better if you stopped worrying about me, and moved on yourself."

He was silent for a long time. When he finally spoke, his tone was subdued, but not resentful.

"All right," he said. "I hope you don't think less of me for trying."

"No," she said, turning back to face him. "And I hope you don't think less of me for saying no."

"That wouldn't be possible," he said with a brave smile.

She squeezed his broad shoulder, marveled briefly at the rock-hard muscles, and then hurried away.

AFTER THE CLOSE DIMNESS of the workshop, the light outside seemed very bright and the noise was deafening. Instead of going straight back to the landing bay, she scoured the streets until she found a food seller she remembered from her previous visits, a wise old Cantrosian who made the best pashi noodles she'd ever tasted. The hit of familiar and very powerful spices cleared her head almost immediately. She was able to push the stricken look in Shyre's eyes out of her mind for long enough to start thinking about the safest route to the Inner Rim. There were so many interdictors stationed on the Hydian Way, pirates and Imperials alike. It wouldn't do to get caught by one of them.

"It's been over a year now. Don't you think it's time to move on?"

As she threaded through the crowd back to the landing bay, she thought she glimpsed Kota's silver topknot standing high above the heads, in a crowd of haggling mercenaries. That was impossible, of course. He had fallen on Cato Neimoidia over a week earlier.

Shaking her head and walking on, she admonished herself severely. When she started hallucinating dead friends, she knew she really *was* stuck in the past.

CHAPTER 9

DAGOBAH WAS A SMALL green-brown world with no moons. It seemed utterly uninhabited, and further examination didn't prove that impression wrong. Starkiller checked the rest of the system, wondering if he'd come to the wrong planet, but there was no doubt. Its sibling worlds were boiling, airless, frozen, or gaseous. There was nowhere else to go but here, assuming he wanted to survive longer than a minute outside.

For the hundredth time, he asked himself what he was doing.

There was no ready answer.

Mon Calamari had been an utter dead end. With an Imperial administration boiling over from recent resistance activity, he had only barely managed to slice into records deeply enough to find out that no one called Juno Eclipse had ever officially come to the planet, let alone in the last week. With no other way to search for her open to him, he had been forced to retreat and think of something else. Unfortunately, another search through the Force had been fruitless. She was either dead, in hyperspace, or hiding somehow. The second was the most likely, of course, but a long wait and then another search had still given him nothing. If she was going somewhere, it was taking her a long time to get there.

Studying a map of the galaxy in frustration, he had stumbled across a name that Kota had used. *Dagobah*. Starkiller had never heard of it before, and the ship's records had nothing to add, beyond its location. All he had to go on was Kota's brief mention of it.

"Go to the forests of Kashyyyk or the caves of Dagobah or wherever you think you'll find what you need, and let the galaxy die."

The forests of Kashyyyk brought back memories of wood smoke and the face of a man who must have been his father. The *original* Starkiller's father. He had found his birth name there, but that wasn't where his quest was leading him now. He was going forward, not backward. His gut told him that there was nothing on Kashyyyk for him now.

What *Kota's* gut was telling him was the issue. Had he mentioned Dagobah for a reason or entirely at random? Was the Force moving him in ways even he didn't understand?

Either way, Starkiller had no other leads to follow. Kota had jumped ship to Commenor long ago, so Starkiller plotted a course to the Sluis sector and raced to the distant world as fast as the *Rogue Shadow* was able.

Now that he was here, he didn't know if he'd found something or gotten more lost than ever.

Skimming over the planet's atmosphere, carefully cloaked in case there was someone watching, he detected no hint of Juno, but he could feel a pervasive aura radiating from the planet. Like Felucia, where the original Starkiller had fought Shaak Ti and her young Zabrak apprentice, this world was rich with the Force. A multitude of life-forms thrived in its rich biosphere, which only made it stranger to him that no one had settled there.

Life was in principle a good thing, he reasoned, but living things weren't always good to one another. Perhaps Dagobah was infested with giant predators, or its vegetable life ate anything that moved, or something he hadn't come close to imagining.

He would have to be careful if he were to land there.

Was he going to do that?

He weighed up the pros and cons as thoroughly as he could. On the one hand, he had no reason to think that anything useful to his quest lay on the planet below. On the other hand, Kota was no fool, and he had deep connections to the Force of his own, connections that might become apparent if explored more deeply.

It was his own original instinct that convinced him. His first thought on leaving Vader had been to seek out Kota. On finding Kota, he had been disappointed that he couldn't tell him anything about Juno's whereabouts, but maybe *this* was why Kota had been important. Turning away now might leave him more lost than ever, even if he couldn't see where this path might lead him. At the very least, he might find a place to meditate, as he had told Kota he was going in search of.

Operating the *Rogue Shadow*'s controls by feel, he followed his instincts down into the atmosphere and sought a safe landing spot.

It wasn't easy. The tree canopy was dense and hid marshy, treacherous soil. Thick clouds clung to promontories and low mountain ranges, making them visible only to radar. He imagined a thousand hungry eyes peering up at him as he circled. Eventually he decided on a narrow strip of isolated land, just visible through a gap in the clouds. The *Rogue Shadow* swooped down with repulsors whining and settled onto the green-furred soil. Nothing lumbered out of the undergrowth to taste it. No huge vegetable jaws closed shut around it. Nothing happened at all, which only made him more nervous.

At least the ground was stable. He shut down the engines and waited as the ship grew quiet around him. A patter of rain rippled across the hull, sounding like asteroid fragments against shields. Streamers of mist blew through the trees.

When he got up and opened the hatch, a powerful smell hit his nostrils. The mixture of pollen, pheromones, and decay originated from all around him, from every living thing on the tiny world. He had never encountered anything like it before. Felucia was more cloying, with a thick fungal edge; Raxus Prime was just rot, all the way through; Kashyyyk's distinctive odor came from wood and its by-products. Dagobah was something else entirely.

Maybe, he thought, that stink was why no one had settled here.

He jumped lightly from the ramp onto the mossy ground. Water dripped from trees and leaves all around him, maintaining a steady patter. There was no wind to raise a sudden tattoo. The air was thick and motionless, as though it never moved, ever.

Juno wasn't there. He was sure of that. But what *was* there? Where were the caves of Dagobah?

He closed his eyes and let the Force tell him what it could.

Life roiled around him, tugging his mind in a dozen directions at once. He let himself be buffeted, tilting his head from one side to the other, testing the flows. There was a hint of something unusual to the east, a knot in the Force unlike any he had felt before. It drew him and repelled him at the same time. The longer he studied it, the more he felt as though it was studying him right back.

He opened his eyes. A large reptilian bird was staring at him from the trees. Its black eyes blinked, but otherwise it didn't move. With a flutter of leathery wings, another of its kind swooped in to join it.

Starkiller reached behind him to seal the *Rogue Shadow*'s hatch. Then he ignited one lightsaber as a precautionary measure. Still the reptavians didn't move.

With every sense alert for danger, he loped off into the swampy forest.

THE GIANT SLUG had twenty-four legs and a mouth full of teeth. Eight meters from snout to tail, it loomed over him, roaring. Its breath was vile.

Starkiller hacked a double line down its belly with both his lightsabers and jumped to avoid the rush of foulness that released. Among the body parts expelled from the creature's stomach was the head of one of the giant reptiles he had encountered farther back. The slug writhed and whined in pain. He left it to die on its own time. His destination was close.

He forced his way through a tangle of long, leg-like roots, scattering a clutch of big, white spiders as he went. The knot he had felt lay dead ahead, at the base of the largest tree he had seen so far. Despite its size, the tree looked sick with a malevolence that surprised him. If Dagobah as a whole was alive with the Force, then this tree had been poisoned by the dark side.

His searching gaze found a deep hole choked with roots and vines at its base. This was undoubtedly the source of the poison that had ruined the tree. A lingering evil lurked here, wedded to the place as firmly as the tree itself. Its roots dug deep and stretched far.

He approached more cautiously, no longer worrying about the planet's more obvious predators. Was this the cave Kota had alluded to? Part of him hoped it wasn't, even as he yearned for this particular part of his mission to be over. Juno wasn't here, and he didn't want to be, either, any longer than he had to.

There was a clearing in front of the cave. He ran to it, and braced himself to enter the cave. His head was thick with foreboding. He felt as though black tendrils were reaching into his mind, stirring up memories that had been mercifully dormant until now. The voices of Darth Vader and Jedi Master Shaak Ti warred within his mind as though fighting over who controlled him.

"The dark side is always with you."

"You are Vader's slave—"

"Your hatred gives you strength—"

"You could be so much more."

"You are at last a master of the dark side."

"Are you prepared to meet your fate?"

A gentle tapping brought him out of his mental deadlock.

He spun around with both lightsabers upraised. Something was watching him—a tiny green creature dressed in swamp-colored rags with green skin, long, pointed ears, and a heavily lined face. It stood on a log with the help of a short cane that it held in both hands, and it was this that made the tapping noise.

The creature didn't flinch at the sight of the lightsabers. Its brown eyes were alive with amusement, if anything. It nodded once at him—in acknowledgment or recognition, Starkiller couldn't tell—and the cane ceased its gentle *tap-tap*.

He lowered his blades and, after a moment, deactivated them as well. He sensed no threat from this unexpected being. Quite the opposite, in fact. The yawning void of the cave seemed to retreat for a moment, clearing his mind of confusion. The being before him might be small in stature, but he was much greater than he looked.

"You guard this place?" Starkiller asked him, gesturing at the cave with the hilt of one of his lightsabers.

The creature chuckled as though pleased by the question. "Oh ho. Only a watcher am I now."

"Then you'll let me pass?"

That earned him a shrug. "Brought you here, the galaxy has. Your path, clearly this is."

Starkiller turned and looked behind him, into the cave mouth. The swamp jungle had fallen utterly silent around them. The air was as thick as glass.

"You know what I'm looking for?"

Something poked the back of his knee. He jumped. The little creature had hopped off the log and approached close enough to test him with his cane—so lightly and silently that Starkiller hadn't noticed.

"Hey!"

The creature persisted, poking his flight suit and lightsabers and gloves, and dissecting him with intense eyes.

"Something lost," he said. "A part of yourself, perhaps?"

Starkiller brushed him away, profoundly unnerved by the accurate and unasked-for reading of his situation.

"Maybe."

"Whatever you seek, only inside you will find."

The creature settled back with his hands on his cane, staring up at Starkiller with so powerful a gaze that for a moment he felt as though he were being looked at from a great height. All trace of humor was gone.

"Inside?" he repeated.

The tip of the cane lifted, pointed at the cave.

Starkiller hesitated. The insidious pressure of the hole in the tree roots grew stronger, and his mind clouded again.

"*Be careful, boy*," said Kota from the past. "*I hear the long shadow of the dark side reaching out to you.*"

Like a diver preparing for a long descent, he took a deep breath and entered the cave.

IT WAS DARK INSIDE, of course, but somehow it managed to be even darker than he had expected. He struggled through thick curtains of roots and vines, resisting the urge to slash at them with his lightsabers. He kept his weapons carefully inactive, intuitively understanding that any aggressive move that he took might be reflected back at him a hundredfold. Intuition was all he had to guide him now.

His groping fingers encountered a wall of stone ahead of him. Instead of a dead end, however, he found that the cave bent sharply to his right. He pressed on, feeling the dark side throbbing in his ears and beating against his useless eyes. The air seemed to vibrate. Every breath made him want to scream—but in dismay or delight, he couldn't tell.

Another wall ahead of him. This time the tunnel turned to his left. His grasping hands were wet with moisture. He could see them now, somehow, reaching ahead of him as he felt his way into the far reaches of the cave. Gradually the vines fell away, leaving just the roots to obstruct him.

Through a dream-like fog, he stumbled into a larger chamber, the outer limits of which were obscured. He looked down at his feet but couldn't see them, either. The ground was hidden by a crawling gray mist.

He realized with a shock that his flight suit was gone. He was now, somehow, wearing the traditional robes of a Jedi Knight. A flash of memory came to him then, of seeing himself exactly like this on Kashyyyk, wielding his father's blade.

He heard himself asking Darth Vader.

"Your spies have located a Jedi?"

"Yes. General Rahm Kota. You will destroy him and bring me his lightsaber."

The voices from his memory seemed to echo through the room, whispering, tugging him on.

". . . at once, Master . . ."

". . . one more test . . ."

". . . as you wish, my Master . . ."

". . . one step closer to your destiny . . ."

". . . will not fail you, Lord . . ."

". . . do not disappoint me . . ."

He emerged into a much larger cave. The fog cleared, revealing muddy walls overgrown with roots. The floor was treacherous underfoot. He walked carefully forward, seeking the source of the whispers, but stopped dead on realizing that the tangled roots ahead of him were moving.

It was too dark to see properly. The time had come to shed some light on his unusual situation. Igniting both his blades, he held them up above his head, crossed in an X.

The light they cast was blue, not red. That was the first unnerving detail. By their cool light, he made out something hidden by the roots—and it was this that was moving, struggling against the winding net. He stepped warily closer, peering into the shadows. Was that an arm he saw, with a hand clutching vainly at freedom? Was this a hallucination, a vision, or something that was really happening?

A face shoved forward through the muddy roots. Starkiller gasped and stepped back, bringing his lightsabers down between him and the figure caught in the roots. He recognized those features. They were his own: lean and desperate and full of hunger.

Movement came from his right. Another body struggled against the grasping vegetation. Another version of him. And another. They were all around him, dozens of them, writhing, twisting, straining, whispering in agony.

"Yes, my Master."

"I am strong, my Master, and I am getting stronger."

"When will *my training be complete, Master?"*

They wore the black uniforms of Kamino. They were clones like him.

"What will you do with me?"

Starkiller shuddered and moaned. He looked about for an exit from the chamber, and saw a narrow crack in the stone. He lunged for it, but not so quickly that he avoided the hands that clutched at him. They gripped his flight uniform with his own strength, trying to hold him back, entrap him with them, where he belonged. He cried out and pulled free, falling back into the chamber. He raised his lightsabers automatically, thinking to hack his way free.

"Kill me and you destroy yourself."

He heard the voice clearly, as he had on Kashyyyk. That time, he had not hesitated to strike down the doppelgänger he had seen in his mind. This time he listened to himself, and once more extinguished his blades. The decision renewed his strength, gave him the courage to continue.

In the near darkness he faced the clutching hands of his other selves, and pushed firmly through them. Their slippery fingers skidded off his flight uniform and fell away. Behind him their whispers became moans and then faded to silence. All he could hear now was his breathing—fast and heavy, as though he had been running. He had been underground for hours, or so it felt. How much farther until he reached the end of the cave and found what he was looking for—or what was looking for him?

Another chamber, this one swirling with shadows. He kept walking, and the shadows rose up around him, forming short-lived figures that loomed and retreated, blocking his path. He tried to force his way past them, as he had with the visions of his other selves, but found himself confused and disoriented. His head spun. Twice he found himself facing the way he had come. He put out both hands to stop the world turning. There had to be a way out somewhere, if only the cave would let him find it.

He could hear rain in the distance, and he stumbled toward it. Thunder boomed—

—and suddenly he was standing in the cloning facility on Kamino, near the hole he had ripped in the wall during his escape. Visible through the hole, the sky hung wild and low, racked by a fierce electrical storm. Spray-slicked metal gleamed even in the gray light. The howl of wind was relentless and eerie.

A figure walked closer to the hole in order to inspect the torn metal. Armored from head to foot in gray and green, with an unfamiliar T-shaped visor and some kind of jetpack affixed to his back, his voice had the inflectionless grate of a vocoder. It was clear, though, that he wasn't a droid. Perhaps his vocal chords had been damaged.

"He has a healthy head start."

Starkiller moved closer. Only when he moved did he recognize the closeness of armor, the heaviness of limb, the sensation of being trapped. He had experienced all these sensations before.

He said in leaden tones, "The Empire will provide whatever you require, bounty hunter."

Starkiller strained to move his former Master's limbs, but he was powerless to do anything other than ride out the vision. He could only see through Darth Vader's eyes and wait for it to end.

"I'll need backup," said the green-armored figure.

Starkiller's black-gloved left hand gestured out the hole, toward the landing pad. There a long line of troopers was marching into two Lambda-class shuttles, followed by a type of droid he had never seen before. It was huge, with long legs, powerful armament, and heavy shielding. It was so big, the full extent of it was hidden behind the buildings near the landing bay.

The bounty hunter turned to Starkiller and said in a satisfied tone, "They'll do."

A flurry of rain obscured the view and—

—he was back in his body, and the shadows were retreating, forming a dense knot in front of him. He reeled away from it, holding his hands in front of him. They were flesh and blood, with no sign of prosthetics. He was himself, wholly and only himself, which came as a great relief even as the knowledge that his former Master was hunting him sank in. That was what the vision had been telling him, beyond all doubt. He thought himself free, but Darth Vader thought otherwise.

The shadows swirled and burst apart, and came rushing at him, filling his head—

—*with an image of PROXY, which surely couldn't be possible, since he had been destroyed by Darth Vader on Corellia. This had to be something from the past, Starkiller decided. But when, and where, and who was he now?*

There was none of the heaviness of Vader, and no sign of an Imperial presence at all. He was on a ship of some kind, a large one, bigger than the Rogue Shadow. *Crew members rushed around him, briskly but without urgency. They wore uniforms identical to the ones he had trained against on Kamino.*

Soldiers of the Rebel Alliance.

A canine-faced officer turned to face him.

"I'm having trouble with the forward sensor array, Captain."

Starkiller looked through the observation canopy, out at the space ahead. A small cluster of ships dotted the view, accompanied by an escort of Y-wings. In the backdrop hung a dense and beautiful nebula, all curls and swirls, glowing every color of the spectrum.

A familiar voice asked, "Interference from the nebula?"

PROXY turned from an instrument he was studying. "Perhaps. I'll try to pin it down."

"Let's not take any chances."

Starkiller barely heard the words. He was stunned by the knowledge that it was Juno speaking. He was experiencing what she was experiencing. Whatever had happened to her would happen to him now.

He punched a button on the console with her hand, not his.

"This is Captain Eclipse." Her voice echoed through the ship.

"Set defensive protocols throughout all ships. Prime your shields and check your scanners for anything that's not one of ours."

The canine-faced officer nodded and checked the screens in front of him. "All clear, Captain."

"Keep looking, Nitram. We can't be too careful."

"Of course, sir."

Starkiller watched the screens with her, searching for any sign of disturbance. His senses prickled. Something was coming. She could feel it, and therefore he could, too.

A voice crackled over the comm. "Captain Eclipse—we're picking up five, no six small warships, coming in fa—"

Explosions puffed alongside a ship ahead. Starkiller didn't see where the attacking vessels had come from, but he could see what they were doing. Four precisely aimed missiles cracked the ship in two, sending crew and air gushing into the void. With one ship down, the focus of the attack turned to the center of the group: the ship containing Juno.

"Shields to full," she called over the intercom. "Open fire, all batteries!"

An impact rocked the deck beneath her. The bridge swayed.

"We've been breached," said her second in command. "Troopers boarding!"

"Send a security detail to the main reactor. Seal off life support."

Another explosion, closer than before. Rebel crew went flying, but Juno held on to her post.

"Get those deflector shields up!"

PROXY leaned into view. "Internal security beacons are going crazy. Captain Eclipse, I think we should—"

The bridge doors blew in. Smoke and burning debris filled the air. Through the cloud stalked two heavily armed troopers, already firing. Juno ducked down, blaster pistol in hand. One precise shot to the throat seal put one of the troopers down. Another barely missed the second.

Four more troopers rushed into the bridge. The maze of blasterfire intensified. Starkiller felt his heart racing as he edged to a better vantage point, picking off troopers as best he could. His crew died around him. First PROXY, blown backward in a shower of sparks, then the dog-faced second in command. Rage rose up in him, pure and clean. He stood up in order to see more clearly through the thickening smoke.

A blaster bolt took him in the shoulder, sending him spinning sideways, falling—

—and when he hit the ground in the cave he realized that, although it had been Juno's heart pounding all along, his still kept perfect time with hers. He was covered in sweat, and the stink of the smoke was thick in his nostrils. The pain of the bolt to Juno's arm hurt all the more for knowing that he hadn't been there to stop it.

The timing of the vision tormented him. Juno hadn't been captain of anything larger than the *Rogue Shadow* while PROXY had lived—or while the original Starkiller had lived, for that matter. She hadn't been shot, either. Was it conceivable that PROXY had been brought back to life—or simply replaced? He had seen other droids of his make on Kamino, so that wasn't impossible. That placed the vision sometime after the events of the Death Star. But when? Had they already happened, or were they still to come? *Could he prevent them from happening?*

He struggled to his hands and knees. The shadows crowded him, made it hard to move. His lightsaber hilts had fallen from his hands and rolled out of sight. He scrabbled about for them in the gloom, but they were nowhere to be found.

"Give them back," he told the shadows. "Give them back!"

All they gave him was another vision.

He was crouched on a metal surface, holding Juno in his arms. Rain pounded them. Her eyes were closed. She was covered in blood. He was covered in blood. She wasn't breathing. He tipped his head back and howled back at the storm.

The image of Juno faded into nothing and he fell face-forward onto the muddy ground of the cave, as though gravity had multiplied a thousand times. In that vision, he had definitely been himself. It was either the future or a past he could no longer remember. Or the work of another clone. Or some equally bizarre possibility he could not for the moment fathom.

"We form a strong team," said her voice out of the past. *"It's unfortunate we can't keep on as we are."*

The memory gave him strength to resist the terrible weight of the shadows. Juno had said that on their return to the *Empirical,* at which time he had expected to help Darth Vader overthrow the Emperor and she, he had assumed, would have been allocated to other duties. She had been wrong then, and this vision might be wrong now. Past, present, future—if anyone could change it, it would be him.

Juno could not die.

The pressure fell away. He leapt to his feet. His lightsabers flew out of the shadows and landed in his hands, and were lit an instant later. They were red once more, as red as the blood in his final vision. The shadows fled.

By the crimson light he could see that there was nowhere else to go. He had reached the end of the caves. The only direction he had left to go was back.

He steeled himself for a repeat of his clawing other selves, just in case the cave wasn't finished with him yet, and pressed on his way.

EVEN THE MURKY SWAMP LIGHT seemed bright and green to his eyes when he finally staggered out of the cave. The air smelled sweet and fresh. He clung to a fall of tangled vines and gave himself a moment to recover. He felt utterly drained by what lay behind him, and utterly daunted by what lay ahead.

Juno could not die.

That was the only thing keeping him going.

The click of a tiny wooden cane brought him out of his

thoughts. His head came up. His searching gaze found the little creature sitting on a rock, calmly watching him.

How he stayed so close to the cave was beyond Starkiller. He could feel the dark side rolling in waves at him. The undertow was powerful. He had only just escaped. To be constantly within range of such an assault, and to remain sane—or what passed for it on this sodden, forgotten world—was utterly inconceivable to him . . .

The little creature possessed a power out of all proportion to his appearance.

"Whatever you have seen," he said, pointing the tip of his cane at Starkiller's heaving chest, "follow it, you must."

Starkiller nodded. If that was wisdom, then he shared it. "To the ends of the galaxy if I have to."

The creature returned his nod and lowered the cane. His eyes closed, and Starkiller knew that his audience, if such it was, had ended.

Leaping out of the clearing, propelled by a sense of urgency that transcended time and space, he ran as fast as he could for the *Rogue Shadow*.

CHAPTER 10

NORDRA WAS ANOTHER HIGH-GRAVITY WORLD, but one that was extremely tectonically active, with numerous precipitous mountain ranges crisscrossed by deadly blue glaciers. From orbit Juno spied several low-altitude lakes of bubbling lava, alongside which the inhabitants had built several heat-devouring cities. She tapped into their local version of the Holonet News, NordFeed, and found a hardy if not particularly lofty race that had learned to live with constant physical threat and danger. Some of the reports were openly critical of the Emperor's policies. Only their isolation saved them, Juno suspected. Although technically on the Hydian Way, the well-traveled hyperroute detoured around a nearby nebula, bypassing Nordra and several other nearby worlds.

Juno bided her time waiting for the Rebel Alliance to pick up her transponder by half watching NordFeed, half staring blankly out her viewport at the vast and beautiful nebula ahead, all the while trying very hard not to think about Berkelium Shyre. She hadn't intended to hurt him. She had thought they were only friends. She had valued his friendship, and was guilty only of wanting everything to stay the same between them, even though she knew now that it could never be . . .

They couldn't go back, but they couldn't go forward, either. She wasn't ready for anything like that, and she didn't *want* to be ready, ever. It seemed stupid even to think it, but if she couldn't have Starkiller then she wouldn't have anyone. His death had left such a huge empty space in her life that no one seemed likely to fill it.

"We have you on our scopes, R-Two-Two," came a voice over the comm. "Identify."

She scanned her own screens but couldn't pin down the source of the transmission. There were five ships in orbit around Nordra, any one of which could belong to the Rebel Alliance. Possibly all of them did.

"Juno Eclipse," she broadcast. "Authorization Onda Cuvran Twenty-three Seventeen Ninety-one. Is the *Solidarity* here?"

"The *Salvation*, too, Captain. Here are the coordinates."

She fed the data into the navicomp, thinking: *Still Captain.* That was a welcome sign.

"These coordinates are on the other side of the nebula," PROXY warned her.

"Ion drive only, I presume?" she checked with the Rebel contact.

"You presume correctly. Itani Nebula is diffuse, for the most part, but it casts a big enough mass shadow to ruin your day."

"Understood. Thanks."

She fired up the ion drives and pulled the starfighter out of orbit. Ion drive would take longer, but it was worth it to ensure that the Alliance fleet couldn't be surprised by ships appearing out of hyperspace right on top of them. Thus far Commodore Viedas had managed to keep one step ahead of the Empire's spies, but it was only a matter of time before something critical leaked.

And that, she told herself, was of much greater concern than a broken heart.

JUNO DOCKED WITH THE *SOLIDARITY* and turned the R-22 back over to the hangar crew. She half expected to find Leia or her droid waiting for her, but the welcoming committee awaiting her consisted solely of an aide asking her to meet the commodore in his quarters, immediately. She said she would. No off-the-record chats in the officers' mess this time, she thought. That could be a good or a bad thing.

"You should consider yourself fortunate, PROXY," she said as they wound their way through the ship's corridors. "Not having a primary program means you don't have to worry about losing it."

"I do not feel fortunate, Captain Eclipse," he said in a mournful tone. "It makes me wonder if droids have a layer of programming even more fundamental than the one I am missing—a layer that makes us feel incomplete without instructions. We are built not just to serve, but to crave to serve. I cannot decide if this is slavery or a form of liberation."

"From choice, you mean?"

"From doubt."

Juno wished she could alleviate her own doubts by undergoing a quick memory wipe and restoring her factory presets.

She saluted the sentry outside Viedas's door and was waved through. The Rodian commodore was sitting behind a desk, studying charts. He half stood when she entered and waved her to a seat, then he sat back down again. PROXY stayed by the door, yellow eyes watching unblinkingly.

"Congratulations, Captain Eclipse," was Viedas's opening remark. "The inquiry found you not guilty of putting Alliance resources and staff in undue peril."

"Thank you, sir," she said, feeling an immediate lightness in her chest.

"As of now you are reinstated to full rank, privileges, and security clearance. But of course you have a whole new hurdle to leap over."

"Sir?"

"There's a meeting of Alliance leadership in half an hour to discuss the situation on Dac. You've been asked to attend."

"By whom?"

"By Mon Mothma."

Juno nodded. "I don't suppose I could get back in my star-fighter and circle the nebula until it's over?"

"Not a chance. And we'll know if you send that droid of yours in your place." Viedas's antenna twitched in something that might have been amusement. "Go freshen up. I'll have someone call your droid when we're ready."

"Thank you, sir."

"Oh, and you might be interested to know, Captain, that your mission to Cato Neimoidia is now being considered a success."

Juno frowned, thinking of Kota. "How is that possible, sir?"

"Baron Tarko was killed during insurgent action shortly after you left. Clearly you started something that someone else chose to finish. That's all."

She returned his salute and left the room, still puzzling over this latest development. There was very little to think of it, though, except to feel fortunate that someone had done her that favor. If she ever found out who it was, she would be sure to express her heartfelt thanks. With Cato Neimoidia now seen in a more positive light, it would be easier to talk about Dac, surely.

The sentry gave her directions to the nearest common area, where she did her best to look as though she had only just stepped off her bridge. She couldn't wait to get back to the *Salvation* and see what kind of mess Nitram had made of her duty rosters.

She studied her face in the mirror for a long time, wondering despite herself what Shyre saw in her. Couldn't he see how wrecked she looked? Was he oblivious to the bags under her eyes and her flight-helmet-hair? Would he still like her if he saw her as she really was, psychological scars and all?

Not for the first time she wished there were someone among the Rebels she could talk to about things other than tactics and starship specifications. If her mother were still alive . . .

A hand touched her shoulder. "Excuse me, Captain Eclipse. The commodore has asked for you."

She tore her eyes away from her face—and saw another version of her standing behind her.

"Thanks, PROXY. You know you're doing it again? Only this time you look like me."

The droid's holographic image shimmered and vanished with a flash. "I'm sorry, Captain Eclipse. I don't know what compels me." He put a hand to his metal forehead. "Perhaps another overhaul is in order."

"Next time we see that handy little droid, I'll put in a request." She took a second to make sure her uniform wasn't out of order. "Come on, or we'll be late."

The meeting was in the same place as before. This time, she and the commodore were the only flesh-and-blood participants. Mon Mothma and Garm Bel Iblis attended via hologram. Their gray-blue forms flickered and crackled, thanks to interference from the looming nebula. Leia Organa was conspicuous by her absence.

"Difficulties arranging transmission," Viedas explained when he saw her glance at the empty projector. "I suggest we begin regardless."

"We've received an overture from the Dac resistance," said Mon Mothma without preamble. "Ackbar has successfully united the Quarren and the Mon Calamari and convinced them to openly stand against the Empire. He promises ships, if we help him liberate the shipyards."

"That's excellent news," said Bel Iblis. "And excellent timing, given our recent conversation on this matter."

"The very thing that makes me suspicious," Mon Mothma said. "Where were you these last two days, Captain Eclipse?"

"I was relieved of command," Juno said, "so I took the opportunity to tie up some loose ends."

"On Dac, perchance?"

"I'm flattered, Senator, if you think I could pull off something like this on my own—"

A third holographic figure flickered into being next to the

others. Instead of Leia, though, it was Bail Organa, looking scruffy and cramped in his miner's disguise.

"Sorry to hold you up," he said. "I had to move to Mon Eron to obtain a secure line. It's a mess here at the moment. You might have heard."

"We were just talking about it," said Mon Mothma, looking unsurprised at his appearance, rather than his daughter's. "Captain Eclipse here denies any involvement."

"Actually," Juno put in, "what I said was that I couldn't have done it alone."

"Indeed." Mon Mothma raised an eyebrow. "I suppose, Bail, your daughter would say the same."

"I don't know what Leia would say," said Organa, "and I'm not sure why you're asking me. Why don't you ask her directly instead of hauling me in out of the cold?"

Mon Mothma's disapproval was a formidable thing, even over a hologram. "She might deny it, but I know that Leia orchestrated this unsanctioned operation, with Captain Eclipse and Ackbar as her conspirators, using confidential, *privileged* information. She acted precipitously and without consideration for the decisions we had made regarding the future direction of the Alliance. She abused her position as your representative and betrayed our trust in the process."

"Perhaps she did, but what do you expect me to do about it? I can't suspend her like you suspended Captain Eclipse."

"I believe it's time for you to come out of hiding and resume your position on this council, before she comes up with yet another wild scheme."

"I thought it was rather a good scheme, myself. That was why I was part of it." He threw Juno a self-deprecatory salute. "If you're going to censure Leia, you'd better censure me, too."

Mon Mothma's lips tightened. She looked around the gathering, taking the measure of everyone present.

"Did you know about this, Garm?"

Bel Iblis looked warily amused. "Not the slightest thing—but

I can't say I disapprove. This is everything Kota believed in: small, strategic strikes employed to great effect. This little action might change the course of the battle, if we follow it up quickly."

"But the *risk*," she said. "We might have lost Ackbar *and* Bail."

"There's no such thing as a risk-free war," Bel Iblis said. "And you can't force people not to fight, if they want to. Isn't that a kind of tyranny, in its own way?"

Mon Mothma stiffened as though physically threatened. Then she sagged. "Yes, I suppose you're right—and even if you're not, it's clear I'm in a minority. So what now? Do you propose we hand control over to an eighteen-year-old girl and let her decide our course?"

"Hardly," said Bail, "but you can listen to her and act on what she says. She speaks with my voice. Trust her judgment, as I do. If her plan on Dac had failed, I might well have died—but it didn't. She's an Organa, remember. We bring more than just our money to the cause."

"Very well," said Mon Mothma. "I shall do as you say. But that doesn't change the situation right now. The Mon Calamari star cruisers are promised but not delivered. Ackbar is in no position to replace Kota, dealing as he is with his own planet's problems. Our resources are precious, and stretched very thin."

"The Rebellion isn't something you can put on hold," said Organa. "It's a living thing. It needs to be *doing* something, not just being."

"A symbolic strike," said Juno, remembering what Organa had told her on Dac's Moon. "That's what we need. Something that will show our own people we still mean business, as well as the Emperor."

"Agreed," said Bel Iblis. "All this skulking around, effective or not, doesn't do much to bring in new recruits."

"All right," said Mon Mothma. "All right. A symbolic strike it is—but against what? There are thousands of potential targets, each as dangerous as the next. What are our criteria? What's our time frame? Who leads the operation?"

"These are important questions," said Organa. "I leave them in your capable hands, Senators. For now, I'd better sign off. The Empire is closely watching every signal that leaves the system. I don't want a squadron of TIEs landing on top of me, just as things are starting to get interesting."

"We understand," said Bel Iblis. "When we've reached a decision, we'll let you know."

"Thank you, Bail," said Mon Mothma. "Be safe."

The third hologram flickered out.

"Leadership is hard," said Bel Iblis to Mon Mothma, not unsympathetically, "when there are three of us trying to lead at once."

"If it were easy," she said, "we would have finished this long ago."

The two remaining Senators signed off, leaving Commodore Viedas, Juno, and PROXY alone.

"I think we just witnessed some progress," said the commodore, standing. "Of a sort."

Juno understood what he meant. Mon Mothma had given ground, but the leadership might still argue for weeks before settling on an appropriate target. And this time, something low-key simply wouldn't do. It would have to be extremely visible to have the effect required.

"I guess being seen to do something is better than doing nothing at all," she said, "even if it's hard to tell the difference sometimes."

"Careful, Captain Eclipse. You're becoming a cynic."

"Politics will do that to you."

"There are few immune to it, unfortunately."

Starkiller would have been, she wanted to say as the door closed between them, but she kept that thought to herself.

ON THE BRIEF SHUTTLE RIDE to the *Salvation,* PROXY changed shape without warning.

Juno looked up from the controls.

"Is that really you, Princess, or is PROXY playing up again?"

"Call me Leia," came the instantaneous reply. Wherever she was transmitting from, the signal was good. "Congratulations on the success of your mission, Captain. How did the meeting go?"

"Well enough, I think," Juno said, glad the shuttle was empty apart from her and PROXY. "I'm relieved your father was part of it."

"Yes. He can handle the others better than I."

"I wouldn't say that," Juno said. "You have the advantage of being young. I think it puts Mon Mothma off her game."

"It doesn't feel like an advantage when you're arguing with some of the old fools I have to deal with here at home. Alderaanian politics makes the Empire look like child's play."

"Still, you got what you wanted. Don't discount that."

"All right. Maybe I softened them up, but Father sealed the deal. And we couldn't have done it without you, of course."

"Happy to serve," Juno said, "although that might be a little more difficult now that I've got my command back—thank goodness."

"There was never any doubt of that. You'll be exactly where we can use you best—in the middle, not too far away from the action that you forget what's at stake, and not so close that you can't see the big picture. And you have a frigate at your disposal, which is nothing to be sniffed at when it comes to winning arguments."

Juno smiled. It didn't sound so bad, the way Leia put it.

"The important thing," Leia went on, "is that we keep fighting on all fronts at once. Big stuff, small stuff, everything in between. The Empire isn't just the Emperor: it's all the people beneath him who serve him willingly. We have to take the fight to them, too."

"Sounds exhausting."

"I get tired just thinking about it."

They laughed together, more out of companionship than at anything particularly funny. Juno couldn't remember the last time she'd had anything at all to laugh about.

"What are your plans now?" she asked.

"Well, the Death Star is still out there," said the Princess. "The Emperor has it well hidden from us, but it's too big a project to keep out of sight forever. We'll find it, one way or another, and we'll do our best to disrupt its construction. That's our number one priority, because if it's ever operational, the entire galaxy will suffer." She shrugged. "Apart from that, life goes on. University, training, all that ridiculous Old House palaver. If my aunts had their way, I'd be paired off to some brainless boy before the year is out—and there'd go any chance I had of doing something *real* ever again."

Juno was forcefully reminded then of how young Leia was. Boy troubles, parental expectations, frustrated ambition—for teenagers some things were universal, even in the middle of a galactic revolution. Leia reminded Juno of herself, not so very long ago.

"My father tried to set me up with the son of a friend once," she told the Princess. "A horrible boy, not much more than a recruit. Thought he was going to be the next High Commander but could barely button up his uniform right. Somehow just being from the right side of the planet mattered more than anything about who he was."

"What did you do?"

"Learned to be the best pilot in my sector and got myself transferred. The kid stayed behind—never made it above corporal, for all his talk. My father probably still thinks I missed my chance."

"Parents have no idea."

They laughed again, even as Juno wondered what was going on. Did the Princess have so little contact with the people around her that she, too, had no one to talk to? That didn't seem possible: She had mentioned the university, after all, where there would be lots of people her age, and Juno was sure Bail Organa wouldn't let his daughter grow up isolated and socially inept.

At least Leia still knew her father, Juno thought. Her own father was so distant and alienated that she didn't even know if he was alive.

"Do you have a boyfriend at the moment?" Juno asked her, testing the moment to see where it led.

To her credit, Leia didn't blush. "No one my aunts would approve of."

"Ah, it's like that. Watch out for the bad ones, Leia. They're the ones who really mess you up."

"Everyone says that."

"Because it's true. Don't learn it the hard way, like I did."

Instead of lumping Juno in with "everyone" and dismissing the advice, Leia nodded soberly. "I guess you did."

Juno sobered, too. She hadn't even been thinking of Starkiller, but now she was. The pain was sharp and piercing, causing her to lower her eyes from the Princess's searching gaze.

And suddenly it was clear just how Leia saw her. Not as a friend or confidante, although she might claim either if directly asked. What else could a Princess of the Royal House of Alderaan with rebellious aspirations see in an independent-minded officer who always seemed to be in the thick of things but a role model?

Now, *that* was a daunting responsibility.

"I'm sorry," said Leia. "I can't imagine what it must feel like to miss someone so badly."

"I hope you'll never know." Juno collected herself and forced a smile. Time to change the subject. "It makes fighting the Emperor and our friends the Senators look easy in comparison. At least they're fights we can win."

Like a good diplomat-in-training, Leia picked up on her signals. "Well, I'm sure we'll find ways to keep you busy. Thanks for your support, Juno. I'll be in touch again soon."

"We won't be sitting on our hands out here, that's for sure. The moment we have a target, the fleet will be ready to move."

Leia smiled and raised her hand as though to hit a switch at her end.

"Oh, before I go," she said, "if your droid is playing up again, have you considered that it might not be a random malfunction? There could be a reason for it, beyond a simple glitch."

"Like deliberate sabotage, you mean?"

"Maybe. Or a message. Or something else entirely." Leia shrugged. "I don't know. It's worth thinking about, though."

Juno nodded. "I will. Thank you."

Leia fizzled out, and suddenly Juno was sitting face-to-face with the droid himself.

"What do you think, PROXY? Are you trying to tell me something?"

"I can't imagine what, Captain Eclipse. When I have something to communicate with you, I use the verbal interface my makers gave me."

"You're all talk, in other words."

"Correct."

"My thoughts exactly." That left sabotage or a message from someone else. But who would go to so much trouble just to send her images of Starkiller and herself? It didn't make sense.

"We have you on approach, Captain Eclipse," said a familiar voice over the comm. "Welcome back."

"Thanks, Nitram," she said, quickly taking stock of the shuttle's location. It was decelerating smoothly on autopilot for the *Salvation*'s mid-spine docking tube. Taking the controls, she adjusted its trim and gave the thrusters an extra nudge. Just seeing the frigate raised her spirits. "Break out the Old Janx Spirit. It's good to be home."

"Uh, seriously, sir?"

Juno smiled at her second in command's tone. Sometimes the Bothan was too easy to tease. "Of course not. We have work to do. The bottle stays in my safe until the Emperor is dead."

"Yes, sir. Understood."

The *Salvation* loomed ahead. Juno put all other thoughts from her mind as she jockeyed the shuttle in to dock.

CHAPTER 11

FROM DAGOBAH TO MALASTARE was a relatively short journey, but it seemed to take forever. With nothing to do but think and worry while the *Rogue Shadow* was in hyperspace, Starkiller paced relentlessly from one end of the ship to the other, turning over everything he had seen and felt on the swampy world receding behind him.

"He has a healthy head start."

"We've been breached. Troopers boarding!"

Juno lying dead in his arms.

"Whatever you have seen, follow it you must."

He had gone to Dagobah hoping for clarity, and all he had received were visions and cryptic advice. Was he closer to Juno or getting farther away? Would he be able to save her, or was she already dead?

The Force reflected his inner turmoil, sending occasional shudders and shakes through the ship. He tried his best to calm down. If his mood disrupted life support or the hyperdrive, he might not make it to Malastare at all.

Finally the navicomp chimed, warning him that his destination was approaching. Leaving the meditation chamber, he hurried to the pilot's seat and took the controls. The moment the stars of realspace ceased streaking, he had the ship under power and accelerating toward the high-gravity world.

Starkiller had visited Port Pixelito just once, while in the service of Darth Vader. A treacherous Imperial aide who had run up gambling debts from podracing had been his target, and one soon dealt with, even in the early days of his apprenticeship. In disguise and with PROXY's help, he had infiltrated the security installation without being detected, then sliced into the mainframe to find his target. From there, he had crawled through ventilation ducts until he was above the target's private chambers, then Force-choked him while he worked at his desk. Escaping had been just as simple. To date, he was sure no one knew what had really happened that night.

Seeing the world brought back memories of his first pilot, a dour old sergeant who rarely spoke and who flew the *Rogue Shadow* like it was an ore barge. Like the murdered aide, he hadn't lasted long. Tardiness wasn't tolerated in Darth Vader's employ.

That mission had been five years ago, but the Starkiller in his mind seemed barely a child to him now. So much had changed since then. He had died at least once, for starters . . .

The crowd on the ground cleared his head of any kind of nostalgia. Spaceports were typically chaotic, but this one broke all the records. Since the collapse of Imperial control, all manner of beings roamed the streets, free to pursue whatever dreams or fancies took them. Starkiller kept his guard up, and his senses tuned for Kota. The old man had said that he was heading here after Commenor, and he had definitely arrived. Starkiller recognized that mix of anger and self-control anywhere.

The trail led him to a market, and from there to a machine repair shop. A cover, he assumed. Kota was very close now.

He went inside. It looked perfectly innocent, from the mess of spare parts to the three-eyed Gran behind the counter. Behind the façade, though, Starkiller could sense something very different.

"The Jedi," he said, exactly as he had on Cato Neimoidia. "Where is he?"

"No Jedi here," said the Gran, blinking its eyes one at a time from right to left. "Got something to fix?"

"I'm not a customer." He raised and passed his hand in front of the Gran's face. "You'll show me the way."

The Gran couldn't resist the Force. Starkiller's suggestion was as implacable as gravity, made all the more irresistible by his urgent need. The Gran pointed hesitantly at the shelves. There was no door visible. Starkiller didn't have the patience for guesswork, not when Juno's life might be at stake.

He faced the wall and Force-pushed, gently at first but with growing insistence. Machine parts rattled and shook. Glass smashed. With a groan and squeak of tortured metal, a section of the wall began to swing back.

There was movement on the far side. Someone fired at him. He deflected the bolt effortlessly into the ground and leapt through the gap, sending what seemed like a mountain of spare parts flying ahead of him.

A green lightsaber flashed toward him. He blocked it with both of his. By the mixed light of their blades, he recognized Kota's face, and Kota recognized his in return.

The general performed a startled double take.

"What's with you, boy?" he asked, deactivating his weapon and stepping away. "You could've knocked."

"I'm in a hurry." Starkiller kept one lightsaber at the ready. The space was large and cluttered—not helped by the mess he had made on the way in—and he hadn't yet pinned down the location of the person who had fired the blaster at him. "I need to find the Alliance fleet."

"You've had a change of heart, then."

"I wouldn't say that. The fleet's about to be attacked. I need to stop that from happening at all cost."

"Lots of people looking for the fleet at the moment," said a voice out of the shadows. "Not all of them friendly."

Starkiller turned. Into the light stepped a broad-shouldered man holding an energy weapon trained at his head. His walked with an unusual gait and a strange whining noise. As he approached, Starkiller realized why.

His legs were gone. In their place were three multi-jointed prosthetics tipped with rubber "feet." They moved with a complicated grace that had nothing to do with the way ordinary humans walked.

"Who are you?"

"I'm the repairman," he said. "The name's Shyre. What's yours?"

"I don't have one anymore. Is that a problem?"

"That depends. Do you vouch for him, General?"

"I do."

"He part of your new squad? A spy, perhaps?"

"Not exactly."

"So how does he know the fleet's about to be attacked?"

"It's a long story," Starkiller said.

"I'm all ears."

"I had a vision," he said, directing his words to Kota. It didn't matter what Shyre thought. "The fleet was near a nebula, one I've never seen before. It was taken by surprise. Several fighters got through the defenses. Juno's ship was hit. She was hurt. Then I saw her die."

"Juno?" asked Shyre, lowering his weapon.

Starkiller glanced at him. "I don't know whether I was seeing something that happened in the past or the future, but every second you hold me up makes it more likely I won't be able to fix it."

"She was here yesterday," Shyre said. "I told her where to find the fleet. It's stationed just off Itani Nebula."

"Thank you," Starkiller said, deactivating his lightsaber. "That's all I need to know."

He turned to leave, but Kota stood in his way. The general's armor was still battered and bloodstained, but he had regained his strength and confidence.

"Just slow down, boy. How do you know this isn't a trap?"

"It might well be," he said. "Vader is hunting me. I saw that, too."

"What if the vision was a fake? You should at least think it through before charging off on your own."

Starkiller saw the sense in that. There were inconsistencies in what he had seen that had bothered him ever since Dagobah. Painful though the events of the vision were, he forced himself to remember them, searching for incriminating details. If it *was* a fake, then maybe the other visions were, too.

"She was the captain of a frigate," he said, "but you told me that. I only got a glimpse of the instruments. It looked like a Nebulon-B. It was called the *Salvation*."

Kota nodded. "That's her ship, all right."

"Her second in command was an alien of some kind."

"Bothan."

"But I saw PROXY," he said, "and that can't be correct, can it?"

"She and Bail Organa found your droid on Corellia. She must have gotten him working again."

Kota and Shyre exchanged glances.

"Sounds real to me," said Shyre. "So what are we going to do about it?"

"You're not doing anything," Starkiller said. "I'll handle this."

"You won't get within a parsec of the fleet without me," said Kota. "You don't have the authorization codes."

"So give them to me."

"Are you ready to expose yourself like this? Have you thought through what'll happen when you turn up in the middle of the fleet as though you've never been away?"

Starkiller hadn't, but he was beginning to now. If the Rebellion was as riven by arguments as Kota had said—and if Kota had told anyone else about the Jedi Starkiller had murdered—then his arrival would be like an anti-matter bomb going off among them. It might take months for the pieces to come back together, if they ever did. Rushing in might end up placing Juno in more peril, in the long run.

"All right," he said. "You're coming with me."

"And if I'm coming, so's my squad. I'll call them and they'll be ready to lift off within the hour."

"I don't know—"

"How many ships did you see in your vision?"

"Seven, maybe eight."

"Let my crew handle them while you look after Juno. Besides, they need to bond. Fighting Imperials is just the thing for that."

Kota held out his hand, and Starkiller, resigned to the sense the general was making, shook it.

"You move fast, old man."

"Stand still too long and you're dead."

Kota left the workshop to call his squad, leaving Starkiller momentarily alone with the repairman.

Shyre was staring at him with an odd expression on his face.

"You're *him*," he said.

A crawling sensation went up Starkiller's spine. "Him who?"

"Juno told me about you. You flew together. She told me she—" A pained expression flashed across Shyre's face. "She told me you died."

Starkiller didn't hesitate. He didn't need people talking about him behind his back, not when Darth Vader was sending bounty hunters across the galaxy in search of him. The wrong word in the wrong ear could bring about a much greater disaster than the one he was trying to prevent.

He took three steps closer to Shyre and raised his left hand.

"You don't know me," he said.

The repairman stiffened and his voice took on a distant tone. "I don't know you."

"I was never here."

"You were never here."

"Neither were Kota and Juno."

"Neither was Kota."

"Or Juno."

Shyre's jaw muscles worked. "Or Juno."

"Good. You've got a lot to clean up and you'd better get on with it."

"Okay, well, I've got a huge mess to clean up here. Guess I'd better get on with it."

Starkiller released his hold over him. Shyre turned and went looking for a broom. Starkiller left him to it.

KOTA'S SQUAD HAD A SHIP, a modified Ghtroc 630 freighter that had seen extensive action, judging by the carbon scoring on the hull and the slightly cockeyed look to its drives. Kota arranged for them to assemble at the ship, a dozen berths up from the *Rogue Shadow*. Starkiller didn't want to meet them, but Kota insisted.

"The medic, at least. There's something you need to hear."

Starkiller grudgingly consented to listen. They found a quiet corner in a smoky cantina where the three of them could talk in private.

"Ni-Ke-Vanz." The medic was a fast-talking Cerean with a high domed skull and amazingly elaborate eyebrows. They rose up and down rapidly as he talked, providing a visual counterpoint to his words. "Kota tells me you want to make a clone."

That was news to him, but he could guess where it was going. "Do you know how it's done?"

"I ought to. For five years I worked with a Khommite. They're the galaxy's experts at this kind of thing."

"Where was this?"

"On Kessel."

"I didn't know they had cloning facilities there."

"They didn't," said Ni-Ke-Vanz. "We were slaves."

Of course. Starkiller indicated that he should continue.

"The Khommites have been cloning themselves for a thousand years and they've got it down to a fine art. It defines their entire culture. They have certain lines they reproduce over and over again—lines that are good at teaching, good at art, good at politics, and so on. Each line is basically the same person made multiple times over. On the whole planet, there might be only a few dozen true individuals. The rest are just repeats, passed on down the generations."

"That's not the kind of thing I'm after," said Starkiller.

"I know, I know. You're after immortality. Everyone is when it comes to clones. Either that or an army, and even the Emperor's worked out that this doesn't work in the long run. It's too expensive and dangerous. An army made up of the same soldier is either one hundred percent loyal or one hundred percent against you. When your enemy has to convince only one mind to turn, you're walking on thin ice."

"I don't want an army," Starkiller assured him. "Tell me what I need to know."

"You need to know that cloning won't make you immortal, either."

"Why not?"

"They've never managed to fix the memory problem. Not even the Khommites. Each clone they make is a new person—one based to a very large degree on the original, but still one that has its own identity, its own memories, its own weird quirks. They don't think they're the same people, just different versions of the same template. And that's not immortality. Sorry."

"I've often wondered," said Kota, leaning into the conversation, "why the Jedi didn't just clone ourselves after Order Sixty-six. I mean, there weren't many of us left. Why not take the ones we *did* have and create some more? It wouldn't matter if we didn't think we were the same person. We wouldn't have to, as long as we could fight."

"Ah, well now, that's an entirely different problem." Ni-Ke-Vanz leaned forward, too. His eyebrows attained a whole new level of animation. "You see, the other thing no one has ever managed to copy is Force sensitivity. Worse than that, it actually gets in the way of the cloning process. We don't know how. It just does. The Khommites are aware of the problem and they do everything they can to stamp it out."

Starkiller's surprise must have shown on his face, for the medic nodded emphatically at him.

"That's right: They *weed out* Force sensitivity. Can you imagine? That's how big a problem it is."

"What would happen if you tried to clone someone Force-sensitive anyway?"

Ni-Ke-Vanz sank back into his seat with a dire look on his long face. "Terrible things. Insanity. Psychosis. Suicidal tendencies. Who wants a crazy Force-sensitive running amok in your lab? No one."

"No one," agreed Starkiller, thinking of Kamino and the damage he'd left in his wake.

"Sorry," said Ni-Ke-Vanz, misreading his grim mood for disappointment. "Looks like you're going to have to ride out the war with the rest of us."

"That's not—" he started to object. Then thought better of it. "Right. No pain, no gain. Guess I'd better get used to it."

THEY LEFT THE CANTINA and headed back to the ships. Starkiller left Kota to organize his squad, not particularly caring about the band of mercenaries and wannabe heroes he'd assembled in little more than a day. They would perhaps be useful in preventing any kind of harm coming to Juno—and Starkiller was more than happy to employ them in that regard—but he doubted their involvement together would extend far beyond the end of the mission, whichever way it went.

Juno's voice spoke to him from his memory.

"We can help each other."

"Nobody can help me."

"I don't think you really mean that. I just think you're afraid to let me try."

"Is that really what you think?" he had asked. *"I'm afraid of you?"*

The very suggestion had seemed preposterous then, but it didn't anymore. Just the thought of Juno had a profound effect on him. He would slash his way through a hundred Emperors to save her, if he had to. There was nothing he wouldn't sacrifice. Not even the very Rebellion that the original Starkiller had created.

That truly *was* a frightening thought, one he kept carefully hidden from Kota.

The engines were warm and ready by the time the general walked up the ramp and into the bridge.

"You don't look terribly reassured," Kota said, taking the copilot's seat.

"Should I be?"

The *Rogue Shadow* lifted off with a louder roar than usual as the repulsors fought the intense gravity of the world. Turning the ship nose-upward, Starkiller aimed for the sky. Over the screaming of the drives, conversation was temporarily impossible.

Blue turned to black, and the first stars appeared. Dodging heavy orbital traffic, Starkiller didn't wait for the squad's disreputable freighter. He would meet them at the other end.

Space stretched and tore. The *Rogue Shadow* leapt into hyperspace and began the flight for the Itani Nebula.

"Of course you should feel reassured," said Kota, with a persistence that shouldn't have surprised him. For more than fifteen years the Emperor and all his minions had been hunting the Jedi. It took a mammoth kind of stubbornness to have survived so long against such odds. "You're on your way to see Juno. You've got reinforcements. And best of all you know you can't be a clone."

"So why haven't you told anyone I'm back?"

"How do you know that?"

"Because the repairman didn't know. And the way he was talking, Juno didn't know, either."

"Well, I figure that's your business, who you tell and who you don't."

"Back in Athega system, you said it was entirely the Alliance's business."

"Maybe you convinced me to stay out of it until you're ready. There are already too many confused people running this Rebellion. Are you saying you're ready now?"

He searched his feelings. "No. Not until Juno is safe."

"And she'll probably need to see you with her own eyes, otherwise she won't believe that you're really back."

"I keep telling you: I'm not him."

The general's blind stare was full of disbelief. "Even now you think that, after everything Ni-Ke-Vanz said?"

"He didn't really tell us anything."

"Only that cloned Jedi can't exist."

"Have never existed in the past. That's an entirely different thing."

"The Khommites have been grappling with the problem for a thousand years! Do you think Vader solved it overnight?"

"With the help of the Kaminoans, maybe. Or they didn't solve it and I am as crazy as I feel sometimes."

"You act no crazier than you originally did." Kota wasn't joking. "A bit more obsessive, perhaps, but who can blame you? You love her. It's only natural to want to save her."

You love her.

Starkiller could say nothing to that for a moment. Those three words hit him harder than he could have anticipated. Not just because it was Kota saying them—Kota, the gruff career soldier who had never displayed the slightest amount of emotional awareness in Starkiller's presence. Because it was the present tense, not the past, and because it was about him.

There was a world of difference between Juno, the woman he loved, and Juno, the woman Starkiller *had* loved.

Perversely, that only deepened the blackness of his mood. Did he have the right to love anyone, if he was only a clone? She had loved the original, not him. What if she rejected him? What if she had put the original behind her and had no room in her life for him now? She was a captain in the Rebel Alliance; she had duties, responsibilities, staff, timetables. She couldn't drop everything and run off with him—and there was no guarantee that the rest of the Rebellion would accept him if he wanted to stay.

"Who wants a crazy Force-sensitive running amok in your lab?"

Acknowledging that he was a psychotic clone who would never be worthy of either Juno or the Rebellion was somehow more acceptable than believing that he was the real Starkiller, who, beyond all kinds of understanding, had managed to return from the dead.

To kill again.

Kota got out of his seat and opened a small wall compartment. He rummaged inside for a moment, then his right fist emerged, tightly holding something in its grip. He returned to Starkiller's side and opened his hand to reveal what he had found. There lay two bright crystals, as blue as Juno's eyes.

"Where did you get these?" Starkiller asked.

"Relics of the Clone War. It doesn't matter. The point is, they're yours if you want them."

Kota pushed his hand toward Starkiller, who made no move to take them.

"Does this mean you believe I'm not a clone?" he asked.

The general exhaled heavily. "Honestly? I don't know. But I'm beginning to think it doesn't matter."

Again the blind eyes pinned him, but for once they revealed more about Kota than the person he was looking at. Starkiller could feel the hatred churning inside the general as powerfully as it ever had. It was part of him that he had learned to live with, like his blindness. Sometimes it gave him strength; sometimes it worked against him. Starkiller couldn't imagine what it must have been like after Order 66, balancing the need to survive against the absolute requirement of all true Jedi Knights—that they never succumb to the dark side.

Kota's hatred was directed at the Emperor, but its focus was Darth Vader. Starkiller didn't know why; there were probably a thousand reasons, reasons Kota himself would never reveal or dwell upon, most likely. The general wasn't one for living in the past, or for worrying about the means as long as the end was in sight. To him, the return of Starkiller was an opportunity to strike at Darth Vader, just as, to Starkiller, Kota was a means of finding and saving Juno.

You love her.

Some obsessions were worth it. Starkiller took the crystals and made his way back to the meditation chamber, seeking a peace he suspected the general would never find.

THEY WERE MET AT NORDRA by outliers of the fleet and given the coordinates they needed. Kota quizzed them about recent traffic. There had been some, but nothing suspicious. Juno herself had come through less than a day earlier.

Starkiller felt all his hopes and fears magnify at that simple confirmation of fact. She was close, so very close. Soon he would be with her. What happened after that, only time and fate would tell.

The squad's freighter wasn't far behind the *Rogue Shadow*. For all its lopsided engines, it could clearly hold its own. The convoy of two headed off toward the nebula, scanners peeled for anything out of the ordinary. Slowly, slowly, the kaleidoscopic view shifted ahead of them.

"This is taking too long," Starkiller said through grinding teeth. "I'm using the hyperdrive."

"The mass shadow of the nebula—"

"I don't care." His hands flew across the controls. "The others can come the long way if you want."

"They'd better. None of them is as good a pilot as you."

Starkiller acknowledged the compliment with a brisk nod. When the navicomp was ready, he sat for a moment with his hands on the controls.

"I've been thinking," he said slowly, "about the Alliance."

"About your place in it?"

He shook his head. "About what it should do next. If I give you the nav coordinates and schematics for a secret cloning facility on Kamino—everything needed to launch a successful assault—will that go some way toward helping them believe in me again?"

Kota chewed this over. "The facility where Vader claims you were made?"

"If his claims are true, then Kamino is much more of a threat than any ordinary stormtrooper factory."

"Maybe. But the Alliance couldn't pull off an attack like this without your help."

"They'll have to," he said. He activated the drives. Realspace smeared and stretched, vanished into the paradoxical light of hyperspace. "They wouldn't trust me to lead anything yet, anyway."

"I would."

"The Alliance is more than just you and your militia, Kota."

Instead of being offended, the general grinned. "If what you saw comes to pass, you'll be glad you picked us up."

Starkiller acknowledged that, but his mind was unchanged. Judging by everything he'd learned from Kota, the Alliance didn't need someone to lead them into battle. It needed to find strong leadership among the leaders it already had.

The ship shook, disturbed by the widely distributed mass of the nebula. He gripped the console, urging it to fly straight by the force of his will. This had to work. He had to arrive on time. There was simply no other option.

The *Rogue Shadow* exploded out of hyperspace, tumbling wildly. He corrected its trim automatically, firing retros even as he searched the scopes for the fleet. The sky was a mess of glowing gas and light. The scanners picked up two minor asteroid fields, a distant protostar with a single gas giant, and, finally, a small scattering of starships.

He brought the ship about, ion engines blazing.

"No sign of attack," he said.

"Stay on guard," said Kota. "A powerful glimpse of the future like you experienced is rarely wrong."

The fleet grew larger and more detailed through the cockpit viewport. Starkiller searched the ships for the one he was after. He recognized the *Salvation* more by instinct than knowledge. Like all Nebulon-B frigates, it was heavy at fore and aft, with a relatively thin spine connecting each end. Engines and reactor were confined to the rear; command and crew quarters were up front, near primary communications and sensor arrays. This example looked old but well maintained, a reliable worker that had found a good home with the Rebel Alliance.

The *Salvation* wasn't the biggest or the newest ship in the fleet. But Juno was inside it. He was sure of it. Finally he had found her.

"*Rogue Shadow*," came a voice over the comm, "please transmit landing codes."

Starkiller froze at the sight of something on the side of the approaching frigate.

"What is it, boy?"

He could only point at the crest adorning the *Salvation*—adorning every ship in the fleet, he saw as they grew nearer. He remembered seeing it only once before, on Kashyyyk, but he knew what it was. It had been an integral part of the life Darth Vader had stolen from him, when he was a child.

"My family's crest," he said. "It's . . . everywhere."

"Yes," said Kota, tapping the chest plate of his armor—where, Starkiller belatedly realized, the same symbol lay buried under a thick layer of muck. "I suppose I should've told you about that."

"What does it mean?"

"That you're part of the Rebel Alliance whether you want to be or not."

"*Rogue Shadow*," came the voice from the fleet a second time, "landing codes immediately."

Four Y-wings were nosing in their direction—to either escort or intercept, Starkiller thought through the fog of surprise.

Kota leaned over and punched the comlink.

"This is General Rahm Kota," he said, "requesting permission to board the *Salvation*. Authorization Talus Haroon Ten Eleven Thirty-eight."

The voice didn't respond immediately. When it did, there was no mistaking the surprise. "Code checks out. Good to have you back, General. You're cleared for docking."

The Y-wings peeled away.

"If you give me the data on Kamino," said Kota, "I'll do what needs to be done."

Starkiller leaned forward and peered through the canopy at the *Salvation*. The crest painted on the hull loomed over him like a shadow.

His father's voice came to him from the deepest refuges of his memory.

"I never wanted this for you."

He sensed the final pieces falling into place, the last of the gaps closing up. He was here, on the brink of seeing Juno again, and his mind was whole. Whoever he was, wherever he had come from, he was complete.

He only hoped, against hope, that he would be enough.

CHAPTER 12

JUNO STOOD ON THE BRIDGE of the *Salvation,* feeling the smooth operation of the ship and crew around her as though they were parts of her physical body. With a change of uniform and a decent meal in the recent past, she felt entirely transformed. Being restored to command had felt like being returned to life. There was indeed something in what Leia had said about having a frigate at her disposal: It was truly nothing to be sniffed at.

At the back of her mind, though, was something her flight instructor had drummed into her all the way through her training. Getting too comfortable was just asking for the universe to provide a kick in the pants. She went through everything that had happened in recent days, searching for the one thing that had gone wrong, for the boot that might already be on its way to shake her out of her complacency.

"Uh, Captain," said Nitram with surprising hesitancy, "we have the *Rogue Shadow* in view."

"Impossible," Juno said automatically, assuming someone had made a mistake. "It was destroyed on Cato Neimoidia."

But even as she said the words, she saw it in the scopes, accelerating smoothly toward her.

"It can't be him," she said to herself through a stab of surprise and guilt in equal measures.

Then a more likely possibility occurred to her: "The Imperials must have captured it and are using it as a disguise. Target it—all weapons!"

The bridge crew jumped into life around her. Alert sirens wailed.

Then Kota's voice boomed out of the comm.

"This is General Rahm Kota, requesting permission to board the Salvation."

"He can't be," she repeated, barely hearing the authorization code he gave. "It *can't* be him."

"Captain?"

She blinked. "If it's a trick, there's only one way to find out. Let him board. We'll greet him with every soldier available."

"Yes, sir."

She stood straighter and kept her hands behind her back. They were clenched into fists.

You abandoned him, she told herself. *You gave up on him. You left him behind.*

Any relief she felt at the possibility of his survival was buried under the crushing weight of remorse.

"Blackguard to Blackout," came Kota's voice over the comm.

"I'll take it," she said, reaching for her comlink.

Nitram patched the transmission directly through to her.

"This is Blackout," she said, taking a deep breath. "What's your status, Blackguard?"

"Back in the game," he said with obvious relish. "I have intel on a major target that I can't take out on my own. Do you think the Alliance will be interested?"

The meeting with Mon Mothma, Garm Bel Iblis, and Bail Organa was still fresh in her mind. "I think they'll be very interested, Kota."

"Good. Here it comes."

A second later the intel arrived on the bridge. She picked up a datapad and scrolled through the files, seeing floor plans, security systems, troop deployments—everything the fleet needed to ensure a victory over what appeared at first to be some kind of Imperial medical base. No, she realized: a *cloning* operation. It was way past the Outer Rim, too far for reinforcements to come in time, but obviously important, or else it wouldn't be hidden so far off the usual hyperroutes. One of many such super-secret facilities supplying stormtroopers for the Emperor's ever-expanding army, she assumed.

"Looks good," she said, hiding a rising excitement. There was only one problem: Without knowing the provenance of the data, she couldn't be entirely sure it wasn't misinformation, even a trap. "Where did you get this intel, Kota?"

There was a pause. She thought she heard movement on the other end of the open line.

"It's best you see for yourself," he finally said. "We'll be aboard in a few minutes. Meet us then."

"Will you also tell me how you killed Baron Tarko and got off Cato Neimoidia?"

There was another pause, shorter than the last.

"You did the right thing, Juno. I would've done the same."

The line disconnected with a *click*.

She looked down at the comlink in her hand, feeling simultaneously drained and buoyed. Kota's return, with or without the data, was a momentous turnaround for the Alliance. The mission to Cato Neimoidia really could be considered a success now. They had lost nothing and succeeded on every front. Mon Mothma would find it much harder to argue against such missions in the future.

If Kota was the boot, it was suspiciously wrapped in velvet.

Nitram was staring at her with an expression that mirrored her own feelings—and she understood, suddenly, that he was the one who had informed the Alliance leadership of her activities with Kota. He, her loyal second in command, was also a loyal Alliance soldier, wanting to do the right thing for the cause. It was only natural that he would experience the same internal conflict she had over helping Kota in his unsanctioned activities: he wasn't an automaton, after all.

Instead of feeling betrayed, Juno felt nothing but sympathy. How long had he agonized over what to do? Why hadn't he come to talk to her first? What was he feeling now that the right thing he *thought* he had done turned out to be utterly baseless?

He opened his mouth as though to say something, but an alarm cut him off. He turned and checked the console in front of him.

"I'm having trouble with the forward sensor array, Captain."

She studied the display screens around her.

"Interference from the nebula?" They had been having the occasional blackout ever since the fleet took up its current station, the result of nothing more sinister than natural forces.

PROXY was examining the problem, too. He looked up with bright yellow eyes. "Perhaps. I'll try to pin it down."

She considered numerous factors at once: the arrival of Kota, the promise of a target, this strange glitch in the sensor array . . .

It added up to something, but she didn't know what it was.

"Let's not take any chances," she said, punching the all-stations button on the console in front of her.

"This is Captain Eclipse," she said. Her voice echoed back at her from throughout the frigate. "Set defensive protocols throughout all ships. Prime your shields and check your scanners for anything that's not one of ours."

Nitram nodded, still checking the screens. "All clear, Captain."

"Keep looking, Nitram. We can't be too careful."

"Of course, sir."

In a secondary screen, she saw the blip representing the *Rogue Shadow* coming in to dock. She watched it, wondering what its arrival foretold. Something nagged at her, an instinct that had for the moment no precise focus. The ground was shifting under her, but the landscape hadn't changed yet. At any moment, she expected her whole world to be overturned.

A light flashed on the display in front of her, signaling a private call from Viedas. He probably wanted to ask about her alert—not that there was anything wrong with reminding the crews of the various ships that they should be on constant guard against discovery and attack. Complacency had killed more soldiers than the craziest battle-lust.

She reached for the comlink to answer the call.

A voice crackling over the comm beat her to it.

"Captain Eclipse—we're picking up five, no, six small warships, coming in fa—"

There it is, she thought, turning her attention to the screens. The *Lexi Dio,* an assault bomber, was under attack. Bright explosions pockmarked its hull. The missiles came from two of seven small vessels darting and weaving across the sky. Whoever was piloting them was good: The next four missiles split the *Lexi Dio* from nose to stern, resulting in the decompression and death of everyone aboard.

Horrified, she gripped the console with both hands. Where had the ships come from? They hadn't come out of hyperspace or the fleet would have noticed them. The same with the nearby asteroid fields—unless they had cloaking systems as sophisticated as the *Rogue Shadow*'s, which meant they weren't standard Imperial manufacture.

Where they came from took second place as all seven vessels turned their attention to the *Salvation* and began attacking.

"Shields to full," she called over the intercom. "Open fire, all batteries."

A coded signal came from Commodore Viedas. Around her, the fleet began to break apart—standard protocol in the event of discovery. A new rendezvous point lay in a code cylinder carried by every ship's commander. The surviving ships would regroup in that location, and the fleet would count its losses. Juno vowed not to be like the poor *Lexi Dio.*

A missile got past the shields and exploded in the engineering section, making the deck shift beneath her. Red lights began to flash, signaling vents and structural damage near the hyperdrive. Four of the seven ships were targeting the main spine but found stiff opposition from the frigate's Y-wing escort. As she watched, one of the remaining three hostiles rammed the *Salvation,* just aft of the surgery suite. The ship didn't explode. Lodged nose-first in the hull of the larger vessel, its engines flickered and shut down.

"We've been breached," barked her second in command. "Troopers boarding!"

"Send a security detail to the main reactor. Seal off life support."

A much more powerful impact sent crew flying. Juno gripped the console for dear life. Diagnostic systems showed red in the forward sensor unit.

"Get those deflector shields up!" she shouted into the intercom. Another hit like that and the frigate would be effectively blind.

She checked internal cameras. They were flickering, full of static. Through thickening smoke she glimpsed her crew fighting both fires and invading troops. The latter flickered and shimmered as though they had cloaking systems of their own. She had never heard of such things. Luckily they were struggling in a complex, ship-bound environment. Only against relatively still backgrounds did they have a clear advantage, and there weren't many of those on the *Salvation* at that moment.

The ship couldn't risk jumping until the hyperdrive was looked at. Their only option now was to fight.

A metal hand took her shoulder. PROXY's yellow eyes filled her vision. "Security beacons are going crazy. Captain Eclipse, I think we should—"

Before he could finish the sentence, the bridge doors blew inward. She raised a hand to protect her face. Burning shards peppered Juno's skin, followed by a wave of intense heat. She ducked instinctively, along with everyone else on the bridge. Blaster bolts speared out of the cloud, fired by two stormtroopers wielding high-powered rifles. Juno's right hand found the blaster at her side. She had never fired it on the frigate before. When she'd strapped it on an hour ago she'd had no conception that she would be doing so now.

The universe's boot was firmly in play now.

She came out from behind the main display console and released two bolts twice, fast, then ducked back down again before she drew return fire. The first shot took out one of the troopers. She heard his respirator wheezing as he went down, showering sparks. The second missed by a margin small enough to spook. She braced herself to fire at him a second time, but the arrival of four more troopers put paid to that plan.

She wasn't the only one defending the ship. Nitram was crouched behind a display like her, peppering the troopers whenever they crossed his line of fire. PROXY had taken the blaster from a fallen navigator and was using it to harass the invaders, his image displaying a flickering form of camouflage of his own. Juno saw her own features come and go, with hints of Mon Mothma and Leia, too. There didn't seem any rhyme or reason to it, but she didn't have the time to think it through just then.

The sound of fighting echoed all through the ship, not just in the bridge. Reports came from soldiers in a steady stream, but went unheard. Two more troopers went down near the entrance, taken out by concentrated fire from three sides. Juno rolled to a new position, covered by Nitram. He may have ratted on her to Mon Mothma, but against the Imperials she could trust him implicitly.

Her goal was to stop the troopers reaching the main console, even if it killed her. That was the symbol of her command. They weren't going to get their hands on it.

Even as she blasted another trooper to oblivion, the smoke swirled oddly between the walls where the bridge doors used to be. The small hairs on her arms stood on end. Ships with cloaking systems, troopers with camouflage—how was she supposed to fight an invisible enemy?

She targeted the swirls, to some effect. One lucky hit killed the camouflage of one of the troopers, and she finished him off with a second shot. But she had no idea how many had arrived with him, how many were left to fight. There could be no others at all, or dozens already in the bridge. Perhaps if she killed the lights, they would all be at a disadvantage . . .

Even as she thought that, PROXY was hit in the chest. He went over backward, showering sparks, innards screeching. She couldn't tell where the shot had come from. Nitram was next, shot from behind by someone he couldn't even see.

The muscles in her jaw were like rock. The unfairness of the fight appalled her. Scrabbling for PROXY's fallen blaster, she stood up tall and began firing at random with both hands, screaming her rage and frustration.

From the corner of the bridge, where the smoke was thinnest, came the shot that put her out of action. The trooper might have been standing there for minutes, unseen, awaiting each opportunity as it came. She had given him one, and he took it.

The shot hit her in the shoulder, almost knocking her down. Her right arm went limp and the blaster she held in that hand went flying. The pain was unbelievable. She fell to one knee, then ground her teeth even tighter and raised her left hand to fire at the trooper who had shot her. Her aim was good. He flickered back into visibility and crumpled forward.

Her satisfaction was short-lived. A bolt of energy flashed past her, and the pistol exploded from her hand. She stared at the hand, momentarily surprised to see that she still had fingers. Some type of stun weapon, obviously. A trooper stepped toward her through the smoke, holding his weapon at the ready, just in case she had another blaster secreted on her somewhere.

She didn't. Neither did anyone on the bridge. They were all dead. The pain in her shoulder peaked, making the world seem gray and distant.

The figure came closer. He seemed enormous. He wasn't a trooper at all, she distantly realized. His armor was green.

"Who—?"

He didn't let her finish the question. His blaster flared again, as bright as a sun, and the world vanished.

CHAPTER 13

STARKILLER HAD JUST SECURED the *Rogue Shadow* when the first of the proximity alarms went off. He watched the initial attack unfold from the bridge, with Kota leaning close over his shoulder. What Kota "saw," exactly, through his heightened senses, Starkiller didn't know. But he was keeping up: that was the important thing.

"The asteroids," Starkiller said, hastily scanning the surrounding space. "That's where they were hiding."

"They must have been lying dormant ever since the fleet arrived." Kota's right hand rested on the grip of his lightsaber. "What brought them out of hiding now?"

There was only one possible answer. "Me," Starkiller said. "It's one of Vader's bounty hunters. He found out where the fleet was due to gather next and, instead of turning it in to the Imperial Navy, waited here until I showed up. Now he's springing his trap."

"We should leave," said Kota. "Give him the slip."

Starkiller shook his head as, on the screen in front of him, a small assault bomber was ripped apart. "I have to get to Juno before she's hurt."

"Even if it means putting yourself at risk?"

"Our bounty hunter friend will find it works the other way around."

Starkiller checked the disposition of the attacking ships. They were homing in on the *Salvation,* exactly as expected now that the *Rogue Shadow* was docked alongside it. One of the larger ships was heaving around to ram. If the move was successful, that would give the hostiles easy access to the frigate.

Around them, the fleet was dispersing, protecting the ships that could be saved before a much larger Imperial presence arrived. Only he and Kota knew that there were no other ships coming.

"Your new squad shouldn't be far away," he told Kota. "Call them by comlink when they're in range. They can keep the fight going outside while we get to Juno. Come on."

He hurried from the bridge and through the air lock. Even as he went, the frigate shook from a massive impact, presumably the ship ramming into its hull. He braced himself to ride out the impact, estimating that it came from the forward half of the ship. If the boarding maneuver had been successful, that meant there would be hostiles between them and the *Salvation*'s bridge.

For a split instant he felt a crippling sense of guilt. He and Kota had had the chance to warn Juno that something was going to happen, while they were approaching her ship, but they hadn't taken it. By not doing so, they might inadvertently have helped the vision he received come true.

The feeling didn't last. The future was always in motion. If willpower alone couldn't change it, then brute force would have to do.

The deck steadied underfoot. He lit both his lightsabers, now brilliant, fiery blue, as they had been on Dagobah, and leapt through the docking tube into the *Salvation.* The lights were flickering relentlessly from on to off, red to black, creating a surreal landscape full of smoke and sparks. Figures moved ahead of them, but it was impossible for the moment to tell who was on what side.

Kota rushed forward, sensing directly through the Force and therefore unimpaired by lack of light or visual distractions.

Starkiller watched his back, happy for him to take the lead. His concentration was taking a hit from more than just the lack of light. Being so close to Juno and yet still separated from her was a

constant distraction. Until they were in the same room together—
better yet, in each other's arms—he would remain on edge.

The figures he had seen at the end of the corridor were Alliance
soldiers, firing around a corner at a trio of Imperial stormtroopers
who had formed a barricade across a major intersection. Wind
whistled around them: Clearly shields and self-repair facilities
hadn't quite sealed off the breach formed by the ramming ship.
Flecks of ash and soot swirled in short-lived eddies as Kota ran
boldly toward the barricade, deflecting every shot that came at him
back to the person who fired it. White-armored limbs flailed as the
troopers went down. Starkiller waved for the Alliance soldiers to
secure the position while he and the general carried on toward the
bridge.

They passed the surgery suite, where medics were patching up
crew members hit during the early strikes. The suite itself had been
hit, creating a chaotic, body-strewn battle hospital where a sterile
environment should have been. Starkiller didn't doubt the surgery
had been deliberately targeted. The ship had a complement of
more than a thousand; the more crew members the attackers could
put permanently out of action, the better for the invaders.

Explosions boomed in the major access tubes leading toward
the forward compartments. Starkiller and Kota headed straight
for them, ignoring the trams that occasionally whizzed overhead.
They were too vulnerable to sabotage and ambush. Better to run,
Starkiller thought. What he lost in speed he more than gained in
the surety of getting where he needed to go. Nothing would stop
him getting to the bridge, to Juno.

They reached the impact site of the ramming ship. No one
guarded it. Clearly the stormtroopers had another way off the
ship, or they expected to take control and fly the frigate itself. Either
way, a blackened trail led forward from the site, cutting through
walls and blast doors, heading in a perfectly straight line through
the ship. Dead Rebels lay everywhere, sprawled or slouched where
they had fallen. There were a lot of them. Too many.

"Juno trained this crew?" Starkiller asked Kota.

"Yes."

"They know how to fight, then—which means they're not fighting ordinary troopers."

Starkiller stooped over a fallen sergeant who clung barely to life.

"Who attacked you? Or what?"

"Out of nowhere," the sergeant breathed. "Invisible."

"Stormtroopers?"

But the Rebel had said his last. His head lolled back to the deck, and Starkiller closed his dead eyes for him.

"Camouflage systems—something new," Kota said. "Keep all your senses alert."

Starkiller nodded, acknowledging another situation in which Kota's odd substitute for sight gave him a unique advantage.

They hurried through the ship with their lightsabers at the ready. Starkiller remembered one of his training sessions, when Darth Vader had placed a blast helmet over his young apprentice's eyes and locked him in a cage with a trio of starved howling rasps. The hunger-maddened birds had pecked and bitten at him until, by sheer necessity, he had learned to listen to what his instincts, not his covered eyes, were telling him. Not one of the birds had survived.

Apart from soldiers clearing away rubble and healing the injured, the way ahead *seemed* clear, but it paid to be too careful.

More explosions came from the decks ahead and below. Their direction of travel became less horizontal, more vertical, as they reached the steeply pitched nose of the ship. He and Kota forwent lifts and descended the dark, booming shafts by their own means. Severed cables snaked around them as they jumped from level to level. The bridge grew rapidly closer.

Blasterfire strobed at them out of a gaping doorway. The lift doors had been blown away and a pair of stormtroopers waited there to make sure no one followed by that means. Starkiller and Kota made short work of them, downing one with his own fire, slashing the other in two once they were in range. Immediately fire came from the next floor down. This time their adversaries weren't visible.

Kota stood over the fallen troopers and pointed down into the shadows. Starkiller could see nothing with his eyes, but he drew the full power of the Force into his hands and blasted the empty air. Blue lightning made short work of the camouflage system of the trooper hiding there. He writhed and sparked until Starkiller released him, letting him drop heavily to the depths below.

They moved more cautiously from then on. The sound of blasterfire echoed around them, but none was aimed at them. The lower decks were where most of the fighting was taking place. Starkiller longed to know what was happening outside, but didn't dare break his concentration to check.

Three invisible troopers guarded the entrance to the bridge level. He blasted his way through them, not giving them the slightest chance to fight back. Four more stood outside the bridge itself. Emergency lighting and smoke made details hard to discern, but it looked like the doors behind them had been blown in.

Starkiller rushed forward. If he was too late—if they had—

Kota cut in front of him, holding him back with one hand on his chest.

"What are you doing?" Starkiller growled as he tried to find a clear line of approach.

"Cool down, boy," said the general. "Fight without hatred, or you'll lose the war."

Starkiller took the advice to heart. He recognized the feelings rising inside him, and he reminded himself where they could lead. He wasn't Darth Vader's servant anymore. He was no instrument of the dark side. He didn't want to find Juno only to have her reject him for being a monster. He needed to be calm, to find himself, to proceed with surety in any direction but toward his doom.

Doing so slowed him down by less than a second. The four troopers fell, sparking and whining, and he was through the shattered doors, into the bridge.

Thick smoke hid the carnage, but he could smell it in the air. A fire was burning and no one was putting it out. He extinguished the flames with one sweep of the Force and sucked the acrid black smoke into the corridor outside. The unnatural wind howled, echoing the tension in his heart.

Bodies everywhere, most in Rebel uniforms. He stepped across them, searching their faces, turning them over when they lay face-down. There—the dog-faced officer he'd seen killed in the vision. No sign of PROXY. Lying in a pool of deep red blood—

Juno.

He ran to her side, stifling a scream growing in his chest. Too late! He had arrived too late! The attack had happened exactly as he had seen it, and now the third of the visions was about to come true. He would hold Juno's body in his arms and—

"Boy," Kota cautioned him. The ship was shaking, echoing his distress. Starkiller tried to rein in his feelings, but they were too overwhelming. If she died, what reason did he have to live?

Juno's eyes opened.

He fell backward in surprise. She stared up at him and tried to lift her head. Only then did he notice that there wasn't a scratch on her, or her uniform. The blood she was been lying in had belonged to someone else.

"Master?"

Sparks flashed through a rent in her skin, and suddenly the illusion failed.

"PROXY!"

"Yes, Master. I—" The droid held his head as though in pain. One of his eyes had shorted, and there was a broad hole in his chest. His left arm was missing from the elbow down. "I was informed that you were dead. So was Captain Eclipse. I believe she will be most surprised to see you."

"She's alive?" Starkiller gripped PROXY by his narrow metal shoulders. "Where? Tell me where!"

The droid's innards ground together, like the workings of a sand-filled machine. His image flickered and changed again, becoming an image of a green-armored man with a T-shaped visor. PROXY's right arm lifted to point at the bridge entrance.

"The Imperials took her toward deck seven," he said, returning to his true form. His arm fell to the deck with a clank. "She is injured."

Starkiller stared at the droid in confusion and alarm. The green armor matched the vision of the bounty hunter he had seen talking to Darth Vader on Kamino, accepting instructions to recapture the missing clone. But what was he playing at? Why invade a ship, effectively destroy its command structure, and not take it over? Why was Juno in particular, the ship's captain, still alive?

Because she was more than just a captain.

She was *bait*.

He stood up, full of a dark and terrible determination.

"Order the attack on Kamino, General," he said, moving for the exit.

Kota looked around him in momentary confusion. "But the crew—"

"Your squad can fly this thing. Inform the rest of the fleet. We need to send Darth Vader the message that we mean business."

"All right, but what about—?"

"Deck seven is the cargo bay. If I hurry, I can cut them off."

Starkiller ignited both his lightsabers and ran out into the smoke.

CHAPTER 14

JUNO STRUGGLED BACK TO CONSCIOUSNESS through thick and suffocating fog. She had been dreaming of the *Empirical*, of being confined to shackles and strung up for weeks on end, with her wrists bleeding and her shoulders aching. The pain seemed utterly immediate and unceasing now, particularly in her left hand and right shoulder. It shouted at her with a voice that was almost audible.

"Wake up, Captain Eclipse. You have to walk now. My troopers are needed elsewhere."

Lights flashed in her eyes. She felt a sharp jab in her neck. Something jetted into her bloodstream with an audible hiss.

Bright alertness rushed through her, accompanied by a sharp taste of metal. She was being held upright by two armored stormtroopers with her head dangling forward and her feet brushing the ground. Her muscles jerked. Pain flared.

Suddenly fully awake, she struggled against the hands holding her, and tried to pull away from the armored figure standing in front of her. His green-gray duraplast visor came closer, filling her vision.

"You are expendable, Captain Eclipse," said the man within. "I warn you against inconveniencing me too much."

The coldness of his tone convinced her more than his words. She stopped pulling against the stormtroopers who held her and stood as straight as she was able. A third trooper affixed binders around her wrists so her hands were held securely in front of her. The movement pulled at her injured shoulder and prompted another flare-up of pain. She remembered being hit by blasterfire and nothing after that. Someone had applied a field bandage to the wound, which was something, but it meant she couldn't tell how severe it was. The fingers of her left hand were burned and red, otherwise undamaged.

"Why haven't you killed me already?" she asked the man in green. He didn't lack the capacity to do so, judging by the impressive array of blades, dart launchers, and flame projectors strategically placed about his person, not to mention the BlasTech EE-3 carbine rifle he carried in one hand. "While I live, I'll do everything in my power to regain control of the ship."

"It's not your ship I'm after." He waved one gloved hand and the troopers fell away. With the other hand he clipped a chain to her binders. "When my employer is done with you, you can have it back for all I care."

"Your employer—?"

He turned and tugged firmly on the chain. The wrench to her shoulder blotted out all other thoughts but to follow him. Sparks danced in her vision for a moment, and when they cleared the troopers had fallen behind. Her captor was leading her through a broad corridor literally blasted through the ship, one of several, if she remembered the data PROXY had shown her right before the bridge was invaded. It was hard to match its trajectory to the ship's original designs, but she thought they might be headed toward the base of the primary communications array.

"If you have an employer, that makes you a bounty hunter," she said, fishing for information. "At least, you don't look like any kind of Imperial I've ever seen. But you use Imperial troops, so you know people in high places. Is Grand Moff Tarkin still ticked off about what we did on Dac? Is that what this is about?"

The bounty hunter said nothing. They turned a corner and arrived at a vertical shaft.

"You've got a jetpack, but I haven't," she said. "Unless you want me to climb tied up like this . . . ?"

He whistled and from above descended a cable and harness, which he wrapped around her, pinning her arms to her body.

She braced herself for the ascent, but even so, when the cable started moving, she almost blacked out. The pain was incredible. Whoever had put the bandage on had cared less about her comfort than merely stopping the blood flow from the wound.

The roar of the bounty hunter's thrusters ruled out any further conversation. She concentrated instead on trying to find a way out of her predicament. The binders were very tight, so tight her hands were already going numb. No chance of wriggling out of them, then. Her blaster was probably still back on the bridge, and she had no way of calling for help, except by shouting. Thus far she had seen no sign of her crew, anywhere along the route. Chances were they were busy elsewhere, with a diversion staged by the bounty hunter's troopers.

Her best chance of escape, then, lay at the other end of their journey, when the binders came off and her hands were free—and even then she had to hope for a distraction to give her an advantage. There was no way she, injured, could take on an exceedingly well-armed bounty hunter in a fair fight and expect to prevail.

The cable jerked to a halt next to a hole carved in the wall of an empty mess. The bounty hunter came up beside her and landed safely on the deck. His thrusters cut out with a hiss. He reached out and bodily hauled her onto the solid deck. Juno didn't struggle. One wrong step when the cable came off and she'd fall to her death below.

From around her came the sounds of fighting: blasterfire, explosions, screams and shouts, feet running in all directions. The air was laced with a thick, dangerous tang, as though the ship itself were wounded. She hoped the guards she'd stationed at its critical points had managed to repel at least some of the boarders. If she were to die, she didn't want her last recorded act in the Alliance to be the destruction of her ship.

"Whatever your employer is paying you," she said, "the Alliance will double it."

He said nothing, pulling her after him along the charred makeshift corridor.

"You're a man of principle, then?"

"It's about repeat business, and your Alliance most likely won't exist long enough to pay my first fee."

"You're overconfident, like the Emperor."

"I have reason to be. His credit's good."

"Is *he* your employer?"

He said nothing.

"It *must* be Tarkin, then," she said, thinking: *Try to get him talking. Sooner or later he's bound to let something slip.* "He's the only one I can think of with a motive for capturing me. He wants me to be his new slave, right?"

He ignored her.

"Who, then? Who would go to so much trouble?"

"It's not about you."

"But you need me. Why?" An idea struck her. "This is all about Kota, for what he and I did on Cato Neimoidia. It must be—but I didn't think Baron Tarko was so well connected—"

"Quiet."

The bounty hunter had slowed as though sensing danger ahead. She listened but could hear only the sounds of distant demolition, communicated through the floors and walls around her. It sounded like a wrecking droid was coming through the ship toward her.

"At least tell me how you found the fleet," she said. "Who did you torture to get that information?"

He didn't answer.

Behind them, metal tore and glass shattered. The bounty hunter turned and raised his rifle. Someone or something was coming up through the floor, ten meters away.

Juno stared in shock as a figure dressed entirely in black leapt out of the new hole in the floor, swinging two bright blue blades through the air. The bounty hunter fired at the figure, three precise shots in quick succession. The energy bolts were deflected into the walls, where they discharged with bright flashes. By their light, Juno saw the face of the man running toward her.

It was *him*.

Time stopped. The universe shattered around her. Natural laws unraveled and everything she thought she knew dissolved to nothing.

It was him, but it couldn't be. It couldn't be, but it was. Her heart leapt even as all the pieces fell into place, forming a terrible new pattern. She knew now who the bounty hunter was really seeking, and who was behind the plan. The pattern made sense in an instant, even as everything else seemed to fall apart. Starkiller was heading into a trap, and she was the lure.

Her mind teetered on the brink of hysteria. First Kota and now him. *Doesn't anyone stay dead anymore?*

More questions flooded in.

He's back—but how? And how did the bounty hunter know about him before I did?

The seconds ticked again. Her heart restarted. There was suddenly no more time to think. The man she had loved began to run toward them, his face a mask of fierce determination, and she knew that he had seen her, too.

She opened her mouth to shout a warning, but the bounty hunter shoved her through a doorway, out of view. She jerked to a halt at the end of the chain and went down to her knees, fighting waves of agony. Behind her, she heard Starkiller call her name, but his voice was drowned out on the second syllable by a massive explosion.

Smoke and debris rushed out of the corridor and filled the room. Even out of the blast's direct line she was still stung by the shrapnel. She covered her mouth and closed her eyes an instant too late. Blinking, coughing, deafened, she fought waves of unconsciousness as the bounty hunter dragged her back to her feet and pulled her into the corridor.

Through streaming eyes she saw a huge hole where Starkiller had been standing. Drips of molten metal rained down on the cavernous space below.

"If you killed him—" she started to say.

"You're as foolish as he is," the bounty hunter said with a sneer in his voice. He hurried along the corridor, pulling her after him. The tugs on the chain were sharp and insistent. Between the pain and trying to maintain her footing on the uneven floor, she had no inclination to talk anymore. Wherever he was taking her, he was in a much greater hurry than he had been before.

They left the burned corridor and entered an area that was relatively undamaged. Juno thought she recognized the location, and that was confirmed when she and her captor reached a large double door, lying open in their path. The cargo bay. It was empty apart from a dozen crates and two dead Rebel crew members. Dim red light flickered and played across the vast space. Again she worried about the reactor's functionality.

The bounty hunter tugged her inside and closed the doors behind them. As they slid shut, she caught something moving in the shadows above, but couldn't make out what it was. Not the cargo arm, that was for sure. It was much too big.

Behind them came the sound of destruction once again. The bounty hunter hurried to the matching double door on the far side of the bay, dragging her behind him like a recalcitrant child.

"You have no idea who you're dealing with," she said, and received only silence in reply.

The doors began to open ahead of them, revealing the orange-yellow vista of the Itani Nebula. The fight continued for control of space around the *Salvation*. Energy weapons flashed and flared. Starlight gleamed off wreckage and combative starships alike.

On the other side of the force field preventing them from being sucked into space was a transport the likes of which Juno had never seen before. Too compact to be a freighter but too stocky to be a starfighter, it was much taller than it was either wide or deep, giving it a slightly long-trunked appearance. It had the same functional and highly customized look as the bounty hunter beside her, and Juno had no doubt at all that it belonged to him.

"Shame it's the other side of the force field," she said. "Now what are you going to do?"

As the sound of rending metal behind them grew louder, the bounty hunter punched another button on his right gauntlet and turned to face the opening.

Figuring that he was never going to be this distracted again, Juno grabbed the chain with both hands and pulled it out of his grasp. Simultaneously, she rocked back on one leg and kicked him in the back with all her strength, propelling him toward the force field. While he was off balance, she ran for the other doors, hoping to get her hand on the activation switch before he recovered.

What came next happened almost too quickly for her to take in.

First, the doors ahead of her burst open, punched by unimaginable force from the far side.

Then the force field collapsed, sending everything in the room rushing toward the endless vacuum of space—including her and the dark figure standing where the inner doors had once been.

She lost her footing and jarred her shoulder. Dazed by pain, she would have tumbled helplessly out of the cargo bay but for a cable that whipped about her waist and dragged her back toward the bounty hunter.

At the same time, a stubby missile protruding from the top of his jetpack launched itself out into the void. Halfway between the cargo bay and the hanging ship outside, its tip unfolded into a grappling hook that an instant later found solid purchase on the side of the ship.

The cable binding Juno brought her within arm's reach of the bounty hunter. Unaffected by the rapidly thinning atmosphere, he slapped a breather across her face and bodily threw himself out of the cargo bay, taking her with him.

She kicked and struggled but his grip and the cable combined were impossible to resist. Her cry of anger and frustration fogged up the mask of the breather, so for a moment she couldn't tell what was happening behind her. They jerked to a halt, and she assumed at first that it was because they had reached the bounty hunter's ship, but a rapid volley of blasterfire back the way they had come, followed by the straining sound of the grapnel retractor, revealed that something very different was happening.

She held her breath, cursing the foggy visor and willing it to clear more quickly. By the fiery light of the nebula she glimpsed the *Salvation* looming ahead of her, sparkling jets indicating where breaches were venting air into the vacuum. Flames burned on the other side of several transparisteel windows. Bodies tumbled like dead stars, too many to count.

Clinging to the edge of the cargo bay door, withstanding the emptiness of space, the doors that were trying to close on him, and the shots fired his way by the bounty hunter, was Starkiller. One hand reached for her, fingers straining as though clutching at something invisible. Through the Force, he was trying to bring her back.

The whining of the grapnel reached a higher pitch. It was only a matter of time before something snapped—either the cable or the motor trying to reel it in. Juno had no doubt of that. Starkiller had shifted whole Star Destroyers. It would be nothing for him to overpower a single motor.

The bounty hunter reached around her to push yet another button on his gauntlet. For a second it had no obvious effect. Then, in the cargo bay behind Starkiller, something vast and angular moved.

Sparks flared. Starkiller turned with lightsabers swinging. The force pulling her back to safety faltered—and then died entirely as the cargo bay doors slammed shut between her and him.

Juno could hold her breath no longer. She raged against her captor, calling him things she hadn't called anyone since her earliest days in the Academy. She kicked and flailed against his chest, not caring how much it hurt her shoulder. The pain she felt ran deeper than flesh. Her entire being was in agony.

He was alive. She had seen him. A thousand questions barraged her—questions she didn't want to ask, but would have to address later, because they weren't ever going to go away.

How did he survive?

Where had he been for the last year?

Why had he stayed away when the Rebel Alliance had needed him so badly?

Why didn't he tell her?

For now it was terrible enough that she was being taken from him, and there was nothing she or anyone could do to stop it.

CHAPTER 15

JUNO.

Her proximity filled his mind, making it hard to deal with anything or anyone else around him. After leaving Kota, his comlink had squawked and blared about distant events and conflicts, so he had switched it off in irritation. He didn't care what happened outside the ship, only what happened to Juno inside it. When stormtroopers had crossed his path, he had blasted them out of the way with disinterested ferocity. Nothing could slow him. Nothing would stop him. The only thing keeping him and Juno apart was distance, and that could easily be overcome.

"Whatever you have seen, follow it you must."

"To the ends of the galaxy if I have to."

But the man in his vision was wilier than Starkiller had anticipated. The trail he had been following led nowhere, and was seeded with numerous traps and troopers designed to slow him down. If Juno *was* being taken to the cargo bay on level seven, then she was going by a very different route.

He forced himself to concentrate, seeking her through the many walls and decks of the *Salvation,* and finally sensed her presence two decks up. They were connected through the Force, by invisible lines that might fade but would never entirely break. Now he saw them clearly, it was just a matter of following them. Forgoing stairwells or lifts, he simply blasted his way through the ship's infrastructure. Metal and plastoid could be repaired. Wires and hydraulics could be rerouted. Human life—*Juno's* life—could not be replaced.

And he had seen her, briefly, face white and spattered with her own blood, eyes wide and staring at him in utter disbelief. What was going through her mind he could not begin to guess. Joy? Confusion? Relief? Doubt? They had only locked stares for a moment before the man who had taken her captive pushed her out of sight. Then he had fired a missile at Starkiller's feet that had blown a massive hole in the frigate. Starkiller had thrown up a Force shield at the last instant, but had still found himself four decks away when the blast dissipated. By the time he had retraced his steps, Juno was gone.

She was nearby, though, and it had taken him less than a minute to catch up, thinking hard all the way. If Juno was bait, why hadn't the trap been sprung? Starkiller was still alive and unfettered, and so, presumably, was Juno. Where did this particular gambit end?

"I do not expect you to survive," the voice of his former Master said in his mind. *"But should you succeed, you will be one step closer to your destiny."*

Starkiller could clearly remember the moment those words had been spoken. It seemed an eternity ago, while receiving orders to kill the mad Jedi droid maker, Kazdan Paratus. He had succeeded in that mission, but his destiny remained as elusive as ever.

What did Darth Vader *want?*

Sometimes it seemed that only Darth Vader could answer that question.

Starkiller reached the cargo bay doors. They were locked, but that didn't slow him for longer than a second. Inert matter was no match for the Force, and therefore no obstacle to him. Had Juno not been on the other side, he would have vaporized it in an instant, sending scalding metal shrapnel flying all through the cargo bay.

She was facing him, being dragged backward by a loop of

cable wrapped around her waist. The armored man blew out the cargo bay's external force field, and the vacuum pulled them with the rushing atmosphere outward into space. Starkiller grabbed hold of the nearest solid object in order to stop himself from sliding out after them. There was a stocky ship hanging just outside the air lock, obviously waiting to scoop them up and take them elsewhere. Juno's captor fired a grappling hook toward it and began to reel him and his struggling prisoner aboard.

Starkiller braved the hurricane pouring past him and skidded to the very edge of the air lock. There he found purchase against the bulkhead and stretched one hand out toward them. Again, he could have wrenched them back into the frigate without great difficulty, were it not for fear of hurting Juno in the process. If he pulled too hard, she might be crushed. Also, the man holding her was armed and unafraid to use his weapon. If he turned the weapon on her, she might be killed before Starkiller could prevent it.

Still he tried, straining against the cable winch and, when that proved too difficult, actually dragging the ship in toward the frigate. Why fight the winch when he could just as easily move the anchor it was attached to? The stocky ship rocked and swayed and began to creep toward him, Juno and her captor with it . . .

Then a shadow fell across him from behind. His concentration wavered. Something was moving toward him. Not a stormtrooper, visible or otherwise. It came from above, and got bigger the more it came into view.

Dying wasn't going to help Juno. He turned, lightsabers upraised to strike whatever it was. A droid of some kind, with multiple glowing photoreceptors and a vast, armored body that towered over him, balanced on eight thick legs.

He had seen it before, in his vision of Kamino. That knowledge didn't help, however, as it raised its forelegs and tried to spear him with four powerful lasers. He jumped, and the orange beams followed him, leaving glowing lines in their wake. It was big but fast, and he barely stayed ahead of its deadly attack. Behind him, the cargo bay doors slammed shut and life support began pumping in air. It smelled scorched and acrid under the giant droid's relentless assault.

Running wasn't helping, either. It was only wasting time. Starkiller took stock and decided to try another tactic.

He leapt into a corner and faced the droid with his lightsabers crossed. The convergent beams hit both blades and were reflected back at their source. The droid's mirror finish bounced them right back at him, doubling the number of attacks he had to deal with. Instead of retreating, he changed the angle of his blades. The four laser beams reflected by him sliced down toward the ground, slicing arcs in the durasteel floor. Metallic smoke rose up around the droid in thick streamers. By the time it realized his intentions, it was too late.

Already straining under the droid's weight, the floor sagged and gave way. The droid's lasers switched off, entirely too late. The sharp tips of its eight legs scrabbled for purchase, leaving deep scratches in the floor, which only gave way further.

With a grinding of metal, the droid dropped out of sight and crashed through the levels below, one after the other.

Almost before it had vanished from sight, Starkiller was moving. The external door was shut, but he forced it open and braved the renewed storm of air to see outside. Juno and her captor were no longer visible. The stocky ship's trio of engines was firing, pulling it away from the frigate. Starkiller reached out to catch it, too late. The craft barely wobbled as it receded into the distance, and vanished into hyperspace.

"No!"

His cry disappeared into the vacuum. He had lost her again, and for all his frustration and fury, there was nothing he could do about it now. The Force couldn't accomplish miracles, even in his hands.

It could, however, help him get revenge.

The dark side rose up in him, seductively powerful. Darth Vader had sent the bounty hunter to capture Juno, knowing that Starkiller would try to save her from him. There was only one place, then, that she could be headed: back to where it had all started. *Kamino.* He *would* go there, but he would not succumb to the trap Darth Vader had undoubtedly prepared. His wrath would know no bounds. All who stood in his way would suffer.

A new vision came to him, rushing out of the void to fill his mind.

Lightning. The Dark Lord on one knee before him, helmet slick and shining in the rain, disarmed. Starkiller's lightsabers formed an X between them, and Vader's neck lay just millimeters from their intersection. With a flick of his wrists, Starkiller could behead the galaxy's greatest monster, and gain revenge for everything he had done.

But what would revenge get him? It couldn't turn back time. It couldn't tell him who the real Starkiller was. It couldn't bring Juno back.

None of those things, he decided, but better than nothing.

His face formed a determined expression. He tensed to execute the man who had made him into what he was: a killing machine, with no hope for anything better.

Before he could complete the move, a red blade erupted from his chest, exactly as it had in a former life, on the Empirical. *Only this time his former Master couldn't have wielded it. He still knelt before him, awaiting the death blow.*

The pain and shock were too great. Starkiller arched backward, lightsabers falling from his hands. With an agonized cry, he crumpled to the ground, and stared up at the man who had killed him.

It was himself.

Darth Vader rose to his feet. Blasterfire erupted around them. Starkiller heard screams and cries and the sound of people falling. The battle was intense but short-lived, and he had eyes only for the pair in black looming over him.

"I lied when I told you that the cloning process had not been perfected."

His former Master's words fell like blows upon his stricken form. The version of himself sanding at the Dark Lord's side was upright and whole in every way. The Sith training uniform he wore was immaculate and lethally adorned. The two red lightsabers held crossed over his chest didn't waver a millimeter as their eyes locked.

Starkiller's breath was growing shallow. The fire that had burned in him was dying, as it always died in the end. The dark side consumed everything. Hatred was never a substitute for love, and the price of pursuing it was life itself.

In the corner of his view, lying drenched in the rain, lay a limp, shattered form. He could not bear to look at it. Instead he clutched the burning hole in his chest and watched the Dark Lord give his new apprentice his first orders.

"You have faced your final test."

The reborn Starkiller knelt at the Dark Lord's feet. "What is thy bidding, my Master?"

"Take the Rogue Shadow. *Scour the far reaches of the galaxy. Find the last of the Rebels and destroy them."*

"As you wish."

"Then, and only then, will you achieve your destiny."

The new apprentice rose and walked away, stepping over Juno's body as he went. Kota's body lay nearby, and PROXY's, sliced neatly in two. Darth Vader looked down at Starkiller's body and, with a contemptuous flick of his wrist, sent it skidding over the edge of the platform and into the sea.

The last thing Starkiller saw was storm clouds and lightning far above, as he had on the first day of his freedom, just days ago.

Thunder boomed, and Starkiller came back to himself with a gasp. The sound echoed around him, disorienting him. It couldn't be real. He had been seeing the future, not something happening in the present.

The deck beneath him shook. The sound came again. Not thunder, he realized, but the giant droid fighting its way back up to him, intending to finish their battle.

He felt weary, then. Weary of hatred and pain and loss and despair. He would fight on, but not by giving in to the dark side. He would find his own way, even as he ran headlong into a trap and put everything at risk.

He reactivated the cargo bay's force fields, and air rushed back in once more. Staring out at the nebula, he pulled the comlink from his belt and switched it on.

"Kota? Come in, Kota."

"I'm here, boy."

"Where's *here*, exactly?"

"On the bridge. We've regained control of the *Salvation* and repaired the hyperdrive. The hostile ships are retreating. What's your status?"

"That doesn't matter. Juno has been captured, and I know exactly where she's going. It has to be Kamino, where it all started. Which means that Darth Vader is there, too. I think he's set another trap."

"For you or the rest of us?"

"Just me, I think."

"Then he won't be ready for the entire Rebel fleet when it arrives on his doorstep. I told the Alliance about this chance to strike. The fleet is converging exactly as you wanted it to."

"Good," said Starkiller with a faint smile, "because if you hadn't sent the order I was going to go without you."

"Prepare for lightspeed, boy," said Kota from the bridge. "Let's hope you know what you're doing."

The booming from below grew louder. Behind it came a new scuttling sound that Starkiller hadn't heard before, as of giant metal insects crawling across a hollow deck.

Outside, the stars stretched and snapped. The angular impossibility of hyperspace filled the cargo bay doors.

Starkiller activated his lightsabers and stood facing the hole in the floor. The dark vision he had just received ate at his confidence. Thus far, three of his visions had come true: The bounty hunter had been sent after him, resulting in Juno being injured and deprived of her command, and his lightsabers had turned blue. That left two visions, the grimmest of them all. Was there any way he could avoid both their deaths? Was the other Starkiller, perfect and deadly in every way, something that already existed, or could he be a mere possibility, or even nothing more than a manifestation of his deepest fears?

"What happens if you do clone someone Force-sensitive?"

"Terrible things. Insanity. Psychosis. Suicidal tendencies."

The list of symptoms Ni-Ke-Vanz had rattled off was frighteningly close to what Starkiller himself was experiencing—but he had begun, perversely, to take hope from that. Perhaps Kota was right, and he had always been this way, even in his first life. Maybe learning to hate the way one felt was part of growing up. Maybe—

The rattling of tiny feet reached a crescendo. Five miniature versions of the huge droid rushed out of the hole on four sharp-tipped feet. He snapped out of his thoughts and ran forward to meet them, wearily grateful for the opportunity to act rather than think. The first two leapt at him, and he sliced them in pieces right out of the air. The other two split up and came for him from opposite sides. He met both advances with a lightsaber outstretched in each hand, using the Force to guide his blows. The droids shot piercing darts of energy in streams at him, trying to get through his guard. They, too, were immune to their own reflected fire, so instead of pursuing that tactic he danced closer to one and sliced its domed midsection in two, then brought his free hand around to blast the other with lightning. The miniature droid went wild, spinning in circles and sending energy darts about the cargo bay. Its green eyes glowed blue, then purple, and then its head exploded. Tiny bits of metal rained all over the hold with an almost musical sound.

More rattling came from the hole. Starkiller approached the lip and peered cautiously over the edge.

No less than a dozen droids were climbing toward him, hopping from deck to deck through the gaps the larger version had created. He reached out for the crates remaining in the cargo hold and sent them tumbling down on the droid's heads. They fell with legs spinning and were crushed far below.

Barely had they been dealt with than more appeared, leaping upward to attack him.

He pulled out his comlink again. "Kota, we have a problem."

"You might be right," came the gruff reply. "PROXY's picking up red lights all through the lower decks. Something you did?"

"We have a droid loose. I think it's headed for the secondary reactor."

"If it takes that out, we could lose the navicomp—and we don't want that to happen out here."

Starkiller glanced at the swirling madness of hyperspace. "Send as many troops as you can spare to defend it."

"That won't be many. The ship took heavy losses, so we're on a skeleton crew."

"All right, all right. I'll be there in a minute."

Starkiller ended the call and leapt feetfirst into the shaft. He lashed out with his lightsabers as he fell, taking out all of the miniature droids, one at a time. When he landed lightly at the bottom, a rain of droid parts fell around him, red-limned and bleeding sparks.

More were waiting for him in the path of the larger version. He glimpsed it far ahead, cutting through bulkheads and beams that lay in its path. The smaller droids seemed to be dropping from its underbelly, unfolding with a snap and hurrying back to confront him. The "parent" droid was definitely heading for the secondary reactor—but why now? The question occupied his mind as he fought his way past the smaller droids. Why not earlier, before the ship entered hyperspace?

The answer lay in the very question, he decided. Losing navicomp midjump would be disastrous. They might be blown to atoms, or never return to realspace. Should the droid even get close to damaging the reactor, then, they would have no choice but to drop out of hyperspace rather than take the risk.

It was a delaying tactic. Just like everything else had been, ever since Starkiller had engaged with the Imperials. Their leader, the bounty hunter, had wanted to grab Juno only in order to lure him elsewhere. He had never intended to engage directly with Starkiller. And that was a good call, for Starkiller would have blown *him* to atoms had he stood between him and her. Instead, the bounty hunter was forcing him to come face-to-face with the only man in the galaxy who had ever killed him.

Starkiller would face his creator and make the choice: live as a monster or die as himself, whoever that was.

Starkiller thought it unlikely that Darth Vader saw the irony in the situation. It was doubtful he saw anything in his plan other than objective methodology. Like Starkiller, Vader had been trained in the art of betrayal by a Sith who somehow expected nothing but ab-solute servitude in return. The finer points of existence—not just irony, but humor, sarcasm, regret, and many more—were com-pletely lost on him. Darth Vader was, for all intents and purposes, the machine he looked like.

He fought like a machine, too, with relentless blows and single-minded aggression. The first time they had dueled, in Starkiller's first life, Vader had displayed no anger at all—just determination, not to kill his apprentice, but to wear him into submission. The fight had raged across the training deck of the *Executor* for hours, with Starkiller never landing a single blow, no matter how he tried. He had gone from excitement at thinking that he had graduated to a new level of mastery to realizing just how much he had left to learn. More fuel had been added to the hatred he had felt for his Master and tormentor, along with a twisted kind of love for the man who made him stronger by showing him how weak he was. The fight had only stopped when Starkiller collapsed unconscious from exhaustion and was dragged by PROXY to his meditation chamber.

And maybe there, Starkiller thought, in that single-mindedness and determination that Darth Vader had handed down to his ap-prentice, lay his own weakness. Machines were exemplary at certain things. They were monomaniacal and focused, as PROXY had been in Starkiller's early life, when his mission had been to protect his charge—while at the same time training him by trying to kill him. Contradictions existed in their worlds, but they caused no conflict. They were simply assimilated and worked around, like the droids Starkiller had fought during his training on Kamino.

The galaxy wasn't a machine, and neither was the Rebellion. It would confound Darth Vader, perhaps even surprise him.

"You can teach me nothing," Darth Vader had told him on the Death Star.

Starkiller vowed to prove him very wrong on that score.

Part 3

RETRIBUTION

CHAPTER 16

JUNO WOKE WITH A START. She was lying on her side in complete darkness. Her hands were unbound, and her right shoulder was numb all the way down to her elbow. There was a sickening throb between her eyes that spoke of another stunning at the hands of her captor. The last thing she remembered was being dragged into his ship and the air lock sliding closed behind them. The *Salvation* had loomed over her like a mountain, glowing red and yellow by the light of the nearby nebula. The remaining TIE fighters had broken off their attack and were retreating back into the asteroid clouds. A smattering of turbolaser fire chased them as they went.

Then, nothing. And now, blackness, with nothing connecting the two periods. Juno wondered when, if ever, she would see her ship again.

That day wouldn't come any sooner by just lying there, she told herself. Reaching out with her left hand, she felt around her and slowly sat up. There was nothing above her head she might bang into, and nothing but empty flatness on the floor in any direction. The surface she had been lying on felt like unadorned plastoid, but there was a distinct smell of duralloy in the air, and a complex whine in the background that spoke of a ship under power. They were under way, wherever they were going. It was probably for the best, she told herself, that they hadn't yet arrived.

The shoulder of her uniform had been cut away and new bandages placed over her blaster wound. It seemed to her questing fingers like a capable job. She supposed bounty hunters would have to learn at least basic medical skills, if they were to keep their prisoners alive long enough to earn a reward. For that she was grateful, if nothing else.

She rose up onto her hands and knees and explored the space around her more thoroughly. She soon learned that it was a cage approximately two meters high, wide, and deep, with horizontal metal bars along two walls and plastoid elsewhere. She searched for a hinge or a lock but found nothing: The bars most likely recessed into the walls and would only retract on the ship's owner's command. With no tools and no light, she could see no way of getting out of the cage, let alone taking control of the ship and turning it around.

She put her head in her hands. That she had to go back was something she didn't doubt, at first. Starkiller had returned. What else was there to worry about? But the unremitting darkness began to get to her, the questions she had asked herself while being dragged from the *Salvation* returned.

Starkiller was undeniably back. How? Why? How long? And where was he now? Could he possibly be dead again?

Time wore on and she began to doubt the evidence of her eyes. She had only glimpsed him on the *Salvation*. It was conceivable that she had mistaken someone else for him—but was it conceivable that there was anyone else in the galaxy with the ability to do what he did?

It had to be him. But the rest of her doubts weren't so easily dismissed. Starkiller *was* alive, and while the part of her that had mourned him rejoiced, the simple fact of his existence wasn't enough to reassure her completely. The ramifications of his return weren't going to go away simply by assuming that he would eventually come for her, or hoping that she could escape, in order that they would be together again.

How *had* he come back? She had seen him consumed in a massive explosion while rescuing the Rebel leaders from the Death

Star—an explosion that Kota had assured her had definitely killed him. She had felt as though part of her had died, and she had moved forward in complete faith that what she had seen was real, that Kota had neither lied nor been mistaken. Starkiller *had* died. But now he was back. The explanation for this apparently simple fact had to lie far beyond what she regarded as normal, perhaps even *possible,* and the source of that explanation worried her.

Had he been alive all this time, or had he only recently returned from the dead? That was another question with powerful undercurrents. If he had been alive the last year, why hadn't he contacted her? What had he been doing? When had Kota learned about it? It was clear to her now that Starkiller had been aboard the *Rogue Shadow* when it docked, and that he was most likely the source of the tactical information Kota had given her. How long had they been in league to keep this knowledge from her? How far, in that light, should she trust the information?

On the latter point, she had no choice. Sealed up in the belly of a bounty hunter's prison ship, she might as well have been in another universe as far as the Rebel Alliance was concerned. They might even think her dead, if the battle went badly and the *Salvation* was destroyed. She might never get the chance to share her concerns, or to ask Kota why he had deceived her.

The painkiller was wearing off. A long, throbbing ache spread outward from her shoulder, down her arm and spine and up into her skull. She embraced the pain at the same time as she hated it. It cleared her thoughts.

She remembered the *Empirical,* the last time she had been a prisoner. Then she had thought Starkiller dead, killed by his Master under the orders of the Emperor. Then, as now, he had returned from the grave. Darth Vader had told him that he had been rescued before his life signs had faded away completely, but that could have been a lie. Had whatever process brought him back then been used now, too? How many times could a man die and be reborn and still remain the same man?

Escape had seemed impossible from the *Empirical*. It was Starkiller himself who had rescued her. His appearance in her cell had seemed a miracle, or a pain-induced fantasy designed to ease her own passage from life. She had put out of her mind what the guards had called him then, but those words came back to her now. They had called him "experiment" and "lab rat." They had feared him long before he had attacked them, for reasons she had never wondered about before.

"I saw you die," she had told him. *"But you've come back."*

All he had said in reply was, *"I have some unfinished business."*

As though that explained everything. She wondered now if he could have used a Jedi mind trick on her in that moment, to assuage her concerns. He had been mostly Vader's tool at that point, so she could readily understand why he might have done so. But those concerns about his survival returned a hundredfold, as though they had compounded at the back of her mind in the time since.

What would she say to him now, if he appeared in the cell with her?

Would he tell her what his unfinished business was, this time? Did it matter?

If it was *her,* perhaps it made all the difference in the universe.

She got up and paced as best she could. The diagonal across a two meter-square cell was less than three meters, but it gave her something to do. She didn't know how soon they would arrive at their destination, wherever that was. It could be hours, yet. She needed a distraction from her thoughts, because they were leading her down a very dark path.

If Starkiller was back because he loved her, why hadn't he revealed himself before now?

If love had nothing to do with his return, what reason did she have to be glad of it?

She thought of PROXY mourning the loss of his primary programming and desperately seeking a new one. For the first time, she truly understood his pain. How simple it would be, if such a thing existed for humans, to plug a module into her head and have all these thoughts erased. To forget Starkiller and all he had meant to her. To finally get on with her life at last. What unimaginable freedom!

But it would be a lie, she knew. She wouldn't be who she was anymore. Starkiller had given her a new and better life. To turn her back on him would be to turn her back on the Alliance as well as everything she had become. That was a betrayal she could never contemplate.

As the ship rushed on through hyperspace, Juno remembered a moment on Felucia when she had been sure Starkiller was about to kiss her. She remembered making that thought come true above the Death Star, and the way her heart had pounded from fear and excitement at once. And she remembered Kota telling her about what he had seen in Starkiller's mind: *"Among all the dark thoughts in his head I glimpsed one bright spot, one beautiful thing that gave me hope—and that he held on to, even at the end."*

She had asked what that was, and Kota hadn't told her, but she had known—and she still knew now. They had been each other's salvation in very dark times. They would be so again.

Come rescue me, she said in her mind, knowing the words would be lost in hyperspace forever but hoping that he would hear her anyway. *Rescue me, Starkiller, so I can return the favor.*

CHAPTER 17

STARKILLER FACED THE GIANT DROID and stared hard into its two remaining eyes. It had lost four of its legs and numerous gaping rents had been carved all across its underbelly and back, but it remained a formidable opponent. It had killed every soldier Kota had thrown at it, leaving only Starkiller between it and the secondary reactor. He could feel the damage already done to the frigate as a deep, irregular vibration that rose and fell in the normally semi-audible rumble of the hyperdrive. There was no doubt in his mind that any more fluctuations in power would result in a catastrophe.

He feinted to his left. The droid shifted right to block him. He feinted in the opposite direction. It shifted again. Internal mechanisms thudded and groaned behind its durasteel shell. It crouched low, preparing to spring, and issued a noise like an antique boiler hissing its last.

Mentally, Starkiller triple-checked the layout of the secondary reactor against the rest of the frigate. He and the droid had been sparring vigorously for what felt like hours, and he was afraid of getting everything back to front. Without a clear landmark, that would have been very easy. Two decks, uncountable rooms and corridors, and one water tank had been completely destroyed during their fight, leaving an immense tangle of wreckage in their wake.

He hoped Juno would forgive him for the damage when he finally found her. It was still her ship, after all, and she might not take kindly to his giving it such a battering.

Still, he thought, shifting a couple of meters to his right, it wasn't as if he had much choice . . .

The droid tracked his movement, and pounced.

He ducked as he had many times before, and gave the droid a solid shove as it went over his head. Its lasers flashed around him, cutting yet another hieroglyphic pattern deep into the metal deck. Its innards whined as it spun to reorient itself, intending to arrest its trajectory against the wall ahead with three feet, and then leap back at him, stabbing with the fourth limb, hoping to impale him on its deadly, sharp tip.

He stayed still just long enough to give the machine the impression that this time, unlike all the other times, its plan might work.

The droid hit the bulkhead with a mighty thud, and kicked its three legs as hard as it could. The bulkhead, strained and scarred by many such impacts, gave way with a shriek. The noise was instantly joined by another, much louder sound—that of atmosphere rushing out into the void.

This was no ordinary bulkhead. It was the outer hull of the frigate, and it had been pushed far beyond its tolerance. The droid, realizing its error, scrambled to withdraw the legs that now stuck through the hull, outside the ship, but Starkiller wasn't having any of that. He braced himself firmly against the interior bulkhead behind him and pushed. The droid sank a meter deeper into the metal, which tore and stretched further in response. Through the rents he glimpsed the abstract angularity of hyperspace rushing by, and he felt the droid's desperation increase. Starkiller didn't know what happened to ordinary matter when it was separated from the hyperdrive that lay at the heart of a starship and left to founder in the unreal spaces beyond. He suspected the droid didn't, either. It was about to find out.

One last flurry of laserfire slashed and burned at him. He

ducked but held his ground, not caring if the droid scored a few light hits at this terminal stage. There was only one possible outcome now.

He pushed again, and the hull bent outward. The droid gave up all attempts to fight back and concentrated solely on survival. Its legs left deep scratches in the metal as they fought to maintain their purchase. But Starkiller's strength was too great, when combined with the strange effects of hyperspace outside. One claw slipped, then another, and then, with a final shriek of metal, it vanished, swept away by forces neither of them could understand.

Starkiller staggered backward, weakened by the effort and feeling giddy from the sudden drop in pressure. He hurried to a hatch leading down to the secondary reactor that had been the cause of all the fuss. It was sealed tight against the vacuum, but with the last of his strength he forced it open and fell through. He landed heavily on his back and stared up at the ceiling. The hatch slammed shut behind him. Deeply, gratefully, he filled his lungs.

Gradually he became aware of alarms and his comlink squawking. He reached down and brought it up to his mouth.

"What is it, Kota?"

"I've been trying to ask you the same question," the general shot back. "The hull breach on deck three—your doing?"

"The reactor's out of danger now," he said. "How's the rest of the ship?"

"Holding together."

"ETA?"

"You might want to get moving if you intend being on the bridge when we arrive."

Starkiller groaned and sat up. Two nervous reactor technicians he hadn't noticed before backed deeper into the corner they occupied.

"It's okay," he said. "I'm one of the good guys."

They didn't look terribly reassured, and he couldn't blame them. His black flight uniform was torn and charred; laser-cauterized wounds covered almost every square centimeter of his exposed skin; his face was smudged and bruised. Favoring his right leg very slightly, he left the technicians to tend the machine in their care, and began the complicated ascent back to the bridge, through damaged decks and past mounds of wreckage and bodies everywhere.

One of the good guys. The technicians hadn't known who he was, and that was undoubtedly for the best. Maybe they had heard of a young man who had played a role in the formation of the Alliance; they might even have heard rumors of his death on the Death Star; they were very unlikely to connect him to that person, and even if they did, who would believe them? People didn't come back from the dead. It just wasn't possible, even for Jedi.

Starkiller wondered if Darth Vader thought *himself* one of the good guys. He wondered if any servant of the Empire did, for long. Juno had been having doubts long before she'd met him. Vader had guided her toward evil the same way he guided everyone he encountered. Anyone who fought back, or tried to, was killed.

He wondered, not for the first time, who the Dark Lord had been before being subsumed by the Emperor's plan for galactic domination. Could he have been a Jedi Knight, perhaps one of the many whose bodies had never been found after the execution of Order 66? Several times Starkiller had strained to detect a hint of Jedi training in his former Master's own teaching techniques—but there was little evidence to pore over from a man who let actions speak louder than words, and whose philosophies concerned only power and domination. The only subtlety Starkiller could discern was that, although the lessons were brutal and the cost of failure high, there was no malicious cruelty. Once the equation was laid down—obey and succeed versus fail and die—the rest was entirely up to him.

The world was black and white through Darth Vader's mask, Starkiller thought. There were no grays. He imposed this view on everyone around him, and people either fell in line or fell by the wayside.

That didn't stop Darth Vader from emulating his own Master,

though. He plotted treachery and had schemes that might take years to unfold. He was smart, and had learned the hard way to be cunning—probably thanks to the long years of his own tutelage under the galaxy's ruling Sith Lord.

But Vader preferred the direct approach, whenever possible. He fought the way he thought. It was easier to lure Starkiller back to him by using Juno as a hostage than any other method, so that was what he did. Instead of negotiating with Starkiller, he would simply kill him. Black, white—open, shut. Vader's mind was a puzzle box from which he let little escape, but the shape of the box said much about him.

I will surprise you, Starkiller promised his former Master, *if it's the last thing I do.*

In this life, he added, *or any other.*

The bridge was scarred with the signs of battle—blood, blaster scoring, burned consoles—but amazingly functional nonetheless. Like any band of mercenaries, Kota's squad had plenty of experience with operating in less-than-perfect conditions. They patched sensors out of spilled components; they rewired control systems by hand. The medic, Ni-Ke-Vanz, was nowhere to be seen. Starkiller assumed he was in the surgery suite, doing what he could to patch the crew back together.

PROXY was helping, too, stabbing at buttons on two consoles at once. After a hasty repair job on his chest and eye, he seemed to be back to his old self, more or less. A flicker of Kota swept across the droid's metal body, and Starkiller wondered why.

"Forget about the cargo bays," Kota shouted into a comlink. "If engine six fails in the next five minutes, we won't care about what stores we've lost."

He glanced up as Starkiller walked to stand next to him. Kota looked as battered as he had on Cato Neimoidia. Clearing out the last of the camouflaged stormtroopers had taken its toll, it seemed.

Kota acknowledged Starkiller with a nod. "We're running slow. The fleet will get there ahead of us at the rate we're moving, but we *will* get there in the end. That I guarantee you."

Starkiller was somewhat reassured, but the anxiety he felt for Juno was unabated. If the fleet had arrived at Kamino, that meant the bounty hunter had arrived, too. She was almost certainly in the hands of Darth Vader right now, suffering in a thousand unknown ways.

To distract himself, he checked on the *Rogue Shadow*. It was still docked along the frigate's spine, seeming undamaged. Its shields had protected it during the dogfight, and it hadn't been boarded. That was something. Just having a solid link to the past nearby helped him settle his thoughts.

Get to Kamino, he told himself. *Find Juno. Free her. Easy.*

"I'm sorry, General Kota," PROXY was saying, "but I have been unable to restore the targeting computer to its full capacity."

"So we'll be firing by hand," Kota said, "which will drain some crew-power. Fighter complement is down to fifteen. Make sure they're ready to launch the moment we come out of hyperspace," he called to one of his squad members.

"How long now?"

"Two minutes." Kota studied Starkiller's face. "Don't worry. We'll find her."

Starkiller acknowledged the general's attempt at reassurance with little more than a grunt. He knew what Kota wanted. He wanted Starkiller back in the fight. Kamino was just a means to that end. Once Juno was free, presumably, Kota hoped to announce Starkiller's return, reunite the Alliance behind him, and storm the Emperor's stronghold on Coruscant.

Perhaps, Starkiller thought, he was being unfair to Kota, but he saw little compassion in the general's blind eyes. Just determination to win—at all costs. If the operation at Kamino was a success, there would be another one, and another one, and another. It would never end, until the Empire itself was ended.

Starkiller didn't know how to tell Kota that what came after finding Juno was a mystery he himself hadn't unraveled yet. He could barely think farther ahead than the next few minutes.

Get to Kamino. Find Juno. Free her.

Everything else could wait. Whether it was his faulty clone brain talking or a clear-eyed certainty that Juno mattered more than anyone else, he was sure of that much. The near future, as glimpsed in his visions, needed to be changed before he would think about what would happen afterward.

A long, slow shudder rolled through the ship in response to a random power fluctuation from the main reactor. Starkiller took hold of a nearby console and rode it out. There was nothing else he could do. This wasn't an enemy he could fight with force. He could only trust the people around him and the machines they maintained to bring him safely to where he needed to be.

When it passed, Kota addressed the makeshift crew.

"We're nearing Kamino. All power to forward deflector shields."

"Yes, General," replied PROXY.

The ship shuddered again, this time in reaction to the drain caused by the shields. Starkiller held his breath, hoping the hyperdrive wouldn't fail just moments before reaching its destination. Or that it would bring them to a point light-years from where they needed to be. There was no guarantee they could get the drives working again, once they were shut down.

Ahead, the tortured topology of hyperspace began to transform into the familiar streaked stars of realspace. The ship was spinning around its long axis, making the view even more disorienting than normal. Metal creaked and decks swayed. Pressure alarms went off in a dozen quarters.

Again, Starkiller wondered what Juno would think of the condition of her ship when she got it back. Again, he relegated that concern to join the others he would worry about later. *After.*

The *Salvation* slammed back into reality with a bone-shaking thud, and suddenly it was in the middle of a war.

Kamino hung dead ahead, its white-streaked blue face looking deceptively placid against the unfamiliar constellations of Wild Space. Starkiller counted a dozen Rebel starships facing off against no less than five Imperial Star Destroyers. Clouds of TIE fighters,

Y-wings, and Z-95 Headhunters engaged in dogfights across the hulls of the larger vessels. Bombers stitched bright trails in their wakes. Energy weapons and shield flashes painted the sky in every wild color imaginable.

Just seconds after it exited hyperspace, the *Salvation* was hit by a blast from one of the Star Destroyers.

"Cannons on those warships!" Kota ordered. "Scramble fighters!"

Starkiller went to leave the bridge, intending to take the *Rogue Shadow* into battle, but Kota took his arm.

"Not you. I want you on the primary forward turbolaser. Whoever's firing down there couldn't hit a planet from low orbit. Operate the controls by remote." He indicated an empty console. "When the planetary shield is down, we'll take the *Rogue Shadow* to the surface together."

Starkiller didn't argue, although he yearned to be out in the thick of it. Being a gunner wasn't the same thing as cutting and weaving through the mess of ships and energy outside, but he could still do good from where he was. A frigate's primary turbolaser wasn't a weapon to be dismissed easily.

He called up the remote controls and settled into a seat. The interface was one he hadn't used before, but it was easily navigated. *Gas charges. Galven coils. Cooling. Tracking.* He smiled. *Trigger.* That was what he wanted.

A holographic display of the battlefield hung in front of him. He swung the targeting reticle from Star Destroyer to Star Destroyer, seeking a weak spot. The weapon was more sluggish than the *Rogue Shadow*'s armaments, but that was only to be expected. He took opportunistic shots at TIE fighters that darted nearby, guided by the steady hand of the Force, and soon made a significant dent in the Imperial numbers.

Targeting ion cannon and bridge towers to great effect, Starkiller brought the *Salvation* to the attention of the Star Destroyers' gunners. The frigate's shields groaned and complained while the Rebel starfighters did their best to retaliate.

With half an ear, Starkiller listened to panicky comm chatter from the pilots.

"We're getting ripped apart up here!" one cried as a concentrated blast of turbolaser fire tore his squadron apart. "Order the retreat!"

Kota's response was immediate. "Hold your position, Antilles." He changed frequencies to broadcast to all ships. "Keep pressing the attack! We won't get another chance to take this target!"

A flickering hologram appeared in front of him. It showed a stocky Rodian in what looked like a commodore's uniform.

"The planetary shield around Kamino is proving stronger than we thought," he said. Static ate up a couple of words. "—ground assault is impossible until they're down."

Kota looked desperate. Starkiller knew what he was feeling. This was the Rebel Alliance's first and best chance to strike the Empire hard. If it failed, the symbolic defeat could be much worse than a mere military setback.

"PROXY," Kota said, "can you slice into the defenses and bring them down from out here?"

"I have been trying, General, but it will take too long. The *Salvation* is suffering heavy damage. We've already lost decks eight through twelve, and can't hold out much longer."

"There has to be a way." Kota gripped the edge of the main display so tightly, his knuckles were pure white. Tiny images of starships danced and whirled in front of him. The commodore waited, image dissolving and firming every second or so. "But what can we do? The ship is falling apart around us. The fleet is being pounded. And we're no closer to the target than we were when we arrived."

Starkiller restored control of the turbolaser to the crew and went to join Kota. An idea was forming in his mind—an idea that ought to be crazy but might, he thought, barely be crazy enough to work.

"Where are the planetary shield generators?" he asked.

PROXY leaned over the main display and pointed out the location on a map of Kamino. Among the domes and towers of the facility, he instantly recognized the familiar lines of the main stormtrooper breeding facilities and, nestled among them, the secret spaces in which Darth Vader had conducted his experiments.

"Here, Master. Both generator and reactor are in the same location, making it exceptionally vulnerable. The shield it creates, however, is strong enough to prevent any form of attack, so we are unable to take advantage of that fact."

Starkiller nodded. Crazy indeed, he told himself, and Juno was certain not to approve, but it was the one plan he could think of that had the slightest chance.

"Head to the *Rogue Shadow*," Starkiller told Kota. "I'm pretty sure those shields can't take a direct hit from a frigate."

Kota's blind eyes stared at Starkiller for a full second. His chin came up as he fully grasped the details of the plan. "You sure about this?"

"It's the only way. Just be ready to clean up."

"All right." Kota's fist slammed into a button on the console. "Abandon ship! Abandon ship!" His gruff voice echoed through the frigate. "All crew, abandon ship!"

He took his hand off the button and reached for Starkiller. They shook hands firmly, without saying anything. Then the general turned and swept with his squad from the bridge.

"You too, PROXY."

"Yes, Master." A re-creation of Starkiller's own face flickered across the droid's features. "Even without primary programming, I remain committed to the principle of self-preservation."

For some time after PROXY was gone, and even as he threw himself into the complicated issue of slaving the ship to his commands, Starkiller wondered at the droid's parting words. They had been stated with great significance, but he didn't think they were intended as an attack on his own motives. PROXY wasn't trying to imply that he was suicidal—he hoped. And he hoped his motives weren't remotely bent that way. The plan wasn't half as crazy as others he had been party to. It was just the voice of Ni-Ke-Vanz again, adding to his uncertainty.

Insanity. Psychosis. Suicidal tendencies.

But for that, he told himself, crashing a frigate from orbit into a planetary shield generator might seem a perfectly sane thing to do.

The image of the Rodian commodore had long flickered out for good. Starkiller assumed Kota had passed on the decision, and the disposition of the fleet bore that out. Starfighters converged on the *Salvation,* offering covering fire while he was distracted with realigning the ion engines and turbolasers. The frigate's shields bore the brunt of everything coming his way, and that situation was certain to worsen when the Star Destroyers' commanders realized what his intentions were.

Slowly, the damaged frigate came about. All seven ion engines flared to full thrust. Every forward turbolaser and cannon fired continuously at the planetary shield below. Starkiller adjusted the *Salvation*'s trim so it was aimed directly at the shield generator. A chron began to count down in the main display, estimating how much time remained before impact.

There would actually be two impacts, Starkiller reflected as the frigate picked up speed. First, against the shield; second, against the surface of the planet itself. There was no way to tell how far apart they would be spaced. It would depend on how successfully the shield managed to keep the *Salvation* at bay. Not long, he estimated, but even a second could significantly reduce its momentum, to the point, perhaps, where the frigate didn't so much ram the generator as simply fall on it.

That would still be enough. He was sure of that much. Nothing was designed to withstand an impact like that.

Not even him.

The planet grew large ahead of him. The Imperials gradually figured out what the frigate accelerating toward them was intending to do. Energy weapons and TIE fighters came in wave after wave, attempting to destroy the *Salvation* before it got anywhere near impacting the shield. The Rebels literally threw themselves between him and the Imperials, taking hits for him in an attempt to ensure the success of his last-ditch gambit. A Star Destroyer rumbled by, too slowly to physically intercept the falling frigate. He wondered who had issued the order to attempt a ram—Darth Vader or the ship's commander. Probably the former. If anyone could guess who was at the controls of the *Salvation,* it would be him.

And Darth Vader, of all people, would know what Starkiller was capable of. On Raxus Prime, he had changed the course of a Star Destroyer using nothing but the Force.

"What is mass?" Kota had asked him. *"Concentrate on what's important."*

Kamino loomed large ahead. Already he felt the faint fringes of atmosphere.

Starkiller clung tightly to the edge of the main display and held an image of Juno's face steady in his mind.

CHAPTER 18

JUNO FELT THE PITCH of the prison ship's engines change beneath her, and she was on her feet in an instant. The hyperdrives had cut out. A second later, ion engines kicked in—three of them, mounted at the base of the craft. That was an unusual configuration, one that would make it easier to identify the ship later. There were no portholes to peer through, and no visits from her captor, either, so she had no way of knowing what, exactly, was happening outside. But she could guess. They had reached their destination and were accelerating into an equatorial insertion trajectory, preparatory to landing.

That guess was confirmed when she heard repulsors kick in. The ship rocked a couple of times and shook from nose to stern. Wherever they were, it was bumpy.

She stayed where she was, riding out the short trip to the surface with an uneasy sensation in her stomach that wasn't motion sickness. She hadn't been face-to-face with Darth Vader since her arrest, the first time Starkiller had "died." His opinion of her was unlikely to have improved since then.

The ship's flight steadied. She imagined it hovering over a pad, preparatory to landing. Gravity shifted minutely as the ship's artificial field gave over to local ambient levels. She lightly jumped twice into the air. There wasn't much change, which didn't help her refine the possibilities at all.

The ship settled with hardly a bump as it touched solid ground. The repulsors eased off, and all the other noises of flight gradually ceased. The hull allowed very little sound from outside into her tiny cell. She heard a faint hiss that wasn't life support, and an incessant, threading whine that might have been wind.

A door she hadn't noticed before slid open to her right, allowing a shaft of natural light into the caged areas. She blinked and raised a hand to shield her eyes. Through the unaccustomed glare she saw straight into the cockpit and out the visor on the far side. The skies were heavily overcast. As she watched, a ribbon of lightning ran from left to right. Thunder followed, muffled to the point of inaudibility.

The ship's pilot—and only crew member, she could now confirm—walked through the hatch and approached her cage. His rifle was slung over his shoulder. She didn't doubt he could have it trained on her in a microsecond.

"Hands," the bounty hunter said, demonstrating with his own how he wanted her to stand.

She slipped her forearms through the bars so he could reach her wrists. He clamped binders around her, not so tightly that it hurt, but leaving no possibility of slipping free. When she was secure, he hit a stud on the wall and the bars retracted.

She didn't run or attack him. There was no point. Better, she had decided long ago, to save her energies for when they were needed. The only thing resistance now could get her was another injury, or worse.

The bounty hunter pressed a second stud, opening the inner door of a small air lock, probably the one through which they had entered the craft. It was just large enough for two.

"Where are we?" she asked.

"Kamino," he said, waving her ahead of him.

That rang a bell. "Imperial cloning facility?"

He shrugged and closed the inner lock behind them. An instant later the outer lock opened and rain poured in.

He took her arm and roughly pulled her from the ship. She understood instantly that this was part of the act. The customer had to see that they were getting their money's worth.

The odd-looking prison ship sat on a landing platform belonging to a high-tech facility mounted on long columns directly over an ocean—an ocean that stretched as far as her eyes could see. A broad walkway connected the platform to a series of tall habitats constructed in a distinctly Imperial style. She must have seen hundreds like them, all across the occupied worlds. At the nearest end of the ramp was a welcoming committee of ten stormtroopers, their white armor slick with rain. The building behind them showed signs of recent construction, or possibly repairs. A tall door opened in its side, and through it stepped Darth Vader.

She tensed without wanting to, and the bounty hunter felt it. Perhaps fearing that she might make a break for the edge of the platform, there to hurl herself into the sea, he tightened his grip and pulled her forward.

"You returned sooner than I expected, bounty hunter," said Vader when they were within earshot.

"I work faster than most." The bounty hunter pushed her forward. "She's all yours."

"And Starkiller?"

"He's your problem, Lord Vader. I know my limitations."

"Our arrangement is not complete until he is in the Kamino system."

"I don't think you'll be waiting long."

Juno swallowed her fear as Vader's attention turned to her.

"Captain Eclipse, you and your fellow subversives in the Rebel Alliance have caused me considerable inconvenience. I should execute you now as the traitor you are, but there is one last service that I would have you perform."

"I will never willingly serve you."

"Your compliance is not required." Vader raised his right hand, but stopped at the sound of footsteps. A signals officer had emerged from the doorway and was proceeding in haste along the ramp, slipping occasionally in the rain.

"Lord Vader," he said. "We are detecting the signatures of several large vessels entering the Kamino system. They lack Imperial transponders and will not reply to our hails."

Vader's hand clenched into a fist. "Excellent. Notify Fleet Commander Touler that it is time." He turned to the man next to her. "You have done well. You will be rewarded handsomely once this matter is concluded."

"But you said—"

"Bring her." Vader stalked off, not waiting around to hear the bounty hunter's objections. Stormtroopers shoved him aside and closed in on Juno.

Gloved hands took her shoulders and elbows. Armored figures blocked her front and back. She could barely see the top of the bounty hunter's broadband antenna as he turned away and trudged back to his ship.

VADER WAS MOVING FAST. The stormtroopers hustled her to keep up, occasionally making her stumble. She hadn't gotten a good look at the facility before they entered it, but it seemed enormous, the furthermost tip of a city-sized structure that covered a significant amount of ocean. They passed long-necked aliens who shied away from Vader with either respect or fear, or both. Native Kaminoans, she assumed: The geneticists responsible for the army of clones that had given the Emperor an unbeatable advantage in his overthrow of the Republic.

She didn't like how fast they were moving. Vader had something in mind. The more she could do to distract him from it, the better.

"He's coming, you know," she called after Vader's back. "Doesn't that worry you?"

He walked on, unchecked.

"I mean, he's beaten you once before. You know it as well as I do. A lesser man would have killed you there and then. Do you really want to give him the chance to change his mind?"

Nothing. Just the grating draw and release of his respirator, as implacable as his heavy footfalls.

"And when you're gone, what chance do you think the Emperor has? *You're* the one everyone's afraid of. Or don't you care about the Empire? You just want to protect your tiny piece of it— the piece your Master lets fall from the table, to keep you compliant."

Still nothing. Grudgingly, she decided that taunting him was probably not going to work, in terms of him letting something slip. But that wasn't the only reason why she kept at it.

"To be honest," she said, "I'm a bit disappointed. Using me as bait shows real desperation. How do you know it'll work? What makes you think he cares a bit what happens to me? He's more likely to come here for you, because you're the one he wants."

She waited a moment, and then added, "Which is odd, when you think about it. The harder you drive him away, the harder he comes back. No matter how you punish him, no matter how many times you betray him, he keeps returning for more. I'm beginning to wonder if he's been on your side the whole time, and just doesn't know it."

They entered a new section of the facility, one containing vast cloning spires studded with growing bodies destined one day to become stormtroopers in the Emperor's army. That prompted her to change tack.

"You probably want me to think that you brought him back," she said. "Well, I don't. You know what I believe? I believe he brought himself back, and you found him while he was weak, convinced him that he owed his life to you, and thought that this way you'd have power over him. Like you didn't learn the first time that no one has power over him. Not you, not me, not the Emperor himself. You're wasting your time trying to control him— but hey, if that's how you want to end it all, don't let me stand in your way."

Without turning, Vader raised a hand and cocked two fingers

to the lead stormtrooper. Their little troupe came to a halt. Juno backed away, expecting to be stunned again. She hated that.

Instead, the stormtrooper produced an armor sealant patch from his thigh pocket and placed it firmly over her mouth.

Fair enough, she thought. Her failure to get a rise out of the Dark Lord was beginning to wear her down, too. But at least now she knew one thing for sure.

He definitely wanted her alive.

Her mouth sealed shut, the long walk resumed. At the base of one of the cloning spires they stopped to wait for a turbolift. Four of the stormtroopers entered with Vader, including the one who had gagged her. The rest stayed behind, improving her odds but not by much.

They went upward, fast. Her ears popped. The only sound was the harsh in–out of Vader's respirator. Not for the first time she wondered what lay inside the black, expressionless helmet. She hoped she would never know.

The lift slowed and she was escorted out again. They were perhaps halfway up the cloning spire, in a section heavily guarded by stormtroopers. The tubes around her were different—larger, darker, connected to more wires and tubes than those below. The figures within were shrouded in shadow.

One moved as she was led to a second turbolift, farther around the tower. Its leg kicked out, blindly. One hand batted against the curved glass. Then it stilled and went back to growing.

They reached the base of the second lift, where they waited for the cab to descend. She had time to study the nearest tube in more detail. The clone within was taller than the average stormtrooper, and leaner. It, too, twitched, as though it could sense her watching it. It rolled over, like a child turning in its womb.

Its face approached the curved glass, and she flinched on seeing its features. They were younger, slighter, not entirely whole, but they definitely belong to just one man.

Starkiller.

She gasped and recoiled from the tank, resisting the explanation even though she admitted to herself, was *forced* to admit, that no other made sense. The only alternative was the one she had offered Vader—that Starkiller was so strong in the Force that he could stave off death itself—and at accepting that she had to balk. As Bail Organa had said, such power was too great to be trusted, in anyone. And if the Emperor ever got his hands on it, there would go all hope for the galaxy.

But cloning was dangerous and unreliable. It was impossible to imagine what was going through the mind of the Starkiller she had seen. Clones had gone mad from identity crises many times in the past. Why would he be any different?

Her shoulders slumped as a new thought sunk in. The clone in the tank before must have come from the real Starkiller's cells—from his corpse's cells—and she didn't want to think about that at all.

But what difference did it make, really? Clone or otherwise, Starkiller was back. He had come to find her. He was following her now. What right did she have to say that his feelings were counterfeit? Who was her captor to suggest that she never give him a chance to at least put them into action?

Behind the gag, Juno's jaw worked. She noticed Vader watching her reaction closely and pulled herself together.

She had to believe Starkiller was himself until proven otherwise. It didn't matter where he came from if he was the same at the end of it. And she would know *that* the moment she saw him, the very second they were standing face-to-face.

You can clone his body, she wanted to tell the Dark Lord, *you can torture him any way you want, but you'll never turn him into a monster.*

The second turbolift led to a section far above the clone tubes and the second Starkiller she had seen. A series of irregular terraces rose upward to the very top of the spire. Water dripped in a steady cascade from the uppermost platform, and she wondered if the building was entirely finished. That would make sense, she supposed, if Vader's cloning experiments were relatively new. For all she knew, Starkiller was merely the test subject. Vader's long-term plans might be to create an army based on himself.

She shuddered at the thought. One of him was bad enough—and he was *damaged*. A copy of Darth Vader, perfect in every way, would be an unstoppable force for evil. Beyond evil, perhaps. Not even the Emperor could withstand him.

They ascended on foot from the last turbolift, right up to the exposed platform. The facility dome was open, allowing in the rain. Juno, the only one not wearing armor and a helmet, felt the full effect of the storm. In a way, she welcomed it. The chill precipitation and swirling wind provided something new to think about, apart from her predicament.

"Bind her," said Vader, pointing to a restraint harness erected on one side the platform.

The stormtroopers did as they were told, attaching her legs first, then undoing her binders and placing her arms in shackles. When they were finished, she could hardly move.

Vader was standing on the far lip of the platform, staring up at the clotted sky as though waiting for something to happen.

Juno followed his gaze and imagined she saw faint streaks and flashes of light through the clouds, as though something momentous in scale were taking place on the far side, something much brighter than lightning.

A space battle.

Abruptly, Vader turned and stalked back to her, his cloak heavy and wet from the rain. He raised a gloved hand as though to strike her, and she didn't pull away. She couldn't fight him; she knew that very well. But she wouldn't cringe before him, either.

"I sense your fear," he said. With a single, surprisingly swift motion, he ripped the patch from her mouth. "Your doubt, too, is clear to me."

The rain was cooling against her red-raw lips. "What doubt?" she asked, attempting to brazen out his uncanny insight into her mind.

He took one step to his right, and turned to face the way he had been before. Ahead of them, in the clouds, was a patch of yellow light. Not the sun, or even a bright moon. This was shifting slightly and growing brighter by the second. A meteor, she thought, coming right at her.

"Is that . . . ?"

Vader put his hands on his hips and nodded in satisfaction.

"He is almost here."

CHAPTER 19

BARELY A MINUTE into the dive, Starkiller knew he had to move. Nebulon-B frigates weren't designed for rapid reentry. Anything over eight hundred kilometers an hour risked tearing off control vanes and external sensors—and the *Salvation* was already doing far in excess of that.

The ship shook and thundered. Strange screeching noises ran from nose to tail, as though it might tear apart at any moment. It would physically hold together long enough—he was sure of that, but the controls in the bridge were already approaching useless. The main display was full of static. He could barely make out the planet, let alone the location he was aiming for.

He needed a better vantage point if he was going to pull this off.

That he was effectively riding in a giant metal coffin was an additional thought he tried to suppress.

The ship could fly itself for a short time. He had patched the navicomp into what remained of targeting computers, leaving him reasonably certain that it could point and thrust effectively while his hands were off the controls. He didn't want to leave it long, though, so he ran for the exit and headed upward as fast as he could, taking turbolift shafts and passages cut by the bounty hunter wherever he could. He ignored bodies, personal effects, fires—everything. Where doors or bulkheads lay in his path, he telekinetically ripped them aside and kept running.

The ship lurched beneath him as he entered the upper decks. That, he presumed, was the result of the primary forward laser cannon being ripped away by the rising atmospheric friction. Its center of gravity perturbed, the ship began to sway from side to side. He tried not to imagine superheated air boiling up through the infrastructure from the hole left behind. He would be exposed to the same soon enough.

He reached the freshwater tanks and began moving horizontally, toward the rear rather than forward. When he reached the surgery suite—even more of a bloody mess than it had been before—he headed upward again, to where the short-range communications array protruded from a bulge on the frigate's upper fore section.

He could hear the air rushing past as he approached the outer hull. It sounded like a mad giant screaming.

The ship lurched again, but less noisily this time. The rupture was more distant—probably the static discharge vanes on the aft section, he decided. That would rob the ship of even more stability.

Even as he thought that, the *Salvation* began slewing from side to side.

"Hang in there," he told the ship. "I'm coming."

He found a maintenance ladder leading to an air lock and leapt up it in two bounds, blowing the inner hatch as he came. He could feel a wild drumming from the far side of the outer door. The ship was moving so fast now that unexposed flesh wouldn't last a microsecond. He would have to rely on a Force shield to keep him safe. A single lapse in concentration would be the end of him.

He took a second to compose himself.

For Juno.

Then he raised a hand and telekinetically burst through the outer hatch.

Instantly the world was fire. The air around the ship consisted of a blinding plasma, hotter than any ordinary flame. He forced his way into it, bracing himself against metal rungs that had turned instantly red on exposure to the outside. His eyes narrowed to slits in order to make out even the nearest outline. He could barely see the fingers in front of his face.

He didn't need to see. The Force guided him, move by move, out onto the hull, where he braced himself with his back to the short-range array and turned to face forward. Like Kota, he would see without eyes.

A trembling shape up and to his left chose that moment to give way, showering molten fragments all along the spine of the ship. The primary array was no great loss: he couldn't have heard anyone anyway over the racket in his ears. But the forward turbolasers and primary sensor unit, the next two chunks to go, were more of a concern. The ship was seriously unbalanced now. It shuddered underfoot, pulling wildly in different directions. If he was going to prevent it slipping into an uncontrollable tumble or tearing apart, he had to act quickly and decisively.

This was where it got difficult. He needed to maintain the Force shield against the sort of heat he might find in the outer layers of a star. He also had to keep in mind the target ahead—a target he couldn't see through the plasma, but had to hit square-on or else the planetary shield generators wouldn't fail. No matter what happened, he had to fly straight.

Starkiller took a deep breath. The cool trapped air behind the shield would last long enough, he hoped. He had been too worried about frying to consider suffocating to death.

He raised his hands and spread his fingers wide. His eyes closed tightly against the fiery brightness of the plasma. With each bucking and shaking of the ship beneath him, he encouraged himself to ride with it instead of fighting it. He was part of the ship, not a passenger. He *was* the ship, not a reckless pilot guiding it to destruction.

In the same way that he could feel his fingers and toes, his mind seeped outward into the metal and plastoid of the frigate, until every joint and weld, every porthole and deck became part of his sense of being. There was no line anymore between Starkiller and the *Salvation*. They were one and the same being, from the perspective of the Force.

He raised his right arm, and the ship followed the movement, listing slowly and heavily to starboard. Some of the headlong shuddering faded, as though it were grateful to have someone at the helm again. Even the wind's shrieking seemed to ebb.

Something tore away at aft of the ship, and he bent his knees slightly to absorb the shock.

The *Salvation* steadied, found a new center of gravity, and roared on.

Confident that his vast metal charge was now under control, he cast his mind outward. He was shocked by how far he had fallen. The *Salvation* must have punctured the planetory shield it-self some time ago, and he simply hadn't noticed in all the turbu-lence. Now the cloud cover was less than a hundred meters below and coming up quickly. Behind the *Salvation*, a long fiery wake stretched across the sky, trailed by starfighters, and, farther back, capital ships on both sides, coming through the hole in the shield. The generators below would soon repair the hole, if he didn't guide his hurtling missile correctly, leaving the Rebel ships on the inside trapped, with him.

Assuming he survived . . .

For Juno.

The frigate slammed into the clouds with a tearing sound. At that speed, individual droplets of water hit like thermal detona-tors. The *Salvation*'s own shields were holding, barely, but even so it lost still more of its mass to the ongoing battering. Several lower decks peeled back and were swept away, including the bridge. Most of the short-range array was gone, leaving him with just the base to hold him steady. He clenched his hands into fists and *willed* the ship to keep going.

Something succumbed to the plasma with a flash. A bright spark tumbled in his wake—the secondary reactor he had spent so much energy saving from the giant droid. He ignored it. The bottom of the cloud layer was approaching, and with it would come his first clear glimpse of the shield generators.

The air became still and relatively quiet when the *Salvation* punched through the clouds. The extra friction had slowed the frigate somewhat, making it a more manageable beast. Starkiller opened his eyes and discovered that he could see over the bulge of the forward decks to his destination. Perhaps some of the hull had been ripped away there, too.

The cloning facility lay spread out ahead of him. Had he wanted to, he could have hit it dead-center and wiped it off the face of Kamino. And had Juno not been inside, he would have been tempted. He felt no sentimental attachment to the place of his rebirth, and if there was any chance of taking out Darth Vader with it, all the better.

His sole target, however, was the shield generator buildings, and at last he saw them, as clear as they had seemed from the bridge, directly ahead.

Carefully, wary of putting too much strain on an already overtaxed chassis, he nudged the *Salvation*'s nose down. If he came in low and hit the ocean first, he could concentrate the damage to one location. If he overreached by so much as a degree, he might miss the ocean completely and scrape a long, fiery line right through the heart of the facility.

The *Salvation* resisted. He pushed harder. The nose descended and held there for ten seconds, strain echoing all through the ship. It wasn't made for anything like this. Nothing larger than a starfighter was. Neither was he.

With a bone-jarring crack, the spine connecting fore and aft sections of the frigate snapped clean through. Starkiller reached out with the Force, trying desperately to keep the two pieces together, but nothing could be done. They were already moving on slightly different trajectories. Air and debris sprayed from the great wound that separated them, providing entirely unpredictable thrust.

Groaning, juddering, the fore section began to lift again. Starkiller didn't fight it. With so much mass already stripped from it, the damage it would do when it hit was negligible. The rear was the priority. The heavy engines and main reactor continued powering forward on the trajectory it had originally been following. Was that the right trajectory or not? Starkiller anxiously studied its fall, projecting it forward to the best of his senses.

It looked good. He felt positive about it. Keeping an eye on the stubby rear section as it passed under him, he braced himself for impact. Barely a minute remained now. If he survived the crash, he would soon know whether he was right or not.

Ahead, a series of cloning towers loomed, standing as upright and tall as wroshyr trees on Kashyyyk. The fore section he stood upon was going to come down among them, doing a considerable amount of damage in the process. Starkiller didn't mind. Until their memories were activated, clones weren't truly alive; they were little more than meat in suspended animation. And the technicians attending them were servants of the Empire, and therefore viable targets. Some of them, perhaps, were responsible for his birth, if clone he truly was, and for their complicity in Vader's twisted plans. He smiled as his fiery steed descended toward them, imagining them fleeing in the face of the meteor as it grew large in the sky.

He could actually see tiny long-necked figures running through the complex, white-armored stormtroopers resolutely standing at their stations, and a black-robed figure looming high above them all, watching him approach.

Vader.

Below and slightly ahead, the engines struck the surface of the sea, sending a wave of superheated steam radiating outward along the wave tops.

Starkiller couldn't take his eyes off his former Master. He was right in his path, and not even moving! For a moment Starkiller couldn't understand why—until, next to Vader, bound in shackles and so small he had barely noticed her, he saw—

Juno.

A huge eruption heralded the impact of the engines into the side of the shield generators. The sky and sea convulsed. A shock wave spread through the facility, making the cloning towers sway. The fore section of the *Salvation* rolled to starboard, but not by enough to miss the cloning towers. Its terminus was fixed.

Just seconds remained before the *Salvation*'s fore section hit Kamino. The facility was in close focus ahead of him, and he imagined he could see Juno's eyes widening on seeing him, haloed with his Force shield on top of her precious ship. Did she know it was him, or did she wonder at this strange apparition? Did she imagine that he was her death coming at last, from the skies instead of Darth Vader's hand?

Starkiller closed his eyes. He didn't have time to wonder what was going through her mind. He had to think of something fast, or Juno was going to die.

There was only one thing he could do, and although he knew he wasn't likely to survive, he didn't hesitate. What was death when the love of his former life was at stake? Besides, anything was possible. Dying, as he had thought once before, always seemed to bring out the best in him.

With his mind and all the power of the Force, Starkiller embraced what remained of the frigate beneath him—and blew it into a billion pieces.

CHAPTER 20

JUNO WAS HYPNOTIZED by the fiery blaze in the sky. Ever since it had broached the cloud cover, two things had become clear. It was a ship, a big ship, and it was going to hit the facility. The roar it made vied with thunder for loudest sound in the sky. Lightning scattered from the disturbed clouds in its wake.

Then the falling ship had split in two, with one half powering down at a steeper angle, and the other continuing onward. Only then had she realized that the second one was coming right for her.

"Was this part of your plan?" she asked Vader, who still stood, unmoving, beside her.

He didn't respond. Neither did he make any move toward the ramp that might take him to safety. Maybe, she thought, he had other means of protecting himself, means that neither she nor the stormtroopers possessed. She could see that they were getting nervous, too. The fiery balls grew brighter and brighter until they were almost too painful to look at. She refused to avert her eyes.

The first came down hard and fast, striking a well-defended portion of the facility outside the dome immediately surrounding her. There was a bright flash of light. The boom followed later, along with a rising sensation that she assumed was the shock wave rolling through the flexible foundations of the ocean-bound facility. She could *see* the cloning towers swaying from side to side. A vast column of flash-boiled steam and wreckage rose up into the sky. Hot, damp air rushed outward in its wake.

Still the other fragment of the ship came toward her. Seconds remained before it hit—not long enough to think anything coherent, barely time even to observe what was happening. The stricken ship was glowing red, with the last shreds of plasma still clinging to it like flames. Its class was almost unrecognizable, but she made out stumps that might once have been a communications array on the upper port side. That made it a Nebulon-B frigate, one of many EF76s in the service of either the Empire or the Rebel Alliance. It could have been any one of them.

So why, then, did she feel a cold stab of certainty in her gut that this was none other than the *Salvation*?

Her own ship was going to kill her.

The irony wasn't lost on her.

At the last instant she made out a tiny human figure standing on the upper hull. The flames and rushing wind swept past him, as though he were impervious to their touch. His arms were upraised in defiance and his head was tipped back so she couldn't see his face. But she knew. Just as she knew that it was the *Salvation,* she knew it was him.

He *would* come for her in flames and smoke, wreaking destruction all around.

Despite the apparent certainty of her death, she smiled. Either he would save her—in which case there was nothing to worry about—or he wouldn't, and she didn't want to live anyway.

The ship was almost upon them when the figure brought his hands down in a fierce, pounding motion, and the last solid fragment of the *Salvation* exploded into fiery pieces.

She had to close her eyes. The conflagration was too intense, and the sound was that of worlds ending. The cloning tower kicked beneath her. She was momentarily afraid that she might be falling with it into the sea. But then she was rising again, and she understood that the structure had survived, somehow, and so had she.

Her eyelids flickered, braving the brightness that only slowly faded around her. A cloud of hot metallic fragments was spreading across the city. Dense splinters rained from it, hissing where they landed. Heavier fragments struck with more substantial thuds, near and far. None struck her. The rain ceased for a moment, and then returned, settling the cloud of dust still further. Of the *Salvation*, nothing at all remained.

Darth Vader lowered the hand he had risen to shield his helmet and took stock around him. Juno did the same. Fires blazed in the wreckage where the rear half of the *Salvation* had come down. Alarms sounded through the facility, loud enough even for Juno's blast-numbed ears to hear them. Ash was settling on every horizontal surface and forming a thick, gray sludge.

Above, the clouds, already disturbed by the *Salvation*'s fiery passage, were being torn apart by a new outrage. Starfighters and capital ships powered down from orbit in large numbers, dodging and firing at one another as they went. Juno recognized more frigates, and dozens of Headhunter, Y-wing, and TIE fighters. There were bombers, cruisers, even Star Destroyers bringing up the rear. An all-out war was taking place above Kamino, between Imperial and Alliance forces, and it, too, was growing ever nearer.

"I ask again, is this part of the plan?"

Instead of answering, Vader stalked off, waving for the stormtroopers to remain where they were. When he was gone, they stationed themselves several paces away from her and carefully watched the perimeter around them. High above their heads, the secure facility's dome began to close.

Juno coughed and wished she could wipe her eyes clear of ash. Her ship had blown itself practically to atoms; she had seen it happen, right in front of her. There was no chance at all that Starkiller could have survived. He had been riding right on top of it.

But she knew as well as they did that this wasn't the end. He had come back from the dead sufficient times now to make anything possible. Anything at all.

CHAPTER 21

THE GIANT REPTILIAN *biped loomed over him, roaring in its own language. He didn't understand what it was saying. Fear made it almost impossible to think. All Starkiller wanted to do was run.*

A bright yellow blade slashed across his vision, and the lizard fell backward, dead. The woman who had wielded the blade rushed to him and enfolded him in her cloak. He tried not to cry, but the fear was too great.

"Take him, Mallie—take him somewhere safe!" His father's voice cut through the screams and shouts that filled the village. "I'll hold them off."

"Don't be a fool, Kento. You can't do it alone."

"I can slow them down while you get into the forest. Go!"

"No." Mallie stood up and faced her husband. "You know Kkowir better than I do."

"All you have to do is get to the Kerritamba, or if they're under attack, try the Myyydril caverns as a last resort—"

"But there's the Sayormi to think about, and the dead area. You're the expert, Kento. If anyone goes, it should be you."

The boy looked up at his parents in anxious confusion, unable to understand what the argument was about. Weren't they both coming? Wasn't it time to run now?

Explosions sent trees tumbling nearby. One of them crushed the hut he had known all his conscious life. There his mother had told him stories of the great Wookiee warriors and showed him how to braid his own friendship band. There his father had thrown him up to the ceiling and held him floating aloft, spinning as though sitting on air. The crushing of the walls sent splinters flying, and he screamed at the thought of everything he loved disappearing in an instant.

More of the big lizards came running out of the trees, firing at the villagers and setting their hair on fire.

His father went to run forward, his blue lightsaber raised, but his mother caught his arm.

"Kento," she said in a soft but firm voice, "you know I'm right."

His anguish was plain to see, even for a very young child. When he sagged, something broke inside him.

"You always are, my love."

They embraced, quickly, and then she ran toward the lizards, shouting a battle cry. Her son cried out, too, wondering where she was going, but his father scooped him up and began running for the trees.

"Don't worry, son," he said as they escaped. "I'll keep you safe. And when she comes back, we'll make a new home. Somewhere safe and special, I promise you."

Behind them, the lizards cried out in surprise and pain. He tried to look, but his father held on too tightly. And when the trees enfolded them, the sound of his mother fighting became muffled and indistinct. Slowly, over the course of many years, it faded into silence.

STARKILLER'S EYES JERKED OPEN. Where was he? All was dark around him. He smelled smoke and his body felt as though it had been hit by an asteroid. The last thing he remembered was tightening the Force shield around him and destroying the *Salvation* so it wouldn't kill Juno. He was somewhere on Kamino, then. But his mind remained full of strange images and feelings that he had never experienced before.

Kashyyyk. Trandoshan slavers. His parents . . . ?

He tried to shrug them off. They had been dead for a long time, and the living mattered more. But he was struck by this brief glimpse of the woman who had given birth to him. Tall, with short brown hair and a physique honed by years of training, she, too, had been a Jedi Knight, like her husband. She had been a warrior, and yet she had loved her son as well. She had loved him and most likely died defending him and the Wookiees they had befriended. And until this moment, he had never known she existed or that his father had made a promise he couldn't keep.

Where had the memory come from?

It didn't matter. *She* didn't matter. Starkiller had to get moving, or the promise he had made to himself would also go unfulfilled.

For Juno.

He reached for his comlink, but it was gone. Lost during the fall, presumably. He sat up and felt around him, seeking the dimensions of the space he found himself in. It was a deep, stone pit—and for a terrible moment he feared that he was back in the training rooms Vader had confined him to ever since his reawakening. But then he found a doorway, not far from the pile of rubble he had brought down with him. Somewhere far above, he was sure, was the hole he had made when he had hit the facility. There was no way of telling now just how far he had tumbled, burning and smoking like a meteor.

He wrenched the door off its hinges. Outside was marginally lighter. A corridor led off into the distance. He loped along it, concentrating on faint sounds of fighting in the distance. Numerous varieties of weapons were in play, and several starfighters screamed overhead. That meant the shields were safely down, and the Rebel forces were making their way into the facility. He allowed himself a small feeling of satisfaction, even though he knew the battle was far from won. The Imperials were well entrenched on Kamino. They wouldn't go down without a fight.

The corridor led to a darkened command room. He flicked a switch and its blast shields opened, letting in the cool gray light of the outside world. Details assaulted him, too many at once. The first thing he needed to do was work out where he was. To his right were the cloning spires where he had seen Juno, now protected behind a clear, curved dome. They were too smoke-blackened to make out if she was still there. A thick column of steam rose up from the shield generators, forming a spreading mushroom cloud high above the facility. Fighters on both sides dodged and weaved around the cloud, while higher up capital ships vied for ascendancy.

Closer at hand, he made out flashpoints of engagement where Rebel forces were trying to penetrate the high-security dome around Darth Vader's restricted area. They were coming under heavy fire from all directions. Troop carriers descended under close escort to provide reinforcements, but for every one that landed two were diverted or destroyed. Bombing runs softened up the Imperial defenses, which had both the advantage and disadvantage of being relatively fixed. TIE bombers returned the favor, attempting to blow the Rebels to pieces whenever they stopped moving too long. Cannon emplacements strafed any Rebel ships that came too close in their attempt to penetrate the dome, while AT-STs patrolled the perimeter, constantly vigilant.

Starkiller needed to get through the same defenses as the Rebels in order to save Juno. He scanned the controls in front of him, looking for maps or hidden routes that he could access. There were maintenance hatches spaced irregularly around the base of the dome, but he didn't have the codes required to open them.

He didn't let that bother him. There were alternatives to codes.

Picking the closest hangar hatch, he memorized the way there, activated his lightsabers, and left the control room.

THE MEMORY OF KASHYYYK stayed with him as he fought his way through the Imperials, occasionally dodging the odd Rebel who thought he was on the Imperials' side. He didn't know the location of his birthplace, and knowing now that both his parents were Jedi made it even more difficult to guess. Their relationship would have been forbidden by the Jedi Council, and then endangered even further by Order 66 and the subsequent slaughter of all their kind. How they had stayed hidden was unknown. Somehow they had ended up on Kashyyyk, where an attack by Trandoshan slavers had forced the two of them to come out of hiding. It was this, probably, that had brought Darth Vader to the planet, in search of Starkiller's surviving father.

The death of his mother was now his earliest memory. And was it really his? That, too, he had no way of knowing. If Vader was telling the truth, his true birthplace lay ahead, under the high security dome, and the memory of Kashyyyk belonged to another man.

He reached the maintenance hatch and cut his way through it. A stormtrooper armed with a flamethrower tried to roast him once he was inside, but a solid Force push threw him back into his squadmates, where his fuel tank exploded. Starkiller took a moment to bring down the ceiling over the hatch, so no one could follow him, then crawled on hands and knees into the secure facility.

He kicked out the vent on the far end of the tunnel and dropped onto a walkway that followed the base of the dome. Inside the dome, the battle was even more difficult for the Rebels. They had no air support and only a handful of limited access points. Several TIE fighters patrolled from above, ready to rain fire on anyone unauthorized. The Rebels desperately needed a way to get their own fighters into play.

Starkiller ducked as shots from a weapon lanced out at him from the far side of the dome. Snipers. He ran along the walkway to his right in order to present a moving target, speeding up and slowing down to make getting a bead even more difficult. There was no sign of Darth Vader, and Starkiller was too far away to see if Juno was on top of the cloning spires.

Down among the Rebel fighters, though, he spotted a familiar white topknot. Kota was fighting his way toward a command center, accompanied by the members of his squad, but sniper fire was making their progress slow. Starkiller looked up and waited for the muzzle flashes. The snipers harrying Kota were situated in a tower not far away, within reach of the walkway he was following.

He ran faster and leapt when he was at the closest point to the tower. For a moment he was in free fall, and then he hit the side of the tower with lightsabers pointing forward. They arrested his downward slide just above an observation window, which he shattered with a quick Force push. Swinging himself down and through the window, he made his way to the nearest stairwell before any of the snipers could turn their high-powered weapons inward.

He burst in the door on the uppermost level and found himself at the center of a web of concentrated blasterfire. Each of the snipers was armed with at least one nonspecialist weapon, and they had all abandoned their harrowing of Kota in order to deal with him. His lightsabers swung like propellers, reflecting every shot back to their source. The air filled with smoke and cries, until finally the last sniper fell, slumped over his weapon.

Just in case another team of Imperials came to reactivate the emplacement, Starkiller ran his blades through each of the sniper weapons, rendering them useless. Then he left the room and went up onto the roof. A passing TIE took a potshot at him, but he jumped before the bolts could hit him. The top of the tower exploded into flame as he dropped in a carefully controlled fall to where Kota and his squad stood below.

They were hunkered down at the entrance to the command center. Kota had his blade deep in the armored door while one of his militia tried to slice through its lock. Both succeeded at the same time, and the squad burst inside with Starkiller hot on their heels. They made short work of the Imperial officers within and immediately took control of the consoles they found.

"Get those hangar doors open," Kota ordered. "Quickly!" He

turned to Starkiller. "Vader's TIE fighters are going to keep us pinned down here until we get air support."

"Good to see you too, General."

"I knew you'd be back." His attention was directed through the curved window and the facility outside, as though he could see without the slightest impediment. "I'm just surprised it took you so long to catch up."

"I need to get to the cloning towers."

"Well, be quick. They'll be coming down around your ears once we get through the dome."

A close strike from one of the TIE bombers made the command center shake.

"Time's running out," Kota growled at one of the Rebels, furiously tapping at his console.

"I almost have control of the hangar doors," was the response. "Just give me—"

A second blast tore one corner of the roof away, taking the Rebel technician with it. Kota cursed and led the dash forward, out of the center and back onto the walkways.

"I'll deal with the hangar doors," Starkiller told him as they dodged fire from snipers and cannon emplacements on all sides. "You just give me time to get Juno before you take everything out."

Kota didn't argue. "Good, good. We'll find the security hub and try to prevent any more lockdowns."

They split up at the next intersection, and Starkiller leapt from ledge to ledge toward another command center near the base of the dome. Behind it was the nearest hangar entrance, and its thick durasteel doors were tightly sealed against the Rebels outside. The Imperials inside the command center saw him coming and took steps to prepare: by the time he had burned his way in, the controls were locked, and when he tried to interfere with them they self-destructed.

There went that plan. But it wasn't the only one he had. Leaving the ruined command center behind, he leapt to the base of the hangar door and, facing it, spread his arms wide, palms forward.

For Juno, he thought, and pushed.

The hangar doors shook in their tracks, but didn't give.

He stepped back, changed his stance, and tried pulling instead. Again, nothing.

A sniper had taken a bead on him. He took a moment to deflect a shot very precisely back to the other side of the dome. The resulting explosion seemed tiny from such a great distance, but had the desired effect. No more shots came his way.

Starkiller turned back to the doors and extended his widespread fingers to the stubborn metal.

Waves of intense electricity surged into the doors, shorting out systems both physical and electromagnetic. He gave them a good twenty seconds before stepping back and trying to pull again.

This time the doors responded as they were supposed to. With a shriek of complaint, the metal buckled and curved inward, allowing access to the outside. When the doors were protruding vertically from the wall, he pushed each side back so it was flush. Barely had he finished when the first Rebel Y-wing swept by, saw the opening, then came around to rush through.

It roared past him, a wave of exhaust hot in its wake. The pilot took in the situation and began firing at the TIE fighters pestering Kota, turning the fight a little more in the Rebels' favor.

Starkiller felt that he had discharged his responsibility to Kota. It was time now to go for Juno. But the spires were on the other side of the dome, and the lower levels were crawling with AT-STs and stormtroopers.

Seeking the best shortcut available, he climbed to the top of the ruined hangar door and waited for the next starfighter to come through.

Two TIE fighters followed the Y-wing, then a Headhunter. He let them go unmolested: There were insufficient handholds on the top of either model's canopy. The fifth was a Y-wing—exactly what he was after.

As it rushed through the open hangar entrance, he jumped

onto it and caught the R2 unit protruding from its exposed chassis tightly about the domed head.

The impact nearly tore his arms off at the shoulders, and the Y-wing dipped sharply under the unexpected weight. The droid squawked in alarm, prompting a barrel roll from the starfighter's pilot. Starkiller hung on tightly as the world turned around him.

"Tell the pilot I'm on your side!" he shouted over the roaring of the Y-wing's twin ion jet engines.

The starfighter banked to avoid the fire-blackened tower where Starkiller had dealt with the snipers, then it leveled out.

"You're not doing any damage back there," crackled a voice from the R2's vocoder, "so I guess you really aren't an Imp. But what *are* you doing? Do you have a death wish or something?"

I hope not, Starkiller thought. "I need a ride. See those spires over to starboard? That's where I have to go."

"Where the firepower's heaviest?"

"If you're not up to it, I'll find myself another ride . . ."

The pilot laughed. "No one's ever called Wedge Antilles a coward. Hold tight and we'll see what this wishbone can do."

The Y-wing began to curve around the inside of the dome, dodging fire from turbolasers and TIE fighters. Starkiller braced himself with both feet and one hand gripping a manipulator extended by the R2 unit. With his free arm, he supplemented the starfighter's energy shields with one lightsaber, bouncing laser blasts up into the dome and Force-pushing ion torpedoes away.

At first it looked as though getting to the spires would be easy, but the more the number of ships under the dome increased, the harder it became to fly in a straight line.

After a tense dogfight with two TIEs flying in tandem—which ended with them colliding thanks to some deft flying from Antilles— the Y-wing rushed the spires head-on, but was driven back by fire too concentrated to fly through.

"Okay, now what?" asked Antilles as he swept them smoothly out of range.

Starkiller thought for a second. "That depends on what kind of odds you like."

"I make my own odds."

"Good. Go down."

"What? We can't go down. There's—"

"There's an opportunity. The facility sits on platforms over the ocean. Find a gap in the platform and you can get under it. Then it's just a matter of finding a way back up near the spires. See?"

"All I can see is my life flashing before my eyes." The pilot laughed again. "But that's okay: I always skip the boring bits. Get ready—here we go!"

The Y-wing's nose suddenly dropped. The R2 unit wailed. Starkiller held on with both hands as the rooftops of the facility rushed up at him. The terrified exhilaration he felt was more intense than when he had surfed the *Salvation* down onto Kamino. He was a passenger now, trusting entirely in the flying abilities of a pilot he'd never met. The chances were he'd misjudge the insertion into the infrastructure and kill both of them. But it was too late to bail now. They were committed.

The Y-wing sped down a gap between two buildings, dodging bridges and walkways. At first Starkiller saw no gap through the rapidly approaching lower levels, but then he caught a gleam of light on wave tops through a square hole. Antilles must have spied it by radar from above. It looked very small, barely enough room to fit the widely spaced twin ion engines, even on the diagonal.

"Keep an eye on that eyeball for me, will you?"

Starkiller looked behind him. A TIE fighter had their tail and fired twice, just missing their port engine. Starkiller didn't know what Antilles expected him to do about it. He couldn't let go, not with a sudden course change just seconds ahead. All he could do was hope the rear deflector shields would last long enough.

The hole rushed for them. The pilot jockeyed the Y-wing from side to side, adjusting its trim by minute degrees. Then suddenly they were through, and Starkiller was wrenched to his right by the violent delta-vee. His legs were swept out from under him, leaving him hanging by his fingertips from the R2 unit. The ion rockets roared. A mist of flash-boiled seawater sprayed him. He swung back and forth violently before the Y-wing found horizontal again and sped off, ducking and weaving around the facility's many deep-sea supports.

Behind them, the TIE fighter clipped the edge of the hole and exploded with a flash of yellow light against the surface of the sea.

Starkiller's knees touched the back of the Y-wing and grate-fully took some of the pressure off his hands. It was dark under the facility, apart from the odd shaft shining down through the lower levels and a distant glimmer shining past its outer edges.

"Good flying," he said breathlessly.

"You're still there? That's a relief. Deesix has gone quiet. I think he's in shock."

The R2 unit made a mournful sound.

"Just hold on a minute longer," Antilles told it, "then we'll get back to shooting bucketheads." The Y-wing curved gracefully around a trio of heavyset columns supporting something weighty above them. "If my guess is right, and it always is, we're coming up on the spires now. All we need is a way in . . ."

"No need to be subtle about it," Starkiller told him, shifting position to see more clearly over the canopy. "What about up there, near that access ladder?"

"Set. Get ready for some more g's, whoever you are!"

The Y-wing surged forward, laser cannon firing in a steady stream. Hot gas and molten metal exploded from the impact site. A new shaft of light beamed through the hole Antilles had made in the lower levels. He hit the retros and swung his starfighter in a complicated maneuver that left it tail-down and nose-up, directly under the hole. Both ion engines roared and they shot upward through what might have been a garbage chute, back into the se-cure facility.

They emerged in the midst of the cloning spires. Turbolaser

emplacements instantly spotted them and began firing. Multiple flashes indicated hits to the Y-wing's shields. Almost immediately, Antilles grew concerned.

"I can take this heat, but not for long. Where do you want me to put you down?"

Starkiller tried to get his bearings, but he had lost them under the facility. His instincts told him that Juno was ahead, and he hoped they spoke truly.

"Keep on as you are. No need to slow down."

"You're not going to jump again, are y—?"

Wedge Antilles's voice was swept away as Starkiller launched himself off the back of the Y-wing and into space. The side of the nearest spire rushed toward him, and he lit his lightsabers an instant before striking the glass wall. He landed in a shower of glass shards, rolled, and stood unscathed.

The Y-wing swooped back to check he was okay, and Starkiller waved his lightsaber blade in thanks. The stubby craft acknowledged him by dipping its nose, then roared away.

HE WAS ALONE. Splinters of glass crunched softly underfoot as he jogged to the end of the corridor in which he had landed. Alarms vied with the sound of explosions and starfighter engines for dominance, creating a dissonant racket all around him. He heard no footsteps or voices. If there had ever been Kaminoan technicians in this area of the spire, they had almost certainly been evacuated now.

He passed through an open doorway and passed into the heart of the spire itself. He stood in the entrance for a moment, eyes tracking upward along a seemingly endless series of cloning tanks, affixed to platforms barely wide enough for droids and technicians to gain access. Stormtroopers patrolled the tanks, but Starkiller didn't think they were specifically stationed to watch for him. More likely they were guarding the beings who would one day swell their own ranks—for these were ordinary stormtrooper clones, nothing experimental or sinister. And as such they were a valid target for an attack by the Rebel Alliance.

Starkiller had his sights set much higher. He was sure now that he had the right spire. He could sense both Juno and Darth Vader in the cavernous spaces above him. It was just a matter of getting to them.

But if he could sense Vader, then the Dark Lord could sense him in return, and that made the game that much more complicated.

The stormtroopers in the cloning tower were too dispersed to take on all at once. Instead, and in order to confuse the trail he would inevitably leave in his wake, he chose a very different strategy.

Once, he had been paralyzed and abandoned in a trench full of bloodwolves, with no way to reach safety except by using the power of his own mind. It was a lesson Darth Vader had made sure his apprentice learned before even beginning combat training. Killing enemies wasn't the same thing as controlling them. Each method had its uses, but they weren't interchangeable.

Running lightly around the base of the tower, he approached the first clutch of sentries from behind. A judicious use of telekinesis triggered a life-support alarm a dozen clone tubes along, prompting a quick inspection by the stormtroopers. While they were distracted, he ran up the stairs they had been guarding, to the next platform.

There he put the thought into the mind of another trooper that he had heard a disturbance some distance away. The moment he and his fellows were busy, Starkiller crept past them, too. The Force absorbed all sound of his movement and shrouded his form in shadow. He didn't just fade into the background: he *became* the background.

Before long, though, the guards became suspicious. They were of course in constant contact via their helmet comlinks, and a plethora of false alarms was itself unlikely to be innocent. So Starkiller turned the screws a little tighter, creating half-seen phantoms in the minds of the troopers that literally ran circles around them. Pressure hoses exploded with the force of grenades when Starkiller blocked them from afar. Clone tubes opened unexpectedly, spilling disoriented, half-minded bodies across the decks.

By the time he had reached the summit of that tower, the stormtroopers were in utter disarray, and he hadn't used his lightsabers once.

Satisfied, he entered a narrow junction between that cloning tower and the one above it. There he met his first real opposition. Camouflaged troopers guarded a bottleneck between the towers. On seeing him, they opened fire immediately. He shocked their armor back into opacity and quickly dealt with them, but the damage had been done. Troopers above and below the junction knew he was there, and they converged on his location en masse.

He fought his way into the second tower against a steady rain of blasterfire, while at the same time defending his back. He buckled lofty platforms, tipping stormtroopers to their deaths far below. He used cloning tubes as flying bombs, turning the floor underfoot slick with spilled amniotic fluids. He peeled plates from the walls and sent them flying into clutches of stormtroopers too time-consuming to confront head-on. Ruination surrounded him.

More death, he thought. Even when he tried, the curse of Darth Vader's training lay heavily upon him. Was this the way it would always be? Would he never shake off that fatal legacy—or was there another way to resist that he hadn't found yet?

Great mastery of the Force *had* to lead to more than just the increased capacity for violence—or else every Jedi would be a Sith, and the galactic civil war would never have happened.

Again he thought of the first time the original Starkiller had faced his Master in a duel. If Vader *had* been a Jedi, what kind of Jedi had he been? A hero or a failure? Starkiller had a hard time believing that such great evil could have come out of indifference or inability—but at the same time he could barely credit that someone with such natural talent could have gone unnoticed, as his own had not. Perhaps the young Darth Vader had been kept secret, too. Perhaps the mask was a matter of habit rather than necessity.

Starkiller reached the top of the second tower unscathed. An open turbolift awaited him there. He faced it for a moment, not knowing where it would take him but sensing it was somewhere he had to go. Whatever awaited him at the other end, he needed to face it.

He supposed his mother had felt this way on Kashyyyk, while fending off the Trandoshan slavers who threatened her family. She, too, had had no choice, but still she had fought—for something greater than her own survival, for love. Her legacy was a powerful one, and Darth Vader had never entirely managed to expunge it from the boy who would be his apprentice. Or even a clone of that boy.

He stepped into the turbolift. The doors closed, and he was taken upward. He readied himself for what was to come both physically, with lightsabers raised and ready, and emotionally, inasmuch as that was possible.

The cab slowed, stopped, and the doors slid open.

The space beyond was gloomy and vast. Starkiller emerged slowly from the lift, keeping all his senses peeled. Darth Vader was close, very close. In the shadows above he made out the faint outlines of platforms much like the ones in the cloning towers below. Beyond them, faint light gleamed on curved glass tubes, but he could not make out what lay within.

The skin of his arms prickled. Something was very close, very close indeed.

"Whatever you seek, only inside you will find."

The words of the wise little creature he had met on Dagobah reassured him, oddly.

"A part of yourself, perhaps?"

The sound of another lightsaber echoed off the metal and glass surfaces around him.

"You have returned."

Starkiller looked around. He couldn't pinpoint the origin of his former Master's voice.

"As you see," he said, moving slowly forward in a confident but wary stance.

"It was only a matter of time."

"Where is Juno?" he asked. The last he had seen of her, she had been on the roof of the spire. She could have been moved anywhere since then.

A dark figure lunged at him from the shadows. Starkiller blocked a powerful slash to his head, and retaliated with a double sweep to Darth Vader's legs. The Dark Lord leapt upward, out of reach of his weapons, and Starkiller followed.

When he landed on the first platform, Darth Vader was nowhere to be seen.

Something moved to his right. He spun to face it, lightsabers upraised.

A slender form stepped out of the shadows.

"I knew you'd come," said Juno, smiling. "At last, we are together again."

Almost, he lowered his weapons. It was *her*. She held out her arms to embrace him. He longed to run to her. But an instinct told him something was wrong.

A flash of memory—a memory of a vision—came to him. He had seen a vision of Juno on the bridge of the *Salvation,* when the bounty hunter had captured her. Everything about that vision had come true, right down to the last detail. PROXY had been taken out, along with her canid second in command. She herself had been shot in the shoulder.

This Juno was uninjured.

"Stay back," he said, tightening his defenses.

Juno's smile faded. Her arms came down. When she moved, she did so with a speed that wasn't human, reaching behind her back with both hands to produce two Q2 hold-out blasters. With blank-faced, depersonalized lethality, she came for him, firing both blasters at once.

Starkiller deflected the shots right back at her, and she staggered backward with a cry. Then he was on her, bisecting her abdomen with his left lightsaber and taking her head off at the neck with his right.

As the body fell in pieces to the metal floor, showering sparks, Starkiller stood over her, breathing heavily.

The illusion died, revealing the wreckage of a PROXY droid at his feet.

"*It's a lot easier to fight the Empire when it's faceless,*" he heard her say from the past, "*when the people whose lives are ending are hidden behind stormtrooper helmets or durasteel hulls. But when they're people we knew, people like we used to be . . .*"

He spun, catching the faintest echo of an in-drawn, artificial breath from behind him, and caught Darth Vader's lightsaber on the downstroke. They stood that way, locked blade-to-blade, for a moment, and then Starkiller pushed the Dark Lord back. He swept one lightsaber on a rising arc that would have taken off Darth Vader's left arm while the other he flicked sideways, hoping to catch his opponent in the chest unit.

Vader blocked both blows, then leapt a second time, the next platform up.

"*How much harder is it going to get?*"

Starkiller scowled.

"*Are you having second thoughts?*" he had asked Juno that same day—the day after he had seen the vision of his father on Kashyyyk. Her answer had been immediate: *No.* But he had sensed an uneasiness within her, just as his former Master had sensed uneasiness within him shortly afterward. Their loyalties were being tested. Principles, too. Such testing was never easy.

Darth Vader was playing a very obvious game now. Starkiller could see it, and he would not be deflected from his course.

He jumped to the second level, and there came face-to-face with Bail Organa, then Kota, then Mon Mothma, then Garm Bel Iblis. When all the leaders of the Rebel Alliance lay dead at his feet, their droid bodies exposed beneath treacherous holograms, Darth

Vader attacked again. His blows were swift and economical, and the threat no less than it had ever been, but Starkiller sensed more was to come. Darth Vader would kill him, yes, without hesitation, but he would rather turn him first.

On the fourth level, he came face-to-face with his own father, and struck him down without hesitation. Dreams and memories had no power over him anymore.

He spun to face the attack he had come to expect from the real Darth Vader, full of confidence and surety. The Dark Lord fell back under his blows, and this time, when he leapt for safety, Starkiller telekinetically pulled him back down. His former Master sprawled before him, lightsaber raised defensively. He slashed the hand holding it away, and then plunged his second lightsaber deep into his chest.

With a gasping, wheezing moan, Darth Vader fell back and dissolved into another PROXY droid.

Unsurprised, Starkiller stepped back and looked around for the real Darth Vader. He could see or hear nothing, but his senses tingled with an acute and insistent message.

Above him.

He somersaulted upward and landed in a crouch, ready for anything.

"You are confident," said Darth Vader. "That will be your downfall."

The Dark Lord was standing out of Starkiller's reach. Instead of attacking, he gestured at the rows of cloning tanks beside him. Lights flickered on inside them, revealing row after row of identical forms. Clad in stripped-down version of his former training suit and attached via tubes to complex feeders and breathers, they hung weightlessly in transparent fluid, twitching occasionally in their sleep.

Starkiller felt a shock of recognition jolt through him. These weren't stormtroopers. They were *him*. Incomplete, and oddly warped from true, but definitely him.

Vader gestured again, and the clones' eyes opened.

In them Starkiller saw nothing but hatred, anger, confusion, betrayal, madness, and loss.

Their glass cages shattered. Amniotic fluid boiled away. They pulled free from their cables and tubes and, with motions faltering at first but quickly growing stronger, climbed free from the wreckage.

Starkiller stood his ground as a circle of failed clones formed around him.

Behind them Darth Vader nodded once.

The clones came forward in one overwhelming rush.

CHAPTER 22

JUNO HUNG PAINFULLY in her shackles, doing her best to follow the fight unfolding around her although she could see little of it directly. Sometimes she closed her eyes to let her ears do the work. There was a music to the explosions and weapons fire that played out in waves and bursts all around her. Thus far none of it had impacted directly upon her, but she could feel it coming steadily closer.

After the crash and disintegration of the *Salvation,* a dome had closed above her, sealing this section of the facility behind a secure bubble. Outside, Rebel and Imperial forces had raged hard. Dogfights and furious standoffs between capital vessels lit up the cloudy skies of Kamino, with the occasional capitulation shining like a sun over the battlefield, albeit briefly. It was hard to determine who was winning, partly because of the clouds. She didn't know how many ships were engaging in orbit, or how many the Emperor and Alliance commanders were holding in reserve. What she saw could be the entirety of the conflict, or the merest hint of it.

At one point, through the dome, she thought she saw the unique outline of the *Rogue Shadow* behind the cloak protecting it from enemy gunners' eyes. Her heart leapt. If it was here, then Kota was here, too. Then it disappeared behind a building, just outside the bubble protecting her from the rain. Moments later, she heard the sounds of a concentrated assault on the bubble's walls. Not long after that, gunfire came from below, within the bubble itself, and she knew the fight was definitely coming her way.

She strained against the shackles, wishing she had some way, any way at all, to join the battle. Her four guards were growing restless, probably feeling the same.

TIE fighters circled the interior of the bubble with engines screaming. The fight had stalled while Kota's ground forces faced off against the aerial defenses, but before long the balance shifted again. Someone got a hangar door open, allowing Rebel forces access at last. Dogfights played out around her, and for the first time it occurred to her that, if the facility as a whole was the target, then she herself might not be safe.

That was a sobering thought. What if her presence was unknown—or worse, completely irrelevant—to the attacking forces? She would be collateral damage if the cloning towers fell, and there was nothing she could do about it.

Starkiller was her only hope. If anyone could get to her in time, it would be him.

Rebel starfighters buzzed the towers, but none of them attacked, yet. They were busy with the TIEs and the cannon emplacements. A series of large explosions suggested that Kota's new squad was attacking the dome itself, hoping to expose the facility to the superior firepower outside. When they managed that, she supposed, that would spell the end for her. Not even Starkiller could fend off a concentrated assault from above.

"I don't know about you," she told her guards, "but I feel like a sitting mynock out here."

They didn't respond, but again she could tell they sympathized.

When warning klaxons began to sound in the spire below her, their uneasiness redoubled.

"There goes your exit strategy," she said. "Bet you wish you'd slept in this morning."

Faintly through their helmets she heard the sound of the

stormtroopers talking to one another, over their comlinks. Maybe discussing the value in shooting her and making a run for it, although she doubted any of them would risk incurring Vader's wrath. Even with such Rebel firepower arrayed against them, they would regard the Dark Lord as the greatest threat. She remembered feeling that way, once.

Something exploded in the spire, making it sway underfoot.

Juno felt breathless, as though the air were growing thinner.

It was *him*. She was certain of it. The stormtroopers knew it, too. They tightened around her, drawing a false sense of security from closer proximity to one another. They looked at her and glanced quickly away, looking more nervous than ever, and she realized only then that she was smiling.

He was so *close* to her.

The spire shook again, more violently than before. She wondered where Darth Vader was and what he was doing. Surely he wouldn't have brought her to Kamino only to leave her dangling in the trap—unless it had sprung already, and she was no longer needed. But in that case, why didn't the troopers just shoot her and be done with it? She didn't understand the finer details of Vader's plan. That was her only uncertainty.

Seven powerful explosions filled the interior of the dome. With a piercing splitting sound, the dome itself began to shatter. Cracks spread across the transparisteel, fissures dozens of meters long that joined one another and branched to create entirely new ones. They reached up from its base and converged on the center, high above. Where they met, gently, in slow motion, the first pieces began to fall. Each was larger than a starfighter, and easily as heavy. They turned as they fell, tumbling with ponderous grace.

When the first piece hit the buildings below, it shattered into a million pieces.

And from the interior of the spire came a terrible scream, as of a hundred voices at once, crying out in despair.

CHAPTER 23

STARKILLER FOUGHT AS he had never fought before. Clones—*his* clones, nightmarishly imperfect but powerful all the same— pressed in on all sides. Darth Vader's vile conditioning had a profound hold on their immature psychologies. The desire to kill consumed their thoughts. It was all they radiated. Together they could easily have turned on their creator and overpowered him. Instead they were driven to destroy their own.

Not their own. Just him. Whether he was the original Starkiller, as Kota believed, or simply the best copy to date didn't matter. He was their target, and they used every power they possessed to bring him down.

On Kashyyyk he had fought a vision of himself, and won.

On Dagobah, he had seen other versions of him, and spared them.

On Kamino, the choice was taken from him. He had to fight if he was to live, and he had to live in order to save Juno. Thought didn't enter into it. The Force rushed through him, and his lightsabers moved as though of their own accord.

His clones screamed as he cut them down.

It quickly became apparent that the first to rush in were the wildest and weakest both. In their eagerness to do battle, they didn't stop to plan their strategies. What they possessed in speed, they lacked in forethought. He was armed and they were not, so for

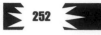

being headstrong beyond all reason these brutish beings paid the ultimate price.

The next wave either learned from the fate of the first or had enough innate caution to stand back a moment and observe the way he fought. They came at him from all sides, using telekinesis to try to knock him off balance on the blood-slicked floor. He was too fast for them, leaping over their heads and attacking from behind, slashing at their overdeveloped shoulders and hunched backs without remorse.

Moving out of the center of the ring of converging clones brought him into contact with the third wave, the most cunning he had encountered so far. Long-armed and long-fingered, with blackened, blistering skin, these employed lightning when attacking him, and then by devious means. They would wait until he was distracted and attack him from behind, or come at him from three directions at once, or even use one of their fellow clones as an impromptu conductor. Deadly currents crackled and sparkled around him, kept barely at bay by the judicious application of a Force shield. Sometimes a lucky strike caused him pain, but he fought through it, found the source, and put the attack quickly to an end.

From above came the sound of lightsabers activating, and he braced himself for another, more dangerous onslaught. These, the most normal looking of all the clones, spun, slashed, hacked, and stabbed at him from all sides, one-handed, two-handed, with all possible variations of lightsaber combat styles. Red-eyed and hate-filled, they fought each other, too, and the ones who had come before. There were no allies, just a sea of individuals.

And yet . . . Confidence, determination, intelligence, and cunning—combined with physical strength and agility—the clones possessed every attribute he did, in greater or lesser degrees. He saw in their faces the same confusion he felt. They were all clones, so who was he to stand out from among them? What special qualities set him apart?

Who *was* Starkiller, in this mass of faces and bodies?

A desperate rage built up inside him. What if what he felt was nothing but a lingering imprint left behind by the first Starkiller? Did he cling to his feelings with all the more desperation because deep down he knew they were counterfeit? *"The memories of a dead man,"* Vader had called them, blaming them for the torment and confusion he had felt. *"They will fade,"* Vader had promised, but they had not. Did the other clones experience the same hopes and fears? Were their experiences any less worthy than his?

"Destroy what he created . . . hate what he loved . . . be strong . . ." That was the command Vader had given him, on threat of death. But who was the deliverer of that death? Wasn't he the one delivering to the clones the very fate that he had feared? Had they all been given the same ultimatum?

"You will receive the same treatment as the others."

Death by lightsaber, at his own hand. Perhaps this macabre free-for-all was Vader's way of weeding out the imperfect stock. The last one left standing would be considered the perfect Starkiller, the one who would take his place at Vader's side. Perhaps *that* was his plan.

"You have faced your final test," Vader had told a victorious version of himself in the vision he had received on the *Salvation*. Maybe the vision he had received on Dagobah had warned him of a very real trial, not the metaphorical one he had imagined it to be.

The dark side awaited his call. But if this *was* his final test, then he would not fail. There was too much riding on it. If he gave in to temptation and became Darth Vader's apprentice once more, then it was clear from the vision that Juno would die. She was the whole reason he had escaped, and then returned. He would not turn his back on that, even to survive.

He sought strength from within himself, and pushed outward with all his might. Clones went flying. The empty tubes from which they had emerged shattered into millions of pieces. Platforms buckled and fell with reverberant crashes. The interior of the cloning tower rang as though struck with a giant hammer. Every muscle in his body shook with the effort of it.

The echoes faded, and he felt a peculiar kind of quiet descend.

The air was misted red, and every surface was slick with blood. He tasted it on his tongue and smelled it in his nose. *His* blood. A veritable ocean of it.

He maintained a defensive pose, breathing rhythmically and deeply, regaining his strength. The tips of his lightsabers shook. He had never felt so exhausted, at every level of his being. He felt simultaneously cleansed and poisoned.

Nothing moved. Slowly, incredulously, he began to believe that it was over.

They were all dead. He had destroyed every last one of them. He was the only one left—of the many Darth Vader had created to do his bidding.

"Why me?" he asked the silent cloning tower.

"Search your feelings," Vader said, stepping into view at the very top of the tower, lightsaber held tightly in his right hand. "The answer lies within you."

Starkiller stared up at his former Master. What did he have that none of the other clones did?

He remembered:

"How long this time?"

"Thirteen days. Impressive."

And he remembered:

"The Force gives me all I need."

"The Force?"

"The dark side, I mean."

Slowly a dark understanding began to form. All the duels, all the tests, all the torturous mind games, had been to ensure his survival against every opponent—bar one. His Master. In a sense, they were still playing out the first time they had faced each other in combat.

He didn't remember the early days of his apprenticeship, when the memories of his parents had been strong and the young boy he had once been resisted Vader's absolute authority, but he was sure the battle had been even then, psychological. The battle would never cease until one of them won.

Was this what it was like to be a Sith? Forever at war with one's own Master?

"Your training made me strong enough to escape you," he said, "not obey you."

"Yet here you are." Darth Vader's words fell on him like heavy weights. "My most deadly creation."

"You lie!" Starkiller jumped up to the next platform, passion stirring him to action. "You never wanted this. You can't have. Once Juno has been rescued, your facility will be destroyed. You with it, if there's any justice."

"There is no justice," said Darth Vader, watching him ascend. "Only power."

Vader made no move to defend himself when Starkiller reached the very top of the cloning tower. Determined to prove him wrong, Starkiller didn't waste time announcing his intentions. He just lunged. Only at the very last moment did Vader raise his blade to block the blow, and even then the move seemed almost casual, disinterested. Starkiller struck again, with both lightsabers. Vader blocked one blade and used telekinesis to throw the other off target. The platform buckled and twisted, sending Starkiller flying.

He rolled and leapt, and came up swinging. Covered in blood—the blood of his fellow clones—and knowing Juno was close, he fought his former Master with single-minded focus. Vader was still testing him; he sensed that more and more keenly, with every passing moment, but to what purpose he still couldn't tell. Vader himself fought more cautiously than he had on the Death Star, the last time they had dueled in earnest. His armor seemed to have improved, too; it was less vulnerable to lightning than it had been just days before.

Vader threw wrecked platforms and cloning tubes at him, while he scored three slashes to the Dark Lord's cape in return. They circled the top of the cloning tower, striking and assessing, then striking again.

Starkiller swore that he would not give in to anger or frustration. If that was what Darth Vader wanted, he wasn't going to get it. The only emotion he would give in to was love.

Finally, Starkiller saw an opportunity. They were exchanging rapid blows along the edge of the buckled platform, blades swinging so fast they were visible only as blurs. Vader's defenses were impenetrable; his lightsaber seemed to arrive a split second before Starkiller's, every time. He may have defeated Vader before, but Vader had learned from that mistake. He knew the measure of his former apprentice now.

But the same was true in reverse. And when Vader forced Starkiller onto his back foot and raised his lightsaber to strike him down, Starkiller fired a lightning blast into the side of Vader's armor that was so concentrated, even the new insulation couldn't absorb it.

The Dark Lord stiffened, betrayed by his extensive prosthetics. The distraction lasted only a moment, but it was enough. Starkiller knocked his blade out of the way and moved in to strike.

Juno lying limp in his arms.

The vision struck him as powerfully as a physical blow. When he tried to push it aside, it returned with even more power.

Juno—dead.

He reeled in shock. Was this what would happen if he killed Vader? He had no choice but to believe so. But if he didn't kill Vader, how would he ever get to her?

The Dark Lord took advantage of his momentary confusion. He delivered a telekinetic shove that threw Starkiller backward off the platform and down to the lower levels of the ruined cloning tower. The blow and the fall had the welcome effect of clearing his mind. He turned in midair and landed on his feet. An instant later he was leaping upward again, his face a mask of determination.

Whatever happened to Juno, he saw no choice but to confront Darth Vader. The Dark Lord had killed his father, betrayed him at least once, and would kill Juno the very second she was of no more use to him. Their time of reckoning was long overdue.

The attainment of his true mastery of the Force—the destiny

Darth Vader so often threatened him with—could only come one way. He saw that now. His final test was to kill Vader himself.

When he reached the top level, Vader was disappearing behind the doors of another turbolift. Starkiller ripped them open, but the cab had already begun to ascend. He had no intention of waiting for it to return. He braced himself on the inside of the shaft, and jumped.

One powerful leap saw him rising almost as fast as the cab. He reached telekinetically for its underside, and caught it. When the cab started to slow, he approached close enough to physically hold on to the underside, and raised one lightsaber to cut his way through.

The cab jerked to a halt. Vader was already gone by the time Starkiller emerged through a circular hole in the floor. Outside the cab wasn't another cloning tower. A short ramp led up to the roof of the spire itself, currently out of sight. Starkiller emerged from the cab, a tightness in his chest telling him that Juno was very close now. Very close indeed. She was exactly where he had last seen her.

It was raining.

The dome had been breached. All around him, the fight between the Rebels and Imperials waged on. Wrecked starfighters tumbled from the sky in flames. Debris gushed out of wounded frigates. A listing Star Destroyer vented air and bodies in huge quantities. Across the facility, dozens of dark columns of smoke formed a thick veil of carbonized ash, choking the air. A constant high-frequency pulsation of energy weapons came from all around him, punctuated by the occasional bass explosion. It was impossible to tell who was winning.

Wary of an ambush, Starkiller walked up the ramp. As he did so, Darth Vader came into view. The Dark Lord stood with his lightsaber extinguished in the center of the roof. Behind him, partially obscured by their lord, were four stormtroopers with weapons held at the ready.

"Get out of my way," he said.

"Your memories betray you," Darth Vader said.

"They make me who I am."

"You must turn your back on them in order to become who you will be."

Starkiller stopped in his tracks. Was *that* why Darth Vader burdened him with everything the original Starkiller had been—to demonstrate his strength and commitment by dismissing it, his former self with it? Or was there still some other motive that he couldn't discern?

Of only one thing was he certain. He wouldn't turn his back on Juno for any incentive.

"Never," he said.

"Then she will die."

Darth Vader stepped aside, revealing Juno in shackles. He gestured, and the four stormtroopers surrounding her raised their weapons and fired as one.

CHAPTER 24

WHEN DARTH VADER WALKED onto the roof, the stormtroopers stood to immediate attention. Juno straightened, too, but not out of respect. She didn't know what was coming, but she swore she would be ready for it. The strange sounds coming from below— the screams and clash of lightsabers—had encouraged her to hope that it would be Starkiller who came to her first, but that was dashed now. If he was dead, then Vader would surely have no reason to keep her alive.

Her guards' comlinks chattered too faintly for her to make out the words. Orders, she assumed, from the Dark Lord. They nodded and took new positions, two on either side of her. Then they all turned to face their Master, and he turned his back on them.

For a second, the world paused. The fighting around the spires seemed to lessen. Even the conflict in the sky grew still. She felt as though everyone in Kamino was looking in her direction— although surely, she knew, they didn't even see her. It was all about Vader and Starkiller—if the man she had loved was still alive.

Footsteps came up the ramp. She strained against her bonds, but Vader was directly in her line of sight. She couldn't see past him.

She could hear, though, and she would recognize his voice under any conditions, just like the *Rogue Shadow*.

"Get out of my way," he said to Vader.

"Your memories betray you."

"They make me who I am."

"You must turn your back on them in order to become who you will be."

"Never," he said.

Vader stepped to one side, and past the swirling of his cloak, Juno saw him—Starkiller—and for an instant she didn't see the blood all over him or the tattered state of his flight uniform. All she saw was his eyes. And they in turn saw nothing but her.

"Then she will die," Vader said, raising one hand in a signal to her guards.

They raised their weapons, took aim, and fired.

It happened so fast she barely had time to flinch. Vader had been keeping her alive for so long now that it didn't seem entirely real that he would dispose of her so suddenly. She jerked forward as far as the shackles allowed her, straining to get away. Every muscle in her body tensed in readiness.

The weapons' muzzles flashed—

—and at that very instant a massive force struck her and the guards, flinging her backward so hard she thought her chains might break her wrists. The stormtroopers effectively disappeared, swept off the top of the spire in an instant. The shots they had fired all missed, deflected by the powerful force, although one burned her right cheek as it went by. The four energy bursts followed wild trajectories, outward across the crowded sky.

"Juno!"

Her shackles fell to the ground with a heavy clatter.

Alive but winded, she couldn't reply. She could barely even believe she was alive. She had caught just the fringe of the push that had killed the guards, and she knew that even so she had almost been killed herself.

A different force gripped her, one no less powerful than the first, but aimed at her, not at anything else. It gripped her cruelly about the throat and lifted her so her feet barely touched the ground.

"Bow before me," said Vader to the man she loved.

Starkiller took a step forward. The force gripped her even more tightly, closing her windpipe. She choked, kicking out and finding no ground at all beneath her now. Her hands pulled at her throat, but there was nothing there to grip, and no way to fight it.

"Juno!"

She heard the furious despair in Starkiller's voice, and understood that he was fighting for her, and losing.

"Bow before me," Vader repeated, "or she dies."

Don't, she wanted to say. *Don't do it. You've been down that path before. You know where it leads you.* But she couldn't speak. She could barely even see him. Black dots were crowding out her vision as her oxygen-starved optic nerve began to fail. *Don't let him trick you again.*

He couldn't possibly hear her, but she suspected it wouldn't make any difference. In his shoes, she would be tempted to give in, too. After all they had been through, after all they might have been but had been denied, they at last had a second chance. Arguably that was worth more than any political movement or philosophy. So long as they survived, their love would survive. Nothing else mattered.

She understood, but she felt no relief as Darth Vader's terrible grip loosened and she fell painfully to the ground. Cool air rushed into her lungs. She coughed as though retching, feeling pain all along her windpipe.

Over the sound of her hacking and wheezing, she heard two metallic clinks and looked up to see what had happened.

Starkiller had deactivated his lightsabers and thrown them at Vader's feet. They rolled across the rooftop, their residual heat making the raindrops steam.

Her vocal cords were red raw. Juno could only shake her head as Starkiller took three steps forward, and went down on one knee at Darth Vader's feet.

"I'll do your bidding," he said. "Just promise me you'll never hurt her again."

"That," said Vader, "depends entirely on you."

Starkiller bowed his head, and Juno fought the urge to weep. She understood the dark place from which his capitulation had come, but submission to Darth Vader was not the way to save her. That way lay nothing but more separation and death. And betrayal. And murder.

She had to find the strength somehow to free Starkiller—just as he, clone or original, had somehow fought his way back from the dead in order to find her again.

Her desperate gaze caught sight of one of Starkiller's lightsabers. It had rolled in her direction and lay just out of her reach. If she was quiet, she might just be able to reach it.

The equation was very simple, really. Once before, she had abandoned her entire life for Starkiller. She could easily abandon this one too if it meant saving him from the horrible fate he had just accepted, thinking that it would save *her*.

Vader's back was to her, and Starkiller's head was still bowed. She raised herself to hands and knees and reached out for the lightsaber.

"You will find and kill General Kota," Vader said. "If you refuse, the woman dies."

Starkiller said nothing. Maybe he nodded, but Juno couldn't see him. Vader had placed himself firmly between them once again, symbolically as well as physically.

"You will return to me and give yourself to the dark side," Vader went on. "If you resist, she dies."

The warm metal hilt slid into Juno's hand. She lifted it gently, afraid of making any noise at all, and raised herself to her knees. This was the first time she had held a lightsaber. She knew all too well that it was probably going to be her last.

"And when your training is complete," Vader said, "you will hunt down and execute the Rebel leaders."

Still winded and aching from head to foot, Juno rose unsteadily to her feet, feeling for the lightsaber's activation switch and hardly daring to take her eyes off Vader's back as she did so. They were less than two paces apart.

"If you fail, she dies."

She pressed the activation switch at the same instant she lunged. The bright blue blade sprang to life with a startling hiss, but she didn't let herself be distracted. She had used vibroblades in her training days; she knew how to wield a sword. It was even simpler than the point-and-shoot quip about blasters.

She stabbed at Vader's back, taking the one chance she had left to reclaim her life with Starkiller.

For an instant, she thought it might actually work. Vader's attention was firmly on Starkiller, and the sounds of battle provided effective cover. What was one more energy weapon over the hundreds in play in the facility?

At the last instant, however, some arcane instinct must have warned him. He turned with inhuman speed. She could barely credit her eyes—black holes didn't spin so fast. The tip of Starkiller's lightsaber grazed the front of his chest panel, producing a shower of sparks. She felt no resistance.

Then he pushed her in exactly the same way Starkiller had pushed the stormtroopers. She felt as though the world moved out from under her, sucking all the air away with it. The lightsaber fell from her hand, and suddenly she was flying. Her head snapped forward, and the rain boiled around her. The air itself seemed to hurt, she was moving so fast. Vader receded into the distance with uncanny speed.

How far he pushed her, she couldn't tell. It seemed to last forever, but she knew she had to hit the ground sometime. She hoped it wouldn't be soon. Landing was going to hurt.

Something slammed into her from behind.

It *did* hurt.

The last thing she felt was rain falling into her open eyes. The last thing she saw were three lightsaber blades painting red and blue shapes against the encroaching black.

CHAPTER 25

STARKILLER RAN PAST DARTH VADER to where Juno lay broken on the edge of the cloning spire's roof. Horror and self-reproach filled his mind. He hadn't seen her crawling for the lightsaber; he hadn't sensed her desperate plan until the very last moment—and it was *his* alarm that had alerted Vader, he was sure of it. He and his former Master had reacted at the same time. If Starkiller had moved an instant faster, had a fraction more of a second to think the problem through, he would have pushed Vader just as Vader had pushed Juno, impaling him on the blade before it was whisked away. Instead, he had thought only of saving Juno—a plan, he feared, that might always have been doomed to failure.

He stopped her before she flew off the edge of the roof, at least, but the grisly crunch of bones when she landed was unmistakable. Her head was bent at an impossible angle, and her eyes didn't track him as he ran toward her.

"Juno!"

A black-gloved hand grabbed his shoulder. He pulled away, howling with rage. His fallen lightsabers snapped into his hands and came instantly to life. With both blades moving in tandem, he struck out at his former Master using all his strength, all his rage, all his grief. Darth Vader blocked the blow, but only just. Starkiller pushed, and the Dark Lord stumbled backward.

Instead of pursuing the attack, Starkiller went to go to Juno, but once again Darth Vader stood in his path.

"Get out of my way."

"Your feelings for her are not real," Vader said, not moving.

"They are real to me."

Starkiller attacked the Dark Lord again, but this time he was the one driven back.

With a sense of piercing despair, he saw exactly how the fight would go. He and his former Master would dance like marionettes while Juno lay dying—if she wasn't already dead—and the war raged around them, unchecked by this minor tragedy. In the context of the galaxy's suffering, Juno was just one freedom fighter who had died that day—one among many on Kamino alone. Only she hadn't given her life in combat or to save someone less fortunate than herself. She had been snuffed out thanks to the manipulations of one single tortured man, a man whose stubbornness would never allow him to give up, admit fault, or compromise.

Starkiller knew nothing about the Dark Lord's origins, but he knew what he had become. More monolith than man, his shadow bestrode the Empire, casting darkness wherever it fell. But what was the source of that scourge? What twisted psychology had brought him to where he stood now—risking his life to prevent the clone of his failed apprentice from coming near the body of the woman he had loved?

Sudden understanding burst in Starkiller's mind. This was what Darth Vader had wanted all along. He had been right to fear that Juno was in danger, but not just from clones like him—from Vader, who would use her death to destabilize Starkiller and lead him headlong back to the dark side via anger and despair. Where Starkiller had seen hope, where Starkiller had been willing to sacrifice his own destiny to give the woman he had loved a chance to live, his former Master had seen only opportunity for betrayal—for without Juno, what did Starkiller have left to live and fight for? He had no family, friends, or allies. Juno was always intended to be the catalyst for his downfall. Her precipitous attack had merely brought the critical moment forward.

Starkiller saw things very differently. It wasn't *Juno* who had to die to complete Starkiller's training. It was Darth Vader himself, and he had brought this moment upon himself. Had he been content to let Starkiller go, none of this would have happened. Were he dead or freely searching for Juno, either way, he would never have willingly come back to Kamino. He would have gone anywhere else, and never returned.

Darth Vader simply wouldn't let go. The massive cloning exercise itself was proof of that. He had raised Starkiller to be a monster, and he would let nothing get in the way of achieving that outcome. Not even Starkiller's own death. Even if it took a thousand reincarnations and the death of trillions of innocent people, Darth Vader would not give up. His persistence, his unwillingness to accept defeat, was both his greatest strength and his greatest weakness.

All the clones were destroyed. As far as Starkiller knew, he was the last one left—so that was one vision averted, at least. No matter what happened, no version of him would fall foul of Darth Vader's vile plan now.

They fought like the Sith Lords of old, raging back and forth across the roof of the spire, uncaring what happened around them. Starkiller maintained his efforts to get to Juno, and Darth Vader did everything in his power to stop him. Neither would capitulate. Neither would be the first to break. Their wills were locked.

They broke apart, lightsabers hissing in the ceaseless rain. Lightning split the sky into a thousand jagged shapes. Thunder rolled. Neither had noticed the battle fading around them.

"Let me go," Starkiller said, sounding much calmer than he felt. His heart was pounding, and his lungs burned. "You've taken everything from me. You must see that I will never serve you now."

"You are wrong. I have given you everything."

"This?" He gestured at Juno's inert form. He couldn't tell if she was breathing, but he still held out a distant hope. "You have done nothing for me."

"It is our destiny to destroy the Emperor. You and me, together."

There it was, Starkiller thought. That promise again. Surely Darth Vader could see that it meant nothing now, after so many times offered in the past, and none of them fulfilled?

Unless . . . A deeper layer of understanding presented itself. Unless Darth Vader felt exactly the same as he did.

What lengths had the Emperor, Darth Vader's Master, gone to in order to create *him*? And how far would Darth Vader go to get revenge? To attain his own destiny as a Sith?

"The Rebels want to destroy the Emperor," Starkiller said. "Why not work with them rather th—?"

Vader attacked before he could finish the sentence, a blistering combination of blows that left Starkiller on his back foot. Clearly he had hit a very deep nerve. For a fleeting moment, the plan had seemed almost inspired. With Darth Vader on Kota's side, what couldn't the Alliance accomplish?

But it was a dream. The Rebels would never trust the Emperor's apprentice, and Vader was making it very clear that he wanted no part of it either. The vehemence of his response left no doubt about that.

Starkiller found himself backed up almost to the edge of the cloning spire's roof. One more step, and he would fall, and to fall would give Vader the high ground. That might not result in his death, but it would certainly end the fight.

It needed to end now, or else it might *never* end.

Blow after blow rained on him, forcing him back. There had to be a way to free himself and avenge Juno at the same time . . . but a stalemate seemed unavoidable. Any move he made was sure to lead him to an indefensible position.

Then it occurred to him. An indefensible position was exactly what he needed.

He lunged. Darth Vader saw him coming and swiped with unbeatable strength, sending Starkiller's left lightsaber flying in pieces. Starkiller lunged again, and his right lightsaber joined his left. He fell back, beaten, and stared up at his former Master.

"This is your last chance," Vader said, standing over him with the unwavering tip of his lightsaber pointed directly at Starkiller's chest.

Starkiller stared up at the black mask, sure of two things. Vader didn't want to kill him, but not out of mercy or sympathy for his lot. The Dark Lord had invested far too much time and energy in re-creating his former apprentice, and he wouldn't want to throw all that away. Not when he seemed on the verge of victory.

Juno was dead or dying. Starkiller was disarmed and helpless. Any rational being would at least consider Vader's offer.

The second thing Starkiller knew was: *The best way to beat Darth Vader is to let him think he's won.*

Thinking of Wedge Antilles, he said, "I make my own chances."

With both hands he sent a wave of lightning into the sparking gash Juno had made in Vader's chest plate.

The Dark Lord staggered backward, transfixed by the unexpected retaliation. Starkiller leapt to his feet and followed him, keeping up the lightning attack and using telekinesis to rip Vader's lightsaber from his temporarily weakened fingers. Sheets of energy spread out across the wet rooftop. Smoke and steam rose up in a tortured spiral. The grating whine of Vader's respirator took on a desperate edge.

He went down on one knee. Starkiller stood over him. Vader's lightsaber swept into his former apprentice's hand. The blade came to rest at his throat.

Starkiller stared into the black mask, breathing heavily. One twitch of the blade and Vader would be dead at last.

"Wait," said a voice from behind him.

Starkiller froze, remembering his vision of being stabbed in the back. But the other clones were dead. And like the owner of this unexpected voice, he didn't need to look to see what was in fact occurring.

Booted feet splashed in the water as Kota and members of his squad ran up the ramp and surrounded him, training their guns on Vader. Starkiller didn't move. He kept the lightsaber at Vader's neck, ready to finish what Vader himself had started.

"Why wait?" he asked. "You want him dead as much as I do."

"Yes, of course." There was no hiding the venom in the general's voice. "But not yet. Not until he's told us the Empire's secrets."

"You want to take him *prisoner*?"

"To a hidden Rebel base where we can interrogate him, put him on trial for crimes against the true Republic." Starkiller felt Kota's hand on his shoulder. "And *then* we'll execute him, to show the galaxy that we don't need to fear him any longer."

For several seconds the only sounds came from Vader's wheezing respirator and the storm around them. Water ran down Starkiller's face in rippling streams. Kota's hand gripped him tightly, and it wasn't entirely a gesture of reassurance. There was warning in it, too.

Kota didn't understand. Starkiller was under no threat of the dark side. He wouldn't turn evil just by killing Vader.

"If I let him live," Starkiller said, "he'll haunt me forever."

The general came in closer and spoke in a whisper only Starkiller could hear. "Remember this: Vader is the only one who knows if and how you survived. He can't tell you if you are the original you if he is dead."

Starkiller looked at Kota. The general's face showed no sign of dissemblance. He meant everything he said, even though it pained him. Under any other circumstances, Kota would have relished killing Vader himself, but here he was arguing against it, with one hand on his lightsaber hilt to show that he meant business.

Starkiller looked at Vader, kneeling in the rain with his own lightsaber at his throat, waiting for Starkiller to complete his training and do what Vader had never been able to do himself: kill his own Master.

Either way, Starkiller thought, *I've beaten him.*

That was the only thing left that mattered.

He deactivated the lightsaber and turned away. Kota instantly took his place, holding his blade at Vader's chest while the Rebel soldiers moved in.

"Get something to hold him," Kota ordered, "quickly!"

"Yes, General."

Starkiller didn't stay to watch. PROXY was kneeling next to Juno's body, checking for signs of vitality. Starkiller ran to them and dropped on his knees at Juno's side. Her eyes had closed. Wet hair lay flat across her forehead, limp and colorless.

"Is she—?"

"I'm sorry, Master," the droid said. "I can't revive her."

Juno's features flickered across PROXY's metal face, and then vanished.

"I have failed you again."

Barely hearing PROXY's words, Starkiller gathered her up into his arms and held her tightly to his chest. She was still warm, despite the rain.

"It's not your fault, PROXY. It's mine."

"Yours, Master? Is your primary program malfunctioning, too?"

All Starkiller could see was smoke and storm clouds and the ruination of war.

"I should never have left here, Juno," he said to her, although she was beyond all words. "I should never have come back . . ."

CHAPTER 26

AT THE SOUND of an unfamiliar energy weapon activating nearby, Juno looked up from her work and reached for the blaster pistol at her side. Putting down her welder, she disengaged the safety on her pistol and inched out from under the ship.

Two men armed with lightsabers leapt and tumbled with inhuman agility across the hangar. When they gestured, metal walls buckled and engine parts flew like bullets. One of the combatants rammed his crimson lightsaber through the chest of his opponent, and things took a decidedly strange turn. The arms, legs, torso, and face of the stricken man flickered and dissolved, revealing the bipedal form of a droid, which fell forward with a clatter of metal on metal.

"Ah, Master. Another excellent duel."

The droid struggled to stand and remain upright.

"Easy, PROXY. You're malfunctioning."

"It's my fault, Master. I had hoped that using an older training module would catch you off guard and allow me to finally kill you. I'm sorry I failed you again."

"I'm sure you'll keep trying."

"Of course, Master. It is my primary programming."

Droid and Master began moving through the maze of debris across the hangar.

"PROXY, who is that?"

"Ah, yes. Your new pilot has finally arrived, Master."

"You know why you're here?" Starkiller asked her.

"Lord Vader gave me my orders himself," she said. *"I am to keep your ship running and fly you wherever your missions require."*

Starkiller seemed neither pleased nor displeased. *"Did Lord Vader tell you that he killed our last pilot?"*

"No. But I can only assume he gave Lord Vader good cause to do so. I will not."

"We'll see. I'm sick of training new pilots."

FOR EVERY ENDING there was a beginning. And for every beginning, a middle.

In the cells of the Empirical, *she stared in amazement not just at Starkiller, but at the slaughter he had meted out to her stormtrooper guards as well.*

"Juno . . ."

Words didn't come easily. The last time she had seen him, he had been floating through space, to all appearances dead. "It's—really you!"

PROXY cut across their reunion.

"Master, hurry! She is part of your past life now. Leave her behind, as Lord Vader commanded!"

"I can't."

Starkiller destroyed the magna locks holding her captive. Weakened by months of confinement, she fell to the ground and had to be helped to her feet.

"I saw you die," she said, staring at him in disbelief. A thousand confused thoughts formed a pileup in her mind. "But you've come back."

"I have some unfinished business."

"Vader?"

"Don't worry about him," he told her.

Easier said than done, *she thought, although the reality of her rescue was slowly sinking in.*

"I've been branded a traitor to the Empire," she said. *"I can't go anywhere, do anything—"*

"I don't care about any of that. I'm leaving the Empire behind." He offered her an expression that might have been a smile. *"And I need a pilot."*

"I hope you have a plan."

He nodded. *"There are two things I want, and I can't get them on my own. The first is revenge. To get that we need to rally the Emperor's enemies behind us."*

"Go on."

"The second thing I want is to learn all the things that Vader couldn't—or wouldn't—teach me about the Force."

"If we're not careful," she had said, *"we might end up in our old job again—hunting Jedi."*

It had been a joke.

AFTER *EMPIRICAL* HAD COME KASHYYYK, and after Kashyyyk had come Felucia.

"Juno, wait, this isn't what—"

"Of course it is," she snapped, pulling away from him. *"You're still loyal to Vader. After all he did to us—branding me a traitor and trying to kill you—you're still his . . . his . . ."*

"His slave."

"Yes. But if that's so . . . why? Why did you defy your Master to rescue me?"

"My being here has never been about my piloting."

He neither denied nor admitted the truth of her accusation.

She went to leave, but on the threshold she stopped.

"I don't know who—or what—you really are. Maybe I'll never know. But sometime soon, you will decide the fate of the Rebellion, not your Master. That's something he can't take away from you. And when you're faced with that moment, remember that I, too, was forced to leave everything I've ever known."

AFTER FELUCIA, Raxus Prime and Corellia.

Juno could see Starkiller's grief visibly turning to anger as he realized exactly how far he had been played for a fool by his Master.

"Yes, you did do what he wanted. There's no point hiding from it—and now the fate of the Alliance rests on your shoulders. The question is, what are you going to do about it?"

He wrestled with his emotions and thoughts. When he raised his head, he was resolved.

"We're going after Vader. And the Rebels."

"Where?"

"I don't know," he admitted. "Not yet."

"Do you know how this is going to end?"

He hesitated, and then shook his head. "No."

BUT THERE HAD TO BE AN ENDING. The only question was: When?

"Juno—"

"Don't say it. Don't say a word." She glanced at him. "Just tell me you're still sure. This is what we have to do, right?"

"It is."

"All right."

The air outside was cold but breathable. As the ramp opened, it rushed in around them, making her shiver.

The view down to the surface of the Death Star was giddying, but she was unable to look away.

"I have a really bad feeling about this."

"Then we must be doing the right thing."

She looked up at him. "Am I going to see you again?"

"Probably not, no."

"Then I guess I'll never need to live this down."

She pulled him closer to her and kissed him hard on the lips.

THAT LOOKED LIKE AN ENDING. It certainly felt like an ending.

"He's at one with the Force NOW," Kota said.

AND WHEN THINGS ENDED, they stayed ended.

"We need a symbol to rally behind," Leia said.

"Agreed," said Garm Bel Iblis.

The Princess wiped dust from the table, revealing Starkiller's family crest etched into the wood. "A symbol of hope."

THEY WERE SUPPOSED TO, anyway.

Juno watched the Rogue Shadow *leave Corellia with a sinking heart, although she knew it would be perfectly safe in Kota and Bail Organa's hands. There were just so many memories attached to it. Letting it go was like losing a part of herself. Unfortunately, she wasn't losing the part of her that still ached for* him. *That re-*

mained exactly where it was, in the center of her chest, pounding like a funeral drum . . .

"I hardly ever see you smile," said Shyre, tapping her dangling boot with one of his metal legs. "You wisecrack and take shots at everyone, but you don't laugh. Is there a reason for that?"

Juno wished she hadn't had that last eyeblaster. It was making her head ache but doing nothing at all to help her forget.

"It's old news," she said, wondering if maybe the problem wasn't having one too many, but not having had enough.

She was beginning to wonder if there would ever be enough.

"Congratulations, Captain," said Commodore Viedas on the bridge of her first command. "The Salvation is a fine ship. It will serve you well, and I know you will return the compliment."

"Thank you, sir." She tried not to stare around the bridge in wonder. The truth was that she felt proud and daunted at the same time. She had come a long way from TIE fighter squadrons and secret missions for Darth Vader.

Her expression fell, as it always did when he came to mind.

"Don't worry," said the commodore, coming closer to whisper a brisk reassurance. "We all feel nervous the first time out."

He had misunderstood her mood, but she didn't correct him. Better to let him believe what he wanted to believe, and to keep her scars hidden.

"Let's not be blinded as Kota was," said Mon Mothma, "by the dream of an easy victory. We learned the hard way that will never be our lot."

"You wouldn't be saying that if Starkiller were here."

Mon Mothmas looked at her sternly. "He's not here, so the point is irrelevant."

* * *

Juno stared, blinking, as a figure dressed entirely in black leapt out of a hole in the floor. The bounty hunter fired three shots in quick succession. The energy bolts were deflected by a pair of spinning lightsabers into the walls, where they discharged brightly. By their light, Juno saw the face of the man running toward her.

Juno stared at the clone in the tube, her jaw working. Through her distress and confusion, one core certainty remained. It didn't matter where Starkiller came from or what he was, just so long as he was the same man she had loved. She would know who he was the moment she saw him. Nothing in the universe could keep that truth from her.

Vader stepped aside. Juno saw Starkiller, and he saw Juno. In that moment she knew.

She knew that she was right and Darth Vader was wrong. Shyre was wrong. Mon Mothma was wrong.

EVERYONE WHO INSISTED STARKILLER's story had ended was wrong.

"Your feelings for her are not real," Vader insisted.

"They are real to me."

NOT EVEN DEATH could stop her from hearing him call her name.

"Juno . . . come back . . ."

CHAPTER 27

JUNO'S FACE WAS WET. From tears or the rain, she couldn't tell. Her entire being felt relieved of a mighty weight—as though an incredible pain had just been taken from her, leaving her not quite of the world.

Kamino.

Memories rushed back in.

Vader.

An echo of that terrible pain swept through her, and then disappeared forever.

Starkiller.

He was holding her. She could smell him. When she opened her eyes, she could see him *right there,* so close to her, that he almost seemed part of her. His forehead pressed firmly against hers. His eyes were closed and his face was wet, too, although perhaps not from only the rain.

She reached up and touched his cheek, felt him start and almost pull away.

Their eyes met.

Weightless, impossible, miraculous—there were no words for how she felt. Time had rolled back, and so many wrongs had been righted, just by being here, now, with him.

She pulled herself up and kissed him properly, without fear, without regret, and without the smallest doubt that it was the most perfect thing to do in that moment.

He held her as though he planned never to let go.

"We're alive," she whispered into his ear. "We are both of us so very alive."

EPILOGUE: Kamino

SOMETIMES, ON EXCEEDINGLY rare occasions, it stopped raining on Kamino. On this occasion, Starkiller thought, there might be a very good, meteorological reason for the relatively fair turn in the weather. Numerous fires burned in the doomed facility, sending hot air rising into the cloud layer, while the upper atmosphere still boiled from the battle that had only recently finished. He wasn't, therefore, entirely surprised by the sudden sunlight that shone weakly down onto the restless ocean. He just knew it wouldn't last.

"The *Rogue Shadow*'s on its way," said Kota. "As far as containment and concealment go, that remains our best bet."

"Agreed," said Juno, all business. She stayed at Starkiller's side, tightly holding his hand, having made it clear several times that she was unwilling to be parted from him. He wasn't remotely inclined to force the point. It still seemed a miracle that they were together again, after all the obstacles the universe had placed in their path.

"And you," said Kota to him in a sharper tone. "Where do you stand now? Are you with us or going off on your own, now that you have what you want?"

Juno glanced anxiously at him. There hadn't been time to talk about how this changed things. He didn't know when they would find time to.

"I'm with you," he said, sure that Juno would have it no other way. Wherever his destiny lay, it would be with her and the Rebellion she served, if they would have him. "One hundred percent."

Kota nodded, although his relief was clouded. They had scored a significant victory against the Empire, but so much more needed to be done. If Kota still wanted him to be a rallying point, then so be it. As long as it got the job done.

In that sense, he supposed, it didn't matter if he was a clone or not. The ends justified the means. And the ultimate end was to defeat the Emperor. He was sure no one would quibble about his pedigree when that day arrived.

Still, the clones he had murdered on Kamino would haunt him forever, he knew. What gave them any less right to live than him? If he was one of them, the stain of fratricide—or suicide—would always be on his hands.

Unless, he suddenly thought to himself, the Starkiller who had died on the Death Star had been a clone, and he *was* the original after all. Maybe then, if that were the case, his doubts would be settled.

Only one person knew the truth. And he wasn't talking.

Juno squeezed his hand, as though sensing his inner conflict and seeking to reassure him. He squeezed back, wishing they had time to be alone. They had so much to talk about, so many events to catch up on. Now that they had both returned from death, it was finally time to start living.

Someone shouted on the other side of the spire roof. Starkiller anxiously glanced in that direction, right hand reaching for the lightsaber hilt at his belt.

It was nothing. Just a slight disagreement over the proper fastening of the harness. Still, his attention was diverted.

"Go help," said Juno. "I've got a meeting to attend, anyway." She kissed him briefly on the lips. "Just don't go too far away."

Starkiller understood that sentiment completely. The power of love had brought her back to him—he could see no other explanation for it. It hadn't been the Force, and it hadn't been medical science, unless there was more happening on Kamino than simple cloning. However it had happened, he couldn't assume that just because it had happened once, it would ever happen again.

Only with great reluctance did he allow his hand to leave hers, telling himself that surely a few meters wouldn't hurt.

Leaving Kota and Juno to discuss Alliance business, he strode over to where the members of Kota's new squad were dealing with the weighty matter of the prisoner.

JUNO WATCHED HIM go and was unable to hold in a smile. She still couldn't believe it had worked out this way. Kota was alive, Vader captured, Starkiller back at her side, and the operation on Kamino a success. She was certain now that the Alliance would see the sense in Kota's approach and ultimately succeed in all its aims.

Feeling Kota's blind-eyed attention on her, she shifted the direction of her own stare. Above them, numerous capital ships orbited, including the gutted remains of the three Star Destroyers stationed in the system to defend the facility. She counted several Alliance cruisers and frigates, among them one whose configuration she didn't recognize.

"Where'd that come from?" she asked, pointing.

"The MC-Eighty?" Kota said. "A friend of yours on Dac heard you were in trouble and sent it to help. Tipped the balance in our favor."

Her smile broadened. *Ackbar.* Things were coming together with incredible speed. Whatever Starkiller had done to bring her back, he seemed to have made everything else right as well.

PROXY came to join them. "I am expecting the transmission at any moment," he said. "There have been some difficulties establishing completely secure protocols but I believe—"

The droid stopped in midsentence. His holoprojectors sparkled and shimmered. With a crackling noise, his appearance and posture changed, and Juno found herself staring at the youthful face of Bail Organa's daughter.

"I received your message, General," Leia said, "but as you're supposed to be dead, I'm not sure how much credence to give it."

"It's true, Your Highness," he told her. "We have him."

"Vader himself?"

"He's being prepared for transport as we speak."

Leia looked as though she still couldn't believe what she was hearing. "This changes everything! When the Emperor hears we've got his prize thug on a leash . . ." She visibly snapped herself out of her thoughts. "That's not for me to decide. Captain Eclipse, I'm relieved to see you in one piece, too."

"Thank you," she said.

"I hope you're not seriously injured."

Juno raised her left forearm, which was encapsulated by a field brace. Her shoulder still bothered her, but she didn't notice the pain anymore. "I'll live." She would indeed.

"My commiserations regarding the *Salvation*. I understand it was lost during the assault on Kamino."

"A small price to pay," she said, although she reminded herself to take Starkiller to task for that, later. If he made a habit of destroying her commands, she would never get anywhere in the Alliance hierarchy. "We'll use the *Rogue Shadow* to ferry Vader to Dantooine."

Kota added, "At the same time, we'll send a dozen freighters in a dozen different directions. Even if someone finds out we have him, they won't know which ship to follow."

"Excellent," said Leia. "And the security detail?"

Juno and Kota exchanged glances.

"We have it covered," she said.

"It's not just the Imperials we have to worry about," Leia said, her face very serious. "As I'm sure you're very aware, General, there are plenty of people on our own side who would like to see Vader dead. The mission to overthrow the Emperor is more important than any personal vendetta."

Kota cleared his throat. It sounded like the growl of a large and dangerous animal.

"Rest assured, Your Highness," he said, "that if Vader dies in custody, it won't be by my hand. And anyone who tries will feel the hot edge of my blade."

Leia nodded. "Thank you, General Kota. I know I can trust you."

Kota nodded stiffly, as he always did when offered a compliment. Leia smiled reassuringly, and Juno was impressed by the deftness with which she handled him. She combined the military understanding of Garm Bel Iblis and the diplomacy of Mon Mothma. Perhaps, Juno thought, *she* might turn out to be the one to marry both means and end and thereby unite the Alliance, not her father or Kota or even Juno. If she only had time to grow up . . .

"I'd like to debrief with you personally, Captain Eclipse," Leia said. "Do you think we'll have the opportunity on Dantooine?"

"I hope so, Princess," Juno said, surprised but pleased that Leia had made the overture.

Kota said, "We'll contact you again once we have Vader safely locked away."

"Good." Leia's expression was cautiously optimistic. After the bickering and confusion of recent weeks, it looked good on her. "This is a turning point for the Alliance. You should both be very proud. May the Force be with you."

Juno saluted and Kota bowed. PROXY's holographic form dissolved, and Leia was gone.

"Keeping him a secret is going to be difficult," said Kota.

"Which 'him'?"

The general inclined his head to where Starkiller was assisting the imprisonment team. "My squad will never tell anyone. You can be sure of that. But they're not the only ones who've seen him. A pilot is asking about someone who hitched a ride on his Y-wing. Some of the survivors of the *Salvation* have been talking, too. I think we can trust Berkelium Shyre, but—"

"Starkiller was on Malastare?"

"Yes, two days ago. Why?"

She shook her head. It didn't matter. They would have plenty of time later to chart their near misses. Hopefully the repairman didn't say anything untoward.

"I thought you wanted him to lead the charge."

Kota sighed. "I do, yes, but our illustrious leaders need to sort themselves out first. He can't keep swooping in and fixing things for them. And the questions—people will insist on asking . . ."

"Is that why you didn't tell me about him?"

He nodded, jaw set like stone, and Juno could tell what was going through his mind. It had been going through hers, in the bounty hunter's prison ship. Until they knew for certain where Starkiller had come from, would the Rebel Alliance ever really believe in him? Would have Juno herself, had she not seen him with her own eyes?

Bail Organa's words came back to her. *"I don't trust that kind of power."* He, at least, would be especially difficult to convince.

Juno felt a faint pang of regret at that. Of the few people she could have talked to about how she was feeling, Leia was the only one she trusted to be completely honest and objective. But her loyalty to the Alliance and her father was fierce, too. This was a bomb Juno couldn't afford to drop in her lap without being sure it wasn't about to go off.

War got in the way of friendship, just as it got in the way of love. The list of casualties wasn't confined just to people. She knew with a sinking feeling that the debriefing session on Dantooine, if it happened at all, would have to be all business, for both of their good.

So much for being a role model, she thought . . .

"I'll encourage him to keep a low profile," she said, confident that Vader and Kota himself would give the Alliance leadership plenty to argue about for now. "What about Kamino? I hope you're not thinking of leaving all this behind for the Emperor to start up again."

"We'll search the databases for any information on the space station the Emperor's building. I'm sure it's all been erased, but it's still worth looking. Then we'll ditch the Star Destroyers into the ocean and wreck the facilities with the resulting tsunami. In an hour or two, there'll be nothing left."

"Good," she said, thinking of Vader's sinister efforts to re-create the perfect—and perfectly evil—apprentice. The sooner they were at the bottom of the ocean, the better.

She thought of Dac, and smiled again. If forest worlds were bad for her, then ocean worlds were the opposite. The sea air suited her, clearly.

A familiar shape swooped overhead. The *Rogue Shadow* had scored some new dents and scratches during the action, but looked unharmed in any significant way. Rebel soldiers had cleared a space for it on the rooftop, and Kota loped off to supervise the next stage in the operation. Juno watched the ship descend lightly on its repulsors, and found herself looking forward to getting behind the controls again.

Just like old times, she thought. With the Empire on their heels, an uncertain future ahead, and fragile hope in their hearts.

"Excuse me, Captain Eclipse."

Juno forced herself to tear her gaze from the ship. "Yes, PROXY, what is it?"

"While ascending through the cloning spire, I couldn't help noticing the remains of several droids of my class. I wonder if, with your permission, I could attempt to salvage some of the components I require to restore my primary programming."

The droid blinked anxiously at her, and Juno could see no reason to refuse. "All right, but don't take too long. Imperial reinforcements will be here soon, and you don't want to be left behind."

"No, I do not. Thank you, Captain Eclipse." PROXY hurried off, dodging and weaving around soldiers and technicians making ready the harness that would keep the *Rogue Shadow*'s new passenger secure.

Juno's mood darkened at that thought. Hardly like old times at all, with *him* aboard. Still, it wouldn't be for long, and if all went well, he'd soon be out of the picture entirely, and she, along with the rest of the galaxy, would breathe a heartfelt sigh of relief.

THE HARNESS SEEMED large enough to hold a rancor, and still the soldiers were nervous. Starkiller stayed nearby, in case of slip-ups or the slightest hint of an escape attempt. Except for one moment, when the harness swung a little too far to the right and threatened to hit the *Rogue Shadow*'s air lock frame, he let the soldiers do their work unimpeded. A slight nudge through the Force put the harness on course again, and no one was the wiser.

Kota followed the harness inside to check that it was firmly secured to the deck and ceiling. Starkiller didn't go with him. He still wasn't certain he had done the right thing.

Twice now, he'd had Vader at his mercy. Twice, Kota had talked him out of it. He wasn't sure if that was wisdom of the highest order, or madness utterly beyond his understanding. If Vader broke free, he knew he'd never get a third chance.

He had to make this one count.

Kota emerged, looking satisfied.

"Did he say anything to you?" Starkiller asked.

"Not a word."

"He never told me anything worth hearing in my entire life. What makes you think he'll talk to anyone on Dantooine?"

"Everyone has their breaking point," said the general. "Even him."

"I think he passed his years ago."

Kota's blind eyes searched Starkiller's face, but he said nothing.

Starkiller told himself to be happy. He had everything he had set out from Kamino to find, and more. The only thing he had forgotten to think about was what happened next.

"*Brought you here, the galaxy has,*" the strange creature on Dagobah had told him. "*Your path clearly this is.*"

Maybe this *was* his path, then. But if so, he remained utterly in the dark as to what lay at the end of it.

PROXY hurried past them and up the ramp into the ship, clutching a tangled mess of droid parts to his chest. He looked like a droid on a mission, and Starkiller took that as his cue to enter the ship, too. He couldn't avoid going up the ramp forever. That was a journey whose end he *was* completely sure about.

He found the droid in the crew quarters, taking out bits and pieces of his own circuitry and plugging new modules in their place, prompting strange responses as he did so. His photoreceptors went from yellow to green and back again. Holographic limbs came and went. Weird buzzes and squeaks issued from his vocabulator.

"What are you doing, PROXY?" asked Starkiller, alarmed.

The droid looked up at him, and didn't seem to recognize him for a moment. He took a half-melted circuit block out of the back of his skull and inserted the original back in place.

"My primary program is still missing, Master," he said. "I am trying to replace it."

"Are these from the droids I killed?" Starkiller asked, stirring the parts with a finger.

"Yes, Master. It is clear now that my line did not end with my manufacture."

PROXY took out another block from his head and replaced it with one from the pile. Instantly his holoprojectors went crazy, shooting electrical arcs around the room. His arms and legs flailed, and Starkiller quickly reached over to remove the offending component.

"I think you should be careful," he said as PROXY settled back down. Thin streamers of smoke rose up from the droid's joints. "Better to have no primary program than no existence at all."

The droid looked disconsolate. "That is what Captain Eclipse says, but I do not understand why. My malfunctions upset her. I fear she may have me melted down if they continue."

"She would never do that," said Starkiller, hoping it wasn't true. "Describe these malfunctions to me. Maybe I can help."

PROXY did so, quickly and clinically, even though it clearly caused him discomfort to admit to his faults.

"Most disturbing," he concluded, "was the period when I looked like you, Master. For some reason I could not return to my normal form. That was when Captain Eclipse shut me down, for her good as well as mine."

"I understand," Starkiller said. He could imagine what Juno had felt with an identical copy of him hanging around, talking like PROXY talked, when he had been supposedly dead and gone. He hated the thought of it as well.

He understood on a deeper level, too.

"Something lost." The voice of the wise little creature on Dagobah returned to him again. *"A part of yourself, perhaps?"*

"I think you're trying to replace the wrong thing," he said, indicating the chips and circuits from the dead droids. "Look at the people you're imitating and ask yourself—do they have something in common? Maybe they possess something you're missing."

PROXY gravely considered the possibility. "Perhaps, but apart from all being human and known to me, I can't see how you, Captain Eclipse, General Kota, Mon Mothma, and Princess Leia are similar at all."

"Well, give it some more thought. That's an order."

"Yes, Master. I will do my best." PROXY began fishing around in the pile of spare parts again, clearly not intending to abandon that pursuit as well.

"Just remember that I need you in one piece, no matter what kind of primary programming you have."

"Yes, Master."

Starkiller stood. He and PROXY were still alone on the ship, apart from the prisoner, but that would soon change. It was time to get it over with.

Leaving PROXY to piece himself together, Starkiller walked

through the ship to the entrance of the meditation chamber. There he took a deep breath and checked that Vader's lightsaber was safely at his side.

The door slid open at his touch. Two small overhead lights illuminated the entrance. More flickered on as he walked into the circular space. He didn't hesitate; his step never faltered. Inside, though, he felt only conflict and confusion.

He stopped in front of the harness. The last of the lights flickered on, revealing the harness and the prisoner contained within. Darth Vader's arms were hidden from the elbows down by thick, durasteel cuffs; his legs below the knees, likewise. Thick magna locks encased his waist, chest, and throat. A cage surrounded his helmet, leaving only the "face" exposed. A faint hum of energy fields pervaded the air. One more step closer, Starkiller knew, and he risked disintegration.

His former Master had no choice but to look down at him. Even Vader, with his prodigious strength and willpower, could barely turn his head. The only sound was the relentless in–out of his respirator.

Starkiller returned the stare, acutely aware that he had initiated this confrontation and that, even in the harness, his Master seemed more imposing and threatening than ever.

He didn't know what he had come to say, exactly, but he could feel his determination fading fast.

"I let you live," he said before he could think about it too much.

He meant it as a provocation, but it emerged more like a question, an expression of disbelief, as though he himself still didn't quite believe what he had done. If he *had* truly cast aside the Sith's notion of destiny—to kill his own Master—what did that leave him now? Did he even *have* a destiny, in this life?

Vader said nothing.

"You tell me I'm a clone—a *failed* clone. But I chose to spare you. Does this prove you right or wrong?"

Still Vader said nothing.

"Maybe Kota is right," he said more softly. "Maybe everything you told me was a trick. Maybe you were trying to get me so confused I'd forget who I really am and become your slave again."

His eyes narrowed as they took in the restraints keeping his former Master utterly helpless.

"Either way, I've finally broken your hold over me."

Vader stared at him, unable to convey anything by expression or body language. It was like talking to a statue.

With a small, disgusted sound, Starkiller turned to leave.

"As long as she lives," Darth Vader said, "I will always control you."

Starkiller stopped and almost turned. What was this? Another empty threat? A last desperate mind game? The truth . . . ?

It didn't deserve a reply. He wouldn't give Vader the satisfaction of seeing his face, and the uncertainty he was sure it displayed.

When he left the room, the lights flickered out and the door slid securely closed behind him.

THERE WERE SURVIVORS of the *Salvation* among the troops on the ground. Juno had no intentions of going anywhere until they were accounted for and provided with berths on Alliance ships. Several Imperial vessels had been commandeered from the landing bays on Kamino; she felt it her duty to ensure at least a couple of them went to "her" crew. She didn't know how long it was going to be before she would be in such a position again. Perhaps when more of the Mon Calamari cruisers came into service . . .

Juno thought of Nitram and how he had betrayed her to Mon Mothma. She couldn't begrudge him that, although it had caused her inconvenience at the time; just like her, he had only been trying to do the right thing. It didn't seem fair that he was dead, while she lived on. Had she been standing where he was on the bridge of the *Salvation,* she would be in his place. Had he had someone like Starkiller to champion him, he might still be alive.

One of the downsides of command, she told herself, was losing good crew to the vagaries of fate. Best she got used to it—just as Vader's bounty hunter would have to get used to the idea that he wouldn't be paid for this particular job, now that his employer was locked up for good . . .

Finally everything was ready for departure. The decoy freighters were loaded with fake cargoes and crewed by people either utterly loyal or, if there was a chance of a traitor among them, at least aware that they were part of a much larger deception. Only a handful of critical personnel knew precisely who was going where. The betrayal of the fleet's location by the Itani Nebula was still fresh in everyone's minds.

"Word will get to the Emperor eventually," she said to Kota as they took their leave of each other on top of the cloning tower. The whining of engines was rising all around them. "We can't avoid it."

"So we get our demands in earlier," the general said, "or we allow him to sweat for a bit. That's Mon Mothma's decision. Just get Vader to Dantooine in one piece and leave the rest to me."

"Of course." She saluted.

He returned the salute. "We'll be waiting for you."

"Not if I get there first."

Kota jumped into a waiting shuttle and ascended immediately in the direction of the new frigate. Juno took one last look around the surface of Kamino, and shivered. The clouds had closed over again. A new storm was brewing on the western horizon.

She was the last one left on the roof of the cloning spire, where so many awful and wonderful things had happened. Soon it would be gone forever. Tightening the collar around her bruised throat, she ran up the ramp and into the *Rogue Shadow,* vowing never to look back.

Darth Vader was standing in the crew compartment, domed head looming high above hers, seeming to fill the whole ship with shadow.

Juno reached for the blaster at her side, heart thudding hard in her chest.

With a flash of light, Vader disappeared.

"PROXY?" Juno lowered the blaster. Her hands were shaking. "What on Coruscant are you playing at?"

"I am experimenting, Captain Eclipse," said the droid, reaching up to tap the back of his head. "My Master suggested that I ask myself what the people I have been imitating have in common. The only detail I can discern is that they have a sense of purpose beyond themselves. They stand for principles, not just self-preservation—as I must, too, in order to be whole."

She remembered what Leia had said about their being a message behind PROXY's manifestations. "Maybe you knew that all along, on that deeper level of programming you talked about, and you've been trying to tell yourself about it."

"That is possible."

"But Darth Vader fits . . . how, exactly?"

"I am as yet unsure. This may be a residue from one of the chips I have salvaged."

"He serves a Master, too, don't forget. And if he has any principles, they're not anything you'd want to follow."

"Assuredly not, Captain Eclipse."

PROXY look pleased, and she didn't have the heart to argue the point.

"Well, good, I guess," she said. "I'm glad your primary program is finally fixed. We're going to need you in full working order."

"I exist to serve, Captain."

Juno brushed past him to the bridge, where Starkiller was sitting in the copilot's seat. A hit of déjà vu struck her as she crossed the threshold.

He looked up. "Anything wrong?"

"Absolutely nothing," she said, coming to sit next to him, at the controls. Although she hadn't been inside the *Rogue Shadow* for more than a year, the layout of the console seemed as familiar to her as the back of her hands. As the battered fatigue on Starkiller's face.

PROXY took his seat behind them. "All systems are fully functional," he assured her.

She placed her hands on the controls. A series of deft touches closed the ramp and brought the repulsors to life. Gently, the *Rogue Shadow* lifted off and rose into the sky.

Starkiller's expression was impassive, but she could tell that he was watching closely as the cloning towers receded below them. Barely had they lifted off when the first of the gutted Star Destroyers hit the ocean several klicks away. There was a flash like the rising of the sun as several megatons of water instantly vaporized. The shock wave radiated outward in a wave of steam hundreds of meters high. In seconds, the tsunami reached the towers, knocking them over and occluding the wreckage from sight.

Ahead, bright stars appeared through the thinning atmosphere. Dotted among them, the shining constellation of the Rebel fleet, all proudly marked with the symbol of the Alliance: Starkiller's family crest, with none of the soldiers or commanders aware that the one who had inspired it was among them again.

The *Rogue Shadow* joined twelve small freighters in orbit above the waterworld.

"You have your orders," said Commodore Viedas to each of them in a firm and steady voice. "May the Force be with you."

One by one, the freighters accelerated, each heading along a different trajectory into hyperspace.

Juno counted them off, double-checking the course for Dantooine. As their numbers dwindled, she glanced at Starkiller, who was still staring back at Kamino. The expanding circular shock wave looked like the pupil of an enormous eye.

He was difficult to read sometimes, and this was no exception. She reached out and placed a hand on his forearm, breaking his concentration.

"Ready for lightspeed," she said.

He managed a smile. "I'm ready for anything."

Her other hand pushed a lever on the console, and the hyper-drives kicked into life. The *Rogue Shadow* flung itself forward. Stars turned to streaks ahead of them. This time, Juno hoped, the past was left far, far behind.

Read on for an excerpt from

Star Wars: The Old Republic: Fatal Alliance

by Sean Williams

Published by Del Rey Books

SHIGAR KONSHI FOLLOWED the sound of blasterfire through Coruscant's old districts. He never stumbled, never slipped, never lost his way, even through lanes that were narrow and crowded with years of detritus that had settled slowly from the levels above. Cables and signs swayed overhead, hanging so low in places that Shigar was forced to duck beneath them. Tall and slender, with one blue chevron on each cheek, the Jedi apprentice moved with grace and surety surprising for his eighteen years.

At the core of his being, however, he seethed. Master Nikil Nobil's decision had cut no less deeply for being delivered by hologram from the other side of the galaxy.

"The High Council finds Shigar Konshi unready for Jedi trials."

The decision had shocked him, but Shigar knew better than to speak. The last thing he wanted to do was convey the shame and resentment he felt in front of the Council.

"Tell him why," said Grand Master Satele Shan, standing at his side with hands folded firmly before her. She was a full head shorter than Shigar but radiated an indomitable sense of self. Even via holoprojector, she made Master Nobil, an immense Thisspiasian with full ceremonial beard, shift uncomfortably on his tail.

"We—that is, the Council—regard your Padawan's training as incomplete."

Shigar flushed. "In what way, Master Nobil?"

His Master silenced him with a gentle but irresistible telepathic nudge. "He is close to attaining full mastery," she assured the Council. "I am certain that it is only a matter of time."

"A Jedi Knight is a Jedi Knight in all respects," said the distant Master. "There are no exceptions, even for you."

Master Satele nodded her acceptance of the decision. Shigar bit his tongue. She said she believed in him, so why did she not overrule the decision? She didn't have to submit to the Council. If he weren't her Padawan, would she have spoken up for him then?

His unsettled feelings were not hidden as well as he would have liked.

"Your lack of self-control reveals itself in many ways," said Master Nobil to him in a stern tone. "Take your recent comments to Senator Vuub regarding the policies of the Resource Management Council. We may all agree that the Republic's handling of the current crisis is less than perfect, but anything short of the utmost political discipline is unforgivable at this time. Do you understand?"

Shigar bowed his head. He should've known that the slippery Neimoidian was after more than just his opinion when she'd sidled up to him and flattered him with praise. When the Empire had invaded Coruscant, it had only handed the world back to the Republic in exchange for a large number of territorial concessions elsewhere. Ever since then, supply lines had been strained. That Shigar was right, and the RMC a hopelessly corrupt mess, putting the lives of billions at risk from something much worse than war— starvation, disease, disillusionment—simply didn't count in some circles.

Master Nobil's forbidding visage softened. "You are naturally disappointed. I understand. Know that the Grand Master has spoken strongly in favor of you for a long time. In all respects but this one do we defer to her judgment. She cannot sway our combined decision, but she has drawn our attention. We will be watching your progress closely, with high expectations."

The holoconference had ended there, and Shigar felt the same conflicted emptiness in the depths of Coruscant as he had then. *Unready? High expectations?* The Council was playing a game with him—or so it felt—batting him backward and forward like a fe-linx in a cage. Would he ever be free to follow his own path?

Master Satele understood his feelings better than he did. "Go for a walk," she had told him, putting a hand on each shoulder and holding his gaze long enough to make sure he understood her intentions. She was giving him an opportunity to cool down, not dismissing him. "I need to talk to Supreme Commander Stantorrs anyway. Let's meet later in Union Cloisters."

"Yes, Master."

And so he was walking and stewing. Somewhere inside him, he knew, had to be the strength to rise above this temporary setback, the discipline to bring the last threads of his talent into a unified design. But on this occasion, his instincts were leading him away from stillness, not toward it.

The sound of blasterfire grew louder ahead of him.

Shigar stopped in an alley that stank like a woodoo's leavings. A swinging light flashed fitfully on and off in the level above, casting rubbish and rot in unwanted relief. An ancient droid watched with blinking red eyes from a filthy niche, rusted fingers protectively gathering wires and servos back into its gaping chest plate. The cold war with the Empire was being conducted far away from this alley and its unhappy resident, but its effects were keenly felt. If he wanted to be angry at the state of the Republic, he couldn't have chosen a better place for it.

The shooting intensified. His hand reached for the grip of his lightsaber.

There is no emotion, he told himself. *There is only peace.*

But how could there be peace without justice? What did the Jedi Council, sitting comfortably in their new Temple on Tython, know about *that*?

The sound of screams broke him out of his contemplative trance. Between one heartbeat and the next he was gone, the emerald fire of his lightsaber lingering a split instant behind him, brilliant in the gloom.

Larin Moxla paused to tighten the belly strap on her armor. The wretched thing kept coming loose, and she didn't want to take any chances. Until the justicars got there, she was the only thing standing between the Black Sun gangsters and the relatively innocent residents of Gnawer's Roost. It sounded like half of it had been shot to pieces already.

Satisfied that nothing too vulnerable was exposed, she peered out from cover and hefted her modified snub rifle. Illegal on Coruscant except for elite special forces commandos, it featured a powerful sniper sight, which she trained on the Black Sun safehouse. The main entrance was deserted, and there was no sign of the roof guard. That was unexpected. Still the blasterfire came from within the fortified building. Could it be a trap of some kind?

Wishing as always that she had backup, she lowered the rifle and lifted her helmeted head into full view. No one took a potshot at her. No one even noticed her. The only people she could see were locals running for cover. But for the commotion coming from within, the street could have been completely deserted.

Trap or no trap, she decided to get closer. Rattling slightly, and ignoring the places where her secondhand armor chafed, Larin hustled low and fast from cover to cover until she was just meters from the front entrance. The weapons-fire was deafening now, and screaming came with it. She tried to identify the weapons. Blaster pistols and rifles of several different makes; at least one floor-mounted cannon; two or three vibrosaws; and beneath all that, a different sound. A roaring, as of superheated gases jetting violently through a nozzle.

A flamethrower.

No gang she'd heard of used fire. The risk of a blaze spreading everywhere was too high. Only someone from outside would employ a weapon like that. Only someone who didn't care what damage he left in his wake.

Something exploded in an upper room, sending a shower of bricks and dust into the street. Larin ducked instinctively, but the wall held. If it had collapsed, she would have been buried under meters of rubble.

Her left hand wanted to count down, and she let it. It felt wrong otherwise. Moving in—in *three . . . two . . . one . . .*

Silence fell.

She froze. It was as though someone had pulled a switch. One minute, nine kinds of chaos had been unfolding inside the building. Now there was nothing.

She pulled her hand in, countdown forgotten. She wasn't going *anywhere* until she knew what had just happened and who was involved.

Something collapsed inside the building. Larin gripped her rifle more tightly. Footsteps crunched toward the entrance. One set of feet: that was all.

She stood up in full view of the entrance, placed herself side-on to reduce the target she made, and trained her rifle on the darkened doorway.

The footsteps came closer—unhurried, confident, heavy. Very heavy.

The moment she saw movement in the doorway, she cried out in a firm voice, "Hold it right there."

Booted feet assumed a standing position. Armored shins in metallic gray and green.

"Move slowly forward, into the light."

The owner of the legs took one step, then two, revealing a Mandalorian so tall his helmeted head brushed the top of the doorway.

"That's far enough."

"For what?"

Larin maintained her cool in the face of that harsh, inhuman voice, although it was difficult. She'd seen Mandalorians in action before, and she knew how woefully equipped she was to deal with one now. "For you to tell me what you were doing in there."

The domed head inclined slightly. "I was seeking information."

"So you're a bounty hunter?"

"Does it matter what I am?"

"It does when you're messing up my people."

"You do not look like a member of the Black Sun syndicate."

"I never said I was."

"You haven't said you aren't, either." The massive figure shifted slightly, finding a new balance. "I'm seeking information concerning a woman called Lema Xandret."

"Never heard of her."

"Are you certain of that?"

"I thought I was the one asking questions here."

"You thought wrong."

The Mandalorian raised one arm to point at her. A hatch in his sleeve opened, revealing the flamethrower she'd heard in action earlier. She steadied her grip and tried desperately to remember where the weak points on Mandalorian armor were—if there were any . . .

"Don't," said a commanding voice to her left.

Larin glanced automatically and saw a young man in robes standing with one hand raised in the universal *stop* signal.

The sight of him dropped her guard momentarily.

A sheet of powerful flame roared at her. She ducked, and it seared the air bare millimeters over her head.

She let off a round that ricocheted harmlessly from the Mandalorian's chest plate and rolled for cover. It was hard to say what surprised her more: a Jedi down deep in the bowels of Coruscant, or the fact that he had the facial tattoos of a Kiffu native, just like she did.

Shigar took in the confrontation with a glance. He'd never fought a Mandalorian before, but he had been carefully instructed in the art by his Master. They were dangerous, very dangerous, and he almost had second thoughts about taking this one on. Even together, he and a single battered-looking soldier would hardly be sufficient.

Then flame arced across the head of the soldier, and his instincts took over. The soldier ducked for cover with admirable speed. Shigar lunged forward, lightsaber raised to slash at the net that inevitably headed his way. The whine of the suit's jetpack drowned out the angry sizzling of Shigar's blade as he cut himself free. Before the Mandalorian had gained barely a meter of altitude, Shigar Force-pushed him sideways into the building beside him, thereby crushing off the jet's exhaust vent.

With a snarl, the Mandalorian landed heavily on both feet and fired two darts in quick succession, both aimed at Shigar's face. Shigar deflected them and moved closer, dancing lightly on his feet. From a distance, he was at a disadvantage. Mandalorians were masters of ranged weaponry, and would do anything to avoid hand-to-hand combat except in one of their infamous gladiatorial pits. If he could get near enough to strike—with the soldier maintaining a distracting cover fire—he might just get lucky . . .

A rocket exploded above his head, then another. They weren't aimed at him, but at the city's upper levels. Rubble rained down on him, forcing him to protect his head. The Mandalorian took advantage of that slight distraction to dive under his guard and grip him tight about the throat. Shigar's confusion was complete—but Mandalorians weren't *supposed* to fight at close quarters! Then he was literally flying through the air, hurled by his assailant's vast physical strength into a wall.

He landed on both feet, stunned but recovering quickly, and readied himself for another attack.

The Mandalorian ran three long steps to his right, leaping one-two-three onto piles of rubbish and from there onto a roof. More rockets arced upward, tearing through the ferrocrete columns of a monorail. Slender spears of metal warped and fell toward Shigar and the soldier. Only with the greatest exertion of the Force that

Shigar could summon was he able to deflect them into the ground around them, where they stuck fast, quivering.

"He's getting away!"

The soldier's cry was followed by another explosion. A grenade hurled behind the escaping Mandalorian destroyed much of the roof in front of him and sent a huge black mushroom rising into the air. Shigar dived cautiously through it, expecting an ambush, but found the area clear on the far side. He turned in a full circle, banishing the smoke with one out-thrust push.

The Mandalorian was gone. Up, down, sideways—there was no way to tell which direction he had chosen to flee. Shigar reached out through the Force. His heart still hammered, but his breathing was steady and shallow. He felt nothing.

The soldier became visible through the smoke just steps away, moving forward in a cautious crouch. She straightened and planted her feet wide apart. The snout of her rifle targeted him, and for a moment Shigar thought she might actually fire.

"I lost him," he said, unhappily acknowledging their failure.

"Not your fault," she said, lowering the rifle. "We did our best."

"Where did he come from?" he asked.

"I thought it was just the usual Black Sun bust-up," she said, indicating the destroyed building. "Then he walked out."

"Why did he attack you?"

"Beats me. Maybe he assumed I was a justicar."

"You're not one?"

"No. I don't like their methods. And they'll be here soon, so you should get out of here before they decide you're responsible for all this."

That was good advice, he acknowledged to himself. The bloodthirsty militia controlling the lower levels was a law unto itself, one that didn't take kindly to incursions on their territory.

"Let's see what happened here, first," he said, moving toward the smoke-blackened doorway with lightsaber at the ready.

"Why? It's not your problem."

Shigar didn't answer that. Whatever was going on here, neither of them could just walk away from it. He sensed that she would be relieved not to be heading into the building alone.

Together they explored the smoking, shattered ruins. Weapons and bodies lay next to one another in equal proportions. Clearly, the inhabitants had taken up arms against the interloper, and in turn every one of them had died. That was grisly, but not surprising. Mandalorians didn't disapprove of illegals per se, but they did take poorly to being shot at.

On the upper floor, Shigar stopped, sensing something living among the carnage. He raised a hand, cautioning the soldier to proceed more slowly, just in case someone thought they were coming to finish the job. She glided smoothly ahead of him, heedless of danger and with her weapon at the ready. He followed soundlessly in her wake, senses tingling.

They found a single survivor huddled behind a shattered crate, a Nawtolan with blaster burns down much of one side and a dart wound to his neck, lying in a pool of his own blood. The blood was spreading fast. He looked up as Shigar bent over him to check his wounds. What Shigar couldn't tourniquet he could cauterize, but he would have to move fast to have any chance at all.

"Dao Stryver." The Nautolan's voice was a guttural growl, not helped by the damage to his throat. "Came out of nowhere."

"The Mandalorian?" said the soldier. "Is that who you're talking about?"

The Nautolan nodded. "Dao Stryver. Wanted what we had. Wouldn't give it to him."

The soldier took off her helmet. She was surprisingly young, with short dark hair, a strong jaw, and eyes as green as Shigar's lightsaber. Most startling were the distinctive black markings of Clan Moxla tattooed across her dirty cheeks.

"What did you have, exactly?" she pressed the Nautolan.

The Nautolan's eyes rolled up into his head. "*Cinzia*," he coughed, spraying dark blood across the front of her armor. "*Cinzia.*"

"And that is. . . ?" she asked, leaning close as his breathing failed. "Hold on—help's coming—just hold on!"

Shigar leaned back. There was nothing he could do, not without a proper medpac. The Nautolan had said his last.

"I'm sorry," he said.

"You've no reason to be," she said, staring down at her hands. "He was a member of the Black Sun, probably a murderer himself."

"Does that make him evil? Lack of food might have done that, or medicine for his family, or a thousand other things."

"Bad choices don't make bad people. Right. But what else do we have to go on down here? Sometimes you have to make a stand, even if you can't tell who the bad guys are anymore."

A desperately fatigued look crossed her face, then, and Shigar thought that he understood her a little better. Justice was important, and so was the way people defended it, even if that meant fighting alone sometimes.

"My name is Shigar," he said in a calming voice.

"Nice to meet you, Shigar," she said, brightening. "And thanks. You probably saved my life back there."

"I can't take any credit for that. I'm sure he didn't consider either of us worthy opponents."

"Or maybe he worked out that we didn't know anything about what he was looking for in the safehouse. Lema Xandret: that was the name he used on me. Ever heard of it?"

"No. Not *Cinzia*, either."

She rose to her feet in one movement and cocked her rifle onto her back. "Larin, by the way."

Her grip was surprisingly strong. "Our clans were enemies, once," Shigar said.

"Ancient history is the least of our troubles. We'd better move out before the justicars get here."

He looked around him, at the Nautolan, the other bodies, and the wrecked building. Dao Stryver. Lema Xandret. *Cinzia*.

"I'm going to talk to my Master," he said. "She should know there's a Mandalorian making trouble on Coruscant."

"All right," she said, hefting her helmet. "Lead the way."

"You're coming with me?"

"Never trust a Konshi. That's what my mother always said. And if we're going to stop a war between Dao Stryver and the Black Sun, we have to do it right. Right?"

He barely caught her smile before it disappeared behind her helmet.

"Right," he said.

ABOUT THE AUTHOR

SEAN WILLIAMS is the #1 *New York Times* bestselling and award-winning author of more than sixty published short stories and thirty novels, including *Star Wars: The Force Unleashed* and the *Star Wars New Jedi Order: Force Heretic* novels (co-written with Shane Dix): *Remnant, Refugee,* and *Reunion.* He is a judge for the Writers of the Future contest, which he won in 1993. He is also a multiple winner of Australia's speculative fiction awards and recently received both the Ditmar and the Aurealis for *The Crooked Letter,* marking the first time in the history of the awards that a fantasy novel has won both. Williams lives with writer Kirsty Brooks in Adelaide, South Australia.

www.seanwilliams.com.au

ABOUT THE TYPE

This book was set in Sabon, a typeface designed by the well-known German typographer Jan Tschichold (1902–74). Sabon's design is based upon the original letter forms of Claude Garamond and was created specifically to be used for three sources: foundry type for hand composition, Linotype, and Monotype. Tschichold named his typeface for the famous Frankfurt typefounder Jacques Sabon, who died in 1580.

SIEGE of
DARKNESS

R. A. Salvatore

SIEGE OF DARKNESS

First Printing: August 1994
Printed in the United States of America
Library of Congress Number: 93-61467

9 8 7 6 5 4 3 2 1

ISBN: 1-56076-888-6

TSR, Inc.   TSR Ltd.
P.O. Box 756   120 Church End, Cherry Hinton
Lake Geneva, WI 53147   Cambridge CB1 3LB
U.S.A.   United Kingdom

Books by
R. A. Salvatore

The Icewind Dale Trilogy
The Crystal Shard
Streams of Silver
The Halfling's Gem

The Dark Elf Trilogy
Homeland
Exile
Sojourn

The Cleric Quintet
Canticle
In Sylvan Shadows
Night Masks
The Fallen Fortress
The Chaos Curse

The Legacy
Starless Night
Siege of Darkness

PROLOGUE

y all appearances, she was too fair a creature to be walking through the swirling sludge of this smoky layer of the Abyss. Too beautiful, her features were sculpted fine and delicate, her shining ebony skin giving her the appearance of animated artwork, an obsidian sculpture come to life.

The monstrous things around her, crawling slugs and bat-winged denizens, monitored her every move, watched her carefully, cautiously. Even the largest and strongest of them, gigantic fiends that could sack a fair-sized city, kept a safe distance, for appearances could be deceiving. While this fine-featured female seemed delicate, even frail by the standards of the gruesome monsters of the Abyss, she could easily destroy any one, any ten, any fifty, of the fiends now watching her.

They knew it, too, and her passage was unhindered. She was Lloth, the Spider Queen, goddess of the drow, the dark elves. She was chaos incarnate, an instrument of destruction, a monster beneath a delicate facade.

R. A. Salvatore

Lloth calmly strolled into a region of tall, thick mushrooms clustered on small islands amid the grimy swirl. She walked from island to island without concern, stepping so lightly about the slurping sludge that not even the bottoms of her delicate black slippers were soiled. She found many of this level's strongest inhabitants, even true tanar'ri fiends, sleeping amid those mushroom groves, and roused them rudely. Inevitably, the irritable creatures came awake snarling and promising eternal torture, and just as inevitably, they were much relieved when Lloth demanded of them only a single answer to a single question.

"Where is he?" she asked each time, and, though none of the monsters knew of the great fiend's exact location, their answers led Lloth on, guided her until at last she found the beast she was looking for, a huge bipedal tanar'ri with a canine maw, the horns of a bull, and tremendous, leathery wings folded behind its huge body. Looking quite bored, it sat in a chair it had carved from one of the mushrooms, its grotesque head resting on the upraised palm of one hand. Dirty, curved claws scratched rhythmically against its pallid cheek. In its other hand the beast held a many-tongued whip and, every so often, snapped it about, lashing at the side of the mushroom chair, where crouched the unfortunate lesser creature it had selected for torture during this point of eternity.

The smaller denizen yelped and whined pitifully, and that drew another stinging crack of the merciless fiend's whip.

The seated beast grunted suddenly, head coming up alert, red eyes peering intently into the smoky veil swirling all about the mushroom throne. Something was about, it knew, something powerful.

Lloth walked into view, not slowing in the least as she regarded this monster, the greatest of this area.

A guttural growl escaped the tanar'ri's lips, lips that curled into an evil smile, then turned down into a frown as it considered the pretty morsel walking into its lair. At first, the fiend thought Lloth a gift, a lost, wandering dark elf far from the Material Plane and her home. It didn't take the fiend long to recognize the truth of this one, though.

It sat up straight in its chair. Then, with incredible speed and fluidity for one its size, it brought itself to its full height, twelve feet, and towered over the intruder.

"Sit, Errtu," Lloth bade it, waving her hand impatiently. "I have

2

not come to destroy you."

A second growl issued from the proud tanar'ri, but Errtu made no move for Lloth, understanding that she could easily do what she had just claimed she had not come here to do. Just to salvage a bit of his pride, Errtu remained standing.

"Sit!" Lloth said suddenly, fiercely, and Errtu, before he registered the movement, found himself back on the mushroom throne. Frustrated, he took up his whip and battered the sniveling beast that groveled at his side.

"Why are you here, drow?" Errtu grumbled, his deep voice breaking into higher, crackling whines, like fingernails on slate.

"You have heard the rumblings of the pantheon?" Lloth asked.

Errtu considered the question for a long moment. Of course he had heard that the gods of the Realms were quarreling, stepping over each other in intrigue-laden power grabs and using intelligent lesser creatures as pawns in their private games. In the Abyss, this meant that the denizens, even greater tanar'ri such as Errtu, were often caught up in unwanted political intrigue.

Which was exactly what Errtu figured, and feared, was happening here.

"A time of great strife is approaching," Lloth explained. "A time when the gods will pay for their foolishness."

Errtu chuckled, a grating, terrible sound. Lloth's red-glowing gaze fell over him scornfully.

"Why would such an event displease you, Lady of Chaos?" the fiend asked.

"This trouble will be beyond me," Lloth explained, deadly serious, "beyond us all. I will enjoy watching the fools of the pantheon jostled about, stripped of their false pride, some perhaps even slain, but any worshipped being who is not cautious will find herself caught in the trouble."

"Lloth was never known for caution," Errtu put in dryly.

"Lloth was never a fool," the Spider Queen quickly replied.

Errtu nodded but sat quietly for a moment on his mushroom throne, digesting it all. "What has this to do with me?" he asked finally, for tanar'ri were not worshipped, and, thus, Errtu did not draw his powers from the prayers of any faithful.

"Menzoberranzan," Lloth replied, naming the fabled city of drow, the largest base of her worshippers in all the Realms.

Errtu cocked his grotesque head.

"The city is in chaos already," Lloth explained.

"As you would have it," Errtu put in, and he snickered. "As you have arranged it."

Lloth didn't refute that. "But there is danger," the beautiful drow went on. "If I am caught in the troubles of the pantheon, the prayers of my priestesses will go unanswered."

"Am I expected to answer them?" Errtu asked incredulously.

"The faithful will need protection."

"I cannot go to Menzoberranzan!" Errtu roared suddenly, his outrage, the outrage of years of banishment, spilling over. Menzoberranzan was a city of Faerun's Underdark, the great labyrinth beneath the world's surface. But, though it was separated from the region of sunlight by miles of thick rock, it was still a place of the Material Plane. Years ago, Errtu had been on that plane, at the call of a minor wizard, and had stayed there in search of Crenshinibon, the Crystal Shard, a mighty artifact, relic of a past and greater age of sorcery. The great tanar'ri had been so close to the relic! He had entered the tower it had created in its image, and had worked with its possessor, a pitiful human who would have died soon enough, leaving the fiend to his coveted treasure. But then Errtu had met a dark elf, a renegade from Lloth's own flock, from Menzoberranzan, the city she now apparently wanted him to protect!

Drizzt Do'Urden had defeated Errtu and, to a tanar'ri, a defeat on the Material Plane meant a hundred years of banishment in the Abyss.

Now Errtu trembled visibly with rage, and Lloth took a step backward, preparing herself in case the beast attacked before she could explain her offer. "You cannot go," she agreed, "but your minions can. I will see that a gate is kept open, if all the priestesses of my domain must tend it continually."

Errtu's thunderous roar drowned out the words.

Lloth understood the source of that agony; a fiend's greatest pleasure was to walk loose on the Material Plane, to challenge the weak souls and weaker bodies of the various races. Lloth understood, but she did not sympathize. Evil Lloth never sympathized with any creature.

"I cannot deny you!" Errtu admitted, and his great, bulbous, bloodshot eyes narrowed wickedly.

His statement was true enough. Lloth could enlist his aid simply by offering him his very existence in return. The Spider Queen was smarter than that, however. If she enslaved Errtu and was, indeed, as she expected, caught up in the coming storm, Errtu might escape her capture or, worse, find a way to strike back at her. Lloth was malicious and merciless in the extreme, but she was, above all else, intelligent. She had in her possession honey for this fly.

"This is no threat," she said honestly to the fiend. "This is an offer."

Errtu did not interrupt, still, the bored and outraged fiend trembled on the edge of catastrophe.

"I have a gift, Errtu," she purred, "a gift that will allow you to end the banishment Drizzt Do'Urden has placed on you."

The tanar'ri did not seem convinced. "No gift," he rumbled. "No magic can break the terms of banishment. Only he who banished me can end the indenture."

Lloth nodded her agreement; not even a goddess had the power to go against that rule. "But that is exactly the point!" the Spider Queen exclaimed. "This gift will make Drizzt Do'Urden want you back on his plane of existence, back within his reach."

Errtu did not seem convinced.

In response, Lloth lifted one arm and clamped her fist tightly, and a signal, a burst of multicolored sparks and a rocking blast of thunder, shook the swirling sludge and momentarily stole the perpetual gray of the dismal level.

Forlorn and beaten, head down—for it did not take one such as Lloth very long to sunder the pride—he walked from the fog. Errtu did not know him, but understood the significance of this gift.

Lloth clamped her fist tight again, another explosive signal sounded, and her captive fell back into the veil of smoke.

Errtu eyed the Spider Queen suspiciously. The tanar'ri was more than a little interested, of course, but he realized that most everyone who had ever trusted the diabolical Lloth had paid greatly for their foolishness. Still, this bait was too great for Errtu to resist. His canine maw turned up into a grotesque, wicked smile.

"Look upon Menzoberranzan," Lloth said, and she waved her arm before the thick stalk of a nearby mushroom. The plant's fibers became glassy, reflecting the smoke, and, a moment later, Lloth and the fiend saw the city of drow. "Your role in this will be small, I assure you," Lloth said, "but vital. Do not fail me, great Errtu!"

It was as much a threat as a plea, the fiend knew.

"The gift?" he asked.

"When things are put aright."

Again a suspicious look crossed Errtu's huge face.

"Drizzt Do'Urden is a pittance," Lloth said. "Daermon N'a'shezbaernon, his family, is no more, so he means nothing to me. Still, it would please me to watch great and evil Errtu pay back the renegade for all the inconveniences he has caused."

Errtu was not stupid, far from it. What Lloth was saying made perfect sense, yet he could not ignore the fact that it was Lloth, the Spider Queen, the Lady of Chaos, who was making these tempting offers.

Neither could he ignore the fact that her gift promised him relief from the interminable boredom. He could beat a thousand minor fiends a day, every day, torture them and send them crawling pitifully into the muck. But if he did that for a million days, it would not equal the pleasure of a single hour on the Material Plane, walking among the weak, tormenting those who did not deserve his vengeance.

The great tanar'ri agreed.

Part 1

RUMBLES OF DISCORD

R. A. Salvatore

 watched the preparations unfolding at Mithril Hall, preparations for war, for, though we, especially Catti-brie, had dealt House Baenre a stinging defeat back in Menzoberranzan, none of us doubted that the dark elves might come our way once more. Above all else, Matron Baenre was likely angry, and having spent my youth in Menzoberranzan, I knew it was not a good thing to make an enemy of the first matron mother.

Still, I liked what I was seeing here in the dwarven stronghold. Most of all, I enjoyed the spectacle of Bruenor Battlehammer.

Bruenor! My dearest friend. The dwarf I had fought beside since my days in Icewind Dale—days that seemed very long ago indeed! I had feared Bruenor's spirit forever broken when Wulfgar fell, that the fire that had guided this most stubborn of dwarves through seemingly insurmountable obstacles in his quest to reclaim his lost homeland had been forever doused. Not so, I learned in those days of preparation. Bruenor's physical scars were deeper now—his left eye was lost, and a bluish line ran diagonally across his face, from forehead to jawbone—but the flames of spirit had been rekindled, burning bright behind his good eye.

Bruenor directed the preparations, from agreeing to the fortification designs being constructed in the lowest tunnels to sending out emissaries to the neighboring settlements in search of allies. He asked for no help in the decision-making, and needed none, for this was Bruenor, Eighth King of Mithril Hall, a veteran of so many adventures, a dwarf who had earned his title.

Now his grief was gone; he was king again, to the joy of his friends and subjects. "Let the damned drow come!" Bruenor growled quite often, and always he nodded in my direction if I was about, as if to remind me that he meant no personal insult.

In truth, that determined war cry from Bruenor Battlehammer was among the sweetest things I had ever heard.

What was it, I wondered, that had brought the grieving dwarf from his despair? And it wasn't just Bruenor; all about me I saw an excitement, in the dwarves, in Catti-brie, even in Regis, the halfling known more for preparing for lunch and nap than for war. I felt it, too. That tingling anticipation, that camaraderie that had me and all the others patting each other on the back, offering praises for the simplest of additions to the common defense, and raising our voices together in cheer whenever good news was announced.

What was it? It was more than shared fear, more than giving thanks for what we had while realizing that it might soon be stolen away. I didn't understand it then, in that time of frenzy, in that euphoria of frantic preparations. Now, looking back, it is an easy thing to recognize.

It was hope.

To any intelligent being, there is no emotion more important than hope. Individually or collectively, we must hope that the future will be better than the past, that our offspring, and theirs after them, will be a bit closer to an ideal society, whatever our perception of that might be. Certainly a warrior barbarian's hope for the future might differ from the ideal fostered in the imagination of a peaceful farmer. And a dwarf would not strive to live in a world that resembled an elf's ideal! But the hope itself is not so different. It is at those times when we feel we are contributing to that ultimate end, as it was in Mithril Hall when we believed the battle with Menzoberranzan would soon come—that we would defeat the dark elves and end, once and for all, the threat from the Underdark city—we feel true elation.

Hope is the key. The future will be better than the past, or the present. Without this belief, there is only the self-indulgent, ultimately empty striving of the present, as in drow society, or simple despair, the time of life wasted in waiting for death.

Bruenor had found a cause—we all had—and never have I been more alive than in those days of preparation in Mithril Hall.

—Drizzt Do'Urden

9

Chapter 1
DIPLOMACY

er thick auburn hair bouncing below her shoulders, Catti-brie worked furiously to keep the drow's whirling scimitars at bay. She was a solidly built woman, a hundred and thirty pounds of muscles finely toned from living her life with Bruenor's dwarven clan. Catti-brie was no stranger to the forge or the sledge.

Or the sword, and this new blade, its white-metal pommel sculpted in the likeness of a unicorn's head, was by far the most balanced weapon she had ever swung. Still, Catti-brie was hard-pressed, indeed, overmatched, by her opponent this day. Few in the Realms could match blades with Drizzt Do'Urden, the drow ranger.

He was no larger than Catti-brie, a few pounds heavier perhaps, with his tight-muscled frame. His white hair hung as low as Catti-brie's mane and was equally thick, and his ebony skin glistened with streaks of sweat, a testament to the young woman's prowess.

Drizzt's two scimitars crossed in front of him (one of them glowing a fierce blue even through the protective padding that covered it), then went back out wide, inviting Catti-brie to thrust straight between.

She knew better than to make the attempt. Drizzt was too quick, and could strike her blade near its tip with one scimitar, while the other alternately parried low, batting the opposite way near the hilt. With a single step diagonally to the side, following his closer-parrying blade, Drizzt would have her beaten.

Catti-brie stepped back instead, and presented her sword in front of her. Her deep blue eyes peeked out around the blade, which had been thickened with heavy material, and she locked stares with the drow's lavender orbs.

"An opportunity missed?" Drizzt teased.

"A trap avoided," Catti-brie was quick to reply.

Drizzt came ahead in a rush, his blades crossing, going wide, and cutting across, one high and one low. Catti-brie dropped her left foot behind her and fell into a crouch, turning her sword to parry the low-rushing blade, dipping her head to avoid the high.

She needn't have bothered, for the cross came too soon, before Drizzt's feet had caught up to the move, and both his scimitars swished through the air, short of the mark.

Catti-brie didn't miss the opening, and darted ahead, sword thrusting.

Back snapped Drizzt's blades, impossibly fast, slamming the sword on both its sides. But Drizzt's feet weren't positioned correctly for him to follow the move, to go diagonally ahead and take advantage of Catti-brie's turned sword.

The young woman went ahead and to the side instead, sliding her weapon free of the clinch and executing the real attack, the slash at Drizzt's hip.

Drizzt's backhand caught her short, drove her sword harmlessly high.

They broke apart again, eyeing each other, Catti-brie wearing a sly smile. In all their months of training, she had never come so close to scoring a hit on the agile and skilled drow.

Drizzt's expression stole her glory, though, and the drow dipped the tips of his scimitars toward the floor, shaking his head in frustration.

"The bracers?" Catti-brie asked, referring to the magical wrist bands, wide pieces of black material lined with gleaming mithril rings. Drizzt had taken them from Dantrag Baenre, the deposed weapon master of Menzoberranzan's first house, after defeating Dantrag in mortal combat. Rumors said those marvelous bracers allowed Dantrag's hands to move incredibly fast, giving him the advantage in combat.

Upon battling the lightning-quick Baenre, Drizzt had come to believe those rumors, and after wearing the bracers in sparring for the last few weeks, he had confirmed their abilities. But Drizzt wasn't convinced that the bracers were a good thing. In the fight with Dantrag, he had turned Dantrag's supposed advantage against the drow, for the weapon master's hands moved too quickly for Dantrag to alter any started move, too quickly for Dantrag to improvise if his opponent made an unexpected turn. Now, in these sparring exercises, Drizzt was learning that the bracers held another disadvantage.

His feet couldn't keep up with his hands.

"Ye'll learn them," Catti-brie assured.

Drizzt wasn't so certain. "Fighting is an art of balance and movement," he explained.

"And faster ye are!" Catti-brie replied.

Drizzt shook his head. "Faster are my hands," he said. "A warrior does not win with his hands. He wins with his feet, by positioning himself to best strike the openings in his opponent's defenses."

"The feet'll catch up," Catti-brie replied. "Dantrag was the best Menzoberranzan had to offer, and ye said yerself that the bracers were the reason."

Drizzt couldn't disagree that the bracers greatly aided Dantrag, but he wondered how much they would benefit one of his skill, or one of Zaknafein's, his father's, skill. It could be, Drizzt realized, that the bracers would aid a lesser fighter, one who needed to depend on the sheer speed of his weapons. But the complete fighter, the master who had found harmony between all his muscles, would be put off balance. Or perhaps the bracers would aid someone wielding a heavier weapon, a mighty warhammer, such as Aegis-fang. Drizzt's scimitars, slender blades of no more than two pounds of metal, perfectly balanced by both workmanship and enchantment, weaved effortlessly, and, even without the bracers, his hands were quicker than his feet.

"Come on then," Catti-brie scolded, waving her sword in front of her, her wide blue eyes narrowing intently, her shapely hips swiveling as she fell into a low balance.

She sensed her chance, Drizzt realized. She knew he was fighting at a disadvantage and finally sensed her chance to pay back one of the many stinging hits he had given her in their sparring.

Drizzt took a deep breath and lifted the blades. He owed it to Catti-brie to oblige, but he meant to make her earn it!

He came forward slowly, playing defensively. Her sword shot out, and he hit it twice before it ever got close, on its left side with his right hand, and on its left side again, bringing his left hand right over the presented blade and batting it with a downward parry.

Catti-brie fell with the momentum of the double block, spinning a complete circle, rotating away from her adversary. When she came around, predictably, Drizzt was in close, scimitars weaving.

Still the patient drow measured his attack, did not come too fast and strong. His blades crossed and went out wide, teasing the young woman.

Catti-brie growled and threw her sword straight out again, determined to find that elusive hole. And in came the scimitars, striking in rapid succession, again both hitting the left side of Catti-brie's sword. As before, Catti-brie spun to the right, but this time Drizzt came in hard.

Down went the young woman in a low crouch, her rear grazing the floor, and she skittered back. Both of Drizzt's blades swooshed through the air above and before her, for again his cuts came before his feet could rightly respond and position him.

Drizzt was amazed to find that Catti-brie was no longer in front of him.

He called the move the "Ghost Step," and had taught it to Catti-brie only a week earlier. The trick was to use the opponent's swinging weapon as an optical shield, to move within the vision-blocked area so perfectly and quickly that your opponent would not know you had come forward and to the side, that you had, in fact, stepped behind his leading hip.

Reflexively, the drow snapped his leading scimitar straight back, blade pointed low, for Catti-brie had gone past in a crouch. He beat the sword to the mark, too quickly, and the momentum of

13

his scimitar sent it sailing futilely in front of the coming attack.

Drizzt winced as the unicorn-handled sword slapped hard against his hip.

For Catti-brie, the moment was one of pure delight. She knew, of course, that the bracers were hindering Drizzt, causing him to make mistakes of balance—mistakes that Drizzt Do'Urden hadn't made since his earliest days of fighting—but even with the uncomfortable bracers, the drow was a powerful adversary, and could likely defeat most swordsmen.

How delicious it was, then, when Catti-brie found her new sword slicing in unhindered!

Her joy was stolen momentarily by an urge to sink the blade deeper, a sudden, inexplicable anger focused directly on Drizzt.

"Touch!" Drizzt called, the signal that he had been hit, and when Catti-brie straightened and sorted out the scene, she found the drow standing a few feet away, rubbing his sore hip.

"Sorry," she apologized, realizing she had struck far too hard.

"Not to worry," Drizzt replied slyly. "Surely your one hit does not equal the combined pains my scimitars have caused you." The dark elf's lips curled up into a mischievous smile. "Or the pains I will surely inflict on you in return!"

"Me thinking's that I'm catching ye, Drizzt Do'Urden," Catti-brie answered calmly, confidently. "Ye'll get yer hits, but ye'll take yer hits as well!"

They both laughed at that, and Catti-brie moved to the side of the room and began to remove her practice gear.

Drizzt slid the padding from one of his scimitars and considered those last words. Catti-brie was indeed improving, he agreed. She had a warrior's heart, tempered by a poet's philosophy, a deadly combination indeed. Catti-brie, like Drizzt, would rather talk her way out of a battle than wage it, but when the avenues of diplomacy were exhausted, when the fight became a matter of survival, then the young woman would fight with conscience clear and passion heated. All her heart and all her skill would come to bear, and in Catti-brie, both of those ingredients were considerable.

And she was barely into her twenties! In Menzoberranzan, had she been a drow, she would be in Arach-Tinilith now, the school of Lloth, her strong morals being assaulted daily by the lies of the

Spider Queen's priestesses. Drizzt shook that thought away; he didn't even want to think of Catti-brie in that awful place. Suppose she had gone to the drow school of fighters, Melee-Magthere, instead, he mused. How would she fare against the likes of young drow?

Well, Drizzt decided, Catti-brie would be near the top of her class, certainly among the top ten or fifteen percent, and her passion and dedication would get her there. How much could she improve under his tutelage? Drizzt wondered, and his expression soured as he considered the limitations of Catti-brie's heritage. He was in his sixties, barely more than a child by drow standards, for they could live to see seven centuries, but when Catti-brie reached his tender age, she would be old, too old to fight well.

That notion pained Drizzt greatly. Unless the blade of an enemy or the claws of a monster shortened his life, he would watch Catti-brie grow old, would watch her pass from this life.

Drizzt looked at her now as she removed the padded baldric and unclasped the metal collar guard. Under the padding above the waist, she wore only a simple shirt of light material. It was wet with perspiration now and clung to her.

She was a warrior, Drizzt agreed, but she was also a beautiful young woman, shapely and strong, with the spirit of a foal first learning to run and a heart filled with passion.

The sound of distant furnaces, the sudden, increased ringing of hammer on steel, should have alerted Drizzt that the room's door had opened, but it simply didn't register in the distracted drow's consciousness.

"Hey!" came a roar from the side of the chamber, and Drizzt turned to see Bruenor storm into the room. He half expected the dwarf, Catti-brie's adoptive, overprotective, father, to demand what in the Nine Hells Drizzt was looking at, and Drizzt's sigh was one of pure relief when Bruenor, his fiery red beard foamed with spittle, instead took up a tirade about Settlestone, the barbarian settlement south of Mithril Hall.

Still, the drow figured he was blushing (and hoped that his ebon-hued skin would hide it) as he shook his head, ran his fingers through his white hair to brush it back from his face, and likewise began to remove the practice gear.

Catti-brie walked over, shaking her thick auburn mane to get the droplets out. "Berkthgar is being difficult?" she reasoned, referring to Berkthgar the Bold, Settlestone's new chieftain.

Bruenor snorted. "Berkthgar can't be anything but difficult!"

Drizzt looked up at beautiful Catti-brie. He didn't want to picture her growing old, though he knew she would do it with more grace than most.

"He's a proud one," Catti-brie replied to her father, "and afraid."

"Bah!" Bruenor retorted. "What's he got to be afraid of? Got a couple hunnerd strong men around him and not an enemy in sight."

"He is afraid he will not stand well against the shadow of his predecessor," Drizzt explained, and Catti-brie nodded.

Bruenor stopped in midbluster and considered the drow's words. Berkthgar was living in Wulfgar's shadow, in the shadow of the greatest hero the barbarian tribes of faraway Icewind Dale had ever known. The man who had killed Dracos Icingdeath, the white dragon; the man who, at the tender age of twenty, had united the fierce tribes and shown them a better way of living.

Bruenor didn't believe any human could shine through the spectacle of Wulfgar's shadow, and his resigned nod showed that he agreed with, and ultimately accepted, the truth of the reasoning. A great sadness edged his expression and rimmed his steel-gray eyes, as well, for Bruenor could not think of Wulfgar, the human who had been a son to him, without that sadness.

"On what point is he being difficult?" Drizzt asked, trying to push past the difficult moment.

"On the whole damned alliance," Bruenor huffed.

Drizzt and Catti-brie exchanged curious expressions. It made no sense, of course. The barbarians of Settlestone and the dwarves of Mithril Hall already were allies, working hand in hand, with Bruenor's people mining the precious mithril and shaping it into valuable artifacts, and the barbarians doing the bargaining with merchants from nearby towns, such as Nesme on the Trollmoors, or Silverymoon to the east. The two peoples, Bruenor's and Wulfgar's, had fought together to clear Mithril Hall of evil gray dwarves, the duergar, and the barbarians had come down from their homes in faraway Icewind Dale, resolved to stay, only because of this solid friendship and alliance with Bruenor's clan. It made no sense that Berkthgar was being difficult, not with the prospect of a drow attack hanging over their heads.

"He wants the hammer," Bruenor explained, recognizing Drizzt and Catti-brie's doubts.

That explained everything. The hammer was Wulfgar's hammer, mighty Aegis-fang, which Bruenor himself had forged as a gift for Wulfgar during the years the young man had been indentured to the red-bearded dwarf. During those years, Bruenor, Drizzt, and Catti-brie had taught the fierce young barbarian a better way.

Of course Berkthgar would want Aegis-fang, Drizzt realized. The warhammer had become more than a weapon, had become a symbol to the hardy men and women of Settlestone. Aegis-fang symbolized the memory of Wulfgar, and if Berkthgar could convince Bruenor to let him wield it, his stature among his people would increase tenfold.

It was perfectly logical, but Drizzt knew Berkthgar would never, ever convince Bruenor to give him the hammer.

The dwarf was looking at Catti-brie then, and Drizzt, in regarding her as well, wondered if she was thinking that giving the hammer to the new barbarian leader might be a good thing. How many emotions must be swirling in the young woman's thoughts! Drizzt knew. She and Wulfgar were to have been wed; she and Wulfgar had grown into adulthood together and had learned many of life's lessons side by side. Could Catti-brie now get beyond that, beyond her own grief, and follow a logical course to seal the alliance?

"No," she said finally, resolutely. "The hammer he cannot have."

Drizzt nodded his agreement, and was glad that Catti-brie would not let go of her memories of Wulfgar, of her love for the man. He, too, had loved Wulfgar, as a brother, and he could not picture anyone else, neither Berkthgar nor the god Tempus himself, carrying Aegis-fang.

"Never thought to give it to him," Bruenor agreed. He wagged an angry fist in the air, the muscles of his arm straining with the obvious tension. "But if that half-son of a reindeer asks again, I'll give him something else, don't ye doubt!"

Drizzt saw a serious problem brewing. Berkthgar wanted the

hammer, that was understandable, even expected, but the young, ambitious barbarian leader apparently did not appreciate the depth of his request. This situation could get much worse than a strain on necessary allies, Drizzt knew. This could lead to open fighting between the peoples, for Drizzt did not doubt Bruenor's claim for a moment. If Berkthgar demanded the hammer as ransom for what he should give unconditionally, he'd be lucky to get back into the sunshine with his limbs attached.

"Me and Drizzt'll go to Settlestone," Catti-brie offered. "We'll get Berkthgar's word and give him nothing in return."

"The boy's a fool!" Bruenor huffed.

"But his people are not foolish," Catti-brie added. "He's wanting the hammer to make himself more the leader. We'll teach him that asking for something he cannot have will make him less the leader."

Strong, and passionate, and so wise, Drizzt mused, watching the young woman. She would indeed accomplish what she had claimed. He and Catti-brie would go to Settlestone and return with everything Catti-brie had just promised her father.

The drow blew a long, low sigh as Bruenor and Catti-brie moved off, the young woman going to retrieve her belongings from the side of the room. He watched the renewed hop in Bruenor's step, the life returned to the fiery dwarf. How many years would King Bruenor Battlehammer rule? Drizzt wondered. A hundred? Two hundred?

Unless the blade of an enemy or the claws of a monster shortened his life, the dwarf, too, would watch Catti-brie grow old and pass away.

It was an image that Drizzt, watching the light step of this spirited young foal, could not bear to entertain.

* * * * *

Khazid'hea, or Cutter, rested patiently on Catti-brie's hip, its moment of anger passed. The sentient sword was pleased by the young woman's progress as a fighter. She was able, no doubt, but still Khazid'hea wanted more, wanted to be wielded by the very finest warrior.

Right now, that warrior seemed to be Drizzt Do'Urden.

The sword had gone after Drizzt when the drow renegade had killed its former wielder, Dantrag Baenre. Khazid'hea had altered its pommel, as it usually did, from the sculpted head of a fiend (which had lured Dantrag) to one of a unicorn, knowing that was the symbol of Drizzt Do'Urden's goddess. Still, the drow ranger had bade Catti-brie take the sword, for he favored the scimitar.

Favored the scimitar!

How Khazid'hea wished that it might alter its blade as it could the pommel! If the weapon could curve its blade, shorten and thicken it . . .

But Khazid'hea could not, and Drizzt would not wield a sword. The woman was good, though, and getting better. She was human, and would not likely live long enough to attain as great a proficiency as Drizzt, but if the sword could compel her to slay the drow . . .

There were many ways to become the best.

* * * * *

Matron Baenre, withered and too old to be alive, even for a drow, stood in the great chapel of Menzoberranzan's first house, her house, watching the slow progress as her slave workers tried to extract the fallen stalactite from the roof of the dome-shaped structure. The place would soon be repaired, she knew. The rubble on the floor had already been cleared away, and the bloodstains of the dozen drow killed in the tragedy had long ago been scoured clean.

But the pain of that moment, of Matron Baenre's supreme embarrassment in front of every important matron mother of Menzoberranzan, in the very moment of the first matron mother's pinnacle of power, lingered. The spearlike stalactite had cut into the roof, but it might as well have torn Matron Baenre's own heart. She had forged an alliance between the warlike houses of the drow city, a joining solidified by the promise of new glory when the drow army conquered Mithril Hall.

New glory for the Spider Queen. New glory for Matron Baenre.

Shattered by the point of a stalactite, by the escape of that renegade Drizzt Do'Urden. To Drizzt she had lost her eldest son,

Dantrag, perhaps the finest weapon master in Menzoberranzan. To Drizzt she had lost her daughter, wicked Vendes. And, most painful of all to the old wretch, she had lost to Drizzt and his friends the alliance, the promise of greater glory. For when the matron mothers, the rulers of Menzoberranzan and priestesses all, had watched the stalactite pierce the roof of this chapel, this most sacred place of Lloth, at the time of high ritual, their confidence that the goddess had sanctioned both this alliance and the coming war had crumbled. They had left House Baenre in a rush, back to their own houses, where they sealed their gates and tried to discern the will of Lloth.

Matron Baenre's status had suffered greatly.

Even with all that had happened, though, the first matron mother was confident she could restore the alliance. On a necklace about her neck she kept a ring carved from the tooth of an ancient dwarven king, one Gandalug Battlehammer, patron of Clan Battlehammer, founder of Mithril Hall. Matron Baenre owned Gandalug's spirit and could exact answers from it about the ways of the dwarven mines. Despite Drizzt's escape, the dark elves could go to Mithril Hall, could punish Drizzt and his friends.

She could restore the alliance, but for some reason that Matron Baenre did not understand, Lloth, the Spider Queen herself, held her in check. The yochlol, the handmaidens of Lloth, had come to Baenre and warned her to forego the alliance and instead focus her attention on her family, to secure her house defenses. It was a demand no priestess of the Spider Queen would dare disobey.

She heard the harsh clicking of hard boots on the floor behind her and the jingle of ample jewelry, and she didn't have to turn about to know that Jarlaxle had entered.

"You have done as I asked?" she questioned, still looking at the continuing work on the domed ceiling.

"Greetings to you as well, First Matron Mother," the always sarcastic male replied. That turned Baenre to face him, and she scowled, as she and so many other of Menzoberranzan's ruling females scowled when they looked at the mercenary.

He was swaggering—there was no other word to describe him. The dark elves of Menzoberranzan, particularly the lowly males, normally donned quiet, practical clothes, dark-hued robes adorned with spiders or webs, or plain black jerkins beneath supple chain mail armor. And, almost always, both male and female drow wore camouflaging *piwafwis*, dark cloaks that could hide them from the probing eyes of their many enemies.

Not so with Jarlaxle. His head was shaven and always capped by an outrageous wide-brimmed hat feathering the gigantic plume of a diatryma bird. In lieu of a cloak or robe, he wore a shimmering cape that flickered through every color of the spectrum, both in light and under the scrutiny of heat-sensing eyes looking in the infrared range. His sleeveless vest was cut high to show the tight muscles of his stomach, and he carried an assortment of rings and necklaces, bracelets, even anklets, that chimed gratingly—but only when the mercenary wanted them to. Like his boots, which had sounded so clearly on the hard chapel floor, the jewelry could be silenced completely.

Matron Baenre noted that the mercenary's customary eye patch was over his left eye this day, but what, if anything, that signified, she could not tell.

For who knew what magic was in that patch, or in those jewels and those boots, or in the two wands he wore tucked under his belt, and the fine sword he kept beside them? Half those items, even one of the wands, Matron Baenre believed, were likely fakes, with little or no magical properties other than, perhaps, the ability to fall silent. Half of everything Jarlaxle did was a bluff, but half of it was devious and ultimately deadly.

That was why the swaggering mercenary was so dangerous.

That was why Matron Baenre hated Jarlaxle so, and why she needed him so. He was the leader of Bregan D'aerthe, a network of spies, thieves, and killers, mostly rogue males made houseless when their families had been wiped out in one of the many inter-house wars. As mysterious as their dangerous leader, Bregan D'aerthe's members were not known, but they were indeed very powerful—as powerful as most of the city's established houses—and very effective.

"What have you learned?" Matron Baenre asked bluntly.

"It would take me centuries to spew it all," the cocky rogue replied.

Baenre's red-glowing eyes narrowed, and Jarlaxle realized she was not in the mood for his flippancy. She was scared, he knew, and, considering the catastrophe at the high ritual, rightly so.

21

"I find no conspiracy," the mercenary honestly admitted.

Matron Baenre's eyes widened, and she swayed back on her heels, surprised by the straightforward answer. She had enacted spells that would allow her to detect any outright lies the mercenary spoke, of course. And of course, Jarlaxle would know that. Those spells never seemed to bother the crafty mercenary leader, who could dance around the perimeters of any question, never quite telling the truth, but never overtly lying.

This time, though, he had answered bluntly, and right to the heart of the obvious question. And as far as Matron Baenre could tell, he was telling the truth.

Baenre could not accept it. Perhaps her spell was not functioning as intended. Perhaps Lloth had indeed abandoned her for her failure, and was thus deceiving her now concerning Jarlaxle's sincerity.

"Matron Mez'Barris Armgo," Jarlaxle went on, referring to the matron mother of Barrison del'Armgo, the city's second house, "remains loyal to you, and to your cause, despite the . . ." He fished about for the correct word. "The disturbance," he said at length, "to the high ritual. Matron Mez'Barris is even ordering her garrison to keep on the ready in case the march to Mithril Hall is resumed. And they are more than eager to go, I can assure you, especially with . . ." The mercenary paused and sighed with mock sadness, and Matron Baenre understood his reasoning.

Logically, Mez'Barris would be eager to go to Mithril Hall, for with Dantrag Baenre dead, her own weapon master, mighty Uthegental, was indisputably the greatest in the city. If Uthegental could get the rogue Do'Urden, what glories House Barrison del'Armgo might know!

Yet that very logic, and Jarlaxle's apparently honest claim, flew in the face of Matron Baenre's fears, for without the assistance of Barrison del'Armgo, no combination of houses in Menzoberranzan could threaten House Baenre.

"The minor shuffling among your surviving children has commenced, of course," Jarlaxle went on. "But they have had little contact, and if any of them plan to move against you, it will be without the aid of Triel, who has been kept busy in the Academy since the escape of the rogue."

Matron Baenre did well to hide her relief at that statement. If Triel, the most powerful of her daughters, and certainly the one most in Lloth's favor, was not planning to rise against her, a coup from within seemed unlikely.

"It is expected that you will soon name Berg'inyon as weapon master, and Gromph will not oppose," Jarlaxle remarked.

Matron Baenre nodded her agreement. Gromph was her elder-boy, and as Archmage of Menzoberranzan, he held more power than any male in the city (except for, perhaps, sly Jarlaxle). Gromph would not disapprove of Berg'inyon as weapon master of House Baenre. The ranking of Baenre's daughters seemed secure as well, she had to admit. Triel was in place as Mistress Mother of Arach-Tinilith in the Academy, and, though those remaining in the house might squabble over the duties and powers left vacant by the loss of Vendes, it didn't seem likely to concern her.

Matron Baenre looked back to the spike Drizzt and his companions had put through the ceiling, and was not satisfied. In cruel and merciless Menzoberranzan, satisfaction and the smugness that inevitably accompanied it too often led to an untimely demise.

Chapter 2

THE GUTBUSTER BRIGADE

e're thinking we'll need the thing?" Catti-brie asked as she and Drizzt made their way along the lower levels of Mithril Hall. They moved along a corridor that opened wide to their left, into the great tiered cavern housing the famed dwarven Undercity.

Drizzt paused and regarded her, then went to the left, drawing Catti-brie behind him. He stepped through the opening, emerging on the second tier up from the huge cavern's floor.

The place was bustling, with dwarves running every which way, shouting to be heard over the continual hum of great pumping bellows and the determined ring of hammer on mithril. This was the heart of Mithril Hall, a huge, open cavern cut into gigantic steps on both its east and west walls, so that the whole place resembled an inverted pyramid. The widest floor area was the lowest level, between the gigantic steps, housing the huge furnaces. Strong dwarves pulled carts laden with ore along prescribed routes, while others worked the many levers of the intricate ovens, and still others tugged smaller carts of finished metals up to the tiers. There the various craftsman pounded the ore into useful items. Normally, a great variety of goods would be produced here—fine silverware, gem-studded chalices, and ornate helmets—gorgeous but of little practical use. Now, though, with war hanging over their heads, the dwarves focused on weapons and true defensive armor. Twenty feet to the side of Drizzt and Catti-brie, a dwarf so soot-covered that the color of his beard was not distinguishable leaned another iron-shafted, mithril-tipped ballista bolt against the wall. The dwarf couldn't even reach the top of the eight-foot spear, but he regarded its barbed and many-edged tip and chuckled. No doubt he enjoyed a fantasy concerning its flight and little drow elves all standing in a row.

On one of the arcing bridges spanning the tiers, perhaps a hundred and fifty feet up from the two friends, a substantial argument broke out. Drizzt and Catti-brie could not make out the words above the general din, but they realized that it had to do with plans for dropping that bridge, and most of the other bridges, forcing any invading dark elves along certain routes if they intended to reach the complex's higher levels.

None of them, not Drizzt, Catti-brie, or any of Bruenor's people, hoped it would ever come to that.

The two friends exchanged knowing looks. Rarely in the long history of Mithril Hall had the Undercity seen this kind of excitement. It bordered on frenzy. Two thousand dwarves rushed about, shouting, pounding their hammers, or hauling loads that a mule wouldn't pull.

All of this because they feared the drow were coming.

Catti-brie understood then why Drizzt had detoured into this place, why he had insisted on finding the halfling Regis before going to Settlestone, as Bruenor had bade them.

"Let's go find the sneaky one," she said to Drizzt, having to yell to be heard. Drizzt nodded and followed her back into the relative quiet of the dim corridors. They moved away from the Undercity then, toward the remote chambers where Bruenor had told them they could find the halfling. Silently they moved along—and Drizzt was impressed with how quietly Catti-brie had learned to move. Like him, she wore a fine mesh armor suit of thin but incredibly strong mithril rings, custom fitted to her by Buster Bracer, the finest armorer in Mithril Hall. Catti-brie's armor did little to diminish the dwarf's reputation, for it was so perfectly crafted and supple that it bent with her movements as easily as a thick shirt.

R. A. Salvatore

Like Drizzt's, Catti-brie's boots were thin and well worn but, to the drow's sharp ears, few humans, even so attired, could move so silently. Drizzt subtly eyed her in the dim, flickering light of the widely spaced torches. He noted that she was stepping like a drow, the ball of her foot touching down first, instead of the more common human heel-toe method. Her time in the Underdark, chasing Drizzt to Menzoberranzan, had served her well.

The drow nodded his approval but made no comment. Catti-brie had already earned her pride points this day, he figured. No sense in puffing up her ego any more.

The corridors were empty and growing increasingly dark. Drizzt did not miss this point. He even let his vision slip into the infrared spectrum, where the varying heat of objects showed him their general shapes. Human Catti-brie did not possess such Underdark vision, of course, but around her head she wore a thin silver chain, set in its front with a green gemstone streaked by a single line of black: a cat's eye agate. It had been given to her by Lady Alustriel herself, enchanted so that its wearer could see, even in the darkest, deepest tunnels, as though she were standing in an open field under a starry sky.

The two friends had no trouble navigating in the darkness, but still, they were not comfortable with it. Why weren't the torches burning? they each wondered. Both had their hands close to weapon hilts; Catti-brie suddenly wished she had brought Taulmaril the Heartseeker, her magical bow, with her.

A tremendous crash sounded, and the floor trembled under their feet. Both were down in a crouch immediately; Drizzt's scimitars appeared in his hands so quickly that Catti-brie didn't even register the movement. At first the young woman thought the impossibly fast maneuver the result of the magical bracers, but, in glancing at Drizzt, she realized he wasn't even wearing them. She likewise drew her sword and took a deep breath, privately scolding herself for thinking she was getting close in fighting skill to the incredible ranger. Catti-brie shook the thought aside—no time for it now—and concentrated on the winding corridor ahead. Side by side, she and Drizzt slowly advanced, looking for shadows where enemies might hide and for lines in the wall that would indicate cunning secret doors to side passages. Such ways were common in the dwarven complex, for most dwarves could make them, and

26

most dwarves, greedy by nature, kept personal treasures hidden away. Catti-brie did not know this little-used section of Mithril Hall very well. Neither did Drizzt.

Another crash came, and the floor trembled again, more than before, and the friends knew they were getting closer. Catti-brie was glad she had been training so hard, and gladder still that Drizzt Do'Urden was by her side.

She stopped moving, and Drizzt did likewise, turning to regard her.

"Guenhwyvar?" she silently mouthed, referring to Drizzt's feline friend, a loyal panther that the drow could summon from the Astral Plane.

Drizzt considered the suggestion for a moment. He tried not to summon Guenhwyvar too often now, knowing there might soon be a time when the panther would be needed often. There were limits on the magic; Guenhwyvar could only remain on the Material Plane for half a day out of every two.

Not yet, Drizzt decided. Bruenor had not indicated what Regis might be doing down here, but the dwarf had given no hint that there might be danger. The drow shook his head slightly, and the two moved on, silent and sure.

A third crash came, followed by a groan.

"Yer head, ye durned fool!" came a sharp scolding. "Ye gots to use yer stinkin' head!"

Drizzt and Catti-brie straightened immediately and relaxed their grips on their weapons. "Pwent," they said together, referring to Thibbledorf Pwent, the outrageous battlerager, the most obnoxious and bad-smelling dwarf south of the Spine of the World (and probably north of it, as well).

"Next ye'll be wantin' to wear a stinkin' helmet!" the tirade continued.

Around the next bend, the two companions came to a fork in the corridor. To the left, Pwent continued roaring in outrage; to the right was a door with torchlight showing through its many cracks. Drizzt cocked his head, catching a slight and familiar chuckle that way.

He motioned for Catti-brie to follow and went through the door without knocking. Regis stood alone inside, leaning on a crank near the left-hand wall. The halfling's smile lit up when he saw his friends, and he waved one hand high to them—relatively high, for

27

Regis was small, even by halfling standards, his curly brown hair barely topping three feet. He had an ample belly, though it seemed to be shrinking of late, as even the lazy halfling took seriously the threat to this place that had become his home.

He put a finger over pursed lips as Drizzt and Catti-brie approached, and he pointed to the "door" before him. It didn't take either of the companions long to understand what was transpiring. The crank next to Regis operated a sheet of heavy metal that ran along runners above and to the side of the door. The wood of the door could hardly be seen now, for the plate was in place right before it.

"Go!" came a thunderous command from the other side, followed by charging footsteps and a grunting roar, then a tremendous explosion as the barreling dwarf hit, and of course bounced off, the barricaded portal.

"Battlerager training," Regis calmly explained.

Catti-brie gave Drizzt a sour look, remembering what her father had told her of Pwent's plans. "The Gutbuster Brigade," she remarked, and Drizzt nodded, for Bruenor had told him, too, that Thibbledorf Pwent meant to train a group of dwarves in the not-so-subtle art of battleraging, his personal Gutbuster Brigade, highly motivated, skilled in frenzy, and not too smart.

Another dwarf hit the barricaded door, probably headfirst, and Drizzt understood how Pwent meant to facilitate the third of his three requirements for his soldiers.

Catti-brie shook her head and sighed. She did not doubt the military value of the brigade—Pwent could outfight anyone in Mithril Hall, except for Drizzt and maybe Bruenor, but the notion of a bunch of little Thibbledorf Pwents running around surely turned her stomach!

Behind the door, Pwent was thoroughly scolding his troops, calling them every dwarven curse name, more than a few that Catti-brie, who had lived among the clan for more than a score of years, had never heard, and more than a few that Pwent seemed to be making up on the spot, such as "mule-kissin', flea-sniffin', water-drinkin', who-thinks-ye-squeeze-the-durned-cow-to-get-the-durned-milk, lumps o' sandstone."

"We are off to Settlestone," Drizzt explained to Regis, the drow suddenly anxious to be out of there. "Berkthgar is being difficult."

Regis nodded. "I was there when he told Bruenor he wanted the warhammer." The halfling's cherubic face turned up into one of his common, wistful smiles. "I truly believed Bruenor would cleave him down the middle!"

"We're needing Berkthgar," Catti-brie reminded the halfling.

Regis pooh-poohed that thought away. "Bluffing," he insisted. "Berkthgar needs us, and his people would not take kindly to his turning his back on the dwarves who have been so good to his folk."

"Bruenor would not really kill him," Drizzt said, somewhat unconvincingly. All three friends paused and looked to each other, each considering the tough dwarf king, the old and fiery Bruenor returned. They thought of Aegis-fang, the most beautiful of weapons, the flanks of its gleaming mithril head inscribed with the sacred runes of the dwarven gods. One side was cut with the hammer and anvil of Moradin the Soulforger, the other with the crossed axes of Clanggedon, dwarven god of battle, and both were covered perfectly by the carving of the gem within the mountain, the symbol of Dumathoin, the Keeper of Secrets. Bruenor had been among the best of the dwarven smiths, but after Aegis-fang, that pinnacle of creative triumph, he had rarely bothered to return to his forge.

They thought of Aegis-fang, and they thought of Wulfgar, who had been like Bruenor's son, the tall, fair-haired youth for whom Bruenor had made the mighty hammer.

"Bruenor *would* really kill him," Catti-brie said, echoing the thoughts of all three.

Drizzt started to speak, but Regis stopped him by holding up a finger.

" . . . now get yer head lower!" Pwent was barking on the other side of the door. Regis nodded and smiled and motioned for Drizzt to continue.

"We thought you might—"

Another crash sounded, then another groan, followed by the flapping of dwarven lips as the fallen would-be battlerager shook his head vigorously.

"Good recovery!" Pwent congratulated.

"We thought you might accompany us," Drizzt said, ignoring Catti-brie's sigh of disgust.

Regis thought about it for a moment. The halfling would have liked to get out of the mines and stretch in the sunshine once more, though the summer was all but over and the autumn chill already began to nip the air.

"I have to stay," the unusually dedicated halfling remarked. "I've much to do."

Both Drizzt and Catti-brie nodded. Regis had changed over the last few months, during the time of crisis. When Drizzt and Catti-brie had gone to Menzoberranzan—Drizzt to end the threat to Mithril Hall, Catti-brie to find Drizzt—Regis had taken command to spur grieving Bruenor into preparing for war. Regis, who had spent most of his life finding the softest couch to lie upon, had impressed even the toughest dwarf generals, even Thibbledorf Pwent, with his fire and energy. Now the halfling would have loved to go, both of them knew, but he remained true to his mission.

Drizzt looked hard at Regis, trying to find the best way to make his request. To his surprise, the halfling saw it coming, and immediately Regis's hands went to the chain about his neck. He lifted the ruby pendant over his head and casually tossed it to Drizzt.

Another testament to the halfling's growth, Drizzt knew, as he stared down at the sparkling ruby affixed to the chain. This was the halfling's most precious possession, a powerful charm Regis had stolen from his old guild master in far-off Calimport. The halfling had guarded it, coveted it, like a mother lion with a single cub, at least until this point.

Drizzt continued to look at the ruby, felt himself drawn by its multiple facets, spiraling down to depths that promised . . .

The drow shook his head and forced himself to look away. Even without one to command it, the enchanted ruby had reached out for him! Never had he witnessed such a powerful charm. And yet, Jarlaxle, the mercenary, had given it back to him, had willingly swapped it when they had met in the tunnels outside Menzoberranzan after Drizzt's escape. It was unexpected and important that Jarlaxle had given it back to Drizzt, but what the significance might be, Drizzt had not yet discerned.

"You should be careful before using that on Berkthgar," Regis said, drawing Drizzt from his thoughts. "He is proud, and if he figures out that sorcery was used against him, the alliance may indeed be dissolved."

"True enough," Catti-brie agreed. She looked to Drizzt.

"Only if we need it," the drow remarked, looping the chain

about his neck. The pendant settled near his breast and the ivory unicorn head, symbol of his goddess, that rested there.

Another dwarf hit the door and bounced off, then lay groaning on the floor.

"Bah!" they heard Pwent snort. "Ye're a bunch o' elf-lickin' pixies! I'll show ye how it's done!"

Regis nodded—that was his cue—and immediately began to turn the crank, drawing the metal plate out from behind the portal.

"Watch out," he warned his two companions, for they stood in the general direction of where Pwent would make his door-busting entrance.

"I'm for leaving," Catti-brie said, starting for the other, normal, door. The young woman had no desire to see Pwent. Likely, he would pinch her cheek with his grubby fingers and tell her to "work on that beard" so that she might be a beautiful woman.

Drizzt didn't take much convincing. He held up the ruby, nodded a silent thanks to Regis, and rushed out into the hall after Catti-brie.

They hadn't gone a dozen steps when they heard the training door explode, followed by Pwent's hysterical laughter and the admiring "oohs" and "aahs" of the naive Gutbuster Brigade.

"We should send the lot of them to Menzoberranzan," Catti-brie said dryly. "Pwent'd chase the whole city to the ends of the world!"

Drizzt—who had grown up among the unbelievably powerful drow houses and had seen the wrath of the high priestesses and magical feats beyond anything he had witnessed in his years on the surface—did not disagree.

*   *   *   *   *

Councilor Firble ran a wrinkled hand over his nearly bald pate, feeling uncomfortable in the torchlight. Firble was a svirfneblin, a deep gnome, eighty pounds of wiry muscles packed into a three-and-a-half-foot frame. Few races of the Underdark could get along as well as the svirfnebli, and no race, except perhaps the rare pech, understood the ways of the deep stone so well.

Still, Firble was more than a bit afraid now, out in the (hopefully) empty corridors beyond the borders of Blingdenstone, the city that was his home. He hated the torchlight, hated any light, but the

R. A. Salvatore

orders from King Schnicktick were final and unarguable: no gnome was to traverse the corridors without a burning torch in his hand.

No gnome except for one. Firble's companion this day carried no torch, for he possessed no hands. Belwar Dissengulp, Most Honored Burrow Warden of Blingdenstone, had lost his hands to drow, to Drizzt Do'Urden's brother Dinin, many years before. Unlike so many other Underdark races, though, the svirfnebli were not without compassion, and their artisans had fashioned marvelous replacements of pure, enchanted mithril: a block-headed hammer capping Belwar's right arm and a two-headed pickaxe on his left.

"Completed the circuit, we have," Firble remarked. "And back to Blingdenstone we go!"

"Not so!" Belwar grumbled. His voice was deeper and stronger than those of most svirfnebli, and was fitting, considering his stout, barrel-chested build.

"There are no drow in the tunnels," Firble insisted. "Not a fight in three weeks!" It was true enough; after months of battling drow from Menzoberranzan in the tunnels near Blingdenstone, the corridors had gone strangely quiet. Belwar understood that Drizzt Do'Urden, his friend, had somehow played a part in this change, and he feared that Drizzt had been captured or killed.

"Quiet, it is," Firble said more softly, as if he had just realized the danger of his own volume. A shudder coursed the smaller svirfneblin's spine. Belwar had forced him out here—it was his turn in the rotation, but normally one as experienced and venerable as Firble would have been excused from scouting duties. Belwar had insisted, though, and for some reason Firble did not understand, King Schnicktick had agreed with the most honored burrow warden.

Not that Firble was unaccustomed to the tunnels. Quite the contrary. He was the only gnome of Blingdenstone with actual contacts in Menzoberranzan, and was more acquainted with the tunnels near the drow city than any other deep gnome. That dubious distinction was causing Firble fits these days, particularly from Belwar. When a disguised Catti-brie had been captured by the svirfnebli, and subsequently recognized as no enemy, Firble, at great personal risk, had been the one to show her quicker, secret ways into Menzoberranzan.

Now Belwar wasn't worried about any drow in the tunnels, Firble knew. The tunnels were quiet. The gnome patrols and other secret allies could find no hint that any drow were about at all, not even along the dark elves' normal routes closer to Menzoberranzan. Something important had happened in the drow city, that much was obvious, and it seemed obvious, too, that Drizzt and that troublesome Catti-brie were somehow involved. That was the real reason Belwar had forced Firble out here, Firble knew, and he shuddered again to think that was why King Schnicktick had so readily agreed with Belwar.

"Something has happened," Belwar said, unexpectedly playing his cards, as though he understood Firble's line of silent reasoning. "Something in Menzoberranzan."

Firble eyed the most honored burrow warden suspiciously. He knew what would soon be asked of him, knew that he would soon be dealing with that trickster Jarlaxle again.

"The stones themselves are uneasy," Belwar went on.

"As if the drow will soon march," Firble interjected dryly.

"*Cosim camman denoctusd,*" Belwar agreed, in an ancient svirfneblin saying that translated roughly into "the settled ground before the earthquake," or, as it was more commonly known to surface dwellers, "the calm before the storm."

"That I meet with my drow informant, King Schnicktick desires," Firble reasoned, seeing no sense in holding back the guess any longer. He knew he would not be suggesting something that Belwar wasn't about to suggest to him.

"*Cosim camman denoctusd,*" Belwar said again, this time more determinedly. Belwar and Schnicktick, and many others in Blingdenstone, were convinced that the drow would soon march in force. Though the most direct tunnels to the surface, to where Drizzt Do'Urden called home, were east of Blingdenstone, beyond Menzoberranzan, the drow first would have to set out west, and would come uncomfortably close to the gnome city. So unsettling was that thought that King Schnicktick had ordered scouting parties far to the east and south, as far from home and Menzoberranzan as the svirfnebli had ever roamed. There were whispers of deserting Blingdenstone altogether, if the rumors proved likely and a new location could be found. No gnome wanted that, Belwar and Firble perhaps least of all. Both were old, nearing their second full century, and both were tied, heart and soul, to this city called Blingdenstone.

But among all the svirfnebli, these two understood the power of a drow march, understood that if Menzoberranzan's army came to

Blingdenstone, the gnomes would be obliterated.

"Set up the meeting, I will," Firble said with a resigned sigh. "He will tell me little, I do not doubt. Never does he, and high always is the price!"

Belwar said nothing, and sympathized little for the cost of such a meeting with the greedy drow informant. The most honored burrow warden understood that the price of ignorance would be much higher. He also realized that Firble understood, as well, and that the councilor's apparent resignation was just a part of Firble's bluster. Belwar had come to know Firble well, and found that he liked the oft-complaining gnome.

Now Belwar, and every other svirfneblin in Blingdenstone, desperately needed Firble and his contacts.

Chapter 3
AT PLAY

rizzt and Catti-brie skipped down the rocky trails, weaving in and out of boulder tumbles as effortlessly and spiritedly as two children at play. Their trek became an impromptu race as each hopped breaks in the stone, leaped to catch low branches, then swung down as far as the small mountain trees would carry them. They came onto one low, level spot together, where each leaped a small pool (though Catti-brie didn't quite clear it) and split up as they approached a slab of rock taller than either of them. Catti-brie went right and Drizzt started left, then changed his mind and headed up the side of the barrier instead.

Catti-brie skidded around the slab, pleased to see that she was first to the other side.

"My lead!" she cried, but even as she spoke she saw her companion's dark, graceful form sail over her head.

"Not so!" Drizzt corrected, touching down so lightly that it seemed as if he had never been off the ground. Catti-brie groaned and kicked into a run again, but pulled up short, seeing that Drizzt had stopped.

"Too fine a day," the dark elf remarked. Indeed, it was as fine a day as the southern spur of the Spine of the World ever offered once the autumn winds began to blow. The air was crisp, the breeze cool, and puffy white clouds—gigantic snowballs, they seemed—raced across the deep blue sky on swift mountain winds.

"Too fine for arguing with Berkthgar," Catti-brie added, thinking that was the direction of the drow's statement. She bent a bit and put her hands to her thighs for support, then turned her head back and up, trying to catch her breath.

"Too fine to leave Guenhwyvar out of it!" Drizzt clarified happily.

Catti-brie's smile was wide when she looked down to see Drizzt take the onyx panther figurine out of his backpack. It was among the most beautiful of artworks Catti-brie had ever seen, perfectly detailed to show the muscled flanks and the true, insightful expression of the great cat. As perfect as it was, though, the figurine paled beside the magnificent creature that it allowed Drizzt to summon.

The drow reverently placed the item on the ground before him. "Come to me, Guenhwyvar," he called softly. Apparently the panther was eager to return, for a gray mist swirled about the item almost immediately, gradually taking shape and solidifying.

Guenhwyvar came to the Material Plane with ears straight up, relaxed, as though the cat understood from the inflections of Drizzt's call that there was no emergency, that she was being summoned merely for companionship.

"We are racing to Settlestone," Drizzt explained. "Do you think you can keep pace?"

The panther understood. A single spring from powerful hind legs sent Guenhwyvar soaring over Catti-brie's head, across the twenty-foot expanse to the top of the rock slab she and Drizzt had just crossed. The cat hit the rock's flat top, backpedaled, and spun to face the duo. Then for no other reason than to give praise to the day, Guenhwyvar reared and stood tall in the air, a sight that sent her friends' hearts racing. Guenhwyvar was six hundred pounds, twice the size of an ordinary panther, with a head almost as wide as Drizzt's shoulders, a paw that could cover a man's face, and spectacular, shining green eyes that revealed an intelligence far beyond what an animal should possess. Guenhwyvar was the most loyal of companions, an unjudging friend, and every time

Drizzt or Catti-brie, or Bruenor or Regis, looked at the cat, their lives were made just a bit warmer.

"Me thinking's that we should get a head start," Catti-brie whispered mischievously.

Drizzt gave a slight, inconspicuous nod, and they broke together, running full-out down the trail. A few seconds later they heard Guenhwyvar roar behind them, still from atop the slab of rock. The trail was relatively clear and Drizzt sprinted out ahead of Catti-brie, though the woman, young and strong, with a heart that would have been more appropriate in the chest of a sturdy dwarf, could not be shaken.

"Ye're not to beat me!" she cried, to which Drizzt laughed. His mirth disappeared as he rounded a bend to find that stubborn and daring Catti-brie had taken a somewhat treacherous shortcut, light-skipping over a patch of broken and uneven stones, to take an unexpected lead.

Suddenly this was more than a friendly competition. Drizzt lowered his head and ran full-out, careening down the uneven ground so recklessly that he was barely able to avoid smacking face first into a tree. Catti-brie paced him, step for step, and kept her lead.

Guenhwyvar roared again, still from the slab, they knew, and they knew, too, that they were being mocked.

Sure enough, barely a few seconds later, a black streak rebounded off a wall of stone to Drizzt's side, crossing level with the drow's head. Guenhwyvar cut back across the trail between the two companions, and passed Catti-brie so quickly and so silently that she hardly realized she was no longer leading.

Sometime later, Guenhwyvar let her get ahead again, then Drizzt took a treacherous shortcut and slipped into the front—only to be passed again by the panther. So it went, with competitive Drizzt and Catti-brie working hard, and Guenhwyvar merely hard at play.

The three were exhausted—at least Drizzt and Catti-brie were; Guenhwyvar wasn't even breathing hard—when they broke for lunch on a small clearing, protected from the wind by a high wall on the north and east, and dropping off fast in a sheer cliff to the south. Several rocks dotted the clearing, perfect stools for the tired companions. A grouping of stones was set in the middle as a fire pit, for this was a usual campsite of the oft-wandering drow.

R. A. Salvatore

Catti-brie relaxed while Drizzt brought up a small fire. Far below she could see the gray plumes of smoke rising lazily into the clear air from the houses of Settlestone. It was a sobering sight, for it reminded the young woman, who had spent the morning at such a pace, of the gravity of her mission and of the situation. How many runs might she and Drizzt and Guenhwyvar share if the dark elves came calling?

Those plumes of smoke also reminded Catti-brie of the man who had brought the tough barbarians to this place from Icewind Dale, the man who was to have been her husband. Wulfgar had died trying to save her, had died in the grasp of a yochlol, a handmaiden of evil Lloth. Both Catti-brie and Drizzt had to bear some responsibility for that loss, yet it wasn't guilt that pained the young woman now, or that pained Drizzt. He, too, had noticed the smoke and had taken a break from his fire-tending to watch and contemplate.

The companions did not smile now, for simple loss, because they had taken so many runs just like this one, except that Wulfgar had raced beside them, his long strides making up for the fact that he could not squeeze through breaks that his two smaller companions could pass at full speed.

"I wish . . . " Catti-brie said, and the words resonated in the ears of the similarly wishing dark elf.

"Our war, if it comes, would be better fought with Wulfgar, son of Beornegar, leading the men of Settlestone," Drizzt agreed, and what both he and Catti-brie silently thought was that all their lives would be better if Wulfgar were alive.

There. Drizzt had said it openly, and there was no more to say. They ate their lunch silently. Even Guenhwyvar lay very still and made not a sound.

Catti-brie's mind drifted from her friends, back to Icewind Dale, to the rocky mountain, Kelvin's Cairn, dotting the otherwise flat tundra. It was so similar to this very place. Colder, perhaps, but the air held the same crispness, the same clear, vital texture. How far she and her friends, Drizzt and Guenhwyvar, Bruenor and Regis, and, of course, Wulfgar, had come from that place! And in so short a time! A frenzy of adventures, a lifetime of excitement and thrills and good deeds. Together they were an unbeatable force.

So they had thought.

Catti-brie had seen the emotions of a lifetime, indeed, and she was barely into her twenties. She had run fast through life, like her run down the mountain trails, free and high-spirited, skipping without care, feeling immortal.

Almost.

Chapter 4
AT THE SEAMS

conspiracy?" the drow's fingers flashed, using the silent hand code of the dark elves, its movements so intricate and varied that nearly every connotation of every word in the drow language could be represented.

Jarlaxle replied with a slight shake of his head. He sighed and seemed sincerely perplexed—a sight not often seen—and motioned for his cohort to follow him to a more secure area.

They crossed the wide, winding avenues of Menzoberranzan, flat, clear areas between the towering stalagmite mounds that served as homes to the various drow families. Those mounds, and a fair number of long stalactites leering down from the huge cavern's ceiling, were hollowed out and sculpted with sweeping balconies and walkways. The clusters within each family compound were often joined by high bridges, most shaped to resemble spiderwebs. And on all the houses, especially those of the older and more established families, the most wondrous designs were highlighted by glowing faerie fire, purple and blue, sometimes outlined in red and, not so often, in green. Menzoberranzan was the most spectacular of cities, breathtaking, surreal, and an ignorant visitor (who would not be ignorant, or likely even alive, for long!) would never guess that the artisans of such beauty were among the most malicious of Toril's races.

Jarlaxle moved without a whisper down the darker, tighter avenues surrounding the lesser houses. His focus was ahead and to the sides, his keen eye (and his eye patch was over his right eye at the time) discerning the slightest of movements in the most distant shadows.

The mercenary leader's surprise was complete when he glanced back at his companion and found, not M'tarl, the lieutenant of Bregan D'aerthe he had set out with, but another, very powerful, drow.

Jarlaxle was rarely without a quick response, but the specter of Gromph Baenre, Matron Baenre's elderboy, the archmage of Menzoberranzan, standing so unexpectedly beside him, surely stole his wit.

"I trust that M'tarl will be returned to me when you are finished," Jarlaxle said, quickly regaining his seldom-lost composure.

Without a word, the archmage waved his arm, and a shimmering green globe appeared in the air, several feet from the floor. A thin silver cord hung down from it, its visible end barely brushing the stone floor.

Jarlaxle shrugged and took up the cord, and as soon as he touched it, he was drawn upward into the globe, into the extradimensional space beyond the shimmering portal.

The casting was impressive, Jarlaxle decided, for he found within not the usual empty space created by such an evocation, but a lushly furnished sitting room, complete with a zombielike servant that offered him a drink of fine wine before he ever sat down. Jarlaxle took a moment to allow his vision to shift into the normal spectrum of light, for the place was bathed in a soft blue glow. This was not unusual for wizards, even drow wizards accustomed to the lightless ways of the Underdark, for one could not read scrolls or spellbooks without light!

"He will be returned if he can survive where I put him long enough for us to complete our conversation," Gromph replied. The wizard seemed not too concerned, as he, too, came into the extradimensional pocket. The mighty Baenre closed his eyes and whispered a word, and his *piwafwi* cloak and other unremarkable attire transformed. Now he looked the part of his prestigious station. His flowing robe showed many pockets and was emblazoned with sigils

41

and runes of power. As with the house structures, faerie fire highlighted these runes, though the archmage could darken the runes with a thought, and then his robe would be more concealing than the finest of *piwafwis*. Two brooches, one a black-legged, red-bodied spider, the other a shining green emerald, adorned the magnificent robe, though Jarlaxle could hardly see them, for the old wizard's long white hair hung down the side of his head and in front of his shoulders and chest.

With his interest in things magical, Jarlaxle had seen the brooches on the city's previous archmage, though Gromph had held the position longer than most of Menzoberranzan's drow had been alive. The spider brooch allowed the archmage to cast the *lingering heat* enchantment into Narbondel, the pillar clock of Menzoberranzan. The heat would rise to the tip of the clock over a twelve-hour period, then diminish back toward the base in a like amount of time, until the stone was again cool, a very obvious and effective clock for heat-sensing drow eyes.

The other brooch gave Gromph perpetual youth. By Jarlaxle's estimation, this one had seen the birth and death of seven centuries, yet so young did he appear that it seemed he might be ready to begin his training at the drow Academy!

Not so, Jarlaxle silently recanted in studying the wizard. There was an aura of power and dignity about Gromph, reflected clearly in his eyes, which showed the wisdom of long and often bitter experience. This one was cunning and devious, able to scrutinize any situation immediately, and in truth, Jarlaxle felt more uncomfortable and more vulnerable standing before Gromph than before Matron Baenre herself.

"A conspiracy?" Gromph asked again, this time aloud. "Have the other houses finally become fed up with my mother and banded together against House Baenre?"

"I have already given a full accounting to Matron—"

"I heard every word," Gromph interrupted, snarling impatiently. "Now I wish to know the truth."

"An interesting concept," Jarlaxle said, smiling wryly at the realization that Gromph was truly nervous. "Truth."

"A rare thing," Gromph agreed, regaining his composure and resting back in his chair, his slender fingers tapping together before him. "But a thing that sometimes keeps meddling fools alive."

Jarlaxle's smile vanished. He studied Gromph intently, surprised at so bold a threat. Gromph was powerful—by all measures of Menzoberranzan, the old wretch was as powerful as any male could become. But Jarlaxle did not operate by any of Menzoberranzan's measures, and for the wizard to take such a risk as to threaten Jarlaxle . . .

Jarlaxle was even more surprised when he realized that Gromph, mighty Gromph Baenre, was beyond nervous. He was truly scared.

"I will not even bother to remind you of the value of this 'meddling fool,' " Jarlaxle said.

"Do spare me."

Jarlaxle laughed in his face.

Gromph brought his hands to his hips, his outer robes opening in front with the movement and revealing a pair of wands set under his belt, one on each hip.

"No conspiracy," Jarlaxle said suddenly, firmly.

"The truth," Gromph remarked in dangerous, low tones.

"The truth," Jarlaxle replied as straightforwardly as he had ever spoken. "I have as much invested in House Baenre as do you, Archmage. If the lesser houses were banding against Baenre, or if Baenre's daughters plotted her demise, Bregan D'aerthe would stand beside her, at least to the point of giving her fair notice of the coming coup."

Gromph's expression became very serious. What Jarlaxle noted most was that the elderboy of House Baenre had taken no apparent notice of his obvious (and intentional) slip in referring to Matron Baenre as merely "Baenre." Errors such as that often cost drow, particularly male drow, their lives.

"What is it then?" Gromph asked, and the very tone of the question, almost an outright plea, caught Jarlaxle off his guard. Never before had he seen the archmage, or heard of the archmage, in so desperate a state.

"You sense it!" Gromph snapped. "There is something wrong about the very air we breathe!"

For centuries untold, Jarlaxle silently added, a notion he knew he would be wise to keep to himself. To Gromph he offered only, "The chapel was damaged."

The archmage nodded, his expression turning sour. The great

43

domed chapel of House Baenre was the holiest place in the entire city, the ultimate shrine to Lloth. In perhaps the most terrible slap in the face the Spider Queen had ever experienced, the renegade Do'Urden and his friends had, upon their escape, dropped a stalactite from the cavern's roof that punctured the treasured dome like a gigantic spear.

"The Spider Queen is angered," Gromph remarked.

"I would be," Jarlaxle agreed.

Gromph snapped an angry glare over the smug mercenary. Not for any insult he had given Lloth, Jarlaxle understood, but simply because of his flippant attitude.

When that glare had no more effect than to bring a smile to Jarlaxle's lips, Gromph sprang from his chair and paced like a caged displacer beast. The zombie host, unthinking and purely programmed, rushed over, drinks in hand.

Gromph growled and held his palm upraised, a ball of flame suddenly appearing atop it. With his other hand Gromph placed something small and red—it looked like a scale—into the flame and began an ominous chant.

Jarlaxle watched patiently as Gromph played out his frustration, the mercenary preferring that the wizard aim that retort at the zombie and not at him.

A lick of flame shot out from Gromph's hand. Lazily, determinedly, like a snake that had already immobilized its prey with poison, the flame wound about the zombie, which, of course, neither moved nor complained. In mere seconds, the zombie was engulfed by this serpent of fire. When Gromph casually sat again, the burning thing followed its predetermined course back to stand impassively. It made it back to its station, but soon crumbled, one of its legs consumed.

"The smell . . . " Jarlaxle began, putting a hand over his nose.

"Is of power!" Gromph finished, his red eyes narrowing, the nostrils of his thin nose flaring. The wizard took a deep breath and basked in the stench.

"It is not Lloth who fosters the wrongness of the air," Jarlaxle said suddenly, wanting to steal the obviously frustrated wizard's bluster and be done with Gromph and out of this reeking place.

"What do you know?" Gromph demanded, suddenly very anxious once more.

"No more than you," Jarlaxle replied. "Lloth is likely angry at Drizzt's escape, and at the damage to the chapel. You above all can appreciate the importance of that chapel." Jarlaxle's sly tone sent Gromph's nostrils flaring once more. The mercenary knew he had hit a sore spot, a weakness in the archmage's armored robes. Gromph had created the pinnacle of the Baenre chapel, a gigantic, shimmering illusion hovering over the central altar. It continually shifted form, going from a beautiful drow female to a huge spider and back again. It was no secret in Menzoberranzan that Gromph was not the most devout of Lloth's followers, no secret that the creation of the magnificent illusion had spared him his mother's unmerciful wrath.

"But there are too many things happening for Lloth to be the sole cause," Jarlaxle went on after savoring the minor victory for a moment. "And too many of them adversely affect Lloth's own base of power."

"A rival deity?" Gromph asked, revealing more intrigue than he intended. "Or an underground revolt?" The wizard sat back suddenly, thinking he had hit upon something, thinking that any underground revolt would certainly fall into the domain of a certain rogue mercenary leader.

But Jarlaxle was in no way cornered, for if either of Gromph's suspicions had any basis, Jarlaxle did not know of it.

"Something," was all the mercenary replied. "Something perhaps very dangerous to us all. For more than a score of years, one house or another has, for some reason, overestimated the worth of capturing the renegade Do'Urden, and their very zeal has elevated his stature and multiplied the troubles he has caused."

"So you believe all of this is tied to Drizzt's escape," Gromph reasoned.

"I believe many matron mothers will believe that," Jarlaxle was quick to reply. "And, thus, Drizzt's escape will indeed play a role in what is to come. But I have not said, and do not believe, that what you sense is amiss is the result of the renegade's flight from House Baenre."

Gromph closed his eyes and let the logic settle. Jarlaxle was right, of course. Menzoberranzan was a place so wound up in its own intrigue that truth mattered less than suspicion, that suspicion often became a self-fulfilling prophecy, and thus, often created truth.

R. A. Salvatore

"I may wish to speak with you again, mercenary," the archmage said quietly, and Jarlaxle noticed a door near where he had entered the extradimensional pocket. Beside it the zombie still burned, now just a crumpled, blackened ball of almost bare bone.

Jarlaxle started for the door.

"Alas," Gromph said dramatically, and Jarlaxle paused. "M'tarl did not survive."

"A pity for M'tarl," Jarlaxle added, not wanting Gromph to think that the loss would in any way wound Bregan D'aerthe.

Jarlaxle went out the door, down the cord, and slipped away silently into the shadows of the city, trying to digest all that had occurred. Rarely had he spoken to Gromph, and even more rarely had Gromph requested, in his own convoluted way, the audience. That fact was significant, Jarlaxle realized. Something very strange was happening here, a slight tingle in the air. Jarlaxle, a lover of chaos (mostly because, within the swirl of chaos, he always seemed to come out ahead), was intrigued. What was even more intriguing was that Gromph, despite his fears and all that he had to lose, was also intrigued!

The archmage's mention of a possible second deity proved that, showed his entire hand. For Gromph was an old wretch, despite the fact that he had come as far in life as any male drow in Menzoberranzan could hope to climb.

No, not despite that fact, Jarlaxle silently corrected himself. Because of that fact. Gromph was bitter, and had been so for centuries, because, in his lofty view of his own worth, he saw even the position of archmage as pointless, as a limit imposed by an accident of gender.

The greatest weakness in Menzoberranzan was not the rivalry of the various houses, Jarlaxle knew, but the strict matriarchal system imposed by Lloth's followers. Half the drow population was subjugated merely because they had been born male.

That was a weakness.

And subjugation inevitably bred bitterness, even—especially!— in one who had gone as far as Gromph. Because from his lofty perch, the archmage could clearly see how much farther he might possibly go if he had been born with a different set of genitals.

Gromph had indicated he might wish to speak with Jarlaxle again; Jarlaxle had a feeling he and the bitter mage would indeed

46

meet, perhaps quite often. He spent the next twenty steps of his walk back across Menzoberranzan wondering what information Gromph might extract from poor M'tarl, for of course the lieutenant was not dead—though he might soon wish he were.

Jarlaxle laughed at his own foolishness. He had spoken truly to Gromph, of course, and so M'tarl couldn't reveal anything incriminating. The mercenary sighed. He wasn't used to speaking truthfully, wasn't used to walking where there were no webs.

That notion dismissed, Jarlaxle turned his attention to the city. Something was brewing. Jarlaxle, the ultimate survivor, could sense it, and so could Gromph. Something important would occur all too soon, and what the mercenary needed to do was figure out how he might profit from it, whatever it might be.

Chapter 5
CATTI-BRIE'S CHAMPION

rizzt called Guenhwyvar to his side when the companions came down to the lower trails. The panther sat quietly, expecting what was to come.

"Ye should bring the cat in," Catti-brie suggested, understanding Drizzt's intent. The barbarians, though they had come far from their tundra homes and their secluded ways, remained somewhat distrustful of magic, and the sight of the panther always unnerved more than a few of Berkthgar's people, and didn't sit so well with Berkthgar himself.

"It is enough for them that I will enter their settlement," Drizzt replied.

Catti-brie had to nod in agreement. The sight of Drizzt, of a dark elf, one of a race noted for magic and evil, was perhaps even more unnerving to the Northmen than the panther. "Still, it'd teach Berkthgar good if ye had the cat sit on him for a while," she remarked.

Drizzt chuckled as he conjured an image of Guenhwyvar stretching comfortably on the back of the large, wriggling man. "The folk of Settlestone will grow accustomed to the panther as

48

they did to my own presence," the drow replied. "Think of how many years it took Bruenor to become comfortable around Guenhwyvar."

The panther gave a low growl, as if she understood their every word.

"It wasn't the years," Catti-brie returned. "It was the number of times Guen pulled me stubborn father's backside out of a hot fire!"

When Guenhwyvar growled again, both Drizzt and Catti-brie had a good laugh at surly Bruenor's expense. The mirth subsided as Drizzt took out the figurine and bade Guenhwyvar farewell, promising to call the panther back as soon as he and Catti-brie were on the trails once more, heading back to Mithril Hall.

The formidable panther, growling low, walked in circles about the figurine. Gradually those growls diminished as Guenhwyvar faded into gray mist, then into nothing at all.

Drizzt scooped up the figurine and looked to the plumes of smoke rising from nearby Settlestone. "Are you ready?" he asked his companion.

"He'll be a stubborn one," Catti-brie admitted.

"We just have to get Berkthgar to understand the depth of Bruenor's distress," Drizzt offered, starting off again for the town.

"We just have to get Berkthgar to imagine Bruenor's axe sweeping in for the bridge of his nose," Catti-brie muttered. "Right between the eyes."

Settlestone was a rocky, windswept cluster of stone houses set in a vale and protected on three sides by the climbing, broken sides of the towering mountains known as the Spine of the World. The rock structures, resembling houses of cards against the backdrop of the gigantic mountains, had been built by the dwarves of Mithril Hall, by Bruenor's ancestors, hundreds of years before, when the place had been called Dwarvendarrow. It had been used as a trading post by Bruenor's people and was the only place for merchants to peek at the wonders that came from Mithril Hall, for the dwarves did not wish to entertain foreigners in their secret mines.

Even one who did not know the history of Dwarvendarrow would reason that this place had been constructed by the bearded folk. Only dwarves could have imbued the rocks with such

49

strength, for, though the settlement had been uninhabited for centuries, and though the wind sweeping down the channel of the tall mountain walls was unrelenting, the structures had remained. In setting the place up for their own use, Wulfgar's people had no more a task than to brace an occasional wall, sweep out the tons of pebbles that had half buried some of the houses, and flush out the animals that had come to live there.

So it was a trading post again, looking much as it had in the heyday of Mithril Hall, but now called Settlestone and now used by humans working as agents for the busy dwarves. The agreement seemed sound and profitable to both parties, but Berkthgar had no idea of how tentative things had suddenly become. If he did not relent on his demand to carry Aegis-fang, both Drizzt and Catti-brie knew, Bruenor would likely order the barbarian and his people off the land.

The proud barbarians would never follow such a command, of course. The land had been granted, not loaned.

The prospect of war, of Bruenor's people coming down from the mountains and driving the barbarians away, was not so outlandish.

All because of Aegis-fang.

"Wulfgar would not be so glad to know the source of the arguing," Catti-brie remarked as she and Drizzt neared the settlement. "'Twas he who bringed them all together. Seems a pity indeed that it's his memory threatening to tear them apart."

A pity and a terrible irony, Drizzt silently agreed. His steps became more determined; put in that light, this diplomatic mission took on even greater significance. Suddenly Drizzt was marching to Settlestone for much more than a petty squabble between two unyielding rulers. The drow was going for Wulfgar's honor.

As they came down to the valley floor, they heard chanting, a rhythmic, solemn recitation of the deeds of a legendary warrior. They crossed into the empty ways, past the open house doors that the hardy folk never bothered to secure. Both knew where the chanting was coming from, and both knew where they would find the men and women and children of Settlestone.

The only addition the barbarian settlers had made to the town was a large structure that could fit all four hundred people of

Settlestone and a like number of visitors. Hengorot, "the Mead Hall," it was called. It was a solemn place of worship, of valor recalled, and ultimately of sharing food and drink.

Hengorot wasn't finished. Half its long, low walls were of stone, but the rest was enclosed by deerskin canopies. That fact seemed fitting to Drizzt, seemed to reflect how far Wulfgar's people had come, and how far they had to go. When they had lived on the tundra of Icewind Dale, they had been nomadic, following the reindeer herd, so all their houses had been of skin, which could be packed up and taken with the wandering tribe.

No longer were the hardy folk nomads; no longer was their existence dependent on the reindeer herd. It was an unreliable source that often led to warring between the various tribes, or with the folk of Ten-Towns, on the three lakes, the only non-barbarians in Icewind Dale.

Drizzt was glad to see the level of peace and harmony that the northmen had attained, but still it pained him to look at the uncompleted part of Hengorot, to view the skins and remember, too, the sacrifices these people had made. Their way of life, which had survived for thousands of years, was no more. Looking at this construction of Hengorot, a mere shade of the glories the mead hall had known, looking at the stone that now enclosed this proud people, the drow could not help but wonder if this way was indeed "progress."

Catti-brie, who had lived most of her young life in Icewind Dale, and who had heard countless tales of the nomadic barbarians, had understood the loss all along. In coming to Settlestone, the barbarians had given away a measure of their freedom and more than a bit of their heritage. They were richer now, far richer than they could have ever dreamt, and no longer would a harsh winter threaten their very existence. But there had been a price. Like the stars. The stars were different here beside the mountains. They didn't come down to the flat horizon, drawing a person's soul into the heavens.

With a resigned sigh, a bit of her own homesickness for Icewind Dale, Catti-brie reminded herself of the pressing situation. She knew that Berkthgar was being stubborn, but knew, too, how pained the barbarian leader was over Wulfgar's fall, and how pained he must be to think that a dwarf held the key to the

51

warhammer that had become the most honored weapon in his tribe's history.

Never mind that the dwarf had been the one to forge that weapon; never mind that the man who had carried it to such glory had, in fact, been like that dwarf's son. To Berkthgar, Catti-brie knew, the lost hero was not the son of Bruenor, but was Wulfgar, son of Beornegar, of the Tribe of the Elk. Wulfgar of Icewind Dale, not of Mithril Hall. Wulfgar, who epitomized all that had been respected and treasured among the barbarian people. Perhaps most of all, Catti-brie appreciated the gravity of the task before them.

Two tall, broad-shouldered guards flanked the skin flap of the mead hall's opening, their beards and breath smelling more than a little of thick mead. They bristled at first, then moved hastily aside when they recognized the visitors. One rushed to the closest end of the long table set in the hall's center to announce Drizzt and Catti-brie, listing their known feats and their heritage (Catti-brie's at least, for Drizzt's heritage would not be a source of glory in Settlestone).

Drizzt and Catti-brie waited patiently at the door with the other man, who easily outweighed the two of them put together. Both of them focused on Berkthgar, seated halfway down the table's right-hand side, and he inevitably looked past the man announcing the visitors to stare back at them.

Catti-brie thought the man a fool in his argument with Bruenor, but neither she nor Drizzt could help but be impressed by the giant barbarian. He was nearly as tall as Wulfgar, fully six and a half towering feet, with broad shoulders and hardened arms the size of a fat dwarf's thighs. His brown hair was shaggy, hanging low over his shoulders, and he was beginning a beard for winter, the thick tufts on his neck and cheeks making him appear all the more fierce and imposing. Settlestone's leaders were picked in contests of strength, in matches of fierce battle, as the barbarians had selected their leaders through their history. No man in Settlestone could defeat Berkthgar—Berkthgar the Bold, he was called—and yet, because of that fact, he lived, more than any of the others, in the shadow of a dead man who had become legend.

"Pray, join us!" Berkthgar greeted warmly, but the set of his expression told the two companions that he had been expecting this visit, and was not so thrilled to see them. The chieftain focused particularly on Drizzt, and Catti-brie read both eagerness and trepidation in the large man's sky-blue eyes.

Stools were offered to Drizzt and Catti-brie (a high honor for Catti-brie, for no other woman was seated at the table, unless upon the lap of a suitor). In Hengorot, and in all this society, the women and children, save for the older male children, were servants. They hustled now, placing mugs of mead before the newest guests.

Both Drizzt and Catti-brie eyed the drinks suspiciously, knowing they had to keep their heads perfectly clear, but when Berkthgar offered a toast to them and held his own mug high, custom demanded they likewise salute. And in Hengorot, one simply did not sip mead!

Both friends downed their mugs to rousing cheers, and both looked to each other despairingly as another full mug quickly replaced the emptied one.

Unexpectedly, Drizzt rose and deftly hopped up on the long table.

"My greetings to the men and women of Settlestone, to the people of Berkthgar the Bold!" he began, and a chorus of deafening cheers went up, roars for Berkthgar, the focus of the town's pride. The huge, shaggy-haired man got slapped on the back a hundred times in the next minute, but not once did he blink, and not once did he take his suspicious gaze from the dark elf.

Catti-brie understood what was going on here. The barbarians had come to grudgingly accept Drizzt, but still he was a scrawny elf, and a dark elf on top of it all! The paradox was more than a little uncomfortable for them. They saw Drizzt as weak—probably no stronger than some of their hardy womenfolk—and yet they realized that not one of them could defeat the drow in combat. Berkthgar was the most uncomfortable of all, for he knew why Drizzt and Catti-brie had come, and he suspected this issue about the hammer would be settled between him and Drizzt.

"Truly we are grateful, nay, thrilled, at your hospitality. None in all the Realms can set a table more inviting!" Again the cheers. Drizzt was playing them well, and it didn't hurt that more than half of them were falling-down drunk.

"But we cannot remain for long," Drizzt said, his voice

suddenly solemn. The effect on those seated near the drow was stunning, as they seemed to sober immediately, seemed to suddenly grasp the weight of the drow's visit.

Catti-brie saw the sparkle of the ruby pendant hanging about Drizzt's neck, and she understood that though Drizzt wasn't actively using the enchanting gem, its mere presence was as intoxicating as any amount of thick mead.

"The heavy sword of war hangs over us all," Drizzt went on gravely. "This is the time of allian—"

Berkthgar abruptly ended the drow's speech by slamming his mug on the table so brutally that it shattered, splattering those nearby with golden-brown mead and glass fragments. Still holding the mug's handle, the barbarian leader unsteadily clambered atop the table to tower over the dark elf.

In the blink of an eye, Hengorot hushed.

"You come here claiming alliance," the barbarian leader began slowly. "You come asking for alliance." He paused and looked around at his anxious people for dramatic effect. "And yet you hold prisoner the weapon that has become a symbol of my people, a weapon brought to glory by Wulfgar, son of Beornegar!"

Thunderous cheers erupted, and Catti-brie looked up to Drizzt and shrugged helplessly. She always hated it when the barbarians referred to Wulfgar by his legacy, as the son of Beornegar. For them to do so was an item of pride, and pride alone never sat well with the pragmatic woman.

Besides, Wulfgar needed no claim of lineage to heighten his short life's achievements. His children, had he sired any, would have been the ones to rightfully speak of their father.

"We are friends of the dwarf king you serve, dark elf," Berkthgar went on, his booming voice resonating off the stone sections of Hengorot's walls. "And we ask the same of Bruenor Battlehammer, son of Bangor, son of Garumn. You shall have your alliance, but not until Aegis-fang is delivered to me.

"I am Berkthgar!" the barbarian leader bellowed.

"Berkthgar the Bold!" several of the man's advisors quickly piped in, and another chorus went up, a toast of mugs lifted high to the mighty chieftain of Settlestone.

"Bruenor would sooner deliver his own axe," Drizzt replied, thoroughly fed up with Berkthgar's glories. The drow understood then that he and Catti-brie had been expected in Settlestone, for Berkthgar's little speech, and the reaction to it, had been carefully planned, even rehearsed.

"And I do not think you would enjoy the way he would deliver that axe," the drow finished quietly, when the roaring had died away. Again came the hush of expectation, for the drow's words could be taken as a challenge, and Berkthgar, blue eyes squinting dangerously, seemed more than ready to pick up the gauntlet.

"But Bruenor is not here," the barbarian leader said evenly. "Will Drizzt Do'Urden champion his cause?"

Drizzt straightened, trying to decide the best course.

Catti-brie's mind, too, was working fast. She held little doubt that Drizzt would accept the challenge and put Berkthgar down at once, and the men of Settlestone surely would not tolerate that kind of embarrassment.

"Wulfgar was to be my husband!" she yelled, rising from her chair just as Drizzt was about to respond. "And I am the daughter of Bruenor—by rights, the princess of Mithril Hall. If anyone here is to champion my father's cause—"

"You will name him," Berkthgar reasoned.

"I will be . . . her," Catti-brie replied grimly.

Roars went up again, all about the mead hall, and more than a few women at the back of the room tittered and nodded hopefully.

Drizzt didn't seem so pleased, and the look he put over Catti-brie was purely plaintive, begging her to calm this situation before things got fully out of hand. He didn't want a fight at all. Neither did Catti-brie, but the room was in a frenzy then, with more than half the voices crying for Berkthgar to "Fight the woman!" as though Catti-brie's challenge had already been launched.

The look that Berkthgar put over Catti-brie was one of pure outrage.

She understood and sympathized with his predicament. She had meant to go on and explain that she would be Bruenor's only champion, if there was to be a champion, but that she had not come here to fight. Events had swept her past that point, however.

"Never!" Berkthgar roared above the din, and the room

calmed somewhat, eager cries dying away to whispers. "Never have I battled a woman!"

That's an attitude Berkthgar had better overcome soon, Drizzt thought, for if the dark elves were indeed marching to Mithril Hall, there would be little room for such inhibitions. Females were typically the strongest of drow warriors, both magically and with weapons.

"Fight her!" cried one man, obviously very drunk, and he was laughing as he called, and so, too, were his fellows about him.

Berkthgar looked from the man to Catti-brie, his huge chest heaving as he tried to take in deep breaths to calm his rage.

He could not win, Catti-brie realized. If they fought, he could not win, even if he battered her. To the hardy men of Settlestone, even lifting a weapon against her would be considered cowardly.

Catti-brie climbed onto the table and gave a slight nod as she passed in front of Drizzt. Hands on hips—and her hip out to the side to accentuate her feminine figure—she gave a wistful smile to the barbarian leader. "Not with weapons, perhaps," she said. "But there are other ways a man and woman might compete."

All the room exploded at that comment. Mugs were lifted so forcefully in toast that little mead remained in them as they came back down to the eager mouths of the men. Several in the back end of Hengorot took up a lewd song, clapping each other on the back at every crescendo.

Drizzt's lavender eyes grew so wide that they seemed as if they would simply roll out of their sockets. When Catti-brie took the moment to regard him, she feared he would draw his weapons and kill everyone in the room. For an instant, she was flattered, but that quickly passed, replaced by disappointment that the drow would think so little of her.

She gave him a look that said just that as she turned and jumped down from the table. A man nearby reached out to catch her, but she slapped his hands away and strode defiantly for the door.

"There's fire in that one!" she heard behind her.

"Alas for poor Berkthgar!" came another rowdy cry.

On the table, the stunned barbarian leader turned this way and that, purposely avoiding the dark elf's gaze. Berkthgar was at a loss; Bruenor's daughter, though a famed adventurer, was not known for such antics. But Berkthgar was also more than a little intrigued. Every man in Settlestone considered Catti-brie, the princess of Mithril Hall, the fairest prize in all the region.

"Aegis-fang will be mine!" Berkthgar finally cried, and the roar behind him, and all about him, was deafening.

The barbarian leader was relieved to see that Drizzt was no longer facing him, was no longer anywhere in sight, when he turned back. One great leap had taken the dark elf from the table, and he strode eagerly for the door.

Outside Hengorot, in a quiet spot near an empty house, Drizzt took Catti-brie by the arm and turned her to face him. She expected him to shout at her, even expected him to slap her.

He laughed at her instead.

"Clever," Drizzt congratulated. "But can you take him?"

"How do ye know that I did not mean what I said?" Catti-brie snapped in reply.

"Because you have more respect for yourself than that," Drizzt answered without hesitation.

It was the perfect answer, the one Catti-brie needed to hear from her friend, and she did not press the point further.

"But can you take him?" the drow asked again, seriously. Catti-brie was good, and getting better with every lesson, but Berkthgar was huge and tremendously strong.

"He's drunk," Catti-brie replied. "And he's slow, like Wulfgar was before ye showed him the better way o' fighting." Her blue eyes, rich as the sky just before the dawn, sparkled. "Like ye showed me."

Drizzt patted her on the shoulder lightly, understanding then that this fight would be as important to her as it was to Berkthgar. The barbarian came storming out of the tent then, leaving a horde of sputtering comrades leering out of the open flap.

"Taking him won't be half the trouble as figuring out how to let him keep his honor," Catti-brie whispered.

Drizzt nodded and patted her shoulder again, then walked away, going in a wide circuit about Berkthgar and back toward the tent. Catti-brie had taken things into hand, he decided, and he owed her the respect to let her see this through.

The barbarians fell back as the drow came into the tent and pointedly closed the flap, taking one last look at Catti-brie as he did, to see her walking side by side with Berkthgar (and he so resembled huge Wulfgar from the back!) down the windswept lane.

For Drizzt Do'Urden, the image was not a pleasant one.

* * * * *

"Ye're not surprised?" Catti-brie asked as she removed the practice padding from her backpack and began sliding it over the fine edge of her sword. She felt a twinge of emotion as she did so, a sudden feeling of disappointment, even anger, which she did not understand.

"I did not believe for a moment that you had brought me out here for the reason you hinted at," Berkthgar replied casually. "Though if you had—"

"Shut yer mouth," Catti-brie sharply interrupted.

Berkthgar's jaw went firm. He was not accustomed to being talked to in that manner, particularly not from a woman. "We of Settlestone do not cover our blades when we fight," he said boastfully.

Catti-brie returned the barbarian leader's determined look, and as she did, she slid the sword back out from its protective sheath. A sudden rush of elation washed over her. As with the earlier feeling, she did not understand it, and so she thought that perhaps her anger toward Berkthgar was more profound than she had dared to admit to herself.

Berkthgar walked away then, to his house, and soon returned wearing a smug smile and a sheath strapped across his back. Above his right shoulder Catti-brie could see the hilt and crosspiece of his sword—a crosspiece nearly as long as her entire blade!—and the bottom portion of the sheath poked out below Berkthgar's left hip, extending almost to the ground.

Catti-brie watched, awestruck, wondering what she had gotten herself into, as Berkthgar solemnly drew the sword to the extent of his arm. The sheath had been cut along its upper side after a foot of leather so that the barbarian could then extract the gigantic blade.

And gigantic indeed was Berkthgar's flamberge! Its wavy blade extended over four feet, and after that came an eight-inch ricasso between the formal crosspiece and a second, smaller one of edged steel.

With one arm, muscles standing taut in ironlike cords, Berkthgar began spinning the blade, creating a great "whooshing" sound in the air above his head. Then he brought its tip to the ground before him and rested his arm on the crosspiece, which was about shoulder height to his six-and-a-half-foot frame.

"Ye meaning to fight with that, or kill fatted cows?" Catti-brie asked, trying hard to steal some of the man's mounting pride.

"I would still allow you to choose the other contest," Berkthgar replied calmly.

Catti-brie's sword snapped out in front of her, at the ready, and she went down in a low, defensive crouch.

The barbarian hooted and went into a similar pose, but then straightened, looking perplexed. "I cannot," Berkthgar began. "If I were to strike you even a glancing blow, King Battlehammer's heart would break as surely as would your skull."

Catti-brie came forward suddenly, jabbing at Berkthgar's shoulder and tearing a line in his furred jerkin.

He looked down at the cut, then his eyes came slowly back to regard Catti-brie, but other than that, he made no move.

"Ye're just afraid because ye're knowing that ye can't move that cow-killer fast enough," the young woman taunted.

Berkthgar blinked very slowly, exaggerated the movement as if to show how boring he thought this whole affair was. "I will show you the mantle where Bankenfuere is kept," he said. "And I will show you the bedding before the mantle."

"The thing's better for a mantle than a swordsman's hands!" Catti-brie growled, tired of this one's juvenile sexual references. She sprang ahead again and slapped the flat of her blade hard against Berkthgar's cheek, then jumped back, still snarling. "If ye're afraid, then admit it!"

Berkthgar's hand went immediately to his wound, and when it came away, the barbarian saw that his fingers were red with blood. Catti-brie winced at that, for she hadn't meant to hit him quite so hard.

Subtle were the intrusions of Khazid'hea.

"I am out of patience with you, foolish woman," snarled the barbarian, and up came the tip of tremendous Bankenfuere, the

R. A. Salvatore

Northern Fury.

Berkthgar growled and leaped ahead, both hands on the hilt this time as he swung the huge blade across in front of him. He attacked with the flat of his blade, as had Catti-brie, but the young woman realized that would hardly matter. Getting hit by the flat of that tremendous flamberge would still reduce her bones to mush!

Catti-brie wasn't anywhere near Berkthgar at that point, the woman in fast retreat (and wondering again if she was in over her head) as soon as the sword went up. The flamberge curled in an arc back over, left to right, then came across a second time, this cut angling down. Faster than Catti-brie expected, Berkthgar reversed the flow, the blade swishing horizontally again, this time left to right, then settled back at the ready beside the barbarian's muscular shoulder.

An impressive display indeed, but Catti-brie had watched the routine carefully, no longer through awestruck eyes, and she noticed more than a few holes in the barbarian's defenses.

Of course, she had to be perfect in her timing. One slip, and Bankenfuere would turn her into worm food.

On came Berkthgar, with another horizontal cut, a predictable attack, for there were only so many ways one could maneuver such a weapon! Catti-brie fell back a step, then an extra step just to make sure, and darted in behind the lumbering sweep of the blade, looking to score a hit on the barbarian's arm. Berkthgar was quicker than that, though, and he had the blade coming around and over so fast that Catti-brie had to abort the attack and scramble hard just to get out of the way.

Still, she had won that pass, she figured, for now she had a better measure of Berkthgar's reach. And by her thinking, every passing moment favored her, for she saw the sweat beading on the drunken barbarian's forehead, his great chest heaving just a bit more than before.

"If ye do other things as poorly as ye fight, then suren I'm glad I chose this contest," Catti-brie said, a taunt that sent proud Berkthgar into another wild-swinging tirade.

Catti-brie dodged and scrambled as Bankenfuere came across in several titanic, and ultimately futile, swipes. Across it came again, the barbarian's fury far from played out, and Catti-brie leaped back. Around and over went the blade, Berkthgar charging ahead, and Catti-brie went far out to the side, just ahead as the great sword came whipping down and across.

"I shall catch up to you soon enough!" Berkthgar promised, turning square to the young woman and whipping his mighty blade left to right once more, bringing it to the ready beside his right shoulder.

Catti-brie started in behind the cut, taking a long stride with her right foot, extending her sword arm toward Berkthgar's exposed hip. She dug her left foot in solidly, though, and had no intention of continuing the move. As soon as Bankenfuere came across to intercept, Catti-brie leaped back, pivoted on her anchor leg, and rushed in behind the blade, going for Berkthgar's right hip instead, and scored a nasty, stinging hit.

The barbarian growled and spun so forcefully that he nearly overbalanced.

Catti-brie stood a few feet away, crouched low, ready. There was no doubt that swinging the heavy weapon was beginning to take a toll on the man, especially after his generous swallows of mead.

"A few more passes," Catti-brie whispered, forcing herself to be patient.

And so she played on as the minutes passed, as Berkthgar's breathing came as loudly as the moaning wind. Through each attack, Catti-brie confirmed her final routine, one that took advantage of the fact that Berkthgar's huge blade and thick arms made a perfect optical barricade.

* * * * *

Drizzt suffered through the half-hour of rude comments.

"Never has he lasted this long!" offered one barbarian.

"Berkthgar the Brauzen!" cried another, the barbarian word for stamina.

"Brauzen!" all the rowdy men shouted together, lifting their mugs in cheer. Some of the women in the back of Hengorot tittered at the bawdy display, but most wore sour expressions.

"Brauzen," the drow whispered, and Drizzt thought the word perfectly fitting for describing his own patience during those

insufferably long minutes. As angry as he was at the rude jokes at Catti-brie's expense, he was more fearful that Berkthgar would harm her, perhaps defeat her in battle and then take her in other ways.

Drizzt worked hard to keep his imagination at bay. For all his boasting, for all of his people's boasting, Berkthgar was an honorable man. But he was drunk . . .

I will kill him, Drizzt decided, and if anything the drow feared had come to pass, he indeed would cut mighty Berkthgar down.

It never got to that point, though, for Berkthgar and Catti-brie walked back into the tent, looking a bit ruffled, the barbarian's stubbly beard darkened in one area with some dried blood, but otherwise seeming okay.

Catti-brie winked subtly as she passed the drow.

Hengorot fell into a hush, the drunken men no doubt expecting some lewd tales of their leader's exploits.

Berkthgar looked to Catti-brie, and she wouldn't blink.

"I will not carry Aegis-fang," the barbarian leader announced.

Moans and hoots erupted, as did speculation about who won the "contest."

Berkthgar blushed, and Drizzt feared there would be trouble.

Catti-brie went up on the table. "Not a better man in Settlestone!" she insisted.

Several barbarians rushed forward to the table's edge, willing to take up that challenge.

"Not a better man!" Catti-brie growled at them, her fury driving them back.

"I'll not carry the warhammer, in honor of Wulfgar," Berkthgar explained. "And for the honor of Catti-brie."

Blank stares came back at him.

"If I am to properly suit the daughter of King Bruenor, our friend and ally," the barbarian leader went on, and Drizzt smiled at that reference, "then it is my own weapon, Bankenfuere, that must become legend." He held high the huge flamberge, and the crowd roared with glee.

The issue was ended, the alliance sealed, and more mead was passed about before Catti-brie even got down from the table, heading for Drizzt. She stopped as she walked beside the barbarian leader, and gave him a sly look.

"If ye ever openly lie," she whispered, taking care that no one could hear, "or if ye ever even hint that ye bedded me, then be knowin' that I'll come back and cut ye down in front o' all yer people."

Berkthgar's expression grew somber at that, and even more somber as he turned to watch Catti-brie depart, to see her deadly drow friend standing easily, hands on scimitar hilts, his lavender eyes telling the barbarian in no uncertain terms his feelings for Catti-brie. Berkthgar didn't want to tangle with Catti-brie again, but he would rather battle her a hundred times than fight the drow ranger.

"You'll come back and cut him down?" Drizzt asked as they exited the town, revealing to Catti-brie that his keen ears had caught her parting words with the barbarian.

"Not a promise I'd ever want to try," Catti-brie replied, shaking her head. "Fighting that one when he's not so full o' mead would be about the same as walking into the cave of a restless bear."

Drizzt stopped abruptly, and Catti-brie, after taking a couple more steps, turned about to regard him.

He stood pointing at her, smiling widely. "I have done that!" he remarked, and so Drizzt had yet another tale to recount as the two (and then three, for Drizzt was quick to recall Guenhwyvar) made their way along the trails, back into the mountains.

Later, as the stars twinkled brightly and the campfire burned low, Drizzt sat watching Catti-brie's prone form, her rhythmic breathing telling the drow that she was fast asleep.

"You know I love her," the drow said to Guenhwyvar.

The panther blinked her shining green eyes, but otherwise did not move.

"Yet, how could I?" Drizzt asked. "And not for the memory of Wulfgar," he quickly added, and he nodded as he heard himself speak the words, knowing that Wulfgar, who loved Drizzt as Drizzt loved him, would not disapprove.

"How could I ever?" the drow reiterated, his voice barely a whisper.

Guenhwyvar issued a long, low growl, but if it had any meaning, other than to convey that the panther was interested in what the drow was saying, it was lost on Drizzt.

"She will not live so long," Drizzt went on quietly. "I will still be a young drow when she is gone." Drizzt looked from Catti-brie to the panther, and a new insight occurred to him. "You must understand such things, my eternal friend," the drow said. "Where will I fall in the span of your life? How many others have you kept as you keep me, my Guenhwyvar, and how many more shall there be?"

Drizzt rested his back against the mountain wall and looked to Catti-brie, then up to the stars. Sad were his thoughts, and yet, in many ways, they were comforting, like an eternal play, like emotions shared, like memories of Wulfgar. Drizzt sent those thoughts skyward, into the heavenly canopy, letting them break apart on the ceaseless and mournful wind.

His dreams were full of images of friends, of Zaknafein, his father, of Belwar, the svirfneblin gnome, of Captain Deudermont, of the good ship *Sea Sprite*, of Regis and Bruenor, of Wulfgar, and most of all, of Catti-brie.

It was as calm and pleasant a sleep as Drizzt Do'Urden had ever known.

Guenhwyvar watched the drow for some time, then rested her great feline head on wide paws and closed her green eyes. Drizzt's comments had hit the mark, except, of course, his intimation that her memory of him would be inconsequential in the centuries ahead. Guenhwyvar had indeed come to the call of many masters, most goodly, some wicked, in the past millennium, and even beyond that. Some the panther remembered, some not, but Drizzt . . .

Forever would Guenhwyvar remember the renegade dark elf, whose heart was so strong and so good and whose loyalty was no less than the panther's own.

Part 2

THE ONSET OF CHAOS

orever after, the bards of the Realms called it the Time of Troubles, the time when the gods were kicked out of the heavens, their avatars walking among the mortals. The time when the Tablets of Fate were stolen, invoking the wrath of Ao, Overlord of the Gods, when magic went awry, and when, as a consequence, social and religious hierarchies, so often based on magical strength, fell into chaos.

I have heard many tales from fanatical priests of their encounters with their particular avatars, frenzied stories from men and women who claim to have looked upon their deities. So many others came to convert to a religion during this troubled time, likewise claiming they had seen the light and the truth, however convoluted it might be.

I do not disagree with the claims, and would not openly attack the premise of their encounters. I am glad for those who have found enrichment amidst the chaos; I am glad whenever another person finds the contentment of spiritual guidance.

But what of faith?

What of fidelity and loyalty? Complete trust? Faith is not granted by tangible proof. It comes from the heart and the soul. If a person needs proof of a god's existence, then the very notion of spirituality is diminished into sensuality and we have reduced what is holy into what is logical.

I have touched the unicorn, so rare and so precious, the symbol of the goddess Mielikki, who holds my heart and soul. This was before the onset of the Time of Troubles, yet were I of a like mind to those who make the claims of viewing avatars, I could say the same. I could say that I have touched Mielikki, that she came to me in a magical glade in the mountains near Dead Orc Pass.

The unicorn was not Mielikki, and yet it was, as is the sunrise and the seasons, as are the birds and the squirrels and the strength of a tree that has lived through the dawn and death of centuries. As are the leaves, blowing on autumn winds and the snow piling deep in cold mountain vales. As are

66

the smell of a crisp night, the twinkle of the starry canopy, and the howl of a distant wolf.

No, I'll not argue openly against one who has claimed to have seen an avatar, because that person will not understand that the mere presence of such a being undermines the very purpose of, and value of, faith. Because if the true gods were so tangible and so accessible, then we would no longer be independent creatures set on a journey to find the truth, but merely a herd of sheep needing the guidance of a shepherd and his dogs, unthinking and without the essence of faith.

The guidance is there, I know. Not in such a tangible form, but in what we know to be good and just. It is our own reactions to the acts of others that show us the value of our own actions, and if we have fallen so far as to need an avatar, an undeniable manifestation of a god, to show us our way, then we are pitiful creatures indeed.

The Time of Troubles? Yes. And even more so if we are to believe the suggestion of avatars, because truth is singular and cannot, by definition, support so many varied, even opposing manifestations.

The unicorn was not Mielikki, and yet it was, for I have touched Mielikki. Not as an avatar, or as a unicorn, but as a way of viewing my place in the world. Mielikki is my heart. I follow her precepts because, were I to write precepts based on my own conscience, they would be the same. I follow Mielikki because she represents what I call truth.

Such is the case for most of the followers of most of the various gods, and if we looked more closely at the pantheon of the Realms, we would realize that the precepts of the "goodly" gods are not so different; it is the worldly interpretations of those precepts that vary from faith to faith.

As for the other gods, the gods of strife and chaos, such as Lloth, the Spider Queen, who possesses the hearts of those priestesses who rule Menzoberranzan . . .

They are not worth mentioning. There is no truth, only worldly gain, and any religion based on such principles is, in fact, no more than a practice of self-indulgence and in no way a measure of spirituality. In worldly terms, the priestesses of the Spider Queen are quite formidable; in spiritual terms, they are empty. Thus, their lives are without love and without joy.

So tell me not of avatars. Show me not your proof that yours is the true god. I grant you your beliefs without question and without judgment, but if you grant me what is in my heart, then such tangible evidence is irrelevant.

— Drizzt Do'Urden

67

Chapter 6

WHEN MAGIC WENT AWRY

erg'inyon Baenre, weapon master of the first house of Menzoberranzan, put his twin swords through a dizzying routine, blades spinning circuits in the air between him and his opponent, an insubordinate drow common soldier.

A crowd of the Baenre house guard, highly trained though mostly males, formed a semicircle about the pair, while other dark elves watched from high perches, tightly saddled astride sticky-footed, huge subterranean lizards, the beasts casually standing along the vertical slopes of nearby stalactites or towering stalagmite mounds.

The soldiers cheered every time Berg'inyon, a magnificent swordsman (though few thought him as good as his brother, Dantrag, had been), scored a minor hit or parried a fast-flying counter, but the cheers were obviously somewhat tempered.

Berg'inyon noticed this, and knew the source. He had been the leader of the Baenre lizard riders, the most elite grouping of the male house guards, for many years. Now, with Dantrag slain, he had become the house weapon master as well. Berg'inyon felt the intense pressure of his dual stations, felt his mother's scrutinizing gaze on his every movement and every decision. He did not doubt that his own actions had intensified as a result. How many fights had he begun, how many punishments had he exacted on his subordinates, since Dantrag's death?

The common drow came ahead with a weak thrust that almost slipped past distracted Berg'inyon's defenses. A sword came up and about at the last moment to drive the enemy's blade aside.

Berg'inyon heard the sudden hush behind him at the near miss, understood that several of the soldiers back there—perhaps all of them—hoped his enemy's next thrust would be quicker, too quick.

The weapon master growled low and came ahead in a flurry, spurred on by the hatred of those around him, of those under his command. Let them hate him! he decided. But while they did, they must also respect him—no, not respect, Berg'inyon decided. They must fear him.

He came forward one step, then a second, his swords snapping alternately, left and right, and each being cleanly picked off. The give and take had become common, with Berg'inyon coming ahead two steps, then retreating. This time, though, the Baenre did not retreat. He shuffled forward two more steps, his swords snapping as his opponent's blades rushed for the parry.

Berg'inyon had the lesser drow up on his heels, so the young Baenre rushed ahead again. His opponent was quick enough with his swords to turn the expected thrusts, but he could not retreat properly, and Berg'inyon was up against him in a clinch, their blades joined to either side, down low, by the hilt.

There was no real danger here—it was more like a break in the battle—but Berg'inyon realized something his opponent apparently did not. With a growl, the young Baenre heaved his off-balance opponent away. The drow skidded back a couple of steps, brought his swords up immediately to fend off any pursuit.

None came; it seemed a simple break of the clinch.

Then the backpedaling drow bumped into the House Baenre fence.

In the city of Menzoberranzan, there was perhaps nothing as spectacular as the twenty-foot-high, web-designed fence ringing House Baenre, anchored on the various stalagmite mounds that ringed the compound. Its silvery metallic cords, thick as a dark elf's leg, were wound into beautiful, symmetrical designs, as intricate as the work of any spider. No weapon could cut through it, no magic, save a single item that Matron Baenre possessed, could get one over it, and the simplest touch or brush against one of those enchanted strands would hold fast a titan.

Berg'inyon's opponent hit the fence hard with the flat of his back. His eyes went wide as he suddenly realized the young Baenre's tactics, as he saw the faces of those gathered brighten in approval of the vicious trick, as he saw devious and wicked Berg'inyon calmly approach.

The drow fell away from the fence and rushed out to meet the weapon master's advance.

The two went through a fast series of attacks and parries, with stunned Berg'inyon on the defensive. Only through his years of superior training was the drow noble able to bring himself back even against his surprising opponent.

Surprising indeed, as every drow face, and all the whispers, confirmed.

"You brushed the fence," Berg'inyon said.

The drow soldier did not disagree. The tips of his weapons drooped as Berg'inyon's drooped, and he glanced over his shoulder to confirm what he, and all the others, knew could not be.

"You hit the fence," Berg'inyon said again, skeptically, as the drow turned back to face him.

"Across the back," he agreed.

Berg'inyon's swords went into their respective scabbards and the young Baenre stormed past his opponent, to stand right before the enchanted web. His opponent and all the other dark elves followed closely, too intrigued to even think of continuing the fight.

Berg'inyon motioned to a nearby female. "Rest your sword against it," he bade her.

The female drew her blade and laid it across one of the thick strands. She looked to Berg'inyon and around to all the others, then easily lifted the blade from the fence.

Another drow farther down the line dared to place his hand on the web. Those around him looked at him incredulously, thinking him dangerously daring, but he had no trouble removing himself from the metal.

Panic rushed through Berg'inyon. The fence, it was said, had been a gift from Lloth herself in millennia past. If it was no longer functioning, it might well mean that House Baenre had fallen out of the Spider Queen's favor. It might well mean that Lloth had dropped House

Baenre's defense to allow for a conspiracy of lower houses.

"To your posts, all of you!" the young Baenre shouted, and the gathered dark elves, sharing Berg'inyon's reasoning and his fears, did not have to be told twice.

Berg'inyon headed for the compound's great central mound to find his mother. He crossed paths with the drow he had just been fighting, and the commoner's eyes widened in sudden fear. Normally Berg'inyon, honorable only by the low standards of dark elves, would have snapped his sword out and through the drow, ending the conflict. Caught up in the excitement of the fence's failure, the commoner was off his guard. He knew it, too, and he expected to be killed.

"To your post," Berg'inyon said to him, for if the young Baenre's suspicions proved correct, that a conspiracy had been launched against House Baenre and Lloth had deserted them, he would need every one of the House's twenty-five hundred soldiers.

* * * * *

King Bruenor Battlehammer had spent the morning in the upper chapel of Mithril Hall, trying to sort out the new hierarchy of priests within the complex. His dear friend Cobble had been the reigning priest, a dwarf of powerful magic and deep wisdom.

That wisdom hadn't gotten poor Cobble out of the way of a nasty drow spell, though, and the cleric had been squashed by a falling wall of iron.

There were more than a dozen remaining acolytes in Mithril Hall. They formed two lines, one on each side of Bruenor's audience chair. Each priest was anxious to impress his (or, in the case of Stumpet Rakingclaw, her) king.

Bruenor nodded to the dwarf at the head of the line to his left. As he did, he lifted a mug of mead, the holy water this particular priest had concocted. Bruenor sipped, then drained the surprisingly refreshing mead in a single swallow as the cleric stepped forward.

"A burst of light in honor of King Bruenor!" the would-be head priest cried, and he waved his arms and began a chanting prayer to Moradin, the Soulforger, god of the dwarves.

"Clean and fresh, and just the slightest twinge of bitterness," Bruenor remarked, running a finger along the rim of the emptied mug and then sucking on it, that he might savor the last drop. The scribe directly behind the throne noted every word. "A hearty bouquet, properly curling nose hairs," Bruenor added. "Seven."

The eleven other clerics groaned. Seven on a scale of ten was the highest grade Bruenor had given any of the five samples of holy water he had already taste-tested.

If Jerbollah, the dwarf now in a frenzy of spellcasting, could perform as well with magic, he would be difficult to beat for the coveted position.

"And the light shall be," Jerbollah cried, the climax of his spell, "red!"

There came a tremendous popping noise, as if a hundred dwarves had just yanked their fingers from puckered mouths. And then . . . nothing.

"Red!" Jerbollah cried in delight.

"What?" demanded Bruenor, who, like those dwarves beside him, saw nothing different about the lighting in the chapel.

"Red!" Jerbollah said again, and when he turned about, Bruenor and the others understood. Jerbollah's face was glowing a bright red—literally, the confused cleric was seeing the world through a rose-colored veil.

Frustrated Bruenor dropped his head into his palm and groaned.

"Makes a good batch o' holy water, though," one of the dwarves nearby remarked, to a chorus of snickers.

Poor Jerbollah, who thought his spell had worked brilliantly, did not understand what was so funny.

Stumpet Rakingclaw leaped forward, seizing the moment. She handed her mug of holy water to Bruenor and rushed out before the throne.

"I had planned something different," she explained quickly, as Bruenor sipped, then swallowed the mead (and the dwarf king's face brightened once more as he declared this batch a nine). "But a cleric of Moradin, of Clanggedon, who knows battle best of all, must be ready to improvise!"

"Do tell us, O Strumpet!" one of the other dwarves roared, and even Bruenor cracked a smile as the laughter exploded about him.

Stumpet, who was used to the nickname and wore it like a badge of honor, took no offense. "Jerbollah called for red," she explained, "so red it shall be!"

"It already *is* red," insisted Jerbollah, who earned a slap on the head from the dwarf behind him for his foolishness.

The fiery young Stumpet ruffled her short red beard and went into a series of movements so exaggerated that it seemed as if she had fallen into convulsions.

"Move it, Strumpet," a dwarf near the throne whispered, to renewed laughter.

Bruenor held up the mug and tapped it with his finger. "Nine," he reminded the wise-cracking dwarf. Stumpet was in the clear lead; if she pulled off this spell where Jerbollah had failed, she would be almost impossible to beat, which would make her the wise-cracking dwarf's boss.

The dwarf behind the humbled jokester slapped him on the back of the head.

"Red!" Stumpet cried with all her might.

Nothing happened.

A few snickers came from the line, but in truth, the gathered dwarves were more curious than amused. Stumpet was a powerful spellcaster and should have been able to throw some light, whatever color, into the room. The feeling began to wash over them all (except Jerbollah, who insisted that his spell had worked perfectly), that something might be wrong here.

Stumpet turned back to the throne, confused and embarrassed. She started to say something, to apologize, when a tremendous explosion rocked the ground so violently that she and half the other dwarves in the room were knocked from their feet.

Stumpet rolled and turned, looking back to the empty area of the chapel. A ball of blue sparks appeared from nowhere, hovered in the air, then shot straight for a very surprised Bruenor. The dwarf king ducked and thrust his arm up to block, and the mug that held Stumpet's batch of holy water shattered, sheared off at the handle. A blue storm of raging sparks burst from the impact, sending dwarves scurrying for cover.

More sparking bursts ignited across the room, glowing balls zipping this way and that, thunderlike booms shaking the floor and walls.

"What in the Nine Hells did ye do?" the dwarf king, a little curled-up ball on his great chair, screamed at poor Stumpet.

The female dwarf tried to respond, tried to disclaim responsibility for this unexpected turn, but a small tube appeared in midair, generally pointed her way, and fired multicolored balls that sent Stumpet scrambling away.

It went on for several long, frightening minutes, dwarves diving every which way, sparks seeming to follow them wherever they hid, burning their backsides and singeing their beards. Then it was over, as suddenly as it had begun, leaving the chapel perfectly quiet and smelling of sulphur.

Gradually Bruenor straightened in his chair and tried to regain some of his lost dignity.

"What in the Nine Hells did ye do?" he demanded again, to which poor Stumpet merely shrugged. A couple of dwarves managed a slight laugh at that.

"At least it's still red," Jerbollah remarked under his breath, but loud enough to be heard. Again he was slapped by the dwarf behind him.

Bruenor shook his head in disgust, then froze in place as two eyeballs appeared in the air before him, scrutinizing him ominously.

Then they dropped to the floor and rolled about haphazardly, coming to rest several feet apart.

Bruenor looked on in disbelief as a spectral hand came out of the air and herded the eyeballs close together and turned them so that they were both facing the dwarf king once more.

"Well, that's never happened before," said a disembodied voice.

Bruenor jumped in fright, then settled and groaned yet again. He hadn't heard that voice in a long time, but never would he forget it. And it explained so much about what was going on in the chapel.

"Harkle Harpell," Bruenor said, and whispers ignited all about him, for most of the other dwarves had heard Bruenor's tales of Longsaddle, a town to the west of Mithril Hall, home of the legendary, eccentric wizard clan, the Harpells. Bruenor and his companions had passed through Longsaddle, had toured the Ivy Mansion, on their way to find Mithril Hall. It was a place the dwarf, no fan of wizardly magic, would never forget, and never remember fondly.

"My greetings, King Bruenor," said the voice, emanating from the floor right below the steadied eyeballs.

"Are ye really here?" the dwarf king asked.

"Hmmm," groaned the floor. "I can hear both you and those who are around me at the Fuzzy Quarterstaff," Harkle replied, referring to the tavern at the Ivy Mansion, back in Longsaddle. "Just a moment, if you please."

The floor "Hmmmm'd" several more times, and the eyeballs blinked once or twice, perhaps the most curious sight Bruenor had ever seen, as an eyelid appeared from nowhere, covered the ball momentarily, then disappeared once more.

"It seems that I'm in both places," Harkle tried to explain. "I'm quite blind back here—of course, my eyes are there. I wonder if I might get them back . . ." The spectral hand appeared again, groping for the eyeballs. It tried to grasp one of them securely, but only wound up turning the ball about on the floor.

"Whoa!" shouted a distressed Harkle. "So that is how a lizard sees the world! I must note it . . ."

"Harkle!" Bruenor roared in frustration.

"Oh, yes, yes, of course," replied Harkle, coming to what little senses he possessed. "Please excuse my distraction, King Bruenor. This has never happened before."

"Well it's happened now," Bruenor said dryly.

"My eyes are there," Harkle said, as though trying to sort things out aloud. "But, of course, I will be there as well, quite soon. Actually, I had hoped to be there now, but didn't get through. Curious indeed. I could try again, or could ask one of my brothers to try—"

"No!" Bruenor bellowed, cringing at the thought that other Harpell body parts might soon rain down on him.

"Of course," Harkle agreed after a moment. "Too dangerous. Too curious. Very well, then. I come in answer to your call, friend dwarf king!"

Bruenor dropped his head into his palm and sighed. He had feared those very words for more than two weeks now. He had sent an emissary to Longsaddle for help in the potential war only because Drizzt had insisted.

To Bruenor, having the Harpells as allies might eliminate the need for enemies.

"A week," Harkle's disembodied voice said. "I will arrive in a week!" There came a long pause. "Err, umm, could you be so kind as to keep safe my eyeballs?"

Bruenor nodded to the side, and several dwarves scrambled ahead, curious and no longer afraid of the exotic items. They battled to scoop up the eyes and finally sorted them out, with two different dwarves each holding one—and each taking obvious pleasure in making faces at the eye.

Bruenor shouted for them to quit playing even before Harkle's voice screamed in horror.

"Please!" pleaded the somewhat absent mage. "Only one dwarf to hold both eyes." Immediately the two dwarves clutched their prizes more tightly.

"Give 'em to Stumpet!" Bruenor roared. "She started this whole thing!"

Reluctantly, but not daring to go against an order from their king, the dwarves handed the eyeballs over.

"And do please keep them moist," Harkle requested, to which, Stumpet immediately tossed one of the orbs into her mouth.

"Not like that!" screamed the voice. "Oh, not like that!"

"I should get them," protested Jerbollah. "My spell worked!" The dwarf behind Jerbollah slapped him on the head.

Bruenor slumped low in his chair, shaking his head. It was going to be a long time in putting his clerical order back together, and longer still would be the preparations for war when the Harpells arrived.

Across the room, Stumpet, who, despite her antics, was the most level-headed of dwarves, was not so lighthearted. Harkle's unexpected presence had deflected the other apparent problems, perhaps, but the weird arrival of the wizard from Longsaddle did not explain the happenings here. Stumpet, several of the other clerics, and even the scribe realized that something was very wrong.

* * * * *

Guenhwyvar was tired by the time she, Drizzt, and Catti-brie came to the high pass leading to Mithril Hall's eastern door. Drizzt had kept the panther on the Material Plane longer than usual, and though it was taxing, Guenhwyvar was glad for the stay. With all the preparations going on in the deep tunnels below the dwarven complex, Drizzt did not get outside much, and consequently, neither did Guenhwyvar.

For a long, long time, the panther figurine had been in the hands of various drow in Menzoberranzan, and, thus, the panther had gone centuries without seeing the out-of-doors on the Material Plane. Still, the out-of-doors was where Guenhwyvar was most at home, where natural panthers lived, and where the panther's first companions on the Material Plane had lived.

Guenhwyvar had indeed enjoyed this romp along mountain trails with Drizzt and Catti-brie, but now was the time to go home, to rest again on the Astral Plane. For all their love of companionship, neither the drow nor the panther could afford that luxury now, with so great a danger looming, an impending war in which Drizzt and Guenhwyvar would likely play a major role, fighting side by side.

The panther paced about the figurine, gradually diminished, and faded to an insubstantial gray mist.

* * * * *

Gone from the material world, Guenhwyvar entered a long, low, winding tunnel, the silvery path that would take her back to the Astral Plane. The panther loped easily, not eager to be gone and too tired to run full out. The journey was not so long anyway, and always uneventful.

Guenhwyvar skidded to a stop as she rounded one long bend, her ears falling flat.

The tunnel ahead was ablaze.

Diabolical forms, fiendish manifestations that seemed unconcerned with the approaching cat, leaped from those flames. Guenhwyvar padded ahead a few short strides. She could feel the intense heat, could see the fiery fiends, and could hear their laughter as they continued to consume the circular tunnel's walls.

A rush of air told Guenhwyvar that the tunnel had been ruptured, somewhere in the emptiness between the planes of existence. Fiery fiends were pulled into elongated shapes, then sucked out; the remaining flames danced wildly, leaping and flickering, seeming to go out altogether, then rising together in a sudden and violent surge. The wind came strong at Guenhwyvar's back, compelling the panther to go forward, compelling everything in the tunnel to fly out through the breach, into nothingness.

Guenhwyvar knew instinctively that if she succumbed to that force, there would be no turning back, that she would become a lost thing, helpless, wandering between the planes.

The panther dug in her claws and backpedaled slowly, fighting the fierce wind every inch of the way. Her black coat ruffled up, sleek fur turning the wrong way.

One step back.

The tunnel was smooth and hard, and there was little for panther claws to dig against. Guenhwyvar's paws pedaled more frantically, but inevitably the cat began to slide forward toward the flames and the breach.

* * * * *

"What is it?" Catti-brie asked, seeing Drizzt's confusion as he picked up the figurine.

"Warm," Drizzt replied. "The figurine is warm."

Catti-brie's expression likewise crinkled with confusion. She had a feeling of sheer dread then, a feeling she could not understand. "Call Guen back," she prompted.

Drizzt, equally fearful, was already doing exactly that. He placed the figurine on the ground and called out to the panther.

* * * * *

Guenhwyvar heard the call, and wanted desperately to answer it, but now the cat was close to the breach. Wild flames danced high, singeing the panther's face. The wind was stronger than ever, and there was nothing, nothing at all, for Guenhwyvar to hold on to.

The panther knew fear, and the panther knew grief. Never again would she come to Drizzt's call; never again would she hunt beside the ranger in the forests near Mithril Hall or race down a mountain with Drizzt and Catti-brie.

Guenhwyvar had known grief before, when some of her previous masters had died. This time, though, there could be no replacement for Drizzt. And none for Catti-brie or Regis, or even Bruenor, that most frustrating of creatures, whose love and hate relationship with Guenhwyvar had provided the panther with many hours of teasing enjoyment.

Guenhwyvar remembered the time Drizzt had bade her lie atop sleeping Bruenor and nap. How the dwarf had roared!

Flames bit at Guenhwyvar's face. She could see through the breach now, see the emptiness that awaited her.

Somewhere far off, beyond the shield of the screeching wind, came Drizzt's call, a call the cat could not answer.

Chapter 7
BAENRE'S FAULT

thegental Armgo, the patron and weapon master of Barrison del'Armgo, Second House of Menzoberranzan, was not Jarlaxle's favorite drow. In fact, Jarlaxle wasn't certain that this one was truly a drow at all. Standing near six feet, with a muscled torso that weighed close to two hundred pounds, Uthegental was the largest dark elf in Menzoberranzan, one of the largest of the normally slender race ever seen in the Underdark. More than size distinguished the fierce weapon master, though. While Jarlaxle was considered eccentric, Uthegental was simply frightening. He cropped his white hair short and spiked it with the thick, gelatinous extract gained by boiling rothe udders. A mithril ring was stuck through Uthegental's angular nose, and a golden pin protruded through each cheek.

His weapon was a trident, black like the fine-fitting mail of jointed plates he wore, and a net—magical, so it was said—hung on his belt, within easy reach.

Jarlaxle was glad that at least Uthegental wasn't wearing his war paint this day, zigzagging streaks of some dye the mercenary did not know that showed yellow and red in both the normal and

79

infrared spectrums. It was common knowledge in Menzoberranzan that Uthegental, in addition to being patron to Matron Mother Mez'Barris, was the consort of many Barrison del'Armgo females. The second house considered him breeding stock, and the thought of dozens of little Uthegentals running around brought a sour expression to Jarlaxle's face.

"The magic is wild, yet I remain strong!" the exotic weapon master growled, his perpetually furrowed brow making him even more imposing. He held one iron-muscled arm to the side and tightened his biceps as he crooked his elbow, the rock-hard muscles of his arm standing high and proud.

Jarlaxle took a moment to remind himself where he was, in the midst of his own encampment, in his own room and seated behind his own desk, secretly surrounded by a dozen highly skilled and undeniably loyal soldiers of Bregan D'aerthe. Even without the concealed allies, Jarlaxle's desk was equipped with more than a few deadly traps for troublesome guests. And, of course, Jarlaxle was no minor warrior himself. A small part of him—a *very* small part of him—wondered how he might measure up in battle against Uthegental.

Few warriors, drow or otherwise, could intimidate the mercenary leader, but he allowed himself a bit of humility in the face of this maniac.

"*Ultrin Sargtlin!*" Uthegental went on, the drow term for "Supreme Warrior," a claim that seemed secure within the city with Dantrag Baenre dead. Jarlaxle often imagined the battle that most of Menzoberranzan's dark elves thought would one day be waged by bitter rivals Uthegental and Dantrag.

Dantrag had been the quicker—quicker than anyone—but with his sheer strength and size, Uthegental had rated as Jarlaxle's favorite in such a contest. It was said that when he went into his battle rage, Uthegental possessed the strength of a giant, and this fearsome weapon master was so tough that when he battled lesser creatures, such as goblin slaves, he always allowed his opponent to swing first, and never tried to parry the attack, accepting the vicious hit, reveling in the pain, before tearing his enemy limb from limb and having the choicest body parts prepared for his supper.

Jarlaxle shuddered at the notion, then put the image from his mind, reminding himself that he and Uthegental had more important business.

"There is no weapon master, no drow at all, in Menzoberranzan to stand against me," Uthegental continued his boasting, for no reason that Jarlaxle could discern beyond the savage's overblown sense of pride.

He went on and on, as was his way, and while Jarlaxle wanted to ask him if there was a point to it all, he kept silent, confident that the emissary from the second house would eventually get around to a serious discussion.

Uthegental stopped his mounting tirade suddenly, and his hand shot out, snatching from the top of the desk a gem that the mercenary used as a paperweight. Uthegental muttered some word that Jarlaxle did not catch, but the mercenary's keen eye did note a slight flicker in the huge drow's brooch, the house emblem of Barrison del'Armgo. Uthegental then held the gem aloft and squeezed it with all his strength. The muscles in his sculpted arm strained and bulged, but the gem held firm.

"I should be able to crush this," Uthegental growled. "Such is the power, the magic, that I have been Lloth-blessed with!"

"The gem would not be worth as much when reduced to powder," Jarlaxle replied dryly. What was Uthegental's point? he wondered. Of course, something strange was going on with magic all over the city. Now Jarlaxle better understood Uthegental's earlier boasting. The exotic weapon master was indeed still strong, but not as strong, a fact that apparently worried Uthegental more than a little.

"Magic is failing," the weapon master said, "failing everywhere. The priestesses kneel in prayer, sacrifice drow after drow, and still nothing they do brings Lloth or her handmaidens to them. Magic is failing, and it is Matron Baenre's fault!"

Jarlaxle took note of the way Uthegental seemed to repeat things. Probably to remind himself of what he was talking about, the mercenary mused, and his sour expression aptly reflected his opinion of Uthegental's intellect. Of course, Uthegental would never catch the subtle indication.

"You cannot know that," the mercenary replied. Uthegental's accusation no doubt came from Matron Mez'Barris herself. Many things were coming clear to the mercenary now, mostly the fact that Mez'Barris had sent Uthegental to feel out Bregan D'aerthe, to see if the time was ripe for a coup against Baenre. Uthegental's words could certainly be considered damning, but not against Barrison del'Armgo, for their weapon master was always running off at the mouth, and never with anything complimentary to anyone but himself.

"It was Matron Baenre who allowed the rogue Do'Urden to escape," Uthegental bellowed. "It was she who presided over the failed high ritual! Failed, as magic is failing."

Say it again, Jarlaxle thought, but wisely kept that derisive reply silent. The mercenary's frustration at that moment wasn't simply with the ignorance revealed by Uthegental. It was with the fact that Uthegental's reasoning was common all over the city. To Jarlaxle's thinking, the dark elves of Menzoberranzan continually limited themselves by their blind insistence that everything was symptomatic of a deeper meaning, that the Spider Queen had some grand design behind their every movement. In the eyes of the priestesses, if Drizzt Do'Urden denied Lloth and ran away, it was only because Lloth wanted House Do'Urden to fall and wanted the challenge of recapturing him presented to the other ambitious houses of the city.

It was a limiting philosophy, one that denied free will. Certainly Lloth might play a hand in the hunt for Drizzt. Certainly she might be angered by the disruption of the high ritual, if she even bothered to take note of the event! But the reasoning that what was happening now was completely tied to that one event—ultimately a minor one in the five-thousand year history of Menzoberranzan—was a view of foolish pride, wherein the dwellers of Menzoberranzan seemed to think that all the multiverse revolved about them.

"Why then is all magic failing every house?" Jarlaxle asked Uthegental. "Why not just House Baenre?"

Uthegental briskly shook his head, not even willing to consider the reasoning. "We have failed Lloth and are being punished," he declared. "If only *I* had met the rogue instead of pitiful Dantrag Baenre!"

Now that was a sight Jarlaxle would wish to see! Drizzt Do'Urden battling Uthegental. The mere thought of it sent a tingle down the mercenary's spine.

"You cannot deny that Dantrag was in Lloth's favor," Jarlaxle reasoned, "while Drizzt Do'Urden most certainly was not. How, then, did Drizzt win?"

Uthegental's brow furrowed so fiercely that his red-glowing eyes nearly disappeared altogether, and Jarlaxle quickly reassessed the prudence of pushing the brute along this line of reasoning. It was one thing to back Matron Baenre; it was another altogether to shake the foundation for this religion-blinded slave's entire world.

"It will sort itself out properly," Jarlaxle assured. "In all of Arach-Tinilith, in all of the Academy, and in every chapel of every house, prayers are being offered to Lloth."

"Their prayers are not being answered," Uthegental promptly reminded. "Lloth is angry with us and will not speak with us until we have punished those who have wronged her."

Their prayers were not being answered, or their prayers were not even being heard, Jarlaxle thought. Unlike most of the other typically xenophobic drow in Menzoberranzan, the mercenary was in touch with the outside world. He knew from his contacts that Blingdenstone's svirfneblin priests were having equal difficulty in their communion, that the deep gnomes' magic had also gone awry. Something had happened to the pantheon itself, Jarlaxle believed, and to the very fabric of magic.

"It is not Lloth," he said boldly, to which Uthegental's eyes went wide. Understanding exactly what was at stake here, the entire hierarchy of the city and perhaps the lives of half of Menzoberranzan's drow, Jarlaxle pressed ahead. "Rather, it is not *solely* Lloth. When you go back into the city, consider Narbondel," he said, referring to the stone pillar clock of Menzoberranzan. "Even now, in what should be the cool dark of night, it glows brighter and hotter than ever before, so hot that its glow can even be viewed without the heat-sensing vision, so hot that any drow near the pillar cannot even allow their vision to slip into the heat-sensing spectrum, lest they be blinded.

"Yet Narbondel is enchanted by a wizard, and not a priestess," Jarlaxle went on, hoping that dim Uthegental would follow the reasoning.

"You doubt that Lloth could affect the clock?" the weapon master growled.

"I doubt she would!" Jarlaxle countered vehemently. "The magic of Narbondel is separate from Lloth, has always been separate from Lloth. Before Gromph Baenre, some of the previous archmages of Menzoberranzan were not even followers of Lloth!" He almost added that Gromph wasn't so devout, either, but decided to keep that bit of information back. No sense in giving the desperate second house additional reasons to think that House Baenre was

83

even more out of the Spider Queen's favor.

"And consider the faerie fires highlighting every structure," Jarlaxle continued. He could tell by the angle of Uthegental's furrowed brow that the brute was suddenly more curious than outraged—not a common sight. "Blinking on and off, or winking out altogether. Wizard's faerie fire, not the magic of a priestess, and decorating every house, not just House Baenre. Events are beyond us, I say, and beyond the high ritual. Tell Matron Mez'Barris, with all my respect, that I do not believe Matron Baenre can be blamed for this, and I do not believe the solution will be found in a war against the first house. Not unless Lloth herself sends us a clear directive."

Uthegental's expression soon returned to its normal scowl. Of course this one was frustrated, Jarlaxle realized. The most intelligent drow of Menzoberranzan, the most intelligent svirfnebli of Blingdenstone, were frustrated, and nothing Jarlaxle might say would change Uthegental's mind, or the war-loving savage's desire to attack House Baenre. But Jarlaxle knew he didn't have to convince Uthegental. He just had to make Uthegental say the right things upon his return to House Barrison del'Armgo. The mere fact that Mez'Barris sent so prominent an emissary, her own patron and weapon master, told Jarlaxle she would not lead a conspiracy against Baenre without the aid of, or at least the approval of, Bregan D'aerthe.

"I go," Uthegental declared, the most welcome words Jarlaxle had heard since the brute had entered his encampment.

Jarlaxle removed his wide-brimmed hat and ran his hands over his bald pate as he slipped back comfortably in his chair. He could not begin to guess the extent of the events. Perhaps within the apparent chaos of the fabric of reality, Lloth herself had been destroyed. Not such a bad thing, Jarlaxle supposed.

Still, he hoped things would sort themselves out soon, and properly, as he had indicated to Uthegental, for he knew this request—and it was a request—to go to war would come again, and again after that, and each time, it would be backed by increasing desperation. Sooner or later, House Baenre would be attacked.

Jarlaxle thought of the encounter he had witnessed between Matron Baenre and K'yorl Odran, matron mother of House Oblodra, the city's third, and perhaps most dangerous, house, when Baenre had first begun to put together the alliance to send a conquering army to Mithril Hall. Baenre had dealt from a position of power then, fully in Lloth's favor. She had openly insulted K'yorl and the third house and forced the unpredictable matron mother into her alliance with bare threats.

K'yorl would never forget that, Jarlaxle knew, and she could possibly be pushing Mez'Barris Armgo in the direction of a war against House Baenre.

Jarlaxle loved chaos, thrived amidst confusion, but this scenario was beginning to worry him more than a little.

* * * * *

Contrary to the usually correct mercenary's belief, K'yorl Odran was not nudging Matron Mez'Barris into a war against House Baenre. Quite the opposite, K'yorl was working hard to prevent such a conflict, meeting secretly with the matron mothers of the six other ruling houses ranked below House Baenre (except for Ghenni'tiroth Tlabbar, Matron of House Faen Tlabbar, the fourth house, whom K'yorl could not stand and would not trust). It wasn't that K'yorl had forgiven Matron Baenre for the insult, and it wasn't that K'yorl was afraid of the strange events. Far from it.

If it hadn't been for their extensive scouting network beyond House Oblodra and the obvious signs such as Narbondel and the winking faerie fire, the members of the third house wouldn't even have known that anything was amiss. For the powers of House Oblodra came not from wizardly magic, nor from the clerical prayers to the Spider Queen. The Oblodrans were psionicists. Their powers were formed by internal forces of the mind, and, thus far, the Time of Troubles had not affected them.

K'yorl couldn't let the rest of the city know that. She had the score of priestesses under her command hard at work, forcing the psionic equivalent of faerie fire highlighting her house to blink, as were the other houses. And to Mez'Barris and the other matron mothers, she seemed as agitated and nervous as they.

She had to keep a lid on things; she had to keep the conspiracy talk quieted. For when K'yorl could be certain that the loss of magic was not a devious trick, her family would strike—alone. She might pay House Faen Tlabbar back first, for all the years she had spent watching their every ambitious move, or she might strike directly against wretched Baenre.

Either way, the wicked matron mother meant to strike alone.

* * * * *

Matron Baenre sat stiffly in a chair on the raised and torch-lit central dais in the great chapel of her house. Her daughter Sos'Umptu, who served as caretaker to this most holy of drow places, sat to her left, and Triel, the eldest Baenre daughter and matron mistress of the drow Academy, was on her right. All three stared upward, to the illusionary image Gromph had put there, and it seemed strangely fitting that the image did not continue its shape-shifting, from drow to arachnid and back again, but rather, had been caught somewhere in the middle of the transformation and suspended there, like the powers that had elevated House Baenre to its preeminent position.

Not far away, goblin and minotaur slaves continued their work in repairing the dome, but Matron Baenre had lost all hope that putting her chapel back together would right the strange and terrible events in Menzoberranzan. She had come to believe Jarlaxle's reasoning that something larger than a failed high ritual and the escape of a single rogue was involved here. She had come to believe that what was happening in Menzoberranzan might be symptomatic of the whole world, of the whole multiverse, and that it was quite beyond her understanding or her control.

That didn't make things easier for Matron Baenre. If the other houses didn't share those beliefs, they would try to use her as a sacrifice to put things aright. She glanced briefly at both her daughters. Sos'Umptu was among the least ambitious drow females she had ever known, and Baenre didn't fear much from that one. Triel, on the other hand, might be more dangerous. Though she always seemed content with her life as matron mistress of the Academy, a position of no minor importance, it was widely accepted that Triel, the eldest daughter, would one day rule the first house.

Triel was a patient one, like her mother, but, like her mother, she was also calculating. If she became convinced that it was necessary to remove her mother from the throne of House Baenre, that such an act would restore the Baenre name and reputation, then she would do so mercilessly.

That is why Matron Baenre had recalled her from the Academy to a meeting and had located that meeting within the chapel. This was Sos'Umptu's place, Lloth's place, and Triel would not dare strike out at her mother here.

"I plan to issue a call from the Academy that no house shall use this troubled time to war against another," Triel offered, breaking the virtual silence—for none of the Baenres had taken note of the hammering and groaning from the slaves working on the curving roof a mere hundred feet away. None of them took note even when a minotaur casually tossed a goblin to its death, for no better reason than enjoyment.

Matron Baenre took a deep breath and considered the words, and the meaning behind the words. Of course Triel would issue such a plea. The Academy was perhaps the most stabilizing force in Menzoberranzan. But why had Triel chosen this moment to tell her mother? Why not just wait until the plea was presented openly and to all?

Was Triel trying to reassure her? Matron Baenre wondered. Or was she merely trying to put her off her guard?

The thoughts circled in Matron Baenre's mind, ran about and collided with one another, leaving her in a trembling, paranoid fit. Rationally, she understood the self-destructive nature of trying to read things into every word, of trying to outguess those who might be less than enemies, who might even be allies. But Matron Baenre was growing desperate. A few weeks before, she had been at the pinnacle of her power, had brought the city together beneath her in readiness for a massive strike at the dwarven complex of Mithril Hall, near the surface.

How fast it had been taken away, as fast as the fall of a stalactite from the ceiling of the cavern above her treasured chapel.

She wasn't done yet, though. Matron Baenre had not lived through more than two thousand years to give up now. Damn Triel, if she was indeed plotting to take the throne. Damn them all!

The matron mother clapped her hands together sharply, and both her daughters started with surprise as a bipedal, man-sized monstrosity popped into view, standing right before them, draped in tremendous flowing crimson robes. The creature's purplish head resembled that of an octopus, except that only four skinny tentacles waved from the perimeter of its round, many-toothed orifice, and its eyes were pupilless and milky white.

The illithid, or mind flayer, was not unknown to the Baenre daughters. Far from it, El-Viddenvelp, or Methil, as he was commonly called, was Matron Baenre's advisor and had been at her side for many years. Recovered from their startlement, both Sos'Umptu and Triel turned curious stares to their surprising mother.

My greetings to you Triel, the illithid imparted telepathically. *And, of course, to you, Sos'Umptu, in this, your place.*

Both daughters nodded and conjured similar mental replies, knowing that Methil would catch the thoughts as clearly as if they had spoken them aloud.

"Fools!" Matron Baenre shouted at both of them. She leaped from her chair and spun about, her withered features fierce. "How are we to survive this time if two of my principle commanders and closest advisors are such fools?"

Sos'Umptu was beside herself with shame, wrought of confusion. She even went so far as to cover her face with the wide sleeve of her thick purple-and-black robe.

Triel, more worldly-wise than her younger sister, initially felt the same shock, but quickly came to understand her mother's point. "The illithid has not lost its powers," she stated, and Sos'Umptu peeked curiously from above her arm.

"Not at all," Matron Baenre agreed, and her tone was not happy.

"But then we have an advantage," Sos'Umptu dared to speak. "For Methil is loyal enough," she said bluntly. There was no use in masking her true feelings behind words of half-truth, for the illithid would read her mind anyway. "And he is the only one of his kind in Menzoberranzan."

"But not the only one who uses such powers!" Matron Baenre roared at her, causing her to shrink back in her chair once more.

"K'yorl," Triel gasped. "If Methil has use of his powers . . ."

"Then so do the Oblodrans," Baenre finished grimly.

They exercise their powers continually, Methil telepathically confirmed to all three. *The highlights of House Oblodra would not be winking were it not for the mental commands of K'yorl's coven.*

"Can we be certain of this?" Triel asked, for there seemed no definite patterns in the failing of magic, just a chaotic mess. Perhaps Methil had not yet been affected, or did not even know that he had been affected. And perhaps Oblodra's faerie fire highlights, though

88

different in creation than the fires glowing about the other houses, were caught in the same chaos.

Psionic powers can be sensed by psionic creatures, Methil assured her. *The third house teems with energy.*

"And K'yorl gives the appearance that this is not so," Matron Baenre added in a nasty tone.

"She wishes to attack by surprise," Triel reasoned.

Matron Baenre nodded grimly.

"What of Methil?" Sos'Umptu offered hopefully. "His powers are great."

"Methil is more than a match for K'yorl," Matron Baenre assured her daughter, though Methil was silently doing the same thing, imparting a sense of undeniable confidence. "But K'yorl is not alone among the Oblodrans with her psionic powers."

"How many?" Triel wanted to know, to which Matron Baenre merely shrugged.

Many, Methil's thoughts answered.

Triel was thinking it, so she knew that Methil was hearing it, and so she said it aloud, suspiciously. "And if the Oblodrans do come against us, which side will Methil take?"

Matron Baenre was, for an instant, shocked by her daughter's boldness, but she understood that Triel had little choice in divulging her suspicions.

"And will he bring in his allies from the illithid cavern not far away?" Triel pressed. "Surely if a hundred illithids came to our side in this, our time of need . . ."

There was nothing from Methil, not a hint of telepathic communication, and that was answer enough for the Baenres.

"Our problems are not the problems of the mind flayers," Matron Baenre said. It was true enough, and she knew so. She had tried to enlist the illithids in the raid on Mithril Hall, promising them riches and a secure alliance, but the motivations of the otherworldly, octopus-headed creatures were not the same as those of the dark elves, or of any race in all the Underdark. Those motivations remained beyond Matron Baenre's understanding, despite her years of dealing with Methil. The most she could get from the illithids for her important raid was Methil and two others agreeing to go along in exchange for a hundred kobolds and a score of drow males, to be used as slaves by the illithid community in their small cavern city.

There was little else to say. The house guards were positioned at full readiness; every spare drow was in prayer for help from the Spider Queen. House Baenre was doing everything it could to avert disaster, and yet, Matron Baenre did not believe they would succeed. K'yorl had come to her unannounced on several occasions, had gotten past her magical fence and past the many magical wards set about the complex. The matron mother of House Oblodra had done so only to taunt Baenre, and, in truth, had little power remaining to do anything more than that by the time her image was revealed to Baenre. But what might K'yorl accomplish with those magical guards down? Baenre had to wonder. How could Matron Baenre resist the psionicist without countering magic of her own?

Her only defense seemed to be Methil, a creature she neither trusted nor understood.

She did not like the odds.

Chapter 8
MAGICAL MANIFESTATIONS

uenhwyvar knew pain, knew agony beyond anything the panther had ever felt. But more than that, the panther knew despair, true despair. Guenhwyvar was a creature formed of magic, the manifestation of the life-force of the animal known on Toril as the panther. The very spark of existence within the great panther depended on magic, as did the conduit that allowed Drizzt and the others before him to bring Guenhwyvar to the Prime Material Plane.

Now that magic had unraveled; the fabric that wove the universal magic into a mystical and predictable pattern was torn.

The panther knew despair.

Guenhwyvar heard Drizzt's continued calling, begging. The drow knew Guen was in trouble; his voice reflected that desperation. In his heart, so connected with his panther companion, Drizzt Do'Urden understood that Guenhwyvar would soon be lost to him forever.

The chilling thought gave the panther a moment of renewed hope and determination. Guenhwyvar focused on Drizzt, conjured an image of the pain she would feel if she could never again return to her beloved master. Growling low in sheer defiance, the panther scraped her back legs so forcefully that more than one claw hooked on the smooth, hard surface and was subsequently yanked out.

The pain did not stop the panther, not when Guenhwyvar measured it against the reality of slipping forward into those flames, of falling out of the tunnel, the only connection to the material world and Drizzt Do'Urden.

The struggle went on for more time than any creature should have resisted. But though Guenhwyvar had not slid any closer to the breach, neither had the panther earned back any ground toward her pleading master.

Finally, exhausted, Guenhwyvar gave a forlorn, helpless look over her shoulder. Her muscles trembled, then gave way.

The panther was swept to the fiery breach.

* * * * *

Matron Baenre paced the small room nervously, expecting a guard to run in at any moment with news that the compound had been overrun, that the entire city had risen against her house, blaming her for the troubles that had befallen them.

Not so long ago, Baenre had dreamt of conquest, had aspired to the pinnacle of power. Mithril Hall had been within her grasp, and, even more than that, the city seemed ready to fall into step behind her lead.

Now she believed she could not hold on to even her own house, to the Baenre empire that had stood for five thousand years.

"Mithril Hall," the wicked drow growled in a damning curse, as though that distant place had been the cause of it all. Her slight chest heaving with forced gasps of air, Baenre reached with both hands to her neck and tore free the chain that lay there.

"Mithril Hall!" she shouted into the ring-shaped pendant, fashioned from the tooth of Gandalug Battlehammer, the patron of Bruenor's clan, the real link to that surface world. Every drow, even those closest to Matron Baenre, thought Drizzt Do'Urden was the catalyst for the invasion, the excuse that allowed Lloth to give her blessing to the dangerous attempt at a conquest so near the surface.

Drizzt was but a part of the puzzle, and a small part, for this little ring was the true impetus. Sealed within it was the tormented spirit of Gandalug, who knew the ways of Mithril Hall and the ways of Clan Battlehammer. Matron Baenre had taken the dwarf king herself centuries before, and it was only blind fate that had brought a rene-gade from Menzoberranzan in contact with Bruenor's clan, blind fate that had provided an excuse for the conquest Matron Baenre had desired for many, many decades.

With a shout of outrage, Baenre hurled the tooth across the room, then fell back in shock as the item exploded.

Baenre stared blankly into the room's corner as the smoke cleared away, at the naked dwarf kneeling there. The matron mother pulled herself to her feet, shaking her head in disbelief, for this was no sum-moned spirit, but Gandalug's physical body!

"You dare to come forth?" Baenre screamed, but her anger masked her fear. When she had previously called Gandalug's physical form forth from the extradimensional prison, he was never truly whole, never corporeal—and never naked. Looking at him now, Baenre knew Gandalug's prison was gone, that Gandalug was returned exactly as he had been the moment Baenre had captured him, except for his clothes.

The battered old dwarf looked up at his captor, his tormentor. Baenre had spoken in the drow tongue, and of course, Gandalug hadn't understood a word. That hardly mattered, though, for the old dwarf wasn't listening. He was, in fact, beyond words.

Struggling, growling, with every pained movement, Gandalug forced his back to straighten, then put one, then the other, leg under him and rose determinedly. He understood that something was differ-ent. After centuries of torment and mostly emptiness, a fugue state in a gray void, Gandalug Battlehammer felt somehow different, felt whole and real. Since his capture, the old dwarf had lived a surreal existence, had lived a dream, surrounded by vivid, frightening images whenever this old wretch had called him forth, encompassed by interminable periods of nothingness, where place and time and thought were one long emptiness.

But now . . . now Gandalug felt different, felt even the creaks and pains of his old bones. And how wonderful those sensations were!

"Go back!" Baenre ordered, this time in the tongue of the surface, the language she always used to communicate with the old dwarf. "Back to your prison until I call you forth!"

Gandalug looked around, to the chain lying on the floor, the tooth ring nowhere in sight.

"I'm not fer tinkin' so," the old dwarf remarked in his heavy, ancient dialect, and he advanced a step.

Baenre's eyes narrowed dangerously. "You dare?" she whispered, drawing forth a slender wand. She knew how dangerous this one could be, and thus she wasted no time in pointing the item and reciting an arcane phrase, meaning to call forth a stream of webbing that would engulf the dwarf and hold him fast.

Nothing happened.

Gandalug took another step, growling like a hungry animal with every inch.

Baenre's steely-eyed gaze fell away, revealing her sudden fear. She was a creature weaned on magic, who relied on magic to protect her and to vanquish her enemies. With the items she possessed (which she carried with her at all times) and her mighty spell repertoire, she could fend off nearly any enemy, could likely crush a battalion of toughened dwarven fighters. But without those items, and with no spells coming to her call, Matron Baenre was a pitiful, bluffing thing, withered and frail.

It wouldn't have mattered to Gandalug had a titan been standing before him. For some reason he could not understand, he was free of the prison, free and in his own body, a sensation he had not felt in two thousand years.

Baenre had other tricks to try, and in truth, some of them, like the pouch that carried a horde of spiders that would rush to her call, had not yet fallen into the chaotic and magical web that was the Time of Troubles. She couldn't chance it, though. Not now, not when she was so very vulnerable.

She turned and ran for the door.

The corded muscles of Gandalug's mighty legs tightened, and the dwarf sprang, clearing the fifteen feet to get to the door before his tormentor.

A fist slammed Baenre's chest, stealing her breath, and before she could respond, she was up in the air, twirling about over the enraged dwarf's head.

Then she was flying, to crash and crumple against the wall across the room.

"I'm to be rippin' yer head off," Gandalug promised as he steadily advanced.

The door burst open, and Berg'inyon rushed into the room. Gandalug spun to face him as Berg'inyon drew his twin blades. Startled by the sight—how had a dwarf come into Menzoberranzan, into his own mother's private chambers?—Berg'inyon got the blades up just as Gandalug grabbed them, one in each hand.

Had the enchantment still been upon the weapon master's fine blades, they would have cut cleanly through the tough dwarven flesh. Even without the enchantment, the magic lost in the swirl of chaos, the swords dug deeply.

Gandalug hardly cared. He heaved Berg'inyon's arms out wide, the slender drow no match for his sheer strength. The dwarf whipped his head forward, crashing it into Berg'inyon's supple armor, slender rings that also relied on enchantment for their strength.

Gandalug repeated the movement over and over, and Berg'inyon's grunts fast became breathless gasps. Soon the young Baenre was out on his feet, hardly conscious as Gandalug yanked the swords from his hands. The dwarf's head came in one more time, and Berg'inyon, no longer connected to, and thus supported by, the dwarf, fell away.

Still ignoring the deep cuts on his hands, Gandalug threw one of Berg'inyon's swords to the side of the room, took the other properly in hand, and turned on Matron Baenre, who was still sitting against the wall, trying to clear her thoughts.

"Where's yer smile?" the dwarf taunted, stalking in. "I'm wantin' a smile on yer stinkin' face when I hold yer head up in me hand fer all t'see!"

The next step was the dwarf king's last, as an octopus-headed monstrosity materialized before him, its grotesque tentacles waving his way.

A stunning blast of mental energy rolled Gandalug over, and he nearly dropped the sword. He shook his head fiercely to keep his wits about him.

He continued to growl, to shake his hairy head, as a second blast, then a third, assaulted his sensibilities. Had he held that wall of rage, Gandalug might have withstood even these, and even the two subsequent attacks from Methil. But that rage melted into confusion, which was not a powerful enough feeling to defeat the mighty illithid's intrusions.

Gandalug didn't hear the drow-made sword fall to the stone, didn't hear Matron Baenre call out for Methil and for the recovering Berg'inyon, as she instructed the pair not to kill the dwarf.

Baenre was scared, scared by these shifts in magic that she could not understand. But that fear did not prevent her from remembering her wicked self. For some unexplained reason, Gandalug had become alive again, in his own body and free of the apparently disintegrated ring.

That mystery would not prevent Baenre from paying this one back for the attack and the insult. Baenre was a master at torturing a spirit, but even her prowess in that fine art paled beside her abilities to torture a living creature.

*   *   *   *   *

"Guenhwyvar!" The figurine was wickedly hot now, but Drizzt held on stubbornly, pressed it close to his chest, his heart, though wisps of smoke were running up from the edge of his cloak and the flesh of his hands was beginning to blister.

He knew, and he would not let go. He knew that Guenhwyvar would be gone from him forever, and like a friend hugging close a dying comrade, Drizzt would not let go, would be there to the end.

His desperate calls began to lessen, not from resignation, but simply because his voice could not get past the lump of grief in his throat. Now his fingers, too, were burning, but he would not let go.

Catti-brie did it for him. On a sudden, desperate impulse, the young woman, herself torn with the pain of grief, grabbed roughly at Drizzt's arm and slapped hard the figurine, knocking it to the ground.

Drizzt's startled expression turned to one of outrage and denial, like the final burst of rage from a mother as she watched her child's casket lowered into the grave. For the moment the figurine hit the ground, Catti-brie drew Khazid'hea from its sheath and leaped to the spot. Up went the sword, over her head, its fine edge still showing the red line of its enchantment.

"No!" Drizzt cried, lunging for her.

He was too late. Tears rimming her blue eyes, her thoughts jumbled, Catti-brie found the courage for a last, desperate try, and she brought the mighty blade to bear. Khazid'hea could cut through stone, and so it did now, at the very instant that Guenhwyvar went through the breach.

There came a flash, and a throbbing pain, a pulsating magic, shot up Catti-brie's arm, hurling her backward and to the ground. Drizzt skidded, pivoted, and ducked low, shielding his head as the figurine's head fell free, loosing a line of raging fire far out into the air.

The flames blew out a moment later and a thick gray smoke

poured from the body of the broken figurine. Gradually Drizzt straightened from his defensive crouch and Catti-brie came back to her senses, both to find a haggard-looking Guenhwyvar, the panther's thick coat still smoking, standing before them.

Drizzt dove to his knees and fell over the panther, wrapping Guenhwyvar in a great hug. They both crawled their way to Catti-brie, who was still sitting on the ground, laughing and sobbing though she was weak from the impact of the magic.

"What have you done?" Drizzt asked her.

She had no immediate answers. She did not know how to explain what had happened when Khazid'hea struck the enchanted figurine. She looked to the blade now, lying quiet at her side, its edge no longer glowing and a burr showing along its previously unblemished length.

"I think I've ruined me sword," Catti-brie replied softly.

* * * * *

Later that same day, Drizzt lounged on the bed in his room in the upper levels of Mithril Hall, looking worriedly at his panther companion. Guenhwyvar was back, and that was a better thing, he supposed, than what his instincts had told him would have happened had Catti-brie not cut the figurine.

A better thing, but not a good thing. The panther was weary, resting by the hearth across the small room, head down and eyes closed. That nap would not suffice, Drizzt knew. Guenhwyvar was a creature of the Astral Plane and could truly rejuvenate only among the stars. On several occasions necessity had prompted Drizzt to keep Guenhwyvar on the Material Plane for extended periods, but even a single day beyond the half the cat usually stayed left Guen exhausted.

Even now the artisans of Mithril Hall, dwarves of no small skill, were inspecting the cut figurine, and Bruenor had sent an emissary out to Silverymoon, seeking help from Lady Alustriel, as skilled as any this side of the great desert Anauroch in the ways of magic.

How long would it take? Drizzt wondered, unsure if any of them could repair the figurine. How long could Guenhwyvar survive?

Unannounced, Catti-brie burst through the door. One look at her tear-streaked face told Drizzt that something was amiss. He rolled from the bed to his feet and stepped toward the mantle, where his twin scimitars hung.

97

R. A. Salvatore

Catti-brie intercepted him before he had completed the step and wrapped him in a powerful hug that knocked them both to the bed.

"All I ever wanted," she said urgently, squeezing tight.

Drizzt likewise held on, confused and overwhelmed. He managed to turn his head so he could look into the young woman's eyes, trying to read some clues.

"I was made for ye, Drizzt Do'Urden," Catti-brie said between sobs. "Ye're all that's been in me thoughts since the day we met."

It was too crazy. Drizzt tried to extract himself, but he didn't want to hurt Catti-brie and her hold was simply too strong and desperate.

"Look at me," she sobbed. "Tell me ye feel the same!"

Drizzt did look at Catti-brie, as deeply as he had ever studied the beautiful young woman. He did care for her—of course he did. He did love her, and had even allowed himself a fantasy or two about this very situation.

But now it seemed simply too weird, too unexpected and with no introduction. He got the distinct feeling that something was out of sorts with the woman, something crazy, like the magic all about them.

"What of Wulfgar?" Drizzt managed to say, though the name got muffled as Catti-brie pressed tightly, her hair thick against Drizzt's face. The poor drow could not deny the woman's allure, the sweet scent of Catti-brie's hair, the warmth of her toned body.

Catti-brie's head snapped as if he had hit her. "Who?"

It was Drizzt's turn to feel as if he had been slapped.

"Take me," Catti-brie implored.

Drizzt's eyes couldn't have gone any wider without falling out of their sockets.

"Wield me!" she cried.

"Wield me?" Drizzt echoed under his breath.

"Make me the instrument of your dance," she went on. "Oh, I beg! It is all I was made for, all I desire." She stopped suddenly and pushed back to arm's length, staring wide-eyed at Drizzt as though some new angle had just popped into her head. "I am better than the others," she promised slyly.

What others? Drizzt wanted to scream, but by this point, the drow couldn't get any words out of his slack-jawed mouth.

"As are yerself," Catti-brie went on. "Better than that woman, I'm now knowing!"

Drizzt had almost found his center again, had almost regained control enough to reply, when the weight of that last statement buried him. Damn the subtlety! the drow determined, and he twisted and pulled free, rolling from the bed and springing to his feet.

Catti-brie dove right behind, wrapped herself about one of his legs, and held on with all her strength.

"Oh, do not deny me, me love!" she screamed, so urgently that Guenhwyvar lifted her head from the hearth and gave a low growl. "Wield me, I'm begging! Only in yer hands might I be whole!"

Drizzt reached down with both hands, meaning to extract his leg from the tight grip. He noticed something then, on Catti-brie's hip, that gave him pause, that stunned him and explained everything all at once.

He noticed the sword Catti-brie had picked up in the Underdark, the sword that had a pommel shaped into the head of a unicorn. Only it was no longer a unicorn.

It was Catti-brie's face.

In one swift movement, Drizzt drew the sword out of its sheath and tugged free, hopping back two steps. Khazid'hea's red line, that enchanted edge, had returned in full and beamed now more brightly than ever before. Drizzt slid back another step, expecting to be tackled again.

There was no pursuit. The young woman remained in place, half sitting, half kneeling on the floor. She threw her head back as if in ecstacy. "Oh, yes!" she cried.

Drizzt stared down at the pommel, watched in blank amazement as it shifted from the image of Catti-brie's face back into a unicorn. He felt an overwhelming warmth from the weapon, a connection as intimate as that of a lover.

Panting for breath, the drow looked back to Catti-brie, who was sitting straighter now, looking around curiously.

"What're ye doing with me sword?" she asked quietly. Again she looked about the room, Drizzt's room, seeming totally confused. She would have asked, "And what am I doing here?" Drizzt realized, except that the question was already obvious from the expression on her beautiful face.

"We have to talk," Drizzt said to her.

Chapter 9
IMPLICATIONS

I t was rare that both Gromph and Triel Baenre would be in audience with their mother at the same time, rarer still that they would be joined by Berg'inyon and Sos'Umptu and the two other notable Baenre daughters, Bladen'Kerst and Quenthel. Six of the seven sat in comfortable chairs about the dais in the chapel. Not Bladen'Kerst, though. Ever seeming the caged animal, the most sadistic drow in the first house paced in circles, her brow furrowed and thin lips pursed. She was the second oldest daughter behind Triel and should have been out of the house by this time, perhaps as a matron in the Academy, or even more likely, as a matron mother of her own, lesser, house. Matron Baenre had not allowed that, however, fearing that her daughter's simple lack of civility, even by drow standards, would disgrace House Baenre.

Triel looked up and shook her head disdainfully at Bladen'Kerst every time she passed. She rarely gave Bladen'Kerst any thought. Like Vendes Baenre, her younger sister who had been killed by Drizzt Do'Urden during the escape, Bladen'Kerst was an instrument of her mother's torture and nothing more. She was a buffoon, a showpiece, and no real threat to anyone in House Baenre above the rank of common soldier.

Quenthel was quite a different matter, and in the long interludes between Bladen'Kerst's passing, Triel's stern and scrutinizing gaze never left that one.

And Quenthel returned the look with open hostility. She had risen to the rank of high priestess in record time and was reputed to be in Lloth's highest favor. Quenthel held no illusions about her tentative position; had it not been for that fact of favor, Triel would have obliterated her long ago. For Quenthel had made no secret of her ambitions, which included the stepping stone as matron mistress of Arach-Tinilith, a position Triel had no intention of abandoning.

"Sit down!" Matron Baenre snapped finally at the annoying Bladen'Kerst. One of Baenre's eyes was swollen shut and the side of her face still showed the welt where she had collided with the wall. She was not used to carrying such scars, nor were others used to seeing her that way. Normally a spell of healing would have cleaned up her face, but these were not normal times.

Bladen'Kerst stopped and stared hard at her mother, focusing on those wounds. They carried a double-edged signal. First, they showed that Baenre's powers were not as they should be, that the matron mother, that all of them, might be very vulnerable. Second, coupled with the scowl that perpetually clouded the worried matron mother's features, those wounds reflected anger.

Anger overweighed the perceived, and likely temporary, vulnerability, Bladen'Kerst wisely decided, and sat down in her appointed chair. Her hard boot, unusual for drow, but effective for kicking males, tapped hard and urgently on the floor.

No one paid her any attention, though. All of them followed Matron Baenre's predictable, dangerous gaze to Quenthel.

"Now is not the time for personal ambitions," Matron Baenre said calmly, seriously.

Quenthel's eyes widened as though she had been caught completely off guard.

"I warn you," Matron Baenre pressed, not the least deterred by the innocent expression.

"As do I!" Triel quickly and determinedly interjected. She wouldn't usually interrupt her mother, knew better than that, but she figured that this matter had to be put down once and for all, and

101

that Baenre would appreciate the assistance. "You have relied on Lloth's favor to protect you these years. But Lloth is away from us now, for some reason that we do not understand. You are vulnerable, my sister, more vulnerable than any of us."

Quenthel came forward in her seat, even managed a smile. "Would you chance that Lloth will return to us, as we both know she shall?" the younger Baenre hissed. "And what might it be that drove the Spider Queen from us?" As she asked the last question her gaze fell over her mother, as daring as anyone had ever been ir the face of Matron Baenre.

"Not what you assume!" Triel snapped. She had expected Quenthel to try to lay blame on Matron Baenre's lap. The removal of the matron mother could only benefit ambitious Quenthel and might indeed restore some prestige to the fast-falling house. In truth, even Triel had considered that course, but she had subsequently dismissed it, no longer believing that Matron Baenre's recent failures had anything to do with the strangeness going on about them. "Lloth has fled every house."

"This goes beyond Lloth," Gromph, the wizard whose magic came from no god or goddess, added pointedly.

"Enough," said Baenre, looking about alternately, her stare calming her children. "We cannot know what has brought about the events. What we must consider is how those events will affect our position."

"The city desires a *pera'dene*," Quenthel reasoned, the drow word for scapegoat. Her unblinking stare at Baenre told the matron mother who she had in mind.

"Fool!" Baenre snapped into the face of that glare. "Do you think they would stop with *my* heart?"

That blunt statement caught Quenthel off guard.

"For some of the lesser houses, there never has been and never will be a better opportunity to unseat this house," Matron Baenre went on, speaking to all of them. "If you think to unseat me, then do so, but know that it will do little to change the rebellion that is rising against us." She huffed and threw her arms up helplessly. "Indeed, you would only be aiding our enemies. I am your tie to Bregan D'aerthe, and know that our enemies have also courted Jarlaxle. And *I* am Baenre! Not Triel, and not Quenthel. Without me, you all would fall to chaos, fighting for control, each with your own factions within the house guard. Where will you be when K'yorl Oblodra enters the compound?"

It was a sobering thought. Matron Baenre had passed word to each of them that the Oblodrans had not lost their powers, and all the Baenres knew the hatred the third house held for them.

"Now is not the time for personal ambitions," Matron Baenre reiterated. "Now is the time for us to hold together and hold our position."

The nods about her were sincere, Baenre knew, though Quenthel was not nodding. "You should hope that Lloth does not come back to me before she returns to you," the ambitious sister said boldly, aiming the remark squarely at Triel.

Triel seemed unimpressed. "You should hope that Lloth comes back at all," she replied casually, "else I will tear off your head and have Gromph place it atop Narbondel, that your eyes may glow when the day is full."

Quenthel went to reply, but Gromph beat her to it.

"A pleasure, my dear sister," he said to Triel. There was no love lost between the two, but while Gromph was ambivalent toward Triel, he perfectly hated Quenthel and her dangerous ambitions. If House Baenre fell, so, too, would Gromph.

The implied alliance between the two elder Baenre children worked wonders in calming the upstart younger sister, and Quenthel said not another word the rest of the meeting.

"May we speak now of K'yorl, and the danger to us all?" Matron Baenre asked. When no dissenting voices came forth (and if there had been, Baenre likely would have run out of patience and had the speaker put to a slow death), the matron mother took up the issue of house defense. She explained that Jarlaxle and his band could still be trusted, but warned that the mercenary would be one to change sides if the battle was going badly for House Baenre. Triel assured them all that the Academy remained loyal, and Berg'inyon's report of the readiness of the house guard was beaming.

Despite the promising news and the well-earned reputation of the Baenre garrison, the conversation ultimately came down to the only apparent way to fully fend off K'yorl and her psionic family. Berg'inyon, who had taken part in the fight with the dwarf Gandalug, voiced it first.

"What of Methil?" he asked. "And the hundred illithids he

represents? If they stand with us, the threat from House Oblodra seems minor."

The others nodded their agreement with the assessment, but Matron Baenre knew that such friends as mind flayers could not be counted on. "Methil remains at our side because he and his people know we are the keystone of security for his people. The illithids do not number one-hundredth the drow in Menzoberranzan. That is the extent of their loyalty. If Methil comes to believe that House Oblodra is the stronger, he will not stand beside us." Baenre gave an ironic, seemingly helpless chuckle.

"The other illithids might even side with K'yorl," she reasoned. "The wretch is akin to them with her powers of the mind. Perhaps they understand one another."

"Should we speak so bluntly?" Sos'Umptu asked. She looked about the dais, concerned, and the others understood that she feared Methil might even be among them, invisibly, hearing every word, reading their every thought.

"It does not matter," Matron Baenre replied casually. "Methil already knows my fears. One cannot hide from an illithid."

"Then what are we to do?" Triel asked.

"We are to muster our strength," Baenre replied determinedly. "We are to show no fear and no weakness. And we are not to do anything that might push Lloth further from us." She aimed that last remark at the rivals, Quenthel and Triel, particularly at Triel, who seemed more than ready to use this Lloth-absent time to be rid of her troublesome sister.

"We must show the illithids we remain the power in Menzoberranzan," Baenre went on. "If they know this, then they will side with us, not wanting House Baenre to be weakened by K'yorl's advances."

"I go to Sorcere," said Gromph, the archmage.

"And I to Arach-Tinilith," added a determined Triel.

"I make no illusions about friendship among my rivals," Gromph added. "But a few promises of repayment when issues sort themselves out will go far in finding allies."

"The students have been allowed no contact outside the school," Triel put in. "They know of the problems in general, of course, but they know nothing of the threat to House Baenre. In their ignorance, they remain loyal."

Matron Baenre nodded to both of them. "And you will meet with the lower houses that we have established," she said to Quenthel, a most important assignment. A large portion of House Baenre's power lay in the dozen minor houses that former Baenre nobles had come to head. So obviously a favorite of Lloth's, Quenthel was the perfect choice for such an assignment.

Her expression revealed that she had been won over—more by Triel and Gromph's threats, no doubt, than by the tidbit that had just been thrown her way.

The most important ingredient in squashing the rivalries, Baenre knew, was to allow both Triel and Quenthel to save face and feel important. Thus, this meeting had been a success and all the power of House Baenre would be coordinated into a single defensive force.

Baenre's smile remained a meager one, though. She knew what Methil could do, and suspected that K'yorl was not so much weaker. All of House Baenre would be ready, but without the Lloth-given clerical magic and Gromph's wizardly prowess, would that be enough?

* * * * *

Just off Bruenor's audience hall on the top level of Mithril Hall was a small room that the dwarf king had set aside for the artisans working on repairing the panther figurine. Inside was a small forge and delicate tools, along with dozens of beakers and flasks containing various ingredients and salves.

Drizzt was eager indeed when he was summoned to that room. He'd gone there a dozen times a day, of course, but without invitation, and every time to find dwarves huddled over the still-broken artifact and shaking their bearded heads. A week had passed since the incident, and Guenhwyvar was so exhausted that she could no longer stand, could barely lift her head from her paws as she lay in front of the hearth in Drizzt's room.

The waiting was the worst part.

Now, though, Drizzt had been called into the room. He knew that an emissary had arrived that morning from Silverymoon; he could only hope that Alustriel had some positive solutions to offer.

Bruenor was watching his approach through the open door of

the audience chamber. The red-bearded dwarf nodded and poked his head to the side, and Drizzt cut the sharp corner, pushing open the door without bothering to knock.

It was among the most curious of sights that Drizzt Do'Urden had ever witnessed. The broken—still broken!—figurine was on a small, round table. Regis stood beside it, working furiously with a mortar and pestle, mushing some blackish substance.

Across the table from Drizzt stood a short, stout dwarf, Buster Bracer, the noted armorer, the one, in fact, who had forged Drizzt's own supple chain mail, back in Icewind Dale. Drizzt didn't dare greet the dwarf now, fearing to upset his obvious concentration. Buster stood with his feet wide apart. Every so often, he took an exaggerated breath, then held perfectly steady, for in his hands, wrapped in wetted cloth of the finest material, he held . . . eyeballs.

Drizzt had no idea of what was going on until a voice, a familiar, bubbly voice, startled him from his shock.

"Greetings, O One of the Midnight Skin!" the disembodied wizard said happily.

"Harkle Harpell?" Drizzt asked.

"Could it be anyone else?" Regis remarked dryly.

Drizzt conceded the point. "What is this about?" he asked, pointedly looking toward the halfling, for he knew that any answer from Harkle would likely shed more dimness on the blurry situation.

Regis lifted the mixing bowl a bit. "A poultice from Silverymoon," he explained hopefully. "Harkle has overseen its mixing."

"Overseen," the absent mage joked, "which means they held my eyes over the bowl!"

Drizzt didn't manage a smile, not with the head of the all-important figurine still lying at the sculpted body's feet.

Regis snickered, more in disdain than humor. "It should be ready," he explained. "But I wanted you to apply it."

"Drow fingers are so dexterous!" Harkle piped in.

"Where are you?" Drizzt demanded, impatient and unnerved by the outrageous arrangement.

Harkle blinked, those eyelids appearing from thin air. "In Nesme," he mage replied. "We will be passing north of the Trollmoors soon."

"And then to Mithril Hall, where you will be reunited with your eyes," Drizzt said.

106

"I am *looking* forward to it!" Harkle roared, but again he laughed alone.

"He keeps that up and I'm throwin' the damned eyes into me forge," Buster Bracer growled.

Regis placed the bowl on the table and retrieved a tiny metal tool. "You'll not need much of the poultice," the halfling said as he handed the delicate instrument to Drizzt. "And Harkle has warned us to try to keep the mixture on the outside of the joined pieces."

"It is only a glue," the mage's voice added. "The magic of the figurine will be the force that truly makes the item whole. The poultice will have to be scraped away in a few day's time. If it works as planned, the figurine will be . . ." He paused, searching for the word. "Will be healed," he finished.

"If it works," Drizzt echoed. He took a moment to feel the delicate instrument in his hands, making sure that the burns he had received when the figurine's magic had gone awry were healed, making sure that he could feel the item perfectly.

"It will work," Regis assured.

Drizzt took a deep, steadying breath and picked up the panther head. He stared into the sculpted eyes, so much like Guenhwyvar's own knowing orbs. With all the care of a parent tending its child, Drizzt placed the head against the body and began the painstaking task of spreading the gluelike poultice about its perimeter.

More than two hours passed before Drizzt and Regis exited the room, moving into the audience hall where Bruenor was still meeting with Lady Alustriel's emissary and several other dwarves.

Bruenor did not appear happy, but Drizzt noted he seemed more at ease than he had since the onset of this strange time.

"It ain't a trick o' the drow," the dwarf king said as soon as Drizzt and Regis approached. "Or the damned drow are more powerful than anyone ever thought! It's all the world, so says Alustriel."

"Lady Alustriel," corrected the emissary, a very tidy-looking dwarf dressed in flowing white robes and with a short and neatly trimmed beard.

"My greetings, Fredegar," Drizzt said, recognizing Fredegar Rockcrusher, better known as Fret, Lady Alustriel's favored bard and advisor. "So at last you have found the opportunity to see the wonders of Mithril Hall."

"Would that the times were better," Fret answered glumly.

R. A. Salvatore

"Pray tell me, how fares Catti-brie?"

"She is well," Drizzt answered. He smiled as he thought of the young woman, who had returned to Settlestone to convey some information from Bruenor.

"It ain't a trick o' the drow," Bruenor said again, more emphatically, making it clear that he didn't consider this the proper time and place for such light and meaningless conversation.

Drizzt nodded his agreement—he had been assuring Bruenor that his people were not involved all along. "Whatever has happened, it has rendered Regis's ruby useless," the drow said. He reached over and lifted the pendant from the halfling's chest. "Now it is but a plain, though undeniably beautiful, stone. And the unknown force has affected Guenhwyvar, and reached all the way to the Harpells. No magic of the drow is this powerful, else they would have long ago conquered the surface world."

"Something new?" Bruenor asked.

"The effects have been felt for several weeks now," Fret interjected. "Though only in the last couple of weeks has magic become so totally unpredictable and dangerous."

Bruenor, never one to care much for magic, snorted loudly.

"It's a good thing, then!" he decided. "The damned drow're more needin' magic than are me own folk, or the men o' Settlestone! Let all the magic drain away, I'm sayin', and then let the drow come on and play!"

Thibbledorf Pwent nearly jumped out of his boots at that thought. He leaped over to stand before Bruenor and Fret, and slapped one of his dirty, smelly hands across the tidy dwarf's back. Few things could calm an excited battlerager, but Fret's horrified, then outraged, look did just that, surprising Pwent completely.

"What?" the battlerager demanded.

"If you ever touch me again, I will crush your skull," Fret, who wasn't half the size of powerful Pwent, promised in an even tone, and for some inexplicable reason, Pwent believed him and backed off a step.

Drizzt, who knew tidy Fret quite well from his many visits to Silverymoon, understood that Fret couldn't stand ten seconds in a fight against Pwent—unless the confrontation centered around dirt. In that instance, with Pwent messing up Fret's meticulous grooming, Drizzt would put all of his money on Fret, as sure a bet as the drow would ever know.

It wasn't an issue, though, for Pwent, boisterous as he was, would never do anything against Bruenor, and Bruenor obviously wanted no trouble with an emissary, particularly a dwarven emissary from friendly Silverymoon. Indeed, all in the room had a good laugh at the confrontation, and all seemed more relaxed at the realization that these strange events were not connected to the mysterious dark elves.

All except for Drizzt Do'Urden. Drizzt would not relax until the figurine was repaired, its magic restored, and poor Guenhwyvar could return to her home on the Astral Plane.

Chapter 10
THE THIRD HOUSE

t wasn't that Jarlaxle, who always thought ahead of others, hadn't been expecting the visit, it was simply the ease with which K'yorl Odran entered his camp, slipped past his guards and walked right through the wall of his private chambers, that so unnerved him. He saw her ghostly outline enter and fought hard to compose himself as she became more substantial and more threatening.

"I had expected you would come many days ago," Jarlaxle said calmly.

"Is this the proper greeting for a matron mother?" K'yorl asked.

Jarlaxle almost laughed, until he considered the female's stance. Too at ease, he decided, too ready to punish, even to kill. K'yorl did not understand the value of Bregan D'aerthe, apparently, and that left Jarlaxle, the master of bluff and the player of intrigue, at somewhat of a disadvantage.

He came up from his comfortable chair, stepped out from behind his desk, and gave a low bow, pulling his wide-brimmed and outrageously plumed hat from his head and sweeping it across the floor. "My greetings, K'yorl Odran, Matron Mother of House

Oblodra, Third House of Menzoberranzan. Not often has my humble home been so graced . . ."

"Enough," K'yorl spat, and Jarlaxle came up and replaced the hat. Never taking his gaze from the female, never blinking, the mercenary went back to his chair and flopped down comfortably, putting both his boots atop his desk with a resounding slam.

It was then Jarlaxle felt the intrusion into his mind, a deeply unsettling probe into his thoughts. He quickly dismissed his many curses at the failure of conventional magic—usually his enchanted eye patch would have protected him from such a mental intrusion—and used his wits instead. He focused his gaze on K'yorl, pictured her with her clothes off, and filled his mind with thoughts so base that the matron mother, in the midst of serious business, lost all patience.

"I could have the skin flailed from your bones for such thoughts," K'yorl informed him.

"Such thoughts?" Jarlaxle said as though he had been wounded. "Surely you are not intruding on my mind, Matron K'yorl! Though I am but a male, such practices are surely frowned on. Lloth would not be pleased."

"Damn Lloth," K'yorl growled, and Jarlaxle was stunned that she had put it so clearly, so bluntly. Of course everyone knew that House Oblodra was not the most religious of drow houses, but the Oblodrans had always kept at least the pretense of piety.

K'yorl tapped her temple, her features stern. "If Lloth was worthy of my praise, then she would have recognized the truth of power," the matron mother explained. "It is the mind that separates us from our lessers, the mind that should determine order."

Jarlaxle offered no response. He had no desire to get into this argument with so dangerous and unpredictable a foe.

K'yorl did not press the point, but simply waved her hand as if throwing it all away. She was frustrated, Jarlaxle could see, and in this one frustration equated with danger.

"It is beyond the Spider Queen now," K'yorl said. "I am beyond Lloth. And it begins this day."

Jarlaxle allowed a look of surprise to cross his features.

"You expected it," K'yorl said accusingly.

That was true enough—Jarlaxle had wondered why the Oblodrans had waited this long with all the other houses so vulnerable—

but he would not concede the point.

"Where in this does Bregan D'aerthe stand?" K'yorl demanded.

Jarlaxle got the feeling that any answer he gave would be moot, since K'yorl was probably going to tell *him* exactly where Bregan D'aerthe stood. "With the victors," he said cryptically and casually.

K'yorl smiled in salute to his cleverness. "I will be the victor," she assured him. "It will be over quickly, this very day, and with few drow dead."

Jarlaxle doubted that. House Oblodra had never shown any regard for life, be it drow or otherwise. The drow numbers within the third house were small mainly because the wild clan members killed as often as they bred. They were renowned for a game that they played, a challenge of the highest stakes called *Khaless*—ironically, the drow word for trust. A globe of darkness and magical silence would be hung in the air above the deepest point in the chasm called the Clawrift. The competing dark elves would then levitate into the globe and, there, unable to see or hear, it would become a challenge of simple and pure courage.

The first one to come out of the globe and back to secure footing was the loser, so the trick was to remain in the globe until the very last second of the levitation enchantment.

More often than not, both stubborn competitors would wait too long and would plunge to their demise.

Now K'yorl, merciless and ultimately wicked, was trying to assure Jarlaxle that the drow losses would be kept at a minimum. By whose standard? the mercenary wondered, and if the answer was K'yorl's, then likely half the city would be dead before the end of the day.

There was little Jarlaxle could do about that, he realized. He and Bregan D'aerthe were as dependent on magic as any other dark elf camps, and without it he couldn't even keep K'yorl out of his private chamber—even his private thoughts!

"This day," K'yorl said again, grimly. "And when it is done, I will call for you, and you will come."

Jarlaxle didn't nod, didn't answer at all. He didn't have to. He could feel the mental intrusion again, and knew that K'yorl understood him. He hated her, and hated what she was about to do, but Jarlaxle was ever pragmatic, and if things went as K'yorl predicted, then he would indeed go to her call.

She smiled again and faded away. Then, like a ghost, she simply walked through Jarlaxle's stone wall.

Jarlaxle rested back in his chair, his fingers tapping nervously together. He had never felt so vulnerable, or so caught in the middle of an uncontrollable situation. He could get word to Matron Baenre, of course, but to what gain? Even House Baenre, so vast and proud, could not stand against K'yorl when her magic worked and theirs did not. Likely, Matron Baenre would be dead soon, and all her family with her, and then where would the mercenary hide?

He would not hide, of course. He would go to K'yorl's call.

Jarlaxle understood why K'yorl had paid him the visit and why it was important to her, who seemed to have everything in her favor, to enlist him in her court. He and his band were the only drow in Menzoberranzan with any true ties outside the city, a crucial factor for anyone aspiring to the position of first matron mother—not that anyone other than Matron Baenre had aspired to that coveted position in close to a thousand years.

Jarlaxle's fingers continued tapping. Perhaps it was time for a change, he thought. He quickly dismissed that hopeful notion, for even if he was right, this change did not seem for the better. Apparently, though, K'yorl believed that the situation with conventional magic was a temporary thing, else she would not have been so interested in enlisting Bregan D'aerthe.

Jarlaxle had to believe, had to pray, that she was right, especially if her coup succeeded (and the mercenary had no reason to believe it would not). He would not survive long, he realized, if First Matron Mother K'yorl, a drow he hated above all others, could enter his thoughts at will.

* * * * *

She was too beautiful to be drow, seemed the perfection of drow features to any, male or female, who looked at her. It was this beauty alone that held in check the deadly lances and crossbows of the House Baenre guard and made Berg'inyon Baenre, after one glance at her, bid her enter the compound.

The magical fence wasn't working and there were no conventional gates in the perimeter of the Baenre household. Normally, the spiderweb of the fence would spiral out, opening a wide hole on command, but now Berg'inyon had to ask the drow to climb over.

She said not a word, but simply approached the fence. Spiral wide it did, one last gasp of magic before this creature, the avatar of the goddess who had created it.

Berg'inyon led the way, though he knew beyond doubt that this one needed no guidance. He understood that she was heading for the chapel—of course she would be heading for the chapel!—so he instructed some of his soldiers to find the matron mother.

Sos'Umptu met them at the door of the chapel, the place that was in her care. She protested for an instant, but just for an instant.

Berg'inyon had never seen his devoted sister so flustered, had never seen her jaw go slack for lack of strength. She fell away from them, to her knees.

The beautiful drow walked past her without a word. She turned sharply—Sos'Umptu gasped—and put her glare over Berg'inyon as he continued to follow.

"You are just a male," Sos'Umptu whispered in explanation. "Be gone from this holy place."

Berg'inyon was too stricken to reply, to even sort out how he felt at that moment. He never turned his back, just gave a series of ridiculous bows, and verily fell through the chapel's door, back out into the courtyard.

Both Bladen'Kerst and Quenthel were out there, but the rest of the group that had gathered in response to the whispered rumors had wisely been dispersed by the sisters.

"Go back to your post," Bladen'Kerst snarled at Berg'inyon. "Nothing has happened!" It wasn't so much a statement as a command.

"Nothing has happened," Berg'inyon echoed, and that became the order of the day, and a wise one, Berg'inyon immediately realized. This was Lloth herself, or some close minion. He knew this in his heart.

He knew it, and the soldiers would whisper it, but their enemies must not learn of this!

Berg'inyon scrambled across the courtyard, passed the word, the command that "nothing had happened." He took up a post that allowed him an overview of the chapel and was surprised to see that his ambitious sisters dared not enter, but rather paced about the main entrance nervously.

Sos'Umptu came out as well and joined their parade. No words were openly exchanged—Berg'inyon didn't even notice any flashes of the silent hand code—as Matron Baenre hustled across the courtyard. She passed by her daughters and scurried into the chapel, and the pacing outside began anew.

For Matron Baenre it was the answer to her prayers and the realization of her nightmares all at once. She knew immediately who and what it was that sat before her on the central dais. She knew, and she believed.

"If I am the offending person, then I offer myself . . ." she began humbly, falling to her knees as she spoke.

"*Wael!*" the avatar snapped at her, the drow word for fool, and Baenre hid her face in her hands with shame.

"*Usstan'sargh wael!*" the beautiful drow went on, calling Matron Baenre an arrogant fool. Baenre trembled at the verbal attack, thought for a moment that she had sunk lower than her worst fears, that her goddess had come personally for no better reason than to shame her to death. Images of her tortured body being dragged through the winding avenues of Menzoberranzan flashed in her mind, thoughts of herself as the epitome of a fallen drow leader.

Yet thoughts such as that were exactly what this creature who was more than a drow had just berated her about, Matron Baenre suddenly realized. She dared look up.

"Do not place so much importance on yourself," the avatar said calmly.

Matron Baenre allowed herself to breathe a sigh of relief. Then this wasn't about her, she understood. All of this, the failure of magic and prayer, was beyond her, beyond all the mortal realms.

"K'yorl has erred," the avatar went on, reminding Baenre that while these catastrophic events might be above her, their ramifications most certainly were not.

"She has dared to believe that she can win without your favor," Matron Baenre reasoned, and her surprise was total when the avatar scoffed at the notion.

"She could destroy you with a thought."

Matron Baenre shuddered and lowered her head once more.

"But she has erred on the side of caution," the avatar went on. "She delayed her attack, and now, when she decided that the advantage was indeed hers to hold, she has allowed a personal feud to

115

delay her most important strike even longer."

"Then the powers have returned!" Baenre gasped. "You are returned."

"*Wael!*" the frustrated avatar screamed. "Did you think I would not return?" Matron Baenre fell flat to the floor and groveled with all her heart.

"The Time of Troubles will end," the avatar said a moment later, calm once more. "And you will know what you must do when all is as it should be."

Baenre looked up just long enough to see the avatar's narrow-eyed glare full upon her. "Do you think I am so resourceless?" the beautiful drow asked.

A horrified expression, purely sincere, crossed Baenre's face, and she began to numbly shake her head back and forth, denying she had ever lost faith.

Again, she lay flat out, groveling, and stopped her prayers only when something hard hit the floor beside her head. She dared to look up, to find a lump of yellow stone, sulphur, lying beside her.

"You must fend off K'yorl for a short while," the avatar explained. "Go join the matron mothers and your eldest daughter and son in the meeting room. Stoke the flames and allow those I have enlisted to come through to your side. Together we will teach K'yorl the truth of power!"

A bright smile erupted on Baenre's face with the realization that she was not out of Lloth's favor, that her goddess had called on her to play a crucial role in this crucial hour. The fact that Lloth had all but admitted she was still rather impotent did not matter. The Spider Queen would return, and Baenre would shine again in her devious eyes.

By the time Matron Baenre mustered the courage to come off the floor, the beautiful drow had already exited the chapel. She crossed the compound without interference, walked through the fence as she had done at her arrival, and disappeared into the shadows of the city.

* * * * *

As soon as she heard the awful rumor that House Oblodra's strange psionic powers had not been too adversely affected by whatever was happening to other magic, Ghenni'tiroth Tlabbar, the matron mother of Faen Tlabbar, Menzoberranzan's Fourth House, knew she was in dire trouble. K'yorl Odran hated the tall, slender Ghenni'tiroth above all others, for Ghenni'tiroth had made no secret of the fact that she believed Faen Tlabbar, and not Oblodra, should rank as Menzoberranzan's third house.

With almost eight hundred drow soldiers, Faen Tlabbar's number nearly doubled that of House Oblodra, and only the little understood powers of K'yorl and her minions had kept Faen Tlabbar back.

How much greater those powers loomed now, with all conventional magic rendered unpredictable at best!

Throughout it all, Ghenni'tiroth remained in the house chapel, a relatively small room near the summit of her compound's central stalagmite mound. A single candle burned upon the altar, shedding minimal light by surface standards, but serving as a beacon to the dark elves whose eyes were more accustomed to blackness. A second source of illumination came from the room's west-facing window, for even from halfway across the city, the wild glow of Narbondel could be clearly seen.

Ghenni'tiroth showed little concern for the pillar clock, other than the significance it now held as an indicator of their troubles. She was among the most fanatical of Lloth's priestesses, a drow female who had survived more than six centuries in unquestioning servitude to the Spider Queen. But she was in trouble now, and Lloth, for some reason she could not understand, would not come to her call.

She reminded herself constantly to keep fast her faith as she knelt and huddled over a platinum platter, the famed Faen Tlabbar Communing Plate. The heart of the latest sacrifice, a not-so-insignificant drow male, sat atop it, an offering to the goddess who would not answer Ghenni'tiroth's desperate prayers.

Ghenni'tiroth straightened suddenly as the heart rose from the bloody platter, came up several inches and hovered in midair.

"The sacrifice is not sufficient," came a voice behind her, a voice she had dreaded hearing since the advent of the Time of Troubles.

She did not turn to face K'yorl Odran.

"There is war in the compound," Ghenni'tiroth stated more than asked.

K'yorl scoffed at the notion. A wave of her hand sent the sacrificial organ flying across the room.

117

Ghenni'tiroth spun about, eyes wide with outrage. She started to scream out the drow word for sacrilege, but stopped, the sound caught in her throat, as another heart floated in the air, from K'yorl toward her.

"The sacrifice was not sufficient," K'yorl said calmly. "Use this heart, the heart of Fini'they."

Ghenni'tiroth slumped back at the mention of the obviously dead priestess, her second in the house. Ghenni'tiroth had taken in Fini'they as her own daughter when Fini'they's family, a lower-ranking and insignificant house, had been destroyed by a rival house. Insignificant indeed had been Fini'they's house—Ghenni'tiroth could not even remember its proper name—but Fini'they had not been so. She was a powerful priestess, and ultimately loyal, even loving, to her adopted mother.

Ghenni'tiroth leaned back further, horrified, as her daughter's heart floated past and settled with a sickening wet sound on the platinum platter.

"Pray to Lloth," K'yorl ordered.

Ghenni'tiroth did just that. Perhaps K'yorl had erred, she thought. Perhaps in death Fini'they would prove most helpful, would prove a suitable sacrifice to bring the Spider Queen to the aid of House Faen Tlabbar.

After a long and uneventful moment, Ghenni'tiroth became aware of K'yorl's laughter.

"Perhaps we are in need of a greater sacrifice," the wicked matron mother of House Oblodra said slyly.

It wasn't difficult for Ghenni'tiroth, the only figure in House Faen Tlabbar greater than Fini'they, to figure out who K'yorl was talking about.

Secretly, barely moving her fingers, Ghenni'tiroth brought her deadly, poisoned dagger out of its sheath under the concealing folds of her spider-emblazoned robes. "Scrag-tooth," the dagger was called, and it had gotten a younger Ghenni'tiroth out of many situations much like this.

Of course, on those occasions, magic had been predictable, reliable, and those opponents had not been as formidable as K'yorl. Even as Ghenni'tiroth locked gazes with the Oblodran, kept K'yorl distracted while she subtly shifted her hand, K'yorl read her thoughts and expected the attack.

Ghenni'tiroth shouted a command word, and the dagger's magic functioned, sending the missile shooting out from under her robes directly at the heart of her adversary.

The magic functioned! Ghenni'tiroth silently cheered. But her elation faded quickly when the blade passed right through the specter of K'yorl Odran to embed itself uselessly in the fabric of a tapestry adorning the room's opposite wall.

"I do so hope the poison does not ruin the pattern," K'yorl, standing far to the left of her image, remarked.

Ghenni'tiroth shifted about and turned a steely-eyed gaze at the taunting creature.

"You cannot outfight me, you cannot outthink me," K'yorl said evenly. "You cannot even hide your thoughts from me. The war is ended before it ever began."

Ghenni'tiroth wanted to scream out a denial, but found herself as silent as Fini'they, whose heart lay on the platter before her.

"How much killing need there be?" K'yorl asked, catching Ghenni'tiroth off her guard. The matron of Faen Tlabbar turned a suspicious, but ultimately curious, expression toward her adversary.

"My house is small," K'yorl remarked, and that was true enough, unless one counted the thousands of kobold slaves said to be running about the tunnels along the edges of the Clawrift, just below House Oblodra. "And I am in need of allies if I wish to depose that wretch Baenre and her bloated family."

Ghenni'tiroth wasn't even conscious of the movement as her tongue came out and licked her thin lips. There was a flicker of hope.

"You cannot beat me," K'yorl said with all confidence. "Perhaps I will accept a surrender."

That word didn't sit well with the proud leader of the third house.

"An alliance then, if that is what you must call it," K'yorl clarified, recognizing the look. "It is no secret that I am not on the best of terms with the Spider Queen."

Ghenni'tiroth rocked back on her legs, considering the implications. If she helped K'yorl, who was not in Lloth's favor, overcome Baenre, then what would be the implications to her house if and when everything was sorted out?

"All of this is Baenre's fault," K'yorl remarked, reading

119

R. A. Salvatore

Ghenni'tiroth's every thought. "Baenre brought about the Spider Queen's abandonment," K'yorl scoffed. "She could not even hold a single prisoner, could not even conduct a proper high ritual."

The words rang true, painfully true, to Ghenni'tiroth, who vastly preferred Matron Baenre to K'yorl Odran. She wanted to deny them, and yet, that surely meant her death and the death of her house, since K'yorl held so obvious an advantage.

"Perhaps I will accept a surren—" K'yorl chuckled wickedly and caught herself in midsentence. "Perhaps an alliance would benefit us both," she said instead.

Ghenni'tiroth licked her lips again, not knowing where to turn. A glance at Fini'they's heart did much to convince her, though. "Perhaps it would," she said.

K'yorl nodded and smiled again that devious and infamous grin that was known throughout Menzoberranzan as an indication that K'yorl was lying.

Ghenni'tiroth returned the grin—until she remembered who it was she was dealing with, until she forced herself, through the temptation of the teasing bait that K'yorl had offered, to remember the reputation of this most wicked drow.

"Perhaps not," K'yorl said calmly, and Ghenni'tiroth was knocked backward suddenly by an unseen force, a physical though invisible manifestation of K'yorl's powerful will.

The matron of Faen Tlabbar jerked and twisted, heard the crack of one of her ribs. She tried to call out against K'yorl, to cry out to Lloth in one final, desperate prayer, but found her words garbled as an invisible hand grasped tightly on her throat, cutting off her air.

Ghenni'tiroth jerked again, violently, and again, and more cracking sounds came from her chest, from intense pressure within her torso. She rocked backward and would have fallen to the floor except that K'yorl's will held her slender form fast.

"I am sorry Fini'they was not enough to bring in your impotent Spider Queen," K'yorl taunted, brazenly blasphemous.

Ghenni'tiroth's eyes bulged and seemed as if they would pop from their sockets. Her back arched weirdly, agonizingly, and gurgling sounds continued to stream from her throat. She tore at the flesh of her own neck, trying to grasp the unseen hand, but only drew lines of her own bright blood.

Then there came a final crackle, a loud snapping, and

120

Ghenni'tiroth resisted no more. The pressure was gone from her throat, for what good that did her. K'yorl's unseen hand grabbed her hair and yanked her head forward so that she looked down at the unusual bulge in her chest, beside her left breast.

Ghenni'tiroth's eyes widened in horror as her robes parted and her skin erupted. A great gout of blood and gore poured from the wound, and Ghenni'tiroth fell limply, lying sidelong to the platinum plate.

She watched the last beat of her own heart on that sacrificial platter.

"Perhaps Lloth will hear this call," K'yorl remarked, but Ghenni'tiroth could no longer understand the words.

K'yorl went to the body and retrieved the potion bottle that Ghenni'tiroth carried, that all House Faen Tlabbar females carried. The mixture, a concoction that forced passionate servitude of drow males, was a potent one—or would be, if conventional magic returned. This bottle was likely the most potent, and K'yorl marked it well for a certain mercenary leader.

K'yorl went to the wall and claimed Scrag-tooth as her own.

To the victor . . .

With a final look to the dead matron mother, K'yorl called on her psionic powers and became less than substantial, became a ghost that could walk through the walls and past the guards of the well-defended compound. Her smile was supreme, as was her confidence, but as Lloth's avatar had told Baenre, Odran had indeed erred. She had followed a personal vengeance, had struck out first against a lesser foe.

Even as K'yorl drifted past the structures of House Faen Tlabbar, gloating over the death of her most hated enemy, Matrons Baenre and Mez'Barris Armgo, along with Triel and Gromph Baenre and the matron mothers of Menzoberranzan's fifth through eighth houses, were gathered in a private chamber at the back of the Qu'ellarz'orl, the raised plateau within the huge cavern that held some of the more important drow houses, including House Baenre. The eight of them huddled, each to a leg, about the spider-shaped brazier set upon the small room's single table. Each had brought their most valuable of flammable items, and Matron Baenre carried the lump of sulphur that the avatar had given her.

None of them mentioned, but all of them knew, that this might be their only chance.

Chapter 11
TRUMP

Normally it pleased Jarlaxle to be in the middle of such a conflict, to be the object of wooing tactics by both sides in a dispute. This time, though, Jarlaxle was uneasy with the position. He didn't like dealing with K'yorl Odran on any account, as friends, and especially not as enemies, and he was uneasy with House Baenre being so desperately involved in any struggle. Jarlaxle simply had too much invested with Matron Baenre. The wary mercenary leader usually didn't count on anything, but he had fully expected House Baenre to rule in Menzoberranzan until at least the end of his life, as it had ruled since the beginning of his life and for millennia before that.

It wasn't that Jarlaxle held any special feelings toward the city's first house. It was just that Baenre offered him an anchor point, a measure of permanence in the continually shifting power struggles of Menzoberranzan.

It would last forever, so he had thought, but after talking with K'yorl—how he hated that one!—Jarlaxle wasn't so sure.

K'yorl wanted to enlist him, most likely wanted Bregan D'aerthe to serve as her connection with the world beyond Menzoberranzan.

They could do that, and do it well, but Jarlaxle doubted that he, who always had a private agenda, could remain in K'yorl's favor for long. At some point, sooner or later, she would read the truth in his mind, and she would dispatch and replace him.

That was the way of the drow.

* * * * *

The fiend was gargantuan, a gigantic, bipedal, doglike creature with four muscled arms, two of which ended in powerful pincers. How it entered Jarlaxle's private cave, along the sheer facing of the Clawrift, some hundred yards below and behind the compound of House Oblodra, none of the drow guards knew.

"*Tanar'ri!*" The warning word, the name of the greatest creatures of the Abyss, known in all the languages of the Realms, was passed in whispers and silent hand signals all through the complex, and the reaction to it was uniformly one of horror.

Pity the two drow guards who first encountered the towering, fifteen-foot monster. Loyal to Bregan D'aerthe, courageous in the belief that others would back their actions, they commanded the great beast to halt, and when it did not, the drow guards attacked.

Had their weapons held their previous enchantment, they might have hurt the beast somewhat. But magic had not returned to the Material Plane in any predictable or reliable manner. Thus, the tanar'ri, too, was deprived of its considerable spell repertoire, but the beast, four thousand pounds of muscle and physical hazards, hardly needed magical assistance.

The two drow were summarily dismembered, and the tanar'ri walked on, seeking Jarlaxle, as Errtu had bade it.

It found the mercenary leader, along with a score of his finest soldiers, around the first bend. Several drow leaped forward to the defense, but Jarlaxle, better understanding the power of this beast, held them at bay, was not so willing to throw away drow lives.

"Glabrezu," he said with all respect, recognizing the beast.

Glabrezu's canine maw curled up in a snarl, and its eyes narrowed as it scrutinized Jarlaxle, privately confirming that it had found the correct dark elf.

"*Baenre cok diemrey nochtero,*" the tanar'ri said in a growl, and without waiting for a response, the gigantic beast lumbered about and waddled away, crouching low so that its head did not scrape the corridor's high ceiling.

Again, several brave, stupid drow moved as if to pursue, and again Jarlaxle, smiling now more widely than he had in many weeks, held them back. The tanar'ri had spoken in the language of the lower planes, a language that Jarlaxle understood perfectly, and it had spoken the words Jarlaxle had longed to hear.

The question was clear on the expressions of all the unnerved drow standing beside him. They did not understand the language and wanted desperately to know what the tanar'ri had said.

"*Baenre cok diemrey nochtero,*" Jarlaxle explained to them. "House Baenre will prevail."

His wry smile, filled with hope, and the eager way he clenched his fists, told his soldiers that such a prediction was a good thing.

*   *   *   *   *

Zeerith Q'Xorlarrin, matron mother of the fifth house, understood the significance of the makeup of the gathering. Triel and Gromph Baenre attended primarily to fill the two vacant spots at the spider-shaped brazier. One of those places rightfully belonged to K'yorl, and since they were gathered to fend off K'yorl, as the avatar of the Spider Queen had bade them, she hadn't been invited.

The other vacant place, the one filled by Gromph, was normally reserved for Zeerith's closest drow friend, Matron Mother Ghenni'tiroth Tlabbar. None had said it aloud, but Zeerith understood the significance of the Baenre son's presence and of the matron mother's failure to appear.

K'yorl hated Ghenni'tiroth—that was no secret—and so Ghenni'tiroth had been left open as a sacrifice to delay the intrusions of House Oblodra. These other supposed allies and the goddess they all served had allowed Zeerith's best friend to perish.

That thought bothered the matron mother for a short while, until she came to realize that she was the third highest-ranking drow in the meeting chamber. If the summoning was successful, if K'yorl and House Oblodra were beaten back, then the hierarchy of the ruling houses would surely shift. Oblodra would fall, leaving vacant the third place, and since Faen Tlabbar was suddenly without a proper matron mother, it was feasible that House Xorlarrin could leap past it into that coveted spot.

Ghenni'tiroth had been given as a sacrifice. Zeerith Q'Xorlarrin smiled widely.

Such were the ways of the drow.

Into the brazier went Gromph's prized spider mask, a most magical item, the only one in all of Menzoberranzan that could get someone over the House Baenre web fence. The flames shot into the air, orange and angry green.

Mez'Barris nodded to Baenre, and the withered old matron mother tossed in the lump of sulphur that the avatar had given her.

If a hundred excited dwarves had pumped a huge bellows, their fire would not have been more furious. The flames shot straight up in a multicolored column that held the eight watchers fast with its unholy glory.

"What is this?" came a question from the front of the room, near the only door. "You dare hold a meeting of council without informing House Oblodra?"

Matron Baenre, at the head of the table and, thus, with her back directly to K'yorl, held up her hand to calm the others gathered about the spider brazier. Slowly she turned to face that most hated drow, and the two promptly locked vicious stares.

"The executioner does not invite her victim to the block," Baenre said evenly. "She takes her there, or lures her in."

Baenre's blunt words made more than a few of the gathered drow uneasy. If K'yorl had been handled more tactfully, some of them might have escaped with their lives.

Matron Baenre knew better, though. Their only hope, her only hope, was to trust the Spider Queen, to believe with all their hearts that the avatar had not steered them wrongly.

When K'yorl's first wave of mental energy rolled over Baenre, she, too, began to foster some doubts. She held her ground for some seconds, a remarkable display of will, but then K'yorl overwhelmed her, pushed her back against the table. Baenre felt her feet coming from the floor, felt as if a gigantic, unseen hand had reached out and grabbed her and was now edging her toward the flames.

"How much grander the call to Lloth will be," K'yorl shrieked happily, "when Matron Baenre is added to the flames!"

The others in the room, particularly the other five matron mothers, did not know how to react. Mez'Barris put her head down and

125

quietly began muttering the words of a spell, praying that Lloth would hear her and grant her this.

Zeerith and the others watched the flames. The avatar had told them to do this, but why hadn't an ally, a tanar'ri or some other fiend, come through?

* * * * *

In the sludge-filled Abyss, perched atop his mushroom throne, Errtu greatly enjoyed the chaotic scene. Even through the scrying device Lloth had prepared for him, the great tanar'ri could feel the fears of the gathered worshippers and could taste the bitter hatred on the lips of K'yorl Odran.

He liked K'yorl, Errtu decided. Here was one of his own heart, purely and deliciously wicked, a murderess who killed for pleasure, a player of intrigue for no better reason than the fun of the game. The great tanar'ri wanted to watch K'yorl push her adversary into the pillar of flame.

But Lloth's instructions had been explicit, and her bartered goods too tempting for the fiend to pass up. Amazingly, given the state of magic at the time, the gate was opening, and opening wide.

Errtu had already sent one tanar'ri, a giant glabrezu, through a smaller gate to act as messenger, but that gate, brought about by the avatar herself, had been tenuous and open for only a fraction of a moment. Errtu had not believed the feat could be duplicated, not now.

The notion of magical chaos gave the fiend a sudden inspiration. Perhaps the old rules of banishment no longer applied. Perhaps he himself might walk through this opening gate, onto the Material Plane once more. Then he would not need to serve as Lloth's lackey; then he might find the renegade Do'Urden on his own, and, after punishing the drow, he could return to the frozen Northland, where the precious Crenshinibon, the legendary Crystal Shard, lay buried!

The gate was opened. Errtu stepped in.

And was summarily rejected, pushed back into the Abyss, the place of his hundred-year banishment.

Several fiends stalked by the great tanar'ri, sensing the opening, heading for the gate, but snarling Errtu, enraged by the defeat, held them back.

Let this wicked drow, K'yorl, push Lloth's favored into the flames, the wretched Errtu decided. The gate would remain open with the sacrifice, might even open wider.

Errtu did not like the banishment, did not like being lackey to any being. Let Lloth suffer; let Baenre be consumed, and only then would he do as the Spider Queen had asked!

*   *   *   *   *

The only thing that saved Baenre from exactly that fate was the unexpected intervention of Methil, the illithid. The glabrezu had gone to Methil after visiting Jarlaxle, bringing the same prediction that House Baenre would prevail, and Methil, serving as ambassador of his people, made it a point to remain on the winning side.

The illithid's psionic waves disrupted K'yorl's telepathic attack, and Matron Baenre slumped back to the side of the table.

K'yorl's eyes went wide, surprised by the defeat—until Methil, who had been standing invisibly and secretly at Matron Baenre's side, came into view.

Wait for this to end, K'yorl's thoughts screamed at the octopus-headed creature. *See who wins and then decide where your alliances lie.*

Methil's assurance that he already knew the outcome did not disturb K'yorl half as much as the sight of the gigantic, batlike wing that suddenly extended from the pillar of flame: a tanar'ri—a true tanar'ri!

Another glabrezu hopped out of the fire to land on the floor between Baenre and her adversary. K'yorl hit it with a psionic barrage, but she was no match for such a creature, and she knew it.

She took note that the pillar was still dancing wildly, that another fiend was forming within the flames. Lloth was against her! she suddenly realized. All the Abyss seemed to be coming to Matron Baenre's call!

K'yorl did the only thing she could, became insubstantial once more and fled across the city, back to her house.

Fiends rushed through the open gate, a hundred of them, and still more. It went on for more than an hour, the minions of Errtu, and, thus, the minions of Lloth, coming to the call of the desperate matron mothers, swooping across the city in frenzied glee to surround House Oblodra.

Smiles of satisfaction, even open cheers, were exchanged in the meeting room at the back of the Qu'ellarz'orl. The avatar had done as promised, and the future of Lloth's faithful seemed deliciously dark once more.

Of the eight gathered, only Gromph wore a grin that was less than sincere. Not that he wanted House Oblodra to win, of course, but the male held no joy at the thought that things might soon be as they had always been, that he, for all his power and devotion to the ways of magic, would, above all else, be a mere male once more.

He took some consolation, as the flames died away and the others began to exit, in noticing that several of the offered items, including his prized spider mask, had not been consumed by the magical flames. Gromph looked to the door, to the matron mothers and Triel, and they were so obsessed with the spectacle of the fiends that they took no notice of him at all.

Quietly and without attracting attention, the covetous drow wizard replaced his precious item under the folds of his robe, then added to his collection some of the most prized artifacts of Menzo-berranzan's greatest houses.

Part 3

RESOLUTION

ow I wanted to go to Catti-brie after I realized the dangers of her sword! How I wanted to stand by her and protect her! The item had possessed her, after all, and was imbued with a powerful and obviously sentient magic.

Catti-brie wanted me by her side—who wouldn't want the supportive shoulder of a friend with such a struggle looming?—and yet she did not want me there, could not have me there, for she knew this battle was hers to fight alone.

I had to respect her conclusion, and in those days when the Time of Troubles began to end and the magics of the world sorted themselves out once more, I came to learn that sometimes the most difficult battles are the ones we are forced not to fight.

I came to learn then why mothers and fathers seldom have fingernails and often carry an expression of forlorn resignation. What agony it must be for a parent in Silverymoon to be told by her offspring, no longer a child, that he or she has decided to head out to the west, to Waterdeep, to sail for adventure along the Sword Coast. Everything within that parent wants to yell out "Stay!" Every instinct within that parent wants to hug the child close, to protect that child forever. And yet, ultimately, those instincts are wrong.

In the heart, there is no sting greater than watching the struggles of one you love, knowing that only through such strife will that person grow and recognize the potential of his or her existence. Too many thieves in the Realms believe the formula for happiness lies in an unguarded treasure trove. Too many wizards seek to circumvent the years of study required for true power. They find a spell on a scroll or an enchanted item that is far beyond their understanding, yet they try it anyway, only to be consumed by the powerful magic. Too many priests in the Realms, and too many religious sects in general, ask of themselves and of their congregations only

130

humble servitude.

All of them are doomed to fail in the true test of happiness. There is one ingredient missing in stumbling upon an unguarded treasure hoard; there is one element absent when a minor wizard lays his hands on an arch-mage's staff; there is one item unaccounted for in humble, unquestioning, and unambitious servitude.

A sense of accomplishment.

It is the most important ingredient in any rational being's formula of happiness. It is the element that builds confidence and allows us to go on to other, greater tasks. It is the item that promotes a sense of self-worth, that allows any person to believe there is value in life itself, that gives a sense of purpose to bolster us as we face life's unanswerable questions.

So it was with Catti-brie and her sword. This battle had found her, and she had determined to fight it. Had I followed my protective instincts, I would have refused to aid her in taking on this quest. My protective instincts told me to go to Bruenor, who would have surely ordered the sen-tient sword destroyed. By doing that, or taking any other course to prevent Catti-brie's battle, I would have, in effect, failed to trust in her, failed to respect her individual needs and her chosen destiny, and, thus, I would have stolen a bit of her freedom. That had been Wulfgar's single failure. In his fears for the woman he so dearly loved, the brave and proud barbarian had tried to smother her in his protective hug.

I think he saw the truth of his error in the moments before his death. I think he remembered then the reasons he loved Catti-brie: her strength and independence. How ironic it is that our instincts often run exactly opposite from what we truly desire for those we love.

In the situation I earlier named, the parents would have to let their child go to Waterdeep and the Sword Coast. And so it was with Catti-brie. She chose to take her sword, chose to explore its sentient side, perhaps at great personal risk. The decision was hers to make, and once she had made it, I had to respect it, had to respect her. I didn't see her much over the next couple of weeks, as she waged her private battle.

But I thought of her and worried for her every waking moment, and even in my dreams.

— Drizzt Do'Urden

131

Chapter 12

WORTH THE TROUBLES

I have tricked tanar'ri to go to your city, Menzoberranzan, and soon I must force them back," the great Errtu roared. "And I cannot even go to this place and join in their havoc, or even to retrieve them!" The balor sat on his mushroom throne, watching the scrying device that showed him the city of drow. Earlier, he was receiving fleeting images only, as this magic, too, struggled against the effects of the strange time. The images had been coming more strongly lately, though, and now the mirrorlike surface was uncloudy, showing a clear scene of House Oblodra, wedged between the fingers of the Clawrift. Fiends great and minor stalked and swooped about the walled compound, banging strong fists against the stone, hurling threats and missiles of rock. The Oblodrans had buttoned the place up tightly, for even with their psionic powers, and the fact that the fiends' magic fared no better than anyone else's, the otherworldly beasts were simply too physically strong, their minds too warped by evil to be much affected by telepathic barrages.

And they were backed by a united army of drow, lying in wait behind the fiendish lines. Hundreds of crossbows and javelins were pointed House Oblodra's way. Scores of drow riding sticky-footed subterranean lizards stalked the walls and ceiling near the doomed house. Any Oblodran that showed her face would be hit by a barrage from every angle.

"Those same fiends are preventing the third house from being attacked," Errtu snarled at Lloth, reminding the Spider Queen whose army was in control here. "Your minions fear my minions, and rightly so!"

The beautiful drow, back in the Abyss once more, understood that Errtu's outburst was one part outrage and nine parts bluster. No tanar'ri ever had to be "tricked" into going to the Material Plane, where it might wreak havoc. That was their very nature, the most profound joy in their miserable existence.

"You ask much, Lady of Spiders," Errtu grumbled on.

"I give much in return," Lloth reminded him.

"We shall see."

Lloth's red-glowing eyes narrowed at the tanar'ri's continuing sarcasm. The payment she had offered Errtu, a gift that could potentially free the fiend from nearly a century more of banishment, was no small thing.

"The four glabrezu will be difficult to retrieve," Errtu went on, feigning exasperation, playing this out to the extreme. "They are always difficult!"

"No more so than a balor," Lloth said in blunt response. Errtu turned on her, his face a mask of hatred.

"The Time of Troubles nears its end," Lloth said calmly into that dangerous visage.

"It has been too long!" Errtu roared.

Lloth ignored the tone of the comment, understanding that Errtu had to act outraged and overburdened to prevent her from concluding that the tanar'ri owed her something more. "It has been longer to my eyes than to your own, fiend," the Spider Queen retorted.

Errtu muttered a curse under his smelly breath.

"But it nears its end," Lloth went on, quietly, calmly. Both she and Errtu looked to the image on the scrying surface just as a great winged tanar'ri soared up out of the Clawrift, clutching a small, wriggling creature in one of its great fists. The pitiful catch could not have been more than three feet tall and seemed less than that in the massive fiend's clutches. It wore a ragged vest that did not hide its rust-colored scales, a vest made even more ragged from the tearing of the tanar'ri's clawed grasp.

"A kobold," Errtu remarked.

"Known allies of House Oblodra," Lloth explained. "Thousands of the wretches run the tunnels along the chasm walls."

The flying tanar'ri gave a hoot, grasped the kobold with its other clawed hand as well, and ripped the squealing thing in half.

"One less ally of House Oblodra," Errtu whispered, and from the pleased look on the balor's face, Lloth understood Errtu's true feelings about this whole event. The great tanar'ri was living vicariously through his minions, was watching their destructive antics and feeding off the scene.

It crossed Lloth's mind to reconsider her offered gift. Why should she repay the fiend for doing something it so obviously wanted to do?

The Spider Queen, never a fool, shook the thoughts from her mind. She had nothing to lose in giving Errtu what she had promised. Her eyes were set on the conquest of Mithril Hall, on forcing Matron Baenre to extend her grasp so that the city of drow would be less secure, and more chaotic, more likely to see interhouse warfare. The renegade Do'Urden was nothing to her, though she surely wanted him dead.

Who better to do that than Errtu? Lloth wondered. Even if the renegade survived the coming war—and Lloth did not believe he would—Errtu could use her gift to force Drizzt to call him from his banishment, to allow him back to the Material Plane. Once there, the mighty balor's first goal would undoubtedly be to exact vengeance on the renegade. Drizzt had beaten Errtu once, but no one ever defeated a balor the second time around.

Lloth knew Errtu well enough to understand that Drizzt Do'Urden would be far luckier indeed if he died swiftly in the coming war.

She said no more about the payment for the fiend's aid, understanding that in giving it to Errtu, she was, in effect, giving herself a present. "When the Time of Troubles has passed, my priestesses will aid you in forcing the tanar'ri back to the Abyss," Lloth said.

Errtu did not hide his surprise well. He knew that Lloth had been planning some sort of campaign, and he assumed his monstrous minions would be sent along beside the drow army. Now that Lloth had clearly stated her intentions, though, the fiend recognized her reasoning. If a horde of tanar'ri marched beside the drow, all the Realms would rise against them, including goodly creatures of great power from the upper planes.

Also, both Lloth and Errtu knew well that the drow priestesses, powerful as they were, would not be able to control such a horde once the rampage of warfare had begun.

"All but one," Errtu corrected.

Lloth eyed him curiously.

"I will need an emissary to go to Drizzt Do'Urden," the fiend explained. "To tell the fool what I have, and what I require in exchange for it."

Lloth considered the words for a moment. She had to play this out carefully. She had to hold Errtu back, she knew, or risk complicating what should be a relatively straightforward conquest of the dwarven halls, but she could not let the fiend know her army's destination. If Errtu thought Lloth's minions would soon put Drizzt Do'Urden, the great fiend's only chance at getting back to the Material Plane anytime soon, in jeopardy, he would covertly oppose her.

"Not yet," the Spider Queen said. "Drizzt Do'Urden is out of the way, and there he shall stay until my city is back in order."

"Menzoberranzan is never in order," Errtu replied slyly.

"In relative order," Lloth corrected. "You will have your gift when I give it, and only then will you send your emissary."

"Lady of Spiders . . ." The balor growled threateningly.

"The Time of Troubles nears its end," Lloth snapped in Errtu's ugly face. "My powers return in full. Beware your threats, balor, else you shall find yourself in a more wretched place than this!"

Her purplish black robes flying furiously behind her, the Spider Queen spun about sharply and moved off, swiftly disappearing into the swirling mist. She smirked at the proper ending to the meeting. Diplomacy went only so far with chaotic fiends. After reaching a point, the time inevitably came for open threats.

Errtu slumped back on his mushroom throne in the realization that Lloth was in full command of this situation. She held the link for his minions to the Material Plane, and she held the gift that might allow Errtu to end his banishment. On top of all of that, Errtu did not doubt the Spider Queen's claims that the pantheon was at last sorting itself out. And if the Time of Troubles was indeed a passing period, and Lloth's powers returned in full, she was far beyond the balor.

Resignedly, Errtu looked back to the image on the scrying surface. Five more kobolds had been pulled up from the Clawrift. They huddled together in a tight group while a host of fiends circled about them, teasing them, tormenting them. The great balor could smell their fear, could taste this torturous kill as sweetly as if he were among those circling fiends.

Errtu's mood brightened immediately.

* * * * *

Belwar Dissengulp and a score of svirfnebli warriors sat on a ledge, overlooking a large chamber strewn with boulders and stalactites. Each held a rope—Belwar's was fastened through a loop on his belt and a mushroom-hide strap set over his pickaxe hand—that they might rappel quickly to the floor. For down below, the gnomish priests were at work, drawing runes of power on the floor with heated dyes and discussing the prior failures and the most effective ways they might combine their powers, both for the summoning, and in case the summoning, as had happened twice already, went bad.

The gnomish priests had heard the call of their god, Segojan, had sensed the returning of priestly magic. For the svirfnebli, no act could greater signify the end of this strange period, no act could better assure them that all was right once more, than the summoning of an elemental earth giant. This was their sphere, their life, and their love. They were attuned to the rock, at one with the stone and dirt that surrounded their dwellings. To call an elemental forth, to share in its friendship, would satisfy the priests that their god was well. Anything less would not suffice.

They had tried several times. The first summoning had brought forth nothing, not a trembling in the ground. The second, third, and fourth had raised tall stone pillars, but they had shown no signs of animation. Three of the stalagmite mounds in this very chamber were testaments to those failures.

On the fifth try, an elemental had come forth, and the gnomish priests had rejoiced—until the monster turned on them in rage, killing a dozen gnomes before Belwar and his troupe had managed to break it apart. That failure was perhaps the very worst thing that could befall the gnomes, for they came to believe not only that Segojan was out of their reach, but that, perhaps, he was angry with them. They had tried again—and again the elemental came forth only to attack them.

Belwar's defenses were better in place that sixth time, as they were now, and the stone-limbed monster was beaten back quickly, with no loss of svirfnebli.

After that second disaster, Belwar had asked that the priests wait a while before trying again, but they had refused, desperate to find Segojan's favor, desperate to know that their god was with them. Belwar was not without influence, though, and he had gone to King Schnicktick and forced a compromise.

Five days had passed since that sixth summoning, five days wherein the gnomish priests and all of Blingdenstone had prayed to Segojan, had begged him to no longer turn against them.

Unknown to the svirfnebli, those five days had also seen the end of the Time of Troubles, the realignment and correction of the pantheon.

Belwar watched now as the robed priests began their dance about the rune-emblazoned circle they had drawn on the ground. Each carried a stone, a small green gem previously enchanted. One by one, they placed a gem on the perimeter of the circle and crushed it with a huge mallet. When that was completed, the high priest walked into the circle, to its very center, placed his gem on the ground, and, crying out a word of completion, smashed it under his mithril mallet.

For a moment there was only silence, then the ground began to tremble slightly. The high priest rushed out of the circle to join his huddling companions.

The trembling increased, multiplied; a large crack ran about the circumference of the enchanted area, separating that circle from the rest of the chamber. Inside the circle, rock split apart, and split again, rolling and roiling into a malleable mud.

Bubbles grew and blew apart with great popping sounds; the

whole chamber warmed.

A great head—a huge head!—poked up from the floor.

On the ledge, Belwar and his cohorts groaned. Never had they seen so tremendous an elemental! Suddenly, they were all plotting escape routes rather than attack routes.

The shoulders came forth from the floor, an arm on each side—an arm that could sweep the lot of the priests into oblivion with a single movement. Curious looks mixed with trepidation on the faces of priests and warriors alike. This creature was not like any elemental they had ever seen. Though its stone was smoother, with no cracks showing, it appeared more unfinished, less in the image of a bipedal creature. Yet, at the same time, it exuded an aura of sheer power and completion beyond anything the gnomes had ever known.

"The glory of Segojan are we witnessing!" one gnome near Belwar squealed in glee.

"Or the end of our people," Belwar added under his breath so that none would hear.

By the girth of the head and shoulders, the gnomes expected the monster to rise twenty feet or more, but when the trembling stopped and all was quiet again, the creature barely topped ten feet—not as tall as many of the elementals even single svirfneblin priests had previously summoned. Still, the gnomes had no doubt that this was a greater achievement, that this creature was more powerful than anything they had ever brought forth. The priests had their suspicions—so did Belwar, who had lived a long time and had listened carefully to the legends that gave his people their identity and their strength.

"Entemoch!" the most honored burrow warden gasped from his perch, and the name, the name of the Prince of Earth Elementals, was echoed from gnome to gnome.

Another name predictably followed, the name of Ogremoch, Entemoch's evil twin, and it was spoken sharply and with open fear. If this was Ogremoch and not Entemoch, then they all were doomed.

The priests fell to their knees, trembling, paying homage, hoping beyond hope that this was indeed Entemoch, who had always been their friend.

Belwar was the first down from the ledge, hitting the ground with a grunt and running off to stand before the summoned creature.

It regarded him from on high, made no move, and offered no sign as to its intentions.

"Entemoch!" Belwar shouted. Behind him, the priests lifted their faces; some found the courage to stand and walk beside the brave burrow warden.

"Entemoch!" Belwar called again. "Answered our call, you have. Are we to take this as a sign that all is right with Segojan, that we are in his favor?"

The creature brought its huge hand to the floor, palm up, before Belwar. The burrow warden looked to the high priest standing at his right.

The priest nodded. "To trust in Segojan is our duty," he said, and he and Belwar stepped onto the hand together.

Up they rose, coming to a stop right before the behemoth's face. And they relaxed and were glad, for they saw compassion there, and friendship. This was indeed Entemoch, they both knew in their hearts, and not Ogremoch, and Segojan was with them.

The elemental prince lifted its hand above its head and melted back into the ground, leaving Belwar and the high priest in the center of the circle, perfectly reformed.

Cheers resounded through the chamber; more than one rough-hewn svirfneblin face was streaked with tears. The priests patted themselves on the back, congratulated themselves and all the gnomes of Blingdenstone. They sang praises to King Schnicktick, whose guidance had led them to this pinnacle of svirfneblin achievement.

For at least one of them, Belwar, the celebration was short-lived. Their god was back with them, it seemed, and their magic was returning, but what did that mean for the drow of Menzoberranzan? the most honored burrow warden wondered. Was the Spider Queen, too, returned? And the powers of the drow wizards as well?

Before all of this had begun, the gnomes had come to believe, and not without reason, that the drow were planning for war. With the onset of this chaotic time, that war had not come, but that was reasonable, Belwar knew, since the drow were more dependent on magic than were the gnomes. If things were indeed aright once more, as the arrival of Entemoch seemed to indicate, then Blingdenstone might soon be threatened.

All about the most honored burrow warden, gnomish priests and warriors danced and cried out for joy. How soon, he wondered, might those cries be screams of pain or shrieks of grief?

Chapter 13
REPAIRING THE DAMAGE

elicately!" Fret whispered harshly, watching Drizzt's hands as the drow scraped and chipped away the dried salve around the neck of the panther figurine. "Oh, do be careful!"

Of course Drizzt was being careful! As careful as the drow had ever been in any task. As important as the figurine appeared to be to Fret, it was a hundred times more important to Drizzt, who treasured and loved his panther companion. Never had the drow taken on a more critical task, not with his wits or his weapons. Now he used the delicate tool Fret had given him, a slender silver rod with a flattened and slightly hooked end.

Another piece of salve fell away—almost a half inch along the side of the panther's neck was clear of the stuff. And clear of any crack, Drizzt noted hopefully. So perfectly had the salve bonded the onyx figurine that not a line could be seen where the break had been.

Drizzt sublimated his excitement, understanding that it would inevitably lead him to rush in his work. He had to take his time. The circumference of the figurine's neck was no more than a few inches, but Drizzt fully expected, and Fret had agreed with the estimate, that he would spend the entire morning at his work.

The drow ranger moved back from the figurine so that Fret could see the cleared area. The tidy dwarf nodded to Drizzt after viewing it, even smiled hopefully. Fret trusted in Lady Alustriel's magic and her ability to mend a tragedy.

With a pat on Drizzt's shoulder, the dwarf moved aside and Drizzt went back to work, slowly and delicately, one tiny fleck at a time.

By noon, the neck was clear of salve. Drizzt turned the figurine over in his hands, studying the area where the break had been, seeing no indication, neither a crack nor any residue from the salve, that the figurine had been damaged. He clasped the item by the head and, after a deep, steadying breath, dared to hold it aloft, with all the pressure of its weight centered on the area of the cut.

It held fast. Drizzt shook his hand, daring it to break apart, but it did not.

"The bonding will be as strong as any other area on the item," Fret assured the drow. "Take heart that the figurine is whole once more."

"Agreed," Drizzt replied, "but what of its magic?"

Fret had no answer.

"The real challenge will be in sending Guenhwyvar home to the Astral Plane," the drow went on.

"Or in calling the panther back," Fret added.

That notion stung Drizzt. The tidy dwarf was right, he knew. He might be able to open a tunnel to allow Guenhwyvar to return home, only to have the panther lost to him forever. Still, Drizzt entertained no thoughts of keeping the cat beside him. Guenhwyvar's condition had stabilized—apparently the panther could indeed remain on the Material Plane indefinitely—but the great cat was not in good health or good spirits. While she seemed no longer in danger of dying, Guenhwyvar roamed about in a state of perpetual exhaustion, muscles slack along her once sleek sides, eyes often closed as the panther tried to find desperately needed sleep.

"Better to dismiss Guenhwyvar to her home," Drizzt said determinedly. "Surely my life will be diminished if I cannot recall Guenhwyvar, but better that than the life Guenhwyvar must now endure."

They went together, the figurine in hand, to Drizzt's room. As usual, Guenhwyvar lay on the rug in front of the hearth, absorbing the heat of the glowing embers. Drizzt didn't hesitate. He marched right up before the panther—who lifted her head sluggishly to regard him—and placed the figurine on the floor before her.

"Lady Alustriel, and good Fret here, have come to our aid, Guenhwyvar," Drizzt announced. His voice quivered a bit as he tried to continue, as the realization hit him that this might be the last time he ever saw the panther.

Guenhwyvar sensed that discomfort and, with great effort, managed to sit up, putting her head in line with kneeling Drizzt's face.

"Go home, my friend," Drizzt whispered, "go home."

The panther hesitated, eyeing the drow intently, as if trying to discern the source of Drizzt's obvious unease. Guenhwyvar, too, got the feeling—from Drizzt and not from the figurine, which seemed whole to the panther once more—that this might be a final parting of dear friends.

But the cat had no control in the matter. In her exhausted state, Guenhwyvar could not have ignored the call of the magic if she tried. Shakily, the cat got to her feet and paced about the figurine.

Drizzt was both thrilled and scared when Guenhwyvar's form began to melt away into gray mist, then into nothing at all.

When the cat was gone, Drizzt scooped up the figurine, taking heart that he felt no warmth coming from it, that apparently whatever had gone wrong the last time he tried to send Guenhwyvar home was not happening again. He realized suddenly how foolish he had been, and looked at Fret, his violet orbs wide with shock.

"What is it?" the tidy dwarf asked.

"I have not Catti-brie's sword!" Drizzt whispered harshly. "If the path is not clear to the Astral Plane . . ."

"The magic is right once more," Fret replied at once, patting his hand soothingly in the air, "in the figurine and in all the world about us. The magic is right once more."

Drizzt held the figurine close. He had no idea of where Catti-brie might be, and knew she had her sword with her. All he could do, then, was sit tight, wait, and hope.

* * * * *

Bruenor sat on his throne, Regis beside him, and the halfling looking much more excited than the dwarf king. Regis had already seen the guests that would soon be announced to Bruenor, and curious Regis was always happy to see the extraordinary Harpells of Longsaddle. Four of them had come to Mithril Hall, four wizards who might play an important role in defending the dwarven complex—if they didn't inadvertently take the place down instead.

Such were the risks of dealing with the Harpells.

The four stumbled into the throne room, nearly running down the poor dwarf who had first entered to announce them. There was Harkle, of course, wearing a bandage about his face, for his eyes were already in Mithril Hall. Guiding him was fat Regweld, who had ridden into the outer hall on a curious mount, the front of which resembled a horse and the back of which had hind legs and a back end more akin to a frog. Regweld had appropriately named the thing Puddlejumper.

The third Harpell Bruenor and Regis did not know, and the wizard did not offer his name. He merely growled low and nodded in their direction.

"I am Bella don DelRoy Harpell," announced the fourth, a short and quite beautiful young woman, except that her eyes did not look in the same direction. Both orbs were green, but one shined with a fierce inner light, while the other was dulled over and grayish. With Bella, though, that seemed to only add to her appearance, to give her fine features a somewhat exotic look.

Bruenor recognized one of the given names, and understood that Bella was probably the leader of this group. "Daughter of Del-Roy, leader of Longsaddle?" the dwarf asked, to which the petite woman dipped low in a bow, so low that her bright blond mane nearly swept the floor.

"Greetings from Longsaddle, Eighth King of Mithril Hall," Bella said politely. "Your call was not unheeded."

A pity, Bruenor thought, but he remained tactfully quiet.

"With me are—"

"Harkle and Regweld," Regis interrupted, knowing the two quite well from a previous stay in Longsaddle. "Well met! And it is good to see that your experiments in crossbreeding a horse and a frog came to fruition."

"Puddlejumper!" the normally forlorn Regweld happily replied.

That name promised a sight that Regis would like to see!

"I am the daughter of DelRoy," Bella said rather sharply, eyeing the halfling squarely. "Please do not interrupt again, or I shall have to turn you into something Puddlejumper would enjoy eating."

The sparkle in her good green eye as she regarded Regis, and the similar glint in the halfling's gray orbs, told Regis that the threat was a hollow one. He heeded it anyway, suddenly anxious to keep on Bella's good side. She wasn't five feet tall, the halfling realized, and a bit on the heavy side, somewhat resembling a slightly larger version of Regis himself—except that there was no mistaking her feminine attributes. At least, not for Regis.

"My third companion is Bidderdoo," Bella went on.

The name sounded curiously familiar to both Bruenor and Regis, and came perfectly clear when Bidderdoo answered the introduction with a bark.

Bruenor groaned; Regis clapped and laughed aloud. When they had gone through Longsaddle, on their way to find Mithril Hall, Bidderdoo, through use of a bad potion, had played the role of the Harpell family dog.

"The transformation is not yet complete," Bella apologized, and she gave Bidderdoo a quick backhand on the shoulder, reminding him to put his tongue back in his mouth.

Harkle cleared his throat loudly and fidgeted about.

"Of course," Bruenor said immediately, taking the cue. The dwarf gave a sharp whistle, and one of his attendants came out of a side room, carrying the disembodied eyes, one in each hand. To his credit, the dwarf tried to keep them as steady as possible, and aimed them both in Harkle's direction.

"Oh, it is so good to see myself again!" the wizard exclaimed, and he spun about. Following what he could see, he started for himself, or for his eyes, or for the back wall, actually, and the door he and his companions had already come through. He cried out, "No, no!" and turned a complete circle, trying to get his bearing, which wasn't an easy thing while viewing himself from across the room.

Bruenor groaned again.

"It is so confusing!" an exasperated Harkle remarked as Regweld grabbed him and tried to turn him aright.

"Ah, yes," the wizard said, and turned back the wrong way once more, heading for the door.

"The other way!" frustrated Regweld cried.

Bruenor grabbed the dwarven attendant and took the eyes,

turning them both to look directly into his own scowling visage.

Harkle screamed.

"Hey!" Bruenor roared. "Turn around."

Harkle calmed himself and did as instructed, his body facing Bruenor once more.

Bruenor looked to Regis, snickered, and tossed one of the eyes Harkle's way, then followed it a split second later with the other, snapping his wrist so the thing spun as it soared through the air.

Harkle screamed again and fainted.

Regweld caught one of the eyes; Bidderdoo went for the other with his mouth. Luckily, Bella cut him off. She missed though, and the eye bounced off her arm, fell to the floor, and rolled about.

"That was very naughty, King Dwarf!" the daughter of DelRoy scolded. "That was . . ." She couldn't maintain the facade, and was soon laughing, as were her companions (though Bidderdoo's chuckles sounded more like a growl). Regis joined in, and Bruenor, too, but only for a second. The dwarf king could not forget the fact that these bumbling wizards might be his only magical defense against an army of dark elves.

It was not a pleasant thought.

* * * * *

Drizzt was out of Mithril Hall at dawn the next morning. He had seen a campfire on the side of the mountain the night before and knew it was Catti-brie's. He still had not tried calling Guenhwyvar back and resisted the urge now, reminding himself to take on one problem at a time.

The problem now was Catti-brie, or, more specifically, her sword.

He found the young woman as he came around a bend in the path, crossing into the shadow between two large boulders. She was almost directly below him, on a small, flat clearing overlooking the wide, rolling terrain east of Mithril Hall. With the rising sun breaking the horizon directly before her, Drizzt could make out only her silhouette. Her movements were graceful as she walked through a practice dance with her sword, waving it in slow, long lines before and above her. Drizzt rested and watched approvingly of both the grace and perfection of the woman's dance. He had shown her this,

146

and, as always, Catti-brie had learned well. She could have been his own shadow, Drizzt realized, so perfect and synchronous were her movements.

He let her continue, both because of the importance of this practice and because he enjoyed watching her.

Finally, after nearly twenty minutes, Catti-brie took a deep breath and held her arms out high and wide, reveling in the rising sun.

"Well done," Drizzt congratulated, walking down to her.

Catti-brie nearly jumped at the sound, and she spun about, a bit embarrassed and annoyed, to see the drow.

"Ye should warn a girl," she said.

"I came upon you quite by accident," Drizzt lied, "but fortunately it would seem."

"I seen the Harpells go into Mithril Hall yesterday," Catti-brie replied. "Have ye speaked with them?"

Drizzt shook his head. "They are not important right now," he explained. "I need only to speak with you."

It sounded serious. Catti-brie moved to slide her sword into its scabbard, but Drizzt's hand came out, motioning for her to stop.

"I have come for the sword," he explained.

"Khazid'hea?" Catti-brie asked, surprised.

"What?" asked the even more surprised drow.

"That is its name," Catti-brie explained, holding the fine blade before her, its razor-sharp edge glowing red once more. "Khazid'hea."

Drizzt knew the word, a drow word! It meant "to cut," or "cutter," and seemed an appropriate name indeed for a blade that could slice through solid stone. But how could Catti-brie know it? the drow wondered, and his face asked the question as plainly as words ever could.

"The sword told me!" Catti-brie answered.

Drizzt nodded and calmed. He shouldn't have been so surprised—he knew the sword was sentient, after all.

"Khazid'hea," the drow agreed. He drew Twinkle from its sheath, flipped it over in his hand, and presented it, hilt-first, to Catti-brie.

She stared at the offering blankly, not understanding.

"A fair exchange," Drizzt explained, "Twinkle for Khazid'hea."

147

"Ye favor the scimitar," Catti-brie said.

"I will learn to use a scimitar and sword in harmony," Drizzt replied. "Accept the exchange. Khazid'hea has begged that I be its wielder, and I will oblige. It is right that the blade and I are joined."

Catti-brie's look went from surprise to incredulity. She couldn't believe Drizzt would demand this of her! She had spent days—weeks!—alone in the mountains, practicing with this sword, connecting with its unnatural intelligence, trying to establish a bond.

"Have you forgotten our encounter?" Drizzt asked, somewhat cruelly. Catti-brie blushed a deep red. Indeed, she had not forgotten, and never would, and what a fool she felt when she realized how she—or at least how her sword, using her body—had thrown herself at Drizzt.

"Give me the sword," Drizzt said firmly, waving Twinkle's hilt before the stunned young woman. "It is right that we are joined."

Catti-brie clutched Khazid'hea defensively. She closed her eyes then, and seemed to sway, and Drizzt got the impression she was communing with the blade, hearing its feelings.

When she opened her eyes once more, Drizzt's free hand moved for the sword, and, to the drow's surprise and satisfaction, the sword tip came up suddenly, nicking his hand and forcing him back.

"The sword does not want ye!" Catti-brie practically growled.

"You would strike me?" Drizzt asked, and his question calmed the young woman.

"Just a reaction," she stammered, trying to apologize.

Just a reaction, Drizzt silently echoed, but exactly the reaction he had hoped to see. The sword was willing to defend her right to wield it; the sword had rejected him in light of its rightful owner.

In the blink of an eye, Drizzt flipped Twinkle over and replaced it on his belt. His smile clued Catti-brie to the truth of the encounter.

"A test," she said. "Ye just gived me a test!"

"It was necessary."

"Ye never had any mind to take Khazid'hea," the woman went on, her volume rising with her ire. "Even if I'd taken yer offer . . ."

"I would have taken the sword," Drizzt answered honestly. "And I would have placed it on display in a secure place in the Hall of Dumathoin."

"And ye would have taken back Twinkle," Catti-brie huffed.

"Ye lyin' drow!"

Drizzt considered the words, then shrugged and nodded his agreement with the reasoning.

Catti-brie gave an impertinent pout and tossed her head, which sent her auburn mane flying over her shoulder. "The sword just knows now that I'm the better fighter," she said, sounding sincere.

Drizzt laughed aloud.

"Draw yer blades, then!" Catti-brie huffed, falling back into a ready posture. "Let me show ye what me and me sword can do!"

Drizzt's smile was wide as his scimitars came into his hands. These would be the last and most crucial tests, he knew, to see if Catti-brie had truly taken control of the sword.

Metal rang out in the clear morning air, the two friends hopping about for position, their breath blowing clouds in the chill air. Soon after the sparring had begun, Drizzt's guard slipped, presenting Catti-brie with a perfect strike.

In came Khazid'hea, but it stopped far short, and the young woman jumped back. "Ye did that on purpose!" she accused, and she was right, and by not going for a vicious hit, she and her sword had passed the second test.

Only one test to go.

Drizzt said nothing as he went back into his crouch. He wasn't wearing the bracers, Catti-brie noticed, and so he wouldn't likely be off balance. She came on anyway, gladly and fiercely, and put up a fine fight as the sun broke clear of the horizon and began its slow climb into the eastern sky.

She couldn't match the drow, though, and, in truth, hadn't seen Drizzt fight with this much vigor in a long time. When the sparring ended, Catti-brie was sitting on her rump, a scimitar resting easily atop each of her shoulders and her own sword lying on the ground several feet away.

Drizzt feared that the sentient sword would be outraged that its wielder had been so clearly beaten. He stepped away from Catti-brie and went to Khazid'hea first, bending low to scoop it up. The drow paused, though, his hand just an inch from the pommel.

No longer did Khazid'hea wear the pommel of a unicorn, nor even the fiendish visage it had taken when in the hands of Dantrag Baenre. That pommel resembled a sleek feline body now, something like Guenhwyvar running flat out, legs extended front and back.

149

More important to Drizzt, though, there was a rune inscribed on the side of that feline, the twin mountains, symbol of Dumathoin, the dwarven god, Catti-brie's god, the Keeper of Secrets Under the Mountain.

Drizzt picked up Khazid'hea, and felt no enmity or any of the desire the sword had previously shown him. Catti-brie was beside him, then, smiling in regard to his obvious approval of her choice for a pommel.

Drizzt handed Khazid'hea back to its rightful owner.

Chapter 14
THE WRATH OF LLOTH

aenre felt strong again. Lloth was back, and Lloth was with her, and K'yorl Odran, that wretched K'yorl, had badly erred. Always before, the Spider Queen had kept House Oblodra in her favor, even though the so-called "priestesses" of the house were not pious and sometimes openly expressed their disdain for Lloth. These strange powers of the Oblodrans, this psionic strength, had intrigued Lloth as much as it had frightened the other houses in Menzoberranzan. None of those houses wanted a war against K'yorl and her clan, and Lloth hadn't demanded one. If Menzoberranzan was ever attacked from the outside, particularly from the illithids, whose cavern lair was not so far away, K'yorl and the Oblodrans would be of great help.

But no more. K'yorl had crossed over a very dangerous line. She had murdered a matron mother, and, while that in itself was not uncommon, she had intended to usurp power from Lloth's priestesses, and not in the name of the Spider Queen.

Matron Baenre knew all of this, felt the will and strength of Lloth within her. "The Time of Troubles has passed," she announced to her family, to everyone gathered in her house, in the nearly repaired chapel.

Mez'Barris Armgo was there as well, in a seat of honor on the central dais, at Matron Baenre's personal invitation.

Matron Baenre took the seat next to the matron mother of the second house as the gathered crowd exploded in cheers, and then, led by Triel, in song to the Spider Queen.

Ended? Mez'Barris asked of Baenre, using the silent hand code, for they could not have been heard above the roar of two thousand Baenre soldiers.

The Time of Troubles has ended, Baenre's delicate fingers responded.

Except for House Oblodra, Mez'Barris reasoned, to which Baenre only chuckled wickedly. It was no secret in Menzoberranzan that House Oblodra was in serious trouble. No secret indeed, for the tanar'ri and other fiends continued to circle the Oblodran compound, plucking kobolds from the ledges along the Clawrift, even attacking with abandon any Oblodran who showed herself.

K'yorl will be forgiven? Mez'Barris asked, popping up her left thumb at the end of the code to indicate a question.

Matron Baenre shook her head once briskly, then pointedly looked away, to Triel, who was leading the gathering in rousing prayers to the Spider Queen.

Mez'Barris tapped a long, curving fingernail against her teeth nervously, wondering how Baenre could be so secure in this decision. Did Baenre plan to go after House Oblodra alone, or did she mean to call Barrison del'Armgo into yet another alliance? Mez'Barris did not doubt that her house and House Baenre could crush House Oblodra, but she wasn't thrilled at the prospect of tangling with K'yorl and those unexplored powers.

Methil, invisible and standing off to the side of the dais, read the visiting matron mother's thoughts easily, and then, in turn, imparted them to Matron Baenre.

"It is the will of Lloth," Matron Baenre said sharply, turning back to regard Mez'Barris. "K'yorl has denounced the Spider Queen, and, thus, she will be punished."

"By the Academy, as is the custom?" Mez'Barris asked, and hoped.

A fiery sparkle erupted behind Matron Baenre's red-glowing eyes. "By me," she answered bluntly, and turned away again, indicating that Mez'Barris would garner no further information.

Mez'Barris was wise enough not to press the point. She slumped back in her chair, trying to sort out this surprising, disturbing information. Matron Baenre had not declared that an alliance of houses would attack Oblodra; she had declared a personal war. Did she truly believe she could defeat K'yorl? Or were those fiends, even the great tanar'ri, more fully under her control than Mez'Barris had been led to believe? That notion scared the matron mother of Barrison del'Armgo more than a little, for, if it were true, what other "punishments" might the angry and ambitious Matron Baenre hand out?

Mez'Barris sighed deeply and let the thoughts pass. There was little she could do now, sitting in the chapel of House Baenre, surrounded by two thousand Baenre soldiers. She had to trust in Baenre, she knew.

No, she silently corrected herself, not trust, never that. Mez'Barris had to hope Matron Baenre would think she was more valuable to the cause—whatever it might now be—alive than dead.

* * * * *

Seated atop a blue-glowing driftdisk, Matron Baenre herself led the procession from House Baenre, down from the Qu'ellarz'orl and across the city, her army singing Lloth's praises every step. The Baenre lizard riders, Berg'inyon in command, flanked the main body, sweeping in and around the other house compounds to ensure that no surprises would block the trail.

It was a necessary precaution whenever the first matron mother went out, but Matron Baenre did not fear any ambush, not now. With the exception of Mez'Barris Armgo, no others had been told of the Baenre march, and certainly the lesser houses, either alone or in unison, would not dare to strike at the first house unless the attack had been perfectly coordinated.

From the opposite end of the great cavern came another procession, also led by a Baenre. Triel, Gromph, and the other mistresses and masters of the drow Academy came from their structures, leading their students, every one. Normally it was this very force, the powerful Academy, that exacted punishment on an individual house for crimes against Menzoberranzan, but this time Triel had informed her charges that they would come only to watch, to see the glory of Lloth revealed.

By the time the two groups joined the gathering already in place at the Clawrift, their numbers had swelled five times over. Nobles and soldiers from every house in the city turned out to watch the spectacle as soon as they came to understand that House Baenre and House Oblodra would finish this struggle once and for all.

When they arrived before the front gates of House Oblodra, the Baenre soldiers formed a defensive semicircle behind Matron Baenre, shielding her, not from K'yorl and the Odran family, but from the rest of the gathering. There was much whispering, drow hands flashed frantically in heated conversations, and the fiends, understanding that some calamity was about to come, whipped into a frenzy, swooping across the Oblodran compound, even exercising their returned magic with an occasional bolt of blue-white lightning or a fireball.

Matron Baenre let the display continue for several minutes, realizing the terror it caused within the doomed compound. She wanted to savor this moment above all others, wanted to bask in the smell of terror emanating from the compound of that most hated family.

Then it was time to begin—or to finish, actually. Baenre knew what she must do. She had seen it in a vision during the ceremony preceding the war, and despite the doubts of Mez'Barris when she had shared it with her, Baenre held faith in the Spider Queen, held faith that it was Lloth's will that House Oblodra be devoured.

She reached under her robes and produced a piece of sulphur, the same yellow lump the avatar had given her to allow the priestesses to open the gate to the Abyss in the small room at the back of the Qu'ellarz'orl. Baenre thrust her hand skyward, and up into the air she floated. There came a great crackling explosion, a rumble of thunder.

All was suddenly silent, all eyes turned to the specter of Matron Baenre, hovering twenty feet off the cavern floor.

Berg'inyon, responsible for his mother's security, looked to Sos'Umptu, his expression sour. He thought his mother was terribly vulnerable up there.

Sos'Umptu laughed at him. He was not a priestess; he could not understand that Matron Baenre was more protected at that moment than at any other time in her long life.

"K'yorl Odran!" Baenre called, and her voice seemed magnified, like the voice of a giant.

* * * * *

Locked in a room in the highest level of the tallest stalagmite mound within the Oblodran compound, K'yorl Odran heard Baenre's call, heard it clearly. Her hands gripped tight on her throne's carved marble arms. She squeezed her eyes shut, as she ordered herself to concentrate.

Now, above any other time, K'yorl needed her powers, and now, for the first time, she could not access them! Something was terribly wrong, she knew, and though she believed that Lloth must somehow be behind this, she sensed, as many of the Spider Queen's priestesses had sensed when the Time of Troubles had begun, that this trouble was beyond even Lloth.

The problems had begun soon after K'yorl had been chased back to her house by the loosed tanar'ri. She and her daughters had gathered to formulate an attack plan to drive off the fiends. As always with the efficient Oblodran meetings, the group shared its thoughts telepathically, the equivalent of holding several understandable conversations at once.

The defense plan was coming together well—K'yorl grew confident that the tanar'ri would be sent back to their own plane of existence, and when that was accomplished, she and her family could go and properly punish Matron Baenre and the others. Then something terrible had happened. One of the tanar'ri had thrown forth a blast of lightning, a searing, blinding bolt that sent a crack running along the outer wall of the Oblodran compound. That in itself was not so bad; the compound, like all the houses of Menzoberranzan, could take a tremendous amount of punishment, but what the blast, what the return of magical powers, signified, was disastrous to the Oblodrans.

At that same moment, the telepathic conversation had abruptly ended, and try as they may, the nobles of the doomed house could not begin it anew.

K'yorl was as intelligent as any drow in Menzoberranzan. Her powers of concentration were unparalleled. She felt the psionic strength within her mind, the powers that allowed her to walk

155

through walls or yank the beating heart from an enemy's chest. They were there, deep in her mind, but she could not bring them forth. She continued to blame herself, her lack of concentration in the face of disaster. She even punched herself on the side of the head, as if that physical jarring would knock out some magical manifestation.

Her efforts were futile. As the Time of Troubles had come to its end, as the tapestry of magic in the Realms had rewoven, many rippling side-effects had occurred. Throughout the Realms, dead magic zones had appeared, areas where no spells would function, or, even worse, where no spells would function as intended. Another of those side-effects involved psionic powers, the magiclike powers of the mind. The strength was still there, as K'yorl sensed, but bringing forth that strength required a different mental route than before.

The illithids, as Methil had informed Matron Baenre, had already discerned that route, and their powers were functioning nearly as completely as before. But they were an entire race of psionicists, and a race possessed of communal intelligence. The illithids had already made the necessary adjustments to accessing their psionic powers, but K'yorl Odran and her once powerful family had not.

So the matron of the third house sat in the darkness, eyes squeezed tightly shut, concentrating. She heard Baenre's call, knew that if she did not go to Baenre, Baenre would soon come to her.

Given time, K'yorl would have sorted through the mental puzzle. Given a month, perhaps, she would have begun to bring forth her powers once more.

K'yorl didn't have a month; K'yorl didn't have an hour.

* * * * *

Matron Baenre felt the pulsing magic within the lump of sulphur, an inner heat, fast-building in intensity. She was amazed as her hand shifted, as the sulphur implored her to change the angle.

Baenre nodded. She understood then that some force from beyond the Material Plane, some creature of the Abyss, and perhaps even Lloth herself, was guiding the movement. Up went her hand, putting the pulsing lump in line with the top level of the highest tower in the Oblodran compound.

"Who are you?" she asked.

I am Errtu, came a reply in her mind. Baenre knew the name, knew the creature was a balor, the most terrible and powerful of all tanar'ri. Lloth had armed her well!

She felt the pure malice of the connected creature building within the sulphur, felt the energy growing to where she thought the lump would explode, probably bringing Errtu to her side.

That could not happen, of course, though she did not know it.

It was the power of the artifact itself she felt, that seemingly innocuous piece of sulphur, imbued with the magic of Lloth, wielded by the highest priestess of the Spider Queen in all of Menzoberranzan.

Purely on instinct, Baenre flattened her hand, and the sulphur sent forth a line of glowing, crackling yellow light. It struck the wall high on the Oblodran tower, the very wall between K'yorl and Baenre. Lines of light and energy encircled the stalagmite mound, crackling, biting into the stone, stealing the integrity of the place.

The sulphur went quiet again, its bolt of seemingly live energy freed, but Baenre did not lower her hand and did not take her awe-struck stare from the tower wall.

Neither did the ten thousand dark elves that stood behind her. Neither did K'yorl Odran, who could suddenly see the yellow lines of destruction as they ate their way through the stone.

All in the city gasped as one as the tower's top exploded into dust and was blown away.

There sat K'yorl, still atop her black marble throne, suddenly in the open, staring down at the tremendous gathering.

Many winged tanar'ri swooped about the vulnerable matron mother, but they did not approach too closely, wisely fearing the wrath of Errtu should they steal even a moment of his fun.

K'yorl, always proud and strong, rose from her throne and walked to the edge of the tower. She surveyed the gathering, and so respectful were many drow, even matron mothers, of her strange powers, that they turned away when they felt her scrutinizing gaze on them, as though she, from on high, was deciding who she would punish for this attack.

Finally K'yorl's gaze settled on Matron Baenre, who did not flinch and did not turn away.

"You dare!" K'yorl roared down, but her voice seemed small.

157

R. A. Salvatore

"You dare!" Matron Baenre yelled back, the power of her voice echoing off the walls of the cavern. "You have forsaken the Spider Queen."

"To the Abyss with Lloth, where she rightly belongs!" stubborn K'yorl replied, the last words she ever spoke.

Baenre thrust her hand higher and felt the next manifestation of power, the opening of an interplanar gate. No yellow light came forth, no visible force at all, but K'yorl felt it keenly.

She tried to call out in protest, but could say nothing beyond a whimper and a gurgle as her features suddenly twisted, elongated. She tried to resist, dug her heels in, and concentrated once more on bringing forth her powers.

K'yorl felt her skin being pulled free of her bones, felt her entire form being stretched out of shape, elongated, as the sulphur pulled at her with undeniable strength. Stubbornly she held on through the incredible agony, through the horrible realization of her doom. She opened her mouth, wanting to utter one more damning curse, but all that came out was her tongue, pulled to its length and beyond.

K'yorl felt her entire body stretching down from the tower, reaching for the sulphur and the gate. She should have been already dead; she knew she should have already died under the tremendous pressure.

Matron Baenre held her hand steady, but could not help closing her eyes, as K'yorl's weirdly elongated form suddenly flew from the top of the broken tower, soaring straight for her.

Several drow, Berg'inyon included, screamed, others gasped again, and still others called to the glory of Lloth, as K'yorl, stretched and narrowed so that she resembled a living spear, entered the sulphur, the gate that would take her to the Abyss, to Errtu, Lloth's appointed agent of torture.

Behind K'yorl came the fiends, with a tremendous fanfare, roaring and loosing bolts of lightning against the Oblodran compound, igniting balls of exploding fire and other blinding displays of their power. Compelled by Errtu, they stretched and thinned and flew into the sulphur, and Matron Baenre held on against her terror, transforming it into a sensation of sheer power.

In a few moments, all the fiends, even the greatest tanar'ri, were gone. Matron Baenre felt their presence still, transformed somehow within the sulphur.

158

Suddenly, it was quiet once more. Many dark elves looked to each other, wondering if the punishment was complete, wondering if House Oblodra would be allowed to survive under a new leader. Nobles from several different houses flashed signals to each other expressing their concern that Baenre would now put one of her own daughters in command of the third house, further sealing her ultimate position within the city.

But Baenre had no such thoughts. This was a punishment demanded by Lloth, a complete punishment, as terrible as anything that had ever been exacted on a house in Menzoberranzan. Again heeding the telepathic instructions of Errtu, Matron Baenre hurled the throbbing piece of sulphur into the Clawrift, and when cheers went up about her, the dark elves thinking the ceremony complete, she raised her arms out wide and commanded them all to witness the wrath of Lloth.

They felt the first rumblings within the Clawrift beneath their feet. A few anxious moments passed, too quiet, too hushed.

One of K'yorl's daughters appeared on the open platform atop the broken tower. She ran to the edge, calling, pleading, to Matron Baenre. A moment later, when Baenre gave no response, she happened to glance to the side, to one of the fingerlike chasms of the great Clawrift.

Wide went her eyes, and her scream was as terrified as any drow had ever heard. From the higher vantage point offered by her levitation spell, Matron Baenre followed the gaze and was next to react, throwing her arms high and wide and crying out to her goddess in ecstasy. A moment later, the gathering understood.

A huge black tentacle snaked over the rim of the Clawrift, wriggling its way behind the Oblodran compound. Like a wave, dark elves fell back, stumbling all over each other, as the twenty-foot-thick monstrosity came around the back, along the side, and then along the front wall, back toward the chasm.

"Baenre!" pleaded the desperate, doomed Oblodran.

"You have denied Lloth," the first matron mother replied calmly. "Feel her wrath!"

The ground beneath the cavern trembled slightly as the tentacle, the angry hand of Lloth, tightened its grasp on the Oblodran compound. The wall buckled and collapsed as the thing began its steady sweep.

K'yorl's daughter leaped from the tower as it, too, began to crumble. She cleared the tentacle, and was still alive, though broken, on the ground when a group of dark elves got to her. Uthegental Armgo was among that group, and the mighty weapon master pushed aside the others, preventing them from finishing the pitiful creature off. He hoisted the Odran in his powerful arms, and, through bleary eyes, the battered female regarded him, even managed a faint smile, as though she expected he had come out to save her.

Uthegental laughed at her, lifted her above his head and ran forward, heaving her over the side of the tentacle, back into the rolling rubble that had been her house.

The cheers, the screams, were deafening, and so was the rumble as the tentacle swept all that had been House Oblodra, all the structures and all the drow, into the chasm.

Chapter 15
GREED

he mercenary shook his bald head, as defiant an act as he had ever made against Matron Baenre. At this moment, so soon after the first matron mother's awesome display of power, and given the fact that she was obviously in the Spider Queen's highest favor, Jarlaxle's questioning of her plans seemed even more dangerous.

Triel Baenre sneered at Jarlaxle, and Berg'inyon closed his eyes; neither of them really wanted to see the useful male beaten to death. Wicked Bladen'Kerst, though, licked her lips anxiously and gripped the five-headed tentacle whip tied on her hip, hoping that her mother would allow her the pleasure.

"I fear it is not the time," Jarlaxle said openly, bluntly.

"Lloth instructs me differently," Baenre replied, and she seemed quite cool and calm, given the defiance of a mere male.

"We cannot be certain that our magic will continue to work as we expect," Jarlaxle reasoned.

Baenre nodded, and the others then realized, to their absolute surprise, that their mother was glad the mercenary was taking a negative role. Jarlaxle's questions were pertinent, and he was, in fact, helping Baenre sort through the details of her proposed new alliance and the march to Mithril Hall.

Triel Baenre eyed her mother suspiciously as all of this sank in. If Matron Baenre had received her instructions directly from the Spider Queen, as she had openly stated, then why would she want, or even tolerate, defiance or questioning at all? Why would Matron Baenre need to have these most basic questions concerning the wisdom of the march answered?

"The magic is secure," Baenre replied.

Jarlaxle conceded the point. Everything he had heard, both within and beyond the drow city, seemed to back that claim. "You will have no trouble forming an alliance after the spectacle of House Oblodra's fall. Matron Mez'Barris Armgo has been supportive all along, and no matron mother would dare even hint that she fears to follow your lead."

"The Clawrift is large enough to hold the rubble of many houses," Baenre said dryly.

Jarlaxle snickered. "Indeed," he said. "And indeed this is the time for alliance, for whatever purpose that alliance must be formed."

"It is time to march to Mithril Hall," Baenre interrupted, her tone one of finality, "time to rise up from despair and bring higher glories to the Spider Queen."

"We have suffered many losses," Jarlaxle dared to press. "House Oblodra and their kobold slaves were to lead the attack, dying in the dwarven traps set for drow."

"The kobolds will be brought up from their holes in the Clawrift," Baenre assured him.

Jarlaxle didn't disagree, but he knew the tunnels below the rim of the chasm better than anyone, now that all of House Oblodra was dead. Baenre would get some kobolds, several hundred perhaps, but House Oblodra could have provided many thousand.

"The city's hierarchy is in question," the mercenary went on. "The third house is no more, and the fourth is without its matron mother. Your own family still has not recovered from the renegade's escape and the loss of Dantrag and Vendes."

Baenre suddenly sat forward in her throne. Jarlaxle didn't flinch, but many of the Baenre children did, fearing that their mother understood the truth of the mercenary's last statement, and that Baenre simply would not tolerate any bickering between her surviving children as they sorted out the responsibilities and opportunities left open by the loss of their brother and sister.

Baenre stopped as quickly as she had started, standing before the throne. She let her dangerous gaze linger over each of her gathered children, then dropped it fully over the impertinent mercenary. "Come with me," she commanded.

Jarlaxle stepped aside to let her pass, and obediently and wisely fell into step right behind her. Triel moved to follow, but Baenre spun about, stopping her daughter in her tracks. "Just him," she growled.

A black column centered the throne room, and a crack appeared along its seemingly perfect and unblemished side as Baenre and the mercenary approached. The crack widened as the cunning door slid open, allowing the two to enter the cylindrical chamber within.

Jarlaxle expected Baenre to yell at him, or to talk to him, even threaten him, once the door closed again, separating them from her family. But the matron mother said nothing, just calmly walked over to a hole in the floor. She stepped into the hole, but did not fall, rather floated down to the next lower level, the great Baenre mound's third level, on currents of magical energy. Jarlaxle followed as soon as the way was clear, but still, when he got to the third level, he had to hurry to keep up with the hustling matron mother, gliding through the floor once more, and then again, and again, until she came to the dungeons beneath the great mound.

Still she offered not a word of explanation, and Jarlaxle began to wonder if he was to be imprisoned down here. Many drow, even drow nobles, had found that grim fate; it was rumored that several had been kept as Baenre prisoners for more than a century, endlessly tortured, then healed by the priestesses, that they might be tortured again.

A wave of Baenre's hand sent the two guards standing beside one cell door scrambling for cover.

Jarlaxle was as relieved as curious when he walked into the cell behind Baenre to find a curious, barrel-chested dwarf chained to the far wall. The mercenary looked back to Baenre, and only then did he realize she was not wearing one of her customary necklaces, the one fashioned of a dwarf's tooth.

"A recent catch?" Jarlaxle asked, though he suspected differently.

"Two thousand years," Baenre replied. "I give to you Gandalug Battlehammer, patron of Clan Battlehammer, founder of Mithril Hall."

Jarlaxle rocked back on his heels. He had heard the rumors, of course, that Baenre's tooth pendant contained the soul of an ancient dwarf king, but never had he suspected such a connection. He realized then, suddenly, that this entire foray to Mithril Hall was not about Drizzt Do'Urden, that the renegade was merely a connection, an excuse, for something Baenre had desired for a very long time.

Jarlaxle looked at Baenre suddenly, curiously. "Two thousand years?" he echoed aloud, while he silently wondered just how old this withered drow really was.

"I have kept his soul through the centuries," Baenre went on, eyeing the old dwarf directly. "During the time Lloth could not hear our call, the item was destroyed and Gandalug came forth, alive again." She walked over, put her snarling visage right up to the battered, naked dwarf's long, pointed nose, and put one hand on his round, solid shoulder. "Alive, but no more free than he was before."

Gandalug cleared his throat as if he meant to spit on Baenre. He stopped, though, when he realized that a spider had crawled out of the ring on her hand, onto his shoulder, and was now making its way along his neck.

Gandalug understood that Baenre would not kill him, that she needed him for her proposed conquest. He did not fear death, but would have preferred it to this torment and weighed against the realization that he might unwittingly aid in the fall of his own people. Baenre's gruesome mind flayer had already scoured Gandalug's thoughts more than once, taking information that no beatings could ever have extracted from the stubborn old dwarf.

Rationally, Gandalug had nothing to fear, but that did little to comfort him now. Gandalug hated spiders above all else, hated and feared them. As soon as he felt the hairy, crawly thing on his neck, he froze, eyes unblinking, sweat beading on his forehead.

Baenre walked away, leaving her pet spider on the dwarf's neck. She turned to Jarlaxle again, a supreme look on her face, as though Gandalug's presence should make all the difference in the world to the doubting mercenary.

It didn't. Jarlaxle never once doubted that Menzoberranzan could defeat Mithril Hall, never once doubted that the conquest would be successful. But what of the aftermath of that conquest? The drow city was in turmoil; there would soon be a fierce struggle, perhaps even an open war, to fill the vacancy left by both House Oblodra's demise and the death of Ghenni'tiroth Tlabbar. Living for centuries on the edge of disaster with his secretive band, the mercenary understood the perils of overextending his grab for power, understood that if one stretched his forces too far, they could simply collapse.

But Jarlaxle knew, too, that he would not convince Matron Baenre. So be it, he decided. Let Baenre march to Mithril Hall with no further questions from him. He would even encourage her. If things went as she planned, then all would be the better for it.

If not . . .

Jarlaxle didn't bother to entertain those possibilities. He knew where Gromph stood, knew the wizard's frustration and the frustrations of Bregan D'aerthe, a band almost exclusively male. Let Baenre go to Mithril Hall, and if she failed, then Jarlaxle would take Baenre's own advice and "rise up from despair."

Indeed.

Chapter 16

OPEN HEARTS

rizzt found her on the same east-facing plateau where she had practiced all those weeks, the very spot where she had at last gained control of her strong-willed sword. Long shadows rolled out from the mountains, the sun low in the sky behind them. The first stars shone clearly, twinkling above Silverymoon, and Sundabar to the east beyond that.

Catti-brie sat unmoving, legs bent and knees pulled in tightly to her chest. If she heard the approach of the almost silent drow, she gave no indication, just rocked gently back and forth, staring into the deepening gloom.

"The night is beautiful," Drizzt said, and when Catti-brie did not jump at the sound of his voice, he realized she had recognized his approach. "But the wind is chill."

"The winter's coming in full," Catti-brie replied softly, not taking her gaze from the darkened eastern sky.

Drizzt sought a reply, wanted to keep talking. He felt awkward here, strangely so, for never in the years he had known Catti-brie had there been such tension between them. The drow walked over

166

and crouched beside Catti-brie, but did not look at her, as she did not look at him.

"I'll call Guenhwyvar this night," Drizzt remarked.

Catti-brie nodded.

Her continued silence caught the drow off guard. His calling of the panther, for the first time since the figurine was repaired, was no small thing. Would the figurine's magic work properly, enabling Guenhwyvar to return to his side? Fret had assured him it would, but Drizzt could not be certain, could not rest easily, until the task was completed and the panther, the healed panther, was back beside him.

It should have been important to Catti-brie as well. She should have cared as much as Drizzt cared, for she and Guenhwyvar were as close as any. Yet she didn't reply, and her silence made Drizzt, anger budding within him, turn to regard her more closely.

He saw tears rimming her blue eyes, tears that washed away Drizzt's anger, that told him that what had happened between himself and Catti-brie had apparently not been so deeply buried. The last time they had met, on this very spot, they had hidden the questions they both wanted to ask behind the energy of a sparring match. Catti-brie's concentration had to be complete on that occasion, and in the days before it, as she fought to master her sword, but now that task was completed. Now, like Drizzt, she had time to think, and in that time, Catti-brie had remembered.

"Ye're knowin' it was the sword?" she asked, almost pleaded.

Drizzt smiled, trying to comfort her. Of course it had been the sentient sword that had inspired her to throw herself at him. Fully the sword, only the sword. But a large part of Drizzt—and possibly of Catti-brie, he thought in looking at her—wished differently. There had been an undeniable tension between them for some time, a complicated situation, and even more so now, after the possession incident with Khazid'hea.

"Ye did right in pushing me away," Catti-brie said, and she snorted and cleared her throat, hiding a sniffle.

Drizzt paused for a long moment, realizing the potential weight of his reply. "I pushed you away only because I saw the pommel," he said, and that drew Catti-brie's attention from the eastern sky, made her look at the drow directly, her deep blue eyes locking with his violet orbs.

R. A. Salvatore

"It was the sword," Drizzt said quietly, "only the sword."

Catti-brie didn't blink, barely drew breath. She was thinking how noble this drow had been. So many other men would not have asked questions, would have taken advantage of the situation. And would that have been such a bad thing? the young woman had to ask herself now. Her feelings for Drizzt were deep and real, a bond of friendship and love. Would it have been such a bad thing if he had made love to her in that room?

Yes, she decided, for both of them, because, while it was her body that had been offered, it was Khazid'hea that was in control. Things were awkward enough between them now, but if Drizzt had relented to the feelings that Catti-brie knew he held for her, if he had not been so noble in that strange situation and had given in to the offered temptation, likely neither of them would have been able to look the other in the eye afterward.

Like they were doing now, on a quiet plateau high in the mountains, with a chill and crisp breeze and the stars glowing ever more brightly above them.

"Ye're a good man, Drizzt Do'Urden," the grateful woman said with a heartfelt smile.

"Hardly a man," Drizzt replied, chuckling, and glad for the relief of tension.

Only a temporary relief, though. The chuckle and the smile died away almost immediately, leaving them in the same place, the same awkward moment, caught somewhere between romance and fear.

Catti-brie looked back to the sky; Drizzt did likewise.

"Ye know I loved him," the young woman said.

"You still do," Drizzt answered, and his smile was genuine when Catti-brie turned back again to regard him.

She turned away almost at once, looked back to the bright stars and thought of Wulfgar.

"You would have married him," Drizzt went on.

Catti-brie wasn't so sure of that. For all the true love she held for Wulfgar, the barbarian carried around the weight of his heritage and a society that valued women not as partners, but as servants. Wulfgar had climbed above many of the narrow-thinking ways of his tribal people, but as his wedding to Catti-brie approached, he had become more protective of her, to the point of being insulting. That, above anything else, proud and capable Catti-brie could not tolerate.

Her doubts were clear on her face, and Drizzt, who knew her better than anyone, read them easily.

"You would have married him," he said again, his firm tone forcing Catti-brie to look back to him.

"Wulfgar was no fool," Drizzt went on.

"Don't ye be blamin' it all on Entreri and the halfling's gem," Catti-brie warned. After the threat of the drow hunting party had been turned away, after Wulfgar's demise, Drizzt had explained to her, and to Bruenor, who perhaps more than anyone else needed to hear the justification, that Entreri, posing as Regis, had used the hypnotic powers of the ruby pendant on Wulfgar. Yet that theory could not fully explain the barbarian's outrageous behavior, because Wulfgar had started down that path long before Entreri had even arrived at Mithril Hall.

"Surely the gem pushed Wulfgar further," Drizzt countered.

"Pushed him where he wanted to go."

"No." The simple reply, spoken with absolute surety, almost caught Catti-brie off guard. She cocked her head to the side, her thick auburn hair cascading over one shoulder, waiting for the drow to elaborate.

"He was scared," Drizzt went on. "Nothing in the world frightened mighty Wulfgar more than the thought of losing his Catti-brie."

"*His* Catti-brie?" she echoed.

Drizzt laughed at her oversensitivity. "His Catti-brie, as he was your Wulfgar," he said, and Catti-brie's smirk fell away as fully as her trap of words.

"He loved you," Drizzt went on, "with all his heart." He paused, but Catti-brie had nothing to say, just sat very still, very quiet, hearing his every word. "He loved you, and that love made him feel vulnerable, and frightened him. Nothing anyone could do to Wulfgar, not torture, not battle, not even death, frightened him, but the slightest scratch on Catti-brie would burn like a hot dagger in his heart.

"So he acted the part of the fool for a short while before you were to be wed," Drizzt said. "The very next time you saw battle, your own strength and independence would have held a mirror up to Wulfgar, would have shown him his error. Unlike so many of his proud people, unlike Berkthgar, Wulfgar admitted his mistakes and

169

never made them again."

As she listened to the words of her wise friend, Catti-brie remembered exactly that incident, the battle in which Wulfgar had been killed. Those very fears for Catti-brie had played a large part in the barbarian's death, but before he was taken from her, he had looked into her eyes and had indeed realized what his foolishness had cost him, had cost them both.

Catti-brie had to believe that now, recalling the scene in light of the drow's words. She had to believe that her love for Wulfgar had been real, very real, and not misplaced, that he was all she had thought him to be.

Now she could. For the first time since Wulfgar's death, Catti-brie could remember him without the pangs of guilt, without the fears that, had he lived, she would not have married him. Because Drizzt was right; Wulfgar would have admitted the error despite his pride, and he would have grown, as he always had before. That was the finest quality of the man, an almost childlike quality, that viewed the world and his own life as getting better, as moving toward a better way in a better place.

What followed was the most sincere smile on Catti-brie's face in many, many months. She felt suddenly free, suddenly complete with her past, reconciled and able to move forward with her life.

She looked at the drow, wide-eyed, with a curiosity that seemed to surprise Drizzt. She could go on, but exactly what did that mean?

Slowly, Catti-brie began shaking her head, and Drizzt came to understand that the movement had something to do with him. He lifted a slender hand and brushed some stray hair back from her cheek, his ebony skin contrasting starkly with her light skin, even in the quiet light of night.

"I do love you," the drow admitted. The blunt statement did not catch Catti-brie by surprise, not at all. "As you love me," Drizzt went on, easily, confident that his words were on the mark. "And I, too, must look ahead now, must find my place among my friends, beside you, without Wulfgar."

"Perhaps in the future," Catti-brie said, her voice barely a whisper.

"Perhaps," Drizzt agreed. "But for now . . ."

"Friends," Catti-brie finished.

Drizzt moved his hand back from her cheek, held it in the air before her face, and she reached up and clasped it firmly.

Friends.

The moment lingered, the two staring, not talking, and it would have gone on much, much longer, except that there came a commotion from the trail behind them, and the sound of voices they both recognized.

"Stupid elf couldn't do this inside!" blustered Bruenor.

"The stars are more fitting for Guenhwyvar," huffed Regis breathlessly. Together they crashed through a bush not far behind the plateau and stumbled and skidded down to join their two friends.

"Stupid elf?" Catti-brie asked her father.

"Bah!" Bruenor snorted. "I'm not for saying . . ."

"Well, actually," Regis began to correct, but changed his mind when Bruenor turned his scarred visage the halfling's way and growled at him.

"So ye're right and I said stupid elf!" Bruenor admitted, speaking mostly to Drizzt, as close to an apology as he ever gave. "But I've got me work to do." He looked back up the trail, in the direction of Mithril Hall's eastern door. "Inside!" he finished.

Drizzt took out the onyx figurine and placed it on the ground, purposely right before the dwarf's heavy boots. "When Guenhwyvar is returned to us, I will explain how inconvenienced you were to come and witness her return," Drizzt said with a smirk.

"Stupid elf," Bruenor muttered under his breath, and he fully expected that Drizzt would have the cat sleep on him again, or something worse.

Catti-brie and Regis laughed, but their mirth was strained and nervous, as Drizzt called quietly for the panther. The pain they would have to bear if the magic of the figurine had not healed, if Guenhwyvar did not return to them, would be no less to the companions than the pain of losing Wulfgar.

They all knew it, even surly, blustery Bruenor, who to his grave would deny his affection for the magical panther. Silence grew around the figurine as the gray smoke came forth, swirled, and solidified.

Guenhwyvar seemed almost confused as she regarded the four companions standing about her, none of them daring to breathe.

Drizzt's grin was the first and the widest, as he saw that his trusted companion was whole again and healed, the black fur

171

glistening in the starlight, the sleek muscles taut and strong.

He had brought Bruenor and Regis out to witness this moment. It was fitting that all four of them stood by when Guenhwyvar returned.

More fitting would it have been had the sixth companion, Wulfgar, son of Beornegar, joined them on that plateau, in the quiet night, under the stars, in the last hours of Mithril Hall's peace.

Part 4

THE DROW MARCH

noticed something truly amazing, and truly heartwarming, as we, all the defenders of Mithril Hall and the immediate region, neared the end of preparations, neared the time when the drow would come.

I am drow. My skin proves that I am different. The ebony hue shows my heritage clearly and undeniably. And yet, not a glare was aimed my way, not a look of consternation from the Harpells and the Longriders, not an angry word from volatile Berkthgar and his warrior people. And no dwarf, not even General Dagna, who did not like anyone who was not a dwarf, pointed an accusing finger at me.

We did not know why the drow had come, be it for me or for the promise of treasure from the rich dwarven complex. Whatever the cause, to the defenders, I was without blame. How wonderful that felt to me, who had worn the burden of self-imposed guilt for many months, guilt for the previous raid, guilt for Wulfgar, guilt that Catti-brie had been forced by friendship to chase me all the way to Menzoberranzan.

I had worn this heavy collar, and yet those around me who had as much to lose as I placed no burden on me.

You cannot understand how special that realization was to one of my past. It was a gesture of sincere friendship, and what made it all the more important is that it was an unintentional gesture, offered without thought or purpose. Too often in the past, my "friends" would make such gestures as if to prove something, more to themselves than to me. They could feel better about themselves because they could look beyond the obvious differences, such as the color of my skin.

Guenhwyvar never did that. Bruenor never did that. Neither did Catti-brie or Regis. Wulfgar at first despised me, openly and without excuse, simply because I was drow. They were honest, and thus, they were always my friends. But in the days of preparation for war, I saw that sphere

174

of friendship expand many times over. I came to know that the dwarves of Mithril Hall, the men and women of Settlestone, and many, many more, truly accepted me.

That is the honest nature of friendship. That is when it becomes sincere, and not self-serving. So in those days, Drizzt Do'Urden came to understand, once and for all, that he was not of Menzoberranzan.

I threw off the collar of guilt. I smiled.

— Drizzt Do'Urden

Chapter 17
BLINGDENSTONE

hey were shadows among the shadows, flickering movements that disappeared before the eye could take them in. And there was no sound. Though three hundred dark elves moved in formation, right flank, left flank, center, there was no sound.

They had come to the west of Menzoberranzan, seeking the easier and wider tunnels that would swing them back toward the east and all the way to the surface, to Mithril Hall. Blingdenstone, the city of svirfnebli, whom the drow hated above all others, was not so far away, another benefit of this roundabout course.

Uthegental Armgo paused in one small, sheltered cubby. The tunnels were wide here, uncomfortably so. Svirfnebli were tacticians and builders; in a fight they would depend on formations, perhaps even on war machines, to compete with the more stealthy and individual-minded drow. The widening of these particular tunnels was no accident, Uthegental knew, and no result of nature. This battlefield had long ago been prepared by his enemies.

So where were they? Uthegental had come into their domain

with three hundred drow, his group leading an army of eight thousand dark elves and thousands of humanoid slaves. And yet, though Blingdenstone itself could not be more than a twenty minute march from his position—and his scouts were even closer than that—there had been no sign of svirfnebli.

The wild patron of Barrison del'Armgo was not happy. Uthegental liked things predictable, at least as far as enemies were concerned, and had hoped that he and his warriors would have seen some action against the gnomes by now. It was no accident that his group, that he, was at the forefront of the drow army. That had been a concession by Baenre to Mez'Barris, an affirmation of the importance of the second house. But with that concession came responsibility, which Matron Mez'Barris had promptly dropped on Uthegental's sturdy shoulders. House Barrison del'Armgo needed to come out of this war with high glory, particularly in light of Matron Baenre's incredible display in the destruction of House Oblodra. When this business with Mithril Hall was settled, the rearrangement of the pecking order in Menzoberranzan would likely begin. Interhouse wars seemed unavoidable, with the biggest holes to be filled those ranks directly behind Barrison del'Armgo.

Thus had Matron Mez'Barris promised full fealty to Baenre, in exchange for being personally excused from the expedition. She remained in Menzoberranzan, solidifying her house's position and working closely with Triel Baenre in forming a web of lies and allies to insulate House Baenre from further accusations. Baenre had agreed with Mez'Barris's offer, knowing that she, too, would be vulnerable if all did not go well in Mithril Hall.

With the matron mother of his house back in Menzoberranzan, the glory of House Barrison del'Armgo was Uthegental's to find. The fierce warrior was glad for the task, but he was edgy as well, filled with nervous energy, wanting a battle, any battle, that he might whet his appetite for what was to come, and might wet the end of his wicked trident with the blood of an enemy.

But where were the ugly little svirfnebli? he wondered. The marching plan called for no attack on Blingdenstone proper—not on the initial journey, at least. If there was to be an assault on the gnome city, it would come on the return from Mithril Hall, after the main objective had been realized. Uthegental had been given permission to test svirfneblin defenses, though, and to skirmish with any gnomes he and his warriors found out in the open tunnels.

Uthegental craved that, and had already determined that if he found and tested the gnome defenses and discovered sufficient holes in them, he would take the extra step, hoping to return to Baenre's side with the head of the svirfneblin king on the end of his trident.

All glory for Barrison del'Armgo.

One of the scouts slipped back past the guards, moved right up to the fierce warrior. Her fingers flashed in the silent drow code, explaining to her leader that she had gone closer, much closer, had even seen the stairway that led up to the level of Blingdenstone's massive front gates. But no sign had she seen of the svirfnebli.

It had to be an ambush; every instinct within the seasoned weapon master told Uthegental that the svirfnebli were lying in wait, in full force. Almost any other dark elf, a race known for caution when dealing with others (mostly because the drow knew they could always win such encounters if they struck at the appropriate time), would have relented. In truth, Uthegental's mission, a scouting expedition, was now complete, and he could return to Matron Baenre with a full report that she would be pleased to hear.

But fierce Uthegental was not like other drow. He was less than relieved, was, in fact boiling with rage.

Take me there, his fingers flashed, to the surprise of the female scout.

You are too valuable, the female's hands replied.

"All of us!" Uthegental roared aloud, his volume surprising every one of the many dark elves about him. But Uthegental wasn't startled, and did not relent. "Send the word along every column," he went on, "to follow my lead to the very gates of Blingdenstone!"

More than a few drow soldiers turned nervous looks to each other. They numbered three hundred, a formidable force, but Blingdenstone held many times that number, and svirfnebli, full of tricks with the stone and often allied with powerful monsters from the Plane of Earth, were not easy foes. Still, not one of the dark elves would argue with Uthegental Armgo, especially since he alone knew what Matron Baenre expected of this point group.

And so they arrived in full, at the stairway and up it they climbed, to the very gates of Blingdenstone—gates that a drow engineer found devilishly trapped, with the entire ceiling above them rigged to fall if they were opened. Uthegental called to a priestess that had been assigned to his group.

You can get one of us past the barrier? his fingers asked her, to which she nodded.

Uthegental's stream of surprises continued when he indicated he would personally enter the svirfneblin city. It was an unheard-of request. No drow leader ever went in first; that's what commoners were for.

But again, who would argue with Uthegental? In truth, the priestess really didn't care if this arrogant male got torn apart. She began her casting at once, a spell that would make Uthegental as insubstantial as a wraith, would make his form melt away into something that could slip through the slightest cracks. When it was done, the brave Uthegental left without hesitation, without bothering to leave instructions in the event that he did not return.

Proud and supremely confident, Uthegental simply did not think that way.

A few minutes later, after passing through the empty guard chambers, crisscrossed with cunningly built trenches and fortifications, Uthegental became only the second drow, after Drizzt Do'Urden, to glance at the rounded, natural houses of the svirfnebli and the winding, unremarkable ways that composed their city. How different Blingdenstone was from Menzoberranzan, built in accord with what the gnomes had found in the natural caverns, rather than sculpted and reformed into an image that a dark elf would consider more pleasing.

Uthegental, who demanded control of everything about him, found the place repulsive. He also found it, this most ancient and hallowed of svirfneblin cities, deserted.

* * * * *

Belwar Dissengulp stared out from the lip of the deep chamber, far to the west of Blingdenstone, and wondered if he had done right in convincing King Schnicktick to abandon the gnomish city. The most honored burrow warden had reasoned that, with magic returned, the drow would surely march for Mithril Hall, and that course, Belwar knew, would take them dangerously close to Blingdenstone.

Though he had little difficulty in convincing his fellows that the dark elves would march, the thought of leaving Blingdenstone, of simply packing up their belongings and deserting their ancient home, had not settled well. For more than two thousand years the gnomes had lived in the ominous shadow of Menzoberranzan, and more than once had they believed the drow would come in full war against them.

This time was different, Belwar reasoned, and he had told them so, his speech full of passion and carrying the weight of his relationship with the renegade drow from that terrible city. Still, Belwar was far from convincing Schnicktick and the others until Councilor Firble piped in on the burrow warden's side.

It was indeed different this time, Firble had told them with all sincerity. This time, the whole of Menzoberranzan would band together, and any attack would not be the ambitious probing of a single house. This time the gnomes, and anyone else unfortunate enough to fall in the path of the drow march, could not depend on interhouse rivalries to save them. Firble had learned of House Oblodra's fall from Jarlaxle; an earth elemental sent secretly under Menzoberranzan and into the Clawrift by svirfneblin priests confirmed it and the utter destruction of the third house. Thus, when, at their last meeting, Jarlaxle hinted "it would not be wise to harbor Drizzt Do'Urden," Firble, with his understanding of drow ways, reasoned that the dark elves would indeed march for Mithril Hall, in a force unified by the fear of the one who had so utterly crushed the third house.

And so, on that ominous note, the svirfnebli had left Blingdenstone, and Belwar had played a critical role in the departure. That responsibility weighed heavily on the burrow warden now, made him second-guess the reasoning that had seemed so sound when he had thought danger imminent. Here to the west the tunnels were quiet, and not eerily so, as though enemy dark elves were slipping from shadow to shadow. The tunnels were quiet with peace; the war Belwar had anticipated seemed a thousand miles or a thousand years away.

The other gnomes felt it, too, and Belwar had overheard more than one complaining that the decision to leave Blingdenstone had been, at best, foolish.

Only when the last of the svirfnebli had left the city, when the long caravan had begun its march to the west, had Belwar realized the gravity of the departure, realized the emotional burden. In leaving, the gnomes were admitting to themselves that they were no match for the drow, that they could not protect themselves or their homes from the dark elves. More than a few svirfnebli, Belwar perhaps most among them, were sick about that fact. Their illusions of security, of the strength of their shamans, of their very god figure, had been shaken, without a single drop of spilled svirfneblin blood.

Belwar felt like a coward.

The most honored burrow warden took some comfort in the fact that eyes were still in place in Blingdenstone. A friendly elemental, blended with the stone, had been ordered to wait and watch, and to report back to the svirfneblin shamans who had summoned it. If the dark elves did come in, as Belwar expected, the gnomes would know of it.

But what if they didn't come? Belwar wondered. If he and Firble were wrong and the march did not come, then what loss had the svirfnebli suffered for the sake of caution?

Could any of them ever feel secure in Blingdenstone again?

*　*　*　*　*

Matron Baenre was not pleased at Uthegental's report that the gnomish city was deserted. As sour as her expression was, though, it could not match the open wrath showing on the face of Berg'inyon, at her side. His eyes narrowed dangerously as he considered the powerful patron of the second house, and Uthegental, seeing a challenge, more than matched that ominous stare.

Baenre understood the source of Berg'inyon's anger, and she, too, was not pleased by the fact that Uthegental had taken it upon himself to enter Blingdenstone. That act reflected clearly the desperation of Mez'Barris. Obviously Mez'Barris felt vulnerable in the shadows of Matron Baenre's display against Oblodra, and thus she had placed a great weight upon Uthegental's broad

181

R. A. Salvatore

shoulders.

Uthegental marched for the glory of Barrison del'Armgo, Matron Baenre knew, marched fanatically, along with his force of more than three hundred drow warriors.

To Berg'inyon, that was not a good thing, for he, and not Matron Baenre, was in direct competition with the powerful weapon master.

Matron Baenre considered all the news in light of her son's expression, and, in the end, she thought Uthegental's daring a good thing. The competition would push Berg'inyon to excellence. And if he failed, if Uthegental was the one who killed Drizzt Do'Urden (for that was obviously the prize both sought), even if Berg'inyon was killed by Uthegental, then so be it. This march was greater than House Baenre, greater than anyone's personal goals—except, of course, for Matron Baenre's own.

When Mithril Hall was conquered, whatever the cost to her son, she would be in the highest glory of the Spider Queen, and her house would be above the schemes of the others, if all the others combined their forces against her!

"You are dismissed," Baenre said to Uthegental. "Back to the forefront."

The spike-haired weapon master smiled wickedly and bowed, never taking his eyes from Berg'inyon. Then he spun on his heel to leave, but spun again immediately as Baenre addressed him once more.

"And if you chance to come upon the tracks of the fleeing svirfnebli," Baenre said, and she paused, looking from Uthegental to Berg'inyon, "do send an emissary to inform me of the chase."

Berg'inyon's shoulders slumped even as Uthegental's grin, showing those filed, pointy teeth, widened so much that it nearly took in his ears. He bowed again and ran off.

"The svirfnebli are mighty foes," Baenre said offhandedly, aiming the remark at Berg'inyon. "They will kill him and all of his party." She didn't really believe the claim, had made it only for Berg'inyon's sake. In looking at her wise son, though, she realized he didn't believe it either.

"And if not," Baenre said, looking the other way, to Quenthel, who stood by impassively, appearing quite bored, and to Methil, who always seemed quite bored, "the gnomes are not so great a prize." The matron mother's gaze snapped back over Berg'inyon. "We know the prize of this march," she said, her voice a feral snarl. She didn't bother to mention that her ultimate goal and Berg'inyon's goal were not the same.

The effect on the young weapon master was instantaneous. He snapped back to rigid attention, and rode off on his lizard as soon as his mother waved her hand to dismiss him.

Baenre turned to Quenthel. *See that spies are put among Uthegental's soldiers*, her fingers subtly flashed. Baenre paused a moment to consider the fierce weapon master, and to reflect on what he would do if such spies were discovered. *Males*, Baenre added to her daughter, and Quenthel agreed.

Males were expendable.

Sitting alone as her driftdisk floated amidst the army, Matron Baenre turned her thoughts to more important issues. The rivalry of Berg'inyon and Uthegental was of little consequence, as was Uthegental's apparent disregard for proper command. More disturbing was the svirfneblin absence. Might the wicked gnomes be planning an assault on Menzoberranzan even as Baenre and her force marched away?

It was a silly thought, one Matron Baenre quickly dismissed. More than half the dark elves remained in Menzoberranzan, under the watchful eyes of Mez'Barris Armgo, Triel, and Gromph. If the gnomes attacked, they would be utterly destroyed, more to the Spider Queen's glory.

But even as she considered those city defenses, the thought of a conspiracy against her nagged at the edges of Baenre's consciousness.

Triel is loyal and in control, came a telepathic assurance from Methil, who remained not so far away and was reading Baenre's every thought.

Baenre took some comfort in that. Before she had left Menzoberranzan, she had bade Methil to scour her daughter's reactions to her plans, and the illithid had come back with a completely positive report. Triel was not pleased by the decision to go to Mithril Hall. She feared her mother might be overstepping her bounds, but she was convinced, as most likely were all the others, that, in the face of the destruction of House Oblodra, Lloth had sanctioned this war. Thus, Triel would not head a coup for control of House Baenre in her mother's absence, would not, in any way, go against her mother at this time.

Baenre relaxed. All was going according to design; it was not important that the cowardly gnomes had fled.

All was going even better than design, Baenre decided, for the rivalry between Uthegental and Berg'inyon would provide much entertainment. The possibilities were intriguing. Perhaps if Uthegental killed Drizzt, and killed Berg'inyon in the process, Matron Baenre would force the spike-haired savage into House Baenre to serve as her own weapon master. Mez'Barris would not dare protest, not after Mithril Hall was conquered.

Chapter 18
UNEASY GATHERINGS

ven now is Regweld, who shall lead us, meeting with Bruenor, who is king," said a rider, a knight wearing the most unusual of armor. There wasn't a smooth spot on the mail; it was ridged and buckled, with grillwork pointing out at various angles, its purpose to turn aside any blows, to deflect rather than absorb.

The man's fifty comrades—a strange-looking group indeed—were similarly outfitted, which could be readily explained by looking at their unusual pennant. It depicted a stick-man, his hair straight up on end and arms held high, standing atop a house and throwing lightning bolts to the sky (or perhaps he was catching lightning hurled down at him from the clouds—one could not be sure). This was the banner of Longsaddle and these were the Longriders, the soldiers of Longsaddle, a capable, if eccentric, group. They had come into Settlestone this cold and gloomy day, chasing the first flakes of the first snow.

"Regweld shall lead *you*," answered another rider, tall and sure on his saddle, carrying the scars of countless battles. He was more conventionally armored, as were his forty companions, riding

185

under the horse-and-spear banner of Nesme, the proud frontier town on the edge of the dreaded Trollmoors. "But not *us*. We are the Riders of Nesme, who follow no lead but our own!"

"Just because you got here first doesn't mean you pick the rules!" whined the Longrider.

"Let us not forget our purpose," intervened a third rider, his horse trotting up, along with two companions, to greet the newest arrivals. When he came closer, the others saw from his angular features, shining golden hair, and similarly colored eyes that he was no man at all, but an elf, though tall for one of his race. "I am Besnell of Silverymoon, come with a hundred soldiers from Lady Alustriel. We shall each find our place when battle is joined, though if there is to be any leader among us, it shall be me, who speaks on behalf of Alustriel."

The man from Nesme and the man from Longsaddle regarded each other helplessly. Their respective towns, particularly Nesme, were surely under the shadow of Silverymoon, and their respective rulers would not challenge Alustriel's authority.

"But you are not in Silverymoon," came a roaring reply from Berkthgar, who had been standing in the shadows of a nearby doorway, listening to the argument, almost hoping it would erupt into something more fun than bandied words. "You are in Settlestone, where Berkthgar rules, and in Settlestone, you are ruled by Berkthgar!"

Everyone tensed, particularly the two Silverymoon soldiers flanking Besnell. The elven warrior sat quietly for a moment, eyeing the huge barbarian as Berkthgar, his gigantic sword strapped across his back, steadily and calmly approached. Besnell was not overly proud, and his rank alone in the Silverymoon detachment proved that he never let pride cloud good judgment.

"Well spoken, Berkthgar the Bold," he politely replied. "And true enough." He turned to the other two mounted leaders. "We have come from Silverymoon, and you from Nesme, and you from Longsaddle, to serve in Berkthgar's cause, and in the cause of Bruenor Battlehammer."

"We came to Bruenor's call," grumbled the Longrider, "not Berkthgar's."

"Would you then take your horse into the dark tunnels beneath Mithril Hall?" reasoned Besnell, who understood from his meetings with Berkthgar and Catti-brie that the dwarves would handle the underground troubles, while the riders would join with the warriors of Settlestone to secure the outlying areas.

"His horse and he might be underground sooner than he expects," Berkthgar piped in, an open threat that shook the Longrider more than a little.

"Enough of this," Besnell was quick to interject. "We have all come together as allies, and allies we shall be, joined in a common cause."

"Joined by fear," the Nesme soldier replied. "We in Nesme once met Bruenor's . . ." He paused, looking to the faces of the other leaders, then to his own grim men for support, as he searched for the proper words. "We have met King Bruenor's dark-skinned friend," he said finally, his tone openly derisive. "What good might come from association with evil drow?"

The words had barely left his mouth before Berkthgar was upon him, reaching up to grab him by a crease in his armor and pull him low in the saddle, that he might look right into the barbarian's snarling visage. The nearby Nesme soldiers had their weapons out and ready, but so, too, did Berkthgar's people, coming out of every stone house and around every corner.

Besnell groaned and the Longriders, every one, shook their heads in dismay.

"If ever again you speak ill of Drizzt Do'Urden," Berkthgar growled, caring nothing of the swords and spears poised not so far away, "you will offer me an interesting choice. Do I cut you in half and leave you dead on the field, or do I bring you in to Drizzt, that he might find the honor of severing your head himself?"

Besnell walked his horse right up to the barbarian and used its heavy press to force Berkthgar back from the stunned Nesme soldier.

"Drizzt Do'Urden would not kill the man for his words," Besnell said with all confidence, for he had met Drizzt on many occasions during the dark elf's frequent visits to Silverymoon.

Berkthgar knew the elf spoke truly, and so the barbarian leader relented, backing off a few steps.

"Bruenor would kill him," Berkthgar did say, though.

"Agreed," said Besnell. "And many others would take up arms in the dark elf's defense. But, as I have said, enough of this. All joined, we are a hundred and ninety calvary, come to aid in the cause." He looked all around as he spoke and seemed taller and more imposing than his elven frame would normally allow. "A hundred and ninety come to join with Berkthgar and his proud warriors. Rarely have four such groups converged as allies. The Longriders, the Riders of Nesme, the Knights in Silver, and the warriors of Settlestone, all joined in common cause. If the war does come—and looking at the allies I have discovered this day, I hope it does—our deeds shall be echoed throughout the Realms! And let the drow army beware!"

He had played perfectly on the pride of all of them, and so they took up the cheer together, and the moments of tension were passed. Besnell smiled and nodded as the shouts continued, but he understood that things were not as solid and friendly as they should be. Longsaddle had sent fifty soldiers, plus a handful of wizards, a very great sacrifice from the town that, in truth, had little stake in Bruenor's well-being. The Harpells looked more to the west, to Waterdeep, for trade and alliance, than to the east, and yet they had come to Bruenor's call, including their leader's own daughter.

Silverymoon was equally committed, both by friendship to Bruenor and Drizzt and because Alustriel was wise enough to understand that if the drow army did march to the surface, all the world would be a sadder place. Alustriel had dispatched a hundred knights to Berkthgar, and another hundred rode independently, skirting the eastern foothills below Mithril Hall, covering the more rugged trails that led around Fourthpeak's northern face, to Keeper's Dale in the west. All told, there were two hundred mounted warriors, fully two-fifths of the famed Knights in Silver, a great contingent and a great sacrifice, especially with the first winds of winter blowing cold in the air.

Nesme's sacrifice was less, Besnell understood, and likely the Riders of Nesme's commitment would be too. This was the town with the most to lose, except of course for Settlestone, and yet Nesme had spared barely a tenth of its seasoned garrison. The strained relations between Mithril Hall and Nesme were no secret, a brewing feud that had begun before Bruenor had ever found his homeland, when the dwarf and his fellow companions had passed near Nesme. Bruenor and his friends had saved several riders from marauding bog blokes, only to have the riders turn on them when the battle had ended. Because of the color of Drizzt's skin and the reputation of his heritage, Bruenor's party had been turned away, and though the dwarf's outrage had been later tempered somewhat by the fact that soldiers from Nesme had joined in the retaking of Mithril Hall, relations had remained somewhat strained.

This time the expected opponents were dark elves and, no doubt, that fact alone had reminded the wary men of Nesme of their distrust for Bruenor's closest friend. But at least they had come, and forty were better than none, Besnell told himself. The elf had openly proclaimed Berkthgar the leader of all four groups, and so it would be (though, if and when battle was joined, each contingent would likely fall into its own tactics, hopefully complementing each other), but Besnell saw a role for himself, less obvious, but no less important. He would be the peacemaker; he would keep the factions in line and in harmony.

If the dark elves did come, his job would be much easier, he knew, for in the face of so deadly an enemy, petty grievances would fast be forgotten.

* * * * *

Belwar didn't know whether to feel relief or fear when word came from the spying elemental that the drow, a single drow at least, had indeed gone into Blingdenstone, and that a drow army had marched past the deserted city, finding the tunnels back to the east, the route to Mithril Hall.

The most honored burrow warden sat again in his now customary perch, staring out at the empty tunnels. He thought of Drizzt, a dear friend, and of the place the dark elf now called home. Drizzt had told Belwar of Mithril Hall when he had passed through Blingdenstone on his way to Menzoberranzan several months earlier. How happy Drizzt had been when he spoke of his friends, this dwarf named Bruenor, and the human woman, Catti-brie, who had crossed through Blingdenstone on Drizzt's heels, and had, according to later reports, aided in Drizzt's wild escape from the drow city.

That very escape had facilitated this march, Belwar knew, and yet the gnome remained pleased that his friend had gotten free of Matron Baenre's clutches. Now Drizzt was home, but the dark elves were going to find him.

Belwar recalled the true sadness in Drizzt's lavender eyes when

189

the drow had recounted the loss of one of his surface-found friends. What tears might Drizzt know soon, the gnome wondered, with a drow army marching to destroy his new home?

"Decisions we have to make," came a voice behind the sturdy gnome. Belwar clapped his mithril "hands" together, more to clear his thoughts than anything else, and turned to face Firble.

One of the good things that had come from all of this confusion was the budding friendship between Firble and Belwar. As two of the older svirfnebli of Blingdenstone, they had known each other, or of each other, a very long time, but only when Belwar's eyes (because of his friendship with Drizzt) had turned to the world outside the gnomish city had Firble truly come into his life. At first the two seemed a complete mismatch, but both had found strength in what the other offered, and a bond had grown between them—though neither had as yet openly admitted it.

"Decisions?"

"The drow have passed," said Firble.

"Likely to return."

Firble nodded. "Obviously," the round-shouldered councilor agreed. "King Schnicktick must decide whether we are to return to Blingdenstone."

The notion hit Belwar like the slap of a cold, wet towel. Return to Blingdenstone? Of course they were to return to their homes! the most honored burrow warden's thoughts screamed out at him. Any other option was too ridiculous to entertain. But as he calmed and considered Firble's grim demeanor, Belwar began to see the truth of it all. The drow would be back, and if they had made a conquest near or at the surface, a conquest of Mithril Hall, as most believed was their intention, then there would likely remain an open route between Menzoberranzan and that distant place, a route that passed too close to Blingdenstone.

"Words, there are, and from many with influence, that we should go farther west, to find a new cavern, a new Blingdenstone," Firble said. From his tone it was obvious the little councilor was not thrilled at that prospect.

"Never," Belwar said unconvincingly.

"King Schnicktick will ask your opinion in this most important matter," Firble said. "Consider it well, Belwar Dissengulp. The lives of us all may hinge on your answer."

190

A long, quiet moment passed, and Firble gave a curt nod and turned to leave.

"What does Firble say?" Belwar asked before he could scurry off.

The councilor turned slowly, determinedly, staring Belwar straight in the eye. "Firble says there is only one Blingdenstone," he answered with more grit than Belwar had ever heard, or ever expected to hear, from him. "To leave as the drow pass by is one thing, a good thing. To stay out is not so good."

"Worth fighting for are some things," Belwar added.

"Worth dying for?" Firble was quick to put in, and the councilor did turn and leave.

Belwar sat alone with his thoughts for his home and for his friend.

Chapter 19

IMPROVISING

atti-brie knew as soon as she saw the dwarven courier's face, his features a mixture of anxiety and battle-lust. She knew, and so she ran off ahead of the messenger, down the winding ways of Mithril Hall, through the Undercity, seeming almost deserted now, the furnaces burning low. Many eyes regarded her, studied the urgency in her stride, and understood her purpose. She knew, and so they all knew.

The dark elves had come.

The dwarves guarding the heavy door leading out of Mithril Hall proper nodded to her as she came through. "Shoot straight, me girl!" one of them yelled at her back, and, though she was terribly afraid, though it seemed as if her worst nightmare was about to come true, that brought a smile to her face.

She found Bruenor, Regis beside him, in a wide cavern, the same chamber where the dwarves had defeated a goblin tribe not so long ago. Now the place had been prepared as the dwarf king's command post, the central brain for the defense of the outer and lower tunnels. Nearly all tunnels leading to this chamber from the wilds of the Underdark had been thoroughly trapped or dropped altogether, or were now heavily guarded, leaving the chamber as secure a place as could be found outside Mithril Hall proper.

"Drizzt?" Catti-brie asked.

Bruenor looked across the cavern, to a large tunnel exiting into the deeper regions. "Out there," he said, "with the cat."

Catti-brie looked around. The preparations had been made; everything had been set into place as well as possible in the time allowed. Not so far away, Stumpet Rakingclaw and her fellow clerics crouched and knelt on the floor, lining up and sorting dozens of small potion bottles and preparing bandages, blankets, and herbal salves for the wounded. Catti-brie winced, for she knew that all those bandages and more would be needed before this was finished.

To the side of the clerics, three of the Harpells—Harkle, Bidderdoo, and Bella don DelRoy—conferred over a small, round table covered with dozens of maps and other parchments.

Bella looked up and motioned to Bruenor, and the dwarf king rushed to her side.

"Are we to sit and wait?" Catti-brie asked Regis.

"For the time," the halfling answered. "But soon Bruenor and I will lead a group out, along with one of the Harpells, to rendezvous with Drizzt and Pwent in Tunult's Cavern. I'm sure Bruenor means for you to come with us."

"Let him try to stop me," Catti-brie muttered under her breath. She silently considered the rendezvous. Tunult's Cavern was the largest chamber outside Mithril Hall, and if they were going to meet Drizzt there, instead of some out-of-the-way place—and if the dark elves were indeed in the tunnels near Mithril Hall—then the anticipated battle would come soon. Catti-brie took a deep breath and took up Taulmaril, her magical bow. She tested its pull, then checked her quiver to make sure it was full, even though the enchantment of the quiver ensured that it was always full.

We are ready, came a thought in her mind, a thought imparted by Khazid'hea, she knew. Catti-brie took comfort in her newest companion. She trusted the sword now, knew that it and she were of like mind. And they were indeed ready; they all were.

Still, when Bruenor and Bidderdoo walked away from the other Harpells, the dwarf motioning to his personal escorts and Regis and Catti-brie, the young woman's heart skipped a few beats.

R. A. Salvatore

*   *   *. *   *

The Gutbuster Brigade rambled and jostled, bouncing off walls and each other. Drow in the tunnels! They had spotted drow in the tunnels, and now they needed a catch or a kill.

To the few dark elves who were indeed so close to Mithril Hall, forward scouts for the wave that would follow, the thunder of Pwent's minions seemed almost deafening. The drow were a quiet race, as quiet as the Underdark itself, and the bustle of surface-dwelling dwarves made them think that a thousand fierce warriors were giving chase. So the dark elves fell back, stretched their lines thin, with the more-important females taking the lead in the retreat and the males forced to hold the line and delay the enemy.

First contact was made in a narrow but high tunnel. The Gut-busters came in hard and fast from the east, and three drow, levitat-ing among the stalactites, fired hand-crossbows, putting poison-tipped darts into Pwent and the two others flanking him in the front rank.

"What!" the battlerager roared, as did his companions, sur-prised by the sudden sting. The ever wary Pwent, cunning and com-prehending, looked around, then he and the other two fell to the floor.

With a scream of surprise, the rest of the Gutbusters turned about and fled, not even thinking to recover their fallen comrades.

Kill two. Take one back for questioning, the most important of the three dark elves signaled as he and his companions began floating back to the floor.

They touched down lightly and drew out fine swords.

Up scrambled the three battleragers, their little legs pumping under them in a wild flurry. No poison, not even the famed drow sleeping poison, could get through the wicked concoctions this group had recently imbibed. Gutbuster was a drink, not just a brigade, and if a dwarf could survive the drink itself, he wouldn't have to worry much about being poisoned (or being cold) for some time.

Closest to the dark elves, Pwent lowered his head, with its long helmet spike, and impaled one elf through the chest, blasting through the fine mesh of drow armor easily and brutally.

The second drow managed to deflect the next battlerager's

194

charge, turning the helmet spike aside with both his swords. But a mailed fist, the knuckles devilishly spiked with barbed points, caught the drow under the chin and tore a gaping hole in his throat. Fighting for breath, the drow managed to score two nasty hits on his opponent's back, but those two strikes did little in the face of the flurry launched by the wild-eyed dwarf.

Only the third drow survived the initial assault. He leaped high in the air, enacting his levitation spell once more, and got just over the remaining dwarf's barreling charge—mostly because the dwarf slipped on the slick blood of Thibbledorf Pwent's quick kill.

Up went the drow, into the stalactite tangle, disappearing from sight.

Pwent straightened, shaking free of the dead drow. "That way!" he roared, pointing farther along the corridor. "Find an open area o' ceiling and take up a watch! We're not to let this one get away!"

Around the eastern bend came the rest of the Gutbusters, whooping and shouting, their armor clattering, the many creases and points on each suit grating and squealing like fingernails on slate.

"Take to lookin'!" Pwent bellowed, indicating the ceiling, and all the dwarves bobbed about eagerly.

One screeched, taking a hand-crossbow hit squarely in the face, but that shout of pain became a cry of joy, for the dwarf had only to backtrack the angle to spot the floating drow. Immediately a globe of darkness engulfed that area of the stalactites, but the dwarves now knew where to find him.

"Lariat!" Pwent bellowed, and another dwarf pulled a rope from his belt and scrambled over to the battlerager. The end of the rope was looped and securely tied in a slip knot, and so the dwarf, misunderstanding Pwent's intent, put the lasso twirling over his head and looked to the darkened area, trying to discern his best shot.

Pwent grabbed him by the wrist and held fast, sending the rope limply to the floor. "Battlerager lariat," Pwent explained.

Other dwarves crowded about, not knowing what their leader had in mind. Smiles widened on every face as Pwent slipped the loop over his foot, tightened it about his ankle, and informed the others that it would take more than one of them to get this drow-catcher flying.

Every eager dwarf grabbed the rope and began tugging wildly, doing no more than to knock Pwent from his feet. Gradually,

195

sobered by the threats of the vicious battlerager commander, they managed to find a rhythm, and soon had Pwent skipping about the floor.

Then they had him up in the air, flying wildly, round and round. But too much slack was given the rope, and Pwent scraped hard against one of the corridor walls, his helmet spike throwing a line of bright sparks.

This group learned fast, though—considering that they were dwarves who spent their days running headlong into steel-reinforced doors—and they soon had the timing of the spin and the length of the rope perfect.

Two turns, five turns, and off flew the battlerager, up into the air, to crash among the stalactites. Pwent grabbed onto one momentarily, but it broke away from the ceiling and down the dwarf and stone tumbled.

Pwent hit hard, then bounced right back to his feet.

"One less barrier to our enemy!" one dwarf roared, and before the dazed Pwent could protest, the others cheered and tugged, bringing the battlerager lariat to bear once more.

Up flew Pwent, to similar, painful results, then a third time, then a fourth, which proved the charm, for the poor drow, blind to the scene, finally dared to come out into the open, edging his way to the west.

He sensed the living lariat coming and managed to scramble behind a long, thin stalactite, but that hardly mattered, for Pwent took the stone out cleanly, wrapped his arms about it, and about the drow behind it, and drow, dwarf, and stone fell together, crashing hard to the floor. Before the drow could recover, half the brigade had fallen over him, battering him into unconsciousness.

It took them another five minutes to get the semiconscious Pwent to let go of the victim.

They were up and moving, Pwent included, soon after, having tied the drow, ankles and wrists to a long pole, supported on the shoulders of two of the group. They hadn't even cleared the corridor, though, when the dwarves farthest to the west, the two Pwent had sent to watch, took up a cry of "Drow!" and spun about at the ready.

Into the passage came a lone, trotting dark elf, and before Pwent could yell out "Not that one!" the two dwarves lowered their heads and roared in.

In a split second, the dark elf cut left, back to the right, spun a complete circuit to the right, then went wide around the end, and the two Gutbusters stumbled and slammed hard into the wall. They realized their foolishness when the great panther came by an instant later, following her drow companion.

Drizzt was back by the dwarves' side, helping them to their feet. "Run on," he whispered, and they paused at the warning long enough to hear the rumble of a not-so-distant charge.

Misunderstanding, the Gutbusters smiled widely and prepared to continue their own charge to the west, headlong into the approaching force, but Drizzt held them firmly.

"Our enemies are upon us in great numbers," he said. "You will get your fight, more than you ever hoped for, but not here."

By the time Drizzt, the two dwarves, and the panther caught up to Pwent, the noise of the coming army was clearly evident.

"I thought ye said the damned drow moved silent," Pwent remarked, double-stepping beside the swift ranger.

"Not drow," Drizzt replied. "Kobolds and goblins."

Pwent skidded to an abrupt halt. "We're runnin' from stinkin' kobolds?" he asked.

"Thousands of stinking kobolds," Drizzt replied evenly, "and bigger monsters, likely with thousands of drow behind them."

"Oh," answered the battlerager, suddenly out of bluster.

In the familiar tunnels, Drizzt and the Gutbusters had no trouble keeping ahead of the rushing army. Drizzt took no detours this time, but ran straight to the east, past the tunnels the dwarves had rigged to fall.

"Run on," the drow ordered the assigned trap-springers, a handful of dwarves standing ready beside cranks that would release the ropes supporting the tunnel structure. Each of them in turn stared blankly at the surprising command.

"They're coming," one remarked, for that is exactly why these dwarves were out in the tunnels.

"All you will catch is kobolds," Drizzt, understanding the drow tactics, informed them. "Run on, and let us see if we cannot catch a few drow as well."

"But none'll be here to spring the traps!" more than one dwarf, Pwent among them, piped in.

Drizzt's wicked grin was convincing, so the dwarves, who had learned many times to trust the ranger, shrugged and fell in line with the retreating Gutbusters.

"Where're we runnin' to?" Pwent wanted to know.

"Another hundred strides," Drizzt informed him. "Tunult's Cavern, where you will get your fight."

"Promises, promises," muttered the fierce Pwent.

Tunult's Cavern, the most open area this side of Mithril Hall, was really a series of seven caverns connected by wide, arching tunnels. Nowhere was the ground even; some chambers sat higher than others, and more than one deep fissure ran across the floors.

Here waited Bruenor and his escorts, along with nearly a thousand of Mithril Hall's finest fighters. The original plan had called for Tunult's Cavern to be set up as an outward command post, used as a send-off point to the remaining, though less direct, tunnels after the drow advance had been stopped cold by the dropped stone.

Drizzt had altered that plan, and he rushed to Bruenor's side, conferring with the dwarf king, and with Bidderdoo Harpell, a wizard that the drow was surely relieved to find.

"Ye gave up the trap-springing positions!" Bruenor bellowed at the ranger as soon as he understood that the tunnels beyond were still intact.

"Not so," Drizzt replied with all confidence. Even as his gaze led Bruenor's toward the eastern tunnel, the first of the kobold ranks rushed in, pouring like water behind a breaking dam into the waiting dwarves. "I merely got the fodder out of the way."

Chapter 20
THE BATTLE OF
TUNULT'S CAVERN

he confusion was immediate and complete, kobolds swarming in by the dozens, and tough dwarves forming into tight battle groups and rushing fast to meet them.

Catti-brie put her magical bow up and fired arrow after arrow, aiming for the main entrance. Lightning flashed with each shot as the enchanted bolt sped off, crackling and sparking every time it skipped off a wall. Kobolds went down in a line, one arrow often killing several, but it hardly seemed to matter, so great was the invading throng.

Guenhwyvar leaped away, Drizzt quick-stepping behind. A score of kobolds had somehow wriggled past the initial fights and were bearing down on Bruenor's position. A shot from Catti-brie felled one; Guenhwyvar's plunge scattered the rest, and Drizzt, moving quicker than ever, slipped in, stabbed one, pivoted and spun to the left, launching the blue-glowing Twinkle against the attempted parry of another. Had Twinkle been a straight blade, the kobold's small sword would have deflected it high, but Drizzt deftly turned the curving weapon over in his hand and slightly

R. A. Salvatore

altered the angle of his attack. Twinkle rolled over the kobold's sword and dove into its chest.

The drow had never stopped his run and now skittered back to the right and slid to one knee. Across came Twinkle, slapping against one kobold blade, driving it hard into a second. Stronger than both the creatures combined, and with a better angle, Drizzt forced their swords and their defense high, and his second scimitar slashed across the other way, disemboweling one and taking the legs out from under the other.

"Damn drow's stealing all the fun," Bruenor muttered, running to catch up to the fray. Between Drizzt, the panther, and Catti-brie's continuing barrage, few of the twenty kobolds still stood by the time he got there, and those few had turned in full flight.

"Plenty more to kill," Drizzt said into Bruenor's scowl, recognizing the sour look.

A line of silver-streaking arrow cut between them as soon as the words had left the drow's mouth. When the spots cleared from before their eyes, the two turned and regarded the scorched and dead kobolds taken down by Catti-brie's latest shot.

Then she, too, was beside them, Khazid'hea in hand, and Regis, holding the little mace Bruenor had long ago forged for him, was beside her. Catti-brie shrugged as her friends regarded the change in weapon, and, looking about, they understood her tactics. With more kobolds pouring in, and more dwarves coming out of the other chambers to meet the charge, it was simply too confusing and congested for the woman to safely continue with her bow.

"Run on," Catti-brie said, a wistful smile crossing her fair features.

Drizzt returned the look, and Bruenor, even Regis, had a sparkle in his eye. Suddenly it seemed like old times.

Guenhwyvar led their charge, Bruenor fighting hard to keep close to the panther's tail. Catti-brie and Regis flanked the dwarf, and Drizzt, speeding and spinning, flanked the group, first on the left, then on the right, seeming to be wherever battle was joined, running too fast to be believed.

*   *   *   *   *

Bidderdoo Harpell knew he had erred. Drizzt had asked him to get to the door, to wait for the first drow to show themselves inside

200

the cavern and then launch a fireball back down the tunnel, where the flames would burn through the supporting ropes and drop the stone.

"Not a difficult task," Bidderdoo had assured Drizzt, and so it should not have been. The wizard had memorized a spell that could put him in position, and knew others to keep him safely hidden until the blast was complete. So when all about him had run off to join in the fracas, they had gone reassured that the traps would be sprung, that the tunnels would be dropped, and that the tide of enemies would be stemmed.

Something went wrong. Bidderdoo had begun casting the spell to get him to the tunnel entrance, had even outlined the extradimensional portal that would reopen at the desired spot, but then the wizard had seen a group of kobolds, and they had seen him. This was not hard to do, for Bidderdoo, a human and not blessed with sight that could extend into the infrared spectrum, carried a shining gemstone. Kobolds were not stupid creatures, not when it came to battle, and they recognized this seemingly out-of-place human for what he was. Even the most inexperienced of kobold fighters understood the value of getting to a wizard, of forcing a dangerous spellcaster into melee combat, keeping his hands tied up with weapons rather than often explosive components.

Still, Bidderdoo could have beaten their charge, could have stepped through the dimensions to get to his appointed position.

For seven years, until the Time of Troubles, Bidderdoo Harpell had lived with the effects of a potion gone awry, had lived as the Harpell family dog. When magic went crazy, Bidderdoo had reverted to his human form—long enough, at least, to get the necessary ingredients together to counteract the wild potion. Soon after, Bidderdoo had gone back to his flea-bitten self, but he had helped his family find the means to get him out of the enchantment. A great debate had followed in the Ivy Mansion as to whether they should "cure" Bidderdoo or not. It seemed that many of the Harpells had grown quite fond of the dog, more so than they had ever loved Bidderdoo as a human.

Bidderdoo had even served as Harkle's seeing-eye dog on a long stretch of the journey to Mithril Hall, when Harkle had no eyes.

But then magic had straightened out, and the debate became moot, for the enchantment had simply gone away.

R. A. Salvatore

Or had it? Bidderdoo had held no doubts about the integrity of his cure until this very moment, until he saw the kobolds approaching. His upper lip curled back in an open snarl; he felt the hair on the back of his neck bristling and felt his tailbone tighten—if he still had a tail, it would be straight out behind him!

He started down into a crouch, and noticed only then that he had not paws, but hands, hands that held no weapons. He groaned, for the kobolds were only ten feet away.

The wizard went for a spell instead. He put the tips of his thumbs together, hands out wide to each side, and chanted frantically.

The kobolds came in, straight ahead and flanking, and the closest of them had a sword high for a strike.

Bidderdoo's hands erupted in flame, jets of scorching, searing fire, arcing out in a semicircle.

Half a dozen kobolds lay dead, and several others blinked in amazement through singed eyelashes.

"Hah!" Bidderdoo cried, and snapped his fingers.

The kobolds blinked again and charged, and Bidderdoo had no spells quick enough to stop them.

*　*　*　*　*

At first the kobolds and goblins seemed a swarming, confused mass, and so it remained for many of the undisciplined brawlers. But several groups had trained for war extensively in the caverns beneath the complex of House Oblodra. One of these, fifty strong, formed into a tight wedge, three large kobolds at the tip and a tight line running back and wide to each side.

They entered the main chamber, avoided combat enough to form up, and headed straight to the left, toward the looming entrance of one of the side caverns. Mostly the dwarves avoided them, with so many other easier kills available, and the kobold group almost got to the side chamber unscathed.

Coming out of that chamber, though, was a group of a dozen dwarves. The bearded warriors hooted and roared and came on fiercely, but the kobold formation did not waver, worked to perfection as it split the dwarven line almost exactly in half, then widened the gap with the lead kobolds pressing to the very entrance of the side chamber. A couple of kobolds went down in that charge, and one dwarf died, but the kobold ranks tightened again immediately, and those dwarves caught along the inside line, caught between the kobolds and the main cavern's low sloping wall, found themselves in dire straights indeed.

Across the way, the "free" half of the dwarven group realized their error, that they had taken the kobolds too lightly and had not expected such intricate tactics. Their kin would be lost, and there was nothing they could do to get through this surprisingly tight, disciplined formation—made even tighter by the fact that, in going near the wall, the kobolds went under some low-hanging stalactites.

The dwarves attacked fiercely anyway, spurred on by the cries of their apparently doomed companions.

Guenhwyvar was low to the ground, low enough to skitter under any stalactites. The panther hit the back of the kobold formation in full stride, blasting two kobolds away and running over a third, claws digging in for a better hold as the cat crossed over.

Drizzt came in behind, sliding to one knee again and killing two kobolds in the first attack routine. Beside him charged Regis, no taller than a kobold and fighting straight up and even against one.

With his great, sweeping style of axe-fighting, Bruenor found the tight quarters uncomfortable at best. Even worse off was Catti-brie, not as agile or quick as Drizzt. If she went down to one knee, as had the drow, she would be at a huge disadvantage indeed.

But standing straight, a stalactite in her face, she wasn't much better off.

Khazid'hea gave her the answer.

It went against every instinct the woman had, was contrary to everything Bruenor (who had spent much of his life repairing damaged weapons) had taught her about fighting. But, hardly thinking, Catti-brie clasped her sword hilt in both hands and brought the magnificent weapon streaking straight across, up high.

Khazid'hea's red line flashed angrily as the sword connected on the hanging stone. Catti-brie's momentum slowed, but only slightly, for Cutter lived up to its name, shearing through the rock. Catti-brie jerked to the side as the sword exited the stalactite, and she would have been vulnerable in that instant—except that the two kobolds in formation right before her were suddenly more concerned that the sky was falling.

One got crushed under the stalactite, and the other's death was

R. A. Salvatore

just as quick, as Bruenor, seeing the opening, rushed in with an overhead chop that nearly took the wretched thing in half.

Those dwarves that had been separated on the outside rank took heart at the arrival of so powerful a group, and they pressed the kobold line fiercely, calling out to their trapped companions to "hold fast!" and promising that help would soon arrive.

Regis hated to fight, at least when his opponent could see him coming. He was needed now, though. He knew that, and would not shirk his responsibilities. Beside him, Drizzt was fighting from his knees; how could the halfling, who would have to get up on his tiptoes to bang his head on a stalactite, justify standing behind his drow friend this time?

Both hands on his mace handle, Regis went in fiercely. He smiled as he actually scored a hit, the well-forged weapon crumbling a kobold arm.

Even as that opponent fell away, though, another squeezed in and struck, its sword catching Regis under his upraised arm. Only fine dwarven armor saved him—he made a note to buy Buster Bracer a few large mugs of mead if he ever got out of this alive.

Tough was the dwarven armor, but the kobold's head was not as tough, as the halfling's mace proved a moment later.

"Well done," Drizzt congratulated, his battle ebbing enough for him to witness the halfling's strike.

Regis tried to smile, but winced instead at the pain of his bruised ribs.

Drizzt noted the look and skittered across in front of Regis, meeting the charge as the kobold formation shifted to compensate for the widening breach. The drow's scimitars went into a wild dance, slashing and chopping, often banging against the low-hanging stalactites, throwing sparks, but more often connecting on kobolds.

To the side, Catti-brie and Bruenor had formed up into an impromptu alliance, Bruenor holding back the enemy, while Catti-brie and Cutter continued to clear a higher path, dropping the hanging stones one at a time.

Across the way, though, the dwarves remained sorely pressed, with two down and the other five taking many hits. None of the friends could get to them in time, they knew, none could cross through the tight formation.

None except Guenhwyvar.

Flying like a black arrow, the panther bored on, running down kobold after kobold, shrugging off many wicked strikes. Blood streamed from the panther's flanks, but Guenhwyvar would not be deterred. She got to the dwarves and bolstered their line, and their cheer at her appearance was of pure delight and salvation.

A song on their lips, the dwarves fought on, the panther fought on, and the kobolds could not finish the task. With the press across the way, the formation soon crumbled, and the dwarven group was reunited, that the wounded could be taken from the cavern.

Drizzt and Catti-brie's concern for Guenhwyvar was stolen by the panther's roar, and its flight, as Guenhwyvar led the five friends off to the next place where they would be needed most.

* * * * *

Bidderdoo closed his eyes, wondering what mysteries death would reveal.

He hoped there would be some, at least.

He heard a roar, then a clash of steel in front of him. Then came a grunt, and the sickening thud of a torn body slapping against the hard floor.

They are fighting over who gets to kill me, the mage thought.

More roars—dwarven roars!—and more grunts; more torn bodies falling to the stone.

Bidderdoo opened his eyes to see the kobold ranks decimated, to see a handful of the dirtiest, smelliest dwarves imaginable hopping up and down about him, pointing this way and that, as they of the Gutbuster Brigade tried to figure out where they might next cause the most havoc.

Bidderdoo took a moment to regard the kobolds, a dozen corpses that had been more than killed. "Shredded," he whispered, and he nodded, deciding that was a better word.

"Ye're all right now," said one of the dwarves—Bidderdoo thought he had heard this one's name as Thibbledorf Pwent or some such thing (not that anyone named Bidderdoo could toss insults regarding names). "And me and me own're off!" the wild battlerager huffed.

Bidderdoo nodded, then realized he still had a serious problem.

205

He had only prepared for one spell that could open such a dimensional door, and that one was wasted, the enchantment expired as he had battled with the kobolds.

"Wait!" he screamed at Pwent, and he surprised himself, and the dwarf, for along with his words came out a caninelike yelp.

Pwent regarded the Harpell curiously. He hopped up right before Bidderdoo and cocked his head to the side, a movement exaggerated by the tilting helmet spike.

"Wait. Pray, do not run off, good and noble dwarf," Bidderdoo said sweetly, needing assistance.

Pwent looked around and behind, as if trying to figure out who this mage was talking to. The other Gutbusters were similarly confused, some standing and staring blankly, scratching their heads.

Pwent poked a stubby, dirty finger into his own chest, his expression showing that he hardly considered himself "good and noble."

"Do not leave me," Bidderdoo pleaded.

"Ye're still alive," Pwent countered. "And there's not much for killin' over here." As though that were explanation enough, the battlerager spun and took a stride away.

"But I've failed!" Bidderdoo wailed, and a howl escaped his lips at the end of the sentence.

"Ye've fail-doooo?" Pwent asked.

"Oh, we are all do-oooo-omed!" the howling mage went on dramatically. "It's too-oooo far."

All the battleragers were around Bidderdoo by this point, intrigued by the strange accent, or whatever it was. The closest enemies, a band of goblins, could have attacked then, but none wanted to go anywhere near this wild troupe, a point made especially clear with the last group of kobolds lying in bloody pieces about the area.

"Ye better be quick and to the point," Pwent, anxious to kill again, barked at Bidderdoo.

"Oooo."

"And stop the damned howlin'!" the battlerager demanded.

In truth, poor Bidderdoo wasn't howling on purpose. In the stress of the situation, the mage who had lived so long as a dog was unintentionally recalling the experience, discovering once more those primal canine instincts. He took a deep breath and pointedly reminded himself he was a man, not a dog. "I must get to the tunnel entrance," he said without a howl, yip, or yelp. "The drow ranger bade me to send a spell down the corridor."

"I'm not for carin' for wizard stuff," Pwent interrupted, and turned away once more.

"Are ye for droppin' the stinkin' tunnel on the stinkin' drow's 'eads?" Bidderdoo asked in his best battlerager imitation.

"Bah!" Pwent snorted, and all the dwarven heads were bobbing eagerly about him. "Me and me own'll get ye there!"

Bidderdoo took care to keep his visage stern, but silently thought himself quite clever for appealing to the wild dwarves' hunger for carnage.

In the blink of a dog's eye, Bidderdoo was swept up in the tide of running Gutbusters. The wizard suggested a roundabout route, skirting the left-hand, or northern, side of the cavern, where the fighting had become less intense.

Silly mage.

The Gutbuster Brigade ran straight through, ran down kobolds and the larger goblins who had come in behind the kobold ranks. They almost buried a couple of dwarves who weren't quick enough in diving aside; they bounced off stalagmites, ricocheting and rolling on. Before Bidderdoo could even begin to protest the tactic, he found himself nearing the appointed spot, the entrance to the tunnel.

He spent a brief moment wondering which was faster, a spell opening a dimensional door or a handful of battle-hungry battleragers. He even entertained the creation of a new spell, *Battlerager Escort*, but he shook that notion away as a more immediate problem, a pair of huge, bull-headed minotaurs and a dark elf behind them, entered the cavern.

"Defensive posture!" cried Bidderdoo. "You must hold them off! Defensive posture!"

Silly mage.

The closest two Gutbusters flew headlong, diving into the feet of the towering, eight-foot monsters. Before they even realized what had hit them, the minotaurs were falling forward. Neither made it unobstructed to the ground, though, as Pwent and another wild-eyed dwarf roared in, butting the minotaurs head-to-head.

A globe of darkness appeared behind the tumble, and the drow was nowhere to be seen.

Bidderdoo wisely began his spellcasting. The drow were here! Just as Drizzt had figured, the dark elves were coming in behind the kobold fodder. If he could get the fireball away now, if he could drop the tunnel. . .

He had to force the words through a guttural, instinctual growl coming from somewhere deep in his throat. He had the urge to join the Gutbusters, who were all clamoring over the fallen minotaurs, taking the brutes apart mercilessly. He had the urge to join in the feast.

"The feast?" he asked aloud.

Bidderdoo shook his head and began again, concentrating on the spell. Apparently hearing the wizard's rhythmic cadence, the drow came out of the darkness, hand-crossbow up and ready.

Bidderdoo closed his eyes, forced the words to flow as fast as possible. He felt the sting of the dart, right in the belly, but his concentration was complete and he did not flinch, did not interrupt the spell.

His legs went weak under him; he heard the drow coming, imagined a shining sword poised for a killing strike.

Bidderdoo's concentration held. He completed the dweomer, and a small, glowing ball of fire leaped out from his hand, soared through the darkness beyond, down the tunnel.

Bidderdoo teetered with weakness. He opened his eyes, but the cavern about him was blurry and wavering. Then he fell backward, felt as though the floor were rushing up to swallow him.

Somewhere in the back of his mind he expected to hit the stone hard, but then the fireball went off.

Then the tunnel fell.

Chapter 21
ONE FOR THE GOOD GUYS

 heavy burden weighed on the most honored burrow warden's strong shoulders, but Belwar did not stoop as he marched through the long, winding tunnels. He had made the decision with a clear mind and definite purpose, and he simply refused to second-guess himself all the way to Mithril Hall.

His opponents in the debate had argued that Belwar was motivated by personal friendship, not the best interests of the svirfnebli. Firble had learned that Drizzt Do'Urden, Belwar's drow friend, had escaped Menzoberranzan, and the drow march, by all indications, was straight for Mithril Hall, no doubt motivated in part by Lloth's proclaimed hatred of the renegade.

Would Belwar lead Blingdenstone to war, then, for the sake of a single drow?

In the end, that vicious argument had been settled not by Belwar, but by Firble, another of the oldest svirfnebli, another of those who had felt the pain most keenly when Blingdenstone had been left behind.

"A clear choice we have," Firble had said. "Go now and see if we can aid the enemies of the dark elves, or a new home we must find, for the drow will surely return, and if we stand then, we stand alone."

It was a terrible, difficult decision for the council and for King Schnicktick. If they followed the dark elves and found their suspicions confirmed, found a war on the surface, could they even count on the alliance of the surface dwarves and the humans, races the deep gnomes did not know?

Belwar assured them they could. With all his heart, the most honored burrow warden believed that Drizzt, and any friends Drizzt had made, would not let him down. And Firble, who knew the outside world so well (but was, by his own admission, somewhat ignorant of the surface), agreed with Belwar, simply on the logic that any race, even not-so-intelligent goblins, would welcome allies against the dark elves.

So Schnicktick and the council had finally agreed, but, like every other decision of the ultimately conservative svirfnebli, they would go only so far. Belwar could march in pursuit of the drow, and Firble with him, along with any gnomes who volunteered. They were scouts, Schnicktick had emphasized, and no marching army. The svirfneblin king and all those who had opposed Belwar's reasoning were surprised to find how many volunteered for the long, dangerous march. So many, in fact, that Schnicktick, for the simple sake of the city operation, had to limit the number to fifteen score.

Belwar knew why the other svirfnebli had come, and knew the truth of his own decision. If the dark elves went to the surface and overwhelmed Mithril Hall, they would not allow the gnomes back into Blingdenstone. Menzoberranzan did not conquer, then leave. No, it would enslave the dwarves and work the mines as its own, then pity Blingdenstone, for the svirfneblin city would be too close to the easiest routes to the conquered land.

So although all of these svirfnebli, Belwar and Firble included, were marching farther from Blingdenstone than they had ever gone before, they knew that they were, in effect, fighting for their homeland.

Belwar would not second-guess that decision, and, keeping that in mind, his burden was lessened.

*　*　*　*　*

Bidderdoo put the fireball far down the tunnel, but the narrow ways could not contain the sheer volume of the blast. A line of fire rushed out of the tunnel, back into the cavern, like the breath of an angry red dragon, and Bidderdoo's own clothes lit up. The mage screamed—as did every dwarf and kobold near him, as did the next line of minotaurs, rushing down for the cavern, as did the skulking dark elves behind them.

In the moment of the wizard's fireball, all of them screamed, and, just as quickly, the cries went away, extinguished, overwhelmed, by hundreds of tons of dropping stone.

Again the backlash swept into the cavern, a blast so strong that the gust of it blew away the fires licking at Bidderdoo's robes. He was flying suddenly, as were all those near him, flying and dazed, pelted with stone, and extremely lucky, for none of the dropping stalactites or the heavy stone displaced in the cavern squashed him.

The ground trembled and bucked; one of the cavern walls buckled, and one of the side chambers collapsed. Then it was done, and the tunnel was gone, just gone, as though it had never been there, and the chamber that had been named for the dwarf Tunult seemed much smaller.

Bidderdoo pulled himself up from the piled dust and debris shakily and brushed the dirt from his glowing gemstone. With all the dust in the air, the light from the enchanted stone seemed meager indeed. The wizard looked at himself, seeing more skin than clothing, seeing dozens of bruises and bright red on one arm, under the clinging dust, where the fires had gotten to his skin.

A helmet spike, bent slightly to the side, protruded from a pile not far away. Bidderdoo was about to speak a lament for the battlerager, who had gotten him to the spot, but Pwent suddenly burst up from the dust, spitting pebbles and smiling crazily.

"Well done!" the battlerager roared. "Do it again!"

Bidderdoo started to respond, but then he swooned, the insidious drow poison defeating the momentary jolt of adrenaline. The next thing the unfortunate wizard knew, Pwent was holding him up and he was gagging on the most foul-tasting concoction ever brewed. Foul but effective, for Bidderdoo's grogginess was no more.

"Gutbuster!" Pwent roared, patting the trusty flask on his broad belt.

As the dust settled, the bodies stirred, one by one. To a dwarf, the Gutbuster Brigade, tougher than the stone, remained, and the few kobolds that had survived were cut down before they could plead.

The way the cavern had collapsed, with the nearest side chamber gone, and the wall opposite that having buckled, this small group found itself cut off from the main force. They weren't trapped, though, for one narrow passage led to the left, back toward the heart of Tunult's Cavern. The fighting in there had resumed, so it seemed from the ring of metal and the calls of both dwarves and kobolds.

Unexpectedly, Thibbledorf Pwent did not lead his force headlong into the fray. The passage was narrow at this end, and seemed to narrow even more just a short way in, so much so that Pwent didn't even think they could squeeze through. Also, the battlerager spotted something over Bidderdoo's shoulder, a deep crack in the wall to the side of the dropped tunnel. As he neared the spot, Pwent felt the stiff breeze rushing out of the crack, as the air pressure in the tunnels beyond adjusted to the catastrophe.

Pwent hooted and slammed the wall below the crack with all his strength. The loose stone gave way and fell in, revealing a passageway angling into the deeper corridors beyond.

"We should go back and report to King Bruenor," Bidderdoo reasoned, "or go as far as the tunnel takes us, to let them know we are in here, that they might dig us out."

Pwent snorted. "Wouldn't be much at scoutin' if we let this tunnel pass," he argued. "If the drow find it, they'll be back quicker than Bruenor's expectin'. Now that's a report worth givin'!"

In truth, it was difficult for the outrageous dwarven warrior to ignore those tempting sounds of battle, but Pwent found his heart seeking the promise of greater enemies, of drow and minotaurs, in the open corridors the other way.

"And if we get stuck in that tunnel there," Pwent continued, pointing back toward what remained of Tunult's Cavern, "the damned drow'll walk right up our backs!"

The Gutbuster Brigade formed up behind their leader, but Bidderdoo shook his head and squeezed into the passage. His worst fears were quickly realized, for it did indeed narrow, and he could not get near the open area beyond, where the fighting continued, could not even get close enough to hope to attract attention above the tumult of battle.

Perhaps he had a spell that would aid him, Bidderdoo reasoned, and he reached into an impossibly deep pocket to retrieve his treasured spellbook. He pulled out a lump of ruffled pages, smeared and singed, many with ink blotched from the intense heat. The glue and stitches in the binding, too, had melted, and when Bidderdoo held the mess up, it fell apart.

The wizard, breathing hard suddenly, feeling as if the world were closing in on him, gathered together as many of the parchments as he could and scrambled back out of the passageway, to find, to his surprise and relief, Pwent and the others still waiting for him.

"Figgered ye'd change yer mind," the battlerager remarked, and he led the Gutbuster Brigade, plus one, away.

*   *   *   *   *

Fifty drow and an entire minotaur grouping, Quenthel Baenre's hands flashed, and from the sharp, jerking movements, her mother knew she was outraged.

Fool, Matron Baenre mused. She wondered then about her daughter's heart for this expedition. Quenthel was a powerful priestess, there could be no denying that, but only then did the withered old matron mother realize that young Quenthel had never really seen battle. House Baenre had not warred in many hundreds of years, and because of her accelerated education through the Academy, Quenthel had been spared the duties of escorting scouting patrols in the wild tunnels outside Menzoberranzan.

It struck Baenre then that her daughter had never even been outside the drow city.

The primary way to Mithril Hall is no more, Quenthel's hands went on. *And several paralleling passages have fallen as well. And worse,* Quenthel stopped abruptly, had to pause and take a deep breath to steady herself. When she began again, her face was locked in a mask of anger. *Many of the dead drow were females, several powerful priestesses and one a high priestess.*

Still the movements were exaggerated, too sharp and too quick. Did Quenthel really believe this conquest would be easy? Baenre wondered. Did she think no drow would be killed?

Baenre wondered, and not for the first time, whether she had erred in bringing Quenthel along. Perhaps she should have brought Triel, the most capable of priestesses.

Quenthel studied the hard look that was coming at her and

213

. A. Salvatore

understood that her mother was not pleased. It took her a moment to realize she was irritating Baenre more than the bad report would warrant.

"The lines are moving?" Baenre asked aloud.

Quenthel cleared her throat. "Bregan D'aerthe has discovered many other routes," she answered, "even corridors the dwarves do not know about, which come close to tunnels leading to Mithril Hall."

Matron Baenre closed her eyes and nodded, approving of her daughter's suddenly renewed optimism. There were indeed tunnels the dwarves did not know about, small passages beneath the lowest levels of Mithril Hall lost as the dwarves continued to shift their mining operations to richer veins. Old Gandalug knew those ancient, secret ways, though, and with Methil's intrusive interrogation, the drow knew them as well. These secret tunnels did not actually connect to the dwarven compound, but wizards could open doors where there were none, and illithids could walk through stone and could take drow warriors with them on their psionic journeys.

Baenre's eyes popped open. "Word from Berg'inyon?" she asked.

Quenthel shook her head. "He exited the tunnels, as commanded, but we have not heard since."

Baenre's features grew cross. She knew that Berg'inyon was outwardly pouting at being sent outside. He led the greatest cohesive unit of all, numerically speaking, nearly a thousand drow and five times that in goblins and kobolds, with many of the dark elves riding huge lizards. But Berg'inyon's duties, though vital to the conquest of Mithril Hall, put him on the mountainside outside the dwarven complex. Very likely, Drizzt Do'Urden would be inside, in the lowest tunnels, working in an environment more suited to a dark elf. Very likely, Uthegental Armgo, not Berg'inyon, would get first try at the renegade.

Baenre's scowl turned to a smile as she considered her son and his tantrum when she had given him his assignment. Of course he had to act angry, even outraged. Of course he had to protest that he, not Uthegental, should spearhead the assault through the tunnels. But Berg'inyon had been Drizzt's classmate and primary rival in their years at Melee-Magthere, the drow school for fighters. Berg'inyon knew Drizzt perhaps better than any living drow in

214

Menzoberranzan. And Matron Baenre knew Berg'inyon.

The truth of it was, Berg'inyon didn't want anything to do with the dangerous renegade.

"Search out your brother with your magic," Baenre said suddenly, startling Quenthel. "If he continues his obstinacy, replace him."

Quenthel's eyes widened with horror. She had been with Berg'inyon when the force had exited the tunnels, crossing out onto a ledge on a mountain overlooking a deep ravine. The sight had overwhelmed her, had dizzied her, and many other drow as well. She felt lost out there, insignificant and vulnerable. This cavern that was the surface world, this great chamber whose black dome sparkled with pinpoints of unknown light, was too vast for her sensibilities.

Matron Baenre did not appreciate the horrified expression. "Go!" she snapped, and Quenthel quietly slipped away.

She was hardly out of sight before the next reporting drow stepped before Baenre's blue-glowing driftdisk.

Her report, of the progress of the force moving secretly in the lower tunnels, was better, but Baenre hardly listened. To her, these details were fast becoming tedious. The dwarves were good, and had many months to prepare, but in the end, Matron Baenre did not doubt the outcome, for she believed that Lloth herself had spoken to her. The drow would win, and Mithril Hall would fall.

She listened to the report, though, and to the next, and the next, and the next after that, a seemingly endless stream, and forced herself to look interested.

Chapter 22

STAR LIGHT, STAR BRIGHT

rom her high perch, her eyesight enhanced by magical dweomers, they seemed an army of ants, swarming over the eastern and steepest side of the mountain, filling every vale, clambering over every rock. Filtering behind in tight formations came the deeper blackness, the tight formations of drow warriors.

Never had the Lady of Silverymoon seen such a disconcerting sight, never had she been so filled with trepidation, though she had endured many wars and many perilous adventures. Alustriel's visage did not reflect those battles. She was as fair as any woman alive, her skin smooth and pale, almost translucent, and her hair long and silvery—not gray with age, though she was indeed very old, but lustrous and rich, the quiet light of night and the sparkling brightness of stars all mixed together. Indeed, the fair lady had endured many wars, and the sorrow of those conflicts was reflected in her eyes, as was the wisdom to despise war.

Across the way toward the southern face, around the bend of the conical mountain, Alustriel could see the banners of the gathered forces, most prominent among them the silver flag of her own

216

knights. They were proud and anxious, Alustriel knew, because most of them were young and did not know grief.

The Lady of Silverymoon shook away the disconcerting thoughts and focused on what likely would transpire, what her role might be.

The bulk of the enemy force was kobolds, and she figured that the huge barbarians and armored riders should have little trouble in scattering them.

But how would they fare against the drow? Alustriel wondered. She brought her flying chariot in a wide loop, watching and waiting.

* * * * *

Skirmishes erupted along the point line, as human scouts met the advancing kobolds.

At the sound of battle, and with reports filtering back, Berkthgar was anxious to loose his forces, to charge off to fight and die with a song to Tempus on his lips.

Besnell, who led the Knights in Silver, was a tempered fighter, and more the strategist. "Hold your men in check," he bade the eager barbarian. "We will see more fighting this night than any of us, even Tempus, your god of battle, would enjoy. Better that we fight them on ground of our choosing." Indeed, the knight had been careful in selecting that very ground, and had argued against both Berkthgar and King Bruenor himself to win over their support for his plan. The forces had been broken into four groups, spaced along the south side of the mountain, Fourthpeak, which held both entrances to Mithril Hall. Northwest around the mountain lay Keeper's Dale, a wide, deep, rock-strewn, and mist-filled valley wherein lay the secret western door to the dwarven complex.

From the soldiers' positions northeast around the mountain, across wide expanses of open rock and narrow, crisscrossing trails, lay the longer, more commonly used path to Mithril Hall's eastern door.

Bruenor's emissaries had wanted the force to split, the riders going to defend Keeper's Dale and the men of Settlestone guarding the eastern trails. Besnell had held firm his position, though, and had enlisted Berkthgar by turning the situation back on the proud dwarves, by insisting that they should be able to conceal and defend

217

their own entrances. "If the drow know where the entrances lie," he had argued, "then that is where they will expect resistance."

Thus, the south side of Fourthpeak was chosen. Below the positions of the defenders the trails were many, but above them the cliffs grew much steeper, so they expected no attack from that direction. The defenders' groups were mixed according to terrain, one position of narrow, broken trails exclusively barbarians, two having both barbarians and riders, and one, a plateau above a wide, smooth, gradually inclined rock face, comprised wholly of the Riders of Nesme.

Besnell and Berkthgar watched and waited now from the second position. They knew the battle was imminent; the men about them could feel the hush, the crouch of the approaching army. The area lower on the mountain, to the east, exploded suddenly in bursts of shining light as a rain of enchanted pellets, gifts from dwarven clerics, came down from the barbarians of the first defense.

How the kobolds scrambled! As did the few dark elves among the diminutive creatures' front ranks. Those monsters highest on the face, near the secret position, were overwhelmed, a horde of mighty barbarians descending over them, splitting them in half with huge swords and battle-axes, or simply lifting the kobolds high over head and hurling them down the mountainside.

"We must go out and meet them!" Berkthgar roared, seeing his kin engaged. He raised huge Bankenfuere high into the air. "To the glory of Tempus!" he roared, a cry repeated by all those barbarians on the second position, and those on the third as well.

"So much for ambush," muttered Regweld Harpell, seated on his horse-frog, Puddlejumper. With a nod to Besnell, for the time drew near, Regweld gave a slight tug on Puddlejumper's rein and the weird beast croaked out a guttural whinny and leaped to the west, clearing thirty feet.

"Not yet," Besnell implored Berkthgar, the barbarian's hand cupping a dozen or so of the magic light-giving pellets. The knight pointed out the movements of the enemy force below, explained to Berkthgar that, while many climbed up to meet the defenders holding the easternmost position, many, many more continued to filter along the lower trails to the west. Also, the light was not so intense anymore, as dark elves used their innate abilities to counter the stingingly bright enchantments.

"What are you waiting for?" Berkthgar demanded.

Besnell continued to hold his hand in the air, continued to delay the charge.

To the east, a barbarian screamed as he saw that his form was outlined suddenly by blue flames, magical fires that did not burn. They weren't truly harmless, though, for in the night, they gave the man's position clearly away. The sound of many crossbows clicked from somewhere below, and the unfortunate barbarian cried out again and again, then he fell silent.

That was more than enough for Berkthgar, and he hurled out the pellets. His nearby kin did likewise, and this second section of the south face brightened with magic. Down charged the men of Settlestone, to Besnell's continuing dismay. The riders should have gone down first, but not yet, not until the bulk of the enemy force had passed.

"We must," whispered the knight behind the elven leader from Silverymoon, and Besnell quietly nodded. He surveyed the scene for just a moment. Berkthgar and his hundred were already engaged, straight down the face, with no hope of linking up with those brave men holding the high ground in the east. Despite his anger at the impetuous barbarian, Besnell marveled at Berkthgar's exploits. Mighty Bankenfuere took out three kobolds at a swipe, launching them, whole or in parts, high into the air.

"The light will not hold," the knight behind Besnell remarked.

"Between the two forces," Besnell replied, speaking loud enough so that all those riders around him could hear. "We must go down at an angle, between the two forces, so that the men in the east can escape behind us."

Not a word of complaint came back to him, though his chosen course was treacherous indeed. The original plan had called for the Knights in Silver to ride straight into the enemy, both from this position and the next position to the west, while Berkthgar and his men linked behind them, the whole of the defending force rolling gradually to the west. Now Berkthgar, in his bloodlust, had abandoned that plan, and the Knights in Silver might pay dearly for the act. But neither man nor elf complained.

"Keep fast your pellets," Besnell commanded, "until the drow counter what light is already available."

He reared his horse once, for effect.

"For the glory of Silverymoon!" he cried.

"And the good of all good folk!" came the unified response.

Their thunder shook the side of Fourthpeak, resonated deep into the dwarven tunnels below the stone. To the blare of horns, down they charged, a hundred riders, lances low, and when those long spears became entangled or snapped apart as they skewered the enemy, out came flashing swords.

More deadly were the sturdy mounts, crushing kobolds under pounding hooves, scattering and terrifying kobolds and goblins and drow alike, for these invaders from the deepest Underdark had never seen such a cavalry charge.

In mere minutes the enemy advance up the mountain was halted and reversed, with only a few of the defenders taken down. And as the dark elves continued to counter the light pellets, Besnell's men countered their spells with still more light pellets.

But the dark force continued its roll along the lower trails, evidenced by the blare of horns to the west, the calls to Tempus and to Longsaddle, and the renewed thunder as the Longriders followed the lead of the Knights in Silver.

The first real throw of magic led the charge from that third position, a lightning bolt from Regweld that split the darkness, causing more horror than destruction.

Surprisingly, there came no magical response from the drow, other than minor darkness spells or faerie fire limning selected defenders.

The remaining barbarian force did as the plan had demanded, angling between the Longriders and the area just below the second position, linking up, not with the Knights in Silver, as was originally planned, but with Berkthgar and his force.

* * * * *

High above the battle, Alustriel used all her discipline and restraint to hold herself in check. The defenders were, as expected, slicing the kobold and goblin ranks to pieces, killing the enemy in a ratio far in excess of fifty to one.

That number would have easily doubled had Alustriel loosed her magic, but she could not. The drow were waiting patiently, and she respected the powers of those evil elves enough to know that her first attack might be her only one.

She whispered to the enchanted horses pulling the aerial chariot and moved lower, nodding grimly as she confirmed that the battle was going as anticipated. The slaughter high on the south face was complete, but the dark mass continued to flow below the struggle to the west.

Alustriel understood that many drow were among the ranks of that lower group.

The chariot swooped to the east, swiftly left the battle behind, and the Lady of Silverymoon took some comfort in the realization that the enemy lines were not so long, not so far beyond the eastern-most of the defensive positions.

She came to understand why when she heard yet another battle, around the mountain, to the east. The enemy had found Mithril Hall's eastern door, had entered the complex, and was battling the dwarves within!

Flashes of lightning and bursts of fire erupted within the shadows of that low door, and the creatures that entered were not diminutive kobolds or stupid goblins. They were dark elves, many, many dark elves.

She wanted to go down there, to rush over the enemy in a magical, explosive fury, but Alustriel had to trust in Bruenor's people. The tunnels had been prepared, she knew, and the attack from outside the mountain had been expected.

Her chariot flew on, around to the north, and Alustriel thought to complete the circuit, to cut low through Keeper's Dale in the east, where the other allies, another hundred of her Knights in Silver, waited.

What she saw did not settle well, did not comfort her.

The northern face of Fourthpeak was a treacherous, barren stretch of virtually unclimbable rock faces and broken ravines that no man could pass.

Virtually unclimbable, but not to the sticky feet of giant subterranean lizards.

Berg'inyon Baenre and his elite force, the four hundred famed lizard riders of House Baenre, scrambled across that northern facing, making swift progress to the west, toward Keeper's Dale.

The waiting knights had been positioned to shore up the final defenses against the force crossing the southern face. Their charge, if it came, would be to open up the last flank, to allow Besnell, the Longriders, and the men of Nesme and Settlestone to get into the dale, which was accessible through only one narrow pass.

The lizard-riders would get there first, Alustriel knew, and they outnumbered the waiting knights—and they were drow.

* * * * *

The easternmost position was surrendered. The barbarians, or what remained of their ranks, ran fast to the west, crossing behind the Knights in Silver to join Berkthgar.

After they had crossed, Besnell turned his force to the west as well, pushing Berkthgar's force, which had swelled to include nearly every living warrior from Settlestone, ahead.

The leader of the Knights in Silver began to think that Berkthgar's error would not be so devastating, that the retreat could proceed as planned. He found a high plateau and surveyed the area, nodding grimly as he noted that the enemy force below had rolled around the first three positions.

Besnell's eyes widened, and he gasped aloud as he realized the exact location of the leading edge of that dark cloud. The Riders of Nesme had missed their call! They had to get down the mountainside quickly, to hold that flank, and yet, for some reason, they had hesitated and the leading edge of the enemy force seemed beyond the fourth, and last, position.

Now the Riders of Nesme did come, and their full-out charge down the smoothest stone of the south face was indeed devastating, the forty horsemen trampling thrice that number of kobolds in mere moments.

But the enemy had that many to spare, Besnell knew, and many more beyond that. The plan had called for an organized retreat to the west, to Keeper's Dale, even in through Mithril Hall's western door if need be.

It was a good plan, but now the flank was lost and the way to the west was closed.

Besnell could only watch in horror.

Part 5

OLD KINGS AND OLD QUEENS

hey came as an army, but not so. *Eight thousand dark elves and a larger number of humanoid slaves, a mighty and massive force, swarmed toward Mithril Hall.*

The descriptions are fitting in terms of sheer numbers and strength, and yet "army" and "force" imply something more, a sense of cohesion and collective purpose. Certainly the drow are among the finest warriors in the Realms, trained to fight from the youngest age, alone or in groups, and certainly the purpose seems clear when the war is racial, when it is drow battling dwarves. Yet, though their tactics are perfect, groups working in unison to support each other, that cohesion among drow ranks remains superficial.

Few, if any, dark elves of Lloth's army would give her or his life to save another, unless she or he was confident that the sacrifice would guarantee a place of honor in the afterlife at the Spider Queen's side. Only a fanatic among the dark elves would take a hit, however minor, to spare another's life, and only because that fanatic thought the act in her own best interest. The drow came crying for the glory of the Spider Queen, but, in reality, they each were looking for a piece of her glory.

Personal gain was always the dark elves' primary precept.

That was the difference between the defenders of Mithril Hall and those who came to conquer. That was the one hope of our side when faced with such horrendous odds, outnumbered by skilled drow warriors!

If a single dwarf came to a battle in which his comrades were being overrun, he would roar in defiance and charge in headlong, however terrible the odds. Yet if we could catch a group of drow, a patrol, perhaps, in an ambush, those supporting groups flanking their unfortunate comrades would not join in unless they could be assured of victory.

We, not they, had true collective purpose. We, not they, understood cohesion, fought for a shared higher principle, and understood and accepted

224

that any sacrifice we might make would be toward the greater good.

There is a chamber—many chambers, actually—in Mithril Hall, where the heroes of wars and past struggles are honored. Wulfgar's hammer is there; so was the bow—the bow of an elf—that Catti-brie put into service once more. Though she has used the bow for years, and has added considerably to its legend, Catti-brie refers to it still as "the bow of Anariel," that long-dead elf. If the bow is put into service again by a friend of Clan Battlehammer centuries hence, it will be called "the bow of Catti-brie, passed from Anariel."

There is in Mithril Hall another place, the Hall of Kings, where the busts of Clan Battlehammer's patrons, the eight kings, have been carved, gigantic and everlasting.

The drow have no such monuments. My mother, Malice, never spoke of the previous matron mother of House Do'Urden, likely because Malice played a hand in her mother's death. In the Academy, there are no plaques of former mistresses and masters. Indeed, as I consider it now, the only monuments in Menzoberranzan are the statues of those punished by Baenre, of those struck by Vendes and her wicked whip, their skin turned to ebony, that they might then be placed on display as testaments of disobedience on the plateau of Tier Breche outside the Academy.

That was the difference between the defenders of Mithril Hall and those who came to conquer. That was the one hope.

— Drizzt Do'Urden

225

Chapter 23

POCKETS OF POWER

idderdoo had never seen anything to match it. Literally, it was raining kobolds and pieces of kobolds all about the terrified Harpell as the Gutbuster Brigade went into full battle lust. They had come into a small, wide chamber and found a force of kobolds many times their own number. Before Bidderdoo could suggest a retreat (or a "tactical flanking maneuver," as he planned to call it, because he knew the word "retreat" was not in Thibbledorf Pwent's vocabulary), Pwent had led the forthright charge.

Poor Bidderdoo had been sucked up in the brigade's wake, the seven frenzied dwarves blindly, happily, following Pwent's seemingly suicidal lead right into the heart of the cavern. Now it was a frenzy, a massacre the likes of which the studious Harpell, who had lived all his life in the sheltered Ivy Mansion (and a good part of that as a family dog) could not believe.

Pwent darted by him, a dead kobold impaled on his helmet spike and flopping limply. Arms wide, the battlerager leaped into a group of kobolds and pulled as many in as possible, hugging them tightly. Then he began to shake, to convulse so violently that Bidderdoo wondered if some agonizing poison had found its way into the dwarf's veins.

Not so, for this was controlled insanity. Pwent shook, and the nasty ridges of his armor took the skin from his hugged enemies, ripped and tore them. He broke away (and three kobolds fell dying) with a left hook that brought his mailed, spiked gauntlet several inches into the forehead of the next unfortunate enemy.

Bidderdoo came to understand that the charge was not suicidal, that the Gutbusters would win easily by overwhelming the greater numbers with sheer fury. He also realized, suddenly, that the kobolds learned fast to avoid the furious dwarves. Six of them bypassed Pwent, giving the battlerager a respectfully wide berth. Six of them swung about and bore down on the one enemy they could hope to defeat.

Bidderdoo fumbled with the shattered remains of his spellbook, flipping to one page where the ink had not smeared so badly. Holding the parchment in one hand, his other hand straight out in front of him, he began a fast chant, waggling his fingers.

A burst of magical energy erupted from each of his fingertips, green bolts rushing out, each darting and weaving to unerringly strike a target.

Five of the kobolds fell dead; the sixth came on with a shriek, its little sword rushing for Bidderdoo's belly.

The parchment fell from the terrified Harpell's hand. He screamed, thinking he was about to die, and reacted purely on instinct, falling forward over the blade, angling his chest down so that he buried the diminutive kobold beneath him. He felt a burning pain as the small creature's sword cut into his ribs, but there was no strength behind the blow and the sword did not dig in deeply.

Bidderdoo, so unused to combat, screamed in terror. And the pain, the pain . . .

Bidderdoo's screams became a howl. He looked down and saw the thrashing kobold, and saw more clearly the thrashing kobold's exposed throat.

Then he tasted warm blood and was not repulsed.

Growling, Bidderdoo closed his eyes and held on. The kobold stopped thrashing.

After some time, the poor Harpell noticed that the sounds of battle had ended about him. He gradually opened his eyes, turned his head slightly to look up at Thibbledorf Pwent, standing over him and nodding his head.

Only then did Bidderdoo realize he had killed the kobold, had bitten the thing's throat out.

"Good technique," Pwent offered, and started away.

* * * * *

While the Gutbuster Brigade's maneuvers were loud and straightforward, wholly dependent on savagery, another party's were a dance of stealth and ambush. Drizzt and Guenhwyvar, Catti-brie, Regis, and Bruenor moved silently from one tunnel to another, the drow and panther leading. Guenhwyvar was the first to detect an approaching enemy, and Drizzt quickly relayed the signals when the panther's ears went flat.

The five worked in unison, setting up so that Catti-brie, with her deadly bow, would strike first, followed by the panther's spring, the drow's impossibly fast rush into the fray, and Bruenor's typically dwarven roaring charge. Regis always found a way to get into the fight, usually moving in behind to slam a drow backside or a kobold's head with his mace when one of his friends became too closely pressed.

This time, though, Regis figured to stay out of the battle altogether. The group was in a wide, high corridor when Guenhwyvar, nearing a bend, fell into a crouch, ears flat. Drizzt slipped into the shadows of an alcove, as did Regis, while Bruenor stepped defensively in front of his archer daughter, so that Catti-brie could use the horns of his helmet to line up her shot.

Around the corner came the enemy, a group of minotaurs and drow, five of each, running swiftly in the general direction of Mithril Hall.

Catti-brie wisely went for the drow. There came a flash of silver, and one fell dead.

Guenhwyvar came out hard and fast, burying another dark elf, clawing and biting and rolling right away to bear down on a third drow.

A second flash came, and another elf fell dead.

But the minotaurs came on hard, and Catti-brie would get no third shot. She went for her sword as Bruenor roared and rushed out to meet the closest monster.

The minotaur lowered its bull-like head; Bruenor dropped his notched battle-axe right behind him over his head, holding the handle tightly in both hands.

In came the minotaur, and over came the axe. The crack sounded like the snapping of a gigantic tree.

Bruenor didn't know what hit him. Suddenly he was flying backward, bowled over by six hundred pounds of minotaur.

* * * * *

Drizzt came out spinning and darting. He hit the first minotaur from the side, a scimitar cutting deep into the back of the creature's thigh, stopping its charge. The ranger spun away and went down to one knee, jabbing straight ahead with Twinkle, hooking the tip of the blue-glowing scimitar over the next monster's kneecap.

The minotaur howled and half-fell, half-dove right for Drizzt, but the drow's feet were already under him, already moving, and the brute slammed hard into the stone.

Drizzt turned back for Catti-brie and Bruenor and the two remaining brutes bearing down on his friends. With incredible speed, he caught up to them almost immediately and his scimitars went to work on one, again going for the legs, stopping the charge.

But the last minotaur caught up to Catti-brie. Its huge club, made of hardened mushroom stalk, came flying about, and Catti-brie ducked fast, whipping her sword above her head.

Khazid'hea sliced right through the club, and as the minotaur stared at the remaining piece dumbfoundedly, Catti-brie countered with a slashing backhand.

The minotaur looked at her curiously. She could not believe she had missed.

* * * * *

Regis watched from the shadows, knowing he was overmatched by any enemy in this fight. He tried to gauge his companions, though, wanting to be ready if needed. Mostly he watched Drizzt, mesmerized by the sheer speed of the drow's charges and dodges. Drizzt had always been quick afoot, but this display was simply amazing, the ranger's feet moving so swiftly that Regis could hardly distinguish them. More than once, Regis tried to anticipate Drizzt's path, only to find himself looking where the drow was not.

For Drizzt had cut to the side, or reversed direction altogether, more quickly than the halfling would have believed possible.

Regis finally just shook his head and filed his questions away for another time, reminding himself that there were other, more important considerations. He glanced about and noticed the last of the enemy drow slipping to the side, out of the way of the panther.

* * * * *

The last drow wanted no part of Guenhwyvar, and was glad indeed that the woman with the killing bow was engaged in close combat. Two of his dark elf companions lay dead from arrows, a third squirmed about on the floor, half her face torn away by the panther's claws, and all five minotaurs were down or engaged. The fourth drow had run off, back around the bend, but that wicked panther was only a couple of strides behind, and the hiding dark elf knew his companion would be down in a matter of moments.

Still, the drow hardly cared, for he saw Drizzt Do'Urden, the renegade, the most hated. The ranger was fully engaged and vulnerable, working furiously to finish the three minotaurs he had wounded. If this drow could seize the opportunity and get Drizzt, then his place of glory, and his house's glory, would be sealed. Even if he was killed by Drizzt's friends, he would have a seat of honor beside Lloth, the Spider Queen.

He loaded his most potent dart, a bolt enchanted with runes of fire and lightning, onto his heavy, two-handed crossbow, an unusual weapon indeed for dark elves, and brought the sights in line.

Something hit the crossbow hard from the side. The drow pulled the trigger instinctively, but the bolt, knocked loose, went nowhere but down, exploding at his feet. The jolt sent him flying; the puff of flames singed his hair and blinded him momentarily.

He rolled over on the floor and managed to get out of his burning *piwafwi*. Dazed, he noticed a small mace lying on the floor, then saw a small, plump hand reaching down to pick it up. The drow tried to react as the bare feet, hairy on top—something the Underdark drow had never seen before—steadily approached.

Then all went dark.

* * * * *

Catti-brie cried out and leaped back, but the minotaur did not charge. Rather, the brute stood perfectly still, eyeing her curiously.

"I didn't miss," Catti-brie said, as if her denial of what seemed obvious would change her predicament. To her surprise, she found she was right.

The minotaur's left leg, severed cleanly by Khazid'hea's passing, caved in under it, and the brute fell sidelong to the floor, its lifeblood pouring out unchecked.

Catti-brie looked to the side to see Bruenor, grumbling and groaning, crawling out from under the minotaur he had killed. The dwarf hopped to his feet, shook his head briskly to clear away the stars, then stared at his axe, hands on hips, head shaking in dismay. The mighty weapon was embedded nearly a foot deep in the minotaur's thick skull.

"How in the Nine Hells am I going to get the damned thing out?" Bruenor asked, looking at his daughter.

Drizzt was done, as was Regis, and Guenhwyvar came back around the corner, dragging the last of the dark elves by the scruff of his broken neck.

"Another win for our side," Regis remarked as the friends regrouped.

Drizzt nodded his agreement but seemed not so pleased. It was a small thing they were doing, he knew, barely scratching at the surface of the force that had come to Mithril Hall. And despite the quickness of this latest encounter, and of the three before it, the friends had been, ultimately, lucky. What would have happened had another group of drow or minotaurs, or even kobolds, come about the corner while the fight was raging?

They had won quickly and cleanly, but their margin of victory was a finer line and a more tentative thing than the rout would indicate.

"Ye're not so pleased," Catti-brie said quietly to the ranger as they started off once more.

"In two hours we have killed a dozen drow, a handful of minotaurs and a score of kobold fodder," Drizzt replied.

"With thousands more to go," the woman added, understanding Drizzt's dismay.

Drizzt said nothing. His only hope, Mithril Hall's only hope, was that they and other groups like them would kill enough drow to take the heart from their enemy. Dark elves were a chaotic and supremely disloyal bunch, and only if the defenders of Mithril Hall could defeat the drow army's will for the war did

231

they have a chance.

Guenhwyvar's ears went flat again, and the panther slipped silently into the darkness. The friends, feeling suddenly weary of it all, moved into position and were relieved indeed when the newest group rambled into sight. No drow this time, no kobolds or minotaurs. A column of dwarves, more than a score, hailed them and approached. This group, too, had seen battle since the fight in Tunult's Cavern. Many showed fresh wounds, and every dwarven weapon was stained with enemy blood.

"How fare we?" Bruenor asked, stepping to the front.

The leader of the dwarven column winced, and Bruenor had his answer. "They're fightin' in the Undercity, me king," said the dwarf. "How they got into the place, we're not for knowin'! And fightin' too, in the upper levels, by all reports. The eastern door's been breached."

Bruenor's shoulders visibly slumped.

"But we're holdin' at Garumn's Gorge!" the dwarf said with more determination.

"Where're ye from and where're ye going?" Bruenor wanted to know.

"From the last guard room," the dwarf explained. "Come out in a short circuit to find yerself, me king. Tunnels're thick with drow scum, and glad we be to see ye standing!" He pointed behind Bruenor, then jabbed his finger to the left. "We're not so far, and the way's still clear to the last guard room . . ."

"But it won't be for long," another dwarf piped in glumly.

"And clear all the way to the Undercity from there," the leader finished.

Drizzt pulled Bruenor to the side and began a whispered conversation. Catti-brie and Regis waited patiently, as did the dwarves.

" . . . keep searching," they heard Drizzt say.

"Me place is with me people!" Bruenor roughly replied. "And yer own is with me!"

Drizzt cut him short with a long stream of words. Catti-brie and the others heard snatches such as "hunting the head" and "roundabout route," and they knew Drizzt was trying to convince Bruenor to let him continue his hunt through the outer, lower tunnels.

Catti-brie decided then and there that if Drizzt and Guenhwyvar were to go on, she, with her Cat's Eye circlet, which Alustriel had given her to allow her to see in the dark, would go with him. Regis, feeling unusually brave and useful, silently came to the same conclusion.

Still, the two were surprised when Drizzt and Bruenor walked back to the group.

"Get ye to the last guard room, and all the way to the Undercity if need be," Bruenor commanded the column leader.

The dwarf's jaw dropped with amazement. "But, me king," he sputtered.

"Get ye!" Bruenor growled.

"And leave yerself alone out here?" the stunned dwarf asked.

Bruenor's smile was wide and wicked as he looked from the dwarf to Drizzt, to Catti-brie, to Regis, and to Guenhwyvar, then finally, back to the dwarf.

"Alone?" Bruenor replied, and the other dwarf, knowing the prowess of his king's companions, conceded the point.

"Get ye back and win," Bruenor said to him. "Me and me friends got some huntin' to do."

The two groups split apart once more, both grimly determined, but neither overly optimistic.

Drizzt whispered something to the panther, and Guenhwyvar took up the lead as before. To this point, the companions had been lying in wait for every enemy group that came their way, but now, with the grim news from the Undercity and the eastern door, Drizzt changed that tactic. If they could not avoid the small groups of drow and other monsters, then they would fight, but otherwise, their path now was more direct. Drizzt wanted to find the priestesses (and he knew it had to be priestesses) who had led this march. The dwarves' only chance was to decapitate the enemy force.

And so the companions were now, as Drizzt had quietly put it to Bruenor, "hunting the head."

Regis, last in line, shook his head and looked more than once back the way the dwarven column had marched. "How do I always get myself into this?" the halfling whispered. Then, looking at the backs of his hardy, sometimes reckless friends, he knew he had his answer.

Catti-brie heard the halfling's resigned sigh, understood its source, and managed to hide her smile.

Chapter 24
FIERY FURY

lustriel watched from her high perch as the southern face of Fourthpeak flickered with light that seemed to be blinking like the stars above. The exchange of enchanted pellets from the defenders and countering dark magic from the invaders was furious. As she brought her chariot around the southwestern cliffs, the Lady of Silverymoon grew terribly afraid, for the defenders had been pushed into a **U** formation, surrounded on all sides by goblins, kobolds, and fierce drow warriors.

Still, the forces of the four armies fought well, practically back to back, and their line was strong. No great number could strike at them from the gap at the top of the **U**, the logical weak spot, because of the almost sheer cliffs, and the defenders were tightly packed enough along the entire line to hold against any concentrated assaults.

Even as Alustriel fostered that thought, her hopes were put to the test. A group of goblins, led by huge bugbears, seven-foot, hairy versions of goblins, formed into a tight diamond and spearheaded into the defenders' eastern flank.

The line wavered; Alustriel almost revealed herself with a flurry of explosive magic.

But amidst the chaos and the press rose one sword above all others, one song above all others.

Berkthgar the Bold, his wild hair flying, sang to Tempus with all his heart, and Bankenfuere hummed as it swept through the air. Berkthgar ignored the lesser goblins and charged straight for the bugbears, and each mighty swipe cut one of them down. The leader of Settlestone took a vicious hit, and another, but no hint of pain crossed his stern visage or slowed his determined march.

Those bugbears who escaped the first furious moments of the huge man's assault fled from him thereafter, and with their leaders so terrified, the goblins quickly lost heart for the press and the diamond disintegrated into a fleeing mob.

Many would be the songs to celebrate Berkthgar, Alustriel knew, but only if the defenders won. If the dark elves succeeded in their conquest, then all such heroics would be lost to the ages, all the songs would be buried beneath a black veil of oppression. That could not happen, the Lady of Silverymoon decided. Even if Mithril Hall were to fall this night, or the next, the war would not be lost. All of Silverymoon would mobilize against the drow, and she would go to Sundabar, in the east, to Citadel Adbar, stronghold of King Harbromme and his dwarves, and all the way to Waterdeep, on the Sword Coast, to muster the necessary forces to push the drow back to Menzoberranzan!

This war was not lost, she reminded herself, and she looked down at the determined defenders, holding against the swarm, fighting and dying.

Then came the tragedy she had expected and feared all along: the magical barrage, bursts of fireballs and lightning, lines of consuming magical energy and spinning bolts of destruction.

The assault focused on the southwestern corner of the U, blew apart the ranks of the Riders of Nesme, consuming horse and man alike. Many humanoid slaves fell as well, mere fodder and of no concern to the wicked drow wizards.

Tears streamed down Alustriel's face as she watched that catastrophe, as she heard the agonized cries of man and beast and saw that corner of the mountain become charred under the sheer power of the barrage. She berated herself for not foreseeing this war, for

R. A. Salvatore

underestimating the intensity of the drow march, for not having her army fully entrenched, warriors, wizards and priests alike, in the defense of Mithril Hall.

The massacre went on for many seconds, seeming like hours to the horrified defenders. It went on and on, the explosions and the cries.

Alustriel found her heart again and looked for the source, and when she saw it, she came to realize that the dark elf wizards, in their ignorance of the surface world, had erred.

They were concentrated within a copse of thick trees, under cover and hurling out their deadly volley of spells.

Alustriel's features brightened into a wicked smile, a smile of vengeance, and she cut her chariot across at a sharp angle, swooping down the mountainside from on high, flying like an arrow for the heart of her enemies.

The drow had erred; they were in the trees.

As she crossed the northern edge of the battlefield, Alustriel cried out a command, and her chariot, and the team of enchanted horses that pulled it, ignited into bright flames.

Below her she heard the cries of fear, from friend and enemy alike, and she heard the trumpets from the Knights in Silver, who recognized the chariot and understood that their leader had come.

Down she streaked, a tremendous fireball leading the way, exploding in the heart of the copse. Alustriel sped right to the trees' edge, then banked sharply and rushed along the thick line, the flames of her chariot igniting branches wherever she passed.

The drow wizards had erred!

She knew the dark elves had likely set up wards against countering magic—perhaps even over themselves—that would defeat even the most intense fires, but they did not understand the flammable nature of trees. Even if the fire did not consume them, the flames would blind them and effectively put them out of the fighting.

And the smoke! The thick copse was damp from previous rains and frost, and billowing black clouds thickened the air. Even worse for the drow, the wizards countered as they had always countered fire, with spells creating water. So great was their response, that the flames would have been quenched, except that Alustriel did not relent, continued to rush about the copse, even cut into the copse wherever she found a break. No water, not the ocean itself, could

236

extinguish the fires of her enchanted chariot. As she continued to fuel the flames, the drenching spells by the wizards added steam to the smoke, thickened the air so that the dark elves could not see at all and could not breathe.

Alustriel trusted in her horses, extensions of her will, to understand her intent and keep the chariot on course, and she watched, her spells ready, for she knew the enemy could not remain within the copse. As she expected, a drow floated up through the trees, rising above the inferno, levitating into the air and trying to orient himself to the scene beyond the copse.

Alustriel's lightning bolt hit him in the back of the head and sent him spinning over and over, and he hung, upside down and dead, until his own spell expired, dropping him back into the trees.

Even as she killed that wizard, though, a ball of flame puffed in the air right before the chariot, and the speeding thing, and Alustriel with it, plunged right through. The Lady of Silverymoon was protected from the flames of her own spell, but not so from the fireball, and she cried out and came through pained, her face bright from burn.

* * * * *

Higher up the mountainside, Besnell and his soldiers witnessed the attack against Alustriel. The elf steeled his golden eyes; his men cried out in outrage. If their earlier exploits had been furious, they were purely savage now, and Berkthgar's men, fighting beside them, needed no prodding.

Goblins and kobolds, bugbears and orcs, even huge minotaurs and skilled drow, died by the score in the next moments of battle.

It hardly seemed to matter. Whenever one died, two took its place, and though the knights and the barbarians could have cut through the enemy lines, there was nowhere for them to go.

Farther to the west, his own Longriders similarly pressed, Regweld understood their only hope. He leaped Puddlejumper to a place where there were no enemies and cast a spell to send a message to Besnell.

To the west! the wizard implored the knight leader.

Then Regweld took up the new lead and turned his men and the barbarians closest to them westward, toward Keeper's Dale, as

R. A. Salvatore

the original plan had demanded. The drow wizards had been silenced, momentarily at least, and now was the only chance Regweld would have.

A lightning bolt split the darkening air. A fireball followed, and Regweld followed that, leaping Puddlejumper over the ranks of his enemies and loosing a barrage of magical missiles below him as he flew.

Confusion hit the enemy ranks, enough so that the Longriders, men who had fought beside the Harpells for all their lives and understood Regweld's tactics, were able to slice through, opening a gap.

Beside them came many of the Settlestone warriors and the few remaining horsemen from Nesme. Behind them came the rest of the barbarian force and the Knights in Silver, mighty Berkthgar bringing up the rear, almost single-handedly keeping the pursuing monsters at bay.

The defenders punched through quickly, but found their momentum halted as another force, mostly drow, cut across in front, forming thick ranks.

Regweld continued his magical barrage, charged ahead with Puddlejumper, expecting to die.

And so he would have, except that Alustriel, forced away from the copse by the increasingly effective counters of the drow wizards, rushed back up the mountainside, right along the dark elf line, low enough so that the drow who did not flee were trampled and burned by her fiery passing.

Besnell and his men galloped to the front of the fleeing force, cried out to Alustriel and for the good of all goodly folk, and plunged into the confusion of the drow ranks, right into the flaming chariot's charred wake.

Many more men died in those few moments of hellish fighting, many men and many drow, but the defenders broke free to the west, ran and rode on, and found the path into Keeper's Dale before the enemy could block it.

Above the battle once more, Alustriel slumped with exhaustion. She had not launched so concentrated a barrage of magic in many, many years, and had not engaged so closely in any conflict since the days before she had come to rule Silverymoon. Now she was tired and wounded, burned and singed, and she had taken several hits by

238

sword and by quarrel as she had rushed along the drow ranks. She knew the disapproval she would find when she returned to Silverymoon, knew that her advisors, and the city's council, and colleagues from other cities, would think her rash, even stupid. Mithril Hall was a minor kingdom not worth her life, her detractors would say. To take such risks against so deadly an enemy was foolish.

So they would say, but Alustriel knew better, knew that the freedoms and rights that applied to Silverymoon were not there simply because of her city's size and strength. They applied to all, to Silverymoon, to Waterdeep, and to the smallest of kingdoms that so desired them, because otherwise the values they promoted were meaningless and selfish.

Now she was wounded, had nearly been killed, and she called off her chariot's flames as she rose high into the sky. To show herself so openly would invite a continuing magical attack that would likely destroy her. She was sorely wounded, she knew, but Alustriel was smiling. Even if she died this night, the Lady of Silverymoon would die smiling, because she was following her heart. She was fighting for something bigger than her life, for values that were eternal and ultimately right.

She watched with satisfaction as the force, led by Besnell and her own knights, broke free and sped for Keeper's Dale, then she climbed higher into the cold sky, angling for the west.

The enemy would pursue, and more enemies were coming fast around the north, and the battle had only just begun.

* * * * *

The Undercity, where two thousand dwarves often labored hard at their most beloved profession, had never seen such bustle and tumult as this day. Not even when the shadow dragon, Shimmergloom, and its host of evil gray dwarves had invaded, when Bruenor's grandfather had been king, had the Undercity been engulfed in such a battle.

Goblins and minotaurs, kobolds and wicked monsters that the dwarves could not name flooded in from the lower tunnels and through the floor itself, areas that had been breached by the magic of the illithids. And the drow, scores of dark elves, struggled and battled along every step and across the wide floor, their dance a

239

macabre mix of swirling shadows in the glow of the many low-burning furnaces.

Still, the main tunnels to the lower levels had not been breached, and the greatest concentration of enemies, particularly the drow force, remained outside Mithril Hall proper. Now the dark elves who had gained the Undercity meant to open that way, to link up with the forces of Uthegental and Matron Baenre.

And the dwarves meant to stop them, knowing that if that joining came to pass, then Mithril Hall would be lost.

Lightning flashed, green and red and sizzling black bolts from below, from the drow, and it was answered from above by Harkle and Bella don DelRoy.

The lowest levels began to grow darker as the drow worked their magic to gain a favorable battlefield.

The fall of light pellets upon the floor sounded like a gentle rain as Stumpet Rakingclaw and her host of dwarven priests countered the magic, brightening the area, loading spell after spell, stealing every shadow from every corner. Dwarves could fight in the dark, but they could fight in the light as well, and the drow and other creatures from the Underdark were not so fond of brightness.

One group of twenty dwarves formed a tight formation on the wide floor and rolled over a band of fleeing goblins. Their boots sounded like a heavy, rolling wheel, a general din, mowing over whatever monster dared to stay in their path.

A handful of dark elves fired stinging crossbow quarrels, but the dwarves shook off the hits—and, since their blood ran thick with potions to counter any poisons, they shook off the infamous drow sleeping drug as well.

Seeing that their attack was ineffective, the drow scattered, and the dwarven wedge rolled toward the next obstacle, two strange-looking creatures that the bearded folk did not know, two ugly creatures with slimy heads that waved tentacles where the mouths should have been, and with milky white eyes that showed no pupils.

The dwarven wedge seemed unstoppable, but when the illithids turned their way and loosed their devastating mental barrage, the wedge wobbled and fell apart, stunned dwarves staggering aimlessly.

"Oh, there they are!" Harkle squealed from the third tier of the Undercity, more than sixty feet from the floor.

Bella don DelRoy's face crinkled with disgust as she looked at mind flayers for the first time. She and Harkle had expected the creatures; Drizzt had told them about Matron Baenre's "pet." Despite her disgust, Bella, like all Harpells, was more curious than afraid. The illithids had been expected—she just hadn't expected them to be so damned ugly!

"Are you sure of this?" the diminutive woman asked Harkle, who had devised the strategy for fighting the squishy-headed things. Her good eye revealed her true hopes, though, for while she talked to Harkle, it remained fixated on the ugly illithids.

"Would I have gone to all the trouble of learning to cast from the different perspective?" Harkle answered, seeming wounded by her doubts.

"Of course," Bella replied. "Well, those dwarves do need our help."

"Indeed."

A quick chant by the daughter of DelRoy brought a shimmering blue, door-shaped field right before the two wizards.

"After you," Bella said politely.

"Oh, rank before beauty," Harkle answered, waving his hand toward the door, indicating that Bella should lead.

"No time for wasting!" came a clear voice behind them, and surprisingly strong hands pressed against both Bella and Harkle's hips, heaving them both for the door. They went through together, and Fret, the tidy dwarf, pushed in right behind them.

The second door appeared on the floor, between the illithids and their stunned dwarven prey, and out popped the three dimensional travelers. Fret skidded to the side, trying to round up the vulnerable dwarves, while Harkle and Bella don DelRoy mustered their nerve and faced the octopus-headed creatures.

"I understand your anger," Harkle began, and he and his companion shuddered as a wave of mental energy rolled across their chests and shoulders and heads, leaving a wake of tingles.

"If I were as ugly as you . . ." Harkle continued, and a second wave came through.

". . . I would be mean, too!" Harkle finished, and a third blast of energy came forth, followed closely by the illithids. Bella screamed and Harkle nearly fainted as the monstrous things pushed in close, tentacles latching onto cheeks and chins. One went straight up

241

R. A. Salvatore

Harkle's nose, in search of brain matter to devour.

"You are sure?" Bella cried out.

But Harkle, deep in the throes of his latest spell, didn't hear her. He didn't struggle against the illithid, for he didn't want the thing to jostle him too severely. It was hard enough to concentrate with wriggling tentacles burrowing under the skin of his face!

Those tentacles swelled now, extracting their prize.

An unmistakably sour look crossed the normally expressionless features of both the creatures.

Harkle's hands came up slowly, palms down, his thumbs touching and his other fingers spread wide. A flash of fire erupted from his hands, searing the confused illithid, burning its robes. It tried to pull away, and Harkle's facial skin bulged weirdly as the tentacles began to slide free.

Harkle was already moving with his next spell. He reached into his robes and extracted a dart, a leaf that had been mushed to powder, and a stringy, slimy thing, a snake's intestine, and squashed them all together as he completed the chant.

From that hand came forth a small bolt, shooting across the two feet to stick into the still-burning illithid's belly.

The creature gurgled something indecipherable and finally fell away, stumbling, grasping at its newest wound, for while the fires still nipped at it in places, this newest attack hurt more.

The enchanted bolt pumped acid into its victim.

Down went the illithid, still clutching at the leaking bolt. It had underestimated its enemy, and it telepathically sent that very message to its immediate companion, who already understood their error, and to Methil, deep in the caverns beside Matron Baenre.

Bella couldn't concentrate. Though her spell of polymorph had been perfect, her brain safely tucked away where the illithid could not find it, she simply couldn't concentrate with the squiggly tentacles probing around her skull. She berated herself, told herself that the daughter of DelRoy should be more in control.

She heard a rumbling sound, a cart rolling near, and opened her eyes to see Fret push the cart right up behind the illithid, a host of drow in pursuit. Holding his nerve, the tidy dwarf leaped atop the cart and drew out a tiny silver hammer.

"Let her go!" Fret cried, bringing the nasty little weapon to bear. To the dwarf's surprise, and disgust, his hammer sank into the engaged illithid's bulbous head and ichor spewed forth, spraying the dwarf and staining his white robes.

Fret knew the drow were bearing down on him; he had resolved to take one attack on the illithid, then turn in defense against the dark elves. But all plans flew away in the face of that gory mess, the one thing that could bring the tidy dwarf into full battle rage.

No woodpecker every hit a log as rapidly. Fret's hammer worked so as to seem a blur, and each hit sent more of the illithid's brain matter spraying, which only heightened the tidy dwarf's frenzy.

Still, that would have been the end of Fret, of all of them, had not Harkle quickly enacted his next spell. He focused on the area in front of the charging drow, threw a bit of lard into the air, and called out his next dweomer.

The floor became slick with grease, and the charge came to a stumbling, tumbling end.

Its head smashed to dripping pulp, the illithid slumped before Bella, the still-clinging tentacles bringing her low as well. She grabbed frantically at those tentacles and yanked them free, then stood straight and shuddered with pure revulsion.

"I told you that was the way to fight mind flayers!" Harkle said happily, for it had been his plan every step of the way.

"Shut up," Bella said to him, her stomach churning. She looked all about, seeing enemies closing in from many directions. "And get us out of here!" she said.

Harkle looked at her, confused and a bit wounded by her disdain. The plan had worked, after all!

A moment later, Harkle, too, became more than a little frightened, as he came to realize that he had forgotten that last little detail, and had no spells left that would transport them back to the higher tiers.

"Ummm," he stammered, trying to find the words to best explain their dilemma.

Relieved he was, and Bella, too, when the dwarven wedge reformed about them, Fret joining the ranks.

"We'll get ye back up," the leader of the grateful dwarves promised, and on they rolled, once more burying everything in their path.

Even more destructive now was their march, for every so often a blast of lightning or a line of searing fire shot out from their ranks as Harkle and Bella joined in the fun.

Still, Bella remained uncomfortable and wanted this all to end so that she could return to her normal physiology. Harkle had studied illithids intently, and knew as much about them as perhaps any wizard in all the Realms. Their mentally debilitating blasts were conical, he had assured her, and so, if he and she could get close, only the top half of their bodies would be affected.

Thus they had enacted the physical transformation enchantment, wherein Harkle and Bella appeared the same, yet had transfigured two areas of their makeup, their brains and their buttocks.

Harkle smiled at his cleverness as the wedge rolled on. Such a transformation had been a delicate thing, requiring many hours of study and preparation. But it had been worth the trouble, every second, the Harpell believed, recalling the sour looks on the ugly illithid faces!

* * * * *

The rumbles from the collapse of the bridges, and of all the antechambers near Garumn's Gorge, were felt in the lowest tunnels of Mithril Hall, even beyond, in the upper passages of the wild Underdark itself. How much work Bruenor's people would have if ever they tried to open the eastern door again!

But the drow advance had been stopped, and was well worth the price. For now General Dagna and his force of defenders were free to go.

But where? the tough, battle-hardened dwarf wondered. Reports came to him that the Undercity was under full attack, but he also realized that the western door, near Keeper's Dale, was vulnerable, with only a few hundred dwarves guarding the many winding tunnels and with no provisions for such catastrophic measures as had been taken here in the east. The tunnels in the west could not be completely dropped; there had not been time to rig them so.

Dagna looked around at his thousand troops, many of them wounded, but all of them eager for more battle, eager to defend their sacred homeland.

"The Undercity," the general announced a moment later. If the western door was breached, the invaders would have to find their way through, no easy task considering the myriad choices they would face. The fighting had already come to the Undercity, so that was where Dagna belonged.

Normally it would have taken many minutes, a half hour or more, for the dwarves to get down to the fighting, even if they went the whole way at a full charge. But this, too, had been foreseen, so Dagna led his charges to the appointed spot, new doors that had been cut into the walls connecting to chimneys running up from the great furnaces. As soon as those doors were opened, Dagna and his soldiers heard the battle, so they went without delay, one after another, onto the heavy ropes that had been set in place.

Down they slid, fearlessly, singing songs to Clanggedon. Down they went, hitting the floor at a full run, rushing out of the warm furnaces and right into the fray, streaming endlessly, it seemed, as were the drow coming in from the lower tunnels.

The fighting in the Undercity grew ever furious.

Chapter 25

KEEPER'S DALE

erg'inyon's force swept into Keeper's Dale, the sticky-footed lizards making trails where none could be found. They came down the northern wall like a sheet of water, into the misty valley, ominous shadows slipping past tall pillars of stone.

Though it was warmer here than on the open northern face, the drow were uncomfortable. There were no formations like this in the Underdark, no misty valleys, except those filled with the toxic fumes of unseen volcanoes. Scouting reports had been complete, though, and had specifically outlined this very spot, the doorstep of Mithril Hall's western door, as safe for passage. Thus, the Baenre lizard riders went into the valley without question, fearing their own volatile matron mother more than any possible toxic fumes.

As they entered the vale, they heard the fighting on the southern side of the mountain. Berg'inyon nodded when he took the moment to notice that the battle was coming closer—all was going as planned. The enemy was in retreat, no doubt, being herded like stupid rothe into the valley, where the slaughter

246

would begin in full.

The moving shadows that were Berg'inyon's force slipped quietly through the mist, past the stone sentinels, trying to get a lay of the valley, trying to find the optimum ambush areas.

Above the mist, a line of fire broke the general darkness of the night sky, streaking fast and angling into the vale. Berg'inyon watched it, as did so many, not knowing what it might be.

As she crossed above the force, Alustriel loosed the last barrage of her magic, a blast of lightning, a rain of greenish pulses of searing energy, and a shower of explosive fireballs that liquified stone.

The alert dark elves responded before the chariot crossed over the northern lip of the vale, hit back with enchanted crossbow quarrels and similar spells of destruction.

The flames of the chariot flared wider, caught in the midst of a fireball, and the whole of the cart jerked violently to the side as a line of lightning blasted against its base.

Alustriel's magic had killed more than a few, and taken the mounts out from under many others, but the real purpose in the wizard's passing had been the part of decoy, for every drow eye was turned heavenward when the second battalion of the Knights in Silver joined the fray, charging through Keeper's Dale, horseshoes clacking deafeningly on the hard stone.

Lances lowered, the knights barreled through the initial ranks of drow, running them down with their larger mounts.

But these were the Baenre lizard riders, the most elite force in all of Menzoberranzan, a complement of warriors and wizards that did not know fear.

Silent commands went out from Berg'inyon, passed from waggling fingers to waggling fingers. Even after the surprise barrage from the sky and the sudden charge of the force that the drow did not know were in Keeper's Dale, the dark elf ranks outnumbered the Knights in Silver by more than three to one. Had those odds been one-to-one, the Knights in Silver still would have had no chance.

The tide turned quickly, with the knights, those who were not taken down, inevitably falling back and regrouping into tight formations. Only the mist and the unfamiliar terrain prevented the slaughter from being wholesale; only the fact that the overwhelming drow force could not find all the targets allowed the valiant knights to continue to resist.

Near the rear of the dark elf ranks, Berg'inyon heard the commotion as one unfortunate human got separated and confused, galloping his mount unintentionally toward the north, away from his comrades.

The Baenre son signaled for his personal guards to follow him, but to stay behind, and took up the chase, his great lizard slinking and angling to intercept. He saw the shadowy figure—and what a magnificent thing Berg'inyon thought the rider to be, so high and tall on his powerful steed.

That image did not deter the weapon master of Menzoberranzan's first house. He came around a pillar of stone, just to the side of the knight, and called out to the man.

The great horse skidded and stopped, the knight wheeling it about to face Berg'inyon. He said something Berg'inyon could not understand, some proclamation of defiance, no doubt, then lowered his long lance and kicked his horse into a charge.

Berg'inyon leveled his own mottled lance and drove his heels into the lizard's flanks, prodding the beast on. He couldn't match the speed of the knight's horse, but the horse couldn't match the lizard's agility. As the opponents neared, Berg'inyon swerved aside, brought his lizard right up the side of a thick stone pillar.

The knight, surprised by the quickness of the evasion, couldn't bring his lance out fast enough for an effective strike, but as the two passed, Berg'inyon managed to prod the running horse in the flank. It wasn't a severe hit, barely a scratch, but this was no ordinary lance. The ten-foot pole that Berg'inyon carried was a devilish death lance, among the most cunning and wicked of drow weapons. As the lance tip connected on the horseflesh, cutting through the metal armor the beast wore as though it were mere cloth, dark, writhing tentacles of black light crawled down its length.

The horse whinnied pitifully, kicked and jumped and came to a skidding stop. Somehow the knight managed to hold his seat.

"Run on!" he cried to his shivering mount, not understanding. "Run on!"

The knight suddenly felt as though the horse was somehow less substantial beneath him, felt the beast's ribs against his calves.

The horse threw its head back and whinnied again, an unearthly, undead cry, and the knight blanched when he looked into the thing's eyes, orbs that burned red with some evil enchantment.

The death lance had stolen the creature's life-force, had turned the proud, strong stallion into a gaunt, skeletal thing, an undead, evil thing. Thinking quickly, the knight dropped his lance, drew his huge sword, and sheared off the monster's head with a single swipe. He rolled aside as the horse collapsed beneath him, and came to his feet, hopping around in confusion.

Dark shapes encircled him; he heard the hiss of nearby lizards, the sucking sounds as sticky feet came free of stone.

Berg'inyon Baenre approached slowly. He, too, lowered his lance. A flick of his wrist freed him from his binding saddle, and he slid off his mount, determined to test one of these surface men in single combat, determined to show those drow nearby the skill of their leader.

Out came the weapon master's twin swords, sharp and enchanted, among the very finest of drow weapons.

The knight, nearly a foot taller than this adversary, but knowing the reputation of dark elves, was rightfully afraid. He swallowed that fear, though, and met Berg'inyon head-on, sword against sword.

The knight was good, had trained hard for all of his adult life, but if he trained for all of his remaining years as well, they would not total the decades the longer-living Berg'inyon had spent with the sword.

The knight was good. He lived for almost five minutes.

*　*　*　*　*

Alustriel felt the chill, moist air of a low cloud brush her face, and it brought her back to consciousness. She moved quickly, trying to right the chariot, and felt the bite of pain all along her side.

She had been hit by spell and by weapon, and her burned and torn robes were wet with her own blood.

What would the world think if she, the Lady of Silverymoon, died here? she wondered. To her haughty colleagues, this was a

R. A. Salvatore

minor war, a battle that had no real bearing on the events of the
world, a battle, in their eyes, that Alustriel of Silverymoon should
have avoided.

Alustriel brushed her long, silvery hair—hair that was also
matted with blood—back from her beautiful face. Anger welled
within her as she thought of the arguments she had fought over
King Bruenor's request for aid. Not a single advisor or councilor
in Silverymoon, with the exception of Fret, wanted to answer that
call, and Alustriel had to wage a long, tiresome battle of words to
get even the two hundred Knights in Silver released to Mithril
Hall.

What was happening to her own city? the lady wondered
now, floating high above the disaster of Fourthpeak. Silverymoon
had earned a reputation as the most generous of places, as a
defender of the oppressed, champion of goodness. The knights
had gone off to war eagerly, but they weren't the problem, and
had never been.

The problem, the wounded Alustriel came to realize, was the
comfortably entrenched bureaucratic class, the political leaders
who had become too secure in the quality of their own lives. That
seemed crystal clear to Alustriel now, wounded and fighting hard
to control her enchanted chariot in the cold night sky above the
battle.

She knew the heart of Bruenor and his people; she knew the
goodness of Drizzt, and the value of the hardy men of Settlestone.
They were worth defending, Alustriel believed. Even if all of Silverymoon were consumed in the war, these people were worth
defending, because, in the end, in the annals future historians
would pen, that would be the measure of Silverymoon; that gen-
erosity would be the greatness of the place, would be what set Silverymoon apart from so many other petty kingdoms.

But what was happening to her city? Alustriel wondered, and
she came to understand the cancer that was growing amidst her
own ranks. She would go back to Silverymoon and purge that disease, she determined, but not now.

Now she needed rest. She had done her part, to the best of her
abilities, and, perhaps at the price of her own life, she realized as
another pain shot through her wounded side.

Her colleagues would lament her death, would call it a waste,

250

considering the minor scale of this war for Mithril Hall.

Alustriel knew better, knew how she, like her city, would be ultimately judged.

She managed to bring the chariot crashing down to a wide ledge, and she tumbled out as the fiery dweomer dissipated into nothingness.

The Lady of Silverymoon sat there against the stone, in the cold, looking down on the distant scramble far below her. She was out of the fight, but she had done her part.

She knew she could die with no guilt weighing on her heart.

* * * * *

Berg'inyon Baenre rode through the ranks of lizard-mounted drow, holding high his twin bloodstained swords. The dark elves rallied behind their leader, filtered from obelisk to obelisk, cutting the battlefield in half and more. The mobility and speed of the larger horses favored the knights, but the dark elves' cunning tactics were quick to steal that advantage.

To their credit, the knights were killing drow at a ratio of one to one, a remarkable feat considering the larger drow numbers and the skill of their enemies. Even so, the ranks of knights were being diminished.

Hope came in the form of a fat wizard riding a half-horse, half-frog beastie and leading the remnants of the defenders of the southern face, hundreds of men, riding and running—from battle and into battle.

Berg'inyon's force was fast pushed across the breadth of Keeper's Dale, back toward the northern wall, and the defending knights rode free once more.

But in came the pursuit from the south, the vast force of drow and humanoid monsters. In came those dark elf wizards who had survived Alustriel's conflagration in the thick copse.

The ranks of the defenders quickly sorted out, with Berkthgar's hardy warriors rallying behind their mighty leader and Besnell's knights linking with the force that had stood firm in Keeper's Dale. Likewise did the Longriders fall into line behind Regweld, and the Riders of Nesme—both of the survivors—joined their brethren from the west.

R. A. Salvatore

Magic flashed and metal clanged and man and beast screamed in agony. The mist thickened with sweat, and the stone floor of the valley darkened with blood.

The defenders would have liked to form a solid line of defense, but to do so would leave them terribly vulnerable to the wizards, so they had followed savage Berkthgar's lead, had plunged into the enemy force headlong, accepting the sheer chaos.

Berg'inyon ran his mount halfway up the northern wall, high above the valley, to survey the glorious carnage. The weapon master cared nothing for his dead comrades, including many dark elves, whose broken bodies littered the valley floor.

This fight would be won easily, Berg'inyon thought, and the western door to Mithril Hall would be his.

All glory for House Baenre.

* * * * *

When Stumpet Rakingclaw came up from the Undercity to Mithril Hall's western door, she was dismayed—not by the reports of the vicious fighting out in Keeper's Dale, but by the fact that the dwarven guards had not gone out to aid the valiant defenders.

Their orders had been explicit: they were to remain inside the complex, to defend the tighter tunnels, and then, if the secret door was found by the enemy and the defenders were pushed back, the dwarves were prepared to drop those tunnels near the door. Those orders, given by General Dagna, Bruenor's second in command, had not foreseen the battle of Keeper's Dale.

Bruenor had appointed Stumpet as High Cleric of Mithril Hall, and had done so publicly and with much fanfare, so that there would be no confusion concerning rank once battle was joined. That decision, that public ceremony, gave Stumpet the power she needed now, allowed her to change the orders, and the five hundred dwarves assigned to guard the western door, who had watched with horror the carnage from afar, were all too happy to hear the new command.

There came a rumbling beneath the ground in all of Keeper's Dale, the grating of stone against stone. On the northern side of

252

the valley, Berg'inyon held tight to his sticky-footed mount and hoped the thing wouldn't be shaken from the wall. He listened closely to the echoes, discerning the pattern, then looked to the southeastern corner of the valley.

A glorious, stinging light flashed there as the western door of Mithril Hall slid open.

Berg'inyon's heart skipped a beat. The dwarves had opened the way!

Out they came, hundreds of bearded folk, rushing to their allies' aid, singing and banging their axes and hammers against their shining shields, pouring from the door that was secret no more. They came up to, and beyond, Berkthgar's line, their tight battle groups slicing holes in the ranks of goblin and kobold and drow alike, pushing deeper into the throng.

"Fools!" the Baenre weapon master whispered, for even if a thousand, or two thousand dwarves came into Keeper's Dale, the course of the battle would not be changed. They had come out because their morals demanded it, Berg'inyon knew. They had opened their door and abandoned their best defenses because their ears could not tolerate the screams of men dying in their defense.

How weak these surface dwellers were, the sinister drow thought, for in Menzoberranzan courage and compassion were never confused.

The furious dwarves came into the battle hard, driving through drow and goblins with abandon. Stumpet Rakingclaw, fresh from her exploits in the Undercity, led their charge. She was out of light pellets but called to her god now, enacting enchantments to brighten Keeper's Dale. The dark elves quickly countered every spell, as the dwarf expected, but Stumpet figured that every drow concentrating on a globe of darkness was out of the fight, at least momentarily. The magic of Moradin, Dumathoin, and Clanggedon flowed freely through the priestess. She felt as though she was a pure conduit, the connection to the surface for the dwarven gods.

The dwarves rallied around her loud prayers as she screamed to her gods with all her heart. Other defenders rallied around the dwarves, and suddenly they were gaining back lost ground. Suddenly the idea of a single line of defense was not so ridiculous.

High on the wall across the way, Berg'inyon chuckled at the futility of it all. This was a temporary surge, he knew, and the defenders of the western door had come together in one final, futile push. All the defense and all the defenders, and Berg'inyon's force still outnumbered them several times over.

The weapon master coaxed his mount back down the wall, gathered his elite troops about him, and determined how to turn back the momentum. When Keeper's Dale fell, so, too, would the western door.

And Keeper's Dale would fall, Berg'inyon assured his companions with all confidence, within the hour.

Chapter 26
SNARL AGAINST SNARL

he main corridors leading to the lower door of Mithril Hall had been dropped and sealed, but that had been expected by the invading army. Even with the largest concentration of drow slowed to a crawl out in the tunnels beyond the door, the dwarven complex was hard pressed. And although no reports had come to Uthegental about the fighting outside the mountain, the mighty weapon master could well imagine the carnage on the slopes, with dwarves and weakling humans dying by the score. Both doors of Mithril Hall were likely breached by now, Uthegental believed, with Berg'inyon's lizard riders flooding the higher tunnels.

That notion bothered the weapon master of Barrison del'Armgo more than a little. If Berg'inyon was in Mithril Hall, and Drizzt Do'Urden was there, the renegade might fall to the son of House Baenre. Thus Uthegental and the small band of a half-dozen elite warriors he took in tow now sought the narrow ways that would get them to the lowest gate of Mithril Hall proper. Those tunnels should be open, with the dark elves filtering out from the Undercity to clear the way.

R. A. Salvatore

The weapon master and his escort came into the cavern that had previously served as Bruenor's command post. It was deserted now, with only a few parchments and scraps from clerical preparations to show that anyone had been in the place. After the fall of the tunnels and the collapse of portions of Tunult's Cavern (and many side tunnels, including the main one that led back to this chamber), Bruenor's lower groups apparently had been scattered, without any central command.

Uthegental passed through the place, hardly giving it a thought. The drow band moved swiftly down the corridors, staying generally east, silently following the weapon master's urgent lead. They came to a wide fork in the trail and noticed the very old bones of a two-headed giant lying against the wall—ironically, a kill Bruenor Battlehammer had made centuries before. Of more concern, though, was the fork in the tunnel.

Frustrated at yet another delay, Uthegental sent scouts left and right, then he and the rest of his group went right, the more easterly course.

Uthegental sighed, relieved that they had at last found the lower door, when his scout and another drow, a priestess, met him a few moments later.

"Greetings, Weapon Master of the Second House," the priestess greeted, affording mighty Uthegental more respect than was normally given to mere males.

"Why are you out in the tunnels?" Uthegental wanted to know. "We are still far from the Undercity."

"Farther than you think," the priestess replied, looking disdainfully back toward the east, down the long tunnel that ended at the lower door. "The way is not clear."

Uthegental issued a low growl. Those dark elves should have taken the Undercity by now, and should have opened the passages. He stepped by the female, his pace revealing his anger.

"You'll not break through," the priestess assured him, and he spun about, scowling as though she had slapped him in the face.

"We have been striking at the door for an hour," the priestess explained. "And we shall spend another week before we get past that barricade. The dwarves defend it well."

"*Ultrin sargtlin!*" Uthegental roared, his favorite title, to remind the priestess of his reputation. Still, despite the fact that Uthegental

256

had earned that banner of "Supreme Warrior," the female did not seem impressed.

"A hundred drow, five wizards, and ten priestesses have not breached the door," she said evenly. "The dwarves strike back against our magic with great spears and balls of flaming pitch. And the tunnel leading to the door is narrow and filled with traps, as well defended as House Baenre itself. Twenty minotaurs went down there, and those dozen that stumbled past the traps found hardy dwarves waiting for them, coming out of concealment from small, secret cubbies. Twenty minotaurs were slain in the span of a few minutes.

"You'll not break through," the priestess said again, her tone matter-of-fact and in no way insulting. "None of us will unless those who have entered the dwarven complex strike at the defenders of the door from behind."

Uthegental wanted to lash out at the female, mostly because he believed her claim.

"Why would you wish to enter the complex?" the female asked unexpectedly, slyly.

Uthegental eyed her with suspicion, wondering if she was questioning his bravery. Why wouldn't he want to find the fighting, after all?

"Whispers say your intended prey is Drizzt Do'Urden," the priestess went on.

Uthegental's expression shifted from suspicion to intrigue.

"Other whispers say the renegade is in the tunnels outside Mithril Hall," she explained, "hunting with his panther and killing quite a few drow."

Uthegental ran a hand through his spiked hair and looked back to the west, to the wild maze of tunnels he had left behind. He felt a surge of adrenaline course through his body, a tingling that tightened his muscles and set his features in a grim lock. He knew that many groups of enemies were operating in the tunnels outside the dwarven complex, scattered bands fleeing the seven-chambered cavern where the first battle had been fought. Uthegental and his companions had met and slain one such group of dwarves on their journey to this point.

Now that he thought about it, it made sense to Uthegental that Drizzt would be out here as well. It was very likely the renegade had been in the battle in the seven-chambered cavern, and, if that

257

was true, then why would Drizzt flee back into Mithril Hall?

Drizzt was a hunter, a former patrol leader, a warrior that had survived a decade alone with his magical panther in the wild Underdark—no small feat, and one that even Uthegental respected.

Yes, now that the priestess had told him the rumor, it made perfect sense to Uthegental that Drizzt Do'Urden would be out there, somewhere back in the tunnels to the west, roaming and killing. The weapon master laughed loudly and started back the way he had come, offering no explanation.

None was needed, to the priestess or to Uthegental's companions, who fell into line behind him.

The weapon master of the second house was hunting.

*   *   *   *   *

"We are winning," Matron Baenre declared.

None of those around her—not Methil or Jarlaxle, not Matron Zeerith Q'Xorlarrin, of the fourth house, or Auro'pol Dyrr, matron mother of House Agrach Dyrr, now the fifth house, not Bladen'Kerst or Quenthel Baenre—argued the blunt statement.

Gandalug Battlehammer, dirty and beaten, his wrists bound tightly by slender shackles so strongly enchanted that a giant could not break them, cleared his throat, a noise that sounded positively gloating. There was more bluster than truth in the dwarf's attitude, for Gandalug carried with him a heavy weight. Even if his folk were putting up a tremendous fight, dark elves had gotten into the Undercity. And they had come to that place because of Gandalug, because of his knowledge of the secret ways. The old dwarf understood that no one could withstand the intrusions of an illithid, but the guilt remained, the notion that he, somehow, had not been strong enough.

Quenthel moved before Bladen'Kerst could react, smacking the obstinate prisoner hard across the back, her fingernails drawing lines of blood.

Gandalug snorted again, and this time Bladen'Kerst whacked him with her five-tonged snake-headed whip, a blow that sent the sturdy dwarf to his knees.

"Enough!" Matron Baenre growled at her daughters, a hint of her underlying frustration showing through.

They all knew—and it seemed Baenre did as well, despite her

258

proclamation—that the war was not going according to plan. Jarlaxle's scouts had informed them of the bottleneck near Mithril Hall's lowest door, and that the eastern door from the surface had been blocked soon after it was breached, at a cost of many drow lives. Quenthel's magical communications with her brother told her that the fighting was still furious on the southern and western slopes of Fourthpeak, and that the western door from the surface had not yet been approached. And Methil, who had lost his two illithid companions, had telepathically assured Matron Baenre that the fight for the Undercity was not yet won, not at all.

Still, there was a measure of truth in Baenre's prediction of victory, they all knew, and her confidence was not completely superficial. The battle outside the mountain was not finished, but Berg'inyon had assured Quenthel that it soon would be—and given the power of the force that had gone out beside Berg'inyon, Quenthel had no reason to doubt his claim.

Many had died in these lower tunnels, but most of the losses had been humanoid slaves, not dark elves. Now those dwarves who had been caught outside their complex after the tunnel collapse had been forced into tactics of hunt and evade, a type of warfare that surely favored the stealthy dark elves.

"All the lower tunnels will soon be secured," Matron Baenre elaborated, a statement made obvious by the simple fact that this group, which would risk no encounters, was on the move once more. The elite force surrounding Baenre was responsible for guiding and guarding the first matron mother. They would not allow Baenre any advancement unless the area in front of them was declared secure.

"The region above the ground around Mithril Hall will also be secured," Baenre added, "with both surface doors to the complex breached."

"And likely dropped," Jarlaxle dared to put in.

"Sealing the dwarves in their hole," Matron Baenre was quick to respond. "We will fight through this lower door, and our wizards and priestesses will find and open new ways into the tunnels of the complex, that we might filter among our enemy's ranks."

Jarlaxle conceded the point, as did the others, but what Baenre was talking about would take quite a bit of time, and a drawn out siege had not been part of the plan. The prospect did not sit well with any of those around Matron Baenre, particularly the other two matron mothers. Baenre had pressured them to come out, so they had, though their houses, and all the city, was in a critical power flux. In exchange for the personal attendance of the matron mothers in the long march, House Xorlarrin and House Agrach Dyrr had been allowed to keep most of their soldiers at home, while the other houses, particularly the other ruling houses, had sent as much as half their complement of dark elves. For the few months that the army was expected to be away, the fourth and fifth Houses seemed secure.

But Zeerith and Auro'pol had other concerns, worries of power struggles within their families. The hierarchy of any drow house, except perhaps for Baenre, was always tentative, and the two matron mothers knew that if they were away for too long, they might return to find they had been replaced.

They exchanged concerned looks now, doubting expressions that ever observant Jarlaxle did not miss.

Baenre's battle group moved along on its slow and determined way, the three matron mothers floating atop their driftdisks, flanked by Baenre's two daughters (dragging the dwarf) and the illithid, who seemed to glide rather than walk, his feet hidden under his long, heavy robes. A short while later, Matron Baenre informed them that they would find an appropriate cavern and set up a central throne room, from which she could direct the continuing fight.

It was another indication that the war would be a long one, and again Zeerith and Auro'pol exchanged disconcerted looks.

Bladen'Kerst Baenre narrowed her eyes at both of them, silently threatening.

Jarlaxle caught it all, every connotation, every hint of where Matron Baenre might find her greatest troubles.

The mercenary leader bowed low and excused himself, explaining that he would join up with his band and try to garner more timely information.

Baenre waved her hand, dismissing him without a second thought. One of her escorts was not so casual.

You and your mercenaries will flee, came an unexpected message in Jarlaxle's mind.

The mercenary's own thoughts whirled in a jumble, and, caught off guard, he couldn't avoid sending the telepathic reply that the notion of deserting the war had indeed crossed his mind. As close to desperation as he had ever been, Jarlaxle looked back over his shoulder at the expressionless face of the intruding illithid.

Beware of Baenre should she return, Methil imparted casually, and he continued on his way with Baenre and the others.

Jarlaxle paused for a long while when the group moved out of sight, scrutinizing the emphasis of the illithid's last communication. He came to realize that Methil would not inform Baenre of his wavering loyalty. Somehow, from the way the message had been given, Jarlaxle knew that.

The mercenary leaned against a stone wall, thinking hard about what his next move should be. If the drow army stayed together, Baenre would eventually win—that much he did not doubt. The losses would be greater than anticipated (they already had been), but that would be of little concern once Mithril Hall was taken, along with all its promised riches.

What, then, was Jarlaxle to do? The disturbing question was still bouncing about the mercenary's thoughts when he found some of his Bregan D'aerthe lieutenants, all bearing news of the continuing bottleneck near the lower door, and information that even more dark elves and slaves were being killed in the outer tunnels, falling prey to roving bands of dwarves and their allies.

The dwarves were defending, and fighting, well.

Jarlaxle made his decision and relayed it silently to his lieutenants in the intricate hand code. Bregan D'aerthe would not desert, not yet. But neither would they continue to spearhead the attack, risking their forward scouts.

Avoid all fights, Jarlaxle's fingers flashed, and the gathered soldiers nodded their accord. *We stay out of the way, and we watch, nothing more.*

Until Mithril Hall is breached, one of the lieutenants reasoned back.

Jarlaxle nodded. *Or until the war becomes futile*, his fingers replied, and from his expression, it was obvious the mercenary leader did not think his last words ridiculous.

* * * * *

Pwent and his band rambled through tunnel after tunnel, growing frustrated, for they found no drow, or even kobolds, to slam.

"Where in the Nine Hells are we?" the battlerager demanded. No answer came in reply, and when he thought about it, Pwent really couldn't expect one. He knew these tunnels better than any in his troupe, and if he had no idea where they were, then certainly the others were lost.

That didn't bother Pwent so much. He and his furious band really didn't care where they were as long as they had something to fight. Lack of enemies was the real problem.

"Start to bangin'!" Pwent roared, and the Gutbusters ran to the walls in the narrow corridor and began slamming hammers against the stone, causing such a commotion that every creature within two hundred yards would easily be able to figure out where they were.

Poor Bidderdoo Harpell, swept up in the wake of the craziest band of suicidal dwarves, stood in the middle of the tunnel, using his glowing gem to try to sort through the few remaining parchments from his blasted spellbook, looking for a spell, any spell (though preferably one that would get him out of this place!).

The racket went on for several minutes, and then, frustrated, Pwent ordered his dwarves to form up, and off they stormed. They went under a natural archway, around a couple of bends in the passage, then came upon a wider and squarer way, a tunnel with worked stone along its walls and an even floor. Pwent snapped his fingers, realizing that they had struck out to the west and south of Mithril Hall. He knew this place, and knew that he would find a dwarven defensive position around the next corner. He bobbed around in the lead, and scrambled over a barricade that reached nearly to the ceiling, hoping to find some more allies to "enlist" into his terror group. As he crested the wall, Pwent stopped short, his smile erased.

Ten dwarves lay dead on the stone floor, amidst a pile of torn goblins and orcs.

Pwent fell over the wall, landed hard, but bounced right back to his feet. He shook his head as he walked among the carnage. This position was strongly fortified, with the high wall behind, and a lower wall in front, where the corridor turned a sharp corner to the left.

Mounted against that left-hand wall, just before the side tunnel, was a curious contraption, a deadly dwarven side-slinger catapult, with a short, strong arm that whipped around to the side, not over the top, as with conventional catapults. The arm was pulled back now, ready to fire, but Pwent noticed immediately that all the ammunition was gone, that the valiant dwarves had held out to the last.

Pwent could smell the remnants of that catapult's missiles and could see flickering shadows from the small fires. He knew before he peeked around the bend that many, many dead enemies would line the corridor beyond.

"They died well," the battlerager said to his minions as they and Bidderdoo crossed the back wall and walked among the bodies.

The charge around the corner came fast and silent, a handful of dark elves rushing out, swords drawn.

Had Bidderdoo Harpell not been on the alert (and had he not found the last remaining usable page of his spellbook), that would have been the swift end of the Gutbuster Brigade, but the wizard got his spell off, enacting a blinding (to the drow) globe of brilliant light.

The surprised dark elves hesitated just an instant, but long enough for the Gutbusters to fall into battle posture. Suddenly it was seven dwarves against five dark elves, the element of surprise gone. Seven battleragers against five dark elves, and what was worse for the drow, these battleragers happened to be standing among the bodies of dead kin.

They punched and kicked, jumped, squealed and head-butted with abandon, ignoring any hits, fighting to make their most wild leader proud. They plowed under two of the drow, and one dwarf broke free, roaring as he charged around the bend.

Pwent got one drow off to the side, caught the dark elf's swinging sword in one metal gauntlet and punched straight out with the other before the drow could bring his second sword to bear.

The drow's head verily exploded under the weight of the spiked gauntlet, furious Pwent driving his fist right through the doomed creature's skull.

He hit the drow again, and a third time, then tossed the broken body beside the other four dead dark elves. Pwent looked around at his freshly bloodied troops, noticed at once that one was missing, and noticed, too, that Bidderdoo was trembling wildly, his jowls flapping noisily. The battlerager would have asked the wizard about it, but then the cry of agony from down the side corridor chilled the marrow in even sturdy Thibbledorf Pwent's bones. He leaped to the corner and looked around.

The carnage along the length of the fifty-foot corridor was even more tremendous than Pwent had expected. Scores of humanoids lay dead, and several small fires still burned, so thick was the pitch from the catapult missiles along the floor and walls.

Pwent watched as a large form entered the other end of the passage, a shadowy form, but the battlerager knew it was a dark elf, though certainly the biggest he had ever seen. The drow carried a large trident, and on the end of the trident, still wriggling in the last moments of his life, was Pwent's skewered Gutbuster. Another drow came out behind the huge weapon master, but Pwent hardly noticed the second form, and hardly cared if a hundred more were to follow.

The battlerager roared in protest, but did not charge. In a rare moment where cleverness outweighed rage, Pwent hopped back around the corner.

"What is it, Most Wild Battlerager?" three of the Gutbusters yelled together.

Pwent didn't answer. He jumped into the basket of the side-slinger and slashed his spiked gauntlet across the trigger rope, cutting it cleanly.

Uthegental Armgo had just shaken free the troublesome kill when the side-slinger went off, shooting the missile Pwent down the corridor. The weapon master's eyes went wide; he screamed as Pwent screamed. Suddenly Uthegental wished he still had the dead dwarf handy, that he might use the body as a shield. Purely on instinct, the warrior drow did the next best thing. He grabbed his drow companion by the collar of his *piwafwi* and yanked him in front.

Pwent's helmet spike, and half his head, blasted the unfortunate dark elf, came through cleanly enough to score a hit on Uthegental as well.

The mighty weapon master extracted himself from the tumble as Pwent tore free of the destroyed drow. They came together in a fit of fury, rage against rage, snarl against snarl, Pwent scoring several hits, but Uthegental, so strong and skilled, countering fiercely.

The butt of the trident slammed Pwent's face, and his eyes crossed. He staggered backward and realized, to his horror, that he had just given this mighty foe enough room to skewer him.

A silver beast, a great wolf running on its hind legs, barreled into Uthegental from the side, knocking him back to the floor.

Pwent shook his head vigorously, clearing his mind, and regarded the newest monster with more than a little apprehension. He glanced back up the corridor to see his Gutbusters approaching fast, all of them pointing to the wolf and howling with glee.

"Bidderdoo," Pwent mumbled, figuring it out.

Uthegental tossed the werewolf Harpell aside and leaped back to his feet. Before he had fully regained his balance, though, Pwent sprang atop him.

A second dwarf leaped atop him, followed by a third, a fourth, the whole of the Gutbuster Brigade.

Uthegental roared savagely, and suddenly, the drow possessed the strength of a giant. He stood tall, dwarves hanging all over him, and threw his arms out wide, plucking dwarves and hurling them as though they were mere rodents.

Pwent slammed him in the chest, a blow that would have killed a fair-sized cow.

Uthegental snarled and gave the battlerager a backhand slap that launched Pwent a dozen feet.

"Ye're good," a shaky Pwent admitted, coming up to one knee as Uthegental stalked in.

For the first time in his insane life (except, perhaps, for when he had inadvertently battled Drizzt), Thibbledorf Pwent knew he was outmatched—knew that his whole brigade was outmatched!—and thought he was dead. Dwarves lay about groaning and none would be able to intercept the impossibly strong drow.

Instead of trying to stand, Pwent cried out and hurled himself forward, scrambling on his knees. He came up at the last second, throwing all of his weight into a right hook.

Uthegental caught the hand in midswing and fully halted Pwent's momentum. The mighty drow's free hand closed over Pwent's face, and Uthegental began bending the poor battlerager over backward.

Pwent could see the snarling visage through the wide-spread fingers. He somehow found the strength to lash out with his free left, and scored a solid hit on the drow's forearm.

Uthegental seemed not to care.

Pwent whimpered.

265

The weapon master threw his head back suddenly.

Pwent thought the drow meant to issue a roar of victory, but no sound came from Uthegental's mouth, no noise at all, until a moment later when he gurgled incoherently.

Pwent felt the drow's grip relax, and the battlerager quickly pulled away. As he straightened, Pwent came to understand. The silver werewolf had come up behind Uthegental and had bitten the drow on the back of the neck. Bidderdoo held on still, all the pressure of his great maw crushing the vertebrae and the nerves.

The two held the macabre pose for many seconds; all the conscious Gutbusters gathered about them marveled at the strength of Bidderdoo's mouth, and at the fact that this tremendous drow warrior was still holding his feet.

There came a loud crack, and Uthegental jerked suddenly, violently. Down he fell, the wolf atop him, holding fast.

Pwent pointed to Bidderdoo. "I got to get him to show me how he did that," the awe-stricken battlerager remarked.

Bidderdoo, clamped tightly on his kill, didn't hear.

Chapter 27
THE LONGEST NIGHT

elwar heard the echoes, subtle vibrations in the thick stone that no surface dweller could ever have noticed. The other three hundred svirfnebli heard them as well. This was the way of the deep gnomes—in the deeper tunnels of the Underdark, they often communicated by sending quiet vibrations through the rock. They heard the echoes now, constant echoes, not like the one huge explosion they had heard a couple of hours before, the rumbling of an entire network of tunnels being dropped. The seasoned svirfnebli fighters considered the newest sound, a peculiar rhythm, and they knew what it meant. Battle had been joined, a great battle, and not so far away.

Belwar conferred with his commanders many times as they inched through the unfamiliar terrain, trying to follow the strongest vibrations. Often one of the svirfnebli on the perimeter, or at the point of the group, would tap his hammer slightly on the stone, trying to get a feel for the density of the rock. Echo hunting was tricky because the density of the stone was never uniform, and vibrations were often distorted. Thus, the svirfnebli, arguably the finest echo followers in all the world, found themselves more than once going the wrong way down a fork in the trail.

A determined and patient bunch, though, they stayed with it, and after many frustrating minutes, a priest named Suntunavick bobbed up to Belwar and Firble and announced with all confidence that this was as close to the sound as these tunnels would allow them to get.

The two followed the priest to the exact spot, alternately putting their ears against the stone. Indeed the noise beyond was loud, relatively speaking.

And constant, Belwar noted with some confusion, for this was not the echoing of give-and-take battle, not the echoes they had heard earlier, or at least, there was more to the sound than that.

Suntunavick assured the burrow warden this was the correct place. Mixed in with this more constant sound was the familiar rhythm of battle joined.

Belwar looked to Firble, who nodded, then to Suntunavick. The burrow warden poked his finger at the spot on the wall, then backed away, so Suntunavick and the other priests could crowd in.

They began their chanting, a grating, rumbling, and apparently wordless sound, and every once in a while one of the priests would throw a handful of some mudlike substance against the stone.

The chanting hit a crescendo; Suntunavick rushed up to the wall, his hands straight out in front of him, palms pressed tightly together. With a cry of ecstacy, the little gnome thrust his fingers straight into the stone. Then he groaned, his arm and shoulder muscles flexing as he pulled the wall apart, opened it as though it were no more solid than a curtain of heavy fabric.

The priest jumped back, and so did all the others, as the echo became a roar and a fine spray, the mist of a waterfall, came in on them.

"The surface, it is," Firble muttered, barely able to find his breath.

And so it was, but this deluge of water was nothing like any of the gnomes had pictured the surface world, was nothing like the descriptions in the many tales they had heard of the strange place. Many in the group harbored thoughts of turning back then and there, but Belwar, who had spoken with Drizzt not so long ago, knew something here was out of the ordinary.

The burrow warden hooked a rope from his belt with his pick-axe hand and held it out to Firble, indicating that the councilor should tie it about his waist. Firble did so and took up the other end, bracing himself securely.

With only the slightest of hesitation, the brave Belwar squeezed through the wall, through the veil of mist. He found the waterfall, and a ledge that led him around it, and Belwar gazed upon stars.

Thousands of stars!

The gnome's heart soared. He was awed and frightened all at once. This was the surface world, that greatest of caverns, under a dome that could not be reached.

The moment of pondering, of awe, was short-lived, defeated by the clear sounds of battle. Belwar was not in Keeper's Dale, but he could see the light of the fight, flames from torches and magical enchantments, and he could hear the ring of metal against metal and the familiar screams of the dying.

With Belwar in their lead, the three hundred svirfnebli filtered out of the caverns and began a quiet march to the east. They came upon many areas that seemed impassable, but a friendly elemental, summoned by gnomish priests, opened the way. In but a few minutes, the battle was in sight, the scramble within the misty vale, of armor-clad horsemen and lizard-riding drow, of wretched goblins and kobolds and huge humans more than twice the height of the tallest svirfneblin.

Now Belwar did hesitate, realizing fully that his force of three hundred would plunge into a battle of thousands, a battle in which the gnomes had no way of discerning who was winning.

"It is why we have come," Firble whispered into the burrow warden's ear.

Belwar looked hard at his uncharacteristically brave companion.

"For Blingdenstone," Firble said.

Belwar led the way.

* * * * *

Drizzt held his breath, they all did, and even Guenhwyvar was wise enough to stifle an instinctive snarl.

R. A. Salvatore

The five companions huddled on a narrow ledge in a high, wide corridor, while a column of drow, many drow, marched past, a line that went on and on and seemed as if it would never end.

Two thousand? Drizzt wondered. Five thousand? He had no way of guessing. There were too many, and he couldn't rightly stick his head out and begin a count. What Drizzt did understand was that the bulk of the drow force had linked together and was marching with a singular purpose. That could mean only that the way had been cleared, at least to Mithril Hall's lower door. Drizzt took heart when he thought of that door, of the many cunning defenses that had been rigged in that region. Even this mighty force would be hard-pressed to get through the portal; the tunnels near the lower door would pile high with bodies, drow and dwarf alike.

Drizzt dared to slowly shift his head, to look past Guenhwyvar, tight against the wall beside him, to Bruenor, stuck uncomfortably between the panther's rear end and the wall. Drizzt almost managed a smile at the sight, and at the thought that he had better move quickly once the drow column passed, for Bruenor would likely heave the panther right over the lip of the ledge, taking Drizzt with her.

But that smile did not come to Drizzt, not in the face of his doubts. Had he done right in leading Bruenor out here? he wondered, not for the first time. They could have gone back to the lower door with the dwarves they had met hours before; the king of Mithril Hall could be in place among his army. Drizzt did not underestimate how greatly Bruenor's fiery presence would bolster the defense of that lower door, and the defense of the Undercity. Every dwarf of Mithril Hall would sing a little louder and fight with a bit more heart in the knowledge that King Bruenor Battlehammer was nearby, joining in the cause, his mighty axe leading the way.

Drizzt's reasoning had kept Bruenor out, and now the drow wondered if his action had been selfish. Could they even find the enemy leaders? Likely the priestesses who had led this army would be well hidden, using magic from afar, directing their forces with no more compassion than if the soldiers were pawns on a gigantic chess board.

The matron mother, or whoever was leading this force, would take no personal risks, because that was the drow way.

Suddenly, up there and crouched on that ledge, Drizzt

Do'Urden felt very foolish. They were hunting the head, as he had explained to Bruenor, but that head would not be easy to find. And, given the size of the force that was marching along below them, toward Mithril Hall, Drizzt and Bruenor and their other companions would not likely get anywhere near the dwarven complex anytime soon.

The ranger put his head down and blew a deep, silent breath, composing himself, reminding himself he had taken the only possible route to winning the day, that though that lower door would not be easily breached, it would eventually come down, whether or not Bruenor Battlehammer was among the defenders. But out here now, with so many drow and so many tunnels, Drizzt began to appreciate the enormity of the task before him. How could he ever hope to find the leaders of the drow army?

What Drizzt did not know was that he was not the only one on a purposeful hunt.

* * * * *

"No word from Bregan D'aerthe."

Matron Baenre sat atop her driftdisk, digesting the words and the meaning behind them. Quenthel started to repeat them, but a threatening scowl from her mother stopped her short.

Still the phrase echoed in Matron Baenre's mind. "No word from Bregan D'aerthe."

Jarlaxle was lying low, Baenre realized. For all his bravado, the mercenary leader was, in fact, a conservative one, very cautious of any risks to the band he had spent centuries putting together. Jarlaxle hadn't been overly eager to march to Mithril Hall, and had, in fact, come along only because he hadn't really been given a choice in the matter.

Like Triel, Baenre's own daughter and closest advisor, the mercenary had hoped for a quick and easy conquest and a fast return to Menzoberranzan, where so many questions were still to be answered. The fact that no word had come lately from the Bregan D'aerthe scouts could be coincidence, but Baenre suspected differently. Jarlaxle was lying low, and that could mean only that he, with the reports that he was constantly receiving from the sly scouts of his network, believed the momentum halted, that he,

271

like Baenre herself, had come to the conclusion that Mithril Hall would not be easily swept away.

The withered old matron mother accepted the news stoically, with confidence that Jarlaxle would be back in the fold once the tide turned again in the dark elves' favor. She would have to come up with a creative punishment for the mercenary leader, of course, one that would let Jarlaxle know the depth of her dismay without costing her a valuable ally.

A short while later, the air in the small chamber Baenre had come to use as her throne room began to tingle with the budding energy of an enchantment. All in the room glanced nervously about and breathed easier when Methil stepped out of thin air into the midst of the drow priestesses.

His expression revealed nothing, just the same passive, observant stare that always came from one of Methil's otherworldly race. Baenre considered that always unreadable face the most frustrating facet of dealing with the illithids. Never did they give even the subtlest clue of their true intentions.

Uthegental Armgo is dead, came a thought in Baenre's mind, a blunt report from Methil.

Now it was Baenre's turn to put on a stoic, unrevealing facade. Methil had given the disturbing thought to her and to her alone, she knew. The others, particularly Zeerith and Auro'pol, who were becoming more and more skittish, did not need to know the news was bad, very bad.

The march to Mithril Hall goes well, came Methil's next telepathic message. The illithid shared it with all in the room, which Matron Baenre realized by the suddenly brightening expressions. *The tunnels are clear all the way to the lower door, where the army gathers and prepares.*

Many nods and smiles came back at the illithid, and Matron Baenre did not have any more trouble than Methil in reading the thoughts behind those expressions. The illithid was working hard to bolster morale—always a tentative thing in dealing with dark elves. But, like Quenthel's report, or lack of report, from Bregan D'aerthe, the first message the illithid had given echoed in Baenre's thoughts disconcertingly. Uthegental Armgo was dead! What might the soldiers of Barrison del'Armgo, a significant force vital to the cause, do when they discovered their leader had been slain?

And what of Jarlaxle? Baenre wondered. If he had learned of the brutish weapon master's fall, that would certainly explain the silence of Bregan D'aerthe. Jarlaxle might be fearing the loss of the Barrison del'Armgo garrison, a desertion that would shake the ranks of the army to its core.

Jarlaxle does not know, nor do the soldiers of the second house, Methil answered her telepathically, obviously reading her thoughts.

Still Baenre managed to keep up the cheery (relatively speaking) front, seeming thrilled at the news of the army's approach to the lower door. She clearly saw a potential cancer growing within her ranks, though, a series of events that could destroy the already shaky integrity of her army and her alliances, and could cost her everything. She felt as though she were falling back to that time of ultimate chaos in Menzoberranzan just before the march, when K'yorl seemed to have the upper hand.

The destruction of House Oblodra had solidified the situation then, and Matron Baenre felt she needed something akin to that now, some dramatic victory that would leave no doubts in the minds of the rank and file. Foster loyalty with fear. She thought of House Oblodra again and toyed with the idea of a similar display against Mithril Hall's lower door. Baenre quickly dismissed it, realizing that what had happened in Menzoberranzan had been a one-time event. Never before (and likely never again—and certainly not so soon afterward!) had Lloth come so gloriously and so fully to the Material Plane. On the occasion of House Oblodra's fall, Matron Baenre had been the pure conduit of the Spider Queen's godly power.

That would not happen again.

Baenre's thoughts swirled in a different direction, a more feasible trail to follow. *Who killed Uthegental?* she thought, knowing that Methil would "hear" her.

The illithid had no answer, but understood what Baenre was implying. Baenre knew what Uthegental had sought, knew the only prize that really mattered to the mighty weapon master. Perhaps he had found Drizzt Do'Urden.

If so, that would mean Drizzt Do'Urden was in the lower tunnels, not behind Mithril Hall's barricades.

You follow a dangerous course, Methil privately warned, before

Baenre could even begin to plot out the spells that would let her find the renegade.

Matron Baenre dismissed that notion with hardly a care. She was the first matron mother of Menzoberranzan, the conduit of Lloth, possessed of powers that could snuff the life out of any drow in the city, any matron mother, any wizard, any weapon master, with hardly an effort. Baenre's course now was indeed dangerous, she agreed—dangerous for Drizzt Do'Urden.

* * * * *

Most devastating was the dwarven force and the center of the blocking line, a great mass of pounding, singing warriors, mulching goblins and orcs under their heavy hammers and axes, leaping in packs atop towering minotaurs, their sheer weight of numbers bringing the brutes down.

But all along the eastern end of Keeper's Dale, the press was too great from every side. Mounted knights rushed back and forth across the barbarian line, bolstering the ranks wherever the enemy seemed to be breaking through, and with their timely support, the line held. Even so, Berkthgar's people found themselves inevitably pushed back.

The bodies of kobolds and goblins piled high in Keeper's Dale; a score dying for every defender. But the drow could afford those losses, had expected them, and Berg'inyon, sitting astride his lizard, calmly watching the continuing battle from afar along with the rest of the Baenre riders, knew that the time for slaughter grew near. The defenders were growing weary, he realized. The minutes had turned into an hour, and that into two, and the assault did not diminish.

Back went the defending line, and the towering eastern walls of Keeper's Dale were not so far behind them. When those walls halted the retreat, the drow wizards would strike hard. Then Berg'inyon would lead the charge, and Keeper's Dale would run even thicker with the blood of humans.

* * * * *

Besnell knew they were losing, knew that a dozen dead goblins were not worth the price of an inch of ground. A resignation began to grow within the elf, tempered only by the fact that never had he seen his knights in finer form. Their tight battle groups rushed to and fro, trampling enemies, and though every man was breathing so hard he could barely sing out a war song, and every horse was lathered in thick sweat, they did not relent, did not pause.

Grimly satisfied, and yet terribly worried—and not just for his own men, for Alustriel had made no further appearance on the field—the elf turned his attention to Berkthgar, then he was truly amazed. The huge flamberge, Bankenfuere, hummed as it swept through the air, each cut obliterating any enemies foolish enough to stand close to the huge man. Blood, much of it his own, covered the barbarian from head to toe, but if Berkthgar felt any pain, he did not show it. His song and his dance were to Tempus, the god of battle, and so he sang, and so he danced, and so his enemies died.

In Besnell's mind, if the drow won here and conquered Mithril Hall, one of the most tragic consequences would be that the tale of the exploits of mighty Berkthgar the Bold would not leave Keeper's Dale.

A tremendous flash to the side brought the elf from his contemplations. He looked down the line to see Regweld Harpell surrounded by a dozen dead or dying, flaming goblins. Regweld and Puddlejumper were also engulfed by the magical flames, dancing licks of green and red, but the wizard and his extraordinary mount did not seem bothered and continued to fight without regard for the fires. Indeed, those fires engulfing the duo became a weapon, an extension of Regweld's fury when the wizard leaped Puddlejumper nearly a dozen yards, to land at the feet of two towering minotaurs. Red and green flames became white hot and leaped out from the wizard's torso, engulfing the towering brutes. Puddlejumper hopped straight up, bringing Regweld even with the screaming minotaurs' ugly faces. Out came a wand, and green blasts of energy tore into the monsters.

Then Regweld was gone, leaping to the next fight, leaving the minotaurs staggering, flames consuming them.

"For the good of all goodly folk!" Besnell cried, holding his sword high. His battle group formed beside him, and the thunder of the charge began anew, this time barreling full stride through a mass of kobolds. They scattered the beasts and came into a thicker throng of larger enemies, where the charge was stopped. Still atop their

275

mounts, the Knights in Silver hacked through the morass, bright swords slaughtering enemies.

Besnell was happy. He felt a satisfaction coursing through his body, a sensation of accomplishment and righteousness. The elf believed in Silverymoon with all his heart, believed in the precept he yelled out at every opportunity.

He was not sad when a goblin spear found a crease at the side of his breastplate, rushed in through his ribs, and collapsed a lung. He swayed in his saddle and somehow managed to knock the spear from his side.

"For the good of all goodly folk!" he said with all the strength he could muster. A goblin was beside his mount, sword coming in.

Besnell winced with pain as he brought his own sword across to block. He felt weak and suddenly cold. He hardly registered the loss as his sword slipped from his hand to clang to the ground.

The goblin's next strike cut solidly against the knight's thigh, the drow-made weapon tearing through Besnell's armor and drawing a line of bright blood.

The goblin hooted, then went flying away, broken apart by the mighty sweep of Bankenfuere.

Berkthgar caught Besnell in his free hand as the knight slid off his mount. The barbarian felt somehow removed from the battle at that moment, as though he and the noble elf were alone, in their own private place. Around them, not so far away, the knights continued the slaughter and no monsters approached.

Berkthgar gently lowered Besnell to the ground. The elf looked up, his golden eyes seeming hollow.

"For the good of all goodly folk," Besnell said, his voice barely a whisper, but, by the grace of Tempus, or whatever god was looking over the battle of Keeper's Dale, Berkthgar heard every syllable.

The barbarian nodded and silently laid the dead elf's head on the stone.

Then Berkthgar was up again, his rage multiplied, and he charged headlong into the enemy ranks, his great sword cutting a wide swath.

* * * * *

Regweld Harpell had never known such excitement. Still in flames that did not harm him or his horse-frog, but attacked any that came near, the wizard single-handedly bolstered the southern end of the defending line. He was quickly running out of spells, but Regweld didn't care, knew that he would find some way to make himself useful, some way to destroy the wretches that had come to conquer Mithril Hall.

A group of minotaurs converged on him, their great spears far out in front to prevent the fires from getting at them.

Regweld smiled and coaxed Puddlejumper into another flying leap, straight up between the circling monsters, higher than even minotaurs and their long spears could reach.

The Harpell let out a shout of victory, then a lightning bolt silenced him.

Suddenly Regweld was free-flying, spinning in the air, and Puddlejumper was spinning the other way just below him.

A second thundering bolt came in from a different angle, and then a third, forking so that it hit both the wizard and his strange mount.

They were each hit again, and again after that as they tumbled, falling very still upon the stone.

The drow wizards had joined the battle.

The invaders roared and pressed on, and even Berkthgar, outraged by the valiant elf's death, could not rally his men to hold the line. Drow lizard riders filtered in through the humanoid ranks, their long lances pushing the mounted knights inevitably back, back toward the blocking wall.

* * * * *

Berg'inyon was among the first to see the next turn of the battle. He ordered a rider up the side of a rock pillar, to gain a better vantage point, then turned his attention to a group nearby, pointing to the northern wall of the valley.

Go up high, the weapon master's fingers signaled to them. *Up high and around the enemy ranks, to rain death on them from above when they are pushed back against the wall.*

277

Evil smiles accompanied the agreeing nods, but a cry from the other side, from the soldier Berg'inyon had sent up high, stole the moment.

The rock pillar had come to life as a great elemental monster. Berg'inyon and the others looked on helplessly as the stone behemoth clapped together great rock arms, splattering the drow and his lizard.

There came a great clamor from behind the drow lines, from the west, and above the thunder of the svirfneblin charge was heard a cry of "Bivrip!" the word Belwar Dissengulp used to activate the magic in his crafted hands.

* * * * *

It was a long time before Berkthgar and the other defenders at the eastern end of Keeper's Dale even understood that allies had come from the west. Those rumors eventually filtered through the tumult of battle, though, heartening defender and striking fear into invader. The goblins and dark elves engaged near that eastern wall began to look back the other way, wondering if disaster approached.

Now Berkthgar did rally what remained of the non-dwarven defenders: two-third of his barbarians, less than a hundred Knights in Silver, a score of Longriders, and only two of the men from Nesme. Their ranks were depleted, but their spirit returned, and the line held again, even made progress in following the dwarven mass back out toward the middle of Keeper's Dale.

Soon after, all semblance of order was lost in the valley; no longer did lines of soldiers define enemies. In the west, the svirfneblin priests battled drow wizards, and Belwar's warriors charged hard into drow ranks. They were the bitterest of enemies, ancient enemies, drow and svirfnebli. No less could be said on the eastern side of the valley, where dwarves and goblins hacked away at each other with abandon.

It went on through the night, a wild and horrible night. Berg'inyon Baenre engaged in little combat and kept the bulk of his elite lizard riders back as well, using his monstrous fodder to weary the defense. Even with the unexpected arrival of the small but powerful svirfneblin force, the drow soon turned the tide back their way.

"We will win," the young Baenre promised those soldiers closest to him. "And then what defense might be left in place beyond the western door of the dwarven complex?

Chapter 28
DIVINATION

uenthel Baenre sat facing a cubby of the small chamber's wall, staring down into a pool of calm water. She squinted as the pool, a scrying pool, brightened, as the dawn broke on the outside world, not so far to the east of Fourthpeak.

Quenthel held her breath, though she wanted to cry out in despair.

Across the small chamber, Matron Baenre was similarly divining. She had used her spells to create a rough map of the area, and then to enchant a single tiny feather. Chanting again, Baenre tossed the feather into the air above the spread parchment and blew softly.

"Drizzt Do'Urden," she whispered in that breath, and she puffed again as the feather flopped and flitted down to the map. A wide, evil grin spread across Baenre's face when the feather, the magical pointer, touched down, its tip indicating a group of tunnels not far away.

It was true, Baenre knew then. Drizzt Do'Urden was indeed in the tunnels outside Mithril Hall.

"We leave," the matron mother said suddenly, startling all in the quiet chamber.

Quenthel looked back nervously over her shoulder, afraid that her mother had somehow seen what was in her scrying pool. The Baenre daughter found that she couldn't see across the room, though, for the view was blocked by a scowling Bladen'Kerst, glaring down at her, and past her, at the approaching spectacle.

"Where are we to go?" Zeerith, near the middle of the room, asked aloud, and from her tone, it was obvious she was hoping Matron Baenre's scrying had found a break in the apparent stalemate.

Matron Baenre considered that tone and the sour expression on the other matron mother's face. She wasn't sure whether Zeerith, and Auro'pol, who was similarly scowling, would have preferred to hear that the way was clear into Mithril Hall, or that the attack had been called off. Looking at the two of them, among the very highest-ranking commanders of the drow army, Baenre couldn't tell whether they preferred victory or retreat.

That obvious reminder of how tentative her alliance was angered Baenre. She would have liked to dismiss both of them, or, better, to have them executed then and there. But Baenre could not, she realized. The morale of her army would never survive that. Besides, she wanted them, or at least one of them, to witness her glory, to see Drizzt Do'Urden given to Lloth.

"You shall go to the lower door, to coordinate and strengthen the attack," Baenre said sharply to Zeerith, deciding that the two of them standing together were becoming too dangerous. "And Auro'pol shall go with me."

Auro'pol didn't dare ask the obvious question, but Baenre saw it clearly anyway from her expression.

"We have business in the outer tunnels," was all Matron Baenre would offer.

Berg'inyon will soon see the dawn, Quenthel's fingers motioned to her sister.

Bladen'Kerst, always angry, but now boiling with rage, turned away from Quenthel and the unwanted images in the scrying pool and looked back to her mother.

Before she could speak, though, a telepathic intrusion came into her mind, and into Quenthel's. *Do not speak ill of other battles*, Methil imparted to them both. *Already, Zeerith and Auro'pol consider desertion.*

Bladen'Kerst considered the message and the implications and

281

R. A. Salvatore

wisely held her information.

The command group split apart, then, with Zeerith and a contingent of the elite soldiers going east, toward Mithril Hall, and Matron Baenre leading Quenthel, Bladen'Kerst, Methil, half a dozen skilled Baenre female warriors, and the chained Gandalug off to the south, in the direction of the spot indicated by her divining feather.

*　*　*　*　*

On another plane, the gray mists and sludge and terrible stench of the Abyss, Errtu watched the proceedings in the glassy mirror Lloth had created on the side of the mushroom opposite his throne.

The great balor was not pleased. Matron Baenre was hunting Drizzt Do'Urden, Errtu knew, and he knew, too, that Baenre would likely find the renegade and easily destroy him.

A thousand curses erupted from the tanar'ri's doglike maw, all aimed at Lloth, who had promised him freedom—freedom that only a living Drizzt Do'Urden could bestow.

To make matters even worse, a few moments later, Matron Baenre was casting yet another spell, opening a planar gate to the Abyss, calling forth a mighty glabrezu to help in her hunting. In his twisted, always suspicious mind, Errtu came to believe that this summoning was enacted only to torment him, to take one of his own kind and use the beast to facilitate the end of the pact. That was the way with tanar'ri, and with all the wretches of the Abyss, Lloth included. These creatures were without trust for others, since they, themselves, could not be trusted by any but a fool. And they were an ultimately selfish lot, every one. In Errtu's eyes, every action revolved around him, because nothing else mattered, and thus, Baenre summoning a glabrezu now was not coincidence, but a dagger jabbed by Lloth into Errtu's black heart.

Errtu was the first to the opening gate. Even if he was not bound to the Abyss by banishment, he could not have gone through, because Baenre, so skilled in this type of summoning, was careful to word the enchantment for a specific tanar'ri only. But Errtu was waiting when the glabrezu appeared through the swirling mists, heading for the opened, flaming portal.

The balor leaped out and lashed out with his whip, catching the glabrezu by the arm. No minor fiend, the glabrezu moved to strike

282

back, but stopped, seeing that Errtu did not mean to continue the attack.

"It is a deception!" Errtu roared.

The glabrezu, its twelve-foot frame hunched low, great pincers nipping anxiously at the air, paused to listen.

"I was to come forth on the Material Plane," Errtu went on.

"You are banished," the glabrezu said matter-of-factly.

"Lloth promised an end!" Errtu retorted, and the glabrezu crouched lower, as if expecting the volatile fiend to leap upon him.

But Errtu calmed quickly. "An end, that I might return, and bring forth behind me an army of tanar'ri." Again Errtu paused. He was improvising now, but a plan was beginning to form in his wicked mind.

Baenre's call came again, and it took all the glabrezu's considerable willpower to keep it from leaping through the flaring portal.

"She will allow you only one kill," Errtu said quickly, seeing the glabrezu's hesitance.

"One is better than none," the glabrezu answered.

"Even if that one prevents my freedom on the Material Plane?" Errtu asked. "Even if it prevents me from going forth, and bringing you forth as my general, that we might wreak carnage on the weakling races?"

Baenre called yet again, and this time it was not so difficult for the glabrezu to ignore her.

Errtu held up his great hands, indicating that the glabrezu should wait here a few moments longer, then the balor sped off, into the swirl, to retrieve something a lesser fiend had given him not so long ago, a remnant of the Time of Troubles. He returned shortly with a metal coffer and gently opened it, producing a shining black sapphire. As soon as Errtu held it up, the flames of the magical portal diminished, and almost went out altogether. Errtu was quick to put the thing back in its case.

"When the time is right, reveal this," the balor instructed, "my general."

He tossed the coffer to the glabrezu, unsure, as was the other fiend, of how this would all play out. Errtu's great shoulders ruffled in a shrug then, for there was nothing else he could do. He could prevent this fiend from going to Baenre's aid, but to what end? Baenre hardly needed a glabrezu to deal with Drizzt Do'Urden, a

283

mere warrior.

The call from the Material Plane came yet again, and this time the glabrezu answered, stepping through the portal to join Matron Baenre's hunting party.

Errtu watched in frustration as the portal closed, another gate lost to the Material Plane, another gate that he could not pass through. Now the balor had done all he could, though he had no way of knowing if it would be enough, and he had so much riding on the outcome. He went back to his mushroom throne then, to watch and wait.

And hope.

* * * * *

Bruenor remembered. In the quiet ways of the tunnels, no enemies to be seen, the eighth king of Mithril Hall paused and reflected. Likely the dawn was soon to come on the outside, another crisp, cold day. But would it be the last day of Clan Battlehammer?

Bruenor looked to his four friends as they took a quick meal and a short rest. Not one of them was a dwarf, not one.

And yet, Bruenor Battlehammer could not name any other friends above these four: Drizzt, Catti-brie, Regis, and even Guenhwyvar. For the first time, that truth struck the dwarf king as curious. Dwarves, though not xenophobic, usually stayed to their own kind. Witness General Dagna, who, if given his way, would kick Drizzt out of Mithril Hall and would take Taulmaril away from Catti-brie, to hang the bow once more in the Hall of Dumathoin. Dagna didn't trust anyone who was not a dwarf.

But here they were, Bruenor and his four non-dwarven companions, in perhaps the most critical and dangerous struggle of all for the defense of Mithril Hall.

Surely their friendship warmed the old dwarf king's heart, but reflecting on that now did something else as well.

It made Bruenor think of Wulfgar, the barbarian who had been like his own son, and who would have married Catti-brie and become his son-in-law, the unlikely seven-foot prince of Mithril Hall. Bruenor had never known such grief as that which bowed his strong shoulders after Wulfgar's fall. Though he should live for more than another century, Bruenor had felt close to death in those weeks of grieving, and had felt as if death would be a welcome thing.

No longer. He missed Wulfgar still—forever would his gray eye mist up at the thought of the noble warrior—but he was the eighth king, the leader of his proud, strong clan. Bruenor's grief had passed the point of resignation and had shifted into the realm of anger. The dark elves were back, the same dark elves who had killed Wulfgar. They were the followers of Lloth, evil Lloth, and now they meant to kill Drizzt and destroy all of Mithril Hall, it seemed.

Bruenor had wetted his axe on drow blood many times during the night, but his rage was far from sated. Indeed, it was mounting, a slow but determined boil. Drizzt had promised they would hunt the head of their enemy, would find the leader, the priestess behind this assault. It was a promise Bruenor needed to see the drow ranger keep.

He had been quiet through much of the fighting, even in preparing for the war. Bruenor was quiet now, too, letting Drizzt and the panther lead, finding his place among the friends whenever battle was joined.

In the few moments of peace and rest, Bruenor saw a wary glance come his way more than once and knew that his friends feared he was brooding again, that his heart was not in the fight. Nothing could have been farther from the truth. Those minor skirmishes didn't matter much to Bruenor. He could kill a hundred—a thousand!—drow soldiers, and his pain and anger would not relent. If he could get to the priestess behind it all, though, chop her down and decapitate the drow invading force . . .

Bruenor might know peace.

The eighth king of Mithril Hall was not brooding. He was biding his time and his energy, coming to a slow boil. He was waiting for the moment when revenge would be most sweet.

*   *   *   *   *

Baenre's group, the giant glabrezu in tow, had just begun moving again, the matron mother guiding them in the direction her scrying had indicated, when Methil telepathically informed her that matrons Auro'pol and Zeerith had been continually entertaining thoughts of her demise. If Zeerith couldn't find a way through

285

Mithril Hall's lower door, she would simply organize a withdrawal. Even now, Auro'pol was considering the potential for swinging the whole army about and leaving Matron Baenre dead behind them, according to Methil.

Do they plot against me? Baenre wanted to know.

No, Methil honestly replied, *but if you are killed, they will be thrilled to turn back for Menzoberranzan without you, that a new hierarchy might arise.*

In truth, Methil's information was not unexpected. One did not have to read minds to see the discomfort and quiet rage on the faces of the matron mothers of Menzoberranzan's fourth and fifth houses. Besides, Baenre had suffered such hatred from her lessers, even from supposed allies such as Mez'Barris Armgo, even from her own daughters, for all her long life. That was an expected cost of being the first matron mother of chaotic and jealous Menzoberranzan, a city continually at war with itself.

Auro'pol's thoughts were to be expected, but the confirmation from the illithid outraged the already nervous Matron Baenre. In her twisted mind, this was no ordinary war, after all. This was the will of Lloth, as Baenre was the Spider Queen's agent. This was the pinnacle of Matron Baenre's power, the height of Lloth-given glory. How dare Auro'pol and Zeerith entertain such blasphemous thoughts? the first matron mother fumed.

She snapped an angry glare over Auro'pol, who simply snorted and looked away—possibly the very worst thing she could have done.

Baenre issued telepathic orders to Methil, who in turn relayed them to the glabrezu. The driftdisks, side by side, were just following Baenre's daughters around a bend in the tunnel when great pincers closed about Auro'pol's slender waist and yanked her from her driftdisk, the powerful glabrezu easily holding her in midair.

"What is this?" Auro'pol demanded, squirming to no avail.

"You wish me dead," Baenre answered.

Quenthel and Bladen'Kerst rushed back to their mother's side, and both were stunned that Baenre had openly moved against Auro'pol.

"She wishes me dead," Baenre informed her daughters. "She and Zeerith believe Menzoberranzan would be a better place without Matron Baenre."

Auro'pol looked to the illithid, obviously the one who had betrayed her. Baenre's daughters, who had entertained similar treasonous thoughts on more than one occasion during this long, troublesome march, looked to Methil as well.

"Matron Auro'pol bears witness to your glory," Quenthel put in. "She will witness the death of the renegade and will know that Lloth is with us."

Auro'pol's features calmed at that statement, and she squirmed again, trying to loosen the tanar'ri's viselike grip.

Baenre eyed her adversary dangerously, and Auro'pol, cocky to the end, matched the intensity of her stare. Quenthel was right, Auro'pol believed. Baenre needed her to bear witness. Bringing her into line behind the war would solidify Zeerith's loyalty as well, so the drow army would be much stronger. Baenre was a wicked old thing, but she had always been a calculating one, not ready to sacrifice an inch of power for the sake of emotional satisfaction. Witness Gandalug Battlehammer, still alive, though Baenre certainly would have enjoyed tearing the heart from his chest many times during the long centuries of his imprisonment.

"Matron Zeerith will be glad to hear of Drizzt Do'Urden's death," Auro'pol said, and lowered her eyes respectfully. The submissive gesture would suffice, she believed.

"The head of Drizzt Do'Urden will be all the proof Matron Zeerith requires," Baenre replied.

Auro'pol's gaze shot up, and Baenre's daughters, too, looked upon their surprising mother.

Baenre ignored them all. She sent a message to Methil, who again relayed it to the glabrezu, and the great pincers began to squeeze about Auro'pol's waist.

"You cannot do this!" Auro'pol objected, gasping for every word. "Lloth is with me! You weaken your own campaign!"

Quenthel wholeheartedly agreed, but kept silent, realizing the glabrezu still had an empty pincer.

"You cannot do this!" Auro'pol shrieked. "Zeerith will . . ." Her words were lost to pain.

"Drizzt Do'Urden killed you before I killed Drizzt Do'Urden," Matron Baenre explained to Auro'pol. "Perfectly believable, and it makes the renegade's death all the sweeter." Baenre nodded to the glabrezu, and the pincers closed, tearing through flesh and bone.

R. A. Salvatore

Quenthel looked away; wicked Bladen'Kerst watched the spectacle with a wide smile.

Auro'pol tried to call out once more, tried to hurl a dying curse Baenre's way, but her backbone snapped and all her strength washed away. The pincers snapped shut, and Auro'pol Dyrr's body fell apart to the floor.

Bladen'Kerst cried out in glee, thrilled by her mother's display of control and power. Quenthel, though, was outraged. Baenre had stepped over a dangerous line. She had killed a matron mother, and had done so to the detriment of the march to Mithril Hall, purely for personal gain. Wholeheartedly devoted to Lloth, Quenthel could not abide such stupidity, and her thoughts were similar indeed to those that had gotten Auro'pol Dyrr chopped in half.

Quenthel snapped a dangerous glare over Methil, realizing the illithid was reading her thoughts. Would Methil betray her next?

She narrowed her thoughts into a tight focus. *It is not Lloth's will!* her mind screamed at Methil. *No longer is the Spider Queen behind my mother's actions.*

That notion held more implications for Methil, the illithid emissary to Menzoberranzan, not to Matron Baenre, than Quenthel could guess, and her relief was great indeed when Methil did not betray her.

*   *   *   *   *

Guenhwyvar's ears flattened, and Drizzt, too, thought he heard a slight, distant scream. They had seen no one, enemies or friends, for several hours, and the ranger believed that any group of dark elves they now encountered would likely include the high priestess leading the army.

He motioned for the others to move with all caution, and the small band crept along, Guenhwyvar leading the way. Drizzt fell into his Underdark instincts now. He was the hunter again, the survivor who had lived alone for a decade in the wilds of the Underdark. He looked back at Bruenor, Regis, and Catti-brie often, for, though they were moving with all the stealth they could manage, they sounded like a marching army of armored soldiers to Drizzt's keen ears. That worried the drow, for he knew their enemies would be far quieter. He considered going a long way ahead with Guenhwyvar, taking up the hunt alone.

It was a passing thought. These were his friends, and no one could ever ask for finer allies.

They slipped down a narrow, unremarkable tunnel and into a chamber that opened wide to the left and right, though the smooth wall directly opposite the tunnel was not far away. The ceiling here was higher than in the tunnel, but stalactites hung down in several areas, nearly to the floor in many places.

Guenhwyvar's ears flattened again, and the panther paused at the entrance. Drizzt came beside her and felt the same tingling sensation.

The enemy was near, very near. That warrior instinct, beyond the normal senses, told the drow ranger the enemy was practically upon them. He signaled back to the three trailing, then he and the panther moved slowly and cautiously into the chamber, along the wall to the right.

Catti-brie came to the entrance next and fell to one knee, bending back her bow. Her eyes, aided by the Cat's Eye circlet, which made even the darkest tunnels seem bathed in bright starlight, scanned the chamber, searching among the stalactite clusters.

Bruenor was soon beside her, and Regis came past her on the left. The halfling spotted a cubby a few feet along the wall. He pointed to himself, then to the cubby, and he inched off toward the spot.

A green light appeared on the wall opposite the door, stealing the darkness. It spiraled out, opening a hole in the wall, and Matron Baenre floated through, her daughters and their prisoner coming in behind her, along with the illithid.

Drizzt recognized the withered old drow and realized his worst fears, knew immediately that he and his friends were badly overmatched. He thought to go straight for Baenre, but realized that he and Guenhwyvar were not alone on this side of the chamber. From the corner of his wary eye Drizzt caught some movement up among the stalactites.

Catti-brie fired a silver-streaking arrow, practically point-blank. The arrow exploded into a shower of multicolored, harmless sparks, unable to penetrate the first matron mother's magical shields.

Regis went into the cubby then and cried out in sudden pain as a ward exploded. Electricity sparked about the halfling, sending

R. A. Salvatore

him jerking this way and that, then dropping him to the floor, his curly brown hair standing straight on end.

Guenhwyvar sprang to the right, burying a drow soldier as she floated down from the stalactites. Drizzt again considered going straight for Baenre, but found himself suddenly engaged as three more elite Baenre guards rushed out of hiding to surround him. Drizzt shook his head in denial. Surprise now worked against him and his friends, not for them. The enemy had expected them, he knew, had hunted them even as they had hunted the enemy. And this was Matron Baenre herself!

"Run!" Drizzt cried to his friends. "Flee this place!"

Chapter 29
KING AGAINST QUEEN

he long night drifted into morning, with the dark elves once again claiming the upper hand in the battle for Keeper's Dale. Berg'inyon's assessment of the futility of the defense, even with the dwarven and svirfneblin reinforcements, seemed correct as the drow ranks gradually engulfed the svirfnebli, then pushed the line in the east back toward the wall once more.

But then it happened.

After an entire night of fighting, after hours of shaping the battle, holding back the wizards, using the lizard riders at precise moments and never fully committing them to the conflict, all the best laid plans of the powerful drow force fell apart.

The rim of the mountains east of Keeper's Dale brightened, a silvery edge that signaled the coming dawn. For the drow and the other monsters of the Underdark, that was no small event.

One drow wizard, intent on a lightning bolt that would defeat the nearest enemies, interrupted his spell and enacted a globe of darkness instead, aiming it at the tip of the sun as it peeked over the horizon, thinking to blot out the light. The spell went off and did nothing more than a put a black dot in the air a long way off, and as the wizard squinted against the glare, wondering what he might try next, those defenders closest charged in and cut him down.

Another drow battling a dwarf had his opponent all but beaten. So intent was he on the kill that he hardly noticed the coming dawn—until the tip of the sun broke the horizon, sending a line of light, a line of agony, to sensitive drow eyes. Blinded and horrified, the dark elf whipped his weapons in a frenzy, but he never got close to hitting the mark.

Then he felt a hot explosion across his ribs.

All these dark elves had seen things in the normal spectrum of light before, but not so clearly, not in such intense light, not with colors so rich and vivid. They had heard of the terrible sunshine—Berg'inyon had witnessed a dawn many years before, had watched it over his shoulder as he and his drow raiding party fled back for the safe darkness of the lower tunnels. Now the weapon master and his charges did not know what to expect. Would the infernal sun burn them as it blinded them? They had been told by their elders that it would not, but had been warned they would be more vulnerable in the sunlight, that their enemies would be bolstered by the brightness.

Berg'inyon called his forces into tight battle formations and tried to regroup. They could still win, the weapon master knew, though this latest development would cost many drow lives. Dark elves could fight blindly, but what Berg'inyon feared here was more than a loss of vision. It was a loss of heart. The rays slanting down from the mountains were beyond his and his troops' experience. And as frightening as it had been to walk under the canopy of unreachable stars, this event, this sunrise, was purely terrifying.

Berg'inyon quickly conferred with his wizards, tried to see if there was some way they could counteract the dawn. What he learned instead distressed him as much as the infernal light. The drow wizards in Keeper's Dale had eyes also in other places, and from those far-seeing mages came the initial whispers that dark elves were deserting in the lower tunnels, that those drow who had been stopped in the tunnels near the eastern door had retreated from Mithril Hall and had fled to the deeper passages on the eastern side of Fourthpeak. Berg'inyon understood that information easily enough; those drow were already on the trails leading back to Menzoberranzan.

Berg'inyon could not ignore the reports' implications. Any alliance between dark elves was tentative, and the weapon master could only guess at how widespread the desertion might be. Despite the dawn, Berg'inyon believed his force would win in Keeper's Dale and would breach the western door, but suddenly he had to wonder what they would find in Mithril Hall once they got there.

Matron Baenre and their allies? King Bruenor and the renegade, Drizzt, and a host of dwarves ready to fight? The thought did not sit well with the worried weapon master.

Thus, it was not greater numbers that won the day in Keeper's Dale. It was not the courage of Berkthgar or Besnell, or the ferocity of Belwar and his gnomes, or the wisdom of Stumpet Rakingclaw. It was the dawn and the distrust among the enemy ranks, the lack of cohesion and the very real fear that supporting forces would not arrive, for every drow soldier, from Berg'inyon to the lowest commoner, understood that their allies would think nothing of leaving them behind to be slaughtered.

Berg'inyon Baenre was not questioned by any of his soldiers when he gave the order to leave Keeper's Dale. The lizard riders, still more than three hundred strong, rode out to the rough terrain of the north, their sticky-footed mounts leaving enemies and allies alike far behind.

The very air of Keeper's Dale tingled from the tragedy and the excitement, but the sounds of battle died away to an eerie stillness, shattered occasionally by a cry of agony. Berkthgar the Bold stood tall and firm, with Stumpet Rakingclaw and Terrien Doucard, the new leader of the Knights in Silver, flanking him, and their victorious soldiers waiting, tensed, behind them.

Ten feet away, Belwar Dissengulp stood point for the depleted svirfneblin ranks. The most honored burrow warden held his strong arms out before him, cradling the body of noble Firble, one of many svirfnebli who had died this day, so far from, but in defense of, their home.

They did not know what to make of each other, this almost-seven-foot barbarian, and the gnome who was barely half his height. They could not talk to each other, and had no comprehensible signs of friendship to offer.

R. A. Salvatore

They found their only common ground among the bodies of hated enemies and beloved friends, piled thick in Keeper's Dale.

* * * * *

Faerie fire erupted along Drizzt's arms and legs, outlining him as a better target. He countered by dropping a globe of darkness over himself, an attempt to steal the enemy's advantage of three-to-one odds.

Out snapped the ranger's scimitars, and he felt a strange urge from one, not from Twinkle, but from the other blade, the one Drizzt had found in the lair of the dragon Dracos Icingdeath, the blade that had been forged as a bane to creatures of fire.

The scimitar was hungry; Drizzt had not felt such an urge from it since . . .

He parried the first attack and groaned, remembering the other time his scimitar had revealed its hunger, when he had battled the balor Errtu. Drizzt knew what this meant.

Baenre had brought friends.

* * * * *

Catti-brie fired another arrow, straight at the withered old matron mother's laughing visage. Again the enchanted arrow merely erupted into a pretty display of useless sparks. The young woman turned to flee, as Drizzt had ordered. She grabbed her father, meaning to pull him along.

Bruenor wouldn't budge. He looked to Baenre and knew she was the source. He looked at Baenre and convinced himself that she had personally killed his boy. Then Bruenor looked past Baenre, to the old dwarf. Somehow Bruenor knew that dwarf. In his heart, the eighth king of Mithril Hall recognized the patron of his clan, though he could not consciously make the connection.

"Run!" Catti-brie yelled at him, taking him temporarily from his thoughts. Bruenor glanced at her, then looked behind, back down the tunnel.

He heard fighting in the distance, from somewhere behind them.

Quenthel's spell went off then, and a wall of fire sprang up in

294

the narrow tunnel, cutting off retreat. That didn't bother determined Bruenor much, not now. He shrugged himself free of Catti-brie's hold and turned back to face Baenre—in his own mind, to face the evil dark elf who had killed his boy.

He took a step forward.

Baenre laughed at him.

* * * * *

Drizzt parried and struck, then, using the cover of the darkness globe, quick-stepped to the side, too quickly for the dark elf coming in at his back to realize the shift. She bored in and struck hard, hitting the same drow that Drizzt had just wounded, finishing her.

Hearing the movement, Drizzt came right back, both his blades whirling. To the female's credit, she registered the countering move in time to parry the first attack, the second and the third, even the fourth.

But Drizzt did not relent. He knew his fury was a dangerous thing. There remained one more enemy in the darkness globe, and for Drizzt to press against a single opponent so forcefully left him vulnerable to the other. But the ranger knew, too, that his friends sorely needed him, that every moment he spent engaged with these warriors gave the powerful priestesses time to destroy them all.

The ranger's fifth attack, a wide-arcing left, was cleanly picked off, as was the sixth, a straightforward right thrust. Drizzt pressed hard, would not relinquish the offensive. He knew, and the female knew, that her only hope would be in her lone remaining ally.

A stifled scream, followed by the growl of a panther ended that hope.

Drizzt's fury increased, and the female continued to fall back, stumbling now in the darkness, suddenly afraid. And in that moment of fear, she banged her head hard against a low stalactite, an obstacle her keen drow senses should have detected. She shook off the blow and managed to straighten her posture, throwing one sword out in front to block another of the ranger's furious thrusts.

She missed.

Drizzt didn't, and Twinkle split the fine drow armor and dove deep into the female's lung.

Drizzt yanked the blade free and spun about.

R. A. Salvatore

His darkness globe went away abruptly, dispelled by the magic of the waiting tanar'ri.

* * * * *

Bruenor took another step, then broke into a run. Catti-brie screamed, thinking him dead, as a line of fire came down on him.

Furious, frustrated, the young woman fired her bow again, and more harmless sparks exploded in the air. Through the tears of outrage that welled in her blue eyes she hardly noticed that Bruenor had shrugged off the stinging hit and broke into a full charge again.

Bladen'Kerst stopped the dwarf, enacting a spell that surrounded Bruenor in a huge block of magical, translucent goo. Bruenor continued to move, but so slowly as to be barely perceptible, while the three drow priestesses laughed at him.

Catti-brie fired again, and this time her arrow hit the block of goo, diving in several feet before stopping and hanging uselessly in place above her father's head.

Catti-brie looked to Bruenor, to Drizzt and the horrid, twelve-foot fiend that had appeared to the right, and to Regis, groaning and trying to crawl at her left. She felt the heat as fires raged in the tunnel behind her, heard the continuing battle back, that way which she did not understand.

They needed a break, a turn in the tide, and Catti-brie thought she saw it then, and a moment of hope came to her. Finished with the kill, Guenhwyvar growled and crouched, ready to spring upon the tanar'ri.

That moment of hope for Catti-brie was short-lived, for as the panther sprang out, one of the priestesses casually tossed something into the air, Guenhwyvar's way. The panther dissipated into gray mist in midleap and was gone, sent back to the Astral Plane.

"And so we die," Catti-brie whispered, for this enemy was too strong. She dropped Taulmaril to the floor and drew Khazid'hea. A deep breath steadied her, reminded her that she had run close to death's door for most of her adult life. She looked to her father and prepared to charge, prepared to die.

A shape wavered in front of the block of goo, between Catti-brie and Bruenor, and the look of determination on the young woman's face turned to one of disgust as a gruesome, octopus-headed monster materialized on this side of the magical block, calmly walking—no, floating—toward her.

Catti-brie raised her sword, then stopped, overwhelmed suddenly by a psionic blast, the likes of which she had never known. Methil waded in.

* * * * *

Berg'inyon's force pulled up and regrouped when they had cleared Keeper's Dale completely, had left the din of battle far behind and were near the last run for the tunnels back to the Underdark. Dimensional doors opened near the lizard riders, and drow wizards (and those other dark elves fortunate enough to have been near the wizards when the spells were enacted) stepped through. Stragglers, infantry drow and a scattering of humanoid allies, struggled to catch up, but they could not navigate the impossible terrain on this sign of the mountain. And they were of no concern to the Baenre weapon master.

All those who had escaped Keeper's Dale looked to Berg'inyon for guidance as the day brightened about them.

"My mother was wrong," Berg'inyon said bluntly, an act of blasphemy in drow society, where the word of any matron mother was Lloth-given law.

Not a drow pointed it out, though, or raised a word of disagreement. Berg'inyon motioned to the east, and the force lumbered on, into the rising sun, miserable and defeated.

"The surface is for surface-dwellers," Berg'inyon remarked to one of his advisors when she walked her mount beside his. "I shall never return."

"What of Drizzt Do'Urden?" the female asked, for it was no secret that Matron Baenre wanted her son to slay the renegade.

Berg'inyon laughed at her, for not once since he had witnessed Drizzt's exploits at the Academy had he entertained any serious thoughts of fighting the renegade.

* * * * *

Drizzt could see little beyond the gigantic glabrezu, and that spectacle was enough, for the ranger knew he was not prepared for such a foe, knew that the mighty creature would likely destroy him.

297

R. A. Salvatore

Even if it didn't defeat him, the glabrezu would surely hold him up long enough for Matron Baenre to kill them all!

Drizzt felt the savage hunger of his scimitar, a blade forged to kill such beasts, but he fought off the urge to charge, knew that he had to find a way around those devilish pincers.

He noted Guenhwyvar's futile leap and disappearance. Another ally lost.

The fight was over before it had begun, Drizzt realized. They had killed a couple of elite guards and nothing more. They had walked headlong into the pinnacle of Menzoberranzan's power, the most high priestesses of the Spider Queen, and they had lost. Waves of guilt washed over Drizzt, but he dismissed them, refused to accept them. He had come out, and his friends had come beside him, because this had been Mithril Hall's only chance. Even if Drizzt had known that Matron Baenre herself was leading this march, he would have come out here, and would not have denied Bruenor and Regis and Catti-brie the opportunity to accompany him.

They had lost, but Drizzt meant to make their enemy hurt.

"Fight on, demon spawn," he snarled at the glabrezu, and he fell into a crouch, waving his blades, eager to give his scimitar the meal it so greatly desired.

The tanar'ri straightened and held out a curious metal coffer.

Drizzt didn't wait for an explanation, and almost unintentionally destroyed the only chance he and his friends had, for as the tanar'ri moved to open the coffer, Drizzt, with the enchanted ankle bracers speeding his rush, yelled and charged, right past the lowered pincers, thrusting his scimitar into the fiend's belly.

He felt the surge of power as the scimitar fed.

* * * * *

Catti-brie was too confused to strike, too overwhelmed to even cry out in protest as Methil came right up to her and the wretched tentacles licked her face. Then, through the confusion, a single voice, the voice of Khazid'hea, her sword, called out in her head.

Strike!

She did, and though her aim was not perfect, Khazid'hea's wicked edge hit Methil on the shoulder, nearly severing the illithid's arm.

Out of her daze, Catti-brie swept the tentacles from her face with her free hand.

Another psionic wave blasted her, crippling her once more, stealing her strength and buckling her legs. Before she went down, she saw the illithid jerk weirdly, then fall away, and saw Regis, staggering, his hair still dancing wildly. The halfling's mace was covered in blood, and he fell sidelong, over the stumbling Methil.

That would have been the end of the illithid, especially when Catti-brie regained her senses enough to join in, except that Methil had anticipated such a disaster and had stored enough psionic energy to get out of the fight. Regis lifted his mace for another strike, but felt himself sinking as the illithid dissipated beneath him. The halfling cried out in confusion, in terror, and swung anyway, but his mace clanged loudly as it hit only the empty stone floor beneath him.

* * * * *

It all happened in a mere instant, a flicker of time in which poor Bruenor had not gained an inch toward his taunting foes.

The glabrezu, in pain greater than anything it had ever known, could have killed Drizzt then. Every instinct within the wicked creature urged it to snap this impertinent drow in half. Every instinct except one: the fear of Errtu's reprisal once the tanar'ri got back to the Abyss—and with that vile scimitar chewing away at its belly, the tanar'ri knew it would soon make that trip.

It wanted so much to snap Drizzt in half, but the fiend had been sent here for a different reason, and evil Errtu would accept no explanations for failure. Growling at the renegade Do'Urden, taking pleasure only in the knowledge that Errtu would soon return to punish this one personally, the glabrezu reached across and tore open the shielding coffer, producing the shining black sapphire.

The hunger disappeared from Drizzt's scimitar. Suddenly, the ranger's feet weren't moving so quickly.

Across the Realms, the most poignant reminder of the Time of Troubles were the areas known as dead zones, wherein all magic ceased to exist. This sapphire contained within it the negative energy of such a zone, possessed the antimagic to steal magical energy, and not Drizzt's scimitars or his bracers, not Khazid'hea or the magic of the drow priestesses, could overcome that negative force.

It happened for only an instant, for a consequence of revealing that sapphire was the release of the summoned tanar'ri from the Material Plane, and the departing glabrezu took with it the sapphire.

For only an instant, the fires stopped in the tunnel behind Catti-brie. For only an instant, the shackles binding Gandalug lost their enchantment. For only an instant, the block of goo surrounding Bruenor was no more.

For only an instant, but that was long enough for Gandalug, teeming with centuries of rage, to tear his suddenly feeble shackles apart, and for Bruenor to surge ahead, so that when the block of goo reappeared, he was beyond its influence, charging hard and scream-ing with all his strength.

Matron Baenre had fallen unceremoniously to the floor, and her driftdisk reappeared when magic returned, hovering above her head.

Gandalug launched a backhand punch to the left, smacking Quenthel in the face and knocking her back against the wall. Then he jumped to the right and caught Bladen'Kerst's five-headed snake whip in his hand, taking more than one numbing bite.

The old dwarf ignored the pain and pressed on, barreling over the surprised Baenre daughter. He reached around her other shoul-der and caught the handle of her whip in his free hand, then pulled the thing tightly against her neck, strangling her with her own wicked weapon.

They fell in a clinch.

* * * * *

In all the Realms there was no creature more protected by magic than Matron Baenre, no creature shielded from blows more effec-tively, not even a thick-scaled ancient dragon. But most of those wards were gone now, taken from her in the moment of antimagic. And in all the Realms there was no creature more consumed by rage than Bruenor Battlehammer, enraged at the sight of the old, tor-mented dwarf he knew he should recognize. Enraged at the realiza-tion that his friends, that his dear daughter, were dead, or soon would be. Enraged at the withered drow priestess, in his mind the personification of the evil that had taken his boy.

He chopped his axe straight overhead, the many-notched blade diving down, shattering the blue light of the driftdisk, blowing the enchantment into nothingness. Bruenor felt the burn as the blade hit one of the few remaining magical shields, energy instantly coursing up the weapon's head and handle, into the furious king.

The axe went from green to orange to blue as it tore through magical defense after magical defense, rage pitted against powerful dweomers. Bruenor felt agony, but would admit none.

The axe drove through the feeble arm that Baenre lifted to block, through Baenre's skull, through her jawbone and neck, and deep into her frail chest.

* * * * *

Quenthel shook off Gandalug's heavy blow and instinctively moved for her sister. Then, suddenly, her mother was dead and the priestess rushed back toward the wall instead, through the green-edged portal, back into the corridor beyond. She dropped some silvery dust as she passed through, enchanted dust that would dispel the portal and make the wall smooth and solid once again.

The stone spiraled in, fast transforming back into a solid barrier.

Only Drizzt Do'Urden, moving with the speed of the enchanted anklets, got through that opening before it snapped shut.

* * * * *

Jarlaxle and his lieutenants were not far away. They knew that a group of wild dwarves and a wolfman had met Baenre's other elite guards in the tunnels across the way, and that the dwarves and their ally had overwhelmed the dark elves and were fast bearing down on the chamber.

From a high vantage point, looking out from a cubby on the tunnel behind that chamber, Jarlaxle knew the approaching band of furious dwarves had already missed the action. Quenthel's appearance, and Drizzt's right behind her, told the watching mercenary leader the conquest of Mithril Hall had come to an abrupt end.

The lieutenant at Jarlaxle's side lifted a hand-crossbow toward Drizzt, and seemed to have a perfect opportunity, for Drizzt's focus was solely on the fleeing Baenre daughter. The ranger would never know what hit him.

Jarlaxle grabbed the lieutenant's wrist and forced the arm down. Jarlaxle motioned to the tunnels behind, and he and his somewhat confused, but ultimately loyal, band slipped silently away.

As they departed, Jarlaxle heard Quenthel's dying scream, a cry of "Sacrilege!" She was yelling out a denial, of course, in Drizzt Do'Urden's—her killer's—face, but Jarlaxle realized she could just as easily, and just as accurately, have been referring to him.

So be it.

* * * * *

The dawn was bright but cold, and it grew colder still as Stumpet and Terrien Doucard, of the Knights in Silver, made their way up the difficult side of Keeper's Dale, climbing hand over hand along the almost vertical wall.

"Ye're certain?" Stumpet asked Terrien, a half-elf with lustrous brown hair and features too fair to be dimmed by even the tragedy of the last night.

The knight didn't bother to reply, other than with a quick nod, for Stumpet had asked the question more than a dozen times in the last twenty minutes.

"This is the right wall?" Stumpet asked, yet another of her redundant questions.

Terrien nodded. "Close," he assured the dwarf.

Stumpet came up on a small ledge and slid over, putting her back against the wall, her feet hanging over the two-hundred-foot drop to the valley floor. She felt she should be down there in the valley, helping tend to the many, many wounded, but if what the knight had told her was true, if Lady Alustriel of Silverymoon had fallen up here, then this trip might be the most important task Stumpet Rakingclaw ever completed in her life.

She heard Terrien struggling below her and bent over, reaching down to hook the half-elf under the shoulder. Stumpet's powerful muscles corded, and she easily hoisted the slender knight over the ledge, guiding him into position beside her against the wall. Both the half-elf and the dwarf breathed heavily, puffs of steam filling the

302

air before them.

"We held the dale," Stumpet said cheerily, trying to coax the agonized expression from the half-elf's face.

"Would the victory have been worth it if you had watched Bruenor Battlehammer die?" the half-elf replied, his teeth chattering a bit from the frigid air.

"Ye're not for knowing that Alustriel died!" Stumpet shot back, and she pulled the pack from her back, fumbling about inside. She had wanted to wait a while before doing this, hopefully to get closer to the spot where Alustriel's chariot had reportedly gone down.

She took out a small bowl shaped of silvery mithril and pulled a bulging waterskin over her head.

"It is probably frozen," the dejected half-elf remarked, indicating the skin.

Stumpet snorted. Dwarven holy water didn't freeze, at least not the kind Stumpet had brewed, dropping in a little ninety-proof to sweeten the mix. She popped the cork from the waterskin and began a rhythmic chant as she poured the golden liquid into the mithril bowl. She was lucky—she knew that—for though the image her spells brought forth was fuzzy and brief, an area some distance away, she knew this region, and knew where to find the indicated ledge.

They started off immediately at a furious and reckless pace, Stumpet not even bothering to collect her bowl and skin. The half-elf slipped more than once, only to be caught by the wrist by Stumpet's strong grasp, and more than once Stumpet found herself falling, and only the quick hands of Terrien Doucard, deftly planting pitons to secure the rope between them, saved her.

Finally, they got to the ledge and found Alustriel lying still and cold. The only indication that her magical chariot had ever been there was a scorch mark where the thing had crashed, on the floor of the ledge and against the mountain wall. Not even debris remained, for the chariot had been wholly a creation of magic.

The half-elf rushed to his fallen leader and gently cradled Alustriel's head in one arm. Stumpet whipped out a small mirror from her belt pouch and stuck it in front of the lady's mouth.

"She's alive!" the dwarf announced, tossing her pack to Terrien. The words seemed to ignite the half-elf. He gently laid Alustriel's head to the ledge, then fumbled in the pack, tearing out several thick blankets, and wrapped his lady warmly, then began briskly rubbing Alustriel's bare, cold hands. All the while, Stumpet called upon her gods for spells of healing and warmth, and gave every ounce of her own energy to this wondrous leader of Silverymoon.

Five minutes later, Lady Alustriel opened her beautiful eyes. She took a deep breath and shuddered, then whispered something neither Stumpet nor the knight could hear, so the half-elf leaned closer, put his ear right up to her mouth.

"Did we hold?"

Terrien Doucard straightened and smiled widely. "Keeper's Dale is ours!" he announced, and Alustriel's eyes sparkled. Then she slept, peacefully, confident that this furiously working dwarven priestess would keep her warm and well, and she was confident that, whatever her own fate, the greater good had been served.

For the good of all goodly folk.

EPILOGUE

erg'inyon Baenre was not surprised to find Jarlaxle and
the soldiers of Bregan D'aerthe waiting for him far
below the surface, far from Mithril Hall. As soon as he
had heard reports of desertion, Berg'inyon realized that
the pragmatic mercenary was probably among those ranks of drow
fleeing the war.

Methil had informed Jarlaxle of Berg'inyon's approach, and
the mercenary leader was indeed surprised to find that Berg'inyon,
the son of Matron Baenre, the weapon master of the first house,
had also run off in desertion. The mercenary had figured that
Berg'inyon would fight his way into Mithril Hall and die as his
mother had died.

Stupidly.

"The war is lost," Berg'inyon remarked. Unsure of himself, he
looked to Methil, for he hadn't anticipated that the illithid would be
out here, away from the matriarch. The illithid's obvious wounds,
one arm hanging limply and a large hole on the side of his octopus
head, grotesque brain matter oozing out, caught Berg'inyon off
guard as well, for he never expected that anyone could catch up to
Methil and harm him so.

"Your mother is dead," Jarlaxle replied bluntly, drawing the young Baenre's attention from the wounded illithid. "As are your two sisters and Auro'pol Dyrr."

Berg'inyon nodded, seeming hardly surprised.

Jarlaxle wondered whether he should mention that Matron Baenre was the one who had murdered the latter. He held the thought in check, figuring he might be able to use that little bit of information against Berg'inyon at a later time.

"Matron Zeerith Q'Xorlarrin led the retreat from Mithril Hall's lower door," the mercenary went on.

"And my own force caught up to those drow who tried, and failed, to get in the eastern door," Berg'inyon added.

"And you punished them?" Jarlaxle wanted to know, for he was still unsure of Berg'inyon's feelings about all of this, still unsure if he and his band were about to fight yet another battle down here in the tunnels.

Berg'inyon scoffed at the notion of punishment, and Jarlaxle breathed a little easier.

Together, they marched on, back for the dark and more comfortable ways of Menzoberranzan. They linked with Zeerith and her force soon after, and many other groups of dark elves and humanoids fell into line as the days wore on. In all, more than two thousand drow, a fourth of them Baenre soldiers, had died in the assault on Mithril Hall, and twice that number of humanoid slaves had been killed, most outside the mountain, on Fourthpeak's southern slopes and in Keeper's Dale. And a like number of humanoids had run off after the battles, fleeing to the surface or down other corridors, taking their chances in the unknown world above or in the wild Underdark rather than return to the tortured life as a slave of the drow.

Things had not gone as Matron Baenre had planned.

Berg'inyon fell into line as the quiet force moved away, letting Zeerith control the procession.

"Menzoberranzan will be many years in healing from the folly of Matron Baenre," Jarlaxle remarked to Berg'inyon later that day, when he came upon the young weapon master alone in a side chamber as the army camped in a region of broken caves and short, connecting tunnels.

Berg'inyon didn't disagree with the statement and showed no anger at all. He understood the truth of Jarlaxle's words, and knew that much trouble would befall House Baenre in the days ahead. Matron Zeerith was outraged, and Mez'Barris Armgo and all the other matron mothers would be, too, when they learned of the disaster.

"The offer remains," Jarlaxle said, and he left the chamber, left Berg'inyon alone with his thoughts.

House Baenre would likely survive, Berg'inyon believed. Triel would assume its rulership, and, though they had lost five hundred skilled soldiers, nearly two thousand remained, including more than three hundred of the famed lizard riders. Matron Baenre had built a huge network of allies outside the house as well, and even this disaster, and the death of Baenre, would not likely topple the first house.

There would indeed be trouble, though. Matron Baenre was the solidifying force. What might House Baenre expect from troublesome Gromph with her gone?

And what of Triel? Berg'inyon wondered. Where would he fit into his sister's designs? Now she would be free to raise children of her own and bring them into power. The first son born to her would either be groomed as the house wizard or as a candidate for Berg'inyon's position as weapon master.

How long, then, did Berg'inyon have? Fifty years? A hundred? Not long in the life span of a dark elf.

Berg'inyon looked to the archway, to the back of the departing mercenary, and considered carefully Jarlaxle's offer for him to join Bregan D'aerthe.

* * * * *

Mithril Hall was a place of mixed emotions: tears for the dead and cheers for the victory. All mourned Besnell and Firble, Regweld Harpell and so many others who had died valiantly. And all cheered for King Bruenor and his mighty friends, for Berkthgar the Bold, for Lady Alustriel, still nursing her grievous wounds, and for Stumpet Rakingclaw, hero of both the Undercity and Keeper's Dale.

And all cheered most of all for Gandalug Battlehammer, the patron of Clan Battlehammer, returned from the grave, it seemed. How strange it was for Bruenor to face his own ancestor, to see the first bust in the Hall of Kings come to life!

The two dwarves sat side by side in the throne room on the upper levels of the dwarven complex, flanked by Alustriel (with Stumpet kneeling beside the Lady of Silverymoon's chair, nagging her to rest!) on the right and Berkthgar on the left.

The celebration was general throughout the dwarven complex, from the Undercity to the throne room, a time of gathering, and of parting, a time when Belwar Dissengulp and Bruenor Battlehammer finally met. Through the magic of Alustriel, an enchantment that sorted out the language problems, the two were able to forge an alliance between Blingdenstone and Mithril Hall that would live for centuries, and they were able to swap tales of their common drow friend, particularly when Drizzt was wandering about, just far enough away to realize they were talking about him.

"It's the damned cat that bothers me," Bruenor huffed on one occasion, loud enough so that Drizzt would hear.

The drow sauntered over, put a foot on the raised dais that held the thrones, and leaned forward on his knee, very close to Belwar. "Guenhwyvar humbles Bruenor," Drizzt said in the Drow tongue, a language Belwar somewhat understood, but which was not translated by Alustriel's spell for Bruenor. "She often uses the dwarf for bedding."

Bruenor, knowing they were talking about him, but unable to understand a word, hooted in protest—and protested louder when Gandalug, who also knew a bit of the Drow tongue, joined in the conversation and the mirth.

"But suren the cat's not fer using me son's son's son's son's son's son's 'ead fer a piller!" the old dwarf howled. "Too hard it be. Too, too!"

"By Moradin, I should've left with the damned dark elves," a defeated Bruenor grumbled.

That notion sobered old Gandalug, took the cheer from his face in the blink of an eye.

Such was the celebration in Mithril Hall, a time of strong emotions, both good and bad.

Catti-brie watched it all from the side, feeling removed and strangely out of place. Surely she was thrilled at the victory, intrigued by the svirfnebli, whom she had met once before, and even more intrigued that the patron of her father's clan had been miraculously returned to the dwarven complex he had founded.

Along with those exciting feelings, though, the young woman felt a sense of completion. The drow threat to Mithril Hall was ended this time, and new and stronger alliances would be forged between Mithril Hall and all its neighbors, even Nesme. Bruenor and Berkthgar seemed old friends now—Bruenor had even hinted on several occasions that he might be willing to let the barbarian wield Aegis-fang.

Catti-brie hoped that would not come to pass, and didn't think it would. Bruenor had hinted at the generous offer mostly because he knew it wouldn't really cost him anything, Catti-brie suspected. After Berkthgar's exploits in Keeper's Dale, his own weapon, Bankenfuere, was well on its way as a legend among the warriors of Settlestone.

No matter what Berkthgar's exploits might be, Bankenfuere would never rival Aegis-fang, in Catti-brie's mind.

Though she was quiet and reflective, Catti-brie was not grim, not maudlin. Like everyone else in Mithril Hall, she had lost some friends in the war. But like everyone else, she was battle-hardened, accepting the ways of the world and able to see the greater good that had come from the battle. She laughed when a group of svirfnebli practically pulled out what little hair they had, so frustrated were they in trying to teach a group of drunken dwarves how to hear vibrations in the stone. She laughed louder when Regis bopped into the throne room, pounds of food tucked under each arm and already so stuffed that the buttons on his waistcoat were near bursting.

And she laughed loudest of all when Bidderdoo Harpell raced past her, Thibbledorf Pwent scrambling on his knees behind the wizard, begging Bidderdoo to bite him!

But there remained a reflective solitude behind that laughter, that nagging sense of completion that didn't sit well on the shoulders of a woman who had just begun to open her eyes to the wide world.

* * * * *

In the smoky filth of the Abyss, the balor Errtu held his breath as the shapely drow, the delicate disaster, approached his mushroom throne.

Errtu didn't know what to expect from Lloth; they had both witnessed the disaster.

The balor watched as the drow came through the mist, the prisoner, the promised gift, in tow. She was smiling, but, on the face of the Lady of Chaos, one could never hope to guess what that meant.

Errtu sat tall and proud, confident he had done as instructed. If Lloth tried to blame him for the disaster, he would argue, he determined, though if she had somehow found out about the antimagic stone he had sent along with the glabrezu . . .

"You have brought my payment?" the balor boomed, trying to sound imposing.

"Of course, Errtu," the Spider Queen replied.

Errtu cocked his tremendous, horned head. There seemed no deception in either her tone or her movements as she pushed the prisoner toward the gigantic, seated balor.

"You seem pleased," Errtu dared to remark.

Lloth's smile nearly took in her ears, and then Errtu understood. She was pleased! The old wretch, the most wicked of the wicked, was glad of the outcome. Matron Baenre was gone, as was all order in Menzoberranzan. The drow city would know its greatest chaos now, thrilling interhouse warfare and a veritable spiderweb of intrigue, layer upon layer of lies and treachery, through each of the ruling houses.

"You knew this would happen from the beginning!" the balor accused.

Lloth laughed aloud. "I did not anticipate the outcome," she assured Errtu. "I did not know Errtu would be so resourceful in protecting the one who might end his banishment."

The balor's eyes widened, and his great leathery wings folded close about him, a symbolic, if ineffective, movement of defense.

"Fear not, my fiendish ally," Lloth cooed. "I will give you a chance to redeem yourself in my eyes."

Errtu growled low. What favor did the Spider Queen now want from him?

"I will be busy these next decades, I fear," Lloth went on, "in trying to end the confusion in Menzoberranzan."

Errtu scoffed. "Never would you desire such a thing," he replied.

"I will be busy watching the confusion then," Lloth was willing to admit. Almost as an afterthought, she added, "And watching what it is you must do for me."

Again came that demonic growl.

"When you are free, Errtu," Lloth said evenly, "when you have Drizzt Do'Urden entangled in the tongs of your merciless whip, do kill him slowly, painfully, that I might hear his every cry!" The Spider Queen swept hers arms up then and disappeared with a flurry of crackling black energy.

Errtu's lip curled up in an evil smile. He looked to the pitiful prisoner, the key to breaking the will and the heart of Drizzt Do'Urden. Sometimes, it seemed, the Spider Queen did not ask for much.

* * * * *

It had been two weeks since the victory, and in Mithril Hall the celebration continued. Many had left—first the two remaining men from Nesme and the Longriders, along with Harkle and Bella don DelRoy (though Pwent finally convinced Bidderdoo to stick around for a while). Then Alustriel and her remaining Knights in Silver, seventy-five warriors, began their journey back to Silverymoon with their heads held high, the lady ready to meet the challenges of her political rivals head-on, confident that she had done right in coming to King Bruenor's aid.

The svirfnebli were in no hurry to leave, though, enjoying the company of Clan Battlehammer, and the men of Settlestone vowed to stay until the last of Mithril Hall's mead was drained away.

Far down the mountain from the dwarven complex, on a cold, windy plain, Catti-brie sat atop a fine roan—one of the horses that had belonged to a slain Silverymoon knight. She sat quietly and confidently, but the sting in her heart as she looked up to Mithril Hall was no less acute. Her eyes scanned the trails to the rocky exit from the mountains, and she smiled, not surprised, in seeing a rider coming down.

"I knew ye'd follow me down here," she said to Drizzt Do'Urden when the ranger approached.

"We all have our place," Drizzt replied.

"And mine's not now in Mithril Hall," Catti-brie said sternly. "Ye'll not change me mind!"

311

R. A. Salvatore

Drizzt paused for a long while, studying the determined young woman. "You've talked with Bruenor?" he asked.

"Of course," Catti-brie retorted. "Ye think I'd leave me father's house without his blessings?"

"Blessings he gave grudgingly, no doubt," Drizzt remarked.

Catti-brie straightened in her saddle and locked her jaw firmly. "Bruenor's got much to do," she said. "And he's got Regis and yer-self . . ." She paused and held that thought, noticing the heavy pack strapped behind Drizzt's saddle. "And Gandalug and Berkthgar beside him," she finished. "They've not even figured which is to rule and which is to watch, though I'm thinking Gandalug's to let Bruenor remain king."

"That would be the wiser course," Drizzt agreed.

A long moment of silence passed between them.

"Berkthgar talks of leaving," Drizzt said suddenly, "of returning to Icewind Dale and the ancient ways of his people."

Catti-brie nodded. She had heard such rumors.

Again came that uncomfortable silence. Catti-brie finally turned her eyes away from the drow, thinking he was judging her, thinking, in her moment of doubt, that she was being a terrible daughter to Bruenor, terrible and selfish. "Me father didn't try to stop me," she blurted with a tone of finality, "and yerself cannot!"

"I never said I came out to try to stop you," Drizzt calmly replied.

Catti-brie paused, not really surprised. When she had first told Bruenor she was leaving, that she had to go out from Mithril Hall for a while and witness the wonders of the world, the crusty dwarf had bellowed so loudly that Catti-brie thought the stone walls would tumble in on both of them.

They had met again two days later, when Bruenor was not so full of dwarven holy water, and, to Catti-brie's surprise and relief, her father was much more reasonable. He understood her heart, he had assured her, though his gruff voice cracked as he delivered the words, and he realized she had to follow it, had to go off and learn who she was and where she fit in the world. Catti-brie had thought the words uncharacteristically understanding and philosophical of Bruenor, and now, facing Drizzt, she was certain of their source. Now she knew who Bruenor had spoken to between their meetings.

"He sent ye," she accused Drizzt.

312

"You were leaving and so was I," Drizzt replied casually.

"I just could not spend the rest o' me days in the tunnels," Catti-brie said, suddenly feeling as if she had to explain herself, revealing the guilt that had weighed heavily on her since her decision to leave home. She looked all around, her eyes scanning the distant horizon. "There's just so much more for me. I'm knowing that in me heart. I've known it since Wulfgar . . ."

She paused and sighed and looked to Drizzt helplessly.

"And more for me," the drow said with a mischievous grin, "much more."

Catti-brie glanced back over her shoulder, back to the west, where the sun was already beginning its descent.

"The days are short," she remarked, "and the road is long."

"Only as long as you make it," Drizzt said to her, drawing her gaze back to him. "And the days are only as short as you allow them to be."

Catti-brie eyed him curiously, not understanding that last statement.

Drizzt was grinning widely as he explained, as full of anticipation as was Catti-brie. "A friend of mine, a blind old ranger, once told me that if you ride hard and fast enough to the west, the sun will never set for you."

By the time he had finished the statement, Catti-brie had wheeled her roan and was in full gallop across the frozen plain toward the west, toward Nesme and Longsaddle beyond that, toward mighty Waterdeep and the Sword Coast. She bent low in the saddle, her mount running hard, her cloak billowing and snapping in the wind behind her, her thick auburn hair flying wildly.

Drizzt opened a belt pouch and looked at the onyx panther figurine. No one could ask for better companions, he mused, and with a final look to the mountains, to Mithril Hall, where his friend was king, the ranger kicked his stallion into a gallop and chased after Catti-brie.

To the west and the adventures of the wide world.